The Abbot

The Abbot
Sir Walter Scott

MINT EDITIONS

The Abbot was first published in 1820.

This edition published by Mint Editions 2021.

ISBN 9781513280448 | E-ISBN 9781513285467

Published by Mint Editions®

 MINT
EDITIONS

minteditionbooks.com

Publishing Director: Jennifer Newens
Design & Production: Rachel Lopez Metzger
Project Manager: Micaela Clark
Typesetting: Westchester Publishing Services

Contents

I

Domum mansit—lanam fecit.

—Ancient Roman Epitaph

She keepit close the hous, and birlit at the quhele.

—Gawain Douglas

The time which passes over our heads so imperceptibly, makes the same gradual change in habits, manners, and character, as in personal appearance. At the revolution of every five years we find ourselves another, and yet the same—there is a change of views, and no less of the light in which we regard them; a change of motives as well as of actions. Nearly twice that space had glided away over the head of Halbert Glendinning and his lady, betwixt the period of our former narrative, in which they played a distinguished part, and the date at which our present tale commences.

Two circumstances only had imbittered their union, which was otherwise as happy as mutual affection could render it. The first of these was indeed the common calamity of Scotland, being the distracted state of that unhappy country, where every man's sword was directed against his neighbour's bosom. Glendinning had proved what Murray expected of him, a steady friend, strong in battle, and wise in counsel, adhering to him, from motives of gratitude, in situations where by his own unbiassed will he would either have stood neuter, or have joined the opposite party. Hence, when danger was near—and it was seldom far distant—Sir Halbert Glendinning, for he now bore the rank of knighthood, was perpetually summoned to attend his patron on distant expeditions, or on perilous enterprises, or to assist him with his counsel in the doubtful intrigues of a half-barbarous court. He was thus frequently, and for a long space, absent from his castle and from his lady; and to this ground of regret we must add, that their union had not been blessed with children, to occupy the attention of the Lady of Avenel, while she was thus deprived of her husband's domestic society.

On such occasions she lived almost entirely secluded from the world, within the walls of her paternal mansion. Visiting amongst neighbors was a matter entirely out of the question, unless on occasions of solemn festival, and then it was chiefly confined to near kindred. Of these the Lady of Avenel had none who survived, and the dames of the neighbouring barons affected to regard her less as the heiress of the house of Avenel than as the wife of a peasant, the son of a church-vassal, raised up to mushroom eminence by the capricious favour of Murray.

The pride of ancestry, which rankled in the bosom of the ancient gentry, was more openly expressed by their ladies, and was, moreover, imbittered not a little by the political feuds of the time, for most of the Southern chiefs were friends to the authority of the Queen, and very jealous of the power of Murray. The Castle of Avenel was, therefore, on all these accounts, as melancholy and solitary a residence for its lady as could well be imagined. Still it had the essential recommendation of great security. The reader is already aware that the fortress was built upon an islet on a small lake, and was only accessible by a causeway, intersected by a double ditch, defended by two draw-bridges, so that without artillery, it might in those days be considered as impregnable. It was only necessary, therefore, to secure against surprise, and the service of six able men within the castle was sufficient for that purpose. If more serious danger threatened, an ample garrison was supplied by the male inhabitants of a little hamlet, which, under the auspices of Halbert Glendinning, had arisen on a small piece of level ground, betwixt the lake and the hill, nearly adjoining to the spot where the causeway joined the mainland. The Lord of Avenel had found it an easy matter to procure inhabitants, as he was not only a kind and beneficent overlord, but well qualified, both by his experience in arms, his high character for wisdom and integrity, and his favour with the powerful Earl of Murray, to protect and defend those who dwelt under his banner. In leaving his castle for any length of time, he had, therefore, the consolation to reflect, that this village afforded, on the slightest notice, a band of thirty stout men, which was more than sufficient for its defence; while the families of the villagers, as was usual on such occasions, fled to the recesses of the mountains, drove their cattle to the same places of shelter, and left the enemy to work their will on their miserable cottages.

One guest only resided generally, if not constantly, at the Castle of Avenel. This was Henry Warden, who now felt himself less able for the stormy task imposed on the reforming clergy; and having by his zeal given personal offence to many of the leading nobles and chiefs, did not consider himself as perfectly safe, unless when within the walls of the strong mansion of some assured friend. He ceased not, however, to serve his cause as eagerly with his pen, as he had formerly done with his tongue, and had engaged in a furious and acrimonious contest, concerning the sacrifice of the mass, as it was termed, with the Abbot Eustatius, formerly the Sub-Prior of Kennaquhair. Answers, replies, duplies, triplies, quadruplies, followed thick upon each other, and displayed, as is not unusual in controversy, fully as much zeal as Christian charity. The disputation very soon became as celebrated as that of John Knox and the Abbot of Crosraguel, raged nearly as fiercely, and, for aught I know, the publications to which it gave rise may be as precious in the eyes of bibliographers.* But the engrossing nature of his occupation rendered the theologian not the most interesting companion for a solitary female; and his grave, stern, and absorbed deportment, which seldom showed any interest, except in that which concerned his religious profession, made his presence rather add to than diminish the gloom which hung over the Castle of Avenel. To superintend the tasks of numerous female domestics, was the principal part of the Lady's daily employment; her spindle and distaff, her Bible, and a solitary walk upon the battlements of the castle, or upon the causeway, or occasionally, but more seldom, upon the banks of the little lake, consumed the rest of the day. But so great was the insecurity of the period, that when she ventured to extend her walk beyond the hamlet, the warder on the watch-tower was directed to keep a sharp look-out in every direction, and four or five men held themselves in readiness to mount and sally forth from the castle on the slightest appearance of alarm.

Thus stood affairs at the castle, when, after an absence of several weeks, the Knight of Avenel, which was now the title most frequently given to Sir Halbert Glendinning, was daily expected to return home. Day after day, however, passed away, and he returned not. Letters in those days were rarely written, and the Knight must have resorted to a secretary to express his intentions in that manner; besides, intercourse of all kinds was precarious and unsafe, and no man cared to give any public intimation of the time and direction of a journey, since, if his route were publicly known, it was always likely he might in that case meet with more enemies than friends upon the road. The precise day, therefore, of Sir Halbert's return, was not fixed, but that which his

---

* The tracts which appeared in the Disputation between the Scottish Reformer and Quentin Kennedy, Abbot of Crosraguel, are among the scarcest in Scottish Bibliography. See M'Crie's *Life of Knox*, p. 258.

lady's fond expectation had calculated upon in her own mind had long since passed, and hope delayed began to make the heart sick.

It was upon the evening of a sultry summer's day, when the sun was half-sunk behind the distant western mountains of Liddesdale, that the Lady took her solitary walk on the battlements of a range of buildings, which formed the front of the castle, where a flat roof of flag-stones presented a broad and convenient promenade. The level surface of the lake, undisturbed except by the occasional dipping of a teal-duck, or coot, was gilded with the beams of the setting luminary, and reflected, as if in a golden mirror, the hills amongst which it lay embossed. The scene, otherwise so lonely, was occasionally enlivened by the voices of the children in the village, which, softened by distance, reached the ear of the Lady, in her solitary walk, or by the distant call of the herdsman, as he guided his cattle from the glen in which they had pastured all day, to place them in greater security for the night, in the immediate vicinity of the village. The deep lowing of the cows seemed to demand the attendance of the milk-maidens, who, singing shrilly and merrily, strolled forth, each with her pail on her head, to attend to the duty of the evening. The Lady of Avenel looked and listened; the sounds which she heard reminded her of former days, when her most important employment, as well as her greatest delight, was to assist Dame Glendinning and Tibb Tackett in milking the cows at Glendearg. The thought was fraught with melancholy.

"Why was I not," she said, "the peasant girl which in all men's eyes I seemed to be? Halbert and I had then spent our life peacefully in his native glen, undisturbed by the phantoms either of fear or of ambition. His greatest pride had then been to show the fairest herd in the Halidome; his greatest danger to repel some pilfering snatcher from the Border; and the utmost distance which would have divided us, would have been the chase of some outlying deer. But, alas! what avails the blood which Halbert has shed, and the dangers which he encounters, to support a name and rank, dear to him because he has it from me, but which we shall never transmit to our posterity! with me the name of Avenel must expire."

She sighed as the reflections arose, and, looking towards the shore of the lake, her eye was attracted by a group of children of various ages, assembled to see a little ship, constructed by some village artist, perform its first voyage on the water. It was launched amid the shouts of tiny voices and the clapping of little hands, and shot bravely forth on its

SIR WALTER SCOTT

voyage with a favouring wind, which promised to carry it to the other side of the lake. Some of the bigger boys ran round to receive and secure it on the farther shore, trying their speed against each other as they sprang like young fawns along the shingly verge of the lake. The rest, for whom such a journey seemed too arduous, remained watching the motions of the fairy vessel from the spot where it had been launched. The sight of their sports pressed on the mind of the childless Lady of Avenel.

"Why are none of these prattlers mine?" she continued, pursuing the tenor of her melancholy reflections. "Their parents can scarce find them the coarsest food—and I, who could nurse them in plenty, I am doomed never to hear a child call me mother!"

The thought sunk on her heart with a bitterness which resembled envy, so deeply is the desire of offspring implanted in the female breast. She pressed her hands together as if she were wringing them in the extremity of her desolate feeling, as one whom Heaven had written childless. A large stag-hound of the greyhound species approached at this moment, and attracted perhaps by the gesture, licked her hands and pressed his large head against them. He obtained the desired caresses in return, but still the sad impression remained.

"Wolf," she said, as if the animal could have understood her complaints, "thou art a noble and beautiful animal; but, alas! the love and affection that I long to bestow, is of a quality higher than can fall to thy share, though I love thee much."

And, as if she were apologizing to Wolf for withholding from him any part of her regard, she caressed his proud head and crest, while, looking in her eyes, he seemed to ask her what she wanted, or what he could do to show his attachment. At this moment a shriek of distress was heard on the shore, from the playful group which had been lately so jovial. The Lady looked, and saw the cause with great agony.

The little ship, the object of the children's delighted attention, had stuck among some tufts of the plant which bears the water-lily, that marked a shoal in the lake about an arrow-flight from the shore. A hardy little boy, who had taken the lead in the race round the margin of the lake, did not hesitate a moment to strip off his *wylie-coat*, plunge into the water, and swim towards the object of their common solicitude. The first movement of the Lady was to call for help; but she observed that the boy swam strongly and fearlessly, and as she saw that one or two villagers, who were distant spectators of the incident, seemed to give themselves no uneasiness on his account, she supposed that he was accustomed to the exercise, and that there was no danger. But whether, in swimming, the boy had struck his breast against a sunken rock, or whether he was suddenly taken with cramp, or whether he had over-calculated his own strength, it so happened, that when he had disembarrassed the little plaything from the flags in which it was entangled, and sent it forward on its course, he had scarce swam a few yards in his way to the shore, than he raised himself suddenly from the water, and screamed aloud, clapping his hands at the same time with an expression of fear and pain.

The Lady of Avenel, instantly taking the alarm, called hastily to the attendants to get the boat ready. But this was an affair of some time. The only boat permitted to be used on the lake, was moored within the second cut which intersected the canal, and it was several minutes ere it could be unmoored and got under way. Meantime, the Lady of Avenel, with agonizing anxiety, saw that the efforts that the poor boy made to keep himself afloat, were now exchanged for a faint struggling, which would soon have been over, but for aid equally prompt and unhoped-for. Wolf, who, like some of that large species of greyhound, was a practised water-dog, had marked the object of her anxiety, and, quitting his mistress's side, had sought the nearest point from which he could with safety plunge into the lake. With the wonderful instinct which these noble animals have so often displayed in the like circumstances, he swam straight to the spot where his assistance was so much wanted, and seizing the child's under-dress in his mouth, he not only kept him afloat, but towed him towards the causeway. The boat having put off with a couple of men, met the dog half-way, and relieved him of his burden. They landed on the causeway, close by the gates of the castle, with their yet lifeless charge, and were there met by the Lady of Avenel, attended by one or two of her maidens, eagerly waiting to administer assistance to the sufferer.

He was borne into the castle, deposited upon a bed, and every mode of recovery resorted to, which the knowledge of the times, and the skill of Henry Warden, who professed some medical science, could dictate. For some time it was all in vain, and the Lady watched, with unspeakable earnestness, the pallid countenance of the beautiful child. He seemed about ten years old. His dress was of the meanest sort, but his long curled hair, and the noble cast of his features, partook not of that poverty of appearance. The proudest noble in Scotland might have been yet prouder could he have called that child his heir. While, with breathless anxiety, the Lady of Avenel gazed on his well-formed and expressive features, a slight shade of colour returned gradually to the cheek; suspended animation became restored by degrees, the child sighed deeply, opened his eyes, which to the human countenance produces the effect of light upon the natural landscape, stretched his arms towards the Lady, and muttered the word "Mother," that epithet, of all others, which is dearest to the female ear.

"God, madam," said the preacher, "has restored the child to your wishes; it must be yours so to bring him up, that he may not one day wish that he had perished in his innocence."

"It shall be my charge," said the Lady; and again throwing her arms around the boy, she overwhelmed him with kisses and caresses, so much was she agitated by the terror arising from the danger in which he had been just placed, and by joy at his unexpected deliverance.

"But you are not my mother," said the boy, recovering his recollection, and endeavouring, though faintly, to escape from the caresses of the Lady of Avenel; "you are not my mother,—alas! I have no mother— only I have dreamt that I had one."

"I will read the dream for you, my love," answered the Lady of Avenel; "and I will be myself your mother. Surely God has heard my wishes, and, in his own marvellous manner, hath sent me an object on which my affections may expand themselves." She looked towards Warden as she spoke. The preacher hesitated what he should reply to a burst of passionate feeling, which, perhaps, seemed to him more enthusiastic than the occasion demanded. In the meanwhile, the large stag-hound, Wolf, which, dripping wet as he was, had followed his mistress into the apartment, and had sat by the bedside, a patient and quiet spectator of all the means used for resuscitation of the being whom he had preserved, now became impatient of remaining any longer unnoticed, and began to whine and fawn upon the Lady with his great rough paws.

"Yes," she said, "good Wolf, and you shall be remembered also for your day's work; and I will think the more of you for having preserved the life of a creature so beautiful."

But Wolf was not quite satisfied with the share of attention which he thus attracted; he persisted in whining and pawing upon his mistress, his caresses rendered still more troublesome by his long shaggy hair being so much and thoroughly wetted, till she desired one of the domestics, with whom he was familiar, to call the animal out of the apartment. Wolf resisted every invitation to this purpose, until his mistress positively commanded him to be gone, in an angry tone; when, turning towards the bed on which the body still lay, half awake to sensation, half drowned in the meanders of fluctuating delirium, he uttered a deep and savage growl, curled up his nose and lips, showing his full range of white and sharpened teeth, which might have matched those of an actual wolf, and then, turning round, sullenly followed the domestic out of the apartment.

"It is singular," said the Lady, addressing Warden; "the animal is not only so good-natured to all, but so particularly fond of children. What can ail him at the little fellow whose life he has saved?"

"Dogs," replied the preacher, "are but too like the human race in their foibles, though their instinct be less erring than the reason of poor mortal man when relying upon his own unassisted powers. Jealousy, my good lady, is a passion not unknown to them, and they often evince it, not only with respect to the preferences which they see given by their masters to individuals of their own species, but even when their rivals are children. You have caressed that child much and eagerly, and the dog considers himself as a discarded favourite."

"It is a strange instinct," said the Lady; "and from the gravity with which you mention it, my reverend friend, I would almost say that you supposed this singular jealousy of my favourite Wolf, was not only well founded, but justifiable. But perhaps you speak in jest?"

"I seldom jest," answered the preacher; "life was not lent to us to be expended in that idle mirth which resembles the crackling of thorns under the pot. I would only have you derive, if it so please you, this lesson from what I have said, that the best of our feelings, when indulged to excess, may give pain to others. There is but one in which we may indulge to the utmost limit of vehemence of which our bosom is capable, secure that excess cannot exist in the greatest intensity to which it can be excited—I mean the love of our Maker."

"Surely," said the Lady of Avenel, "we are commanded by the same authority to love our neighbour?"

"Ay, madam," said Warden, "but our love to God is to be unbounded— we are to love him with our whole heart, our whole soul, and our whole strength. The love which the precept commands us to bear to our neighbour, has affixed to it a direct limit and qualification—we are to love our neighbour as ourself; as it is elsewhere explained by the great commandment, that we must do unto him as we would that he should do unto us. Here there is a limit, and a bound, even to the most praiseworthy of our affections, so far as they are turned upon sublunary and terrestrial objects. We are to render to our neighbour, whatever be his rank or degree, that corresponding portion of affection with which we could rationally expect we should ourselves be regarded by those standing in the same relation to us. Hence, neither husband nor wife, neither son nor daughter, neither friend nor relation, are lawfully to be made the objects of our idolatry. The Lord our God is a jealous God, and will not endure that we bestow on the creature that extremity of devotion which He who made us demands as his own share. I say to you, Lady, that even in the fairest, and purest, and most honourable feelings of our nature, there is that original taint of sin which ought to make us pause and hesitate, ere we indulge them to excess."

"I understand not this, reverend sir," said the Lady; "nor do I guess what I can have now said or done, to draw down on me an admonition which has something a taste of reproof."

"Lady," said Warden, "I crave your pardon, if I have urged aught beyond the limits of my duty. But consider, whether in the sacred promise to be not only a protectress, but a mother, to this poor child, your purpose may meet the wishes of the noble knight your husband. The fondness which you have lavished on the unfortunate, and, I own, most lovely child, has met something like a reproof in the bearing of your household dog.—Displease not your noble husband. Men, as well as animals, are jealous of the affections of those they love."

"This is too much, reverend sir," said the Lady of Avenel, greatly offended. "You have been long our guest, and have received from the Knight of Avenel and myself that honour and regard which your character and profession so justly demand. But I am yet to learn that we have at any time authorized your interference in our family arrangements, or placed you as a judge of our conduct towards each other. I pray this may be forborne in future."

"Lady," replied the preacher, with the boldness peculiar to the clergy of his persuasion at that time, "when you weary of my admonitions— when I see that my services are no longer acceptable to you, and the noble knight your husband, I shall know that my Master wills me no longer to abide here; and, praying for a continuance of his best blessings on your family I will then, were the season the depth of winter, and the hour midnight, walk out on yonder waste, and travel forth through these wild mountains, as lonely and unaided, though far more helpless, than when I first met your husband in the valley of Glendearg. But while I remain here, I will not see you err from the true path, no, not a hair's-breadth, without making the old man's voice and remonstrance heard."

"Nay, but," said the Lady, who both loved and respected the good man, though sometimes a little offended at what she conceived to be an exuberant degree of zeal, "we will not part this way, my good friend. Women are quick and hasty in their feelings; but, believe me, my wishes and my purposes towards this child are such as both my husband and you will approve of." The clergyman bowed, and retreated to his own apartment.

II

How steadfastly he fix'd his eyes on me—
His dark eyes shining through forgotten tears—
Then stretch'd his little arms, and call'd me mother!
What could I do? I took the bantling home—
I could not tell the imp he had no mother.

—Count Basil

When Warden had left the apartment, the Lady of Avenel gave way to the feelings of tenderness which the sight of the boy, his sudden danger, and his recent escape, had inspired; and no longer awed by the sternness, as she deemed it, of the preacher, heaped with caresses the lovely and interesting child. He was now, in some measure, recovered from the consequences of his accident, and received passively, though not without wonder, the tokens of kindness with which he was thus loaded. The face of the lady was strange to him, and her dress different and far more sumptuous than any he remembered. But the boy was naturally of an undaunted temper; and indeed children are generally acute physiognomists, and not only pleased by that which is beautiful in itself, but peculiarly quick in distinguishing and replying to the attentions of those who really love them. If they see a person in company, though a perfect stranger, who is by nature fond of children, the little imps seem to discover it by a sort of free-masonry, while the awkward attempts of those who make advances to them for the purpose of recommending themselves to the parents, usually fail in attracting their reciprocal attention. The little boy, therefore, appeared in some degree sensible of the lady's caresses, and it was with difficulty she withdrew herself from his pillow, to afford him leisure for necessary repose.

"To whom belongs our little rescued varlet?" was the first question which the Lady of Avenel put to her handmaiden Lilias, when they had retired to the hall.

"To an old woman in the hamlet," said Lilias, "who is even now come so far as the porter's lodge to inquire concerning his safety. Is it your pleasure that she be admitted?"

"Is it my pleasure?" said the Lady of Avenel, echoing the question with a strong accent of displeasure and surprise; "can you make any doubt of it? What woman but must pity the agony of the mother, whose heart is throbbing for the safety of a child so lovely!"

"Nay, but, madam," said Lilias, "this woman is too old to be the mother of the child; I rather think she must be his grandmother, or some more distant relation."

"Be she who she will, Lilias," replied the Lady, "she must have an aching heart while the safety of a creature so lovely is uncertain. Go instantly and bring her hither. Besides, I would willingly learn something concerning his birth."

Lilias left the hall, and presently afterwards returned, ushering in a tall female very poorly dressed, yet with more pretension to decency and cleanliness than was usually combined with such coarse garments. The Lady of Avenel knew her figure the instant she presented herself. It was the fashion of the family, that upon every Sabbath, and on two evenings in the week besides, Henry Warden preached or lectured in the chapel at the castle. The extension of the Protestant faith was, upon principle, as well as in good policy, a primary object with the Knight of Avenel. The inhabitants of the village were therefore invited to attend upon the instructions of Henry Warden, and many of them were speedily won to the doctrine which their master and protector approved. These sermons, homilies, and lectures, had made a great impression on the mind of the Abbot Eustace, or Eustatius, and were a sufficient spur to the severity and sharpness of his controversy with his old fellow-collegiate; and, ere Queen Mary was dethroned, and while the Catholics still had considerable authority in the Border provinces, he more than once threatened to levy his vassals, and assail and level with the earth that stronghold of heresy the Castle of Avenel. But notwithstanding the Abbot's impotent resentment, and notwithstanding also the disinclination of the country to favour the new religion, Henry Warden proceeded without remission in his labours, and made weekly converts from the faith of Rome to that of the reformed church. Amongst those who gave most earnest and constant attendance on his ministry, was the aged woman, whose form, tall, and otherwise too remarkable to be forgotten, the Lady had of late observed frequently as being conspicuous among the little audience. She had indeed more than once desired to know who that stately-looking woman was, whose appearance was so much above the poverty of her vestments. But the reply had always been, that she was an Englishwoman, who was tarrying for a season at the hamlet, and that no one knew more concerning her. She now asked her after her name and birth.

"Magdalen Graeme is my name," said the woman; "I come of the Graemes of Heathergill, in Nicol Forest,* a people of ancient blood."

"And what make you," continued the Lady, "so far distant from your home?"

"I have no home," said Magdalen Graeme, "it was burnt by your Border-riders—my husband and my son were slain—there is not a drop's blood left in the veins of any one which is of kin to mine."

"That is no uncommon fate in these wild times, and in this unsettled land," said the Lady; "the English hands have been as deeply dyed in our blood as ever those of Scotsmen have been in yours."

"You have right to say it, Lady," answered Magdalen Graeme; "for men tell of a time when this castle was not strong enough to save your father's life, or to afford your mother and her infant a place of refuge. And why ask ye me, then, wherefore I dwell not in mine own home, and with mine own people?"

"It was indeed an idle question," answered the Lady, "where misery so often makes wanderers; but wherefore take refuge in a hostile country?"

"My neighbours were Popish and mass-mongers," said the old woman; "it has pleased Heaven to give me a clearer sight of the gospel, and I have tarried here to enjoy the ministry of that worthy man Henry Warden, who, to the praise and comfort of many, teacheth the Evangel in truth and in sincerity."

"Are you poor?" again demanded the Lady of Avenel.

"You hear me ask alms of no one," answered the Englishwoman.

Here there was a pause. The manner of the woman was, if not disrespectful, at least much less than gracious; and she appeared to give no encouragement to farther communication. The Lady of Avenel renewed the conversation on a different topic.

"You have heard of the danger in which your boy has been placed?"

"I have, Lady, and how by an especial providence he was rescued from death. May Heaven make him thankful, and me!"

"What relation do you bear to him?"

"I am his grandmother, lady, if it so please you; the only relation he hath left upon earth to take charge of him."

---

* A district of Cumberland, lying close to the Scottish border.

"The burden of his maintenance must necessarily be grievous to you in your deserted situation?" pursued the Lady.

"I have complained of it to no one," said Magdalen Graeme, with the same unmoved, dry, and unconcerned tone of voice, in which she had answered all the former questions.

"If," said the Lady of Avenel, "your grandchild could be received into a noble family, would it not advantage both him and you?"

"Received into a noble family!" said the old woman, drawing herself up, and bending her brows until her forehead was wrinkled into a frown of unusual severity; "and for what purpose, I pray you?—to be my lady's page, or my lord's jackman, to eat broken victuals, and contend with other menials for the remnants of the master's meal? Would you have him to fan the flies from my lady's face while she sleeps, to carry her train while she walks, to hand her trencher when she feeds, to ride before her on horseback, to walk after her on foot, to sing when she lists, and to be silent when she bids?—a very weathercock, which, though furnished in appearance with wings and plumage, cannot soar into the air—cannot fly from the spot where it is perched, but receives all its impulse, and performs all its revolutions, obedient to the changeful breath of a vain woman? When the eagle of Helvellyn perches on the tower of Lanercost, and turns and changes his place to show how the wind sits, Roland Graeme shall be what you would make him."

The woman spoke with a rapidity and vehemence which seemed to have in it a touch of insanity; and a sudden sense of the danger to which the child must necessarily be exposed in the charge of such a keeper, increased the Lady's desire to keep him in the castle if possible.

"You mistake me, dame," she said, addressing the old woman in a soothing manner; "I do not wish your boy to be in attendance on myself, but upon the good knight my husband. Were he himself the son of a belted earl, he could not better be trained to arms, and all that befits a gentleman, than by the instructions and discipline of Sir Halbert Glendinning."

"Ay," answered the old woman, in the same style of bitter irony, "I know the wages of that service;—a curse when the corslet is not sufficiently brightened,—a blow when the girth is not tightly drawn,—to be beaten because the hounds are at fault,—to be reviled because the foray is unsuccessful,—to stain his hands for the master's bidding in the blood alike of beast and of man,—to be a butcher of harmless deer, a murderer and defacer of God's own image, not at his own pleasure, but at that of his lord,—to live a brawling ruffian, and a common stabber—exposed to heat, to cold, to want of food, to all the privations of an anchoret, not for the love of God, but for the service of Satan,—to die by the gibbet, or in some obscure skirmish,—to sleep out his brief life in carnal security, and to awake in the eternal fire, which is never quenched."

"Nay," said the Lady of Avenel, "but to such unhallowed course of life your grandson will not be here exposed. My husband is just and kind to those who live under his banner; and you yourself well know, that youth have here a strict as well as a good preceptor in the person of our chaplain."

The old woman appeared to pause.

"You have named," she said, "the only circumstance which can move me. I must soon onward, the vision has said it—I must not tarry in the same spot—I must on,—I must on, it is my weird.—Swear, then, that you will protect the boy as if he were your own, until I return hither and claim him, and I will consent for a space to part with him. But especially swear, he shall not lack the instruction of the godly man who hath placed the gospel-truth high above those idolatrous shavelings, the monks and friars."

"Be satisfied, dame," said the Lady of Avenel; "the boy shall have as much care as if he were born of my own blood. Will you see him now?"

"No," answered the old woman sternly; "to part is enough. I go forth on my own mission. I will not soften my heart by useless tears and wailings, as one that is not called to a duty."

"Will you not accept of something to aid you in your pilgrimage?" said the Lady of Avenel, putting into her hands two crowns of the sun. The old woman flung them down on the table.

"Am I of the race of Cain," she said, "proud Lady, that you offer me gold in exchange for my own flesh and blood?"

"I had no such meaning," said the Lady, gently; "nor am I the proud woman you term me. Alas! my own fortunes might have taught me humility, even had it not been born with me."

The old woman seemed somewhat to relax her tone of severity.

"You are of gentle blood," she said, "else we had not parleyed thus long together.—You are of gentle blood, and to such," she added, drawing up her tall form as she spoke, "pride is as graceful as is the plume upon the bonnet. But for these pieces of gold, lady, you must needs resume them. I need not money. I am well provided; and I may not care for myself, nor think how, or by whom, I shall be sustained. Farewell, and keep your word. Cause your gates to be opened, and your bridges to be lowered. I will set forward this very night. When I come again, I will demand from you a strict account, for I have left with you the jewel of my life! Sleep will visit me but in snatches, food will not refresh me, rest will not restore my strength, until I see Roland Graeme. Once more, farewell."

"Make your obeisance, dame," said Lilias to Magdalen Graeme, as she retired, "make your obeisance to her ladyship, and thank her for her goodness, as is but fitting and right."

The old woman turned short around on the officious waiting-maid. "Let her make her obeisance to me then, and I will return it. Why should I bend to her?—is it because her kirtle is of silk, and mine of blue lockeram?—Go to, my lady's waiting-woman. Know that the rank of the man rates that of the wife, and that she who marries a churl's son, were she a king's daughter, is but a peasant's bride."

Lilias was about to reply in great indignation, but her mistress imposed silence on her, and commanded that the old woman should be safely conducted to the mainland.

"Conduct her safe!" exclaimed the incensed waiting-woman, while Magdalen Graeme left the apartment; "I say, duck her in the loch, and then we will see whether she is witch or not, as every body in the village of Lochside will say and swear. I marvel your ladyship could bear so long with her insolence." But the commands of the Lady were obeyed, and the old dame, dismissed from the castle, was committed to her fortune. She kept her word, and did not long abide in that place, leaving the hamlet on the very night succeeding the interview, and wandering no one asked whither. The Lady of Avenel inquired under what circumstances she had appeared among them, but could only learn that she was believed to be the widow of some man of consequence among the Graemes who then inhabited the Debateable Land, a name given to a certain portion of territory which was the frequent subject of dispute betwixt Scotland and England—that she had suffered great wrong in some of the frequent forays by which that unfortunate district was wasted, and had been driven from her dwelling-place. She had arrived in the hamlet no one knew for what purpose, and was held by some to be a witch, by others a zealous Protestant, and by others again a Catholic devotee. Her language was mysterious, and her manners repulsive; and all that could be collected from her conversation seemed to imply that she was under the influence either of a spell or of a vow,—there was no saying which, since she talked as one who acted under a powerful and external agency.

Such were the particulars which the Lady's inquiries were able to collect concerning Magdalen Graeme, being far too meagre and contradictory to authorize any satisfactory deduction. In truth, the miseries of the time, and the various turns of fate incidental to a frontier country, were perpetually chasing from their habitations those who had not the means of defence or protection. These wanderers in the land were too often seen, to excite much attention or sympathy. They received the cold relief which was extorted by general feelings of humanity; a little excited in some breasts, and perhaps rather chilled in others, by the recollection that they who gave the charity to-day might themselves want it to-morrow. Magdalen Graeme, therefore, came and departed like a shadow from the neighbourhood of Avenel Castle.

The boy whom Providence, as she thought, had thus strangely placed under her care, was at once established a favourite with the Lady of the castle. How could it be otherwise? He became the object of those affectionate feelings, which, finding formerly no object on which to expand themselves, had increased the gloom of the castle, and imbittered the solitude of its mistress. To teach him reading and writing as far as her skill went, to attend to his childish comforts, to watch his boyish sports, became the Lady's favourite amusement. In her circumstances, where the ear only heard the lowing of the cattle from the distant hills, or the heavy step of the warder as he walked upon his post, or the half-envied laugh of her maiden as she turned her wheel, the appearance of the blooming and beautiful boy gave an interest which can hardly be conceived by those who live amid gayer and busier scenes. Young Roland was to the Lady of Avenel what the flower, which occupies the window of some solitary captive, is to the poor wight by whom it is nursed and cultivated,—something which at once excited and repaid her care; and in giving the boy her affection, she felt, as it were, grateful to him for releasing her from the state of dull apathy in which she had usually found herself during the absence of Sir Halbert Glendinning.

But even the charms of this blooming favourite were unable to chase the recurring apprehensions which arose from her husband's procrastinated return. Soon after Roland Graeme became a resident at the castle, a groom, despatched by Sir Halbert, brought tidings that business still delayed the Knight at the Court of Holyrood. The more distant period which the messenger had assigned for his master's arrival at length glided away, summer melted into autumn, and autumn was about to give place to winter, and yet he came not.

III

The waning harvest-moon shone broad and bright,
The warder's horn was heard at dead of night,
And while the portals-wide were flung,
With trampling hoofs the rocky pavement rung.

—LEYDEN

And you, too, would be a soldier, Roland?" said the Lady of Avenel to her young charge, while, seated on a stone chair at one end of the battlements, she saw the boy attempt, with a long stick, to mimic the motions of the warder, as he alternately shouldered, or ported, or sloped pike.

"Yes, Lady," said the boy,—for he was now familiar, and replied to her questions with readiness and alacrity,-"a soldier will I be; for there ne'er was gentleman but who belted him with the brand."

"Thou a gentleman!" said Lilias, who, as usual, was in attendance; "such a gentleman as I would make of a bean-cod with a rusty knife."

"Nay, chide him not, Lilias," said the Lady of Avenel, "for, beshrew me, but I think he comes of gentle blood—see how it musters in his face at your injurious reproof."

"Had I my will, madam," answered Lilias, "a good birchen wand should make his colour muster to better purpose still."

"On my word, Lilias," said the Lady, "one would think you had received harm from the poor boy—or is he so far on the frosty side of your favour because he enjoys the sunny side of mine?"

"Over heavens forbode, my Lady!" answered Lilias; "I have lived too long with gentles, I praise my stars for it, to fight with either follies or fantasies, whether they relate to beast, bird, or boy."

Lilias was a favourite in her own class, a spoiled domestic, and often accustomed to take more licence than her mistress was at all times willing to encourage. But what did not please the Lady of Avenel, she did not choose to hear, and thus it was on the present occasion. She resolved to look more close and sharply after the boy, who had hitherto been committed chiefly to the management of Lilias. He must, she thought, be born of gentle blood; it were shame to think otherwise of a form so noble, and features so fair;—the very wildness in which he occasionally indulged, his contempt of danger, and impatience of restraint, had in them something noble;—assuredly the child was born of high rank. Such was her conclusion, and she acted upon it accordingly. The domestics around her, less jealous, or less scrupulous than Lilias, acted as servants usually do, following the bias, and flattering, for their own purposes, the humour of the Lady; and the boy soon took on him those airs of superiority, which the sight of habitual deference seldom fails to inspire. It seemed, in truth, as if to command were his natural sphere, so easily did he use himself to exact and receive compliance with his humours. The chaplain, indeed, might have interposed to check the air of assumption which Roland Graeme so readily indulged, and most probably would have willingly rendered him that favour; but the necessity of adjusting with his brethren some disputed points of church discipline had withdrawn him for some time from the castle, and detained him in a distant part of the kingdom.

Matters stood thus in the castle of Avenel, when a winded bugle sent its shrill and prolonged notes from the shore of the lake, and was replied to cheerily by the signal of the warder. The Lady of Avenel knew the sounds of her husband, and rushed to the window of the apartment in which she was sitting. A band of about thirty spearmen, with a pennon displayed before them, winded along the indented shores of the lake, and approached the causeway. A single horseman rode at the head of the party, his bright arms catching a glance of the October sun as he moved steadily along. Even at that distance, the Lady recognized the lofty plume, bearing the mingled colours of her own liveries and those of Glendonwyne, blended with the holly-branch; and the firm seat and dignified demeanour of the rider, joined to the stately motion of the dark-brown steed, sufficiently announced Halbert Glendinning.

The Lady's first thought was that of rapturous joy at her husband's return—her second was connected with a fear which had sometimes intruded itself, that he might not altogether approve the peculiar distinction with which she had treated her orphan ward. In this fear there was implied a consciousness, that the favour she had shown him was excessive; for Halbert Glendinning was at least as gentle and indulgent, as he was firm and rational in the intercourse of his household; and to her in particular, his conduct had ever been most affectionately tender.

Yet she did fear, that, on the present occasion, her conduct might incur Sir Halbert's censure; and hastily resolving that she would not mention, the anecdote of the boy until the next day, she ordered him to be withdrawn from the apartment by Lilias.

"I will not go with Lilias, madam," answered the spoiled child, who had more than once carried his point by perseverance, and who, like his betters, delighted in the exercise of such authority,—"I will not go to Lilias's gousty room—I will stay and see that brave warrior who comes riding so gallantly along the drawbridge."

"You must not stay, Roland," said the Lady, more positively than she usually spoke to her little favourite.

"I will," reiterated the boy, who had already felt his consequence, and the probable chance of success.

"You *will*, Roland!" answered the Lady, "what manner of word is that? I tell you, you must go."

"*Will*," answered the forward boy, "is a word for a man, and *must* is no word for a lady."

"You are saucy, sirrah," said the Lady—"Lilias, take him with you instantly."

"I always thought," said Lilias, smiling, as she seized the reluctant boy by the arm, "that my young master must give place to my old one."

"And you, too, are malapert, mistress!" said the Lady; "hath the moon changed, that ye all of you thus forget yourselves?"

Lilias made no reply, but led off the boy, who, too proud to offer unavailing resistance, darted at his benefactress a glance, which intimated plainly, how willingly he would have defied her authority, had he possessed the power to make good his point.

The Lady of Avenel was vexed to find how much this trifling circumstance had discomposed her, at the moment when she ought naturally to have been entirely engrossed by her husband's return. But we do not recover composure by the mere feeling that agitation is mistimed. The glow of displeasure had not left the Lady's cheek, her ruffled deportment was not yet entirely composed, when her husband, unhelmeted, but still wearing the rest of his arms, entered the apartment. His appearance banished the thoughts of every thing else; she rushed to him, clasped his iron-sheathed frame in her arms, and kissed his martial and manly face with an affection which was at once evident and sincere. The warrior returned her embrace and her caress with the same fondness; for the time which had passed since their union had diminished its romantic ardour, perhaps, but it had rather increased its rational tenderness, and Sir Halbert Glendinning's long and frequent absences from his castle had prevented affection from degenerating by habit into indifference.

When the first eager greetings were paid and received, the Lady gazed fondly on her husband's face as she remarked, "You are altered, Halbert—you have ridden hard and far to-day, or you have been ill?"

"I have been well, Mary," answered the Knight, "passing well have I been; and a long ride is to me, thou well knowest, but a thing of constant custom. Those who are born noble may slumber out their lives within the walls of their castles and manor-houses; but he who hath achieved nobility by his own deeds must ever be in the saddle, to show that he merits his advancement."

While he spoke thus, the Lady gazed fondly on him, as if endeavouring to read his inmost soul; for the tone in which he spoke was that of melancholy depression.

Sir Halbert Glendinning was the same, yet a different person from what he had appeared in his early years. The fiery freedom of the aspiring youth had given place to the steady and stern composure of the approved soldier and skilful politician. There were deep traces of care on those noble features, over which each emotion used formerly to pass, like light clouds across a summer sky. That sky was now, not perhaps clouded, but still and grave, like that of the sober autumn evening. The forehead was higher and more bare than in early youth, and the locks which still clustered thick and dark on the warrior's head, were worn away at the temples, not by age, but by the constant pressure of the steel cap, or helmet. His beard, according to the fashion of the time, grew short and thick, and was turned into mustaches on the upper lip, and peaked at the extremity. The cheek, weather-beaten and embrowned, had lost the glow of youth, but showed the vigorous complexion of active and confirmed manhood. Halbert Glendinning was, in a word, a knight to ride at a king's right hand, to bear his banner in war, and to be his counsellor in time of peace; for his looks expressed the considerate firmness which can resolve wisely and dare boldly. Still, over these noble features, there now spread an air of dejection, of which, perhaps, the owner was not conscious, but which did not escape the observation of his anxious and affectionate partner.

"Something has happened, or is about to happen," said the Lady of Avenel; "this sadness sits not on your brow without cause—misfortune, national or particular, must needs be at hand."

"There is nothing new that I wot of," said Halbert Glendinning; "but there is little of evil which can befall a kingdom, that may not be apprehended in this unhappy and divided realm."

"Nay, then," said the Lady, "I see there hath really been some fatal work on foot. My Lord of Murray has not so long detained you at Holyrood, save that he wanted your help in some weighty purpose."

"I have not been at Holyrood, Mary," answered the Knight; "I have been several weeks abroad."

"Abroad! and sent me no word?" replied the Lady.

"What would the knowledge have availed, but to have rendered you unhappy, my love?" replied the Knight; "your thoughts would have converted the slightest breeze that curled your own lake, into a tempest raging in the German ocean."

"And have you then really crossed the sea?" said the Lady, to whom the very idea of an element which she had never seen conveyed notions of terror and of wonder,—"really left your own native land, and trodden distant shores, where the Scottish tongue is unheard and unknown?"

"Really, and really," said the Knight, taking her hand in affectionate playfulness, "I have done this marvellous deed—have rolled on the ocean for three days and three nights, with the deep green waves dashing by the side of my pillow, and but a thin plank to divide me from it."

"Indeed, my Halbert," said the Lady, "that was a tempting of Divine Providence. I never bade you unbuckle the sword from your side, or lay the lance from your hand—I never bade you sit still when your honour called you to rise and ride; but are not blade and spear dangers enough for one man's life, and why would you trust rough waves and raging seas?"

"We have in Germany, and in the Low Countries, as they are called," answered Glendinning, "men who are united with us in faith, and with whom it is fitting we should unite in alliance. To some of these I was despatched on business as important as it was secret. I went in safety, and I returned in security; there is more danger to a man's life betwixt this and Holyrood, than are in all the seas that wash the lowlands of Holland."

"And the country, my Halbert, and the people," said the Lady, "are they like our kindly Scots? or what bearing have they to strangers?"

"They are a people, Mary, strong in their wealth, which renders all other nations weak, and weak in those arts of war by which other nations are strong."

"I do not understand you," said the Lady.

"The Hollander and the Fleming, Mary, pour forth their spirit in trade, and not in war; their wealth purchases them the arms of foreign soldiers, by whose aid they defend it. They erect dikes on the sea-shore to protect the land which they have won, and they levy regiments of the stubborn Switzers and hardy Germans to protect the treasures which they have amassed. And thus they are strong in their weakness; for the very wealth which tempts their masters to despoil them, arms strangers in their behalf."

"The slothful hinds!" exclaimed Mary, thinking and feeling like a Scotswoman of the period; "have they hands, and fight not for the land which bore them? They should be notched off at the elbow!"

"Nay, that were but hard justice," answered her husband; "for their hands serve their country, though not in battle, like ours. Look at these barren hills, Mary, and at that deep winding vale by which the cattle are even now returning from their scanty browse. The hand of the industrious Fleming would cover these mountains with wood, and raise corn where we now see a starved and scanty sward of heath and ling. It grieves me, Mary, when I look on that land, and think what benefit it might receive from such men as I have lately seen—men who seek not the idle fame derived from dead ancestors, or the bloody renown won in modern broils, but tread along the land, as preservers and improvers, not as tyrants and destroyers."

"These amendments would here be but a vain fancy, my Halbert," answered the Lady of Avenel; "the trees would be burned by the English foemen, ere they ceased to be shrubs, and the grain that you raised would be gathered in by the first neighbour that possessed more riders than follow your train. Why should you repine at this? The fate that made you Scotsman by birth, gave you head, and heart, and hand, to uphold the name as it must needs be upheld."

"It gave *me* no name to uphold," said Halbert, pacing the floor slowly; "my arm has been foremost in every strife—my voice has been heard in every council, nor have the wisest rebuked me. The crafty Lethington, the deep and dark Morton, have held secret council with me, and Grange and Lindsay have owned, that in the field I did the devoir of a gallant knight—but let the emergence be passed when they need my head and hand, and they only know me as son of the obscure portioner of Glendearg."

This was a theme which the Lady always dreaded; for the rank conferred on her husband, the favour in which he was held by the powerful Earl of Murray, and the high talents by which he vindicated his right to that rank and that favour, were qualities which rather increased than diminished the envy which was harboured against Sir Halbert Glendinning among a proud aristocracy, as a person originally of inferior and obscure birth, who had risen to his present eminence solely by his personal merit. The natural firmness of his mind did not enable him to despise the ideal advantages of a higher pedigree, which were held in such universal esteem by all with whom he conversed; and so open are the noblest minds to jealous inconsistencies, that there were moments in which he felt mortified that his lady should possess those advantages of birth and high descent which he himself did not enjoy, and regretted that his importance as the proprietor of Avenel was qualified by his possessing it only as the husband of the heiress. He was not so unjust as to permit any unworthy feelings to retain permanent possession of his mind, but yet they recurred from time to time, and did not escape his lady's anxious observation.

"Had we been blessed with children," she was wont on such occasions to say to herself, "had our blood been united in a son who might have joined my advantages of descent with my husband's personal worth, these painful and irksome reflections had not disturbed our union even for a moment. But the existence of such an heir, in whom our affections, as well as our pretensions, might have centred, has been denied to us."

With such mutual feelings, it cannot be wondered that it gave the Lady pain to hear her husband verging towards this topic of mutual discontent. On the present, as on other similar occasions, she endeavoured to divert the knight's thoughts from this painful channel.

"How can you," she said, "suffer yourself to dwell upon things which profit nothing? Have you indeed no name to uphold? You, the good and the brave, the wise in council, and the strong in battle, have you not to support the reputation your own deeds have won, a reputation more honourable than mere ancestry can supply? Good men love and honour you, the wicked fear, and the turbulent obey you; and is it not necessary you should exert yourself to ensure the endurance of that love, that honour, and wholesome fear, and that necessary obedience?"

As she thus spoke, the eye of her husband caught from hers courage and comfort, and it lightened as he took her hand and replied, "It is most true, my Mary, and I deserve thy rebuke, who forget what I am, in repining because I am not what I cannot be. I am now what the most famed ancestors of those I envy were, the mean man raised into eminence by his own exertions; and sure it is a boast as honourable to have those capacities which are necessary to the foundation of a family, as to be descended from one who possessed them some centuries before. The Hay of Loncarty, who bequeathed his bloody yoke to his lineage,— the 'dark gray man,' who first founded the house of Douglas, had yet less of ancestry to boast than I have. For thou knowest, Mary, that my name derives itself from a line of ancient warriors, although my immediate forefathers preferred the humble station in which thou didst first find them; and war and counsel are not less proper to the house of Glendonwyne, even, in its most remote descendants, than to the proudest of their baronage."*

He strode across the hall as he spoke; and the Lady smiled internally to observe how much his mind dwelt upon the prerogatives of birth, and endeavoured to establish his claims, however remote, to a share in them, at the very moment when he affected to hold them in contempt. It will easily be guessed, however, that she permitted no symptom to escape her that could show she was sensible of the weakness of her husband, a perspicacity which perhaps his proud spirit could not very easily have brooked.

As he returned from the extremity of the hall, to which he had stalked while in the act of vindicating the title of the house of Glendonwyne in its most remote branches to the full privileges of aristocracy, "Where," he said, "is Wolf? I have not seen him since my return, and he was usually the first to welcome my home-coming."

---

* This was a house of ancient descent and superior consequence, including persons who fought at Bannockburn and Otterburn, and closely connected by alliance and friendship with the great Earls of Douglas. The Knight in this story argues as most Scotsmen would do in his situation, for all of the same clan are popularly considered as descended from the same stock, and as having a right to the ancestral honor of the chief branch. This opinion, though sometimes ideal, is so strong even at this day of innovation, that it may be observed as a national difference between my countrymen and the English. If you ask an Englishman of good birth, whether a person of the same name be connected with him, he answers (if *in dubio.*) "No—he is a mere namesake." Ask a similar question of a Scot, (I mean a Scotsman,) he replies—"He is one of our clan; I daresay there is a relationship, though I do not know how distant." The Englishman thinks of discountenancing a species of rivalry in society; the Scotsman's answer is grounded on the ancient idea of strengthening the clan.

"Wolf," said the Lady, with a slight degree of embarrassment, for which perhaps, she would have found it difficult to assign any reason even to herself, "Wolf is chained up for the present. He hath been surly to my page."

"Wolf chained up—and Wolf surly to your page!" answered Sir Halbert Glendinning; "Wolf never was surly to any one; and the chain will either break his spirit or render him savage—So ho, there—set Wolf free directly."

He was obeyed; and the huge dog rushed into the hall, disturbing, by his unwieldy and boisterous gambols, the whole economy of reels, rocks, and distaffs, with which the maidens of the household were employed when the arrival of their lord was a signal to them to withdraw, and extracting from Lilias, who was summoned to put them again in order, the natural observation, "That the Laird's pet was as troublesome as the lady's page."

"And who is this page, Mary?" said the Knight, his attention again called to the subject by the observation of the waiting-woman,—"Who is this page, whom every one seems to weigh in the balance with my old friend and favourite, Wolf?—When did you aspire to the dignity of keeping a page, or who is the boy?"

"I trust, my Halbert," said the Lady, not without a blush, "you will not think your wife entitled to less attendance than other ladies of her quality?"

"Nay, Dame Mary," answered the Knight, "it is enough you desire such an attendant.—Yet I have never loved to nurse such useless menials—a lady's page—it may well suit the proud English dames to have a slender youth to bear their trains from bower to hall, fan them when they slumber, and touch the lute for them when they please to listen; but our Scottish matrons were wont to be above such vanities, and our Scottish youth ought to be bred to the spear and the stirrup."

"Nay, but, my husband," said the Lady, "I did but jest when I called this boy my page; he is in sooth a little orphan whom we saved from perishing in the lake, and whom I have since kept in the castle out of charity.—Lilias, bring little Roland hither."

Roland entered accordingly, and, flying to the Lady's side, took hold of the plaits of her gown, and then turned round, and gazed with an attention not unmingled with fear, upon the stately form of the Knight.—"Roland," said the Lady, "go kiss the hand of the noble Knight, and ask him to be thy protector."—But Roland obeyed not, and, keeping his station, continued to gaze fixedly and timidly on Sir Halbert Glendinning.—"Go to the Knight, boy," said the Lady; "what dost thou fear, child? Go, kiss Sir Halbert's hand."

"I will kiss no hand save yours, Lady," answered the boy.

"Nay, but do as you are commanded, child," replied the Lady.—"He is dashed by your presence," she said, apologizing to her husband; "but is he not a handsome boy?"

"And so is Wolf," said Sir Halbert, as he patted his huge four-footed favourite, "a handsome dog; but he has this double advantage over your new favourite, that he does what he is commanded, and hears not when he is praised."

"Nay, now you are displeased with me," replied the Lady; "and yet why should you be so? There is nothing wrong in relieving the distressed orphan, or in loving that which is in itself lovely and deserving of affection. But you have seen Mr. Warden at Edinburgh, and he has set you against the poor boy."

"My dear Mary," answered her husband, "Mr. Warden better knows his place than to presume to interfere either in your affairs or mine. I neither blame your relieving this boy, nor your kindness for him. But, I think, considering his birth and prospects, you ought not to treat him with injudicious fondness, which can only end in rendering him unfit for the humble situation to which Heaven has designed him."

"Nay, but, my Halbert, do but look at the boy," said the Lady, "and see whether he has not the air of being intended by Heaven for something nobler than a mere peasant. May he not be designed, as others have been, to rise out of a humble situation into honour and eminence?"

Thus far had she proceeded, when the consciousness that she was treading upon delicate ground at once occurred to her, and induced her to take the most natural, but the worst of all courses in such occasions, whether in conversation or in an actual bog, namely, that of stopping suddenly short in the illustration which she had commenced. Her brow crimsoned, and that of Sir Halbert Glendinning was slightly overcast. But it was only for an instant; for he was incapable of mistaking his lady's meaning, or supposing that she meant intentional disrespect to him.

"Be it as you please, my love," he replied; "I owe you too much to contradict you in aught which may render your solitary mode of life more endurable. Make of this youth what you will, and you have my full authority for doing so. But remember he is your charge, not mine—

remember he hath limbs to do man's service, a soul and a tongue to worship God; breed him, therefore, to be true to his country and to Heaven; and for the rest, dispose of him as you list—it is, and shall rest, your own matter."

This conversation decided the fate of Roland Graeme, who from thence-forward was little noticed by the master of the mansion of Avenel, but indulged and favoured by its mistress.

This situation led to many important consequences, and, in truth, tended to bring forth the character of the youth in all its broad lights and deep shadows. As the Knight himself seemed tacitly to disclaim alike interest and control over the immediate favourite of his lady, young Roland was, by circumstances, exempted from the strict discipline to which, as the retainer of a Scottish man of rank, he would otherwise have been subjected, according to all the rigour of the age. But the steward, or master of the household—such was the proud title assumed by the head domestic of each petty baron—deemed it not advisable to interfere with the favourite of the Lady, and especially since she had brought the estate into the present family. Master Jasper Wingate was a man experienced, as he often boasted, in the ways of great families, and knew how to keep the steerage even when the wind and tide chanced to be in contradiction.

This prudent personage winked at much, and avoided giving opportunity for farther offence, by requesting little of Roland Graeme beyond the degree of attention which he was himself disposed to pay; rightly conjecturing, that however lowly the place which the youth might hold in the favour of the Knight of Avenel, still to make an evil report of him would make an enemy of the Lady, without securing the favour of her husband. With these prudential considerations, and doubtless not without an eye to his own ease and convenience, he taught the boy as much, and only as much, as he chose to learn, readily admitting whatever apology it pleased his pupil to allege in excuse for idleness or negligence. As the other persons in the castle, to whom such tasks were delegated, readily imitated the prudential conduct of the major-domo, there was little control used towards Roland Graeme, who, of course, learned no more than what a very active mind, and a total impatience of absolute idleness led him to acquire upon his own account, and by dint of his own exertions. The latter were especially earnest, when the Lady herself condescended to be his tutress, or to examine his progress.

It followed also from his quality as my Lady's favourite, that Roland was viewed with no peculiar good-will by the followers of the Knight, many of whom, of the same age, and apparently similar origin, with the fortunate page, were subjected to severe observance of the ancient and rigorous discipline of a feudal retainer. To these, Roland Graeme was of course an object of envy, and, in consequence, of dislike and detraction; but the youth possessed qualities which it was impossible to depreciate. Pride, and a sense of early ambition, did for him what severity and constant instruction did for others. In truth, the youthful Roland displayed that early flexibility both of body and mind, which renders exercise, either mental or bodily, rather matter of sport than of study; and it seemed as if he acquired accidentally, and by starts, those accomplishments, which earnest and constant instruction, enforced by frequent reproof and occasional chastisement, had taught to others. Such military exercises, such lessons of the period, as he found it agreeable or convenient to apply to, he learned so perfectly, as to confound those who were ignorant how often the want of constant application is compensated by vivacity of talent and ardent enthusiasm. The lads, therefore, who were more regularly trained to arms, to horsemanship, and to other necessary exercises of the period, while they envied Roland Graeme the indulgence or negligence with which he seemed to be treated, had little reason to boast of their own superior acquirements; a few hours, with the powerful exertion of a most energetic will, seemed to do for him more than the regular instruction of weeks could accomplish for others.

Under these advantages, if, indeed, they were to be termed such, the character of young Roland began to develope itself. It was bold, peremptory, decisive, and overbearing; generous, if neither withstood nor contradicted; vehement and passionate, if censured or opposed. He seemed to consider himself as attached to no one, and responsible to no one, except his mistress, and even over her mind he had gradually acquired that species of ascendancy which indulgence is so apt to occasion. And although the immediate followers and dependents of Sir Halbert Glendinning saw his ascendancy with jealousy, and often took occasion to mortify his vanity, there wanted not those who were willing to acquire the favour of the Lady of Avenel by humouring and taking part with the youth whom she protected; for although a favourite, as the poet assures us, has no friend, he seldom fails to have both followers and flatterers.

The partisans of Roland Graeme were chiefly to be found amongst the inhabitants of the little hamlet on the shore of the lake. These villagers, who were sometimes tempted to compare their own situation with that of the immediate and constant followers of the Knight, who attended him on his frequent journeys to Edinburgh and elsewhere, delighted in considering and representing themselves as more properly the subjects of the Lady of Avenel than of her husband. It is true, her wisdom and affection on all occasions discountenanced the distinction which was here implied; but the villagers persisted in thinking it must be agreeable to her to enjoy their peculiar and undivided homage, or at least in acting as if they thought so; and one chief mode by which they evinced their sentiments, was by the respect they paid to young Roland Graeme, the favourite attendant of the descendant of their ancient lords. This was a mode of flattery too pleasing to encounter rebuke or censure; and the opportunity which it afforded the youth to form, as it were, a party of his own within the limits of the ancient barony of Avenel, added not a little to the audacity and decisive tone of a character, which was by nature bold, impetuous, and incontrollable.

Of the two members of the household who had manifested an early jealousy of Roland Graeme, the prejudices of Wolf were easily overcome; and in process of time the noble dog slept with Bran, Luath, and the celebrated hounds of ancient days. But Mr. Warden, the chaplain, lived, and retained his dislike to the youth. That good man, single-minded and benevolent as he really was, entertained rather more than a reasonable idea of the respect due to him as a minister, and exacted from the inhabitants of the castle more deference than the haughty young page, proud of his mistress's favour, and petulant from youth and situation, was at all times willing to pay. His bold and free demeanour, his attachment to rich dress and decoration, his inaptitude to receive instruction, and his hardening himself against rebuke, were circumstances which induced the good old man, with more haste than charity, to set the forward page down as a vessel of wrath, and to presage that the youth nursed that pride and haughtiness of spirit which goes before ruin and destruction. On the other hand, Roland evinced at times a marked dislike, and even something like contempt, of the chaplain. Most of the attendants and followers of Sir Halbert Glendinning entertained the same charitable thoughts as the reverend Mr. Warden; but while Roland was favoured by their lady, and endured by their lord, they saw no policy in making their opinions public.

Roland Graeme was sufficiently sensible of the unpleasant situation in which he stood; but in the haughtiness of his heart he retorted upon the other domestics the distant, cold, and sarcastic manner in which they treated him, assumed an air of superiority which compelled the most obstinate to obedience, and had the satisfaction at least to be dreaded, if he was heartily hated.

The chaplain's marked dislike had the effect of recommending him to the attention of Sir Halbert's brother, Edward, who now, under the conventual appellation of Father Ambrose, continued to be one of the few monks who, with the Abbot Eustatius, had, notwithstanding the nearly total downfall of their faith under the regency of Murray, been still permitted to linger in the cloisters at Kennaquhair. Respect to Sir Halbert had prevented their being altogether driven out of the Abbey, though their order was now in a great measure suppressed, and they were interdicted the public exercise of their ritual, and only allowed for their support a small pension out of their once splendid revenues. Father Ambrose, thus situated, was an occasional, though very rare visitant, at the Castle of Avenel, and was at such times observed to pay particular attention to Roland Graeme, who seemed to return it with more depth of feeling than consisted with his usual habits.

Thus situated, years glided on, during which the Knight of Avenel continued to act a frequent and important part in the convulsions of his distracted country; while young Graeme anticipated, both in wishes and personal accomplishments, the age which should enable him to emerge from the obscurity of his present situation.

IV

Amid their cups that freely flow'd,
Their revelry and mirth,
A youthful lord tax'd Valentine
With base and doubtful birth.

—Valentine and Orson

When Roland Graeme was a youth about seventeen years of age, he chanced one summer morning to descend to the mew in which Sir Halbert Glendinning kept his hawks, in order to superintend the training of an eyas, or young hawk, which he himself, at the imminent risk of neck and limbs, had taken from the celebrated eyry in the neighborhood, called Gledscraig. As he was by no means satisfied with the attention which had been bestowed on his favourite bird, he was not slack in testifying his displeasure to the falconer's lad, whose duty it was to have attended upon it.

"What, ho! sir knave," exclaimed Roland, "is it thus you feed the eyas with unwashed meat, as if you were gorging the foul brancher of a worthless hoodie-crow? by the mass, and thou hast neglected its castings also for these two days! Think'st thou I ventured my neck to bring the bird down from the crag, that thou shouldst spoil him by thy neglect?" And to add force to his remonstrances, he conferred a cuff or two on the negligent attendant of the hawks, who, shouting rather louder than was necessary under all the circumstances, brought the master falconer to his assistance.

Adam Woodcock, the falconer of Avenel, was an Englishman by birth, but so long in the service of Glendinning, that he had lost much of his notional attachment in that which he had formed to his master. He was a favourite in his department, jealous and conceited of his skill, as masters of the game usually are; for the rest of his character he was a jester and a parcel poet, (qualities which by no means abated his natural conceit,) a jolly fellow, who, though a sound Protestant, loved a flagon of ale better than a long sermon, a stout man of his hands when need required, true to his master, and a little presuming on his interest with him.

Adam Woodcock, such as we have described him, by no means relished the freedom used by young Graeme, in chastising his assistant.

"Hey, hey, my Lady's page," said he, stepping between his own boy and Roland, "fair and softly, an it like your gilt jacket—hands off is fair play—if my boy has done amiss, I can beat him myself, and then you may keep your hands soft."

"I will beat him and thee too," answered Roland, without hesitation, "an you look not better after your business. See how the bird is cast away between you. I found the careless lurdane feeding him with unwashed flesh, and she an eyas."*

"Go to," said the falconer, "thou art but an eyas thyself, child Roland.—What knowest thou of feeding? I say that the eyas should have her meat unwashed, until she becomes a brancher—'twere the ready way to give her the frounce, to wash her meat sooner, and so knows every one who knows a gled from a falcon."

"It is thine own laziness, thou false English blood, that dost nothing but drink and sleep," retorted the page, "and leaves that lither lad to do the work, which he minds as little as thou."

"And am I so idle then," said the falconer, "that have three cast of hawks to look after, at perch and mew, and to fly them in the field to boot?—and is my Lady's page so busy a man that he must take me up short?—and am I of false English blood?—I marvel what blood thou art—neither Englander nor Scot—fish nor flesh—a bastard from the Debateable Land, without either kith, kin, or ally!—Marry, out upon thee, foul kite, that would fain be a tercel gentle!"

The reply to this sarcasm was a box on the ear, so well applied, that it overthrew the falconer into the cistern in which water was kept for the benefit of the hawks. Up started Adam Woodcock, his wrath no way appeased by the cold immersion, and seizing on a truncheon which stood by, would have soon requited the injury he had received, had not Roland laid his hand on his poniard, and sworn by all that was sacred, that if he offered a stroke towards him, he would sheath the blade in his bowels. The noise was now so great, that more than one of the household came in, and amongst others the major-domo, a grave personage, already mentioned, whose gold chain and white wand intimated his authority. At the appearance of this dignitary, the strife was for the present appeased. He embraced, however, so favourable an opportunity, to read Roland Graeme a shrewd lecture on the impropriety

---

* There is a difference amongst authorities how long the nestling hawk should be fed with flesh which has previously been washed.

of his deportment to his fellow-menials, and to assure him, that, should he communicate this fray to his master, (who, though now on one of his frequent expeditions, was speedily expected to return,) which but for respect to his Lady he would most certainly do, the residence of the culprit in the Castle of Avenel would be but of brief duration. "But, however," added the prudent master of the household, "I will report the matter first to my Lady."

"Very just, very right, Master Wingate," exclaimed several voices together; "my Lady will consider if daggers, are to be drawn on us for every idle word, and whether we are to live in a well-ordered household, where there is the fear of God, or amidst drawn dirks and sharp knives."

The object of this general resentment darted an angry glance around him, and suppressing with difficulty the desire which urged him to reply in furious or in contemptuous language, returned his dagger into his scabbard, looked disdainfully around upon the assembled menials, turned short upon his heel, and pushing aside those who stood betwixt him and the door, left the apartment.

"This will be no tree for my nest," said the falconer, "if this cock-sparrow is to crow over us as he seems to do."

"He struck me with his switch yesterday," said one of the grooms, "because the tail of his worship's gelding was not trimmed altogether so as suited his humour."

"And I promise you," said the laundress, "my young master will stick nothing to call an honest woman slut and quean, if there be but a speck of soot upon his band-collar."

"If Master Wingate do not his errand to my Lady," was the general result, "there will be no tarrying in the same house with Roland Graeme."

The master of the household heard them all for some time, and then, motioning for universal silence, he addressed them with all the dignity of Malvolio himself.—"My masters,—not forgetting you, my mistresses,—do not think the worse of me that I proceed with as much care as haste in this matter. Our master is a gallant knight, and will have his sway at home and abroad, in wood and field, in hall and bower, as the saying is. Our Lady, my benison upon her, is also a noble person of long descent, and rightful heir of this place and barony, and she also loves her will; as for that matter, show me the woman who doth not. Now, she hath favoured, doth favour, and will favour, this jack-an-ape,— for what good part about him I know not, save that as one noble lady will love a messan dog, and another a screaming popinjay, and a third a

Barbary ape, so doth it please our noble dame to set her affections upon this stray elf of a page, for nought that I can think of, save that she— was the cause of his being saved (the more's the pity) from drowning." And here Master Wingate made a pause.

"I would have been his caution for a gray groat against salt water or fresh," said Roland's adversary, the falconer; "marry, if he crack not a rope for stabbing or for snatching, I will be content never to hood hawk again."

"Peace, Adam Woodcock," said Wingate, waving his hand; "I prithee, peace man—Now, my Lady liking this springald, as aforesaid, differs therein from my Lord, who loves never a bone in his skin. Now, is it for me to stir up strife betwixt them, and put as'twere my finger betwixt the bark and the tree, on account of a pragmatical youngster, whom, nevertheless, I would willingly see whipped forth of the barony? Have patience, and this boil will break without our meddling. I have been in service since I wore a beard on my chin, till now that that beard is turned gray, and I have seldom known any one better themselves, even by taking the lady's part against the lord's; but never one who did not dirk himself, if he took the lord's against the lady's."

"And so," said Lilias, "we are to be crowed over, every one of us, men and women, cock and hen, by this little upstart?—I will try titles with him first, I promise you.—I fancy, Master Wingate, for as wise as you look, you will be pleased to tell what you have seen to-day, if my lady commands you?"

"To speak the truth when my lady commands me," answered the prudential major-domo, "is in some measure my duty, Mistress Lilias; always providing for and excepting those cases in which it cannot be spoken without breeding mischief and inconvenience to myself or my fellow-servants; for the tongue of a tale-bearer breaketh bones as well as Jeddart-staff."*

"But this imp of Satan is none of your friends or fellow-servants," said Lilias; "and I trust you mean not to stand up for him against the whole family besides?"

"Credit me, Mrs. Lilias," replied the senior, "should I see the time fitting, I would, with right good-will give him a lick with the rough side of my tongue."

---

* A species of battle-axe, so called as being in especial use in that ancient burgh, whose armorial bearing still represent an armed horseman brandishing such a weapon.

SIR WALTER SCOTT

"Enough said, Master Wingate," answered Lilias; "then trust me his song shall soon be laid. If my mistress does not ask me what is the matter below stairs before she be ten minutes of time older, she is no born woman, and my name is not Lilias Bradbourne."

In pursuance of her plan, Mistress Lilias failed not to present herself before her mistress with all the exterior of one who is possessed of an important secret,—that is, she had the corners of her mouth turned down, her eyes raised up, her lips pressed as fast together as if they had been sewed up, to prevent her babbling, and an air of prim mystical importance diffused over her whole person and demeanour, which seemed to intimate, "I know something which I am resolved not to tell you!"

Lilias had rightly read her mistress's temper, who, wise and good as she was, was yet a daughter of grandame Eve, and could not witness this mysterious bearing on the part of her waiting-woman without longing to ascertain the secret cause. For a space, Mrs. Lilias was obdurate to all inquiries, sighed, turned her eyes up higher yet to heaven, hoped for the best, but had nothing particular to communicate. All this, as was most natural and proper, only stimulated the Lady's curiosity; neither was her importunity to be parried with,—"Thank God, I am no makebate—no tale-bearer,—thank God, I never envied any one's favour, or was anxious to propale their misdemeanour-only, thank God, there has been no bloodshed and murder in the house—that is all."

"Bloodshed and murder!" exclaimed the Lady, "what does the quean mean?—if you speak not plain out, you shall have something you will scarce be thankful for."

"Nay, my Lady," answered Lilias, eager to disburden her mind, or, in, Chaucer's phrase, to "unbuckle her mail," "if you bid me speak out the truth, you must not be moved with what might displease you—Roland Graeme has dirked Adam Woodstock—that is all."

"Good Heaven!" said the Lady, turning pale as ashes, "is the man slain?"

"No, madam," replied Lilias, "but slain he would have been, if there had not been ready help; but may be, it is your Ladyship's pleasure that this young esquire shall poniard the servants, as well as switch and baton them."

"Go to, minion," said the Lady, "you are saucy-tell the master of the household to attend me instantly."

Lilias hastened to seek out Mr. Wingate, and hurry him to his lady's presence, speaking as a word in season to him on the way, "I have set the stone a-trowling, look that you do not let it stand still."

The steward, too prudential a person to commit himself otherwise, answered by a sly look and a nod of intelligence, and presently after stood in the presence of the Lady of Avenel, with a look of great respect for his lady, partly real, partly affected, and an air of great sagacity, which inferred no ordinary conceit of himself.

"How is this, Wingate," said the Lady, "and what rule do you keep in the castle, that the domestics of Sir Halbert Glendinning draw the dagger on each other, as in a cavern of thieves and murderers?—is the wounded man much hurt? and what—what hath become of the unhappy boy?"

"There is no one wounded as yet, madam," replied he of the golden chain; "it passes my poor skill to say how many may be wounded before Pasche,* if some rule be not taken with this youth—not but the youth is a fair youth," he added, correcting himself, "and able at his exercise; but somewhat too ready with the ends of his fingers, the butt of his riding-switch, and the point of his dagger."

"And whose fault is that," said the Lady, "but yours, who should have taught him better discipline, than to brawl or to draw his dagger."

"If it please your Ladyship so to impose the blame on me," answered the steward, "it is my part, doubtless, to bear it—only I submit to your consideration, that unless I nailed his weapon to the scabbard, I could no more keep it still, than I could fix quicksilver, which defied even the skill of Raymond Lullius."

"Tell me not of Raymond Lullius," said the Lady, losing patience, "but send me the chaplain hither. You grow all of you too wise for me, during your lord's long and repeated absences. I would to God his affairs would permit him to remain at home and rule his own household, for it passes my wit and skill!"

"God forbid, my Lady!" said the old domestic, "that you should sincerely think what you are now pleased to say: your old servants might well hope, that after so many years' duty, you would do their service more justice than to distrust their gray hairs, because they cannot rule the peevish humour of a green head, which the owner carries, it may be, a brace of inches higher than becomes him."

---

* Easter.

"Leave me," said the Lady; "Sir Halbert's return must now be expected daily, and he will look into these matters himself—leave me, I say, Wingate, without saying more of it. I know you are honest, and I believe the boy is petulant; and yet I think it is my favour which hath set all of you against him."

The steward bowed and retired, after having been silenced in a second attempt to explain the motives on which he acted.

The chaplain arrived; but neither from him did the Lady receive much comfort. On the contrary, she found him disposed, in plain terms, to lay to the door of her indulgence all the disturbances which the fiery temper of Roland Graeme had already occasioned, or might hereafter occasion, in the family. "I would," he said, "honoured Lady, that you had deigned to be ruled by me in the outset of this matter, sith it is easy to stem evil in the fountain, but hard to struggle against it in the stream. You, honoured madam, (a word which I do not use according to the vain forms of this world, but because I have ever loved and honoured you as an honourable and elect lady,)—you, I say, madam, have been pleased, contrary to my poor but earnest counsel, to raise this boy from his station, into one approaching to your own."

"What mean you, reverend sir?" said the Lady; "I have made this youth a page—is there aught in my doing so that does not become my character and quality?"

"I dispute not, madam," said the pertinacious preacher, "your benevolent purpose in taking charge of this youth, or your title to give him this idle character of page, if such was your pleasure; though what the education of a boy in the train of a female can tend to, save to ingraft foppery and effeminacy on conceit and arrogance, it passes my knowledge to discover. But I blame you more directly for having taken little care to guard him against the perils of his condition, or to tame and humble a spirit naturally haughty, overbearing, and impatient. You have brought into your bower a lion's cub; delighted with the beauty of his fur, and the grace of his gambols, you have bound him with no fetters befitting the fierceness of his disposition. You have let him grow up as unawed as if he had been still a tenant of the forest, and now you are surprised, and call out for assistance, when he begins to ramp, rend, and tear, according to his proper nature."

"Mr. Warden," said the Lady, considerably offended, "you are my husband's ancient friend, and I believe your love sincere to him and to his household. Yet let me say, that when I asked you for counsel, I expected not this asperity of rebuke. If I have done wrong in loving this poor orphan lad more than others of his class, I scarce think the error merited such severe censure; and if stricter discipline were required to keep his fiery temper in order, it ought, I think, to be considered, that I am a woman, and that if I have erred in this matter, it becomes a friend's part rather to aid than to rebuke me. I would these evils were taken order with before my lord's return. He loves not domestic discord or domestic brawls; and I would not willingly that he thought such could arise from one whom I favoured—What do you counsel me to do?"

"Dismiss this youth from your service, madam," replied the preacher.

"You cannot bid me do so," said the Lady; "you cannot, as a Christian and a man of humanity, bid me turn away an unprotected creature against whom my favour, my injudicious favour if you will, has reared up so many enemies."

"It is not necessary you should altogether abandon him, though you dismiss him to another service, or to a calling better suiting his station and character," said the preacher; "elsewhere he maybe an useful and profitable member of the commonweal—here he is but a makebate, and a stumbling-block of offence. The youth has snatches of sense and of intelligence, though he lacks industry. I will myself give him letters commendatory to Olearius Schinderhausen, a learned professor at the famous university of Leyden, where they lack an under-janitor—where, besides gratis instruction, if God give him the grace to seek it, he will enjoy five merks by the year, and the professor's cast-off suit, which he disparts with biennially."

"This will never do, good Mr. Warden," said the Lady, scarce able to suppress a smile; "we will think more at large upon this matter. In the meanwhile, I trust to your remonstrances with this wild boy and with the family, for restraining these violent and unseemly jealousies and bursts of passion; and I entreat you to press on him and them their duty in this respect towards God, and towards their master."

"You shall be obeyed, madam," said Warden. "On the next Thursday I exhort the family, and will, with God's blessing, so wrestle with the demon of wrath and violence, which hath entered into my little flock, that I trust to hound the wolf out of the fold, as if he were chased away with bandogs."

This was the part of the conference from which Mr. Warden derived the greatest pleasure. The pulpit was at that time the same powerful

SIR WALTER SCOTT

engine for affecting popular feeling which the press has since become, and he had been no unsuccessful preacher, as we have already seen. It followed as a natural consequence, that he rather over-estimated the powers of his own oratory, and, like some of his brethren about the period, was glad of an opportunity to handle any matters of importance, whether public or private, the discussion of which could be dragged into his discourse. In that rude age the delicacy was unknown which prescribed time and place to personal exhortations; and as the court-preacher often addressed the King individually, and dictated to him the conduct he ought to observe in matters of state, so the nobleman himself, or any of his retainers, were, in the chapel of the feudal castle, often incensed or appalled, as the case might be, by the discussion of their private faults in the evening exercise, and by spiritual censures directed against them, specifically, personally, and by name. The sermon, by means of which Henry Warden purposed to restore concord and good order to the Castle of Avenel, bore for text the well-known words, *"He who striketh with the sword shall perish by the sword,"* and was a singular mixture of good sense and powerful oratory with pedantry and bad taste. He enlarged a good deal on the word striketh, which he assured his hearers comprehended blows given with the point as well as with the edge, and more generally, shooting with hand-gun, cross-bow, or long-bow, thrusting with a lance, or doing any thing whatever by which death might be occasioned to the adversary. In the same manner, he proved satisfactorily, that the word sword comprehended all descriptions, whether backsword or basket-hilt, cut-and-thrust or rapier, falchion, or scimitar. "But if," he continued, with still greater animation, "the text includeth in its anathema those who strike with any of those weapons which man hath devised for the exercise of his open hostility, still more doth it comprehend such as from their form and size are devised rather for the gratification of privy malice by treachery, than for the destruction of an enemy prepared and standing upon his defence. Such," he proceeded, looking sternly at the place where the page was seated on a cushion at the feet of his mistress, and wearing in his crimson belt a gay dagger with a gilded hilt,—"such, more especially, I hold to be those implements of death, which, in our modern and fantastic times, are worn not only by thieves and cut-throats, to whom they most properly belong, but even by those who attend upon women, and wait in the chambers of honourable ladies. Yes, my friends,—every species of this unhappy weapon, framed for all evil and for no good, is comprehended under this deadly denunciation, whether it be a stillet, which we have borrowed from the treacherous Italian, or a dirk, which is borne by the savage Highlandman, or a whinger, which is carried by our own Border thieves and cut-throats, or a dudgeon-dagger, all are alike engines invented by the devil himself, for ready implements of deadly wrath, sudden to execute, and difficult to be parried. Even the common sword-and-buckler brawler despises the use of such a treacherous and malignant instrument, which is therefore fit to be used, not by men or soldiers, but by those who, trained under female discipline, become themselves effeminate hermaphrodites, having female spite and female cowardice added to the infirmities and evil passions of their masculine nature."

The effect which this oration produced upon the assembled congregation of Avenel cannot very easily be described. The lady seemed at once embarrassed and offended; the menials could hardly contain, under an affectation of deep attention, the joy with which they heard the chaplain launch his thunders at the head of the unpopular favourite, and the weapon which they considered as a badge of affectation and finery. Mrs. Lilias crested and drew up her head with all the deep-felt pride of gratified resentment; while the steward, observing a strict neutrality of aspect, fixed his eyes upon an old scutcheon on the opposite side of the wall, which he seemed to examine with the utmost accuracy, more willing, perhaps, to incur the censure of being inattentive to the sermon, than that of seeming to listen with marked approbation to what appeared so distasteful to his mistress.

The unfortunate subject of the harangue, whom nature had endowed with passions which had hitherto found no effectual restraint, could not disguise the resentment which he felt at being thus directly held up to the scorn, as well as the censure, of the assembled inhabitants of the little world in which he lived. His brow grew red, his lip grew pale, he set his teeth, he clenched his hand, and then with mechanical readiness grasped the weapon of which the clergyman had given so hideous a character; and at length, as the preacher heightened the colouring of his invective, he felt his rage become so ungovernable, that, fearful of being hurried into some deed of desperate violence, he rose up, traversed the chapel with hasty steps, and left the congregation.

The preacher was surprised into a sudden pause, while the fiery youth shot across him like a flash of lightning, regarding him as he passed, as if he had wished to dart from his eyes the same power of blighting

SIR WALTER SCOTT

and of consuming. But no sooner had he crossed the chapel, and shut with violence behind him the door of the vaulted entrance by which it communicated with the castle, than the impropriety of his conduct supplied Warden with one of those happier subjects for eloquence, of which he knew how to take advantage for making a suitable impression on his hearers. He paused for an instant, and then pronounced, in a slow and solemn voice, the deep anathema: "He hath gone out from us because he was not of us—the sick man hath been offended at the wholesome bitter of the medicine—the wounded patient hath flinched from the friendly knife of the surgeon—the sheep hath fled from the sheepfold and delivered himself to the wolf, because he could not assume the quiet and humble conduct demanded of us by the great Shepherd. Ah! my brethren, beware of wrath—beware of pride— beware of the deadly and destroying sin which so often shows itself to our frail eyes in the garments of light! What is our earthly honour? Pride, and pride only—What our earthly gifts and graces? Pride and vanity. Voyagers speak of Indian men who deck themselves with shells, and anoint themselves with pigments, and boast of their attire as we do of our miserable carnal advantages—Pride could draw down the morning-star from Heaven even to the verge of the pit—Pride and self-opinion kindled the flaming sword which waves us off from Paradise— Pride made Adam mortal, and a weary wanderer on the face of the earth, which he had else been at this day the immortal lord of—Pride brought amongst us sin, and doubles every sin it has brought. It is the outpost which the devil and the flesh most stubbornly maintain against the assaults of grace; and until it be subdued, and its barriers levelled with the very earth, there is more hope of a fool than of the sinner. Rend, then, from your bosoms this accursed shoot of the fatal apple; tear it up by the roots, though it be twisted with the chords of your life. Profit by the example of the miserable sinner that has passed from us, and embrace the means of grace while it is called to-day 'ere your conscience is seared as with a fire-brand, and your ears deafened like those of the adder, and your heart hardened like the nether mill-stone. Up, then, and be doing—wrestle and overcome; resist, and the enemy shall flee from you—Watch and pray, lest ye fall into temptation, and let the stumbling of others be your warning and your example. Above all, rely not on yourselves, for such self-confidence is even the worst symptom of the disorder itself. The Pharisee, perhaps, deemed himself humble while he stooped in the Temple, and thanked God that he was not as other men, and even as the publican. But while his knees touched the marble pavement, his head was as high as the topmost pinnacle of the Temple. Do not, therefore, deceive yourselves, and offer false coin, where the purest you can present is but as dross—think not that such—will pass the assay of Omnipotent Wisdom. Yet shrink not from the task, because, as is my bounden duty, I do not disguise from you its difficulties. Self-searching can do much—Meditation can do much— Grace can do all."

And he concluded with a touching and animating exhortation to his hearers to seek divine grace, which is perfected in human wakness.

The audience did not listen to this address without being considerably affected; though it might be doubted whether the feelings of triumph, excited by the disgraceful retreat of the favourite page, did not greatly qualify in the minds of many the exhortations of the preacher to charity and to humility. And, in fact, the expression of their countenances much resembled the satisfied triumphant air of a set of children, who, having just seen a companion punished for a fault in which they had no share, con their task with double glee, both because they themselves are out of the scrape, and because the culprit is in it.

With very different feelings did the Lady of Avenel seek her own apartment. She felt angry at Warden having made a domestic matter, in which she took a personal interest, the subject of such public discussion. But this she knew the good man claimed as a branch of his Christian liberty as a preacher, and also that it was vindicated by the universal custom of his brethren. But the self-willed conduct of her protegé afforded her yet deeper concern. That he had broken through in so remarkable a degree, not only the respect due to her presence, but that which was paid to religious admonition in those days with such peculiar reverence, argued a spirit as untameable as his enemies had represented him to possess. And yet so far as he had been under her own eye, she had seen no more of that fiery spirit than appeared to her to become his years and his vivacity. This opinion might be founded in some degree on partiality; in some degree, too, it might be owing to the kindness and indulgence which she had always extended to him; but still she thought it impossible that she could be totally mistaken in the estimate she had formed of his character. The extreme of violence is scarce consistent with a course of continued hypocrisy, (although Lilias charitably hinted, that in some instances they were happily united,) and there fore she could not exactly trust the report of others against her own experience and observation. The thoughts of this orphan boy clung to her heartstrings with a fondness for which she herself was unable to account. He seemed to have been sent to her by Heaven, to fill up those intervals of languor and vacuity which deprived her of much enjoyment. Perhaps he was not less dear to her, because she well saw that he was a favourite with no one else, and because she felt, that to give him up was to afford the judgment of her husband and others a triumph over her own; a circumstance not quite indifferent to the best of spouses of either sex.

In short, the Lady of Avenel formed the internal resolution, that she would not desert her page while her page could be rationally protected; and, with a view of ascertaining how far this might be done, she caused him to be summoned to her presence.

V

—In the wild storm,
The seaman hews his mast down, and the merchant
Heaves to the billows wares he once deem'd precious;
So prince and peer, 'mid popular contentions,
Cast off their favourites.

—OLD PLAY

I t was some time ere Roland Graeme appeared. The messenger (his old friend Lilias) had at first attempted to open the door of his little apartment with the charitable purpose, doubtless, of enjoying the confusion, and marking the demeanour of the culprit. But an oblong bit of iron, ycleped a bolt, was passed across the door on the inside, and prevented her benign intentions. Lilias knocked and called at intervals. "Roland—Roland Graeme—*Master* Roland Graeme" (an emphasis on the word Master,) "will you be pleased to undo the door?—What ails you?—are you at your prayers in private, to complete the devotion which you left unfinished in public?—Surely we must have a screened seat for you in the chapel, that your gentility may be free from the eyes of common folks!" Still no whisper was heard in reply. "Well, master Roland," said the waiting-maid, "I must tell my mistress, that if she would have an answer, she must either come herself, or send those on errand to you who can beat the door down."

"What says your Lady?" answered the page from within.

"Marry, open the door, and you shall hear," answered the waiting-maid. "I trow it becomes my Lady's message to be listened to face to face; and I will not for your idle pleasure, whistle it through a key-hole."

"Your mistress's name," said the page, opening the door, "is too fair a cover for your impertinence—What says my Lady?"

"That you will be pleased to come to her directly, in the withdrawing-room," answered Lilias. "I presume she has some directions for you concerning the forms to be observed in leaving chapel in future."

"Say to my Lady, that I will directly wait on her," answered the page; and returning into his apartment, he once more locked the door in the face of the waiting-maid.

"Rare courtesy!" muttered Lilias; and, returning to her mistress, acquainted her that Roland Graeme would wait on her when it suited his convenience.

"What, is that his addition, or your own phrase, Lilias?" said the Lady, coolly.

"Nay, madam," replied the attendant, not directly answering the question, "he looked as if he could have said much more impertinent things than that, if I had been willing to hear them.—But here he comes to answer for himself."

Roland Graeme entered the apartment with a loftier mien, and somewhat a higher colour than his wont; there was embarrassment in his manner, but it was neither that of fear nor of penitence.

"Young man," said the Lady, "what trow you I am to think of your conduct this day?"

"If it has offended you, madam, I am deeply grieved," replied the youth.

"To have offended me alone," replied the Lady, "were but little—You have been guilty of conduct which will highly offend your master—of violence to your fellow-servants, and of disrespect to God himself, in the person of his ambassador."

"Permit me again to reply," said the page, "that if I have offended my only mistress, friend, and benefactress, it includes the sum of my guilt, and deserves the sum of my penitence—Sir Halbert Glendinning calls me not servant, nor do I call him master—he is not entitled to blame me for chastising an insolent groom—nor do I fear the wrath of Heaven for treating with scorn the unauthorized interference of a meddling preacher."

The Lady of Avenel had before this seen symptoms in her favourite of boyish petulance, and of impatience of censure or reproof. But his present demeanour was of a graver and more determined character, and she was for a moment at a loss how she should treat the youth, who seemed to have at once assumed the character not only of a man, but of a bold and determined one. She paused an instant, and then assuming the dignity which was natural to her, she said, "Is it to me, Roland, that you hold this language? Is it for the purpose of making me repent the favour I have shown you, that you declare yourself independent both of an earthly and a Heavenly master? Have you forgotten what you were, and to what the loss of my protection would speedily again reduce you?"

"Lady," said the page, "I have forgot nothing, I remember but too much. I know, that but for you, I should have perished in yon blue waves," pointing, as he spoke, to the lake, which was seen through the window, agitated by the western wind. "Your goodness has gone farther, madam—you have protected me against the malice of others, and against my own folly. You are free, if you are willing, to abandon the orphan you have reared. You have left nothing undone by him, and he complains of nothing. And yet, Lady, do not think I have been ungrateful—I have endured something on my part, which I would have borne for the sake of no one but my benefactress."

"For my sake!" said the Lady; "and what is it that I can have subjected you to endure, which can be remembered with other feelings than those of thanks and gratitude?"

"You are too just, madam, to require me to be thankful for the cold neglect with which your husband has uniformly treated me—neglect not unmingled with fixed aversion. You are too just, madam, to require me to be grateful for the constant and unceasing marks of scorn and malevolence with which I have been treated by others, or for such a homily as that with which your reverend chaplain has, at my expense, this very day regaled the assembled household."

"Heard mortal ears the like of this!" said the waiting-maid, with her hands expanded and her eyes turned up to heaven; "he speaks as if he were son of an earl, or of a belted knight the least penny!"

The page glanced on her a look of supreme contempt, but vouchsafed no other answer. His mistress, who began to feel herself seriously offended, and yet sorry for the youth's folly, took up the same tone.

"Indeed, Roland, you forget yourself so strangely," said she, "that you will tempt me to take serious measures to lower you in your own opinion by reducing you to your proper station in society."

"And that," added Lilias, "would be best done by turning him out the same beggar's brat that your ladyship took him in."

"Lilias speaks too rudely," continued the Lady, "but she has spoken the truth, young man; nor do I think I ought to spare that pride which hath so completely turned your head. You have been tricked up with fine garments, and treated like the son of a gentleman, until you have forgot the fountain of your churlish blood."

"Craving your pardon, most honourable madam, Lilias hath *not* spoken truth, nor does your ladyship know aught of my descent, which should entitle you to treat it with such decided scorn. I am no beggar's brat—my grandmother begged from no one, here nor elsewhere—she would have perished sooner on the bare moor. We were harried out and driven from our home—a chance which has happed elsewhere, and to others. Avenel Castle, with its lake and its towers, was not at all times able to protect its inhabitants from want and desolation."

"Hear but his assurance!" said Lilias, "he upbraids my Lady with the distresses of her family!"

"It had indeed been a theme more gratefully spared," said the Lady, affected nevertheless with the allusion.

"It was necessary, madam, for my vindication," said the page, "or I had not even hinted at a word that might give you pain. But believe, honoured Lady, I am of no churl's blood. My proper descent I know not; but my only relation has said, and my heart has echoed it back and attested the truth, that I am sprung of gentle blood, and deserve gentle usage."

"And upon an assurance so vague as this," said the Lady, "do you propose to expect all the regard, all the privileges, befitting high rank and distinguished birth, and become a contender for concessions which are only due to the noble? Go to, sir, know yourself, or the master of the household shall make you know you are liable to the scourge as a malapert boy. You have tasted too little the discipline fit for your age and station."

"The master of the household shall taste of my dagger, ere I taste of his discipline," said the page, giving way to his restrained passion. "Lady, I have been too long the vassal of a pantoufle, and the slave of a silver whistle. You must henceforth find some other to answer your call; and let him be of birth and spirit mean enough to brook the scorn of your menials, and to call a church vassal his master."

"I have deserved this insult," said the Lady, colouring deeply, "for so long enduring and fostering your petulance. Begone, sir. Leave this castle to-night—I will send you the means of subsistence till you find some honest mode of support, though I fear your imaginary grandeur will be above all others, save those of rapine and violence. Begone, sir, and see my face no more."

The page threw himself at her feet in an agony of sorrow. "My dear and honoured mistress," he said, but was unable to bring out another syllable.

"Arise, sir," said the Lady, "and let go my mantle—hypocrisy is a poor cloak for ingratitude."

"I am incapable of either, madam," said the page, springing up with the hasty start of passion which belonged to his rapid and impetuous temper. "Think not I meant to implore permission to reside here; it has been long my determination to leave Avenel, and I will never forgive myself for having permitted you to say the word begone, ere I said, 'I leave you.' I did but kneel to ask your forgiveness for an ill-considered word used in the height of displeasure, but which ill became my mouth, as addressed to you. Other grace I asked not—you have done much for me—but I repeat, that you better know what you yourself have done, than what I have suffered."

"Roland," said the Lady, somewhat appeased, and relenting towards her favourite, "you had me to appeal to when you were aggrieved. You were neither called upon to suffer wrong, nor entitled to resent it, when you were under my protection."

"And what," said the youth, "if I sustained wrong from those you loved and favoured, was I to disturb your peace with idle tale-bearings and eternal complaints? No, madam; I have borne my own burden in silence, and without disturbing you with murmurs; and the respect with which you accuse me of wanting, furnishes the only reason why I have neither appealed to you, nor taken vengeance at my own hand in a manner far more effectual. It is well, however, that we part. I was not born to be a stipendiary, favoured by his mistress, until ruined by the calumnies of others. May Heaven multiply its choicest blessings on your honoured head; and, for your sake, upon all that are dear to you!"

He was about to leave the apartment, when the Lady called upon him to return. He stood still, while she thus addressed him: "It was not my intention, nor would it be just, even in the height of my displeasure, to dismiss you without the means of support; take this purse of gold."

"Forgive me, Lady," said the boy, "and let me go hence with the consciousness that I have not been degraded to the point of accepting alms. If my poor services can be placed against the expense of my apparel and my maintenance, I only remain debtor to you for my life, and that alone is a debt which I can never repay; put up then that purse, and only say, instead, that you do not part from me in anger."

"No, not in anger," said the Lady, "in sorrow rather for your wilfulness; but take the gold, you cannot but need it."

"May God evermore bless you for the kind tone and the kind word! but the gold I cannot take. I am able of body, and do not lack friends so wholly as you may think; for the time may come that I may yet show myself more thankful than by mere words." He threw himself on his knees, kissed the hand which she did not withdraw, and then, hastily left the apartment.

Lilias, for a moment or two, kept her eye fixed on her mistress, who looked so unusually pale, that she seemed about to faint; but the Lady instantly recovered herself, and declining the assistance which her attendant offered her, walked to her own apartment.

VI

Thou hast each secret of the household, Francis.
I dare be sworn thou hast been in the buttery,
Steeping thy curious humour in fat ale,
And in thy butler's tattle—ay, or chatting
With the glib waiting-woman o'er her comfits—
These bear the key to each domestic mystery.

—OLD PLAY

U pon the morrow succeeding the scene we have described, the disgraced favourite left the castle; and at breakfast-time the cautious old steward and Mrs. Lilias sat in the apartment of the latter personage, holding grave converse on the important event of the day, sweetened by a small treat of comfits, to which the providence of Mr. Wingate had added a little flask of racy canary.

"He is gone at last," said the abigail, sipping her glass; "and here is to his good journey."

"Amen," answered the steward, gravely; "I wish the poor deserted lad no ill."

"And he is gone like a wild-duck, as he came," continued Mrs. Lilias; "no lowering of drawbridges, or pacing along causeways, for him. My master has pushed off in the boat which they call the little Herod, (more shame to them for giving the name of a Christian to wood and iron,) and has rowed himself by himself to the farther side of the loch, and off and away with himself, and left all his finery strewed about his room. I wonder who is to clean his trumpery out after him—though the things are worth lifting, too."

"Doubtless, Mistress Lilias," answered the master of the household, "in the which case, I am free to think, they will not long cumber the floor."

"And now tell me, Master Wingate," continued the damsel, "do not the very cockles of your heart rejoice at the house being rid of this upstart whelp, that flung us all into shadow?"

"Why, Mistress Lilias," replied Wingate, "as to rejoicing—those who have lived as long in great families as has been my lot, will be in no hurry to rejoice at any thing. And for Roland Graeme, though he may be a good riddance in the main, yet what says the very sooth proverb, 'Seldom comes a better.'"

"Seldom comes a better, indeed!" echoed Mrs. Lilias. "I say, never can come a worse, or one half so bad. He might have been the ruin of our poor dear mistress," (here she used her kerchief,) "body and soul, and estate too; for she spent more coin on his apparel than on any four servants about the house."

"Mistress Lilias," said the sage steward, "I do opine that our mistress requireth not this pity at your hands, being in all respects competent to take care of her own body, soul, and estate into the bargain."

"You would not mayhap have said so," answered the waiting-woman, "had you seen how like Lot's wife she looked when young master took his leave. My mistress is a good lady, and a virtuous, and a well-doing lady, and a well-spoken of—but I would not Sir Halbert had seen her last evening for two and a plack."

"Oh, foy! foy! foy!" reiterated the steward; "servants should hear and see, and say nothing. Besides that, my lady is utterly devoted to Sir Halbert, as well she may, being, as he is, the most renowned knight in these parts."

"Well, well," said the abigail, "I mean no more harm; but they that seek least renown abroad, are most apt to find quiet at home, that's all; and my Lady's lonesome situation is to be considered, that made her fain to take up with the first beggar's brat that a dog brought her out of the loch."

"And, therefore," said the steward, "I say, rejoice not too much, or too hastily, Mistress Lilias; for if your Lady wished a favourite to pass away the time, depend upon it, the time will not pass lighter now that he is gone. So she will have another favourite to choose for herself; and be assured, if she wishes such a toy, she will not lack one."

"And where should she choose one, but among her own tried and faithful servants," said Mrs. Lilias, "who have broken her bread, and drunk her drink, for so many years? I have known many a lady as high as she is, that never thought either of a friend or favourite beyond their own waiting-woman—always having a proper respect, at the same time, for their old and faithful master of the household, Master Wingate."

"Truly, Mistress Lilias," replied the steward, "I do partly see the mark at which you shoot, but I doubt your bolt will fall short. Matters being with our Lady as it likes you to suppose, it will neither be your crimped pinners, Mrs. Lilias, (speaking of them with due respect,) nor my silver hair, or golden chain, that will fill up the void which Roland Graeme must needs leave in our Lady's leisure. There will be a learned young divine with some new doctrine—a learned leech with some new drug—a bold cavalier, who will not be refused the favour of wearing her colours at a running at the ring—a cunning harper that could harp the heart out of woman's breast, as they say Signer David Rizzio did to our poor Queen;—these are the sort of folk who supply the loss of a well-favoured favourite, and not an old steward, or a middle-aged waiting-woman."

"Well," replied Lilias, "you have experience, Master Wingate, and truly I would my master would leave off his picking hither and thither, and look better after the affairs of his household. There will be a papestrie among us next, for what should I see among master's clothes but a string of gold beads! I promise you, *aves* and *credos* both!—I seized on them like a falcon."

"I doubt it not, I doubt it not," said the steward, sagaciously nodding his head; "I have often noticed that the boy had strange observances which savoured of popery, and that he was very jealous to conceal them. But you will find the Catholic under the Presbyterian cloak as often as the knave under the Friar's hood—what then? we are all mortal—Right proper beads they are," he added, looking attentively at them, "and may weigh four ounces of fine gold."

"And I will have them melted down presently," she said, "before they be the misguiding of some poor blinded soul."

"Very cautious, indeed, Mistress Lilias," said the steward, nodding his head in assent.

"I will have them made," said Mrs. Lilias, "into a pair of shoe-buckles; I would not wear the Pope's trinkets, or whatever has once borne the shape of them, one inch above my instep, were they diamonds instead of gold.—But this is what has come of Father Ambrose coming about the castle, as demure as a cat that is about to steal cream."

"Father Ambrose is our master's brother," said the steward gravely.

"Very true, Master Wingate," answered the Dame; "but is that a good reason why he should pervert the king's liege subjects to papistrie?"

"Heaven forbid, Mistress Lilias," answered the sententious major-domo; "but yet there are worse folk than the Papists."

"I wonder where they are to be found," said the waiting-woman, with some asperity; "but I believe, Master Wingate, if one were to speak to

SIR WALTER SCOTT

you about the devil himself, you would say there were worse people than Satan."

"Assuredly I might say so," replied the steward, "supposing that I saw Satan standing at my elbow."

The waiting-woman started, and having exclaimed, "God bless us!" added, "I wonder, Master Wingate, you can take pleasure in frightening one thus."

"Nay, Mistress Lilias, I had no such purpose," was the reply; "but look you here—the Papists are but put down for the present, but who knows how long this word *present* will last? There are two great Popish earls in the north of England, that abominate the very word reformation; I mean the Northumberland and Westmoreland Earls, men of power enough to shake any throne in Christendom. Then, though our Scottish king be, God bless him, a true Protestant, yet he is but a boy; and here is his mother that was our queen—I trust there is no harm to say, God bless her too—and she is a Catholic; and many begin to think she has had but hard measure, such as the Hamiltons in the west, and some of our Border clans here, and the Gordons in the north, who are all wishing to see a new world; and if such a new world should chance to come up, it is like that the Queen will take back her own crown, and that the mass and the cross will come up, and then down go pulpits, Geneva-gowns, and black silk skull-caps."

"And have you, Master Jasper Wingate, who have heard the word, and listened unto pure and precious Mr. Henry Warden, have you, I say, the patience to speak, or but to think, of popery coming down on us like a storm, or of the woman Mary again making the royal seat of Scotland a throne of abomination? No marvel that you are so civil to the cowled monk, Father Ambrose, when he comes hither with his downcast eyes that he never raises to my Lady's face, and with his low sweet-toned voice, and his benedicites, and his benisons; and who so ready to take them kindly as Master Wingate?"

"Mistress Lilias," replied the butler, with an air which was intended to close the debate, "there are reasons for all things. If I received Father Ambrose debonairly, and suffered him to steal a word now and then with this same Roland Graeme, it was not that I cared a brass bodle for his benison or malison either, but only because I respected my master's blood. And who can answer, if Mary come in again, whether he may not be as stout a tree to lean to as ever his brother hath proved to us? For down goes the Earl of Murray when the Queen comes by her own again; and good is his luck if he can keep the head on his own shoulders. And down goes our Knight, with the Earl, his patron; and who so like to mount into his empty saddle as this same Father Ambrose? The Pope of Rome can so soon dispense with his vows, and then we should have Sir Edward the soldier, instead of Ambrose the priest."

Anger and astonishment kept Mrs. Lilias silent,—while her old friend, in his self-complacent manner, was making known to her his political speculations. At length her resentment found utterance in words of great ire and scorn. "What, Master Wingate! have you eaten my mistress's bread, to say nothing of my master's, so many years, that you could live to think of her being dispossessed of her own Castle of Avenel, by a wretched monk, who is not a drop's blood to her in the way of relation? I, that am but a woman, would try first whether my rock or his cowl was the better metal. Shame on you, Master Wingate! I If I had not held you as so old an acquaintance, this should have gone to my Lady's ears though I had been called pickthank and tale-pyet for my pains, as when I told of Roland Graeme shooting the wild swan."

Master Wingate was somewhat dismayed at perceiving, that the details which he had given of his far-sighted political views had produced on his hearer rather suspicion of his fidelity, than admiration of his wisdom, and endeavoured, as hastily as possible, to apologize and to explain, although internally extremely offended at the unreasonable view, as he deemed it, which it had pleased Mistress Lilias Bradbourne to take of his expressions; and mentally convinced that her disapprobation of his sentiments arose solely out of the consideration, that though Father Ambrose, supposing him to become the master of the castle, would certainly require the services of a steward, yet those of a waiting-woman would, in the supposed circumstances, be altogether superfluous.

After his explanation had been received as explanations usually are, the two friends separated; Lilias to attend the silver whistle which called her to her mistress's chamber, and the sapient major-domo to the duties of his own department. They parted with less than their usual degree of reverence and regard; for the steward felt that his worldly wisdom was rebuked by the more disinterested attachment of the waiting-woman, and Mistress Lilias Bradbourne was compelled to consider her old friend as something little better than a time-server.

SIR WALTER SCOTT

VII

When I hae a saxpence under my thumb,
Then I get credit in ilka town;
But when I am puir they bid me gae by—
Oh, poverty parts good company!

—OLD SONG

While the departure of the page afforded subject for the conversation which we have detailed in our last chapter, the late favourite was far advanced on his solitary journey, without well knowing what was its object, or what was likely to be its end. He had rowed the skiff in which he left the castle, to the side of the lake most distant from the village, with the desire of escaping from the notice of the inhabitants. His pride whispered, that he would be in his discarded state, only the subject of their wonder and compassion; and his generosity told him, that any mark of sympathy which his situation should excite, might be unfavourably reported at the castle. A trifling incident convinced him he had little to fear for his friends on the latter score. He was met by a young man some years older than himself, who had on former occasions been but too happy to be permitted to share in his sports in the subordinate character of his assistant. Ralph Fisher approached to greet him, with all the alacrity of an humble friend.

"What, Master Roland, abroad on this side, and without either hawk or hound?"

"Hawk or hound," said Roland, "I will never perhaps hollo to again. I have been dismissed—that is, I have left the castle."

Ralph was surprised. "What! you are to pass into the Knight's service, and take the black jack and the lance?"

"Indeed," replied Roland Graeme, "I am not—I am now leaving the service of Avenel for ever."

"And whither are you going, then?" said the young peasant.

"Nay, that is a question which it craves time to answer—I have that matter to determine yet," replied the disgraced favourite.

"Nay, nay," said Ralph, "I warrant you it is the same to you which way you go—my Lady would not dismiss you till she had put some lining into the pouches of your doublet."

"Sordid slave!" said Roland Graeme, "dost thou think I would have accepted a boon from one who was giving me over a prey to detraction and to ruin, at the instigation of a canting priest and a meddling serving-woman? The bread that I had bought with such an alms would have choked me at the first mouthful."

Ralph looked at his quondam friend with an air of wonder not unmixed with contempt. "Well," he said, at length, "no occasion for passion—each man knows his own stomach best—but, were I on a black moor at this time of day, not knowing whither I was going, I should be glad to have a broad piece or two in my pouch, come by them as I could.—But perhaps you will go with me to my father's—that is, for a night, for to-morrow we expect my uncle Menelaus and all his folk; but, as I said, for one night—"

The cold-blooded limitation of the offered shelter to one night only, and that tendered most unwillingly, offended the pride of the discarded favourite.

"I would rather sleep on the fresh heather, as I have done many a night on less occasion," said Roland Graeme, "than in the smoky garret of your father, that smells of peat smoke and usquebaugh like a Highlander's plaid."

"You may choose, my master, if you are so nice," replied Ralph Fisher; "you may be glad to smell a peat-fire, and usquebaugh too, if you journey long in the fashion you propose. You might have said God-a-mercy for your proffer, though—it is not every one that will put themselves in the way of ill-will by harbouring a discarded serving-man."

"Ralph," said Roland Graeme, "I would pray you to remember that I have switched you before now, and this is the same riding-wand which you have tasted."

Ralph, who was a thickset clownish figure, arrived at his full strength, and conscious of the most complete personal superiority, laughed contemptuously at the threats of the slight-made stripling.

"It may be the same wand," he said, "but not the same hand; and that is as good rhyme as if it were in a ballad. Look you, my Lady's page that was, when your switch was up, it was no fear of you, but of your betters, that kept mine down—and I wot not what hinders me from clearing old scores with this hazel rung, and showing you it was your Lady's livery-coat which I spared, and not your flesh and blood, Master Roland."

In the midst of his rage, Roland Graeme was just wise enough to see, that by continuing this altercation, he would subject himself to very rude treatment from the boor, who was so much older and stronger than himself; and while his antagonist, with a sort of jeering laugh of defiance, seemed to provoke the contest, he felt the full bitterness of his own degraded condition, and burst into a passion of tears, which he in vain endeavoured to conceal with both his hands.

Even the rough churl was moved with the distress of his quondam companion.

"Nay, Master Roland," he said, "I did but as 'twere jest with thee—I would not harm thee, man, were it but for old acquaintance sake. But ever look to a man's inches ere you talk of switching—why, thine arm, man, is but like a spindle compared to mine.—But hark, I hear old Adam Woodcock hollowing to his hawk—Come along, man, we will have a merry afternoon, and go jollily to my father's in spite of the peat-smoke and usquebaugh to boot. Maybe we may put you into some honest way of winning your bread, though it's hard to come by in these broken times."

The unfortunate page made no answer, nor did he withdraw his hands from his face, and Fisher continued in what he imagined a suitable tone of comfort.

"Why, man, when you were my Lady's minion, men held you proud, and some thought you a Papist, and I wot not what; and so, now that you have no one to bear you out, you must be companionable and hearty, and wait on the minister's examinations, and put these things out of folk's head; and if he says you are in fault, you must jouk your head to the stream; and if a gentleman, or a gentleman's gentleman, give you a rough word, or a light blow, you must only say, thank you for dusting my doublet, or the like, as I have done by you.—But hark to Woodcock's whistle again. Come, and I will teach you all the trick on't as we go on."

"I thank you," said Roland Graeme, endeavouring to assume an air of indifference and of superiority; "but I have another path before me, and were it otherwise, I could not tread in yours."

"Very true, Master Roland," replied the clown; "and every man knows his own matters best, and so I will not keep you from the path, as you say. Give us a grip of your hand, man, for auld lang syne.—What! not clap palms ere we part?—well, so be it—a wilful man will have his way, and so farewell, and the blessing of the morning to you."

"Good-morrow—good-morrow," said Roland, hastily; and the clown walked lightly off, whistling as he went, and glad, apparently, to be rid of an acquaintance, whose claims might be troublesome, and who had no longer the means to be serviceable to him.

Roland Graeme compelled himself to walk on while they were within sight of each other that his former intimate might not augur any vacillation of purpose, or uncertainty of object, from his remaining on the same spot; but the effort was a painful one. He seemed stunned, as it were, and giddy; the earth on which he stood felt as if unsound, and quaking under his feet like the surface of a bog; and he had once or twice nearly fallen, though the path he trode was of firm greensward. He kept resolutely moving forward, in spite of the internal agitation to which these symptoms belonged, until the distant form of his acquaintance disappeared behind the slope of a hill, when his heart failed at once; and, sitting down on the turf, remote from human ken, he gave way to the natural expressions of wounded pride, grief, and fear, and wept with unrestrained profusion and unqualified bitterness.

When the first violent paroxysm of his feelings had subsided, the deserted and friendless youth felt that mental relief which usually follows such discharges of sorrow. The tears continued to chase each other down his cheeks, but they were no longer accompanied by the same sense of desolation; an afflicting yet milder sentiment was awakened in his mind, by the recollection of his benefactress, of the unwearied kindness which had attached her to him, in spite of many acts of provoking petulance, now recollected as offences of a deep dye, which had protected him against the machinations of others, as well as against the consequences of his own folly, and would have continued to do so, had not the excess of his presumption compelled her to withdraw her protection.

"Whatever indignity I have borne," he said, "has been the just reward of my own ingratitude. And have I done well to accept the hospitality, the more than maternal kindness, of my protectress, yet to detain from her the knowledge of my religion?—but she shall know that a Catholic has as much gratitude as a Puritan—that I have been thoughtless, but not wicked—that in my wildest moments I have loved, respected, and honoured her—and that the orphan boy might indeed be heedless, but was never ungrateful!"

He turned, as these thoughts passed through his mind, and began hastily to retread his footsteps towards the castle. But he checked the first eagerness of his repentant haste, when he reflected on the scorn and contempt with which the family were likely to see the return of

SIR WALTER SCOTT

the fugitive, humbled, as they must necessarily suppose him, into a supplicant, who requested pardon for his fault, and permission to return to his service. He slackened his pace, but he stood not still.

"I care not," he resolutely determined; "let them wink, point, nod, sneer, speak of the conceit which is humbled, of the pride which has had a fall—I care not; it is a penance due to my folly, and I will endure it with patience. But if she also, my benefactress, if she also should think me sordid and weak-spirited enough to beg, not for her pardon alone, but for a renewal of the advantages which I derived from her favour—*her* suspicion of my meanness I cannot—I will not brook."

He stood still, and his pride rallying with constitutional obstinacy against his more just feeling, urged that he would incur the scorn of the Lady of Avenel, rather than obtain her favour, by following the course which the first ardour of his repentant feelings had dictated to him.

"If I had but some plausible pretext," he thought, "some ostensible reason for my return, some excuse to allege which might show I came not as a degraded supplicant, or a discarded menial, I might go thither—but as I am, I cannot—my heart would leap from its place and burst."

As these thoughts swept through his mind, something passed in the air so near him as to dazzle his eyes, and almost to brush the plume in his cap. He looked up—it was the favourite falcon of Sir Halbert, which, flying around his head, seemed to claim his attention, as that of a well-known friend. Roland extended his arm, and gave the accustomed whoop, and the falcon instantly settled on his wrist, and began to prune itself, glancing at the youth from time to time an acute and brilliant beam of its hazel eye, which seemed to ask why he caressed it not with his usual fondness.

"Ah, Diamond!" he said, as if the bird understood him, "thou and I must be strangers henceforward. Many a gallant stoop have I seen thee make, and many a brave heron strike down; but that is all gone and over, and there is no hawking more for me!"

"And why not, Master Roland," said Adam Woodcock the falconer, who came at that instant from behind a few alder bushes which had concealed him from view, "why should there be no more hawking for you? Why, man, what were our life without our sports?—thou know'st the jolly old song—

> "And rather would Allan in dungeon lie,
> Than live at large where the falcon cannot fly;

And Allan would rather lie in Sexton's pound,
Than live where he followed not the merry hawk and hound."

The voice of the falconer was hearty and friendly, and the tone in which he half-sung half-recited his rude ballad, implied honest frankness and cordiality. But remembrance of their quarrel, and its consequences, embarrassed Roland, and prevented his reply. The falconer saw his hesitation, and guessed the cause.

"What now," said he, "Master Roland? do you, who are half an Englishman, think that I, who am a whole one, would keep up anger against you, and you in distress? That were like some of the Scots, (my master's reverence always excepted,) who can be fair and false, and wait their time, and keep their mind, as they say, to themselves, and touch pot and flagon with you, and hunt and hawk with you, and, after all, when time serves, pay off some old feud with the point of the dagger. Canny Yorkshire has no memory for such old sores. Why, man, an you had hit me a rough blow, maybe I would rather have taken it from you, than a rough word from another; for you have a good notion of falconry, though you stand up for washing the meat for the eyases. So give us your hand, man, and bear no malice."

Roland, though he felt his proud blood rebel at the familiarity of honest Adam's address, could not resist its downright frankness. Covering his face with the one hand, he held out the other to the falconer, and returned with readiness his friendly grasp.

"Why, this is hearty now," said Woodcock; "I always said you had a kind heart, though you have a spice of the devil in your disposition, that is certain. I came this way with the falcon on purpose to find you, and yon half-bred lubbard told me which way you took flight. You ever thought too much of that kestril-kite, Master Roland, and he knows nought of sport after all, but what he caught from you. I saw how it had been betwixt you, and I sent him out of my company with a wanion—I would rather have a rifler on my perch than a false knave at my elbow—and now, Master Roland, tell me what way wing ye?"

"That is as God pleases," replied the page, with a sigh which he could not suppress.

"Nay, man, never droop a feather for being cast off," said the falconer; "who knows but you may soar the better and fairer flight for all this yet?—Look at Diamond there, 'tis a noble bird, and shows gallantly with his hood, and bells, and jesses; but there is many a wild falcon in

SIR WALTER SCOTT

Norway that would not change properties with him—And that is what I would say of you. You are no longer my Lady's page, and you will not clothe so fair, or feed so well, or sleep so soft, or show so gallant—What of all that? if you are not her page, you are your own man, and may go where you will, without minding whoop or whistle. The worst is the loss of the sport, but who knows what you may come to? They say that Sir Halbert himself, I speak with reverence, was once glad to be the Abbot's forester, and now he has hounds and hawks of his own, and Adam Woodcock for a falconer to the boot."

"You are right, and say well, Adam," answered the youth, the blood mantling in his cheeks, "the falcon will soar higher without his bells than with them, though the bells be made of silver."

"That is cheerily spoken," replied the falconer; "and whither now?"

"I thought of going to the Abbey of Kennaquhair," answered Roland Graeme, "to ask the counsel of Father Ambrose."

"And joy go with you," said the falconer, "though it is likely you may find the old monks in some sorrow; they say the commons are threatening to turn them out of their cells, and make a devil's mass of it in the old church, thinking they have forborne that sport too long; and troth I am clear of the same opinion."

"Then will Father Ambrose be the better of having a friend beside him!" said the page, manfully.

"Ay, but, my young fearnought," replied the falconer, "the friend will scarce be the better of being beside Father Ambrose—he may come by the redder's lick, and that is ever the worst of the battle."

"I care not for that," said the page, "the dread of a lick should not hold me back; but I fear I may bring trouble between the brothers by visiting Father Ambrose. I will tarry to-night at Saint Cuthbert's cell, where the old priest will give me a night's shelter; and I will send to Father Ambrose to ask his advice before I go down to the convent."

"By Our Lady," said the falconer, "and that is a likely plan—and now," he continued, exchanging his frankness of manner for a sort of awkward embarrassment, as if he had somewhat to say that he had no ready means to bring out—"and now, you wot well that I wear a pouch for my hawk's meat,* and so forth; but wot you what it is lined with, Master Roland?"

---

* This same hag, like every thing belonging to falconry, was esteemed an honourable distinction, and worn often by the nobility and gentry. One of the Sommervilles of

"With leather, to be sure," replied Roland, somewhat surprised at the hesitation with which Adam Woodcock asked a question apparently so simple.

"With leather, lad?" said Woodcock; "ay, and with silver to the boot of that. See here," he said, showing a secret slit in the lining of his bag of office—"here they are, thirty good Harry groats as ever were struck in bluff old Hal's time, and ten of them are right heartily at your service; and now the murder is out."

Roland's first idea was to refuse his assistance; but he recollected the vows of humility which he had just taken upon him, and it occurred that this was the opportunity to put his new-formed resolution to the test. Assuming a strong command of himself, he answered Adam Woodcock with as much frankness as his nature permitted him to wear, in doing what was so contrary to his inclinations, that he accepted thankfully of his kind offer, while, to soothe his own reviving pride, he could not help adding, "he hoped soon to requite the obligation."

"That as you list—that as you list, young man," said the falconer, with glee, counting out and delivering to his young friend the supply he had so generously offered, and then adding, with great cheerfulness,— "Now you may go through the world; for he that can back a horse, wind a horn, hollow a greyhound, fly a hawk, and play at sword and buckler, with a whole pair of shoes, a green jacket, and ten lily-white groats in his pouch, may bid Father Care hang himself in his own jesses. Farewell, and God be with you!"

So saying, and as if desirous to avoid the thanks of his companion, he turned hastily round, and left Roland Graeme to pursue his journey alone.

Camnethan was called *Sir John with the red bag*, because it was his wont to wear his hawking pouch covered with satin of that colour.

SIR WALTER SCOTT

VIII

The sacred tapers lights are gone.
Gray moss has clad the altar stone,
The holy image is o'erthrown,
The bell has ceased to toll,
The long ribb'd aisles are burst and shrunk,
The holy shrines to ruin sunk,
Departed is the pious monk,
God's blessing on his soul!

—Rediviva

The cell of Saint Cuthbert, as it was called, marked, or was supposed to mark, one of those resting-places, which that venerable saint was pleased to assign to his monks, when his convent, being driven from Lindisfern by the Danes, became a peripatetic society of religionists, and bearing their patron's body on their shoulders, transported him from place to place through Scotland and the borders of England, until he was pleased at length to spare them the pain of carrying him farther, and to choose his ultimate place of rest in the lordly towers of Durham. The odour of his sanctity remained behind him at each place where he had granted the monks a transient respite from their labours; and proud were those who could assign, as his temporary resting-place, any spot within their vicinity. There were few cells more celebrated and honoured than that of Saint Cuthbert, to which Roland Graeme now bent his way, situated considerably to the north-west of the great Abbey of Kennaquhair, on which it was dependent. In the neighbourhood were some of those recommendations which weighed with the experienced priesthood of Rome, in choosing their sites for places of religion.

There was a well, possessed of some medicinal qualities, which, of course, claimed the saint for its guardian and patron, and occasionally produced some advantage to the recluse who inhabited his cell, since none could reasonably expect to benefit by the fountain who did not extend their bounty to the saint's chaplain. A few rods of fertile land afforded the monk his plot of garden ground; an eminence well clothed with trees rose behind the cell, and sheltered it from, the north and the east, while the front, opening to the south-west, looked up a wild but pleasant valley, down which wandered a lively brook, which battled with every stone that interrupted its passage.

The cell itself was rather plainly than rudely constructed—a low Gothic building with two small apartments, one of which served the priest for his dwelling-place, the other for his chapel. As there were few of the secular clergy who durst venture to reside so near the Border, the assistance of this monk in spiritual affairs had not been useless to the community, while the Catholic religion retained the ascendancy; as he could marry, christen, and administer the other sacraments of the Roman church. Of late, however, as the Protestant doctrines gained ground, he had found it convenient to live in close retirement, and to avoid, as much as possible, drawing upon himself observation or animadversion. The appearance of his habitation, however, when Roland Graeme came before it in the close of the evening, plainly showed that his caution had been finally ineffectual.

The page's first movement was to knock at the door, when he observed, to his surprise, that it was open, not from being left unlatched, but because, beat off its upper hinge, it was only fastened to the door-post by the lower, and could therefore no longer perform its functions. Somewhat alarmed at this, and receiving no answer when he knocked and called, Roland began to look more at leisure upon the exterior of the little dwelling before he ventured to enter it. The flowers, which had been trained with care against the walls, seemed to have been recently torn down, and trailed their dishonoured garlands on the earth; the latticed window was broken and dashed in. The garden, which the monk had maintained by his constant labour in the highest order and beauty, bore marks of having been lately trod down and destroyed by the hoofs of animals, and the feet of men.

The sainted spring had not escaped. It was wont to rise beneath a canopy of ribbed arches, with which the devotion of elder times had secured and protected its healing waters. These arches were now almost entirely demolished, and the stones of which they were built were tumbled into the well, as if for the purpose of choking up and destroying the fountain, which, as it had shared in other days the honour of the saint, was, in the present, doomed to partake his unpopularity. Part of the roof had been pulled down from the house itself, and an attempt had been made with crows and levers upon one of the angles, by which several large corner-stones had been forced out of their place; but the solidity of ancient mason-work had proved too great for the time or patience of the assailants, and they had relinquished their task of destruction. Such dilapidated buildings, after the lapse of years, during which nature has gradually covered the effects of violence with creeping plants, and with weather-stains, exhibit, amid their decay, a melancholy beauty. But when the visible effects of violence appear raw and recent, there is no feeling to mitigate the sense of devastation with which they impress the spectators; and such was now the scene on which the youthful page gazed, with the painful feelings it was qualified to excite.

When his first momentary surprise was over, Roland Graeme was at no loss to conjecture the cause of these ravages. The destruction of the Popish edifices did not take place at once throughout Scotland, but at different times, and according to the spirit which actuated the reformed clergy; some of whom instigated their hearers to these acts of demolition, and others, with better taste and feeling, endeavoured to protect the ancient shrines, while they desired to see them purified from the objects which had attracted idolatrous devotion. From time to time, therefore, the populace of the Scottish towns and villages, when instigated either by their own feelings of abhorrence for Popish superstition, or by the doctrines of the more zealous preachers, resumed the work of destruction, and exercised it upon some sequestered church, chapel, or cell, which had escaped the first burst of their indignation against the religion of Rome. In many places, the vices of the Catholic clergy, arising out of the wealth and the corruption of that tremendous hierarchy, furnished too good an apology for wreaking vengeance upon the splendid edifices which they inhabited; and of this an old Scottish historian gives a remarkable instance.

"Why mourn ye," said an aged matron, seeing the discontent of some of the citizens, while a stately convent was burnt by the multitude,— "why mourn ye for its destruction? If you knew half the flagitious wickedness which has been perpetrated within that house, you would rather bless the divine judgment, which permits not even the senseless walls that screened such profligacy, any longer to cumber Christian ground."

But although, in many instances, the destruction of the Roman Catholic buildings might be, in the matron's way of judging, an act of justice, and in others an act of policy, there is no doubt that the humour of demolishing monuments of ancient piety and munificence, and that in a poor country like Scotland, where there was no chance of their being replaced, was both useless, mischievous, and barbarous.

In the present instance, the unpretending and quiet seclusion of the monk of Saint Cuthbert's had hitherto saved him from the general wreck; but it would seem ruin had now at length reached him. Anxious to discover if he had at least escaped personal harm, Roland Graeme entered the half ruined cell.

The interior of the building was in a state which fully justified the opinion he had formed from its external injuries. The few rude utensils of the solitary's hut were broken down, and lay scattered on the floor, where it seemed as if a fire had been made with some of the fragments to destroy the rest of his property, and to consume, in particular, the rude old image of Saint Cuthbert, in its episcopal habit, which lay on the hearth like Dagon of yore, shattered with the axe and scorched with the flames, but only partially destroyed. In the little apartment which served as a chapel, the altar was overthrown, and the four huge stones of which it had been once composed lay scattered around the floor. The large stone crucifix which occupied the niche behind the altar, and fronted the supplicant while he paid his devotion there, had been pulled down and dashed by its own weight into three fragments. There were marks of sledge-hammers on each of these; yet the image had been saved from utter demolition by the size and strength of the remaining fragments, which, though much injured, retained enough of the original sculpture to show what it had been intended to represent.*

Roland Graeme, secretly nursed in the tenets of Rome, saw with horror the profanation of the most sacred emblem, according to his creed, of our holy religion.

---

* I may here observe, that this is entirely an ideal scene. Saint Cuthbert, a person of established sanctity, had, no doubt, several places of worship on the Borders, where he flourished whilst living; but Tillmouth Chapel is the only one which bears some resemblance to the hermitage described in the text. It has, indeed, a well, famous for gratifying three wishes for every worshipper who shall quaff the fountain with sufficient belief in its efficacy. At this spot the Saint is said to have landed in his stone coffin, in which he sailed down the Tweed from Melrose and here the stone coffin long lay, in evidence of the fact. The late Sir Francis Blake Delaval is said to have taken the exact measure of the coffin, and to have ascertained, by hydrostatic principles, that it might have actually swum. A profane farmer in the neighborhood announced his intention of converting this last bed of the Saint into a trough for his swine; but the profanation was rendered impossible, either by the Saint, or by some pious votary in his behalf, for on the following morning the stone sarcophargus was found broken in two fragments.

Tillmouth Chapel, with these points of resemblance, lies, however, in exactly the opposite direction as regards Melrose, which the supposed cell of St. Cuthbert is said to have borne towards Kennaquhair.

SIR WALTER SCOTT

"It is the badge of our redemption," he said, "which the felons have dared to violate—would to God my weak strength were able to replace it—my humble strength, to atone for the sacrilege!"

He stooped to the task he first meditated, and with a sudden, and to himself almost an incredible exertion of power, he lifted up the one extremity of the lower shaft of the cross, and rested it upon the edge of the large stone which served for its pedestal. Encouraged by this success, he applied his force to the other extremity, and, to his own astonishment, succeeded so far as to erect the lower end of the limb into the socket, out of which it had been forced, and to place this fragment of the image upright.

While he was employed in this labour, or rather at the very moment when he had accomplished the elevation of the fragment, a voice, in thrilling and well-known accents, spoke behind him these words:— "Well done, thou good and faithful servant! Thus would I again meet the child of my love—the hope of my aged eyes."

Roland turned round in astonishment, and the tall commanding form of Magdalen Graeme stood beside him. She was arrayed in a sort of loose habit, in form like that worn by penitents in Catholic countries, but black in colour, and approaching as near to a pilgrim's cloak as it was safe to wear in a country where the suspicion of Catholic devotion in many places endangered the safety of those who were suspected of attachment to the ancient faith. Roland Graeme threw himself at her feet. She raised and embraced him, with affection indeed, but not unmixed with gravity which amounted almost to sternness.

"Thou hast kept well," she said, "the bird in thy bosom.* As a boy, as a youth, thou hast held fast thy faith amongst heretics—thou hast kept thy secret and mine own amongst thine enemies. I wept when I parted from you—I who seldom weep, then shed tears, less for thy death than for thy spiritual danger—I dared not even see thee to bid thee a last farewell—my grief, my swelling grief, had betrayed me to these heretics. But thou hast been faithful—down, down on thy knees before the holy sign, which evil men injure and blaspheme; down, and praise saints and angels for the grace they have done thee, in preserving thee from the leprous plague which cleaves to the house in which thou wert nurtured."

---

* An expression used by Sir Ralph Percy, slain in the battle of Hedgly-moor in 1464, when dying, to express his having preserved unstained his fidelity to the house of Lancaster.

"If, my mother—so I must ever call you" replied Graeme,—"if I am returned such as thou wouldst wish me, thou must thank the care of the pious father Ambrose, whose instructions confirmed your early precepts, and taught me at once to be faithful and to be silent."

"Be he blessed for it," said she; "blessed in the cell and in the field, in the pulpit and at the altar—the saints rain blessings on him!—they are just, and employ his pious care to counteract the evils which his detested brother works against the realm and the church,—but he knew not of thy lineage?"

"I could not myself tell him that," answered Roland. "I knew but darkly from your words, that Sir Halbert Glendinning holds mine inheritance, and that I am of blood as noble as runs in the veins of any Scottish Baron—these are things not to be forgotten, but for the explanation I must now look to you."

"And when time suits, thou shalt not look for it in vain. But men say, my son, that thou art bold and sudden; and those who bear such tempers are not lightly to be trusted with what will strongly move them."

"Say rather, my mother," returned Roland Graeme, "that I am laggard and cold-blooded—what patience or endurance can you require of which *he* is not capable, who for years has heard his religion ridiculed and insulted, yet failed to plunge his dagger into the blasphemer's bosom!"

"Be contented, my child," replied Magdalen Graeme; "the time, which then and even now demands patience, will soon ripen to that of effort and action—great events are on the wing, and thou,—thou shalt have thy share in advancing them. Thou hast relinquished the service of the Lady of Avenel?"

"I have been dismissed from it, my mother—I have lived to be dismissed, as if I were the meanest of the train."

"It is the better, my child," replied she; "thy mind will be the more hardened to undertake that which must be performed."

"Let it be nothing, then, against the Lady of Avenel," said the page, "as thy look and words seem to imply. I have eaten her bread—I have experienced her favour—I will neither injure nor betray her."

"Of that hereafter, my son," said she; "but learn this, that it is not for thee to capitulate in thy duty, and to say this will I do, and that will I leave undone—No, Roland! God and man will no longer abide the wickedness of this generation. Seest thou these fragments—knowest thou what they represent?—and canst thou think it is for thee to make distinctions amongst a race so accursed by Heaven, that they renounce, violate, blaspheme, and destroy, whatsoever we are commanded to believe in, whatsoever we are commanded to reverence?"

As she spoke, she bent her head towards the broken image, with a countenance in which strong resentment and zeal were mingled with an expression of ecstatic devotion; she raised her left hand aloft as in the act of making a vow, and thus proceeded; "Bear witness for me, blessed symbol of our salvation, bear witness, holy saint, within whose violated temple we stand, that as it is not for vengeance of my own that my hate pursues these people, so neither, for any favour or earthly affection towards any amongst them, will I withdraw my hand from the plough, when it shall pass through the devoted furrow! Bear witness, holy saint, once thyself a wanderer and fugitive as we are now—bear witness, Mother of Mercy, Queen of Heaven—bear witness, saints and angels!"

In this high train of enthusiasm, she stood, raising her eyes through the fractured roof of the vault, to the stars which now began to twinkle through the pale twilight, while the long gray tresses which hung down over her shoulders waved in the night-breeze, which the chasm and fractured windows admitted freely.

Roland Graeme was too much awed by early habits, as well as by the mysterious import of her words, to ask for farther explanation of the purpose she obscurely hinted at. Nor did she farther press him on the subject; for, having concluded her prayer or obtestation, by clasping her hands together with solemnity, and then signing herself with the cross, she again addressed her grandson, in a tone more adapted to the ordinary business of life.

"Thou must hence," she said, "Roland, thou must hence, but not till morning—And now, how wilt thou shift for thy night's quarters?— thou hast been more softly bred than when we were companions in the misty hills of Cumberland and Liddesdale."

"I have at least preserved, my good mother, the habits which I then learned—can lie hard, feed sparingly, and think it no hardship. Since I was a wanderer with thee on the hills, I have been a hunter, and fisher, and fowler, and each of these is accustomed to sleep freely in a worse shelter than sacrilege has left us here."

"Than sacrilege has left us here!" said the matron, repeating his words, and pausing on them. "Most true, my son; and God's faithful children are now worst sheltered, when they lodge in God's own house and the demesne of his blessed saints. We shall sleep cold here, under the nightwind, which whistles through the breaches which heresy has made. They shall lie warmer who made them—ay, and through a long hereafter."

Notwithstanding the wild and singular expression of this female, she appeared to retain towards Roland Graeme, in a strong degree, that affectionate and sedulous love which women bear to their nurslings, and the children dependent on their care. It seemed as if she would not permit him to do aught for himself which in former days her attention had been used to do for him, and that she considered the tall stripling before her as being equally dependent on her careful attention as when he was the orphan child, who had owed all to her affectionate solicitude.

"What hast thou to eat now?" she said, as, leaving the chapel, they went into the deserted habitation of the priest; "or what means of kindling a fire, to defend thee from this raw and inclement air? Poor child! thou hast made slight provision for a long journey; nor hast thou skill to help thyself by wit, when means are scanty. But Our Lady has placed by thy side one to whom want, in all its forms, is as familiar as plenty and splendour have formerly been. And with want, Roland, come the arts of which she is the inventor."

With an active and officious diligence, which strangely contrasted with her late abstracted and high tone of Catholic devotion, she set about her domestic arrangements for the evening. A pouch, which was hidden under her garment, produced a flint and steel, and from the scattered fragments around (those pertaining to the image of Saint Cuthbert scrupulously excepted) she obtained splinters sufficient to raise a sparkling and cheerful fire on the hearth of the deserted cell.

"And now," she said, "for needful food."

"Think not of it, mother," said Roland, "unless you yourself feel hunger. It is a little thing for me to endure a night's abstinence, and a small atonement for the necessary transgression of the rules of the Church upon which I was compelled during my stay in the castle."

"Hunger for myself!" answered the matron—"Know, youth, that a mother knows not hunger till that of her child is satisfied." And with affectionate inconsistency, totally different from her usual manner, she added, "Roland, you must not fast; you have dispensation; you are young, and to youth food and sleep are necessaries not to be dispensed with. Husband your strength, my child,—your sovereign, your religion, your country, require it. Let age macerate by fast and vigil a body which can only suffer; let youth, in these active times, nourish the limbs and the strength which action requires."

While she thus spoke, the scrip, which had produced the means of striking fire, furnished provision for a meal; of which she herself scarce partook, but anxiously watched her charge, taking a pleasure, resembling that of an epicure, in each morsel which he swallowed with a youthful appetite which abstinence had rendered unusually sharp. Roland readily obeyed her recommendations, and ate the food which she so affectionately and earnestly placed before him. But she shook her head when invited by him in return to partake of the refreshment her own cares had furnished; and when his solicitude became more pressing, she refused him in a loftier tone of rejection.

"Young man," she said, "you know not to whom or of what you speak. They to whom Heaven declares its purpose must merit its communication by mortifying the senses; they have that within which requires not the superfluity of earthly nutriment, which is necessary to those who are without the sphere of the Vision. To them the watch spent in prayer is a refreshing slumber, and the sense of doing the will of Heaven is a richer banquet than the tables of monarchs can spread before them!—But do thou sleep soft, my son," she said, relapsing from the tone of fanaticism into that of maternal affection and tenderness; "do thou sleep sound while life is but young with thee, and the cares of the day can be drowned in the slumbers of the evening. Different is thy duty and mine, and as different the means by which we must qualify and strengthen ourselves to perform it. From thee is demanded strength of body—from me, strength of soul."

When she thus spoke, she prepared with ready address a pallet-couch, composed partly of the dried leaves which had once furnished a bed to the solitary, and the guests who occasionally received his hospitality, and which, neglected by the destroyers of his humble cell, had remained little disturbed in the corner allotted for them. To these her care added some of the vestures which lay torn and scattered on the floor. With a zealous hand she selected all such as appeared to have made any part of the sacerdotal vestments, laying them aside as sacred from ordinary purposes, and with the rest she made, with dexterous promptness, such a bed as a weary man might willingly stretch himself on; and during the time she was preparing it, rejected, even with acrimony, any attempt which the youth made to assist her, or any entreaty which he urged, that she would accept of the place of rest for her own use. "Sleep thou," said she, "Roland Graeme, sleep thou—the persecuted, the disinherited orphan—the son of an ill-fated mother—sleep thou! I go to pray in the chapel beside thee."

The manner was too enthusiastically earnest, too obstinately firm, to permit Roland Graeme to dispute her will any farther. Yet he felt some shame in giving way to it. It seemed as if she had forgotten the years that had passed away since their parting; and expected to meet, in the tall, indulged, and wilful youth, whom she had recovered, the passive obedience of the child whom she had left in the Castle of Avenel. This did not fail to hurt her grandson's characteristic and constitutional pride. He obeyed, indeed, awed into submission by the sudden recurrence of former subordination, and by feelings of affection and gratitude. Still, however, he felt the yoke.

"Have I relinquished the hawk and the hound," he said, "to become the pupil of her pleasure, as if I were still a child?—I, whom even my envious mates allowed to be superior in those exercises which they took most pains to acquire, and which came to me naturally, as if a knowledge of them had been my birthright? This may not, and must not be. I will be no reclaimed sparrow-hawk, who is carried hooded on a woman's wrist, and has his quarry only shown to him when his eyes are uncovered for his flight. I will know her purpose ere it is proposed to me to aid it."

These, and other thoughts, streamed through the mind of Roland Graeme; and although wearied with the fatigues of the day, it was long ere he could compose himself to rest.

IX

Kneel with me—swear it—'tis not in words I trust,
Save when they're fenced with an appeal to Heaven.

—Old Play

After passing the night in that sound sleep for which agitation and fatigue had prepared him, Roland was awakened by the fresh morning air, and by the beams of the rising sun. His first feeling was that of surprise; for, instead of looking forth from a turret window on the Lake of Avenel, which was the prospect his former apartment afforded, an unlatticed aperture gave him the view of the demolished garden of the banished anchorite. He sat up on his couch of leaves, and arranged in his memory, not without wonder, the singular events of the preceding day, which appeared the more surprising the more he considered them. He had lost the protectress of his youth, and, in the same day, he had recovered the guide and guardian of his childhood. The former deprivation he felt ought to be matter of unceasing regret, and it seemed as if the latter could hardly be the subject of unmixed self-congratulation. He remembered this person, who had stood to him in the relation of a mother, as equally affectionate in her attention, and absolute in her authority. A singular mixture of love and fear attended upon his early remembrances as they were connected with her; and the fear that she might desire to resume the same absolute control over his motions—a fear which her conduct of yesterday did not tend much to dissipate—weighed heavily against the joy of this second meeting.

"She cannot mean," said his rising pride, "to lead and direct me as a pupil, when I am at the age of judging of my own actions?—this she cannot mean, or meaning it, will feel herself strangely deceived."

A sense of gratitude towards the person against whom his heart thus rebelled, checked his course of feeling. He resisted the thoughts which involuntarily arose in his mind, as he would have resisted an actual instigation of the foul fiend; and, to aid him in his struggle, he felt for his beads. But, in his hasty departure from the Castle of Avenel, he had forgotten and left them behind him.

"This is yet worse," he said; "but two things I learned of her under the most deadly charge of secrecy—to tell my beads, and to conceal that I did so; and I have kept my word till now; and when she shall ask me for the rosary, I must say I have forgotten it! Do I deserve she should believe me when. I say I have kept the secret of my faith, when I set so light by its symbol?"

He paced the floor in anxious agitation. In fact, his attachment to his faith was of a nature very different from that which animated the enthusiastic matron, but which, notwithstanding, it would have been his last thought to relinquish.

The early charges impressed on him by his grandmother, had been instilled into a mind and memory of a character peculiarly tenacious. Child as he was, he was proud of the confidence reposed in his discretion, and resolved to show that it had not been rashly intrusted to him. At the same time, his resolution was no more than that of a child, and must, necessarily, have gradually faded away under the operation both of precept and example, during his residence at the Castle of Avenel, but for the exhortations of Father Ambrose, who, in his lay estate, had been called Edward Glendinning. This zealous monk had been apprized, by an unsigned letter placed in his hand by a pilgrim, that a child educated in the Catholic faith was now in the Castle of Avenel, perilously situated, (so was the scroll expressed,) as ever the three children who were cast into the fiery furnace of persecution. The letter threw upon Father Ambrose the fault, should this solitary lamb, unwillingly left within the demesnes of the prowling wolf, become his final prey. There needed no farther exhortation to the monk than the idea that a soul might be endangered, and that a Catholic might become an apostate; and he made his visits more frequent than usual to the castle of Avenel, lest, through want of the private encouragement and instruction which he always found some opportunity of dispensing, the church should lose a proselyte, and, according to the Romish creed, the devil acquire a soul.

Still these interviews were rare; and though they encouraged the solitary boy to keep his secret and hold fast his religion, they were neither frequent nor long enough to inspire him with any thing beyond a blind attachment to the observances which the priest recommended. He adhered to the forms of his religion rather because he felt it would be dishonourable to change that of his fathers, than from any rational conviction or sincere belief of its mysterious doctrines. It was a principal part of the distinction which, in his own opinion, singled him out from those with whom he lived, and gave him an additional, though an internal and concealed reason, for contemning those of the household

SIR WALTER SCOTT

who showed an undisguised dislike of him, and for hardening himself against the instructions of the chaplain, Henry Warden.

"The fanatic preacher," he thought within himself, during some one of the chaplain's frequent discourses against the Church of Rome, "he little knows whose ears are receiving his profane doctrine, and with what contempt and abhorrence they hear his blasphemies against the holy religion by which kings have been crowned, and for which martyrs have died!"

But in such proud feelings of defiance of heresy, as it was termed, and of its professors, which associated the Catholic religion with a sense of generous independence, and that of the Protestants with the subjugation of his mind and temper to the direction of Mr. Warden, began and ended the faith of Roland Graeme, who, independently of the pride of singularity, sought not to understand, and had no one to expound to him, the peculiarities of the tenets which he professed. His regret, therefore, at missing the rosary which had been conveyed to him through the hands of Father Ambrose, was rather the shame of a soldier who has dropped his cockade, or badge of service, than that of a zealous votary who had forgotten a visible symbol of his religion.

His thoughts on the subject, however, were mortifying, and the more so from apprehension that his negligence must reach the ears of his relative. He felt it could be no one but her who had secretly transmitted these beads to Father Ambrose for his use, and that his carelessness was but an indifferent requital of her kindness.

"Nor will she omit to ask me about them," said he to himself; "for hers is a zeal which age cannot quell; and if she has not quitted her wont, my answer will not fail to incense her."

While he thus communed with himself, Magdalen Graeme entered the apartment. "The blessing of the morning on your youthful head, my son," she said, with a solemnity of expression which thrilled the youth to the heart, so sad and earnest did the benediction flow from her lips, in a tone where devotion was blended with affection. "And thou hast started thus early from thy couch to catch the first breath of the dawn? But it is not well, my Roland. Enjoy slumber while thou canst; the time is not far behind when the waking eye must be thy portion, as well as mine."

She uttered these words with an affectionate and anxious tone, which showed, that devotional as were the habitual exercises of her mind, the thoughts of her nursling yet bound her to earth with the cords of human affection and passion.

But she abode not long in a mood which she probably regarded as a momentary dereliction of her imaginary high calling—"Come," she said, "youth, up and be doing—It is time that we leave this place."

"And whither do we go?" said the young man; "or what is the object of our journey?"

The matron stepped back, and gazed on him with surprise, not unmingled with displeasure.

"To what purpose such a question?" she said; "is it not enough that I lead the way? Hast thou lived with heretics till thou hast learned to instal the vanity of thine own private judgment in place of due honour and obedience?"

"The time," thought Roland Graeme within himself, "is already come, when I must establish my freedom, or be a willing thrall for ever—I feel that I must speedily look to it."

She instantly fulfilled his foreboding, by recurring to the theme by which her thoughts seemed most constantly engrossed, although, when she pleased, no one could so perfectly disguise her religion.

"Thy beads, my son—hast thou told thy beads?"

Roland Graeme coloured high; he felt the storm was approaching, but scorned to avert it by a falsehood.

"I have forgotten my rosary," he said, "at the Castle of Avenel."

"Forgotten thy rosary!" she exclaimed; "false both to religion and to natural duty, hast thou lost what was sent so far, and at such risk, a token of the truest affection, that should have been, every bead of it, as dear to thee as thine eyeballs?"

"I am grieved it should have so chanced, mother," replied the youth, "and much did I value the token, as coming from you. For what remains, I trust to win gold enough, when I push my way in the world; and till then, beads of black oak, or a rosary of nuts, must serve the turn."

"Hear him!" said his grandmother; "young as he is, he hath learned already the lessons of the devil's school! The rosary, consecrated by the Holy Father himself, and sanctified by his blessing, is but a few knobs of gold, whose value may be replaced by the wages of his profane labour, and whose virtue may be supplied by a string of hazel-nuts!—This is heresy—So Henry Warden, the wolf who ravages the flock of the Shepherd, hath taught thee to speak and to think."

"Mother," said Roland Graeme, "I am no heretic; I believe and I pray according to the rules of our church—This misfortune I regret, but I cannot amend it."

"Thou canst repent it, though," replied his spiritual directress, "repent it in dust and ashes, atone for it by fasting, prayer, and penance, instead of looking on me with a countenance as light as if thou hadst lost but a button from thy cap."

"Mother," said Roland, "be appeased; I will remember my fault in the next confession which I have space and opportunity to make, and will do whatever the priest may require of me in atonement. For the heaviest fault I can do no more.—But, mother," he added, after a moment's pause, "let me not incur your farther displeasure, if I ask whither our journey is bound, and what is its object. I am no longer a child, but a man, and at my own disposal, with down upon my chin, and a sword by my side—I will go to the end of the world with you to do your pleasure; but I owe it to myself to inquire the purpose and direction of our travels."

"You owe it to yourself, ungrateful boy?" replied his relative, passion rapidly supplying the colour which age had long chased from her features,—"to yourself you owe nothing—you can owe nothing—to me you owe every thing—your life when an infant—your support while a child—the means of instruction, and the hopes of honour—and, sooner than thou shouldst abandon the noble cause to which I have devoted thee, would I see thee lie a corpse at my feet!"

Roland was alarmed at the vehement agitation with which she spoke, and which threatened to overpower her aged frame; and he hastened to reply,—"I forget nothing of what I owe to you, my dearest mother— show me how my blood can testify my gratitude, and you shall judge if I spare it. But blindfold obedience has in it as little merit as reason."

"Saints and angels!" replied Magdalen, "and do I hear these words from the child of my hopes, the nursling by whose bed I have kneeled, and for whose weal I have wearied every saint in heaven with prayers? Roland, by obedience only canst thou show thy affection and thy gratitude. What avails it that you might perchance adopt the course I propose to thee, were it to be fully explained? Thou wouldst not then follow my command, but thine own judgment; thou wouldst not do the will of Heaven, communicated through thy best friend, to whom thou owest thine all; but thou wouldst observe the blinded dictates of thine own imperfect reason. Hear me, Roland! a lot calls thee—solicits thee—demands thee—the proudest to which man can be destined, and it uses the voice of thine earliest, thy best, thine only friend—Wilt thou resist it? Then go thy way—leave me here—my hopes on earth are gone and withered—I will kneel me down before yonder profaned altar, and when the raging heretics return, they shall dye it with the blood of a martyr."

"But, my dearest mother," said Roland Graeme, whose early recollections of her violence were formidably renewed by these wild expressions of reckless passion, "I will not forsake you—I will abide with you—worlds shall not force me from your side—I will protect—I will defend you—I will live with you, and die for you!"

"One word, my son, were worth all these—say only, 'I will obey you.'"

"Doubt it not, mother," replied the youth, "I will, and that with all my heart; only—"

"Nay, I receive no qualifications of thy promise," said Magdalen Graeme, catching at the word, "the obedience which I require is absolute; and a blessing on thee, thou darling memory of my beloved child, that thou hast power to make a promise so hard to human pride! Trust me well, that in the design in which thou dost embark, thou hast for thy partners the mighty and the valiant, the power of the church, and the pride of the noble. Succeed or fail, live or die, thy name shall be among those with whom success or failure is alike glorious, death or life alike desirable. Forward, then, forward! life is short, and our plan is laborious—Angels, saints, and the whole blessed host of heaven, have their eyes even now on this barren and blighted land of Scotland—What say I? on Scotland? their eye is on *us*, Roland—on the frail woman, on the inexperienced youth, who, amidst the ruins which sacrilege hath made in the holy place, devote themselves to God's cause, and that of their lawful Sovereign. Amen, so be it! The blessed eyes of saints and martyrs, which see our resolve, shall witness the execution; or their ears, which hear our vow, shall hear our death-groan, drawn in the sacred cause!"

While thus speaking, she held Roland Graeme firmly with one hand, while she pointed upward with the other, to leave him, as it were, no means of protest against the obtestation to which he was thus made a party. When she had finished her appeal to Heaven, she left him no leisure for farther hesitation, or for asking any explanation of her purpose; but passing with the same ready transition as formerly, to the solicitous attentions of an anxious parent, overwhelmed him with questions concerning his residence in the Castle of Avenel, and the qualities and accomplishments he had acquired.

"It is well," she said, when she had exhausted her inquiries, "my gay goss-hawk* hath been well trained, and will soar high; but those who bred him will have cause to fear as well as to wonder at his flight.—Let us now," she said, "to our morning meal, and care not though it be a scanty one. A few hours' walk will bring us to more friendly quarters."

They broke their fast accordingly, on such fragments as remained of their yesterday's provision, and immediately set out on their farther journey. Magdalen Graeme led the way, with a firm and active step much beyond her years, and Roland Graeme followed, pensive and anxious, and far from satisfied with the state of dependence to which he seemed again to be reduced.

"Am I for ever," he said to himself, "to be devoured with the desire of independence and free agency, and yet to be for ever led on, by circumstances, to follow the will of others?"

---

* The comparison is taken from some beautiful verses in an old ballad, entitled Fause Foodrage, published in the "Minstrelsy of the Scottish Border." A deposed queen, to preserve her infant son from the traitors who have slain his father, exchanges him with the female offspring of a faithful friend, and goes on to direct the education of the children, and the private signals by which the parents are to hear news each of her own offspring.

> *"And you shall learn my gay goss-hawk*
> *Right well to breast a steed;*
> *And so will I your turtle dow,*
> *As well to write and read.*
>
> *And ye shall learn my gay goss-hawk*
> *To wield both bow and brand;*
> *And so will I your turtle dow,*
> *To lay gowd with her hand.*
>
> *At kirk or market when we meet,*
> *We'll dare make no avow,*
> *But, 'Dame, how does my gay goss-hawk?'*
> *'Madame, how does my dow?'"*

X

She dwelt unnoticed and alone,
Beside the springs of Dove:
A maid whom there was none to praise,
And very few to love.

—WORDSWORTH

In the course of their journey the travellers spoke little to each other.
Magdalen Graeme chanted, from time to time, in a low voice, a
part of some one of those beautiful old Latin hymns which belong to
the Catholic service, muttered an Ave or a Credo, and so passed on,
lost in devotional contemplation. The meditations of her grandson
were more bent on mundane matters; and many a time, as a moor-fowl
arose from the heath, and shot along the moor, uttering his bold crow
of defiance, he thought of the jolly Adam Woodcock, and his trusty
goss-hawk; or, as they passed a thicket where the low trees and bushes
were intermingled with tall fern, furze, and broom, so as to form a
thick and intricate cover, his dreams were of a roebuck and a brace
of gaze-hounds. But frequently his mind returned to the benevolent
and kind mistress whom he had left behind him, offended justly, and
unreconciled by any effort of his.

"My step would be lighter," he thought, "and so would my heart,
could I but have returned to see her for one instant, and to say, Lady,
the orphan boy was wild, but not ungrateful!"

Travelling in these divers moods, about the hour of noon they
reached a small straggling village, in which, as usual, were seen one or
two of those predominating towers, or peel houses, which, for reasons
of defence elsewhere detailed, were at that time to be found in every
Border hamlet. A brook flowed beside the village, and watered the valley
in which it stood. There was also a mansion at the end of the village, and a
little way separated from it, much dilapidated, and in very bad order, but
appearing to have been the abode of persons of some consideration. The
situation was agreeable, being an angle formed by the stream, bearing
three or four large sycamore trees, which were in full leaf, and served to
relieve the dark appearance of the mansion, which was built of a deep
red stone. The house itself was a large one, but was now obviously too

SIR WALTER SCOTT

big for the inmates; several windows were built up, especially those which opened from the lower story; others were blockaded in a less substantial manner. The court before the door, which had once been defended with a species of low outer-wall, now ruinous, was paved, but the stones were completely covered with long gray nettles, thistles, and other weeds, which, shooting up betwixt the flags, had displaced many of them from their level. Even matters demanding more peremptory attention had been left neglected, in a manner which argued sloth or poverty in the extreme. The stream, undermining a part of the bank near an angle of the ruinous wall, had brought it down, with a corner turret, the ruins of which lay in the bed of the river. The current, interrupted by the ruins which it had overthrown, and turned yet nearer to the site of the tower, had greatly enlarged the breach it had made, and was in the process of undermining the ground on which the house itself stood, unless it were speedily protected by sufficient bulwarks.

All this attracted Roland Graeme's observation, as they approached the dwelling by a winding path, which gave them, at intervals, a view of it from different points.

"If we go to yonder house," he said to his mother, "I trust it is but for a short visit. It looks as if two rainy days from the north-west would send the whole into the brook."

"You see but with the eyes of the body," said the old woman; "God will defend his own, though it be forsaken and despised of men. Better to dwell on the sand, under his law, than fly to the rock of human trust."

As she thus spoke, they entered the court before the old mansion, and Roland could observe that the front of it had formerly been considerably ornamented with carved work, in the same dark-coloured freestone of which it was built. But all these ornaments had been broken down and destroyed, and only the shattered vestiges of niches and entablatures now strewed the place which they had once occupied. The larger entrance in front was walled up, but a little footpath, which, from its appearance, seemed to be rarely trodden, led to a small wicket, defended by a door well clenched with iron-headed nails, at which Magdalen Graeme knocked three times, pausing betwixt each knock, until she heard an answering tap from within. At the last knock, the wicket was opened by a pale thin female, who said, "*Benedicti qui venient in nomine Domini.*" They entered, and the portress hastily shut behind them the wicket, and made fast the massive fastenings by which it was secured.

The female led the way through a narrow entrance, into a vestibule of some extent, paved with stone, and having benches of the same solid material ranged around. At the upper end was an oriel window, but some of the intervals formed by the stone shafts and mullions were blocked up, so that the apartment was very gloomy.

Here they stopped, and the mistress of the mansion, for such she was, embraced Magdalen Graeme, and greeting her by the title of sister, kissed her with much solemnity, on either side of the face.

"The blessing of Our Lady be upon you, my sister," were her next words; and they left no doubt upon Roland's mind respecting the religion of their hostess, even if he could have suspected his venerable and zealous guide of resting elsewhere than in the habitation of an orthodox Catholic. They spoke together a few words in private, during which he had leisure to remark more particularly the appearance of his grandmother's friend.

Her age might be betwixt fifty and sixty; her looks had a mixture of melancholy and unhappiness that bordered on discontent, and obscured the remains of beauty which age had still left on her features. Her dress was of the plainest and most ordinary description, of a dark colour, and, like Magdalen Graeme's, something approaching to a religious habit. Strict neatness and cleanliness of person, seemed to intimate, that if poor, she was not reduced to squalid or heart-broken distress, and that she was still sufficiently attached to life to retain a taste for its decencies, if not its elegancies. Her manner, as well as her features and appearance, argued an original condition and education far above the meanness of her present appearance. In short, the whole figure was such as to excite the idea, "That female must have had a history worth knowing." While Roland Graeme was making this very reflection, the whispers of the two females ceased, and the mistress of the mansion, approaching him, looked on his face and person with much attention, and, as it seemed, some interest.

"This, then," she said, addressing his relative, "is the child of thine unhappy daughter, sister Magdalen; and him, the only shoot from your ancient tree, you are willing to devote to the Good Cause?"

"Yes, by the rood," answered Magdalen Graeme, in her usual tone of resolved determination, "to the good cause I devote him, flesh and fell, sinew and limb, body and soul."

"Thou art a happy woman, sister Magdalen," answered her companion, "that, lifted so high above human affection and human feeling, thou

SIR WALTER SCOTT

canst bind such a victim to the horns of the altar. Had I been called to make such a sacrifice—to plunge a youth so young and fair into the plots and bloodthirsty dealings of the time, not the patriarch Abraham, when he led Isaac up the mountain, would have rendered more melancholy obedience."

She then continued to look at Roland with a mournful aspect of compassion, until the intentness of her gaze occasioned his colour to rise, and he was about to move out of its influence, when he was stopped by his grand-mother with one hand, while with the other she divided the hair upon his forehead, which was now crimson with bashfulness, while she added, with a mixture of proud affection and firm resolution,—"Ay, look at him well, my sister, for on a fairer face thine eye never rested. I too, when I first saw him, after a long separation, felt as the worldly feel, and was half shaken in my purpose. But no wind can tear a leaf from the withered tree which has long been stripped of its foliage, and no mere human casualty can awaken the mortal feelings which have long slept in the calm of devotion."

While the old woman thus spoke, her manner gave the lie to her assertions, for the tears rose to her eyes while she added, "But the fairer and the more spotless the victim, is it not, my sister, the more worthy of acceptance?"

She seemed glad to escape from the sensations which agitated her, and instantly added, "He will escape, my sister—there will be a ram caught in the thicket, and the hand of our revolted brethren shall not be on the youthfull Joseph. Heaven can defend its own rights, even by means of babes and sucklings, of women and beardless boys."

"Heaven hath left us," said the other female; "for our sins and our fathers' the succours of the blessed Saints have abandoned this accursed land. We may win the crown of Martyrdom, but not that of earthly triumph. One, too, whose prudence was at this deep crisis so indispensable, has been called to a better world. The Abbot Eustatius is no more."

"May his soul have mercy!" said Magdalen Graeme, "and may Heaven, too, have mercy upon us, who linger behind in this bloody land! His loss is indeed a perilous blow to our enterprise; for who remains behind possessing his far-fetched experience, his self-devoted zeal, his consummate wisdom, and his undaunted courage! He hath fallen with the church's standard in his hand, but God will raise up another to lift the blessed banner. Whom have the Chapter elected in his room?"

"It is rumoured no one of the few remaining brethren dare accept the office. The heretics have sworn that they will permit no future election, and will heavily punish any attempt to create a new Abbot of Saint Mary's. *Conjuraverunt inter se principes, dicentes, Projiciamus laqueos ejus.*"

"*Quousque, Domine!*"—exclaimed Magdalen; "this, my sister, were indeed a perilous and fatal breach in our band; but I am firm in my belief, that another will arise in the place of him so untimely removed. Where is thy daughter Catharine?"

"In the parlour," answered the matron, "but"—She looked at Roland Graeme, and muttered something in the ear of her friend.

"Fear it not," answered Magdalen Graeme, "it is both lawful and necessary—fear nothing from him—I would he were as well grounded in the faith by which alone comes safety, as he is free from thought, deed, or speech of villany. Therein is the heretics' discipline to be commended, my sister, that they train up their youth in strong morality, and choke up every inlet to youthful folly."

"It is but a cleansing the outside of the cup," answered her friend, "a whitening of the sepulchre; but he shall see Catharine, since you, sister, judge it safe and meet.—Follow us, youth," she added, and led the way from the apartment—with her friend. These were the only words which the matron had addressed to Roland Graeme, who obeyed them in silence. As they paced through several winding passages and waste apartments with a very slow step, the young page had leisure to make some reflections on his situation,—reflections of a nature which his ardent temper considered as specially disagreeable. It seemed he had now got two mistresses, or tutoresses, instead of one, both elderly women, and both, it would seem, in league to direct his motions according to their own pleasure, and for the accomplishment of plans to which he was no party. This, he thought, was too much; arguing reasonably enough, that whatever right his grandmother and benefactress had to guide his motions, she was neither entitled to transfer her authority or divide it with another, who seemed to assume, without ceremony, the same tone of absolute command over him.

"But it shall not long continue thus," thought Roland; "I will not be all my life the slave of a woman's whistle, to go when she bids, and come when she calls. No, by Saint Andrew! the hand that can hold the lance is above the control of the distaff. I will leave them the slipp'd collar in their hands on the first opportunity, and let them execute their own devices by their own proper force. It may save them both from peril, for

SIR WALTER SCOTT

I guess what they meditate is not likely to prove either safe or easy—the Earl of Murray and his heresy are too well rooted to be grubbed up by two old women."

As he thus resolved, they entered a low room, in which a third female was seated. This apartment was the first he had observed in the mansion which was furnished with moveable seats, and with a wooden table, over which was laid a piece of tapestry. A carpet was spread on the floor, there was a grate in the chimney, and, in brief, the apartment had the air of being habitable and inhabited.

But Roland's eyes found better employment than to make observations on the accommodations of the chamber; for this second female inhabitant of the mansion seemed something very different from any thing he had yet seen there. At his first entry, she had greeted with a silent and low obeisance the two aged matrons, then glancing her eyes towards Roland, she adjusted a veil which hung back over her shoulders, so as to bring it over her face; an operation which she performed with much modesty, but without either affected haste or embarrassed timidity.

During this manoeuvre Roland had time to observe, that the face was that of a girl apparently not much past sixteen, and that the eyes were at once soft and brilliant. To these very favourable observations was added the certainty that the fair object to whom they referred possessed an excellent shape, bordering perhaps on *enbonpoint*, and therefore rather that of a Hebe than of a Sylph, but beautifully formed, and shown to great advantage by the close jacket and petticoat which she wore after a foreign fashion, the last not quite long enough to conceal a very pretty foot, which rested on a bar of the table at which she sate; her round arms and taper fingers very busily employed in repairing— the piece of tapestry which was spread on it, which exhibited several deplorable fissures, enough to demand the utmost skill of the most expert seamstress.

It is to be remarked, that it was by stolen glances that Roland Graeme contrived to ascertain these interesting particulars; and he thought he could once or twice, notwithstanding the texture of the veil, detect the damsel in the act of taking similar cognizance of his own person. The matrons in the meanwhile continued their separate conversation, eyeing from time to time the young people, in a manner which left Roland in no doubt that they were the subject of their conversation. At length he distinctly heard Magdalen Graeme say these words—"Nay, my sister, we must give them opportunity to speak together, and to become acquainted; they must be personally known to each other, or how shall they be able to execute what they are intrusted with?"

It seemed as if the matron, not fully satisfied with her friend's reasoning, continued to offer some objections; but they were borne down by her more dictatorial friend.

"It must be so," she said, "my dear sister; let us therefore go forth on the balcony, to finish our conversation.—And do you," she said, addressing Roland and the girl, "become acquainted with each other."

With this she stepped up to the young woman, and raising her veil, discovered features which, whatever might be their ordinary complexion, were now covered with a universal blush.

"*Licitum sit*," said Magdalen, looking at the other matron.

"*Vix licitum*," replied the other, with reluctant and hesitating acquiescence; and again adjusting the veil of the blushing girl, she dropped it so as to shade, though not to conceal her countenance, and whispered to her, in a tone loud enough for the page to hear, "Remember, Catharine, who thou art, and for what destined."

The matron then retreated with Magdalen Graeme through one of the casements of the apartment, that opened on a large broad balcony, which, with its ponderous balustrade, had once run along the whole south front of the building which faced the brook, and formed a pleasant and commodious walk in the open air. It was now in some places deprived of the balustrade, in others broken and narrowed; but, ruinous as it was, could still be used as a pleasant promenade. Here then walked the two ancient dames, busied in their private conversation; yet not so much so, but that Roland could observe the matrons, as their thin forms darkened the casement in passing or repassing before it, dart a glance into the apartment, to see how matters were going on there.

XI

Life hath its May, and is mirthful then:
The woods are vocal, and the flowers all odour;
Its very blast has mirth in't,—and the maidens,
The while they don their cloaks to screen their kirtles,
Laugh at the rain that wets them.

—OLD PLAY

C atherine was at the happy age of innocence and buoyancy of spirit, when, after the first moment of embarrassment was over, a situation of awkwardness, like that in which she was suddenly left to make acquaintance with a handsome youth, not even known to her by name, struck her, in spite of herself, in a ludicrous point of view. She bent her beautiful eyes upon the work with which she was busied, and with infinite gravity sate out the two first turns of the matrons upon the balcony; but then, glancing her deep blue eye a little towards Roland, and observing the embarrassment under which he laboured, now shifting on his chair, and now dangling his cap, the whole man evincing that he was perfectly at a loss how to open the conversation, she could keep her composure no longer, but after a vain struggle broke out into a sincere, though a very involuntary fit of laughing, so richly accompanied by the laughter of her merry eyes, which actually glanced through the tears which the effort filled them with, and by the waving of her rich tresses, that the goddess of smiles herself never looked more lovely than Catherine at that moment. A court page would not have left her long alone in her mirth; but Roland was country-bred, and, besides, having some jealousy as well as bashfulness, he took it into his head that he was himself the object of her inextinguishable laughter. His endeavours to sympathize with Catherine, therefore, could carry him no farther than a forced giggle, which had more of displeasure than of mirth in it, and which so much enhanced that of the girl, that it seemed to render it impossible for her ever to bring her laughter to an end, with whatever anxious pains she laboured to do so. For every one has felt, that when a paroxysm of laughter has seized him at a misbecoming time and place, the efforts which he made to suppress it, nay, the very sense of the impropriety of giving way to it, tend only to augment and prolong the irresistible impulse.

It was undoubtedly lucky for Catherine, as well as for Roland, that the latter did not share in the excessive mirth of the former. For, seated as she was, with her back to the casement, Catherine could easily escape the observation of the two matrons during the course of their promenade; whereas Graeme was so placed, with his side to the window, that his mirth, had he shared that of his companion, would have been instantly visible, and could not have failed to give offence to the personages in question. He sate, however, with some impatience, until Catherine had exhausted either her power or her desire of laughing, and was returning with good grace to the exercise of her needle, and then he observed with some dryness, that "there seemed no great occasion to recommend to them to improve their acquaintance, as it seemed, that they were already tolerably familiar."

Catherine had an extreme desire to set off upon a fresh score, but she repressed it strongly, and fixing her eyes on her work, replied by asking his pardon, and promising to avoid future offence.

Roland had sense enough to feel, that an air of offended dignity was very much misplaced, and that it was with a very different bearing he ought to meet the deep blue eyes which had borne such a hearty burden in the laughing scene. He tried, therefore, to extricate himself as well as he could from his blunder, by assuming a tone of correspondent gaiety, and requesting to know of the nymph, "how it was her pleasure that they should proceed in improving the acquaintance which had commenced so merrily."

"That," she said, "you must yourself discover; perhaps I have gone a step too far in opening our interview."

"Suppose," said Roland Graeme, "we should begin as in a tale-book, by asking each other's names and histories?"

"It is right well imagined," said Catherine, "and shows an argute judgment. Do you begin, and I will listen, and only put in a question or two at the dark parts of the story. Come, unfold then your name and history, my new acquaintance."

"I am called Roland Graeme, and that tall woman is my grandmother."

"And your tutoress?—good. Who are your parents?"

"They are both dead," replied Roland.

"Ay, but who were they? you *had* parents, I presume?"

"I suppose so," said Roland, "but I have never been able to learn much of their history. My father was a Scottish knight, who died gallantly in his stirrups—my mother was a Graeme of Hathergill, in the

Debateable Land—most of her family were killed when the Debateable country was burned by Lord Maxwell and Herries of Caerlaverock."

"Is it long ago?" said the damsel.

"Before I was born," answered the page.

"That must be a great while since," said she, shaking her head gravely; "look you, I cannot weep for them."

"It needs not," said the youth, "they fell with honour."

"So much for your lineage, fair sir," replied his companion, "of whom I like the living specimen (a glance at the casement) far less than those that are dead. Your much honoured grandmother looks as if she could make one weep in sad earnest. And now, fair sir, for your own person— if you tell not the tale faster, it will be cut short in the middle; Mother Bridget pauses longer and longer every time she passes the window, and with her there is as little mirth as in the grave of your ancestors."

"My tale is soon told—I was introduced into the castle of Avenel to be page to the lady of the mansion."

"She is a strict Huguenot, is she not?" said the maiden.

"As strict as Calvin himself. But my grandmother can play the puritan when it suits her purpose, and she had some plan of her own, for quartering me in the Castle—it would have failed, however, after we had remained several weeks at the hamlet, but for an unexpected master of ceremonies—"

"And who was that?" said the girl.

"A large black dog, Wolf by name, who brought me into the castle one day in his mouth, like a hurt wild-duck, and presented me to the lady."

"A most respectable introduction, truly," said Catherine; "and what might you learn at this same castle? I love dearly to know what my acquaintances can do at need."

"To fly a hawk, hollow to a hound, back a horse, and wield lance, bow, and brand."

"And to boast of all this when you have learned it," said Catherine, "which, in France at least, is the surest accomplishment of a page. But proceed, fair sir; how came your Huguenot lord and your no less Huguenot lady to receive and keep in the family so perilous a person as a Catholic page?"

"Because they knew not that part of my history, which from infancy I have been taught to keep secret—and because my grand-dame's former zealous attendance on their heretic chaplain, had laid all this suspicion to sleep, most fair Callipolis," said the page; and in so saying, he edged his chair towards the seat of the fair querist.

"Nay, but keep your distance, most gallant sir," answered the blue-eyed maiden, "for, unless I greatly mistake, these reverend ladies will soon interrupt our amicable conference, if the acquaintance they recommend shall seem to proceed beyond a certain point—so, fair sir, be pleased to abide by your station, and reply to my questions.—By what achievements did you prove the qualities of a page, which you had thus happily acquired?"

Roland, who began to enter into the tone and spirit of the damsel's conversation, replied to her with becoming spirit.

"In no feat, fair gentlewoman, was I found inexpert, wherein there was mischief implied. I shot swans, hunted cats, frightened serving-women, chased the deer, and robbed the orchard. I say nothing of tormenting the chaplain in various ways, for that was my duty as a good Catholic."

"Now, as I am a gentlewoman," said Catherine, "I think these heretics have done Catholic penance in entertaining so all-accomplished a serving-man! And what, fair sir, might have been the unhappy event which deprived them of an inmate altogether so estimable?"

"Truly, fair gentlewoman," answered the youth, "your real proverb says that the longest lane will have a turning, and mine was more—it was, in fine, a turning off."

"Good!" said the merry young maiden, "it is an apt play on the word—and what occasion was taken for so important a catastrophe?—Nay, start not for my learning, I do know the schools—in plain phrase, why were you sent from service?"

The page shrugged his shoulders while he replied,—"A short tale is soon told—and a short horse soon curried. I made the falconer's boy taste of my switch—the falconer threatened to make me brook his cudgel—he is a kindly clown as well as a stout, and I would rather have been cudgelled by him than any man in Christendom to choose—but I knew not his qualities at that time—so I threatened to make him brook the stab, and my Lady made me brook the 'Begone;' so adieu to the page's office and the fair Castle of Avenel—I had not travelled far before I met my venerable parent—And so tell your tale, fair gentlewoman, for mine is done."

"A happy grandmother," said the maiden, "who had the luck to find the stray page just when his mistress had slipped his leash, and a most lucky page that has jumped at once from a page to an old lady's gentleman-usher!"

"All this is nothing of your history," answered Roland Graeme, began to be much interested in the congenial vivacity of this facetious young gentlewoman,—"tale for tale is fellow-traveller's justice."

"Wait till we are fellow-travellers, then," replied Catherine.

"Nay, you escape me not so," said the page; "if you deal not justly by me, I will call out to Dame Bridget, or whatever your dame be called, and proclaim you for a cheat."

"You shall not need," answered the maiden—"my history is the counterpart of your own; the same words might almost serve, change but dress and name. I am called Catherine Seyton, and I also am an orphan."

"Have your parents been long dead?"

"This is the only question," said she, throwing down her fine eyes with a sudden expression of sorrow, "that is the only question I cannot laugh at."

"And Dame Bridget is your grandmother?"

The sudden cloud passed away like that which crosses for an instant the summer sun, and she answered with her usual lively expression, "Worse by twenty degrees—Dame Bridget is my maiden aunt."

"Over gods forbode!" said Roland—"Alas! that you have such a tale to tell! and what horror comes next?"

"Your own history, exactly. I was taken upon trial for service—"

"And turned off for pinching the duenna, or affronting my lady's waiting-woman?"

"Nay, our history varies there," said the damsel—"Our mistress broke up house, or had her house broke up, which is the same thing, and I am a free woman of the forest."

"And I am as glad of it as if any one had lined my doublet with cloth of gold," said the youth.

"I thank you for your mirth," said she, "but the matter is not likely to concern you."

"Nay, but go on," said the page, "for you will be presently interrupted; the two good dames have been soaring yonder on the balcony, like two old hooded crows, and their croak grows hoarser as night comes on; they will wing to roost presently.—This mistress of yours, fair gentlewoman, who was she, in God's name?"

"Oh, she has a fair name in the world," replied Catherine Seyton. "Few ladies kept a fairer house, or held more gentlewomen in her household; my aunt Bridget was one of her housekeepers. We never saw our mistress's blessed face, to be sure, but we heard enough of her; were up early and down late, and were kept to long prayers and light food."

"Out upon the penurious old beldam!" said the page.

"For Heaven's sake, blaspheme not!" said the girl, with an expression of fear.—"God pardon us both! I meant no harm. I speak of our blessed Saint Catherine of Sienna!—may God forgive me that I spoke so lightly, and made you do a great sin and a great blasphemy. This was her nunnery, in which there were twelve nuns and an abbess. My aunt was the abbess, till the heretics turned all adrift."

"And where are your companions?" asked the youth.

"With the last year's snow," answered the maiden; "east, north, south, and west—some to France, some to Flanders, some, I fear, into the world and its pleasures. We have got permission to remain, or rather our remaining has been connived at, for my aunt has great relations among the Kerrs, and they have threatened a death-feud if any one touches us; and bow and spear are the best warrant in these times."

"Nay, then, you sit under a sure shadow," said the youth; "and I suppose you wept yourself blind when Saint Catherine broke up housekeeping before you had taken arles* in her service?"

"Hush! for Heaven's sake," said the damsel, crossing herself; "no more of that! but I have not quite cried my eyes out," said she, turning them upon him, and instantly again bending them upon her work. It was one of those glances which would require the threefold plate of brass around the heart, more than it is needed by the mariners, to whom Horace recommends it. Our youthful page had no defence whatever to offer.

"What say you, Catherine," he said, "if we two, thus strangely turned out of service at the same time, should give our two most venerable duennas the torch to hold, while we walk a merry measure with each other over the floor of this weary world?"

"A goodly proposal, truly," said Catherine, "and worthy the mad-cap brain of a discarded page!—And what shifts does your worship propose we should live by?—by singing ballads, cutting purses, or swaggering on the highway? for there, I think, you would find your most productive exchequer."

---

* *Anglice*—Earnest-money

"Choose, you proud peat!" said the page, drawing off in huge disdain at the calm and unembarrassed ridicule with which his wild proposal was received. And as he spoke the words, the casement was again darkened by the forms of the matrons—it opened, and admitted Magdalen Graeme and the Mother Abbess, so we must now style her, into the apartment.

XII

Nay, hear me, brother—I am elder, wiser,
And holier than thou—And age, and wisdom,
And holiness, have peremptory claims,
And will be listen'd to.

—Old Play

When the matrons re-entered, and put an end to the conversation—which we have detailed in the last chapter, Dame Magdalen Graeme thus addressed her grandson and his pretty companion: "Have you spoke together, my children?—Have you become known to each other as fellow-travellers on the same dark and dubious road, whom chance hath brought together, and who study to learn the tempers and dispositions of those by whom their perils are to be shared?"

It was seldom the light-hearted Catharine could suppress a jest, so that she often spoke when she would have acted more wisely in holding her peace.

"Your grandson admires the journey which you propose so very greatly, that he was even now preparing for setting out upon it instantly."

"This is to be too forward, Roland," said the dame, addressing him, "as yesterday you were over slack—the just mean lies in obedience, which both waits for the signal to start, and obeys it when given.—But once again, my children, have you so perused each other's countenances, that when you meet, in whatever disguise the times may impose upon you, you may recognize each in the other the secret agent of the mighty work in which you are to be leagued?—Look at each other, know each line and lineament of each other's countenance. Learn to distinguish by the step, by the sound of the voice, by the motion of the hand, by the glance of the eye, the partner whom Heaven hath sent to aid in working its will.—Wilt thou know that maiden, whensoever, or wheresoever you shall again meet her, my Roland Graeme?"

As readily as truly did Roland answer in the affirmative. "And thou, my daughter, wilt thou again remember the features of this youth?"

"Truly, mother," replied Catherine Seyton, "I have not seen so many men of late, that I should immediately forget your grandson, though I mark not much about him that is deserving of especial remembrance."

"Join hands, then, my children," said Magdalen Graeme; but, in saying so, was interrupted by her companion, whose conventual prejudices had been gradually giving her more and more uneasiness, and who could remain acquiescent no longer.

"Nay, my good sister, you forget," said she to Magdalen, "Catharine is the betrothed bride of Heaven—these intimacies cannot be."

"It is in the cause of Heaven that I command them to embrace," said Magdalen, with the full force of her powerful voice; "the end, sister, sanctifies the means we must use."

"They call me Lady Abbess, or Mother at the least, who address me," said Dame Bridget, drawing herself up, as if offended at her friend's authoritative manner—"the Lady of Heathergill forgets that she speaks to the Abbess of Saint Catherine."

"When I was what you call me," said Magdalen, "you indeed were the Abbess of Saint Catherine, but both names are now gone, with all the rank that the world and that the church gave to them; and we are now, to the eye of human judgment, two poor, despised, oppressed women, dragging our dishonoured old age to a humble grave. But what are we in the eye of Heaven?—Ministers, sent forth to work his will,—in whose weakness the strength of the church shall be manifested-before whom shall be humbled the wisdom of Murray, and the dark strength of Morton,—And to such wouldst thou apply the narrow rules of thy cloistered seclusion?—or, hast thou forgotten the order which I showed thee from thy Superior, subjecting thee to me in these matters?"

"On thy head, then, be the scandal and the sin," said the Abbess, sullenly.

"On mine be they both," said Magdalen. "I say, embrace each other, my children."

But Catherine, aware, perhaps, how the dispute was likely to terminate, had escaped from the apartment, and so disappointed the grandson, at least as much as the old matron.

"She is gone," said the Abbess, "to provide some little refreshment. But it will have little savour to those who dwell in the world; for I, at least, cannot dispense with the rules to which I am vowed, because it is the will of wicked men to break down the sanctuary in which they wont to be observed."

"It is well, my sister," replied Magdalen, "to pay each even the smallest tithes of mint and cummin which the church demands, and I blame not thy scrupulous observance of the rules of thine order. But they were established by the church, and for the church's benefit; and reason it is that they should give way when the salvation of the church herself is at stake."

The Abbess made no reply.

One more acquainted with human nature than the inexperienced page, might have found amusement in comparing the different kinds of fanaticisms which these two females exhibited. The Abbess, timid, narrowminded, and discontented, clung to ancient usages and pretensions which were ended by the Reformation; and was in adversity, as she had been in prosperity, scrupulous, weak-spirited, and bigoted. While the fiery and more lofty spirit of her companion suggested a wider field of effort, and would not be limited by ordinary rules in the extraordinary schemes which were suggested by her bold and irregular imagination. But Roland Graeme, instead of tracing these peculiarities of character in the two old damps, only waited with great anxiety for the return of Catherine, expecting probably that the proposal of the fraternal embrace would be renewed, as his grandmother seemed disposed to carry matters with a high hand.

His expectations, or hopes, if we may call them so, were, however, disappointed; for, when Catherine re-entered on the summons of the Abbess, and placed on the table an earthen pitcher of water, and four wooden platters, with cups of the same materials, the Dame of Heathergill, satisfied with the arbitrary mode in which she had borne down the opposition of the Abbess, pursued her victory no farther—a moderation for which her grandson, in his heart, returned her but slender thanks.

In the meanwhile, Catherine continued to place upon the table the slender preparations for the meal of a recluse, which consisted almost entirely of colewort, boiled and served up in a wooden platter, having no better seasoning than a little salt, and no better accompaniment than some coarse barley-bread, in very moderate quantity. The water-pitcher, already mentioned, furnished the only beverage. After a Latin grace, delivered by the Abbess, the guests sat down to their spare entertainment. The simplicity of the fare appeared to produce no distaste in the females, who ate of it moderately, but with the usual appearance of appetite. But Roland Graeme had been used to better cheer. Sir Halbert Glendinning, who affected even an unusual degree of nobleness in his housekeeping, maintained it in a style of genial hospitality, which rivalled that of the Northern Barons of England. He might think, perhaps, that by doing so, he acted yet more completely the part for which he was born—that of a great Baron and a leader. Two bullocks, and six sheep, weekly, were the allowance when the Baron was at home, and the number was not greatly diminished during his absence. A boll of malt was weekly brewed into ale, which was used by the household at discretion. Bread was baked in proportion for the consumption of his domestics and retainers; and in this scene of plenty had Roland Graeme now lived for several years. It formed a bad introduction to lukewarm greens and spring-water; and probably his countenance indicated some sense of the difference, for the Abbess observed, "It would seem, my son, that the tables of the heretic Baron, whom you have so long followed, are more daintily furnished than those of the suffering daughters of the church; and yet, not upon the most solemn nights of festival, when the nuns were permitted to eat their portion at mine own table, did I consider the cates, which were then served up, as half so delicious as these vegetables and this water, on which I prefer to feed, rather than do aught which may derogate from the strictness of my vow. It shall never be said that the mistress of this house made it a house of feasting, when days of darkness and of affliction were hanging over the Holy Church, of which I am an unworthy member."

"Well hast thou said, my sister," replied Magdalen Graeme; "but now it is not only time to suffer in the good cause, but to act in it. And since our pilgrim's meal is finished, let us go apart to prepare for our journey tomorrow, and to advise on the manner in which these children shall be employed, and what measures we can adopt to supply their thoughtlessness and lack of discretion."

Notwithstanding his indifferent cheer, the heart of Roland Graeme bounded high at this proposal, which he doubted not would lead to another *tête-à-tête* betwixt him and the pretty novice. But he was mistaken. Catherine, it would seem, had no mind so far to indulge him; for, moved either by delicacy or caprice, or some of those indescribable shades betwixt the one and the other, with which women love to tease, and at the same time to captivate, the ruder sex, she reminded the Abbess that it was necessary she should retire an hour before vespers; and, receiving the ready and approving nod of her Superior, she arose to withdraw. But before leaving the apartment, she made obeisance to the matrons, bending herself till her hands touched her knees, and then made a lesser reverence to Roland, which consisted in a slight bend of the body and gentle depression of the head. This she performed very demurely; but the party on whom the salutation was conferred, thought he could discern in her manner an arch and mischievous exultation over his secret disappointment.—"The devil take the saucy girl," he thought in his heart, though the presence of the Abbess should have repressed all such profane imaginations,—"she is as hard-hearted as the laughing hyaena that the story-books tell of—she has a mind that I shall not forget her this night at least."

The matrons now retired also, giving the page to understand that he was on no account to stir from the convent, or to show himself at the windows, the Abbess assigning as a reason, the readiness with which the rude heretics caught at every occasion of scandalizing the religious orders.

"This is worse than the rigour of Mr. Henry Warden, himself," said the page, when he was left alone; "for, to do him justice, however strict in requiring the most rigid attention during the time of his homilies, he left us to the freedom of our own wills afterwards—ay, and would take a share in our pastimes, too, if he thought them entirely innocent. But these old women are utterly wrapt up in gloom, mystery and self-denial.—Well, then, if I must neither stir out of the gate nor look out at window, I will at least see what the inside of the house contains that may help to pass away one's time—peradventure I may light on that blue-eyed laugher in some corner or other."

Going, therefore, out of the chamber by the entrance opposite to that through which the two matrons had departed, (for it may be readily supposed that he had no desire to intrude on their privacy.) he wandered from one chamber to another, through the deserted edifice, seeking, with boyish eagerness, some source of interest and amusement. Here he passed through a long gallery, opening on either hand into the little cells of the nuns, all deserted, and deprived of the few trifling articles of furniture which the rules of the order admitted.

"The birds are flown," thought the page; "but whether they will find themselves worse off in the open air than in these damp narrow cages, I leave my Lady Abbess and my venerable relative to settle betwixt them. I think the wild young lark whom they have left behind them, would like best to sing under God's free sky."

A winding stair, strait and narrow, as if to remind the nuns of their duties of fast and maceration, led down to a lower suite of apartments, which occupied the ground story of the house. These rooms were even more ruinous than those which he had left; for, having encountered the first fury of the assailants by whom the nunnery had been wasted, the windows had been dashed in, the doors broken down, and even the

SIR WALTER SCOTT

partitions betwixt the apartments, in some places, destroyed. As he thus stalked from desolation to desolation, and began to think of returning from so uninteresting a research to the chamber which he had left, he was surprised to hear the low of a cow very close to him. The sound was so unexpected at the time and place, that Roland Graeme started as if it had been the voice of a lion, and laid his hand on his dagger, while at the same moment the light and lovely form of Catherine Seyton presented itself at the door of the apartment from which the sound had issued.

"Good even to you, valiant champion!" said she: "since the days of Guy of Warwick, never was one more worthy to encounter a dun cow."

"Cow?" said Roland Graeme, "by my faith, I thought it had been the devil that roared so near me. Who ever heard of a convent containing a cow-house?"

"Cow and calf may come hither now," answered Catherine, "for we have no means to keep out either. But I advise you, kind sir, to return to the place from whence you came."

"Not till I see your charge, fair sister," answered Roland, and made his way into the apartment, in spite of the half serious half laughing remonstrances of the girl.

The poor solitary cow, now the only severe recluse within the nunnery, was quartered in a spacious chamber, which had once been the refectory of the convent. The roof was graced with groined arches, and the wall with niches, from which the images had been pulled down. These remnants of architectural ornaments were strangely contrasted with the rude crib constructed for the cow in one corner of the apartment, and the stack of fodder which was piled beside it for her food.*

---

* This, like the cell of Saint Cuthbert, is an imaginary scene, but I took one or two ideas of the desolation of the interior from a story told me by my father. In his youth—it may be near eighty years since, as he was born in 1729—he had occasion to visit an old lady who resided in a Border castle of considerable renown. Only one very limited portion of the extensive ruins sufficed for the accommodation of the inmates, and my father amused himself by wandering through the part that was untenanted. In a dining-apartment, having a roof richly adorned with arches and drops, there was deposited a large stack of hay, to which calves were helping themselves from opposite sides. As my father was scaling a dark ruinous turnpike staircase, his greyhound ran up before him, and probably was the means of saving his life, for the animal fell through a trap-door, or aperture in the stair, thus warning the owner of the danger of the ascent. As the dog continued howling from a great depth, my father got the old butler, who alone knew most of the localities about the castle, to unlock a sort of stable, in which Kill-buck was found safe and sound, the place being filled with the same commodity which littered the stalls of Augeas, and which had rendered the dog's fall an easy one.

"By my faith," said the page, "Crombie is more lordly lodged than any one here!"

"You had best remain with her," said Catherine, "and supply by your filial attentions the offspring she has had the ill luck to lose."

"I will remain, at least, to help you to prepare her night's lair, pretty Catherine," said Roland, seizing upon a pitch-fork.

"By no means," said Catherine; "for, besides that you know not in the least how to do her that service, you will bring a chiding my way, and I get enough of that in the regular course of things."

"What! for accepting my assistance?" said the page,—"for accepting *my* assistance, who am to be your confederate in some deep matter of import? That were altogether unreasonable—and, now I think on it, tell me if you can, what is this mighty emprise to which I am destined?"

"Robbing a bird's nest, I should suppose," said Catherine, "considering the champion whom they have selected."

"By my faith," said the youth, "and he that has taken a falcon's nest in the Scaurs of Polmoodie, has done something to brag of, my fair sister.—But that is all over now—a murrain on the nest, and the eyases and their food, washed or unwashed, for it was all anon of cramming these worthless kites that I was sent upon my present travels. Save that I have met with you, pretty sister, I could eat my dagger-hilt for vexation at my own folly. But, as we are to be fellow-travellers—"

"Fellow-labourers! not fellow-travellers!" answered the girl; "for to your comfort be it known, that the Lady Abbess and I set out earlier than you and your respected relative to-morrow, and that I partly endure your company at present, because it may be long ere we meet again."

"By Saint Andrew, but it shall not though," answered Roland; "I will not hunt at all unless we are to hunt in couples."

"I suspect, in that and in other points, we must do as we are bid," replied the young lady.—"But, hark! I hear my aunt's voice."

The old lady entered in good earnest, and darted a severe glance at her niece, while Roland had the ready wit to busy himself about the halter of the cow.

"The young gentleman," said Catherine, gravely, "is helping me to tie the cow up faster to her stake, for I find that last night when she put her head out of window and lowed, she alarmed the whole village; and—we shall be suspected of sorcery among the heretics, if they do not discover the cause of the apparition, or lose our cow if they do."

SIR WALTER SCOTT

"Relieve yourself of that fear," said the Abbess, somewhat ironically; "the person to whom she is now sold, comes for the animal presently."

"Good night, then, my poor companion," said Catherine, patting the animal's shoulders; "I hope thou hast fallen into kind hands, for my happiest hours of late have been spent in tending thee—I would I had been born to no better task!"

"Now, out upon thee, mean-spirited wench!" said the Abbess; "is that a speech worthy of the name of Seyton, or of the mouth of a sister of this house, treading the path of election—and to be spoken before a stranger youth, too?—Go to my oratory, minion—there read your Hours till I come thither, when I will read you such a lecture as shall make you prize the blessings which you possess."

Catherine was about to withdraw in silence, casting a half sorrowful half comic glance at Roland Graeme, which seemed to say—"You see to what your untimely visit has exposed me," when, suddenly changing her mind, she came forward to the page, and extended her hand as she bid him good evening. Their palms had pressed each other ere the astonished matron could interfere, and Catherine had time to say— "Forgive me, mother; it is long since we have seen a face that looked with kindness on us. Since these disorders have broken up our peaceful retreat, all has been gloom and malignity. I bid this youth kindly farewell, because he has come hither in kindness, and because the odds are great, that we may never again meet in this world. I guess better than he, that the schemes on which you are rushing are too mighty for your management, and that you are now setting the stone a-rolling, which must surely crush you in its descent. I bid fare-well," she added, "to my fellow-victim!"

This was spoken with a tone of deep and serious feeling, altogether different from the usual levity of Catherine's manner, and plainly showed, that beneath the giddiness of extreme youth and total inexperience, there lurked in her bosom a deeper power of sense and feeling, than her conduct had hitherto expressed.

The Abbess remained a moment silent after she had left the room. The proposed rebuke died on her tongue, and she appeared struck with the deep and foreboding, tone in which her niece had spoken her good-even. She led the way in silence to the apartment which they had formerly occupied, and where there was prepared a small refection, as the Abbess termed it, consisting of milk and barley-bread. Magdalen Graeme, summoned to take share in this collation, appeared from an adjoining apartment, but Catherine was seen no more. There was little said during the hasty meal, and after it was finished, Roland Graeme was dismissed to the nearest cell, where some preparations had been made for his repose.

The strange circumstances in which he found himself, had their usual effect in preventing slumber from hastily descending on him, and he could distinctly hear, by a low but earnest murmuring in the apartment which he had left, that the matrons continued in deep consultation to a late hour. As they separated he heard the Abbess distinctly express herself thus: "In a word, my sister, I venerate your character and the authority with which my Superiors have invested you; yet it seems to me, that, ere entering on this perilous course, we should consult some of the Fathers of the Church."

"And how and where are we to find a faithful Bishop or Abbot at whom to ask counsel? The faithful Eustatius is no more—he is withdrawn from a world of evil, and from the tyranny of heretics. May Heaven and our Lady assoilzie him of his sins, and abridge the penance of his mortal infirmities!—Where shall we find another, with whom to take counsel?"

"Heaven will provide for the Church," said the Abbess; "and the faithful fathers who yet are suffered to remain in the house of Kennaquhair, will proceed to elect an Abbot. They will not suffer the staff to fall down, or the mitre to be unfilled, for the threats of heresy."

"That will I learn to-morrow," said Magdalen Graeme; "yet who now takes the office of an hour, save to partake with the spoilers in their work of plunder?—to-morrow will tell us if one of the thousand saints who are sprung from the House of Saint Mary's continues to look down on it in its misery.—Farewell, my sister—we meet at Edinburgh."

"Benedicito!" answered the Abbess, and they parted.

"To Kennaquhair and to Edinburgh we bend our way." thought Roland Graeme. "That information have I purchased by a sleepless hour—it suits well with my purpose. At Kennaquhair I shall see Father Ambrose;—at Edinburgh I shall find the means of shaping my own course through this bustling world, without burdening my affectionate relation—at Edinburgh, too, I shall see again the witching novice, with her blue eyes and her provoking smile."—He fell asleep, and it was to dream of Catherine Seyton.

SIR WALTER SCOTT

XIII

What, Dagon up again!—I thought we had hurl'd him
Down on the threshold, never more to rise.
Bring wedge and axe; and, neighbours, lend your hands
And rive the idol into winter fagots!

—Athelstane, or the Converted Dane

Roland Graeme slept long and sound, and the sun was high over the horizon, when the voice of his companion summoned him to resume their pilgrimage; and when, hastily arranging his dress, he went to attend her call, the enthusiastic matron stood already at the threshold, prepared for her journey. There was in all the deportment of this remarkable woman, a promptitude of execution, and a sternness of perseverance, founded on the fanaticism which she nursed so deeply, and which seemed to absorb all the ordinary purposes and feelings of mortality. One only human affection gleamed through her enthusiastic energies, like the broken glimpses of the sun through the rising clouds of a storm. It was her maternal fondness for her grandson—a fondness carried almost to the verge of dotage, in circumstances where the Catholic religion was not concerned, but which gave way instantly when it chanced either to thwart or come in contact with the more settled purpose of her soul, and the more devoted duty of her life. Her life she would willingly have laid down to save the earthly object of her affection; but that object itself she was ready to hazard, and would have been willing to sacrifice, could the restoration of the Church of Rome have been purchased with his blood. Her discourse by the way, excepting on the few occasions in which her extreme love of her grandson found opportunity to display itself in anxiety for his health and accommodation, turned entirely on the duty of raising up the fallen honours of the Church, and replacing a Catholic sovereign on the throne. There were times at which she hinted, though very obscurely and distantly, that she herself was foredoomed by Heaven to perform a part in this important task; and that she had more than mere human warranty for the zeal with which she engaged in it. But on this subject she expressed herself in such general language, that it was not easy to decide whether she made any actual pretensions to a direct and supernatural call, like the celebrated Elizabeth Barton, commonly called the Nun of Kent;* or whether she dwelt upon the general duty which was incumbent on all Catholics of the time, and the pressure of which she felt in an extraordinary degree.

Yet though Magdalen Graeme gave no direct intimation of her pretensions to be considered as something beyond the ordinary class of mortals, the demeanour of one or two persons amongst the travellers whom they occasionally met, as they entered the more fertile and populous part of the valley, seemed to indicate their belief in her superior attributes. It is true, that two clowns, who drove before them a herd of cattle—one or two village wenches, who seemed bound for some merry-making—a strolling soldier, in a rusted morion, and a wandering student, as his threadbare black cloak and his satchel of books proclaimed him—passed our travellers without observation, or with a look of contempt; and, moreover, that two or three children, attracted by the appearance of a dress so nearly resembling that of a pilgrim, joined in hooting and calling "Out upon the mass-monger!" But one or two, who nourished in their bosoms respect for the downfallen hierarchy—casting first a timorous glance around, to see that no one observed them—hastily crossed themselves—bent their knee to Sister Magdalen, by which name they saluted her—kissed her hand, or even the hem of her dalmatique—received with humility the Benedicite with which she repaid their obeisance; and then starting up, and again looking timidly round to see that they had been unobserved, hastily resumed their journey. Even while within sight of persons of the prevailing faith, there were individuals bold enough, by folding their arms and bending their head, to give distant and silent intimation that they recognized Sister Magdalen, and honoured alike her person and her purpose.

She failed not to notice to her grandson these marks of honour and respect which from time to time she received. "You see," she said, "my son, that the enemies have been unable altogether to suppress the good spirit, or to root out the true seed. Amid heretics and schismatics,

---

* A fanatic nun, called the Holy Maid of Kent, who pretended to the gift of prophecy and power of miracles. Having denounced the doom of speedy death against Henry VIII for his marriage with Anne Boleyn, the prophetess was attainted in Parliament, and executed with her accomplices. Her imposture was for a time so successful, that even Sir Thomas More was disposed to be a believer.

spoilers of the church's lands, and scoffers at saints and sacraments, there is left a remnant."

"It is true, my mother," said Roland Graeme; "but methinks they are of a quality which can help us but little. See you not all those who wear steel at their side, and bear marks of better quality, ruffle past us as they would past the meanest beggars? for those who give us any marks of sympathy, are the poorest of the poor, and most outcast of the needy, who have neither bread to share with us, nor swords to defend us, nor skill to use them if they had. That poor wretch that last kneeled to you with such deep devotion, and who seemed emaciated by the touch of some wasting disease within, and the grasp of poverty without—that pale, shivering, miserable caitiff, how can he aid the great schemes you meditate?"

"Much, my son," said the Matron, with more mildness than the page perhaps expected. "When that pious son of the church returns from the shrine of Saint Ringan, whither he now travels by my counsel, and by the aid of good Catholics,—when he returns, healed, of his wasting malady, high in health, and strong in limb, will not the glory of his faithfulness, and its miraculous reward, speak louder in the ears of this besotted people of Scotland, than the din which is weekly made in a thousand heretical pulpits?"

"Ay, but, mother, I fear the Saint's hand is out. It is long since we have heard of a miracle performed at St. Ringan's."

The matron made a dead pause, and, with a voice tremulous with emotion, asked, "Art thou so unhappy as to doubt the power of the blessed Saint?"

"Nay, mother," the youth hastened to reply, "I believe as the Holy Church commands, and doubt not Saint Ringan's power of healing; but, be it said with reverence, he hath not of late showed the inclination."

"And has this land deserved it?" said the Catholic matron, advancing hastily while she spoke, until she attained the summit of a rising ground, over which the path led, and then standing again still. "Here," she said, "stood the Cross, the limits of the Halidome of Saint Mary's—here—on this eminence—from which the eye of the holy pilgrim might first catch a view of that ancient monastery, the light of the land, the abode of Saints, and the grave of monarchs—Where is now that emblem of our faith? It lies on the earth—a shapeless block, from which the broken fragments have been carried off, for the meanest uses, till now no semblance of its original form remains. Look towards the east, my son, where the sun was wont to glitter on stately spires—from which crosses and bells have now been hurled, as if the land had been invaded once more by barbarous heathens.—Look at yonder battlements, of which we can, even at this distance, descry the partial demolition; and ask if this land can expect from the blessed saints, whose shrines and whose images have been profaned, any other miracles but those of vengeance? How long," she exclaimed, looking upward, "How long shall it be delayed?" She paused, and then resumed with enthusiastic rapidity, "Yes, my son, all on earth is but for a period—joy and grief, triumph and desolation, succeed each other like cloud and sunshine;—the vineyard shall not be forever trodden down, the gaps shall be amended, and the fruitful branches once more dressed and trimmed. Even this day—ay, even this hour, I trust to hear news of importance. Dally not—let us on—time is brief, and judgment is certain."

She resumed the path which led to the Abbey—a path which, in ancient times, was carefully marked out by posts and rails, to assist the pilgrim in his journey—these were now torn up and destroyed. A half-hour's walk placed them in front of the once splendid Monastery, which, although the church was as yet entire, had not escaped the fury of the times. The long range of cells and of apartments for the use of the brethren, which occupied two sides of the great square, were almost entirely ruinous, the interior having been consumed by fire, which only the massive architecture of the outward walls had enabled them to resist. The Abbot's house, which formed the third side of the square, was, though injured, still inhabited, and afforded refuge to the few brethren, who yet, rather by connivance than by actual authority,—were permitted to remain at Kennaquhair. Their stately offices—their pleasant gardens—the magnificent cloisters constructed for their recreation, were all dilapidated and ruinous; and some of the building materials had apparently been put into requisition by persons in the village and in the vicinity, who, formerly vassals of the Monastery, had not hesitated to appropriate to themselves a part of the spoils. Roland saw fragments of Gothic pillars richly carved, occupying the place of door-posts to the meanest huts; and here and there a mutilated statue, inverted or laid on its side, made the door-post, or threshold, of a wretched cow-house. The church itself was less injured than the other buildings of the Monastery. But the images which had been placed in the numerous niches of its columns and buttresses, having all fallen under the charge of idolatry, to which the superstitious devotion of the Papists had justly

SIR WALTER SCOTT

exposed them, had been broken and thrown down, without much regard to the preservation of the rich and airy canopies and pedestals on which they were placed; nor, if the devastation had stopped short at this point, could we have considered the preservation of these monuments of antiquity as an object to be put in the balance with the introduction of the reformed worship.

Our pilgrims saw the demolition of these sacred and venerable representations of saints and angels—for as sacred and venerable they had been taught to consider them—with very different feelings. The antiquary may be permitted to regret the necessity of the action, but to Magdalen Graeme it seemed a deed of impiety, deserving the instant vengeance of heaven,—a sentiment in which her relative joined for the moment as cordially as herself. Neither, however, gave vent to their feelings in words, and uplifted hands and eyes formed their only mode of expressing them. The page was about to approach the great eastern gate of the church, but was prevented by his guide. "That gate," she said, "has long been blockaded, that the heretical rabble may not know there still exist among the brethren of Saint Mary's men who dare worship where their predecessors prayed while alive, and were interred when dead—follow me this way, my son."

Roland Graeme followed accordingly; and Magdalen, casting a hasty glance to see whether they were observed, (for she had learned caution from the danger of the times,) commanded her grandson to knock at a little wicket which she pointed out to him. "But knock gently," she added, with a motion expressive of caution. After a little space, during which no answer was returned, she signed to Roland to repeat his summons for admission; and the door at length partially opening, discovered a glimpse of the thin and timid porter, by whom the duty was performed, skulking from the observation of those who stood without; but endeavouring at the same time to gain a sight of them without being himself seen. How different from the proud consciousness of dignity with which the porter of ancient days offered his important brow, and his goodly person, to the pilgrims who repaired to Kennaquhair! His solemn *"Intrate, mei filii,"* was exchanged for a tremulous "You cannot enter now—the brethren are in their chambers." But, when Magdalen Graeme asked, in an under tone of voice, "Hast thou forgotten me, my brother?" he changed his apologetic refusal to "Enter, my honoured sister, enter speedily, for evil eyes are upon us."

They entered accordingly, and having waited until the porter had, with jealous haste, barred and bolted the wicket, were conducted by him through several dark and winding passages. As they walked slowly on, he spoke to the matron in a subdued voice, as if he feared to trust the very walls with the avowal which he communicated.

"Our Fathers are assembled in the Chapter-house, worthy sister—yes, in the Chapter-house—for the election of an Abbott.—Ah, Benedicite! there must be no ringing of bells—no high mass—no opening of the great gates now, that the people might see and venerate their spiritual Father! Our Fathers must hide themselves rather like robbers who choose a leader, than godly priests who elect a mitred Abbot."

"Regard not that, my brother," answered Magdalen Graeme; "the first successors of Saint Peter himself were elected, not in sunshine, but in tempests—not in the halls of the Vatican, but in the subterranean vaults and dungeons of heathen Rome—they were not gratulated with shouts and salvos of cannon-shot and of musketry, and the display of artificial fire—no, my brother—but by the hoarse summons of Lictors and Praetors, who came to drag the Fathers of the Church to martyrdom. From such adversity was the Church once raised, and by such will it now be purified.—And mark me, brother! not in the proudest days of the mitred Abbey, was a Superior ever chosen, whom his office shall so much honour, as *he* shall be honoured, who now takes it upon him in these days of tribulation. On whom, my brother, will the choice fall?"

"On whom can it fall—or, alas! who would dare to reply to the call, save the worthy pupil of the Sainted Eustatius—the good and valiant Father Ambrose?"

"I know it," said Magdalen; "my heart told me long ere your lips had uttered his name. Stand forth, courageous champion, and man the fatal breach!—Rise, bold and experienced pilot, and seize the helm while the tempest rages!—Turn back the battle, brave raiser of the fallen standard!—Wield crook and slang, noble shepherd of a scattered flock!"

"I pray you, hush, my sister!" said the porter, opening a door which led into the great church, "the brethren will be presently here to celebrate their election with a solemn mass—I must marshal them the way to the high altar—all the offices of this venerable house have now devolved on one poor decrepit old man."

He left the church, and Magdalen and Roland remained alone in that great vaulted space, whose style of rich, yet chaste architecture, referred its origin to the early part of the fourteenth century, the best

SIR WALTER SCOTT

period of Gothic building. But the niches were stripped of their images in the inside as well as the outside of the church; and in the pell-mell havoc, the tombs of warriors and of princes had been included in the demolition of the idolatrous shrines. Lances and swords of antique size, which had hung over the tombs of mighty warriors of former days, lay now strewed among relics, with which the devotion of pilgrims had graced those of their peculiar saints; and the fragments of the knights and dames, which had once lain recumbent, or kneeled in an attitude of devotion, where their mortal relics were reposed, were mingled with those of the saints and angels of the Gothic chisel, which the hand of violence had sent headlong from their stations.

The most fatal symptom of the whole appeared to be, that, though this violence had now been committed for many months, the Fathers had lost so totally all heart and resolution, that they had not adventured even upon clearing away the rubbish, or restoring the church to some decent degree of order. This might have been done without much labour. But terror had overpowered the scanty remains of a body once so powerful, and, sensible they were only suffered to remain in this ancient seat by connivance and from compassion, they did not venture upon taking any step which might be construed into an assertion of their ancient rights, contenting themselves with the secret and obscure exercise of their religious ceremonial, in as unostentatious a manner as was possible.

Two or three of the more aged brethren had sunk under the pressure of the times, and the ruins had been partly cleared away to permit their interment. One stone had been laid over Father Nicholas, which recorded of him in special, that he had taken the vows during the incumbency of Abbot Ingelram, the period to which his memory so frequently recurred. Another flag-stone, yet more recently deposited, covered the body of Philip the Sacristan, eminent for his aquatic excursion with the phantom of Avenel, and a third, the most recent of all, bore the outline of a mitre, and the words *Hic jacet Eustatius Abbas*; for no one dared to add a word of commendation in favour of his learning, and strenuous zeal for the Roman Catholic faith.

Magdalen Graeme looked at and perused the brief records of these monuments successively, and paused over that of Father Eustace. "In a good hour for thyself," she said, "but oh! in an evil hour for the Church, wert thou called from us. Let thy spirit be with us, holy man—encourage thy successor to tread in thy footsteps—give him thy bold and inventive capacity, thy zeal and thy discretion—even *thy* piety exceeds not his." As she spoke, a side door, which closed a passage from the Abbot's house into the church, was thrown open, that the Fathers might enter the choir, and conduct to the high altar the Superior whom they had elected.

In former times, this was one of the most splendid of the many pageants which the hierarchy of Rome had devised to attract the veneration of the faithful. The period during which the Abbacy remained vacant, was a state of mourning, or, as their emblematical phrase expressed it, of widowhood; a melancholy term, which was changed into rejoicing and triumph when a new Superior was chosen. When the folding doors were on such solemn occasions thrown open, and the new Abbot appeared on the threshold in full-blown dignity, with ring and mitre, and dalmatique and crosier, his hoary standard-bearers and his juvenile dispensers of incense preceding him, and the venerable train of monks behind him, with all besides which could announce the supreme authority to which he was now raised, his appearance was a signal for the magnificent *jubilate* to rise from the organ and music-loft, and to be joined by the corresponding bursts of Alleluiah from the whole assembled congregation. Now all was changed. In the midst of rubbish and desolation, seven or eight old men, bent and shaken as much by grief and fear as by age, shrouded hastily in the proscribed dress of their order, wandered like a procession of spectres, from the door which had been thrown open, up through the encumbered passage, to the high altar, there to instal their elected Superior a chief of ruins. It was like a band of bewildered travellers choosing a chief in the wilderness of Arabia; or a shipwrecked crew electing a captain upon the barren island on which fate has thrown them.

They who, in peaceful times, are most ambitious of authority among others, shrink from the competition at such eventful periods, when neither ease nor parade attend the possession of it, and when it gives only a painful pre-eminence both in danger and in labour, and exposes the ill-fated chieftain to the murmurs of his discontented associates, as well as to the first assault of the common enemy. But he on whom the office of the Abbot of Saint Mary's was now conferred, had a mind fitted for the situation to which he was called. Bold and enthusiastic, yet generous and forgiving—wise and skilful, yet zealous and prompt—he wanted but a better cause than the support of a decaying superstition, to have raised him to the rank of a truly great man. But as the end crowns the work, it also forms the rule by which it must be ultimately judged; and those who, with sincerity and generosity, fight and fall in an evil cause, posterity can only compassionate as victims of a generous but fatal error. Amongst these, we must rank Ambrosius, the last Abbot of Kennaqubair, whose designs must be condemned, as their success would have riveted on Scotland the chains of antiquated superstition and spiritual tyranny; but whose talents commanded respect, and whose virtues, even from the enemies of his faith, extorted esteem.

The bearing of the new Abbot served of itself to dignify a ceremonial which was deprived of all other attributes of grandeur. Conscious of the peril in which they stood, and recalling, doubtless, the better days they had seen, there hung over his brethren an appearance of mingled terror, and grief, and shame, which induced them to hurry over the office in which they were engaged, as something at once degrading and dangerous.

But not so Father Ambrose. His features, indeed, expressed a deep melancholy, as he walked up the centre aisle, amid the ruin of things which he considered as holy, but his brow was undejected, and his step firm and solemn. He seemed to think that the dominion which he was about to receive, depended in no sort upon the external circumstances under which it was conferred; and if a mind so firm was accessible to sorrow or fear, it was not on his own account, but on that of the Church to which he had devoted himself.

At length he stood on the broken steps of the high altar, barefooted, as was the rule, and holding in his hand his pastoral staff, for the gemmed ring and jewelled mitre had become secular spoils. No obedient vassals came, man after man, to make their homage, and to offer the tribute which should provide their spiritual Superior with palfrey and trappings. No Bishop assisted at the solemnity, to receive into the higher ranks of the Church nobility a dignitary, whose voice in the legislature was as potential as his own. With hasty and maimed rites, the few remaining brethren stepped forward alternately to give their new Abbot the kiss of peace, in token of fraternal affection and spiritual homage. Mass was then hastily performed, but in such precipitation as if it had been hurried over rather to satisfy the scruples of a few youths, who were impatient to set out on a hunting party, than as if it made the most solemn part of a solemn ordination. The officiating priest faltered as he spoke the service, and often looked around, as if he expected to be interrupted in the midst of his office; and the brethren listened to that which, short as it was, they wished yet more abridged.*

These symptoms of alarm increased as the ceremony proceeded, and, as it seemed, were not caused by mere apprehension alone; for, amid the pauses of the hymn, there were heard without sounds of a very different sort, beginning faintly and at a distance, but at length approaching close to the exterior of the church, and stunning with dissonant clamour those engaged in the service. The winding of horns, blown with no regard to harmony or concert; the jangling of bells, the thumping of drums, the squeaking of bagpipes, and the clash of cymbals—the shouts of a multitude, now as in laughter, now as in anger—the shrill tones of female voices, and of those of children, mingling with the deeper clamour of men, formed a Babel of sounds, which first drowned, and then awed into utter silence, the official hymns of the Convent. The cause and result of this extraordinary interruption will be explained in the next chapter.

---

* In Catholic countries, in order to reconcile the pleasures of the great with the observances of religion, it was common, when a party was bent for the chase, to celebrate mass, abridged and maimed of its rites, called a hunting-mass, the brevity of which was designed to correspond with the impatience of the audience.

SIR WALTER SCOTT

XIV

Not the wild billow, when it breaks its barrier—
Not the wild wind, escaping from its cavern—
Not the wild fiend, that mingles both together,
And pours their rage upon the ripening harvest,
Can match the wild freaks of this mirthful meeting—
Comic, yet fearful—droll, and yet destructive.

—THE CONSPIRACY

The monks ceased their song, which, like that of the choristers in the legend of the Witch of Berkley, died away in a quaver of consternation; and, like a flock of chickens disturbed by the presence of the kite, they at first made a movement to disperse and fly in different directions, and then, with despair, rather than hope, huddled themselves around their new Abbot; who, retaining the lofty and undismayed look which had dignified him through the whole ceremony, stood on the higher step of the altar, as if desirous to be the most conspicuous mark on which danger might discharge itself, and to save his companions by his self-devotion, since he could afford them no other protection.

Involuntarily, as it were, Magdalen Graeme and the page stepped from the station which hitherto they had occupied unnoticed, and approached to the altar, as desirous of sharing the fate which approached the monks, whatever that might be. Both bowed reverently low to the Abbot; and while Magdalen seemed about to speak, the youth, looking towards the main entrance, at which the noise now roared most loudly, and which was at the same time assailed with much knocking, laid his hand upon his dagger.

The Abbot motioned to both to forbear: "Peace, my sister," he said, in a low tone, but which, being in a different key from the tumultuary sounds without, could be distinctly heard, even amidst the tumult;— "Peace," he said, "my sister; let the new Superior of Saint Mary's himself receive and reply to the grateful acclamations of the vassals, who come to celebrate his installation.—And thou, my son, forbear, I charge thee, to touch thy earthly weapon;—if it is the pleasure of our protectress, that her shrine be this day desecrated by deeds of violence, and polluted by blood-shedding, let it not, I charge thee, happen through the deed of a Catholic son of the church."

The noise and knocking at the outer gate became now every moment louder; and voices were heard impatiently demanding admittance. The Abbot, with dignity, and with a step which even the emergency of danger rendered neither faltering nor precipitate, moved towards the portal, and demanded to know, in a tone of authority, who it was that disturbed their worship, and what they desired?

There was a moment's silence, and then a loud laugh from without. At length a voice replied, "We desire entrance into the church; and when the door is opened you will soon see who we are."

"By whose authority do you require entrance?" said the Father.

"By authority of the right reverend Lord Abbot of Unreason."* replied the voice from without; and, from the laugh—which followed, it seemed as if there was something highly ludicrous couched under this reply.

---

* We learn from no less authority than that of Napoleon Bonaparte, that there is but a single step between the sublime and ridiculous; and it is a transition from one extreme to another; so very easy, that the vulgar of every degree are peculiarly captivated with it. Thus the inclination to laugh becomes uncontrollable, when the solemnity and gravity of time, place, and circumstances, render it peculiarly improper. Some species of general license, like that which inspired the ancient Saturnalia, or the modern Carnival, has been commonly indulged to the people at all times and in almost all countries. But it was, I think, peculiar to the Roman Catholic Church, that while they studied how to render their church rites imposing and magnificent, by all that pomp, music, architecture, and external display could add to them, they nevertheless connived, upon special occasions, at the frolics of the rude vulgar, who, in almost all Catholic countries, enjoyed, or at least assumed, the privilege of making: some Lord of the revels, who, under the name of the Abbot of Unreason, the Boy Bishop, or the President of Fools, occupied the churches, profaned the holy places by a mock imitation of the sacred rites, and sung indecent parodies on hymns of the church. The indifference of the clergy, even when their power was greatest, to the indecent exhibitions which they always tolerated, and sometimes encouraged, forms a strong contrast to the sensitiveness with which they regarded any serious attempt, by preaching or writing, to impeach any of the doctrines of the church. It could only be compared to the singular apathy with which they endured, and often admired the gross novels which Chaucer, Dunbar, Boccacio, Bandello, and others, composed upon the bad morals of the clergy. It seems as if the churchmen in both instances had endeavoured to compromise with the laity, and allowed them occasionally to gratify their coarse humour by indecent satire, provided they would abstain from any grave question concerning the foundation of the doctrines on which was erected such an immense fabric of ecclesiastical power.

But the sports thus licensed assumed a very different appearance, so soon as the Protestant doctrines began to prevail; and the license which their forefathers had exercised in mere gaiety of heart, and without the least intention of dishonouring religion by their

SIR WALTER SCOTT

"I know not, and seek not to know, your meaning," replied the Abbot, "since it is probably a rude one. But begone, in the name of God, and leave his servants in peace. I speak this, as having lawful authority to command here."

---

frolics, were now persevered in by the common people as a mode of testifying their utter disregard for the Roman priesthood and its ceremonies.

I may observe, for example, the case of an apparitor sent to Borthwick from the Primate of Saint Andrews, to cite the lord of that castle, who was opposed by an Abbot of Unreason, at whose command the officer of the spiritual court was appointed to be ducked in a mill-dam, and obliged to eat up his parchment citation.

The reader may be amused with the following whimsical details of this incident, which took place in the castle of Borthwick, in the year 1517. It appears, that in consequence of a process betwixt Master George Hay de Minzeane and the Lord Borthwick, letters of excommunication had passed against the latter, on account of the contumacy of certain witnesses. William Langlands, an apparitor or macer (*bacularius*) of the See of St Andrews, presented these letters to the curate of the church of Borthwick, requiring him to publish the same at the service of high mass. It seems that the inhabitants of the castle were at this time engaged in the favourite sport of enacting the Abbot of Unreason, a species of high jinks, in which a mimic prelate was elected, who, like the Lord of Misrule in England, turned all sort of lawful authority, and particularly the church ritual, into ridicule. This frolicsome person with his retinue, notwithstanding of the apparitor's character, entered the church, seized upon the primate's officer without hesitation, and, dragging him to the mill-dam on the south side of the castle, compelled him to leap into the water. Not contented with this partial immersion, the Abbot of Unreason pronounced, that Mr. William Langlands was not yet sufficiently bathed, and therefore caused his assistants to lay him on his back in the stream, and duck him in the most satisfactory and perfect manner. The unfortunate apparitor was then conducted back to the church, where, for his refreshment after his bath, the letters of excommunication were torn to pieces, and steeped in a bowl of wine; the mock abbot being probably of opinion that a tough parchment was but dry eating, Langlands was compelled to eat the letters, and swallow the wine, and dismissed by the Abbot of Unreason, with the comfortable assurance, that if any more such letters should arrive during the continuance of his office, "they should a' gang the same gate," *i. e.* go the same road.

A similar scene occurs betwixt a sumner of the Bishop of Rochester, and Harpool, the servant of Lord Cobham, in the old play of Sir John Oldcastle, when the former compels the church-officer to eat his citation. The dialogue, which may be found in the note, contains most of the jests which may be supposed, appropriate to such an extraordinary occasion:

HARPOOL: Marry, sir, is, this process parchment?

SUMNER: Yes, marry is it.

HARPOOL: And this seal wax?

SUMNER: It is so.

HARPOOL: If this be parchment, and this be wax, eat you this parchment and wax, or I will make parchment of your skin, and beat your brains into wax. Sirrah Sumner, despatch—devour, sirrah, devour.

SUMNER: I am my Lord of Rochester's sumner; I came to do my office, and thou shall answer it.

"Open the door," said another rude voice, "and we will try titles with you, Sir Monk, and show you a superior we must all obey."

"Break open the doors if he dallies any longer," said a third, "and down with the carrion monks who would bar us of our privilege!" A general shout followed. "Ay, ay, our privilege! our privilege! down with the doors, and with the lurdane monks, if they make opposition!"

The knocking was now exchanged for blows with great, hammers, to which the doors, strong as they were, must soon have given way. But the Abbot, who saw resistance would be in vain, and who did not wish to incense the assailants by an attempt at offering it, besought silence earnestly, and with difficulty obtained a hearing. "My children," said he, "I will save you from committing a great sin. The porter will presently undo the gate—he is gone to fetch the keys—meantime I pray you to consider with yourselves, if you are in a state of mind to cross the holy threshold."

"Tillyvally for your papistry!" was answered from without; "we are in the mood of the monks when they are merriest, and that is when they sup beef-brewis for lanten-kail. So, if your porter hath not the gout, let him come speedily, or we heave away readily.—Said I well, comrades?"

HARPOOL: Sirrah, no railing, but, betake thyself to thy teeth. Thou shalt, eat no worse than thou bringest with thee. Thou bringest it for my lord; and wilt thou bring my lord worse than thou wilt eat thyself?

SUMNER: Sir. I brought it not my lord to eat.

HARPOOL: O, do you Sir me now? All's one for that; I'll make you eat it for bringing it.

SUMNER: I cannot eat it.

HARPOOL: Can you not? 'Sblood, I'll beat you till you have a stomach! (*Beats him.*)

SUMNER: Oh, hold, hold, good Mr. Servingman; I will eat it.

HARPOOL: Be champing, be chewing, sir, or I will chew you, you rogue. Tough wax is the purest of the honey.

SUMNER: The purest of the honey?—O Lord, sir, oh! oh!

HARPOOL: Feed, feed; 'tis wholesome, rogue, wholesome. Cannot you, like an honest sumner, walk with the devil your brother, to fetch in your bailiff's rents, but you must come to a nobleman's house with process! If the seal were broad as the lead which covers Rochester Church, thou shouldst eat it.

SUMNER: Oh, I am almost choked—I am almost choked!

HARPOOL: Who's within there? Will you shame my lord? Is there no beer in the house? Butler, I say.

Enter BUTLER.

BUTLER: Here, here.

HARPOOL: Give him beer. Tough old sheep skin's but dry meat.

First Part of Sir John Oldcastle, Act II. Scene I.

"Bravely said, and it shall be as bravely done," said the multitude; and had not the keys arrived at that moment, and the porter in hasty terror performed his office, throwing open the great door, the populace would have saved him the trouble. The instant he had done so, the affrighted janitor fled, like one who has drawn the bolts of a flood-gate, and expects to be overwhelmed by the rushing inundation. The monks, with one consent, had withdrawn themselves behind the Abbot, who alone kept his station, about three yards from the entrance, showing no signs of fear or perturbation. His brethren—partly encouraged by his devotion, partly ashamed to desert him, and partly animated by a sense of duty.—remained huddled close together, at the back of their Superior. There was a loud laugh and huzza when the doors were opened; but, contrary to what might have been expected, no crowd of enraged assailants rushed into the church. On the contrary, there was a cry of "A halt!-a halt—to order, my masters! and let the two reverend fathers greet each other, as beseems them."

The appearance of the crowd who were thus called to order, was grotesque in the extreme. It was composed of men, women, and children, ludicrously disguised in various habits, and presenting groups equally diversified and grotesque. Here one fellow with a horse's head painted before him, and a tail behind, and the whole covered with a long foot-cloth, which was supposed to hide the body of the animal, ambled, caracoled, pranced, and plunged, as he performed the celebrated part of the hobby-horse,* so often alluded to in our ancient drama; and

---

* This exhibition, the play-mare of Scotland, stood high among holyday gambols. It must be carefully separated from the wooden chargers which furnish out our nurseries. It gives rise to Hamlet's ejaculation,—

But oh, but oh, the hobby-horse is forgot!

There is a very comic scene in Beaumont and Fletcher's play of "Woman Pleased," where Hope-on-high Bombye, a puritan cobbler, refuses to dance with the hobby-horse. There was much difficulty and great variety in the motions which the hobby-horse was expected to exhibit.

The learned Mr. Douce, who has contributed so much to the illustration of our theatrical antiquities, has given us a full account of this pageant, and the burlesque horsemanship which it practised.

"The hobby-horse," says Mr. Douce, "was represented by a man equipped with as much pasteboard as was sufficient to form the head and hinder parts of a horse, the quadrupedal defects being concealed by a long mantle or footcloth that nearly touched the ground. The former, on this occasion, exerted all his skill in burlesque horsemanship.

which still flourishes on the stage in the battle that concludes Bayes's tragedy. To rival the address and agility displayed by this character, another personage advanced in the more formidable character of a huge dragon, with gilded wings, open jaws, and a scarlet tongue, cloven at the end, which made various efforts to overtake and devour a lad, dressed as the lovely Sabaea, daughter of the King of Egypt, who fled before him; while a martial Saint George, grotesquely armed with a goblet for a helmet, and a spit for a lance, ever and anon interfered, and compelled the monster to relinquish his prey. A bear, a wolf, and one or two other wild animals, played their parts with the discretion of Snug the joiner; for the decided preference which they gave to the use of their hind legs, was sufficient, without any formal annunciation, to assure the most timorous spectators that they had to do with habitual bipeds. There was a group of outlaws with Robin Hood and Little John at their head* the best representation exhibited at the time; and no great

---

In Sympson's play of the Law-breakers, 1636, a miller personates the hobby-horse, and being angry that the Mayor of the city is put in competition with him, exclaims, 'Let the mayor play the hobby-horse among his brethren, an he will; I hope our town-lads cannot want a hobby-horse. Have I practised my reins, my careers, my prankers, my ambles, my false trots, my smooth ambles, and Canterbury paces, and shall master mayor put me beside the hobby-horse? Have I borrowed the fore-horse bells, his plumes, his braveries; nay, had his mane new shorn and frizzled, and shall the mayor put me beside the hobby-horse?"—*Douce's Illustrations*, vol. II. p. 468

* The representation of Robin Hood was the darling Maygame both in England and Scotland, and doubtless the favourite personification was often revived, when the Abbot of Unreason, or other pretences of frolic, gave an unusual decree of license.

The Protestant clergy, who had formerly reaped advantage from the opportunities which these sports afforded them of directing their own satire and the ridicule of the lower orders against the Catholic church, began to find that, when these purposes were served, their favourite pastimes deprived them of the wish to attend divine worship, and disturbed the frame of mind in which it can be attended to advantage. The celebrated Bishop Latimer gives a very *naive* account of the manner in which, bishop as he was, he found himself compelled to give place to Robin Hood and his followers.

"I came once myselfe riding on a journey homeward from London, and I sent word over night into the towne that I would preach there in the morning, because it was holiday, and me thought it was a holidayes worke. The church stood in my way, and I took my horse and my company, and went thither, (I thought I should have found a great company in the church,) and when I came there the church doore was fast locked. I tarryed there halfe an houre and more. At last the key was found, and one of the parish comes to me and said,—'Sir, this is a busie day with us, we cannot hear you; it is Robin Hood's day. The parish are gone abroad to gather for Robin Hood. I pray you let them not.' I was faine there to give place to Robin Hood. I thought my rochet should have been regarded, though I were

wonder, since most of the actors were, by profession, the banished men and thieves whom they presented. Other masqueraders there were, of a less marked description. Men were disguised as women, and women as

---

not: but it would not serve, it was faine to give place to Robin Hood's men. It is no laughing matter, my friends, it is a weeping matter, a heavie matter, a heavie matter. Under the pretence for gathering for Robin Hood, a traytour, and a theif, to put out a preacher; to have his office lesse esteemed; to preferre Robin Hood before the ministration of God's word; and all this hath come of unpreaching prelates. This realme hath been ill provided for, that it hath had such corrupt judgments in it, to prefer Robin Hood to God's word."

—Bishop Latimer's sixth Sermon before King Edward

While the English Protestants thus preferred the outlaw's pageant to the preaching of their excellent Bishop, the Scottish calvinistic clergy, with the celebrated John Knox at their head, and backed by the authority of the magistrates of Edinburgh, who had of late been chosen exclusively from this party, found it impossible to control the rage of the populace, when they attempted to deprive them of the privilege of presenting their pageant of Robin Hood.

(Note on old Scottish spelling: leading y = modern 'th'; leading v = modern 'u')

(561) "Vpon the xxi day of Junij. Archibalde Dowglas of Kilspindie, Provest of Edr., David Symmer and Adame Fullartoun, baillies of the samyne, causit ane cordinare servant, callit James Gillion takin of befoir, for playing in Edr. with Robene Hude, to wnderly the law, and put him to the knawlege of ane assyize qlk yaij haid electit of yair favoraris, quha with schort deliberatioun condemnit him to be hangit for ye said cryme. And the deaconis of ye craftismen fearing vproare, maid great solistatuis at ye handis of ye said provost and baillies, and als requirit John Knox, minister, for eschewing of tumult, to superceid ye execution of him, vnto ye tyme yai suld adverteis my Lord Duke yairof. And yan, if it wes his mynd and will yat he should be disponit vpoun, ye said deaconis and craftismen sould convey him yaire; quha answerit, yat yai culd na way stope ye executioun of justice. Quhan ye time of ye said pouer mans hanging approchit, and yat ye hangman wes cum to ye jibbat with ye ledder, vpoune ye qlk ye said cordinare should have bene hangit, ane certaine and remanent craftischilder, quha wes put to ye horne with ye said Gillione, ffor ye said Robene Huide's *playes*, and vyris yair assistaris and favoraris, past to wappinis, and yai brak down ye said jibbat, and yan chacit ye said provest, baillies, and Alexr. Guthrie, in ye said Alexander's writing buith, and held yame yairin; and yairefter past to ye tolbuyt, and becaus the samyne was steiket, and onnawayes culd get the keyes thairof, thai brak the said tolbuith dore with foure harberis, per force, (the said provost and baillies luckand thairon.) and not onlie put thar the said Gillione to fredome and libertie, and brocht him furth of the said tolbuit, bot alsua the remanent presonaris being thairintill; and this done, the said craftismen's servands, with the said condempnit cordonar, past doun to the Netherbow, to have past furth thairat; bot becaus the samyne on thair coming thairto wes closet, thai past vp agane the Hie streit of the said bourghe to the Castellhill, and in this menetymne the saidis provest and baillies, and thair

men—children wore the dress of aged people, and tottered with crutch-sticks in their hands, furred gowns on their little backs, and caps on their round heads—while grandsires assumed the infantine tone as well as the dress of children. Besides these, many had their faces painted, and wore their shirts over the rest of their dress; while coloured pasteboard and ribbons furnished out decorations for others. Those who wanted all these properties, blacked their faces, and turned their jackets inside out; and thus the transmutation of the whole assembly into a set of mad grotesque mummers, was at once completed.

The pause which the masqueraders made, waiting apparently for some person of the highest authority amongst them, gave those within the Abbey Church full time to observe all these absurdities. They were at no loss to comprehend their purpose and meaning.

Few readers can be ignorant, that at an early period, and during the plenitude of her power, the Church of Rome not only connived at,

---

assistaris being in the writing buith of the said Alexr. Guthrie, past and enterit in the said tolbuyt, and in the said servandes passage vp the Hie streit, then schote furth thairof at thame ane dog, and hurt ane servand of the said childer. This being done, thair wes nathing vthir but the one partie schuteand out and castand stanes furth of the said tolbuyt, and the vther pairtie schuteand hagbuttis in the same agane. Aund sua the craftismen's servandis, aboue written, held and inclosit the said provest and baillies continewallie in the said tolbuyth, frae three houris efternone, quhill aught houris at even, and na man of the said town prensit to relieve their said provest and baillies. And than thai send to the maisters of the Castell, to caus tham if thai mycht stay the said servandis, quha maid ane maner to do the same, bot thai could not bring the same to ane finall end, ffor the said servands wold on noways stay fra, quhill thai had revengit the hurting of ane of them; and thairefter the constable of the castell come down thairfra, and he with the said maisters treatet betwix the said pties in this maner:—That the said provost and baillies sall remit to the said craftischilder, all actioun, cryme, and offens that thai had committit aganes thame in any tyme bygane; and band and oblast thame never to pursew them thairfor; and als commandit thair maisters to resaue them agane in thair services, as thai did befoir. And this being proclainit at the mercat cross, thai scalit, and the said provest and bailies come furth of the same tolbouyth." &c. &c. &c.

John Knox, who writes at large upon this tumult, informs us it was inflamed by the deacons of craftes, who, resenting; the superiority assumed over them by the magistrates, would yield no assistance to put down the tumult. "They will be magistrates alone," said the recusant deacons, "e'en let them rule the populace alone;" and accordingly they passed quietly to take *their four-hours penny*, and left the magistrates to help themselves as they could. Many persons were excommunicated for this outrage, and not admitted to church ordinances till they had made satisfaction.

SIR WALTER SCOTT

but even encouraged, such Saturnalian licenses as the inhabitants of Kennaquhair and the neighbourhood had now in hand, and that the vulgar, on such occasions, were not only permitted but encouraged by a number of gambols, sometimes puerile and ludicrous, sometimes immoral and profane, to indemnify themselves for the privations and penances imposed on them at other seasons. But, of all other topics for burlesque and ridicule, the rites and ceremonial of the church itself were most frequently resorted to; and, strange to say, with the approbation of the clergy themselves.

While the hierarchy flourished in full glory, they do not appear to have dreaded the consequences of suffering the people to become so irreverently familiar with things sacred; they then imagined the laity to be much in the condition of the labourer's horse, which does not submit to the bridle and the whip with greater reluctance, because, at rare intervals, he is allowed to frolic at large in his pasture, and fling out his heels in clumsy gambols at the master who usually drives him. But, when times changed—when doubt of the Roman Catholic doctrine, and hatred of their priesthood, had possessed the reformed party, the clergy discovered, too late, that no small inconvenience arose from the established practice of games and merry-makings, in which they themselves, and all they held most sacred, were made the subject of ridicule. It then became obvious to duller politicians than the Romish churchmen, that the same actions have a very different tendency when done in the spirit of sarcastic insolence and hatred, than when acted merely in exuberance of rude and uncontrollable spirits. They, therefore, though of the latest, endeavoured, where they had any remaining influence, to discourage the renewal of these indecorous festivities. In this particular, the Catholic clergy were joined by most of the reformed preachers, who were more shocked at the profanity and immorality of many of these exhibitions, than disposed to profit by the ridiculous light in which they placed the Church of Rome and her observances. But it was long ere these scandalous and immoral sports could be abrogated;—the rude multitude continued attached to their favourite pastimes, and, both in England and Scotland, the mitre of the Catholic—the rochet of the reformed bishop—and the cloak and band of the Calvinistic divine—were, in turn, compelled to give place to those jocular personages, the Pope of Fools, the Boy-Bishop, and the Abbot of Unreason.*

---

* From the interesting novel entitled Anastasius, it seems the same burlesque ceremonies were practised in the Greek Church.

It was the latter personage who now, in full costume, made his approach to the great door of the church of St. Mary's, accoutred in such a manner as to form a caricature, or practical parody, on the costume and attendants of the real Superior, whom he came to beard on the very day of his installation, in the presence of his clergy, and in the chancel of his church. The mock dignitary was a stout-made under-sized fellow, whose thick squab form had been rendered grotesque by a supplemental paunch, well stuffed. He wore a mitre of leather, with the front like a grenadier's cap, adorned with mock embroidery, and trinkets of tin. This surmounted a visage, the nose of which was the most prominent feature, being of unusual size, and at least as richly gemmed as his head-gear. His robe was of buckram, and his cope of canvass, curiously painted, and cut into open work. On one shoulder was fixed the painted figure of an owl; and he bore in the right hand his pastoral staff, and in the left a small mirror having a handle to it, thus resembling a celebrated jester, whose adventures, translated into English, were whilom extremely popular, and which may still be procured in black letter, for about one sterling pound per leaf.

The attendants of this mock dignitary had their proper dresses and equipage, bearing the same burlesque resemblance to the officers of the Convent which their leader did to the Superior. They followed their leader in regular procession, and the motley characters, which had waited his arrival, now crowded into the church in his train, shouting as they came,—"A hall, a hall! for the venerable Father Howleglas, the learned Monk of Misrule, and the Right Reverend Abbot of Unreason!"

The discordant minstrelsy of every kind renewed its din; the boys shrieked and howled, and the men laughed and hallooed, and the women giggled and screamed, and the beasts roared, and the dragon wallopped and hissed, and the hobby-horse neighed, pranced, and capered, and the rest frisked and frolicked, clashing their hobnailed shoes against the pavement, till it sparkled with the marks of their energetic caprioles.

It was, in fine, a scene of ridiculous confusion, that deafened the ear, made the eyes giddy, and must have altogether stunned any indifferent spectator; the monks, whom personal apprehension and a consciousness that much of the popular enjoyment arose from the ridicule being directed against them, were, moreover, little comforted by the reflection, that, bold in their disguise, the mummers who whooped and capered around them, might, on slight provocation, turn their jest into earnest,

SIR WALTER SCOTT

or at least proceed to those practical pleasantries, which at all times arise so naturally out of the frolicsome and mischievous disposition of the populace. They looked to their Abbot amid the tumult, with such looks as landsmen cast upon the pilot when the storm is at the highest—looks which express that they are devoid of all hope arising from their own exertions, and not very confident in any success likely to attend those of their Palinurus.

The Abbot himself seemed at a stand; he felt no fear, but he was sensible of the danger of expressing his rising indignation, which he was scarcely able to suppress. He made a gesture with his hand as if commanding silence, which was at first only replied to by redoubled shouts, and peals of wild laughter. When, however, the same motion, and as nearly in the same manner, had been made by Howleglas, it was immediately obeyed by his riotous companions, who expected fresh food for mirth in the conversation betwixt the real and mock Abbot, having no small confidence in the vulgar wit and impudence of their leader. Accordingly, they began to shout, "To it, fathers—to it I"— "Fight monk, fight madcap—Abbot against Abbot is fair play, and so is reason against unreason, and malice against monkery!"

"Silence, my mates!" said Howleglas; "cannot two learned Fathers of the Church hold communion together, but you must come here with your bear-garden whoop and hollo, as if you were hounding forth a mastiff upon a mad bull? I say silence! and let this learned Father and me confer, touching matters affecting our mutual state and authority."

"My children"—said Father Ambrose.

"*My* children too,—and happy children they are!" said his burlesque counterpart; "many a wise child knows not its own father, and it is well they have two to choose betwixt."

"If thou hast aught in thee, save scoffing and ribaldry," said the real Abbot, "permit me, for thine own soul's sake, to speak a few words to these misguided men."

"Aught in me but scoffing, sayest thou?" retorted the Abbot of Unreason; "why, reverend brother, I have all that becomes mine office at this time a-day—I have beef, ale, and brandy-wine, with other condiments not worth mentioning; and for speaking, man—why, speak away, and we will have turn about, like honest fellows."

During this discussion the wrath of Magdalen Graeme had risen to the uttermost; she approached the Abbot, and placing herself by his side, said in a low and yet distinct tone-"Wake and arouse thee,

Father—the sword of Saint Peter is in thy hand—strike and avenge Saint Peter's patrimony!—Bind them in the chains which, being riveted by the church on earth, are riveted in Heaven—"

"Peace, sister!" said the Abbot; "let not their madness destroy our discretion—I pray thee, peace, and let me do mine office. It is the first, peradventure it may be the last time, I shall be called on to discharge it."

"Nay, my holy brother!" said Howleglas, "I rede you, take the holy sister's advice—never throve convent without woman's counsel."

"Peace, vain man!" said the Abbot; "and you, my brethren—"

"Nay, nay!" said the Abbot of Unreason, "no speaking to the lay people, until you have conferred with your brother of the cowl. I swear by bell, book, and candle, that no one of my congregation shall listen to one word you have to say; so you had as well address yourself to me who will."

To escape a conference so ludicrous, the Abbot again attempted an appeal to what respectful feelings might yet remain amongst the inhabitants of the Halidome, once so devoted to their spiritual Superiors. Alas! the Abbot of Unreason had only to nourish his mock crosier, and the whooping, the hallooing, and the dancing, were renewed with a vehemence which would have defied the lungs of Stentor.

"And now, my mates," said the Abbot of Unreason, "once again dight your gabs and be hushed-let us see if the Cock of Kennaquhair will fight or flee the pit."

There was again a dead silence of expectation, of which Father Ambrose availed himself to address his antagonist, seeing plainly that he could gain an audience on no other terms. "Wretched man!" said he, "hast thou no better employment for thy carnal wit, than to employ it in leading these blind and helpless creatures into the pit of utter darkness?"

"Truly, my brother," replied Howleglas, "I can see little difference betwixt your employment and mine, save that you make a sermon of a jest, and I make a jest of a sermon."

"Unhappy being," said the Abbot, "who hast no better subject of pleasantry than that which should make thee tremble—no sounder jest than thine own sins, and no better objects for laughter than those who can absolve thee from the guilt of them!"

"Verily, my reverend brother," said the mock Abbot, "what you say might be true, if, in laughing at hypocrites, I meant to laugh at religion.— Oh, it is a precious thing to wear a long dress, with a girdle and a cowl—

SIR WALTER SCOTT

we become a holy pillar of Mother Church, and a boy must not play at ball against the walls for fear of breaking a painted window!"

"And will you, my friends," said the Abbot, looking round and speaking with a vehemence which secured him a tranquil audience for some time,—"will you suffer a profane buffoon, within the very church of God, to insult his ministers? Many of you—all of you, perhaps—have lived under my holy predecessors, who were called upon to rule in this church where I am called upon to suffer. If you have worldly goods, they are their gift; and, when you scorned not to accept better gifts—the mercy and forgiveness of the church—were they not ever at your command?—did we not pray while you were jovial—wake while you slept?"

"Some of the good wives of the Halidome were wont to say so," said the Abbot of Unreason; but his jest met in this instance but slight applause, and Father Ambrose, having gained a moment's attention, hastened to improve it.

"What!" said he; "and is this grateful—is it seemly—is it honest—to assail with scorn a few old men, from whose predecessors you hold all, and whose only wish is to die in peace among these fragments of what was once the light of the land, and whose daily prayer is, that they may be removed ere that hour comes when the last spark shall be extinguished, and the land left in the darkness which it has chosen rather than light? We have not turned against you the edge of the spiritual sword, to revenge our temporal persecution; the tempest of your wrath hath despoiled us of land, and deprived us almost of our daily food, but we have not repaid it with the thunders of excommunication—we only pray your leave to live and die within the church which is our own, invoking God, our Lady, and the Holy Saints to pardon your sins, and our own, undisturbed by scurril buffoonery and blasphemy."

This speech, so different in tone and termination from that which the crowd had expected, produced an effect upon their feelings unfavourable to the prosecution of their frolic. The morris-dancers stood still—the hobby-horse surceased his capering—pipe and tabor were mute, and "silence, like a heavy cloud," seemed to descend on the once noisy rabble. Several of the beasts were obviously moved to compunction; the bear could not restrain his sobs, and a huge fox was observed to wipe his eyes with his tail. But in especial the dragon, lately so formidably rampant, now relaxed the terror of his claws, uncoiled his tremendous rings, and grumbled out of his fiery throat in a repentant tone, "By the mass, I thought no harm in exercising our old pastime, but an I had thought the good Father would have taken it so to heart, I would as soon have played your devil, as your dragon."

In this momentary pause, the Abbot stood amongst the miscellaneous and grotesque forms by which he was surrounded, triumphant as Saint Anthony, in Callot's Temptations; but Howleglas would not so resign his purpose.

"And how now, my masters!" said he, "is this fair play or no? Have you not chosen me Abbot of Unreason, and is it lawful for any of you to listen to common sense to-day? Was I not formally elected by you in solemn chapter, held in Luckie Martin's change-house, and will you now desert me, and give up your old pastime and privilege? Play out the play—and he that speaks the next word of sense or reason, or bids us think or consider, or the like of that, which befits not the day, I will have him solemnly ducked in the mill-dam!"

The rabble, mutable as usual, huzzaed, the pipe and tabor struck up, the hobby-horse pranced, the beasts roared, and even the repentant dragon began again to coil up his spires, and prepare himself for fresh gambols. But the Abbot might still have overcome, by his eloquence and his entreaties, the malicious designs of the revellers, had not Dame Magdalen Graeme given loose to the indignation which she had long suppressed.

"Scoffers," she said, "and men of Belial—Blasphemous heretics, and truculent tyrants—"

"Your patience, my sister, I entreat and I command you!" said the Abbot; "let me do my duty—disturb me not in mine office!"

But Dame Magdalen continued to thunder forth her threats in the name of Popes and Councils, and in the name of every Saint, from St. Michael downward.

"My comrades!" said the Abbot of Unreason, "this good dame hath not spoken a single word of reason, and therein may esteem herself free from the law. But what she spoke was meant for reason, and, therefore, unless she confesses and avouches all which she has said to be nonsense, it shall pass for such, so far as to incur our statutes. Wherefore, holy dame, pilgrim, or abbess, or whatever thou art, be mute with thy mummery or beware the mill-dam. We will have neither spiritual nor temporal scolds in our Diocese of Unreason!"

As he spoke thus, he extended his hand towards the old woman, while his followers shouted, "A doom—a doom!" and prepared to second his purpose, when lo! it was suddenly frustrated. Roland Graeme had witnessed with indignation the insults offered to his old spiritual preceptor, but yet had wit enough to reflect he could render him no assistance, but might well, by ineffective interference, make matters worse. But when he saw his aged relative in danger of personal violence, he gave way to the natural impetuosity of his temper, and, stepping forward, struck his poniard into the body of the Abbot of Unreason, whom the blow instantly prostrated on the pavement.

XV

As when in tumults rise the ignoble crowd,
Mad are their motions, and their tongues are loud,
And stones and brands in rattling furies fly,
And all the rustic arms which fury can supply—
Then if some grave and pious man appear,
They hush their noise, and lend a listening ear.

—DRYDEN'S VIRGIL

A dreadful shout of vengeance was raised by the revellers, whose sport was thus so fearfully interrupted; but for an instant, the want of weapons amongst the multitude, as well as the inflamed features and brandished poniard of Roland Graeme, kept them at bay, while the Abbot, horror-struck at the violence, implored, with uplifted hands, pardon for blood-shed committed within the sanctuary. Magdalen Graeme alone expressed triumph in the blow her descendant had dealt to the scoffer, mixed, however, with a wild and anxious expression of terror for her grandson's safety. "Let him perish," she said, "in his blasphemy—let him die on the holy pavement which he has insulted!"

But the rage of the multitude, the grief of the Abbot, the exultation of the enthusiastic Magdalen, were all mistimed and unnecessary. Howleglas, mortally wounded as he was supposed to be, sprung alertly up from the floor, calling aloud, "A miracle, a miracle, my masters! as brave a miracle as ever was wrought in the kirk of Kennaquhair. And I charge you, my masters, as your lawfully chosen Abbot, that you touch no one without my command—You, wolf and bear, will guard this pragmatic youth, but without hurting him—And you, reverend brother, will, with your comrades, withdraw to your cells; for our conference has ended like all conferences, leaving each of his own mind, as before; and if we fight, both you, and your brethren, and the Kirk, will have the worst on't—Wherefore, pack up you pipes and begone."

The hubbub was beginning again to awaken, but still Father Ambrose hesitated, as uncertain to what path his duty called him, whether to face out the present storm, or to reserve himself for a better moment. His brother of Unreason observed his difficulty, and said, in a tone more natural and less affected than that with which he had hitherto sustained

SIR WALTER SCOTT

his character, "We came hither, my good sir, more in mirth than in mischief—our bark is worse than our bite—and, especially, we mean you no personal harm—wherefore, draw off while the play is good; for it is ill whistling for a hawk when she is once on the soar, and worse to snatch the quarry from the ban-dog—Let these fellows once begin their brawl, and it will be too much for madness itself, let alone the Abbot of Unreason, to bring them back to the lure."

The brethren crowded around Father Ambrosius, and joined in urging him to give place to the torrent. The present revel was, they said, an ancient custom which his predecessors had permitted, and old Father Nicholas himself had played the dragon in the days of the Abbot Ingelram.

"And we now reap the fruit of the seed which they have so unadvisedly sown," said Ambrosius; "they taught men to make a mock of what is holy, what wonder that the descendants of scoffers become robbers and plunderers? But be it as you list, my brethren—move towards the dortour—And you, dame, I command you, by the authority which I have over you, and by your respect for that youth's safety, that you go with us without farther speech—Yet, stay—what are your intentions towards that youth whom you detain prisoner?—Wot ye," he continued, addressing Howleglas in a stern tone of voice, "that he bears the livery of the House of Avenel? They who fear not the anger of Heaven, may at least dread the wrath of man."

"Cumber not yourself concerning him," answered Howleglas, "we know right well who and what he is."

"Let me pray," said the Abbot, in a tone of entreaty, "that you do him no wrong for the rash deed—which he attempted in his imprudent zeal."

"I say, cumber not yourself about it, father," answered Howleglas, "but move off with your train, male and female, or I will not undertake to save yonder she-saint from the ducking-stool—And as for bearing of malice, my stomach has no room for it; it is," he added, clapping his hand on his portly belly, "too well bumbasted out with straw and buckram—gramercy to them both—they kept out that madcap's dagger as well as a Milan corslet could have done."

In fact, the home-driven poniard of Roland Graeme had lighted upon the stuffing of the fictitious paunch, which the Abbot of Unreason wore as a part of his characteristic dress, and it was only the force of the blow which had prostrated that reverend person on the ground for a moment.

Satisfied in some degree by this man's assurances, and compelled—to give way to superior force, the Abbot Ambrosius retired from the Church at the head of the monks, and left the court free for the revellers to work their will. But, wild and wilful as these rioters were, they accompanied the retreat of the religionists with none of those shouts of contempt and derision with which they had at first hailed them. The Abbot's discourse had affected some of them with remorse, others with shame, and all with a transient degree of respect. They remained silent until the last monk had disappeared through the side-door which communicated with their dwelling-place, and even then it cost some exhortations on the part of Howleglas, some caprioles of the hobby-horse, and some wallops of the dragon, to rouse once more the rebuked spirit of revelry.

"And how now, my masters?" said the Abbot of Unreason; "and wherefore look on me with such blank Jack-a-Lent visages? Will you lose your old pastime for an old wife's tale of saints and purgatory? Why, I thought you would have made all split long since—Come, strike up, tabor and harp, strike up, fiddle and rebeck—dance and be merry to-day, and let care come to-morrow. Bear and wolf, look to your prisoner—prance, hobby—hiss, dragon, and halloo, boys—we grow older every moment we stand idle, and life is too short to be spent in playing mumchance."

This pithy exhortation was attended with the effect desired. They fumigated the Church with burnt wool and feathers instead of incense, put foul water into the holy-water basins, and celebrated a parody on the Church-service, the mock Abbot officiating at the altar; they sung ludicrous and indecent parodies, to the tunes of church hymns; they violated whatever vestments or vessels belonging to the Abbey they could lay their hands upon; and, playing every freak which the whim of the moment could suggest to their wild caprice, at length they fell to more lasting deeds of demolition, pulled down and destroyed some carved wood-work, dashed out the painted windows which had escaped former violence, and in their rigorous search after sculpture dedicated to idolatry, began to destroy what ornaments yet remained entire upon the tombs, and around the cornices of the pillars.

The spirit of demolition, like other tastes, increases by indulgence; from these lighter attempts at mischief, the more tumultuous part of the meeting began to meditate destruction on a more extended scale—"Let us heave it down altogether, the old crow's nest," became a general

SIR WALTER SCOTT

cry among them; "it has served the Pope and his rooks too long;" and up they struck a ballad which was then popular among the lower classes.*

> *"The Paip, that pagan full of pride,*
> *Hath blinded us ower lang.*
> *For where the blind the blind doth lead,*
> *No marvel baith gae wrang.*
> *Like prince and king,*
> *He led the ring*
> *Of all iniquity.*
> *Sing hay trix, trim-go-trix,*
> *Under the greenwood tree.*

> *"The Bishop rich, he could not preach*
> *For sporting with the lasses;*
> *The silly friar behoved to fleech*
> *For awmous as he passes:*
> *The curate his creed*
> *He could not read,—*
> *Shame fa' company!*
> *Sing hay trix, trim-go-trix,*
> *Under the greenwood tree."*

Thundering out this chorus of a notable hunting song, which had been pressed into the service of some polemical poet, the followers of the Abbot of Unreason were turning every moment more tumultuous, and getting beyond the management even of that reverend prelate himself, when a knight in full armour, followed by two or three men-at-arms, entered the church, and in a stern voice commanded them to forbear their riotous mummery.

His visor was up, but if it had been lowered, the cognizance of the holly-branch sufficiently distinguished Sir Halbert Glendinning, who,

---

* These rude rhymes are taken, with some trifling alterations, from a ballad called Trim-go-trix. It occurs in a singular collection, entitled; "A Compendious Book of Godly and Spiritual Songs, collected out of sundrie parts of the Scripture, with sundry of other ballatis changed out of prophane sanges for avoyding of sin and harlotrie, with Augmentation of sundrie Gude and Godly Ballates. Edinburgh, printed by Andro Hart." This curious collection has been reprinted in Mr. John. Grahame Dalyell's Scottish Poems of the 16th century Edin. 1801, 2 vols.

on his homeward road, was passing through the village of Kennaquhair; and moved, perhaps, by anxiety for his brother's safety, had come directly to the church on hearing of the uproar.

"What is the meaning of this," he said, "my masters? are ye Christian men, and the king's subjects, and yet waste and destroy church and chancel like so many heathens?"

All stood silent, though doubtless there were several disappointed and surprised at receiving chiding instead of thanks from so zealous a protestant.

The dragon, indeed, did at length take upon him to be spokesman, and growled from the depth of his painted maw, that they did but sweep Popery out of the church with the besom of destruction.

"What! my friends," replied Sir Halbert Glendinning, "think you this mumming and masking has not more of Popery in it than have these stone walls? Take the leprosy out of your flesh, before you speak of purifying stone walls—abate your insolent license, which leads but to idle vanity and sinful excess; and know, that what you now practise, is one of the profane and unseemly sports introduced by the priests of Rome themselves, to mislead and to brutify the souls which fell into their net."

"Marry come up—are you there with your bears?" muttered the dragon, with a draconic sullenness, which was in good keeping with his character, "we had as good have been Romans still, if we are to have no freedom in our pastimes!"

"Dost thou reply to me so?" said Halbert Glendinning; "or is there any pastime in grovelling on the ground there like a gigantic kail-worm?—Get out of thy painted case, or, by my knighthood, I will treat you like the beast and reptile you have made yourself."

"Beast and reptile?" retorted the offended dragon, "setting aside your knighthood, I hold myself as well a born man as thyself."

The Knight made no answer in words, but bestowed two such blows with the butt of his lance on the petulant dragon, that had not the hoops which constituted the ribs of the machine been pretty strong, they would hardly have saved those of the actor from being broken. In all haste the masker crept out of his disguise, unwilling to abide a third buffet from the lance of the enraged Knight. And when the ex-dragon stood on the floor of the church, he presented to Halbert Glendinning the well-known countenance of Dan of the Howlet-hirst, an ancient comrade of his own, ere fate had raised him so high above the rank to which he was born. The clown looked sulkily upon the Knight, as if to upbraid him for his violence towards an old acquaintance, and Glendinning's own good-nature reproached him for the violence he had acted upon him.

"I did wrong to strike thee," he said, "Dan; but in truth, I knew thee not—thou wert ever a mad fellow—come to Avenel Castle, and we shall see how my hawks fly."

"And if we show him not falcons that will mount as merrily as rockets," said the Abbot of Unreason, "I would your honour laid as hard on my bones as you did on his even now."

"How now, Sir Knave," said the Knight, "and what has brought you hither?"

The Abbot, hastily ridding himself of the false nose which mystified his physiognomy, and the supplementary belly which made up his disguise, stood before his master in his real character, of Adam Woodcock, the falconer of Avenel.

"How, varlet!" said the Knight; "hast thou dared to come here and disturb the very house my brother was dwelling in?"

"And it was even for that reason, craving your honour's pardon, that I came hither—for I heard the country was to be up to choose an Abbot of Unreason, and sure, thought I, I that can sing, dance, leap backwards over a broadsword, and am as good a fool as ever sought promotion, have all chance of carrying the office; and if I gain my election, I may stand his honour's brother in some stead, supposing things fall roughly out at the Kirk of Saint Mary's."

"Thou art but a cogging knave," said Sir Halbert, "and well I wot, that love of ale and brandy, besides the humour of riot and frolic, would draw thee a mile, when love of my house would not bring thee a yard. But, go to—carry thy roisterers elsewhere—to the alehouse if they list, and there are crowns to pay your charges—make out the day's madness without doing more mischief, and be wise men to-morrow—and hereafter learn to serve a good cause better than by acting like buffoons or ruffians."

Obedient to his master's mandate, the falconer was collecting his discouraged followers, and whispering into their ears—"Away, away—*tace* is Latin for a candle—never mind the good Knight's puritanism—we will play the frolic out over a stand of double ale in Dame Martin the Brewster's barn-yard—draw off, harp and tabor—bagpipe and drum—mum till you are out of the church-yard, then let the welkin ring again—move on, wolf and bear—keep the hind legs till you cross the kirk-stile, and then show yourselves beasts of mettle—what devil sent him here to spoil our holiday!—but anger him not, my hearts; his lance is no goose-feather, as Dan's ribs can tell."

"By my soul," said Dan, "had it been another than my ancient comrade, I would have made my father's old fox* fly about his ears!"

"Hush! hush! man," replied Adam Woodcock, "not a word that way, as you value the safety of your bones—what man? we must take a clink as it passes, so it is not bestowed in downright ill-will."

"But I will take no such thing," said Dan of the Howlet-hirst, suddenly resisting the efforts of Woodcock, who was dragging him out of the church; when the quick military eye of Sir Halbert Glendinning detecting Roland Graeme betwixt his two guards, the Knight exclaimed, "So ho! falconer,—Woodcock,—knave, hast thou brought my Lady's page in mine own livery, to assist at this hopeful revel of thine, with your wolves and bears? Since you were at such mummings, you might, if you would, have at least saved the credit of my household, by dressing him up as a jackanapes—bring him hither, fellows!"

Adam Woodcock was too honest and downright, to permit blame to light upon the youth, when it was undeserved. "I swear," he said, "by Saint Martin of Bullions—"†

"And what hast thou to do with Saint Martin?"

"Nay, little enough, sir, unless when he sends such rainy days that we cannot fly a hawk—but I say to your worshipful knighthood, that as I am, a true man—"

"As you are a false varlet, had been the better obtestation."

"Nay, if your knighthood allows me not to speak," said Adam, "I can hold my tongue—but the boy came not hither by my bidding, for all that."

"But to gratify his own malapert pleasure, I warrant me," said Sir Halbert Glendinning—"Come hither, young springald, and tell me whether you have your mistress's license to be so far absent from the castle, or to dishonour my livery by mingling in such a May-game?"

"Sir Halbert Glendinning," answered Roland Graeme with steadiness, "I have obtained the permission, or rather the commands, of your lady, to

---

* *Fox*, An old-fashioned broadsword was often so called.
† The Saint Swithin, or weeping Saint of Scotland. If his festival (fourth July) prove wet, forty days of rain are expected.

dispose of my time hereafter according to my own pleasure. I have been a most unwilling spectator of this May-game, since it is your pleasure so to call it; and I only wear your livery until I can obtain clothes which bear no such badge of servitude."

"How am I to understand this, young man?" said Sir Halbert Glendinning; "speak plainly, for I am no reader of riddles.—That my lady favoured thee, I know. What hast thou done to disoblige her, and occasion thy dismissal?"

"Nothing to speak of," said Adam Woodcock, answering for the boy—"a foolish quarrel with me, which was more foolishly told over again to my honoured lady, cost the poor boy his place. For my part, I will say freely, that I was wrong from beginning to end, except about the washing of the eyas's meat. There I stand to it that I was right."

With that, the good-natured falconer repeated to his master the whole history of the squabble which had brought Roland Graeme into disgrace with his mistress, but in a manner so favourable for the page, that Sir Halbert could not but suspect his generous motive.

"Thou art a good-natured fellow," he said, "Adam Woodcock."

"As ever had falcon upon fist," said Adam; "and, for that matter, so is Master Roland; but, being half a gentleman by his office, his blood is soon up, and so is mine."

"Well," said Sir Halbert, "be it as it will, my lady has acted hastily, for this was no great matter of offence to discard the lad whom she had trained up for years; but he, I doubt not, made it worse by his prating— it jumps well with a purpose, however, which I had in my mind. Draw off these people, Woodcock,—and you, Roland Graeme, attend me."

The page followed him in silence into the Abbot's house, where, stepping into the first apartment which he found open, he commanded one of his attendants to let his brother, Master Edward Glendinning, know that he desired to speak with him. The men-at-arms went gladly off to join their comrade, Adam Woodcock, and the jolly crew whom he had assembled at Dame Martin's, the hostler's wife, and the Page and Knight were left alone in the apartment. Sir Halbert Glendinning paced the floor for a moment in silence and then thus addressed his attendant—

"Thou mayest have remarked, stripling, that I have but seldom distinguished thee by much notice;—I see thy colour rises, but do not speak till thou nearest me out. I say I have never much distinguished thee, not because I did not see that in thee which I might well have praised, but because I saw something blameable, which such praises might have made worse. Thy mistress, dealing according to her pleasure in her own household, as no one had better reason or title, had picked thee from the rest, and treated thee more like a relation than a domestic; and if thou didst show some vanity and petulance under such distinction, it were injustice not to say that thou hast profited both in thy exercises and in thy breeding, and hast shown many sparkles of a gentle and manly spirit. Moreover, it were ungenerous, having bred thee up freakish and fiery, to dismiss thee to want or wandering, for showing that very peevishness and impatience of discipline which arose from thy too delicate nurture. Therefore, and for the credit of my own household, I am determined to retain thee in my train, until I can honourably dispose of thee elsewhere, with a fair prospect of thy going through the world with credit to the house that brought thee up."

If there was something in Sir Halbert Glendinning's speech which flattered Roland's pride, there was also much that, according to his mode of thinking, was an alloy to the compliment. And yet his conscience instantly told him that he ought to accept, with grateful deference, the offer which was made him by the husband of his kind protectress; and his prudence, however slender, could not but admit he should enter the world under very different auspices as a retainer of Sir Halbert Glendinning, so famed for wisdom, courage, and influence, from those under which he might partake the wanderings, and become an agent in the visionary schemes, for such they appeared to him, of Magdalen, his relative. Still, a strong reluctance to re-enter a service from which he had been dismissed with contempt, almost counterbalanced these considerations.

Sir Halbert looked on the youth with surprise, and resumed—"You seem to hesitate, young man. Are your own prospects so inviting, that you should pause ere you accept those which I should offer to you? or, must I remind you that, although you have offended your benefactress, even to the point of her dismissing you, yet I am convinced, the knowledge that you have gone unguided on your own wild way, into a world so disturbed as ours of Scotland, cannot, in the upshot, but give her sorrow and pain; from which it is, in gratitude, your duty to preserve her, no less than it is in common wisdom your duty to accept my offered protection, for your own sake, where body and soul are alike endangered, should you refuse it."

SIR WALTER SCOTT

Roland Graeme replied in a respectful tone, but at the same time with some spirit, "I am not ungrateful for such countenance as has been afforded me by the Lord of Avenel, and I am glad to learn, for the first time, that I have not had the misfortune to be utterly beneath his observation, as I had thought—And it is only needful to show me how I can testify my duty and my gratitude towards my early and constant benefactress with my life's hazard, and I will gladly peril it." He stopped.

"These are but words, young man," answered Glendinning, "large protestations are often used to supply the place of effectual service. I know nothing in which the peril of your life can serve the Lady of Avenel; I can only say, she will be pleased to learn you have adopted some course which may ensure the safety of your person, and the weal of your soul—What ails you, that you accept not that safety when it is offered you?"

"My only relative who is alive," answered Roland, "at least the only relative whom I have ever seen, has rejoined me since I was dismissed from the Castle of Avenel, and I must consult with her whether I can adopt the line to which you now call me, or whether her increasing infirmities, or the authority which she is entitled to exercise over me, may not require me to abide with her."

"Where is this relation?" said Sir Halbert Glendinning.

"In this house," answered the page.

"Go then, and seek her out," said the Knight of Avenel; "more than meet it is that thou shouldst have her approbation, yet worse than foolish would she show herself in denying it."

Roland left the apartment to seek for his grandmother; and, as he retreated, the Abbot entered.

The two brothers met as brothers who loved each other fondly, yet meet rarely together. Such indeed was the case. Their mutual affection attached them to each other; but in every pursuit, habit or sentiment, connected with the discords of the times, the friend and counsellor of Murray stood opposed to the Roman Catholic priest; nor, indeed, could they have held very much society together, without giving cause of offence and suspicion to their confederates on each side. After a close embrace on the part of both, and a welcome on that of the Abbot, Sir Halbert Glendinning expressed his satisfaction that he had come in time to appease the riot raised by Howleglas and his tumultuous followers.

"And yet," he said, "when I look on your garments, brother Edward,

I cannot help thinking there still remains an Abbot of Unreason within the bounds of the Monastery."

"And wherefore carp at my garments, brother Halbert?" said the Abbot; "it is the spiritual armour of my calling, and, as such, beseems me as well as breastplate and baldric becomes your own bosom."

"Ay, but there were small wisdom, methinks, in putting on armour where we have no power to fight; it is but a dangerous temerity to defy the foe whom we cannot resist."

"For that, my brother, no one can answer," said the Abbot, "until the battle be fought; and, were it even as you say, methinks a brave man, though desperate of victory, would rather desire to fight and fall, than to resign sword and shield on some mean and dishonourable composition with his insulting antagonist. But, let not you and I make discord of a theme on which we cannot agree, but rather stay and partake, though a heretic, of my admission feast. You need not fear, my brother, that your zeal for restoring the primitive discipline of the church will, on this occasion, be offended with the rich profusion of a conventual banquet. The days of our old friend Abbot Boniface are over; and the Superior of Saint Mary's has neither forests nor fishings, woods nor pastures, nor corn-fields;—neither flocks nor herds, bucks nor wild-fowl—granaries of wheat, nor storehouses of oil and wine, of ale and of mead. The refectioner's office is ended; and such a meal as a hermit in romance can offer to a wandering knight, is all we have to set before you. But, if you will share it with us, we shall eat it with a cheerful heart, and thank you, my brother, for your timely protection against these rude scoffers."

"My dearest brother," said the Knight, "it grieves me deeply I cannot abide with you; but it would sound ill for us both were one of the reformed congregation to sit down at your admission feast; and, if I can ever have the satisfaction of affording you effectual protection, it will be much owing to my remaining unsuspected of countenancing or approving your religious rites and ceremonies. It will demand whatever consideration I can acquire among my own friends, to shelter the bold man, who, contrary to law and the edicts of parliament, has dared to take up the office of Abbot of Saint Mary's."

"Trouble not yourself with the task, my brother," replied Father Ambrosius. "I would lay down my dearest blood to know that you defended the church for the church's sake; but, while you remain unhappily her enemy, I would not that you endangered your own safety, or diminished your own comforts, for the sake of my individual protection.—But who comes hither to disturb the few minutes of fraternal communication which our evil fate allows us?"

The door of the apartment opened as the Abbot spoke, and Dame Magdalen entered.

"Who is this woman?" said Sir Halbert Glendinning, somewhat sternly, "and what does she want?"

"That you know me not," said the matron, "signifies little; I come by your own order, to give my free consent that the stripling, Roland Graeme, return to your service; and, having said so, I cumber you no longer with my presence. Peace be with you!" She turned to go away, but was stopped by inquiries of Sir Halbert Glendinning.

"Who are you?—what are you?—and why do you not await to make me answer?"

"I was," she replied, "while yet I belonged to the world, a matron of no vulgar name; now I am Magdalen, a poor pilgrimer, for the sake of Holy Kirk."

"Yea," said Sir Halbert, "art thou a Catholic? I thought my dame said that Roland Graeme came of reformed kin.'

"His father," said the matron, "was a heretic, or rather one who regarded neither orthodoxy or heresy—neither the temple of the church or of antichrist. I, too, for the sins of the times make sinners, have seemed to conform to your unhallowed rites—but I had my dispensation and my absolution."

"You see, brother," said Sir Halbert, with a smile of meaning towards his brother, "that we accuse you not altogether without grounds of mental equivocation."

"My brother, you do us injustice," replied the Abbot; "this woman, as her bearing may of itself warrant you, is not in her perfect mind. Thanks, I must needs say, to the persecution of your marauding barons, and of your latitudinarian clergy."

"I will not dispute the point," said Sir Halbert; "the evils of the time are unhappily so numerous, that both churches may divide them, and have enow to spare." So saying, he leaned from the window of the apartment, and winded his bugle.

"Why do you sound your horn, my brother?" said the Abbot; "we have spent but few minutes together."

"Alas!" said the elder brother, "and even these few have been sullied by disagreement. I sound to horse, my brother—the rather that, to avert the consequences of this day's rashness on your part, requires hasty efforts on mine.—Dame, you will oblige me by letting your young relative know that we mount instantly. I intend not that he shall return to Avenel with me—it would lead to new quarrels betwixt him and my household; at least to taunts which his proud heart could ill brook, and my wish is to do him kindness. He shall, therefore, go forward to Edinburgh with one of my retinue, whom I shall send back to say what has chanced here.—You seem rejoiced at this?" he added, fixing his eyes keenly on Magdalen Graeme, who returned his gaze with calm indifference.

"I would rather," she said, "that Roland, a poor and friendless orphan, were the jest of the world at large, than of the menials at Avenel."

"Fear not, dame—he shall be scorned by neither," answered the Knight.

"It may be," she replied—"it may well be—but I will trust more to his own bearing than to your countenance." She left the room as she spoke.

The Knight looked after her as she departed, but turned instantly to his brother, and expressing, in the most affectionate terms, his wishes for his welfare and happiness, craved his leave to depart. "My knaves," he said, "are too busy at the ale-stand, to leave their revelry for the empty breath of a bugle-horn."

"You have freed them from higher restraint, Halbert," answered the Abbot, "and therein taught them to rebel against your own."

"Fear not that, Edward," exclaimed Halbert, who never gave his brother his monastic name of Ambrosius; "none obey the command of real duty so well as those who are free from the observance of slavish bondage."

He was turning to depart, when the Abbot said,—"Let us not yet part, my brother—here comes some light refreshment. Leave not the house which I must now call mine, till force expel me from it, until you have at least broken bread with me."

The poor lay brother, the same who acted as porter, now entered the apartment, bearing some simple refreshment, and a flask of wine. "He had found it," he said with officious humility, "by rummaging through every nook of the cellar."

The Knight filled a small silver cup, and, quaffing it off, asked his brother to pledge him, observing, the wine was Bacharac, of the first vintage, and great age.

"Ay," said the poor lay brother, "it came out of the nook which old brother Nicholas, (may his soul be happy!) was wont to call Abbot

Ingelram's corner; and Abbot Ingelram was bred at the Convent of Wurtzburg, which I understand to be near where that choice wine grows."

"True, my reverend sir," said Sir Halbert; "and therefore I entreat my brother and you to pledge me in a cup of this orthodox vintage."

The thin old porter looked with a wishful glance towards the Abbot. "*Do veniam*," said his Superior; and the old man seized, with a trembling hand, a beverage to which he had been long unaccustomed; drained the cup with protracted delight, as if dwelling on the flavour and perfume, and set it down with a melancholy smile and shake of the head, as if bidding adieu in future to such delicious potations. The brothers smiled. But when Sir Halbert motioned to the Abbot to take up his cup and do him reason, the Abbot, in turn, shook his head, and replied—"This is no day for the Abbot of Saint Mary's to eat the fat and drink the sweat. In water from our Lady's well," he added, filling a cup with the limpid element, "I wish you, brother, all happiness, and above all, a true sight of your spiritual errors."

"And to you, my beloved Edward," replied Glendinning, "I wish the free exercise of your own free reason, and the discharge of more important duties than are connected with the idle name which you have so rashly assumed."

The brothers parted with deep regret; and yet, each confident in his opinion, felt somewhat relieved by the absence of one whom he respected so much, and with whom he could agree so little.

Soon afterwards the sound of the Knight of Avenel's trumpets was heard, and the Abbot went to the top of the tower, from whose dismantled battlements he could soon see the horsemen ascending the rising ground in the direction of the drawbridge. As he gazed, Magdalen Graeme came to his side.

"Thou art come," he said, "to catch the last glimpse of thy grandson, my sister. Yonder he wends, under the charge of the best knight in Scotland, his faith ever excepted."

"Thou canst bear witness, my father, that it was no wish either of mine or of Roland's," replied the matron, "which induced the Knight of Avenel, as he is called, again to entertain my grandson in his household—Heaven, which confounds the wise with their own wisdom, and the wicked with their own policy, hath placed him where, for the services of the Church, I would most wish him to be."

"I know not what you mean, my sister," said the Abbot.

"Reverend father," replied Magdalen, "hast thou never heard that there are spirits powerful to rend the walls of a castle asunder when once admitted, which yet cannot enter the house unless they are invited, nay, dragged over the threshold?*

---

* There is a popular belief respecting evil spirits, that they cannot enter an inhabited house unless invited, nay, dragged over the threshold. There is an instance of the same superstition in the Tales of the Genii, where an enchanter is supposed to have intruded himself into the Divan of the Sultan.

"'Thus,' said the illustrious Misnar, 'let the enemies of Mahomet be dismayed! but inform me, O ye sages! under the semblance of which of your brethren did that foul enchanter gain admittance here?'—'May the lord of my heart,' answered Balihu, the hermit of the faithful from Queda, 'triumph over all his foes! As I travelled on the mountains from Queda, and saw neither the footsteps of beasts, nor the flight of birds, behold, I chanced to pass through a cavern, in whose hollow sides I found this accursed sage, to whom I unfolded the invitation of the Sultan of India, and we, joining, journeyed towards the Divan; but ere we entered, he said unto me. 'Put thy hand forth, and pull me towards thee into the Divan, calling on the name of Mahomet, for the evil spirits are on me and vex me.'"

I have understood that many parts of these fine tales, and in particular that of the Sultan Misnar, were taken from genuine Oriental sources by the editor, Mr. James Ridley.

But the most picturesque use of this popular belief occurs in Coleridge's beautiful and tantalizing fragment of Christabel. Has not our own imaginative poet cause to fear that future ages will desire to summon him from his place of rest, as Milton longed

> *"To call him up, who left half told*
> *The story of Cambuscan bold?"*

The verses I refer to are when Christabel conducts into her father's castle a mysterious and malevolent being, under the guise of a distressed female stranger.

> *'They cross'd the moat, and Christabel*
> *Took the key that fitted well;*
> *A little door she open'd straight,*
> *All in the middle of the gate;*
> *The gate that was iron'd within and without,*
> *Where an army in battle array had march'd out.*

> *"The lady sank, belike through pain,*
> *And Christabel with might and main*
> *Lifted her up, a weary weight,*
> *Over the threshold of the gate:*
> *Then the lady rose again,*
> *And moved as she were not in pain.*

> *"So free from danger, free from fear,*
> *They cross'd the court;—right glad they were,*

Twice hath Roland Graeme been thus drawn into the household of Avenel by those who now hold the title. Let them look to the issue."

So saying she left the turret; and the Abbot, after pausing a moment on her words, which he imputed to the unsettled state of her mind, followed down the winding stair to celebrate his admission to his high office by fast and prayer instead of revelling and thanksgiving.

And Christabel devoutly cried
To the lady by her side:
'Praise we the Virgin, all divine,
Who hath rescued thee from this distress.'
'Alas, alas!' said Geraldine,
'I cannot speak from weariness.'
So free from danger, free from fear,
They cross'd the court: right glad they were

XVI

Youth! thou wear'st to manhood now,
Darker lip and darker brow,
Statelier step, more pensive mien,
In thy face and gate are seen:
Thou must now brook midnight watches,
Take thy food and sport by snatches;
For the gambol and the jest,
Thou wert wont to love the best,
Graver follies must thou follow,
But as senseless, false, and hollow.

—LIFE, A POEM

Young Roland Graeme now trotted gaily forward in the train of Sir Halbert Glendinning. He was relieved from his most galling apprehension,—the encounter of the scorn and taunt which might possibly hail his immediate return to the Castle of Avenel. "There will be a change ere they see me again," he thought to himself; "I shall wear the coat of plate, instead of the green jerkin, and the steel morion for the bonnet and feather. They will be bold that may venture to break a gibe on the man-at-arms for the follies of the page; and I trust, that ere we return I shall have done something more worthy of note than hallooing a hound after a deer, or scrambling a crag for a kite's nest." He could not, indeed, help marvelling that his grandmother, with all her religious prejudices, leaning, it would seem, to the other side, had consented so readily to his re-entering the service of the House of Avenel; and yet more, at the mysterious joy with which she took leave of him at the Abbey.

"Heaven," said the dame, as she kissed her young relation, and bade him farewell, "works its own work, even by the hands of those of our enemies who think themselves the strongest and the wisest. Thou, my child, be ready to act upon the call of thy religion and country; and remember, each earthly bond which thou canst form is, compared to the ties which bind thee to them, like the loose flax to the twisted cable. Thou hast not forgot the face or form of the damsel Catherine Seyton?"

Roland would have replied in the negative, but the word seemed to stick in his throat and Magdalen continued her exhortations.

"Thou must not forget her, my son; and here I intrust thee with a token, which I trust thou wilt speedily find an opportunity of delivering with care and secrecy into her own hand."

She put here into Roland's hand a very small packet, of which she again enjoined him to take the strictest care, and to suffer it to be seen by no one save Catherine Seyton, who, she again (very unnecessarily) reminded him, was the young lady he had met on the preceding day. She then bestowed on him her solemn benediction, and bade God speed him.

There was something in her manner and her conduct which implied mystery; but Roland Graeme was not of an age or temper to waste much time in endeavoring to decipher her meaning. All that was obvious to his perception in the present journey, promised pleasure and novelty. He rejoiced that he was travelling towards Edinburgh, in order to assume the character of a man, and lay aside that of a boy. He was delighted to think that he would have an opportunity of rejoining Catherine Seyton, whose bright eyes and lively manners had made so favourable an impression on his imagination; and, as an experienced, yet high-spirited youth, entering for the first time upon active life, his heart bounded at the thought, that he was about to see all those scenes of courtly splendour and warlike adventures, of which the followers of Sir Halbert used to boast on their occasional visits to Avenel, to the wonderment and envy of those who, like Roland, knew courts and camps only by hearsay, and were condemned to the solitary sports and almost monastic seclusion of Avenel, surrounded by its lonely lake, and embossed among its pathless mountains. "They shall mention my name," he said to himself, "if the risk of my life can purchase me opportunities of distinction, and Catherine Seyton's saucy eye shall rest with more respect on the distinguished soldier, than that with which she laughed to scorn the raw and inexperienced page."—There was wanting but one accessary to complete the sense of rapturous excitation, and he possessed it by being once more mounted on the back of a fiery and active horse, instead of plodding along on foot, as had been the case during the preceding days.

Impelled by the liveliness of his own spirits, which so many circumstances tended naturally to exalt, Roland Graeme's voice and his laughter were soon distinguished amid the trampling of the horses of the retinue, and more than once attracted the attention of the leader, who remarked with satisfaction, that the youth replied with good-humoured raillery to such of the train as jested with him on his dismissal and return to the service of the House of Avenel.

"I thought the holly-branch in your bonnet had been blighted, Master Roland?" said one of the men-at-arms.

"Only pinched with half an hour's frost; you see it flourishes as green as ever."

"It is too grave a plant to flourish on so hot a soil as that headpiece of thine, Master Roland Graeme," retorted the other, who was an old equerry of Sir Halbert Glendinning.

"If it will not flourish alone," said Roland, "I will mix it with the laurel and the myrtle—and I will carry them so near the sky, that it shall make amends for their stinted growth."

Thus speaking, he dashed his spurs into his horse's sides, and, checking him at the same time, compelled him to execute a lofty caracole. Sir Halbert Glendinning looked at the demeanour of his new attendant with that sort of melancholy pleasure with which those who have long followed the pursuits of life, and are sensible of their vanity, regard the gay, young, and buoyant spirits to whom existence, as yet, is only hope and promise.

In the meanwhile, Adam Woodcock, the falconer, stripped of his masquing habit, and attired, according to his rank and calling, in a green jerkin, with a hawking-bag on the one side, and a short hanger on the other, a glove on his left hand which reached half way up his arm, and a bonnet and feather upon his head, came after the party as fast as his active little galloway-nag could trot, and immediately entered into parley with Roland Graeme.

"So, my youngster, you are once more under shadow of the holly-branch?"

"And in case to repay you, my good friend," answered Roland, "your ten groats of silver."

"Which, but an hour since," said the falconer, "you had nearly paid me with ten inches of steel. On my faith, it is written in the book of our destiny, that I must brook your dagger after all."

"Nay, speak not of that, my good friend," said the youth, "I would rather have broached my own bosom than yours; but who could have known you in the mumming dress you wore?"

"Yes," the falconer resumed,—for both as a poet and actor he had his own professional share of self-conceit,—"I think I was as good a

SIR WALTER SCOTT

Howleglas as ever played part at a Shrovetide revelry, and not a much worse Abbot of Unreason. I defy the Old Enemy to unmask me when I choose to keep my vizard on. What the devil brought the Knight on us before we had the game out? You would have heard me hollo my own new ballad with a voice should have reached to Berwick. But I pray you, Master Roland, be less free of cold steel on slight occasions; since, but for the stuffing of my reverend doublet, I had only left the kirk to take my place in the kirkyard."

"Nay, spare me that feud," said Roland Graeme, "we shall have no time to fight it out; for, by our lord's command, I am bound for Edinburgh."

"I know it," said Adam Woodcock, "and even therefore we shall have time to solder up this rent by the way, for Sir Halbert has appointed me your companion and guide."

"Ay? and with what purpose?" said the page.

"That," said the falconer, "is a question I cannot answer; but I know, that be the food of the eyases washed or unwashed, and, indeed, whatever becomes of perch and mew, I am to go with you to Edinburgh, and see you safely delivered to the Regent at Holyrood."

"How, to the Regent?" said Roland, in surprise.

"Ay, by my faith, to the Regent," replied Woodcock; "I promise you, that if you are not to enter his service, at least you are to wait upon him in the character of a retainer of our Knight of Avenel."

"I know no right," said the youth, "which the Knight of Avenel hath to transfer my service, supposing that I owe it to himself."

"Hush, hush!" said the falconer; "that is a question I advise no one to stir in until he has the mountain or the lake, or the march of another kingdom, which is better than either, betwixt him and his feudal superior."

"But Sir Halbert Glendinning," said the youth, "is not my feudal superior; nor has he aught of authority—"

"I pray you, my son, to rein your tongue," answered Adam Woodcock; "my lord's displeasure, if you provoke it, will be worse to appease than my lady's. The touch of his least finger were heavier than her hardest blow. And, by my faith, he is a man of steel, as true and as pure, but as hard and as pitiless. You remember the Cock of Capperlaw, whom he hanged over his gate for a mere mistake—a poor yoke of oxen taken in Scotland, when he thought he was taking them in English land? I loved the Cock of Capperlaw; the Kerrs had not an honester man in their clan, and they have had men that might have been a pattern to the Border—men that would not have lifted under twenty cows at once, and would have held themselves dishonoured if they had taken a drift of sheep, or the like, but always managed their raids in full credit and honour.—But see, his worship halts, and we are close by the bridge. Ride up—ride up—we must have his last instructions."

It was as Adam Woodcock said. In the hollow way descending towards the bridge, which was still in the guardianship of Peter Bridgeward, as he was called, though he was now very old, Sir Halbert Glendinning halted his retinue, and beckoned to Woodcock and Graeme to advance to the head of the train.

"Woodcock," said he, "thou knowest to whom thou art to conduct this youth. And thou, young man, obey discreetly and with diligence the orders that shall be given thee. Curb thy vain and peevish temper. Be just, true, and faithful; and there is in thee that which may raise thee many a degree above thy present station. Neither shalt thou—always supposing thine efforts to be fair and honest—want the protection and countenance of Avenel."

Leaving them in front of the bridge, the centre tower of which now began to cast a prolonged shade upon the river, the Knight of Avenel turned to the left, without crossing the river, and pursued his way towards the chain of hills within whose recesses are situated the Lake and Castle of Avenel. There remained behind, the falconer, Roland Graeme, and a domestic of the Knight, of inferior rank, who was left with them to look after their horses while on the road, to carry their baggage, and to attend to their convenience.

So soon as the more numerous body of riders had turned off to pursue their journey westward, those whose route lay across the river, and was directed towards the north, summoned the Bridgeward, and demanded a free passage.

"I will not lower the bridge," answered Peter, in a voice querulous with age and ill-humour.—"Come Papist, come Protestant, ye are all the same. The Papist threatened us with Purgatory, and fleeched us with pardons—the Protestant mints at us with his sword, and cuttles us with the liberty of conscience; but never a one of either says, 'Peter, there is your penny.' I am well tired of all this, and for no man shall the bridge fall that pays me not ready money; and I would have you know I care as little for Geneva as for Rome—as little for homilies as for pardons; and the silver pennies are the only passports I will hear of."

"Here is a proper old chuff!" said Woodcock to his companion; then raising his voice, he exclaimed, "Hark thee, dog—Bridgeward, villain, dost thou think we have refused thy namesake Peter's pence to Rome, to pay thine at the bridge of Kennaquhair? Let thy bridge down instantly to the followers of the house of Avenel, or by the hand of my father, and that handled many a bridle rein, for he was a bluff Yorkshireman—I say, by my father's hand, our Knight will blow thee out of thy solan-goose's nest there in the middle of the water, with the light falconet which we are bringing southward from Edinburgh to-morrow."

The Bridgeward heard, and muttered, "A plague on falcon and falconet, on cannon and demicannon, and all the barking bull-dogs whom they halloo against stone and lime in these our days! It was a merry time when there was little besides handy blows, and it may be a flight of arrows that harmed an ashler wall as little as so many hailstones. But we must jouk and let the jaw gang by." Comforting himself in his state of diminished consequence with this pithy old proverb, Peter Bridgeward lowered the drawbridge, and permitted them to pass over. At the sight of his white hair, albeit it discovered a visage equally peevish through age and misfortune, Roland was inclined to give him an alms, but Adam Woodcock prevented him. "E'en let him pay the penalty of his former churlishness and greed," he said; "the wolf, when he has lost his teeth, should be treated no better than a cur."

Leaving the Bridgeward to lament the alteration of times, which sent domineering soldiers and feudal retainers to his place of passage, instead of peaceful pilgrims, and reduced him to become the oppressed, instead of playing the extortioner, the travellers turned them northward; and Adam Woodcock, well acquainted with that part of the country, proposed to cut short a considerable portion of the road, by traversing the little vale of Glendearg, so famous for the adventures which befell therein during the earlier part of the Benedictine's manuscript. With these, and with the thousand commentaries, representations, and misrepresentations, to which they had given rise, Roland Graeme was, of course, well acquainted; for in the Castle of Avenel, as well as in other great establishments, the inmates talked of nothing so often, or with such pleasure, as of the private affairs of their lord and lady. But while Roland was viewing with interest these haunted scenes, in which things were said to have passed beyond the ordinary laws of nature, Adam Woodcock was still regretting in his secret soul the unfinished revel and the unsung ballad, and kept every now and then, breaking out with some such verses as these:—

> "The Friars of Fail drank berry-brown ale,
> The best that e'er was tasted;
> The Monks of Melrose made gude kale
> On Fridays, when they fasted.
> Saint Monance' sister.
> The gray priest kist her—
> Fiend save the company!
> Sing hay trix, trim-go-trix.
> Under the greenwood tree."

"By my hand, friend Woodcock," said the page, "though I know you for a hardy gospeller, that fear neither saint nor devil, yet, if I were you, I would not sing your profane songs in this valley of Glendearg, considering what has happened here before our time."

"A straw for your wandering spirits!" said Adam Woodcock; "I mind them no more than an earn cares for a string of wild-geese—they have all fled since the pulpits were filled with honest men, and the people's ears with sound doctrine. Nay, I have a touch at them in my ballad, an I had but had the good luck to have it sung to end;" and again he set off in the same key:

> From haunted spring and grassy ring,
> Troop goblin, elf, and fairy;
> And the kelpie must flit from the black bog-pit,
> And the brownie must not tarry;
> To Limbo-lake,
> Their way they take,
> With scarce the pith to flee.
> Sing hay trix, trim-go-trix,
> Under the greenwood tree.

"I think," he added, "that could Sir Halbert's patience have stretched till we came that length, he would have had a hearty laugh, and that is what he seldom enjoys."

"If it be all true that men tell of his early life," said Roland, "he has less right to laugh at goblins than most men."

"Ay, *if* it be all true," answered Adam Woodcock; "but who can ensure us of that? Moreover, these were but tales the monks used to gull us simple laymen withal; they knew that fairies and hobgoblins brought aves and paternosters into repute; but, now we have given up worship of images in wood and stone, methinks it were no time to be afraid of bubbles in the water, or shadows in the air."

"However," said Roland Graeme, "as the Catholics say they do not worship wood or stone, but only as emblems of the holy saints, and not as things holy in themselves—"

"Pshaw! pshaw!" answered the falconer; "a rush for their prating. They told us another story when these baptized idols of theirs brought pike-staves and sandalled shoon from all the four winds, and whillied the old women out of their corn and their candle ends, and their butter, bacon, wool, and cheese, and when not so much as a gray groat escaped tithing."

Roland Graeme had been long taught, by necessity, to consider his form of religion as a profound secret, and to say nothing whatever in its defence when assailed, lest he should draw on himself the suspicion of belonging to the unpopular and exploded church. He therefore suffered Adam Woodcock to triumph without farther opposition, marvelling in his own mind whether any of the goblins, formerly such active agents, would avenge his rude raillery before they left the valley of Glendearg. But no such consequences followed. They passed the night quietly in a cottage in the glen, and the next day resumed their route to Edinburgh.

XVII

Edina! Scotia's darling seat,
All hail thy palaces and towers,
Where once, beneath a monarch's feet,
Sate legislation's sovereign powers.

—Burns

This, then, is Edinburgh?" said the youth, as the fellow-travellers arrived at one of the heights to the southward, which commanded a view of the great northern capital—"This is that Edinburgh of which we have heard so much!"

"Even so," said the falconer; "yonder stands Auld Reekie—you may see the smoke hover over her at twenty miles' distance, as the gosshawk hangs over a plump of young wild-ducks—ay, yonder is the heart of Scotland, and each throb that she gives is felt from the edge of Solway to Duncan's-bay-head. See, yonder is the old Castle; and see to the right, on yon rising ground, that is the Castle of Craigmillar, which I have known a merry place in my time."

"Was it not there," said the page in a low voice, "that the Queen held her court?"

"Ay, ay," replied the falconer, "Queen she was then, though you must not call her so now. Well, they may say what they will—many a true heart will be sad for Mary Stewart, e'en if all be true men say of her; for look you, Master Roland—she was the loveliest creature to look upon that I ever saw with eye, and no lady in the land liked better the fair flight of a falcon. I was at the great match on Roslin Moor betwixt Bothwell—he was a black sight to her that Bothwell—and the Baron of Roslin, who could judge a hawk's flight as well as any man in Scotland—a butt of Rhenish and a ring of gold was the wager, and it was flown as fairly for as ever was red gold and bright wine. And to see her there on her white palfrey, that flew as if it scorned to touch more than the heather blossom; and to hear her voice, as clear and sweet as the mavis's whistle, mix among our jolly whooping and whistling; and to mark all the nobles dashing round her; happiest he who got a word or a look—tearing through moss and hagg, and venturing neck and limb to gain the praise of a bold rider, and the blink of a bonny Queen's bright

SIR WALTER SCOTT

eye!—she will see little hawking where she lies now—ay, ay, pomp and pleasure pass away as speedily as the wap of a falcon's wing."

"And where is this poor Queen now confined?" said Roland Graeme, interested in the fate of a woman whose beauty and grace had made so strong an impression even on the blunt and careless character of Adam Woodcock.

"Where is she now imprisoned?" said honest Adam; "why, in some castle in the north, they say—I know not where, for my part, nor is it worth while to vex one's sell anent what cannot be mended—An she had guided her power well whilst she had it, she had not come to so evil a pass. Men say she must resign her crown to this little baby of a prince, for that they will trust her with it no longer. Our master has been as busy as his neighbours in all this work. If the Queen should come to her own again, Avenel Castle is like to smoke for it, unless he makes his bargain all the better." "In a castle in the north Queen Mary is confined?" said the page. "Why, ay—they say so, at least—In a castle beyond that great river which comes down yonder, and looks like a river, but it is a branch of the sea, and as bitter as brine."

"And amongst all her subjects," said the page, with some emotion, "is there none that will adventure anything for her relief?"

"That is a kittle question," said the falconer; "and if you ask it often, Master Roland, I am fain to tell you that you will be mewed up yourself in some of those castles, if they do not prefer twisting your head off, to save farther trouble with you—Adventure any thing? Lord, why, Murray has the wind in his poop now, man, and flies so high and strong, that the devil a wing of them can match him—No, no; there she is, and there she must lie, till Heaven send her deliverance, or till her son has the management of all—But Murray will never let her loose again, he knows her too well.—And hark thee, we are now bound for Holyrood, where thou wilt find plenty of news, and of courtiers to tell it—But, take my counsel, and keep a calm sough, as the Scots say—hear every man's counsel, and keep your own. And if you hap to learn any news you like, leap not up as if you were to put on armour direct in the cause—Our old Mr. Wingate says—and he knows court-cattle well—that if you are told old King Coul is come alive again, you should turn it off with, 'And is he in truth?—I heard not of it,' and should seem no more moved, than if one told you, by way of novelty, that old King Coul was dead and buried. Wherefore, look well to your bearing, Master Roland, for, I promise you, you come among a generation that are keen as a hungry hawk—And never be dagger out of sheath at every wry word you hear spoken; for you will find as hot blades as yourself, and then will be letting of blood without advice either of leech or almanack."

"You shall see how staid I will be, and how cautious, my good friend," said Graeme; "but, blessed Lady, what goodly house is that which is lying all in ruins so close to the city? Have they been playing at the Abbot of Unreason here, and ended the gambol by burning the church?"

"There again now," replied his companion, "you go down the wind like a wild haggard, that minds neither lure nor beck—that is a question you should have asked in as low a tone as I shall answer it."

"If I stay here long," said Roland Graeme, "it is like I shall lose the natural use of my voice—but what are the ruins then?"

"The Kirk of Field," said the falconer, in a low and impressive whisper, laying at the same time his finger on his lip; "ask no more about it—somebody got foul play, and somebody got the blame of it; and the game began there which perhaps may not be played out in our time.—Poor Henry Darnley! to be an ass, he understood somewhat of a hawk; but they sent him on the wing through the air himself one bright moonlight night."

The memory of this catastrophe was so recent, that the page averted his eyes with horror from the scathed ruins in which it had taken place; and the accusations against the Queen, to which it had given rise, came over his mind with such strength as to balance the compassion he had begun to entertain for her present forlorn situation.

It was, indeed, with that agitating state of mind which arises partly from horror, but more from anxious interest and curiosity, that young Graeme found himself actually traversing the scene of those tremendous events, the report of which had disturbed the most distant solitudes in Scotland, like the echoes of distant thunder rolling among the mountains.

"Now," he thought, "now or never shall I become a man, and bear my part in those deeds which the simple inhabitants of our hamlets repeat to each other, as if they were wrought by beings of a superior order to their own. I will know now, wherefore the Knight of Avenel carries his crest so much above those of the neighbouring baronage, and how it is that men, by valour and wisdom, work their way from the hoddin-gray coat to the cloak of scarlet and gold. Men say I have not much wisdom to recommend me; and if that be true, courage must do it; for I will be a man amongst living men, or a dead corpse amongst the dead."

From these dreams of ambition he turned his thoughts to those of pleasure, and began to form many conjectures, when and where he should see Catherine Seyton, and in what manner their acquaintance was to be renewed. With such conjectures he was amusing himself, when he found that they had entered the city, and all other feelings were suspended in the sensation of giddy astonishment with which an inhabitant of the country is affected, when, for the first time, he finds himself in the streets of a large and populous city, a unit in the midst of thousands.

The principal street of Edinburgh was then, as now, one of the most spacious in Europe. The extreme height of the houses, and the variety of Gothic gables and battlements, and balconies, by which the sky-line on each side was crowned and terminated, together with the width of the street itself, might have struck with surprise a more practised eye than that of young Graeme. The population, close packed within the walls of the city, and at this time increased by the number of the lords of the King's party who had thronged to Edinburgh to wait upon the Regent Murray, absolutely swarmed like bees on the wide and stately street. Instead of the shop-windows, which are now calculated for the display of goods, the traders had their open booths projecting on the street, in which, as in the fashion of the modern bazaars, all was exposed which they had upon sale. And though the commodities were not of the richest kinds, yet Graeme thought he beheld the wealth of the whole world in the various bales of Flanders cloths, and the specimens of tapestry; and, at other places, the display of domestic utensils and pieces of plate struck him with wonder. The sight of cutlers' booths, furnished with swords and poniards, which were manufactured in Scotland, and with pieces of defensive armour, imported from Flanders, added to his surprise; and, at every step, he found so much to admire and gaze upon, that Adam Woodcock had no little difficulty in prevailing on him to advance through such a scene of enchantment.

The sight of the crowds which filled the streets was equally a subject of wonder. Here a gay lady, in her muffler, or silken veil, traced her way delicately, a gentleman-usher making way for her, a page bearing up her train, and a waiting gentlewoman carrying her Bible, thus intimating that her purpose was towards the church—There he might see a group of citizens bending the same way, with their short Flemish cloaks, wide trowsers, and high-caped doublets, a fashion to which, as well as to their bonnet and feather, the Scots were long faithful. Then, again, came the clergyman himself, in his black Geneva cloak and band, lending a grave and attentive ear to the discourse of several persons who accompanied him, and who were doubtless holding serious converse on the religious subject he was about to treat of. Nor did there lack passengers of a different class and appearance.

At every turn, Roland Graeme might see a gallant ruffle along in the newer or French mode, his doublet slashed, and his points of the same colours with the lining, his long sword on one side, and his poniard on the other, behind him a body of stout serving men, proportioned to his estate and quality, all of whom walked with the air of military retainers, and were armed with sword and buckler, the latter being a small round shield, not unlike the Highland target, having a steel spike in the centre. Two of these parties, each headed by a person of importance, chanced to meet in the very centre of the street, or, as it was called, "the crown of the cause-way," a post of honour as tenaciously asserted in Scotland, as that of giving or taking the wall used to be in the more southern part of the island. The two leaders being of equal rank, and, most probably, either animated by political dislike, or by recollection of some feudal enmity, marched close up to each other, without yielding an inch to the right or the left; and neither showing the least purpose of giving way, they stopped for an instant, and then drew their swords. Their followers imitated their example; about a score of weapons at once flashed in the sun, and there was an immediate clatter of swords and bucklers, while the followers on either side cried their master's name; the one shouting "Help, a Leslie! a Leslie!" while the others answered with shouts of "Seyton! Seyton!" with the additional punning slogan, "Set on, set on— bear the knaves to the ground!"

If the falconer found difficulty in getting the page to go forward before, it was now perfectly impossible. He reined up his horse, clapped his hands, and, delighted with the fray, cried and shouted as fast as any of those who were actually engaged in it.

The noise and cries thus arising on the Highgate, as it was called, drew into the quarrel two or three other parties of gentlemen and their servants, besides some single passengers, who, hearing a fray betwixt these two distinguished names, took part in it, either for love or hatred.

The combat became now very sharp, and although the sword-and-buckler men made more clatter and noise than they did real damage, yet several good cuts were dealt among them; and those who wore rapiers, a more formidable weapon than the ordinary Scottish swords, gave and received dangerous wounds. Two men were already stretched on the causeway, and the party of Seyton began to give ground, being much inferior in number to the other, with which several of the citizens had united themselves, when young Roland Graeme, beholding their leader, a noble gentleman, fighting bravely, and hard pressed with numbers, could withhold no longer. "Adam Woodcock," he said, "an you be a man, draw, and let us take part with the Seyton." And, without waiting a reply, or listening to the falconer's earnest entreaty, that he would leave alone a strife in which he had no concern, the fiery youth sprung from his horse, drew his short sword, and shouting like the rest, "A Seyton! a Seyton! Set on! set on!" thrust forward into the throng, and struck down one of those who was pressing hardest upon the gentleman whose cause he espoused. This sudden reinforcement gave spirit to the weaker party, who began to renew the combat with much alacrity, when four of the magistrates of the city, distinguished by their velvet cloaks and gold chains, came up with a guard of halberdiers and citizens, armed with long weapons, and well accustomed to such service, thrust boldly forward, and compelled the swordsmen to separate, who immediately retreated in different directions, leaving such of the wounded on both sides, as had been disabled in the fray, lying on the street.

The falconer, who had been tearing his beard for anger at his comrade's rashness, now rode up to him with the horse which he had caught by the bridle, and accosted him with "Master Roland—master goose—master mad-cap—will it please you to get on horse, and budge? or will you remain here to be carried to prison, and made to answer for this pretty day's work?"

The page, who had begun his retreat along with the Seytons, just as if he had been one of their natural allies, was by this unceremonious application made sensible that he was acting a foolish part; and, obeying Adam Woodcock with some sense of shame, he sprung actively on horseback, and upsetting with the shoulder of the animal a city-officer, who was making towards him, he began to ride smartly down the street, along with his companion, and was quickly out of the reach of the hue and cry. In fact, rencounters of the kind were so common in Edinburgh at that period, that the disturbance seldom excited much attention after the affray was over, unless some person of consequence chanced to have fallen, an incident which imposed on his friends the duty of avenging his death on the first convenient opportunity. So feeble, indeed, was the arm of the police, that it was not unusual for such skirmishes to last for hours, where the parties were numerous and well matched. But at this time the Regent, a man of great strength of character, aware of the mischief which usually arose from such acts of violence, had prevailed with the magistrates to keep a constant guard on foot for preventing or separating such affrays as had happened in the present case.

The falconer and his young companion were now riding down the Canongate, and had slackened their pace to avoid attracting attention, the rather that there seemed to be no appearance of pursuit. Roland hung his head as one who was conscious his conduct had been none of the wisest, whilst his companion thus addressed him:

"Will you be pleased to tell me one thing, Master Roland Graeme, and that is, whether there be a devil incarnate in you or no?"

"Truly, Master Adam Woodcock," answered the page, "I would fain hope there is not."

"Then," said Adam, "I would fain know by what other influence or instigation you are perpetually at one end or the other of some bloody brawl? What, I pray, had you to do with these Seytons and Leslies, that you never heard the names of in your life before?"

"You are out there, my friend," said Roland Graeme, "I have my own reasons for being a friend to the Seytons."

"They must have been very secret reasons then," answered Adam Woodcock, "for I think I could have wagered, you had never known one of the name; and I am apt to believe still, that it was your unhallowed passion for that clashing of cold iron, which has as much charm for you as the clatter of a brass pan hath for a hive of bees, rather than any care either for Seyton or for Leslie, that persuaded you to thrust your fool's head into a quarrel that no ways concerned you. But take this for a warning, my young master, that if you are to draw sword with every man who draws sword on the Highgate here, it will be scarce worth your while to sheathe bilbo again for the rest of your life, since, if I guess rightly, it will scarce endure on such terms for many hours—all which I leave to your serious consideration."

"By my word, Adam, I honour your advice; and I promise you, that I will practise by it as faithfully as if I were sworn apprentice to you, to the trade and mystery of bearing myself with all wisdom and safety through the new paths of life that I am about to be engaged in."

"And therein you will do well," said the falconer; "and I do not quarrel with you, Master Roland, for having a grain over much spirit, because I know one may bring to the hand a wild hawk which one never can a dung-hill hen—and so betwixt two faults you have the best on't. But besides your peculiar genius for quarrelling and lugging out your side companion, my dear Master Roland, you have also the gift of peering under every woman's muffler and screen, as if you expected to find an old acquaintance. Though were you to spy one, I should be as much surprised at it, well wotting how few you have seen of these same wild-fowl, as I was at your taking so deep an interest even now in the Seyton."

"Tush, man! nonsense and folly," answered Roland Graeme, "I but sought to see what eyes these gentle hawks have got under their hood."

"Ay, but it's a dangerous subject of inquiry," said the falconer; "you had better hold out your bare wrist for an eagle to perch upon.—Look you, Master Roland, these pretty wild-geese cannot be hawked at without risk—they have as many divings, boltings, and volleyings, as the most gamesome quarry that falcon ever flew at—And besides, every woman of them is manned with her husband, or her kind friend, or her brother, or her cousin, or her sworn servant at the least—But you heed me not, Master Roland, though I know the game so well—your eye is all on that pretty damsel who trips down the gate before us—by my certes, I will warrant her a blithe dancer either in reel or revel—a pair of silver morisco bells would become these pretty ankles as well as the jesses would suit the fairest Norway hawk."

"Thou art a fool, Adam," said the page, "and I care not a button about the girl or her ankles—But, what the foul fiend, one must look at something!"

"Very true, Master Roland Graeme," said his guide, "but let me pray you to choose your objects better. Look you, there is scarce a woman walks this High-gate with a silk screen or a pearlin muffler, but, as I said before, she has either gentleman-usher before her, or kinsman, or lover, or husband, at her elbow, or it may be a brace of stout fellows with sword and buckler, not so far behind but what they can follow close— But you heed me no more than a goss-hawk minds a yellow yoldring."

"O yes, I do—I do mind you indeed," said Roland Graeme; "but hold my nag a bit—I will be with you in the exchange of a whistle." So saying, and ere Adam Woodcock could finish the sermon which was dying on his tongue, Roland Graeme, to the falconer's utter astonishment, threw him the bridle of his jennet, jumped off horseback, and pursued down one of the closes or narrow lanes, which, opening under a vault, terminate upon the main-street, the very maiden to whom his friend had accused him of showing so much attention, and who had turned down the pass in question.

"Saint Mary, Saint Magdalen, Saint Benedict, Saint Barnabas!" said the poor falconer, when he found himself thus suddenly brought to a pause in the midst of the Canongate, and saw his young charge start off like a madman in quest of a damsel whom he had never, as Adam supposed, seen in his life before,—"Saint Satan and Saint Beelzebub—for this would make one swear saint and devil—what can have come over the lad, with a wanion! And what shall I do the whilst!—he will have his throat cut, the poor lad, as sure as I was born at the foot of Roseberry-Topping. Could I find some one to hold the horses! but they are as sharp here north-away as in canny Yorkshire herself, and quit bridle, quit titt, as we say. An I could but see one of our folks now, a holly-sprig were worth a gold tassel; or could I but see one of the Regent's men—but to leave the horses to a stranger, that I cannot—and to leave the place while the lad is in jeopardy, that I wonot."

We must leave the falconer, however, in the midst of his distress, and follow the hot-headed youth who was the cause of his perplexity.

The latter part of Adam Woodcock's sage remonstrance had been in a great measure lost upon Roland, for whose benefit it was intended; because, in one of the female forms which tripped along the street, muffled in a veil of striped silk, like the women of Brussels at this day, his eye had discerned something which closely resembled the exquisite shape and spirited bearing of Catherine Seyton.—During all the grave advice which the falconer was dinning in his ears, his eye continued intent upon so interesting an object of observation; and at length, as the damsel, just about to dive under one of the arched passages which afforded an outlet to the Canongate from the houses beneath, (a passage, graced by a projecting shield of arms, supported by two huge foxes of stone,) had lifted her veil for the purpose perhaps of descrying who the horseman was who for some time had eyed her so closely, young Roland saw, under the shade of the silken plaid, enough of the bright azure eyes, fair locks, and blithe features, to induce him, like an inexperienced and rash madcap, whose wilful ways never had been traversed by contradiction, nor much subjected to consideration, to throw the bridle of his horse into Adam Woodcock's hand, and leave

SIR WALTER SCOTT

him to play the waiting gentleman, while he dashed down the paved court after Catherine Seyton—all as aforesaid.

Women's wits are proverbially quick, but apparently those of Catherine suggested no better expedient than fairly to betake herself to speed of foot, in hopes of baffling the page's vivacity, by getting safely lodged before he could discover where. But a youth of eighteen, in pursuit of a mistress, is not so easily outstripped. Catherine fled across a paved court, decorated with large formal vases of stone, in which yews, cypresses, and other evergreens, vegetated in sombre sullenness, and gave a correspondent degree of solemnity to the high and heavy building in front of which they were placed as ornaments, aspiring towards a square portion of the blue hemisphere, corresponding exactly in extent to the quadrangle in which they were stationed, and all around which rose huge black walls, exhibiting windows in rows of five stories, with heavy architraves over each, bearing armorial and religious devices.

Through this court Catherine Seyton flashed like a hunted doe, making the best use of those pretty legs which had attracted the commendation even of the reflective and cautious Adam Woodcock. She hastened towards a large door in the centre of the lower front of the court, pulled the bobbin till the latch flew up, and ensconced herself in the ancient mansion. But, if she fled like a doe, Roland Graeme followed with the speed and ardour of a youthful stag-hound, loosed for the first time on his prey. He kept her in view in spite of her efforts; for it is remarkable what an advantage, in such a race, the gallant who desires to see, possesses over the maiden who wishes not to be seen—an advantage which I have known counterbalance a great start in point of distance. In short, he saw the waving of her screen, or veil, at one corner, heard the tap of her foot, light as that was, as it crossed the court, and caught a glimpse of her figure just as she entered the door of the mansion.

Roland Graeme, inconsiderate and headlong as we have described him, having no knowledge of real life but from the romances which he had read, and not an idea of checking himself in the midst of any eager impulse; possessed, besides, of much courage and readiness, never hesitated for a moment to approach the door through which the object of his search had disappeared. He, too, pulled the bobbin, and the latch, though heavy and massive, answered to the summons, and arose. The page entered with the same precipitation which had marked his whole proceeding, and found himself in a large hall, or vestibule, dimly enlightened by latticed casements of painted glass, and rendered yet dimmer through the exclusion of the sunbeams, owing to the height of the walls of those buildings by which the court-yard was enclosed. The walls of the hall were surrounded with suits of ancient and rusted armour, interchanged with huge and massive stone scutcheons, bearing double tressures, fleured and counter-fleured, wheat-sheaves, coronets, and so forth, things to which Roland Graeme gave not a moment's attention.

In fact, he only deigned to observe the figure of Catherine Seyton, who, deeming herself safe in the hall, had stopped to take breath after her course, and was reposing herself for a moment on a large oaken settle which stood at the upper end of the hall. The noise of Roland's entrance at once disturbed her; she started up with a faint scream of surprise, and escaped through one of the several folding-doors which opened into this apartment as a common centre. This door, which Roland Graeme instantly approached, opened on a large and well-lighted gallery, at the upper end of which he could hear several voices, and the noise of hasty steps approaching towards the hall or vestibule. A little recalled to sober thought by an appearance of serious danger, he was deliberating whether he should stand fast or retire, when Catherine Seyton re-entered from a side door, running towards him with as much speed as a few minutes since she had fled from him.

"Oh, what mischief brought you hither?" she said; "fly—fly, or you are a dead man,—or stay—they come—flight is impossible—say you came to ask for Lord Seyton."

She sprung from him and disappeared through the door by which she had made her second appearance; and, at the same instant, a pair of large folding-doors at the upper end of the gallery flew open with vehemence, and six or seven young gentlemen, richly dressed, pressed forward into the apartment, having, for the greater part, their swords drawn.

"Who is it," said one, "dare intrude on us in our own mansion?"

"Cut him to pieces," said another; "let him pay for this day's insolence and violence—he is some follower of the Rothes."

"No, by Saint Mary," said another; "he is a follower of the arch-fiend and ennobled clown Halbert Glendinning, who takes the style of Avenel—once a church-vassal, now a pillager of the church."

"It is so," said a fourth; "I know him by the holly-sprig, which is their cognizance. Secure the door, he must answer for this insolence."

Two of the gallants, hastily drawing their weapons, passed on to the door by which Roland had entered the hall, and stationed themselves there as if to prevent his escape. The others advanced on Graeme, who had just sense enough to perceive that any attempt at resistance would be alike fruitless and imprudent. At once, and by various voices, none of which sounded amicably, the page was required to say who he was, whence he came, his name, his errand, and who sent him hither. The number of the questions demanded of him at once, afforded a momentary apology for his remaining silent, and ere that brief truce had elapsed, a personage entered the hall, at whose appearance those who had gathered fiercely around Roland, fell back with respect.

This was a tall man, whose dark hair was already grizzled, though his high and haughty features retained all the animation of youth. The upper part of his person was undressed to his Holland shirt, whose ample folds were stained with blood. But he wore a mantle of crimson, lined with rich fur, cast around him, which supplied the deficiency of his dress. On his head he had a crimson velvet bonnet, looped up on one side with a small golden chain of many links, which, going thrice around the hat, was fastened by a medal, agreeable to the fashion amongst the grandees of the time.

"Whom have you here, sons and kinsmen," said he, "around whom you crowd thus roughly?—Know you not that the shelter of this roof should secure every one fair treatment, who shall come hither either in fair peace, or in open and manly hostility?"

"But here, my lord," answered one of the youths, "is a knave who comes on treacherous espial!"

"I deny the charge!" said Roland Graeme, boldly, "I came to inquire after my Lord Seyton."

"A likely tale," answered his accusers, "in the mouth of a follower of Glendinning."

"Stay, young men," said the Lord Seyton, for it was that nobleman himself, "let me look at this youth—By heaven, it is the very same who came so boldly to my side not very many minutes since, when some of my own knaves bore themselves with more respect to their own worshipful safety than to mine! Stand back from him, for he well deserves honour and a friendly welcome at your hands, instead of this rough treatment."

They fell back on all sides, obedient to Lord Seyton's commands, who, taking Roland Graeme by the hand, thanked him for his prompt and gallant assistance, adding, that he nothing doubted, "the same interest which he had taken in his cause in the affray, brought him hither to inquire after his hurt."

Roland bowed low in acquiescence.

"Or is there any thing in which I can serve you, to show my sense of your ready gallantry?"

But the page, thinking it best to abide by the apology for his visit which the Lord Seyton had so aptly himself suggested, replied, "that to be assured of his lordship's safety, had been the only cause of his intrusion. He judged," he added, "he had seen him receive some hurt in the affray."

"A trifle," said Lord Seyton; "I had but stripped my doublet, that the chirurgeon might put some dressing on the paltry scratch, when these rash boys interrupted us with their clamour."

Roland Graeme, making a low obeisance, was now about to depart, for, relieved from the danger of being treated as a spy, he began next to fear, that his companion, Adam Woodcock, whom he had so unceremoniously quitted, would either bring him into some farther dilemma, by venturing into the hotel in quest of him, or ride off and leave him behind altogether. But Lord Seyton did not permit him to escape so easily. "Tarry," he said, "young man, and let me know thy rank and name. The Seyton has of late been more wont to see friends and followers shrink from his side, than to receive aid from strangers-but a new world may come around, in which he may have the chance of rewarding his well-wishers."

"My name is Roland Graeme, my lord," answered the youth, "a page, who, for the present, is in the service of Sir Halbert Glendinning."

"I said so from the first," said one of the young men; "my life I will wager, that this is a shaft out of the heretic's quiver-a stratagem from first to last, to injeer into your confidence some espial of his own. They know how to teach both boys and women to play the intelligencers."

"That is false, if it be spoken of me," said Roland; "no man in Scotland should teach me such a foul part!"

"I believe thee, boy," said Lord Seyton, "for thy strokes were too fair to be dealt upon an understanding with those that were to receive them. Credit me, however, I little expected to have help at need from one of your master's household; and I would know what moved thee in my quarrel, to thine own endangering?"

"So please you, my lord," said Roland, "I think my master himself would not have stood by, and seen an honourable man borne to earth by odds, if his single arm could help him. Such, at least, is the lesson we were taught in chivalry, at the Castle of Avenel."

"The good seed hath fallen into good ground, young man," said Seyton; "but, alas! if thou practise such honourable war in these dishonourable days, when right is every where borne down by mastery, thy life, my poor boy, will be but a short one."

"Let it be short, so it be honourable," said Roland Graeme; "and permit me now, my lord, to commend me to your grace, and to take my leave. A comrade waits with my horse in the street."

"Take this, however, young man," said Lord Seyton,* undoing from his bonnet the golden chain and medal, "and wear it for my sake."

---

* George, fifth Lord Seton, was immovably faithful to Queen Mary during all the mutabilities of her fortune. He was grand master of the household, in which capacity he had a picture painted of himself, with his official baton, and the following motto:

> *In adversitate, patiens;*
> *In prosperitate, benevolus.*
> *Hazard, yet forward.*

On various parts of his castle he inscribed, as expressing his religious and political creed, the legend:

> *Un Dieu, un Foy, un Roy, un Loy.*

He declined to be promoted to an earldom, which Queen Mary offered him at the same time when she advanced her natural brother to be Earl of Mar, and afterwards of Murray.

On his refusing this honour, Mary wrote, or caused to be written, the following lines in Latin and French:

> *Sunt comites, ducesque alii; sunt denique reges;*
> *Sethom dominum sit satis esse mihi.*
>
> *Il y a des comptes, des roys, des ducs; ainsi*
> *C'est assez pour moy d'estre Seigneur de Seton.*

Which may be thus rendered:—

> *Earl, duke, or king, be thou that list to be:*
> *Seton, thy lordship is enough for me.*

This distich reminds us of the "pride which aped humility," in the motto of the house of Couci:

With no little pride Roland Graeme accepted the gift, which he hastily fastened around his bonnet, as he had seen gallants wear such an ornament, and renewing his obeisance to the Baron, left the hall, traversed the court, and appeared in the street, just as Adam Woodcock, vexed and anxious at his delay, had determined to leave the horses to their fate, and go in quest of his youthful comrade. "Whose barn hast thou broken next?" he exclaimed, greatly relieved by his appearance, although his countenance indicated that he had passed through an agitating scene.

"Ask me no questions," said Roland, leaping gaily on his horse; "but see how short time it takes to win a chain of gold," pointing to that which he now wore.

"Now, God forbid that thou hast either stolen it, or reft it by violence," said the falconer; "for, otherwise, I wot not how the devil thou couldst compass it. I have been often here, ay, for months at an end, and no one gave me either chain or medal."

"Thou seest I have got one on shorter acquaintance with the city," answered the page, "but set thine honest heart at rest; that which is fairly won and freely given, is neither reft nor stolen."

"Marry, hang thee, with thy fanfarona* about thy neck!" said the falconer; "I think water will not drown, nor hemp strangle thee. Thou hast been discarded as my lady's page, to come in again as my lord's squire; and for following a noble young damsel into some great household, thou gettest a chain and medal, where another would have had the baton across his shoulders, if he missed having the dirk in his body. But here we come in front of the old Abbey. Bear thy good luck with you when you cross these paved stones, and, by our Lady, you may brag Scotland."

Je suis ni roy, ni prince aussi;
Je suis le Seigneur de Coucy.

After the battle of Langside, Lord Seton was obliged to retire abroad for safety, and was an exile for two years, during which he was reduced to the necessity of driving a waggon in Flanders for his subsistence. He rose to favour in James VI's reign, and assuming his paternal property, had himself painted in his waggoner's dress, and in the act of driving a wain with four horses, on the north end of a stately gallery at Seton Castle.

* A name given to the gold chains worn by the military men of the period. It is of Spanish origin: for the fashion of wearing these costly ornaments was much followed amongst the conquerors of the New World.

SIR WALTER SCOTT

As he spoke, they checked their horses, where the huge old vaulted entrance to the Abbey or Palace of Holyrood crossed the termination of the street down which they had proceeded. The courtyard of the palace opened within this gloomy porch, showing the front of an irregular pile of monastic buildings, one wing of which is still extant, forming a part of the modern palace, erected in the days of Charles I.

At the gate of the porch the falconer and page resigned their horses to the serving-man in attendance; the falconer commanding him with an air of authority, to carry them safely to the stables. "We follow," he said, "the Knight of Avenel—We must bear ourselves for what we are here," said he in a whisper to Roland, "for every one here is looked on as they demean themselves; and he that is too modest must to the wall, as the proverb says; therefore cock thy bonnet, man, and let us brook the causeway bravely."

Assuming, therefore, an air of consequence, corresponding to what he supposed to be his master's importance and quality, Adam Woodcock led the way into the courtyard of the Palace of Holyrood.

He appears to have been fond of the arts; for there exists a beautiful family-piece of him in the centre of his family. Mr. Pinkerton, in his Scottish Iconographia, published an engraving of this curious portrait. The original is the property of Lord Somerville, nearly connected with the Seton family, and is at present at his lordship's fishing villa of the Pavilion, near Melrose.

XVIII

—The sky is clouded, Gaspard,
And the vexed ocean sleeps a troubled sleep,
Beneath a lurid gleam of parting sunshine.
Such slumber hangs o'er discontented lands,
While factions doubt, as yet, if they have strength
To front the open battle.

—ALBION—A POEM

The youthful page paused on the entrance of the court-yard, and implored his guide to give him a moment's breathing space. "Let me but look around me, man," said he; "you consider not I have never seen such a scene as this before.—And this is Holyrood—the resort of the gallant and gay, and the fair, and the wise, and the powerful!"

"Ay, marry, is it!" said Woodcock; "but I wish I could hood thee as they do the hawks, for thou starest as wildly as if you sought another fray or another fanfarona. I would I had thee safely housed, for thou lookest wild as a goss-hawk."

It was indeed no common sight to Roland, the vestibule of a palace traversed by its various groups,—some radiant with gaiety—some pensive, and apparently weighed down by affairs concerning the state, or concerning themselves. Here the hoary statesman, with his cautious yet commanding look, his furred cloak and sable pantoufles; there the soldier in buff and steel, his long sword jarring against the pavement, and his whiskered upper lip and frowning brow, looking an habitual defiance of danger, which perhaps was not always made good; there again passed my lord's serving-man, high of heart, and bloody of hand, humble to his master and his master's equals, insolent to all others. To these might be added, the poor suitor, with his anxious look and depressed mien—the officer, full of his brief authority, elbowing his betters, and possibly his benefactors, out of the road—the proud priest, who sought a better benefice—the proud baron, who sought a grant of church lands—the robber chief, who came to solicit a pardon for the injuries he had inflicted on his neighbors—the plundered franklin, who came to seek vengeance for that which he had himself received. Besides there was the mustering and disposition of guards and soldiers—the despatching of messengers, and the receiving them—the trampling and neighing of horses without the gate—the flashing of arms, and rustling of plumes, and jingling of spurs, within it. In short, it was that gay and splendid confusion, in which the eye of youth sees all that is brave and brilliant, and that of experience much that is doubtful, deceitful, false, and hollow—hopes that will never be gratified—promises which will never be fulfilled—pride in the disguise of humility—and insolence in that of frank and generous bounty.

As, tired of the eager and enraptured attention which the page gave to a scene so new to him, Adam Woodcock endeavoured to get him to move forward, before his exuberance of astonishment should attract the observation of the sharp-witted denizens of the court, the falconer himself became an object of attention to a gay menial in a dark-green bonnet and feather, with a cloak of a corresponding colour, laid down, as the phrase then went, by six broad bars of silver lace, and welted with violet and silver. The words of recognition burst from both at once. "What! Adam Woodcock at court!" and "What! Michael Wing-the-wind—and how runs the hackit greyhound bitch now?"

"The waur for the wear, like ourselves, Adam—eight years this grass—no four legs will carry a dog forever; but we keep her for the breed, and so she 'scapes Border doom—But why stand you gazing there? I promise you my lord has wished for you, and asked for you."

"My Lord of Murray asked for me, and he Regent of the kingdom too!" said Adam. "I hunger and thirst to pay my duty to my good lord;—but I fancy his good lordship remembers the day's sport on Carnwath-moor; and my Drummelzier falcon, that beat the hawks from the Isle of Man, and won his lordship a hundred crowns from the Southern baron whom they called Stanley."

"Nay, not to flatter thee, Adam," said his court-friend, "he remembers nought of thee, or of thy falcon either. He hath flown many a higher flight since that, and struck his quarry too. But come, come hither away; I trust we are to be good comrades on the old score."

"What!" said Adam, "you would have me crush a pot with you; but I must first dispose of my eyas, where he will neither have girl to chase, nor lad to draw sword upon."

"Is the youngster such a one?" said Michael.

"Ay, by my hood, he flies at all game," replied Woodcock.

"Then had he better come with us," said Michael Wing-the-wind; "for we cannot have a proper carouse just now, only I would wet my lips, and so must you. I want to hear the news from Saint Mary's before you see my lord, and I will let you know how the wind sits up yonder."

While he thus spoke, he led the way to a side door which opened into the court; and threading several dark passages with the air of one who knew the most secret recesses of the palace, conducted them to a small matted chamber, where he placed bread and cheese and a foaming flagon of ale before the falconer and his young companion, who immediately did justice to the latter in a hearty draught, which nearly emptied the measure. Having drawn his breath, and dashed the froth from his whiskers, he observed, that his anxiety for the boy had made him deadly dry.

"Mend your draught," said his hospitable friend, again supplying the flagon from a pitcher which stood beside. "I know the way to the butterybar. And now, mind what I say—this morning the Earl of Morton came to my lord in a mighty chafe."

"What! they keep the old friendship, then?" said Woodcock.

"Ay, ay, man, what else?" said Michael; "one hand must scratch the other. But in a mighty chafe was my Lord of Morton, who, to say truth, looketh on such occasions altogether uncanny, and, as it were, fiendish; and he says to my lord,—for I was in the chamber taking orders about a cast of hawks that are to be fetched from Darnoway—they match your long-winged falcons, friend Adam."

"I will believe that when I see them fly as high a pitch," replied Woodcock, this professional observation forming a sort of parenthesis.

"However," said Michael, pursuing his tale, "my Lord of Morton, in a mighty chafe, asked my Lord Regent whether he was well dealt with— 'for my brother,' said he, 'should have had a gift to be Commendator of Kennaqubair, and to have all the temporalities erected into a lordship of regality for his benefit; and here,' said he, 'the false monks have had the insolence to choose a new Abbot to put his claim in my brother's way; and moreover, the rascality of the neighbourhood have burnt and plundered all that was left in the Abbey, so that my brother will not have a house to dwell in, when he hath ousted the lazy hounds of priests.' And my lord, seeing him chafed, said mildly to him, 'These are shrewd tidings, Douglas, but I trust they be not true; for Halbert Glendinning went southward yesterday, with a band of spears, and assuredly, had either of these chances happened, that the monks had presumed to choose an Abbot, or that the Abbey had been burnt, as you say, he had taken order on the spot for the punishment of such insolence, and had despatched us a messenger.' And the Earl of Morton replied—now I pray you, Adam, to notice, that I say this out of love to you and your lord, and also for old comradeship, and also because Sir Halbert hath done me good, and may again—and also because I love not the Earl of Morton, as indeed more fear than like him—so then it were a foul deed in you to betray me.—'But,' said the Earl to the Regent, 'take heed, my lord, you trust not this Glendinning too far—he comes of churl's blood, which was never true to the nobles'—by Saint Andrew, these were his very words.—'And besides,' he said, 'he hath a brother, a monk in Saint Mary's, and walks all by his guidance, and is making friends on the Border with Buccleuch and with Ferniehirst,* and will join hand with them, were there likelihood of a new world.' And my lord answered, like a free noble lord as he is; 'Tush! my Lord of Morton, I will be warrant for Glendinning's faith; and for his brother, he is a dreamer, that thinks of nought but book and breviary—and if such hap have chanced as you tell of, I look to receive from Glendinning the cowl of a hanged monk, and the head of a riotous churl, by way of sharp and sudden justice.'—And my Lord of Morton left the place, and, as it seemed to me, somewhat malecontent. But since that time, my lord has asked me more than once whether there has arrived no messenger from the Knight of Avenel. And all this I have told you, that you may frame your discourse to the best purpose, for it seems to me that my lord will not be well-pleased, if aught has happened like what my Lord of Morton said, and if your lord hath not ta'en strict orders with it."

There was something in this communication which fairly blanked the bold visage of Adam Woodcock, in spite of the reinforcement which his natural hardihood had received from the berry-brown ale of Holyrood.

"What was it he said about a churl's head, that grim Lord of Morton?" said the discontented falconer to his friend.

"Nay, it was my Lord Regent, who said that he expected, if the Abbey was injured, your Knight would send him the head of the ringleader among the rioters."

"Nay, but is this done like a good Protestant," said Adam Woodcock, "or a true Lord of the Congregation? We used to be their white-boys and darlings when we pulled down the convents in Fife and Perthshire."

"Ay, but that," said Michael, "was when old mother Rome held her own,

---

* Both these Border Chieftains were great friends of Queen Mary.

and our great folks were determined she should have no shelter for her head in Scotland. But, now that the priests are fled in all quarters, and their houses and lands are given to our grandees, they cannot see that we are working the work of reformation in destroying the palaces of zealous Protestants."

"But I tell you Saint Mary's is not destroyed!" said Woodcock, in increasing agitation; "some trash of painted windows there were broken—things that no nobleman could have brooked in his house— some stone saints were brought on their marrow-bones, like old Widdrington at Chevy-Chase; but as for fire-raising, there was not so much as a lighted lunt amongst us, save the match which the dragon had to light the burning tow withal, which he was to spit against Saint George; nay, I had caution of that."

"How! Adam Woodcock," said his comrade, "I trust thou hadst no hand in such a fair work? Look you, Adam, I were loth to terrify you, and you just come from a journey; but I promise you, Earl Morton hath brought you down a Maiden from Halifax, you never saw the like of her—and she'll clasp you round the neck, and your head will remain in her arms."

"Pshaw!" answered Adam, "I am too old to have my head turned by any maiden of them all. I know my Lord of Morton will go as far for a buxom lass as anyone; but what the devil took him to Halifax all the way? and if he has got a gamester there, what hath she to do with my head?"

"Much, much!" answered Michael. "Herod's daughter, who did such execution with her foot and ankle, danced not men's heads off more cleanly than this maiden of Morton.* 'Tis an axe, man,—an axe which falls of itself like a sash window, and never gives the headsmen the trouble to wield it."

"By my faith, a shrewd device," said Woodcock; "heaven keep us free on't!"

The page, seeing no end to the conversation betwixt these two old comrades, and anxious from what he had heard, concerning the fate of the Abbot, now interrupted their conference.

---

* Maiden of Morton—a species of Guillotine which the Regent Morton brought down from Halifax, certainly at a period considerably later than intimated in the tale. He was himself the first who suffered by the engine.

SIR WALTER SCOTT

"Methinks," he said, "Adam Woodcock, thou hadst better deliver thy master's letter to the Regent; questionless he hath therein stated what has chanced at Kennaquhair, in the way most advantageous for all concerned."

"The boy is right," said Michael Wing-the-wind, "my lord will be very impatient."

"The child hath wit enough to keep himself warm," said Adam Woodcock, producing from his hawking-bag his lord's letter, addressed to the Earl of Murray, "and for that matter so have I. So, Master Roland, you will e'en please to present this yourself to the Lord Regent; his presence will be better graced by a young page than by an old falconer."

"Well said, canny Yorkshire!" replied his friend; "and but now you were so earnest to see our good lord!—Why, wouldst thou put the lad into the noose that thou mayst slip tether thyself?—or dost thou think the maiden will clasp his fair young neck more willingly than thy old sunburnt weasand?"

"Go to," answered the falconer; "thy wit towers high an it could strike the quarry. I tell thee, the youth has nought to fear—he had nothing to do with the gambol—a rare gambol it was, Michael, as mad-caps ever played; and I had made as rare a ballad, if we had had the luck to get it sung to an end. But mum for that—*tace*, as I said before, is Latin for a candle. Carry the youth to the presence, and I will remain here, with bridle in hand, ready to strike the spurs up to the rowel-heads, in case the hawk flies my way.—I will soon put Soltraedge, I trow, betwixt the Regent and me, if he means me less than fair play."

"Come on then, my lad," said Michael, "since thou must needs take the spring before canny Yorkshire." So saying, he led the way through winding passages, closely followed by Roland Graeme, until they arrived at a large winding stone stair, the steps of which were so long and broad, and at the same time so low, as to render the ascent uncommonly easy. When they had ascended about the height of one story, the guide stepped aside, and pushed open the door of a dark and gloomy antechamber; so dark, indeed, that his youthful companion stumbled, and nearly fell down upon a low step, which was awkwardly placed on the very threshold.

"Take heed," said Michael Wing-the-wind, in a very low tone of voice, and first glancing cautiously round to see if any one listened— "Take heed, my young friend, for those who fall on these boards seldom rise again—Seest thou that," he added, in a still lower voice, pointing to some dark crimson stains on the floor, on which a ray of light, shot through a small aperture, and traversing the general gloom of the apartment, fell with mottled radiance—"Seest thou that, youth?—walk warily, for men have fallen here before you."

"What mean you?" said the page, his flesh creeping, though he scarce knew why; "Is it blood?"

"Ay, ay," said the domestic, in the same whispering tone, and dragging the youth on by the arm—"Blood it is,—but this is no time to question, or even to look at it. Blood it is, foully and fearfully shed, as foully and fearfully avenged. The blood," he added, in a still more cautious tone, "of Seignior David."

Roland Graeme's heart throbbed when he found himself so unexpectedly in the scene of Rizzio's slaughter, a catastrophe which had chilled with horror all even in that rude age, which had been the theme of wonder and pity through every cottage and castle in Scotland, and had not escaped that of Avenel. But his guide hurried him forward, permitting no farther question, and with the manner of one who has already tampered too much with a dangerous subject. A tap which he made at a low door at one end of the vestibule, was answered by a huissier or usher, who, opening it cautiously, received Michael's intimation that a page waited the Regent's leisure, who brought letters from the Knight of Avenel.

"The Council is breaking up," said the usher; "but give me the packet; his Grace the Regent will presently see the messenger."

"The packet," replied the page, "must be delivered into the Regent's own hands; such were the orders of my master."

The usher looked at him from head to foot, as if surprised at his boldness, and then replied, with some asperity, "Say you so, my young master? Thou crowest loudly to be but a chicken, and from a country barn-yard too."

"Were it a time or place," said Roland, "thou shouldst see I can do more than crow; but do your duty, and let the Regent know I wait his pleasure."

"Thou art but a pert knave to tell me of my duty," said the courtier in office; "but I will find a time to show you you are out of yours; meanwhile, wait there till you are wanted." So saying, he shut the door in Roland's face.

Michael Wing-the-wind, who had shrunk from his youthful companion during this altercation, according to the established maxim of courtiers of all ranks, and in all ages, now transgressed their prudential line of conduct so far as to come up to him once more. "Thou art a hopeful young springald," said he, "and I see right well old Yorkshire had reason in his caution. Thou hast been five minutes in the court, and hast employed thy time so well, as to make a powerful and a mortal enemy out of the usher of the council-chamber. Why, man, you might almost as well have offended the deputy butler!"

"I care not what he is," said Roland Graeme; "I will teach whomever I speak with to speak civilly to me in return. I did not come from Avenel to be browbeaten in Holyrood."

"Bravo, my lad!" said Michael; "it is a fine spirit if you can but hold it—but see, the door opens."

The usher appeared, and, in a more civil tone of voice and manner, said, that his Grace the Regent would receive the Knight of Avenel's message; and accordingly marshalled Roland Graeme the way into the apartment, from which the Council had been just dismissed, after finishing their consultations. There was in the room a long oaken table, surrounded by stools of the same wood, with a large elbow chair, covered with crimson velvet, at the head. Writing materials and papers were lying there in apparent disorder; and one or two of the privy counsellors who had lingered behind, assuming their cloaks, bonnets, and swords, and bidding farewell to the Regent, were departing slowly by a large door, on the opposite side to that through which the page entered. Apparently the Earl of Murray had made some jest, for the smiling countenances of the statesmen expressed that sort of cordial reception which is paid by courtiers to the condescending pleasantries of a prince.

The Regent himself was laughing heartily as he said, "Farewell, my lords, and hold me remembered to the Cock of the North."

He then turned slowly round towards Roland Graeme, and the marks of gaiety, real or assumed, disappeared from his countenance, as completely as the passing bubbles leave the dark mirror of a still profound lake into which a traveller has cast a stone; in the course of a minute his noble features had assumed their natural expression of deep and even melancholy gravity.

This distinguished statesman, for as such his worst enemies acknowledged him, possessed all the external dignity, as well as almost all the noble qualities, which could grace the power that he enjoyed; and had he succeeded to the throne as his legitimate inheritance, it is probable he would have been recorded as one of Scotland's wisest and greatest kings. But that he held his authority by the deposition and imprisonment of his sister and benefactress, was a crime which those only can excuse who think ambition an apology for ingratitude. He was dressed plainly in black velvet, after the Flemish fashion, and wore in his high-crowned hat a jewelled clasp, which looped it up on one side, and formed the only ornament of his apparel. He had his poniard by his side, and his sword lay on the council table.

Such was the personage before whom Roland Graeme now presented himself, with a feeling of breathless awe, very different from the usual boldness and vivacity of his temper. In fact, he was, from education and nature, forward, but not impudent, and was much more easily controlled by the moral superiority, arising from the elevated talents and renown of those with whom he conversed, than by pretensions founded only on rank or external show. He might have braved with indifference the presence of an earl, merely distinguished by his belt and coronet; but he felt overawed in that of the eminent soldier and statesman, the wielder of a nation's power, and the leader of her armies.—The greatest and wisest are flattered by the deference of youth—so graceful and becoming in itself; and Murray took, with much courtesy, the letter from the hands of the abashed and blushing page, and answered with complaisance to the imperfect and half-muttered greeting, which he endeavoured to deliver to him on the part of Sir Halbert of Avenel. He even paused a moment ere he broke the silk with which the letter was secured, to ask the page his name—so much he was struck with his very handsome features and form.

"Roland Graeme," he said, repeating the words after the hesitating page. "What! of the Grahams of the Lennox?"

"No, my lord," replied Roland; "my parents dwelt in the Debateable Land."

Murray made no further inquiry, but proceeded to read his dispatches; during the perusal of which his brow began to assume a stern expression of displeasure, as that of one who found something which at once surprised and disturbed him. He sat down on the nearest seat, frowned till his eyebrows almost met together, read the letter twice over, and was then silent for several minutes. At length, raising his head, his eye encountered that of the usher, who in vain endeavoured to exchange the look of eager and curious observation with which he had been perusing the Regent's features, for that open and unnoticing expression

SIR WALTER SCOTT

of countenance, which, in looking at all, seems as if it saw and marked nothing—a cast of look which may be practised with advantage by all those, of whatever degree, who are admitted to witness the familiar and unguarded hours of their superiors. Great men are as jealous of their thoughts as the wife of King Candaules was of her charms, and will as readily punish those who have, however involuntarily, beheld them in mental deshabille and exposure.

"Leave the apartment, Hyndman," said the Regent, sternly, "and carry your observation elsewhere. You are too knowing, sir, for your post, which, by special order, is destined for men of blunter capacity. So! now you look more like a fool than you did,"—(for Hyndman, as may easily be supposed, was not a little disconcerted by this rebuke)—"keep that confused stare, and it may keep your office. Begone, sir!"

The usher departed in dismay, not forgetting to register, amongst his other causes of dislike to Roland Graeme, that he had been the witness of this disgraceful chiding. When he had left the apartment, the Regent again addressed the page.

"Your name, you say, is Armstrong?"

"No," replied Roland, "my name is Graeme, so please you—Roland Graeme, whose forbears were designated of Heathergill, in the Debateable Land."

"Ay, I knew it was a name from the Debateable Land. Hast thou any acquaintance in Edinburgh?"

"My lord," replied Roland, willing rather to evade this question than to answer it directly, for the prudence of being silent with respect to Lord Seyton's adventure immediately struck him, "I have been in Edinburgh scarce an hour, and that for the first time in my life."

"What! and thou Sir Halbert Glendinning's page?" said the Regent.

"I was brought up as my Lady's page," said the youth, "and left Avenel Castle for the first time in my life—at least since my childhood—only three days since."

"My Lady's page!" repeated the Earl of Murray, as if speaking to himself; "it was strange to send his Lady's page on a matter of such deep concernment—Morton will say it is of a piece with the nomination of his brother to be Abbot; and yet in some sort an inexperienced youth will best serve the turn.—What hast thou been taught, young man, in thy doughty apprenticeship?"

"To hunt, my lord, and to hawk," said Roland Graeme.

"To hunt coneys, and to hawk at ouzels!" said the Regent, smiling; "for such are the sports of ladies and their followers."

Graeme's cheek reddened deeply as he replied, not without some emphasis, "To hunt red-deer of the first head, and to strike down herons of the highest soar, my lord, which, in Lothian speech, may be termed, for aught I know, coneys and ouzels;-also I can wield a brand and couch a lance, according to our Border meaning; in inland speech these may be termed water-flags and bulrushes."

"Thy speech rings like metal," said the Regent, "and I pardon the sharpness of it for the truth.—Thou knowest, then, what belongs to the duty of a man-at-arms?"

"So far as exercise can teach—it without real service in the field," answered Roland Graeme; "but our Knight permitted none of his household to make raids, and I never had the good fortune to see a stricken field."

"The good fortune!" repeated the Regent, smiling somewhat sorrowfully, "take my word, young man, war is the only game from which both parties rise losers."

"Not always, my lord!" answered the page, with his characteristic audacity, "if fame speaks truth."

"How, sir?" said the Regent, colouring in his turn, and perhaps suspecting an indiscreet allusion to the height which he himself had attained by the hap of civil war.

"Because, my lord," said Roland Graeme, without change of tone, "he who fights well, must have fame in life, or honour in death; and so war is a game from which no one can rise a loser."

The Regent smiled and shook his head, when at that moment the door opened, and the Earl of Morton presented himself.

"I come somewhat hastily," he said, "and I enter unannounced because my news are of weight—It is as I said; Edward Glendinning is named Abbot, and—"

"Hush, my lord!" said the Regent, "I know it, but—"

"And perhaps you knew it before I did, my Lord of Murray," answered Morton, his dark red brow growing darker and redder as he spoke.

"Morton," said Murray, "suspect me not—touch not mine honour—I have to suffer enough from the calumnies of foes, let me not have to contend with the unjust suspicions of my friends.—We are not alone," said he, recollecting himself, "or I could tell you more."

He led Morton into one of the deep embrasures which the windows formed in the massive wall, and which afforded a retiring place for their

SIR WALTER SCOTT

conversing apart. In this recess, Roland observed them speak together with much earnestness, Murray appearing to be grave and earnest, and Morton having a jealous and offended air, which seemed gradually to give way to the assurances of the Regent.

As their conversation grew more earnest, they became gradually louder in speech, having perhaps forgotten the presence of the page, the more readily as his position in the apartment placed him put of sight, so that he found himself unwillingly privy to more of their discourse than he cared to hear. For, page though he was, a mean curiosity after the secrets of others had never been numbered amongst Roland's failings; and moreover, with all his natural rashness, he could not but doubt the safety of becoming privy to the secret discourse of these powerful and dreaded men. Still he could neither stop his ears, nor with propriety leave the apartment; and while he thought of some means of signifying his presence, he had already heard so much, that, to have produced himself suddenly would have been as awkward, and perhaps as dangerous, as in quiet to abide the end of their conference. What he overheard, however, was but an imperfect part of their communication; and although an expert politician, acquainted with the circumstances of the times, would have had little difficulty in tracing the meaning, yet Roland Graeme could only form very general and vague conjectures as to the import of their discourse.

"All is prepared," said Murray, "and Lindsay is setting forward—She must hesitate no longer—thou seest I act by thy counsel, and harden myself against softer considerations."

"True, my lord," replied Morton, "in what is necessary to gain power, you do not hesitate, but go boldly to the mark. But are you as careful to defend and preserve what you have won?—Why this establishment of domestics around her?—has not your sister men and maidens enough to tend her, but you must consent to this superfluous and dangerous retinue?"

"For shame, Morton!—a Princess, and my sister, could I do less than allow her due attendance?"

"Ay," replied Morton, "even thus fly all your shafts—smartly enough loosened from the bow, and not unskilfully aimed—but a breath of foolish affection ever crosses in the mid volley, and sways the arrow from the mark."

"Say not so, Morton," replied Murray, "I have both dared and done—"

"Yes, enough to gain, but not enough to keep—reckon not that she will think and act thus—you have wounded her deeply, both in pride and in power—it signifies nought, that you would tent now the wound with unavailing salves—as matters stand with you, you must forfeit the title of an affectionate brother, to hold that of a bold and determined statesman."

"Morton!" said Murray, with some impatience, "I brook not these taunts—what I have done I have done—what I must farther do, I must and will—but I am not made of iron like thee, and I cannot but remember—Enough of this-my purpose holds."

"And I warrant me," said Morton, "the choice of these domestic consolations will rest with—"

Here he whispered names which escaped Roland Graeme's ear. Murray replied in a similar tone, but so much raised towards the conclusion, of the sentence, that the page heard these words—"And of him I hold myself secure, by Glendinning's recommendation."

"Ay, which may be as much trustworthy as his late conduct at the Abbey of Saint Mary's—you have heard that his brother's election has taken place. Your favourite Sir Halbert, my Lord of Murray, has as much fraternal affection as yourself."

"By heaven, Morton, that taunt demanded an unfriendly answer, but I pardon it, for your brother also is concerned; but this election shall be annulled. I tell you, Earl of Morton, while I hold the sword of state in my royal nephew's name, neither Lord nor Knight in Scotland shall dispute my authority; and if I bear—with insults from my friends, it is only while I know them to be such, and forgive their follies for their faithfulness."

Morton muttered what seemed to be some excuse, and the Regent answered him in a milder tone, and then subjoined, "Besides, I have another pledge than Glendinning's recommendation, for this youth's fidelity—his nearest relative has placed herself in my hands as his security, to be dealt withal as his doings shall deserve."

"That is something," replied Morton; "but yet in fair love and goodwill, I must still pray you to keep on your guard. The foes are stirring again, as horse-flies and hornets become busy so soon as the storm-blast is over. George of Seyton was crossing the causeway this morning with a score of men at his back, and had a ruffle with my friends of the house of Leslie—they met at the Tron, and were fighting hard, when the provost, with his guard of partisans, came in thirdsman, and staved them asunder with their halberds, as men part dog and bear."

SIR WALTER SCOTT

"He hath my order for such interference," said the Regent—"Has any one been hurt?"

"George of Seyton himself, by black Ralph Leslie—the devil take the rapier that ran not through from side to side! Ralph has a bloody coxcomb, by a blow from a messan-page whom nobody knew—Dick Seyton of Windygowl is run through the arm, and two gallants of the Leslies have suffered phlebotomy. This is all the gentle blood which has been spilled in the revel; but a yeoman or two on both sides have had bones broken and ears chopped. The ostlere-wives, who are like to be the only losers by their miscarriage, have dragged the knaves off the street, and are crying a drunken coronach over them."

"You take it lightly, Douglas," said the Regent; "these broils and feuds would shame the capital of the great Turk, let alone that of a Christian and reformed state. But, if I live, this gear shall be amended; and men shall say, when they read my story, that if it were my cruel hap to rise to power by the dethronement of a sister, I employed it, when gained, for the benefit of the commonweal."

"And of your friends," replied Morton; "wherefore I trust for your instant order annulling the election of this lurdane Abbot, Edward Glendinning."

"You shall be presently satisfied." said the Regent; and stepping forward, he began to call, "So ho, Hyndman!" when suddenly his eye lighted on Roland Graeme—"By my faith, Douglas," said he, turning to his friend, "here have been three at counsel!"

"Ay, but only two can keep counsel," said Morton; "the galliard must be disposed of."

"For shame, Morton—an orphan boy!—Hearken thee, my child—Thou hast told me some of thy accomplishments—canst thou speak truth?" "Ay, my lord, when it serves my turn," replied Graeme.

"It shall serve thy turn now," said the Regent; "and falsehood shall be thy destruction. How much hast thou heard or understood of what we two have spoken together?"

"But little, my lord," replied Roland Graeme boldly, "which met my apprehension, saving that it seemed to me as if in something you doubted the faith of the Knight of Avenel, under whose roof I was nurtured."

"And what hast thou to say on that point, young man?" continued the Regent, bending his eyes upon him with a keen and strong expression of observation.

"That," said the page, "depends on the quality of those who speak against his honour whose bread I have long eaten. If they be my inferiors, I say they lie, and will maintain what I say with my baton; if my equals, still I say they lie, and will do battle in the quarrel, if they list, with my sword; if my superiors"—he paused.

"Proceed boldly," said the Regent—"What if thy superiors said aught that nearly touched your master's honour?"

"I would say," replied Graeme, "that he did ill to slander the absent, and that my master was a man who could render an account of his actions to any one who should manfully demand it of him to his face."

"And it were manfully said," replied the Regent—"what thinkest thou, my Lord of Morton?"

"I think," replied Morton, "that if the young galliard resemble a certain ancient friend of ours, as much in the craft of his disposition as he does in eye and in brow, there may be a wide difference betwixt what he means and what he speaks."

"And whom meanest thou that he resembles so closely?" said Murray.

"Even the true and trusty Julian Avenel," replied Morton.

"But this youth belongs to the Debateable Land," said Murray.

"It may be so; but Julian was an outlaying striker of venison, and made many a far cast when he had a fair doe in chase."

"Pshaw!" said the Regent, "this is but idle talk—Here, thou Hyndman—thou curiosity," calling to the usher, who now entered,—"conduct this youth to his companion—You will both," he said to Graeme, "keep yourselves in readiness to travel on short notice."—And then motioning to him courteously to withdraw, he broke up the interview.

XIX

It is and is not—'tis the thing I sought for,
Have kneel'd for, pray'd for, risk'd my fame and life for,
And yet it is not—no more than the shadow
Upon the hard, cold, flat, and polished mirror,
Is the warm, graceful, rounded, living substance
Which it presents in form and lineament.

—OLD PLAY

The usher, with gravity which ill concealed a jealous scowl, conducted Roland Graeme to a lower apartment, where he found his comrade the falconer. The man of office then briefly acquainted them that this would be their residence till his Grace's farther orders; that they were to go to the pantry, to the buttery, to the cellar, and to the kitchen, at the usual hours, to receive the allowances becoming their station,—instructions which Adam Woodcock's old familiarity with the court made him perfectly understand—"For your beds," he said, "you must go to the hostelry of Saint Michael's, in respect the palace is now full of the domestics of the greater nobles."

No sooner was the usher's back turned than Adam exclaimed with all the glee of eager curiosity, "And now, Master Roland, the news—the news—come unbutton thy pouch, and give us thy tidings—What says the Regent? asks he for Adam Woodcock?—and is all soldered up, or must the Abbot of Unreason strap for it?"

"All is well in that quarter," said the page; "and for the rest—But, hey-day, what! have you taken the chain and medal off from my bonnet?"

"And meet time it was, when yon usher, vinegar-faced rogue that he is, began to inquire what Popish trangam you were wearing.—By the mass, the metal would have been confiscated for conscience-sake, like your other rattle-trap yonder at Avenel, which Mistress Lilias bears about on her shoes in the guise of a pair of shoe-buckles—This comes of carrying Popish nicknackets about you."

"The jade!" exclaimed Roland Graeme, "has she melted down my rosary into buckles for her clumsy hoofs, which will set off such a garnish nearly as well as a cow's might?—But, hang her, let her keep them—many a dog's trick have I played old Lilias, for want of having something better to do, and the buckles will serve for a remembrance. Do you remember the verjuice I put into the comfits, when old Wingate and she were to breakfast together on Easter morning?"

"In troth do I, Master Roland—the major-domo's mouth was as crooked as a hawk's beak for the whole morning afterwards, and any other page in your room would have tasted the discipline of the porter's lodge for it. But my Lady's favour stood between your skin and many a jerking—Lord send you may be the better for her protection in such matters!"

"I am least grateful for it, Adam! and I am glad you put me in mind of it."

"Well, but the news, my young master," said Woodcock, "spell me the tidings—what are we to fly at next?—what did the Regent say to you?"

"Nothing that I am to repeat again," said Roland Graeme, shaking his head.

"Why, hey-day," said Adam, "how prudent we are become all of a sudden! You have advanced rarely in brief space, Master Roland. You have well nigh had your head broken, and you have gained your gold chain, and you have made an enemy, Master Usher to wit, with his two legs like hawks' perches, and you have had audience of the first man in the realm, and bear as much mystery in your brow, as if you had flown in the court-sky ever since you were hatched. I believe, in my soul, you would run with a piece of the egg-shell on your head like the curlews, which (I would we were after them again) we used to call whaups in the Halidome and its neighbourhood. But sit thee down, boy; Adam Woodcock was never the lad to seek to enter into forbidden secrets—sit thee down, and I will go and fetch the vivers—I know the butler and the pantler of old."

The good-natured falconer set forth upon his errand, busying himself about procuring their refreshment; and, during his absence, Roland Graeme abandoned himself to the strange, complicated, and yet heart-stirring reflections, to which the events of the morning had given rise. Yesterday he was of neither mark nor likelihood; a vagrant boy, the attendant on a relative, of whose sane judgment he himself had not the highest opinion; but now he had become, he knew not why, or wherefore, or to what extent, the custodier, as the Scottish phrase went, of some important state secret, in the safe keeping of which the Regent himself was concerned. It did not diminish from, but rather added to the interest of a situation so unexpected, that Roland himself did not perfectly understand wherein he stood committed by the state secrets, in which he had unwittingly become participator. On the contrary, he felt like one who looks on a romantic landscape, of which he sees the features for the first time, and then obscured with mist and driving tempest. The imperfect glimpse which the eye catches of rocks, trees, and other objects around him, adds double dignity to these shrouded mountains and darkened abysses, of which the height, depth, and extent, are left to imagination.

But mortals, especially at the well-appetized age which precedes twenty years, are seldom so much engaged either by real or conjectural subjects of speculation, but that their earthly wants claim their hour of attention. And with many a smile did our hero, so the reader may term him if he will, hail the re-appearance of his friend Adam Woodcock, bearing on one platter a tremendous portion of boiled beef, and on another a plentiful allowance of greens, or rather what the Scotch call lang-kale. A groom followed with bread, salt, and the other means of setting forth a meal; and when they had both placed on the oaken table what they bore in their hands, the falconer observed, that since he knew the court, it had got harder and harder every day to the poor gentlemen and yeoman retainers, but that now it was an absolute flaying of a flea for the hide and tallow. Such thronging to the wicket, and such churlish answers, and such bare beef-bones, such a shouldering at the buttery-hatch and cellarage, and nought to be gained beyond small insufficient single ale, or at best with a single straike of malt to counterbalance a double allowance of water—"By the mass, though, my young friend," said he, while he saw the food disappearing fast under Roland's active exertions, "it is not so to well to lament for former times as to take the advantage of the present, else we are like to lose on both sides."

So saying, Adam Woodcock drew his chair towards the table, unsheathed his knife, (for every one carried that minister of festive distribution for himself,) and imitated his young companion's example, who for the moment had lost his anxiety for the future in the eager satisfaction of an appetite sharpened by youth and abstinence.

In truth, they made, though the materials were sufficiently simple, a very respectable meal, at the expense of the royal allowance; and Adam Woodcock, notwithstanding the deliberate censure which he had passed on the household beer of the palace, had taken the fourth deep draught of the black jack ere he remembered him that he had spoken in its dispraise. Flinging himself jollily and luxuriously back in an old danske elbow-chair, and looking with careless glee towards the page, extending at the same time his right leg, and stretching the other easily over it, he reminded his companion that he had not yet heard the ballad which he had made for the Abbot of Unreason's revel. And accordingly he struck merrily up with

> "The Pope, that pagan full of pride,
> Has blinded us full lang."—

Roland Graeme, who felt no great delight, as may be supposed, in the falconer's satire, considering its subject, began to snatch up his mantle, and fling it around his shoulders, an action which instantly interrupted the ditty of Adam Woodcock.

"Where the vengeance are you going now," he said, "thou restless boy?—Thou hast quicksilver in the veins of thee to a certainty, and canst no more abide any douce and sensible communing, than a hoodless hawk would keep perched on my wrist!"

"Why, Adam," replied the page, "if you must needs know, I am about to take a walk and look at this fair city. One may as well be still mewed up in the old castle of the lake, if one is to sit the live-long night between four walls, and hearken to old ballads."

"It is a new ballad—the Lord help thee!" replied Adam, "and that one of the best that ever was matched with a rousing chorus."

"Be it so," said the page, "I will hear it another day, when the rain is dashing against the windows, and there is neither steed stamping, nor spur jingling, nor feather waving in the neighbourhood to mar my marking it well. But, even now, I want to be in the world, and to look about me."

"But the never a stride shall you go without me," said the falconer, "until the Regent shall take you whole and sound off my hand; and so, if you will, we may go to the hostelrie of Saint Michael's, and there you will see company enough, but through the casement, mark you me; for as to rambling through the street to seek Seytons and Leslies, and having a dozen holes drilled in your new jacket with rapier and poniard, I will yield no way to it."

"To the hostelrie of Saint Michael's, then, with all my heart," said the page; and they left the palace accordingly, rendered to the sentinels at the gate, who had now taken their posts for the evening, a strict

SIR WALTER SCOTT

account of their names and business, were dismissed through a small wicket of the close-barred portal, and soon reached the inn or hostelrie of Saint Michael, which stood in a large court-yard, off the main street, close under the descent of the Calton-hill. The place, wide, waste, and uncomfortable, resembled rather an Eastern caravansary, where men found shelter indeed, but were obliged to supply themselves with every thing else, than one of our modern inns;

> *Where not one comfort shall to those be lost,*
> *Who never ask, or never feel, the cost.*

But still, to the inexperienced eye of Roland Graeme, the bustle and confusion of this place of public resort, furnished excitement and amusement. In the large room, into which they had rather found their own way than been ushered by mine host, travellers and natives of the city entered and departed, met and greeted, gamed or drank together, forming the strongest contrast to the stern and monotonous order and silence with which matters were conducted in the well-ordered household of the Knight of Avenel. Altercation of every kind, from brawling to jesting, was going on amongst the groups around them, and yet the noise and mingled voices seemed to disturb no one and indeed to be noticed by no others than by those who composed the group to which the speaker belonged.

The falconer passed through the apartment to a projecting latticed window, which formed a sort of recess from the room itself; and having here ensconced himself and his companion, he called for some refreshments; and a tapster, after he had shouted for the twentieth time, accommodated him with the remains of a cold capon and a neat's tongue, together with a pewter stoup of weak French vin-de-pays. "Fetch a stoup of brandy-wine, thou knave—We will be jolly to-night, Master Roland," said he, when he saw himself thus accommodated, "and let care come to-morrow."

But Roland had eaten too lately to enjoy the good cheer; and feeling his curiosity much sharper than his appetite, he made it his choice to look out of the lattice, which overhung a large yard, surrounded by the stables of the hostelrie, and fed his eyes on the busy sight beneath, while Adam Woodcock, after he had compared his companion to the "Laird of Macfarlane's geese, who liked their play better than their meat," disposed of his time with the aid of cup and trencher, occasionally humming the burden of his birth-strangled ballad, and beating time to it with his fingers on the little round table. In this exercise he was frequently interrupted by the exclamations of his companion, as he saw something new in the yard beneath, to attract and interest him.

It was a busy scene, for the number of gentlemen and nobles who were now crowded into the city, had filled all spare stables and places of public reception with their horses and military attendants. There were some score of yeomen, dressing their own or their masters' horses in the yard, whistling, singing, laughing, and upbraiding each other, in a style of wit which the good order of Avenel Castle rendered strange to Roland Graeme's ears. Others were busy repairing their own arms, or cleaning those of their masters. One fellow, having just bought a bundle of twenty spears, was sitting in a corner, employed in painting the white staves of the weapons with yellow and vermillion. Other lacqueys led large stag-hounds, or wolf-dogs, of noble race, carefully muzzled to prevent accidents to passengers. All came and went, mixed together and separated, under the delighted eye of the page, whose imagination had not even conceived a scene so gaily diversified with the objects he had most pleasure in beholding; so that he was perpetually breaking the quiet reverie of honest Woodcock, and the mental progress which he was making in his ditty, by exclaiming, "Look here, Adam—look at the bonny bay horse—Saint Anthony, what, a gallant forehand he hath got!—and see the goodly gray, which yonder fellow in the frieze-jacket is dressing as awkwardly as if he had never touched aught but a cow—I would I were nigh him to teach him his trade!—And lo you, Adam, the gay Milan armour that the yeoman is scouring, all steel and silver, like our Knight's prime suit, of which old Wingate makes such account—And see to yonder pretty wench, Adam, who comes tripping through them all with her milk-pail—I warrant me she has had a long walk from the loaning; she has a stammel waistcoat, like your favourite Cicely Sunderland, Master Adam!"

"By my hood, lad," answered the falconer, "it is well for thee thou wert brought up where grace grew. Even in the Castle of Avenel thou wert a wild-blood enough, but hadst thou been nurtured here, within a flight-shot of the Court, thou hadst been the veriest crack-hemp of a page that ever wore feather in thy bonnet or steel by thy side: truly, I wish it may end well with thee."

"Nay, but leave thy senseless humming and drumming, old Adam, and come to the window ere thou hast drenched thy senses in the pint-pot there. See here comes a merry minstrel with his crowd, and a wench with him, that dances with bells at her ankles; and see, the yeomen and pages leave their horses and the armour they were cleaning, and gather round, as is very natural, to hear the music. Come, old Adam, we will thither too."

"You shall call me cutt if I do go down," said Adam; "you are near as good minstrelsy as the stroller can make, if you had but the grace to listen to it."

"But the wench in the stammel waistcoat is stopping too, Adam— by heaven, they are going to dance! Frieze-jacket wants to dance with stammel waistcoat, but she is coy and recusant."

Then suddenly changing his tone of levity into one of deep interest and surprise, he exclaimed, "Queen of Heaven! what is it that I see!" and then remained silent.

The sage Adam Woodcock, who was in a sort of languid degree amused with the page's exclamations, even while he professed to despise them, became at length rather desirous to set his tongue once more a-going, that he might enjoy the superiority afforded by his own intimate familiarity with all the circumstances which excited in his young companion's mind so much wonderment.

"Well, then," he said at last, "what is it you do see, Master Roland, that you have become mute all of a sudden?"

Roland returned no answer.

"I say, Master Roland Graeme," said the falconer, "it is manners in my country for a man to speak when he is spoken to."

Roland Graeme remained silent.

"The murrain is in the boy," said Adam Woodcock, "he has stared out his eyes, and talked his tongue to pieces, I think."

The falconer hastily drank off his can of wine, and came to Roland, who stood like a statue, with his eyes eagerly bent on the court-yard, though Adam Woodcock was unable to detect amongst the joyous scenes which it exhibited aught that could deserve such devoted attention.

"The lad is mazed!" said the falconer to himself.

But Roland Graeme had good reasons for his surprise, though they were not such as he could communicate to his companion.

The touch of the old minstrel's instrument, for he had already begun to play, had drawn in several auditors from the street when one entered the gate of the yard, whose appearance exclusively arrested the attention of Roland Graeme. He was of his own age, or a good deal younger, and from his dress and bearing might be of the same rank and calling, having all the air of coxcombry and pretension, which accorded with a handsome, though slight and low figure, and an elegant dress, in part hid by a large purple cloak. As he entered, he cast a glance up towards the windows, and, to his extreme astonishment, under the purple velvet bonnet and white feather, Roland recognized the features so deeply impressed on his memory, the bright and clustered tresses, the laughing full blue eyes, the well-formed eyebrows, the nose, with the slightest possible inclination to be aquiline, the ruby lip, of which an arch and half-suppressed smile seemed the habitual expression—in short, the form and face of Catherine Seyton; in man's attire, however, and mimicking, as it seemed, not unsuccessfully, the bearing of a youthful but forward page.

"Saint George and Saint Andrew!" exclaimed the amazed Roland Graeme to himself, "was there ever such an audacious quean!—she seems a little ashamed of her mummery too, for she holds the lap of her cloak to her face, and her colour is heightened—but Santa Maria, how she threads the throng, with as firm and bold a step as if she had never tied petticoat round her waist!—Holy Saints! she holds up her riding-rod as if she would lay it about some of their ears, that stand most in her way—by the hand of my father! she bears herself like the very model of pagehood.—Hey! what! sure she will not strike friezejacket in earnest?" But he was not long left in doubt; for the lout whom he had before repeatedly noticed, standing in the way of the bustling page, and maintaining his place with clownish obstinacy or stupidity, the advanced riding-rod was, without a moment's hesitation, sharply applied to his shoulders, in a manner which made him spring aside, rubbing the part of the body which had received so unceremonious a hint that it was in the way of his betters. The party injured growled forth an oath or two of indignation, and Roland Graeme began to think of flying down stairs to the assistance of the translated Catherine; but the laugh of the yard was against frieze-jacket, which indeed had, in those days, small chance of fair play in a quarrel with velvet and embroidery; so that the fellow, who was menial in the inn, slunk back to finish his task of dressing the bonny gray, laughed at by all, but most by the wench in the stammel waistcoat, his fellow-servant, who, to crown his disgrace, had the cruelty to cast an applauding smile upon the author of the injury, while, with a freedom more like the milk-maid of the town than she of the plains, she accosted him with—"Is there any one you want here, my pretty gentleman, that you seem in such haste?"

"I seek a sprig of a lad," said the seeming gallant, "with a sprig of holly in his cap, black hair, and black eyes, green jacket, and the air of a country coxcomb—I have sought him through every close and alley in the Canongate, the fiend gore him!"

"Why, God-a-mercy, Nun!" muttered Roland Graeme, much bewildered.

"I will inquire him presently out for your fair young worship," said the wench of the inn.

"Do," said the gallant squire, "and if you bring me to him, you shall have a groat to-night, and a kiss on Sunday when you have on a cleaner kirtle."

"Why, God-a-mercy, Nun!" again muttered Roland, "this is a note above E La."

In a moment after, the servant entered the room, and ushered in the object of his surprise.

While the disguised vestal looked with unabashed brow, and bold and rapid glance of her eye, through the various parties in the large old room, Roland Graeme, who felt an internal awkward sense of bashful confusion, which he deemed altogether unworthy of the bold and dashing character to which he aspired, determined not to be browbeaten and put down by this singular female, but to meet her with a glance of recognition so sly, so penetrating, so expressively humorous, as should show her at once he was in possession of her secret and master of her fate, and should compel her to humble herself towards him, at least into the look and manner of respectful and deprecating observance.

This was extremely well planned; but just as Roland had called up the knowing glance, the suppressed smile, the shrewd intelligent look, which was to ensure his triumph, he encountered the bold, firm, and steady gaze of his brother or sister-page, who, casting on him a falcon glance, and recognizing him at once as the object of his search, walked up with the most unconcerned look, the most free and undaunted composure, and hailed him with "You, Sir Holly-top, I would speak with you."

The steady coolness and assurance with which these words were uttered, although the voice was the very voice he had heard at the old convent, and although the features more nearly resembled those of Catharine when seen close than when viewed from a distance, produced, nevertheless, such a confusion in Roland's mind, that he became uncertain whether he was not still under a mistake from the beginning; the knowing shrewdness which should have animated his visage faded into a sheepish bashfulness, and the half-suppressed but most intelligible smile, became the senseless giggle of one who laughs to cover his own disorder of ideas.

"Do they understand a Scotch tongue in thy country, Holly-top?" said this marvellous specimen of metamorphosis. "I said I would speak with thee."

"What is your business with my comrade, my young chick of the game?" said Adam Woodcock, willing to step in to his companion's assistance, though totally at a loss to account for the sudden disappearance of all Roland's usual smartness and presence of mind.

"Nothing to you, my old cock of the perch," replied the gallant; "go mind your hawk's castings. I guess by your bag and your gauntlet that you are squire of the body to a sort of kites."

He laughed as he spoke, and the laugh reminded Roland so irresistibly of the hearty fit of risibility, in which Catherine had indulged at his expense when they first met in the old nunnery, that he could scarce help exclaiming, "Catherine Seyton, by Heavens!"—He checked the exclamation, however, and only said, "I think, sir, we two are not totally strangers to each other."

"We must have met in our dreams then" said the youth; "and my days are too busy to remember what I think on at nights."

"Or apparently to remember upon one day those whom you may have seen on the preceding eve" said Roland Graeme.

The youth in his turn cast on him a look of some surprise, as he replied, "I know no more of what you mean than does the horse I ride on—if there be offence in your words, you shall find me ready to take it as any lad in Lothian."

"You know well," said Roland, "though it pleases you to use the language of a stranger, that with you I have no purpose to quarrel."

"Let me do mine errand, then, and be rid of you," said the page. "Step hither this way, out of that old leathern fist's hearing."

They walked into the recess of the window, which Roland had left upon the youth's entrance into the apartment. The messenger then turned his back on the company, after casting a hasty and sharp glance around to see if they were observed. Roland did the same, and the page in the purple mantle thus addressed him, taking at the same time from under his cloak a short but beautifully wrought sword, with the hilt and ornaments upon the sheath of silver, massively chased and over-gilded—"I bring you this weapon from a friend, who gives it you under the solemn condition, that you will not unsheath it until you are commanded by your rightful Sovereign. For your warmth of temper is known, and the presumption with which you intrude yourself into the quarrels of others; and, therefore, this is laid upon you as a penance by those who wish you well, and whose hand will influence your destiny for good or for evil. This is what I was charged to tell you. So if you will give a fair word for a fair sword, and pledge your promise, with hand and glove, good and well; and if not, I will carry back Caliburn to those who sent it."

"And may I not ask who these are?" said Roland Graeme, admiring at the same time the beauty of the weapon thus offered him.

"My commission in no way leads me to answer such a question," said he of the purple mantle.

"But if I am offended" said Roland, "may I not draw to defend myself?"

"Not *this* weapon," answered the sword-bearer; "but you have your own at command, and, besides, for what do you wear your poniard?"

"For no good," said Adam Woodcock, who had now approached close to them, "and that I can witness as well as any one."

"Stand back, fellow," said the messenger, "thou hast an intrusive curious face, that will come by a buffet if it is found where it has no concern."

"A buffet, my young Master Malapert?" said Adam, drawing back, however; "best keep down fist, or, by Our Lady, buffet will beget buffet!"

"Be patient, Adam Woodcock," said Roland Graeme; "and let me pray you, fair sir, since by such addition you choose for the present to be addressed, may I not barely unsheathe this fair weapon, in pure simplicity of desire to know whether so fair a hilt and scabbard are matched with a befitting blade?"

"By no manner of means," said the messenger; "at a word, you must take it under the promise that you never draw it until you receive the commands of your lawful Sovereign, or you must leave it alone."

"Under that condition, and coming from your friendly hand, I accept of the sword," said Roland, taking it from his hand; "but credit me, if we are to work together in any weighty emprise, as I am induced to believe, some confidence and openness on your part will be necessary to give the right impulse to my zeal—I press for no more at present, it is enough that you understand me."

"I understand you!" said the page, exhibiting the appearance of unfeigned surprise in his turn,—"Renounce me if I do!—here you stand jiggeting, and sniggling, and looking cunning, as if there were some mighty matter of intrigue and common understanding betwixt you and me, whom you never set your eyes on before!"

"What!" said Roland Graeme, "will you deny that we have met before?"

"Marry that I will, in any Christian court," said the other page.

"And will you also deny," said Roland, "that it was recommended to us to study each other's features well, that in whatever disguise the time might impose upon us, each should recognize in the other the secret agent of a mighty work? Do not you remember, that Sister Magdalen and Dame Bridget—"

The messenger here interrupted him, shrugging up his shoulders, with a look of compassion, "Bridget and Magdalen! why, this is madness and dreaming! Hark ye, Master Holly-top, your wits are gone on wool-gathering; comfort yourself with a caudle, and thatch your brain-sick noddle with a woollen night-cap, and so God be with you!"

As he concluded this polite parting address, Adam Woodcock, who was again seated by the table on which stood the now empty can, said to him, "Will you drink a cup, young man, in the way of courtesy, now you have done your errand, and listen to a good song?" and without waiting for an answer, he commenced his ditty,—

> "The Pope, that pagan full of pride,
> Hath blinded us full lang—"

It is probable that the good wine had made some innovation in the falconer's brain, otherwise he would have recollected the danger of introducing any thing like political or polemical pleasantry into a public assemblage at a time when men's minds were in a state of great irritability. To do him justice, he perceived his error, and stopped short so soon as he saw that the word Pope had at once interrupted the separate conversations of the various parties which were assembled in the apartment; and that many began to draw themselves up, bridle, look big, and prepare to take part in the impending brawl; while others, more decent and cautious persons, hastily paid down their lawing, and prepared to leave the place ere bad should come to worse.

And to worse it was soon likely to come; for no sooner did Woodcock's ditty reach the ear of the stranger page, than, uplifting his riding-rod, he exclaimed, "He who speaks irreverently of the Holy Father of the church in my presence, is the cub of a heretic wolf-bitch, and I will switch him as I would a mongrel-cur."

"And I will break thy young pate," said Adam, "if thou darest to lift a finger to me." And then, in defiance of the young Drawcansir's threats, with a stout heart and dauntless accent, he again uplifted the stave.

> *"The Pope, that pagan full of pride.*
> *Hath blinded—"*

But Adam was able to proceed no farther, being himself unfortunately blinded by a stroke of the impatient youth's switch across his eyes. Enraged at once by the smart and the indignity, the falconer started up, and darkling as he was, for his eyes watered too fast to permit his seeing any thing, he would soon have been at close grips with his insolent adversary, had not Roland Graeme, contrary to his nature, played for once the prudent man and the peacemaker, and thrown himself betwixt them, imploring Woodcock's patience. "You know not," he said, "with whom you have to do.—And thou," addressing the messenger, who stood scornfully laughing at Adam's rage, "get thee gone, whoever thou art; if thou be'st what I guess thee, thou well knowest there are earnest reasons why thou shouldst."

"Thou hast hit it right for once, Holly-top," said the gallant, "though I guess you drew your bow at a venture.—Here, host, let this yeoman have a bottle of wine to wash the smart out of his eyes—and there is a French crown for him." So saying, he threw the piece of money on the table, and left the apartment, with a quick yet steady pace, looking firmly at right and left, as if to defy interruption: and snapping his fingers at two or three respectable burghers, who, declaring it was a shame that any one should be suffered to rant and ruffle in defence of the Pope, were labouring to find the hilts of their swords, which had got for the present unhappily entangled in the folds of their cloaks. But, as the adversary was gone ere any of them had reached his weapon, they did not think it necessary to unsheath cold iron, but merely observed to each other, "This is more than masterful violence, to see a poor man stricken in the face just for singing a ballad against the whore of Babylon! If the Pope's champions are to be bangsters in our very change-houses, we shall soon have the old shavelings back again."

"The provost should look to it," said another, "and have some five or six armed with partisans, to come in upon the first whistle, to teach these gallants their lesson. For, look you, neighbour Lugleather, it is not for decent householders like ourselves to be brawling with the godless grooms and pert pages of the nobles, that are bred up to little else save bloodshed and blasphemy."

"For all that, neighbour," said Lugleather, "I would have curried that youngster as properly as ever I curried a lamb's hide, had not the hilt of my bilbo been for the instant beyond my grasp; and before I could turn my girdle, gone was my master!"

"Ay," said the others, "the devil go with him, and peace abide with us—I give my rede, neighbours, that we pay the lawing, and be stepping homeward, like brother and brother; for old Saint Giles's is tolling curfew, and the street grows dangerous at night."

With that the good burghers adjusted their cloaks, and prepared for their departure, while he that seemed the briskest of the three, laying his hand on his Andrea Ferrara, observed, "that they that spoke in the praise of the Pope on the High-gate of Edinburgh, had best bring the sword of Saint Peter to defend them."

While the ill-humour excited by the insolence of the young aristocrat was thus evaporating in empty menace, Roland Graeme had to control the far more serious indignation of Adam Woodcock. "Why, man, it was but a switch across the mazzard—blow your nose, dry your eyes, and you will see all the better for it."

"By this light, which I cannot see," said Adam Woodcock, "thou hast been a false friend to me, young man—neither taking up my rightful quarrel, nor letting me fight it out myself."

"Fy for shame, Adam Woodcock," replied the youth, determined to turn the tables on him, and become in turn the counsellor of good order and peaceable demeanour—"I say, fy for shame!—Alas, that you will speak thus! Here are you sent with me, to prevent my innocent youth getting into snares—"

"I wish your innocent youth were cut short with a halter, with all my heart," said Adam, who began to see which way the admonition tended.—"And instead of setting before me," continued Roland, "an

SIR WALTER SCOTT

example of patience and sobriety becoming the falconer of Sir Halbert Glendinning, you quaff me off I know not how many flagons of ale, besides a gallon of wine, and a full measure of strong waters."

"It was but one small pottle," said poor Adam, whom consciousness of his own indiscretion now reduced to a merely defensive warfare.

"It was enough to pottle you handsomely, however," said the page—"And then, instead of going to bed to sleep off your liquor, must you sit singing your roistering songs about popes and pagans, till you have got your eyes almost switched out of your head; and but for my interference, whom your drunken ingratitude accuses of deserting you, yon galliard would have cut your throat, for he was whipping out a whinger as broad as my hand, and as sharp as a razor—And these are lessons for an inexperienced youth!—Oh, Adam! out upon you! out upon you!"

"Marry, amen, and with all my heart," said Adam; "out upon my folly for expecting any thing but impertinent raillery from a page like thee, that if he saw his father in a scrape, would laugh at him, instead of lending him aid.

"Nay, but I will lend you aid," said the page, still laughing, "that is, I will lend thee aid to thy chamber, good Adam, where thou shalt sleep off wine and ale, ire and indignation, and awake the next morning with as much fair wit as nature has blessed thee withal. Only one thing I will warn thee, good Adam, that henceforth and for ever, when thou railest at me for being somewhat hot at hand, and rather too prompt to out with poniard or so, thy admonition shall serve as a prologue to the memorable adventure of the switching of Saint Michael's."

With such condoling expressions he got the crest-fallen falconer to his bed, and then retired to his own pallet, where it was some time ere he could fall asleep. If the messenger whom he had seen were really Catherine Seyton, what a masculine virago and termagant must she be! and stored with what an inimitable command of insolence and assurance!—The brass on her brow would furbish the front of twenty pages; "and I should know," thought Roland, "what that amounts to—And yet, her features, her look, her light gait, her laughing eye, the art with which she disposed the mantle to show no more of her limbs than needs must be seen—I am glad she had at least that grace left—the voice, the smile—it must have been Catherine Seyton, or the devil in her likeness! One thing is good, I have silenced the eternal predications of that ass, Adam Woodcock, who has set up for being a preacher and a governor, over me, so soon as he has left the hawks' mew behind him."

And with this comfortable reflection, joined to the happy indifference which youth hath for the events of the morrow, Roland Graeme fell fast asleep.

XX

Now have you reft me from my staff, my guide,
Who taught my youth, as men teach untamed falcons,
To use my strength discreetly—I am reft
Of comrade and of counsel.

—OLD PLAY

In the gray of the next morning's dawn, there was a loud knocking at the gate of the hostelrie; and those without, proclaiming that they came in the name of the Regent, were instantly admitted. A moment or two afterwards, Michael Wing-the-wind stood by the bedside of our travellers.

"Up! up!" he said, "there is no slumber where Murray hath work ado."

Both sleepers sprung up, and began to dress themselves.

"You, old friend," said Wing-the-wind to Adam Woodcock, "must to horse instantly, with this packet to the Monks of Kennaquhair; and with this," delivering them as he spoke, "to the Knight of Avenel."

"As much as commanding the monks to annul their election, I'll warrant me, of an Abbot," quoth Adam Woodcock, as he put the packets into his bag, "and charging my master to see it done—To hawk at one brother with another, is less than fair play, methinks."

"Fash not thy beard about it, old boy," said Michael, "but betake thee to the saddle presently; for if these orders are not obeyed, there will be bare walls at the Kirk of Saint Mary's, and it may be at the Castle of Avenel to boot; for I heard my Lord of Morton loud with the Regent, and we are at a pass that we cannot stand with him anent trifles."

"But," said Adam, "touching the Abbot of Unreason—what say they to that outbreak—An they be shrewishly disposed, I were better pitch the packets to Satan, and take the other side of the Border for my bield."

"Oh, that was passed over as a jest, since there was little harm done.—But, hark thee, Adam," continued his comrade, "if there was a dozen vacant abbacies in your road, whether of jest or earnest, reason or unreason, draw thou never one of their mitres over thy brows.—The time is not fitting, man!—besides, our Maiden longs to clip the neck of a fat churchman."

"She shall never sheer mine in that capacity," said the falconer, while he knotted the kerchief in two or three double folds around his sunburnt bull-neck, calling out at the same time, "Master Roland, Master Roland, make haste! we must back to perch and mew, and, thank Heaven, more than our own wit, with our bones whole, and without a stab in the stomach."

"Nay, but," said Wing-the-wind, "the page goes not back with you; the Regent has other employment for him."

"Saints and sorrows!" exclaimed the falconer—"Master Roland Graeme to remain here, and I to return to Avenel!—Why, it cannot be—the child cannot manage himself in this wide world without me, and I question if he will stoop to any other whistle than mine own; there are times I myself can hardly bring him to my lure."

It was at Roland's tongue's end to say something concerning the occasion they had for using mutually each other's prudence, but the real anxiety which Adam evinced at parting with him, took away his disposition to such ungracious raillery. The falconer did not altogether escape, however, for, in turning his face towards the lattice, his friend Michael caught a glimpse of it, and exclaimed, "I prithee, Adam Woodcock, what hast thou been doing with these eyes of thine? They are swelled to the starting from the socket!"

"Nought in the world," said he, after casting a deprecating glance at Roland Graeme, "but the effect of sleeping in this d—ned truckle without a pillow."

"Why, Adam Woodcock, thou must be grown strangely dainty," said his old companion; "I have known thee sleep all night with no better pillow than a bush of ling, and start up with the sun, as glegg as a falcon; and now thine eyes resemble—"

"Tush, man, what signifies how mine eyes look now?" said Adam—"let us but roast a crab-apple, pour a pottle of ale on it, and bathe our throats withal, thou shalt see a change in me."

"And thou wilt be in heart to sing thy jolly ballad about the Pope," said his comrade.

"Ay, that I will," replied the falconer, "that is, when we have left this quiet town five miles behind us, if you will take your hobby and ride so far on my way."

"Nay, that I may not," said Michael—"I can but stop to partake your morning draught, and see you fairly to horse—I will see that they saddle them, and toast the crab for thee, without loss of time."

During his absence the falconer took the page by the hand—"May I never hood hawk again," said the good-natured fellow, "if I am not as sorry to part with you as if you were a child of mine own, craving pardon for the freedom—I cannot tell what makes me love you so much, unless it be for the reason that I loved the vicious devil of a brown galloway nag whom my master the Knight called Satan, till Master Warden changed his name to Seyton; for he said it was over boldness to call a beast after the King of Darkness—"

"And," said the page, "it was over boldness in him, I trow, to call a vicious brute after a noble family."

"Well," proceeded Adam, "Seyton or Satan, I loved that nag over every other horse in the stable-—There was no sleeping on his back— he was for ever fidgeting, bolting, rearing, biting, kicking, and giving you work to do, and maybe the measure of your back on the heather to the boot of it all. And I think I love you better than any lad in the castle, for the self-same qualities."

"Thanks, thanks, kind Adam. I regard myself bound to you for the good estimation in which you hold me."

"Nay, interrupt me not," said the falconer—"Satan was a good nag— But I say I think I shall call the two eyases after you, the one Roland, and the other Graeme; and while Adam Woodcock lives, be sure you have a friend—Here is to thee, my dear son."

Roland most heartily returned the grasp of the hand, and Woodcock, having taken a deep draught, continued his farewell speech.

"There are three things I warn you against, Roland, now that you art to tread this weary world without my experience to assist you. In the first place, never draw dagger on slight occasion—every man's doublet is not so well stuffed as a certain abbot's that you wot of. Secondly, fly not at every pretty girl, like a merlin at a thrush—you will not always win a gold chain for your labour—and, by the way, here I return to you your fanfarona—keep it close, it is weighty, and may benefit you at a pinch more ways than one. Thirdly, and to conclude, as our worthy preacher says, beware of the pottle-pot—it has drenched the judgment of wiser men than you. I could bring some instances of it, but I dare say it needeth not; for if you should forget your own mishaps, you will scarce fail to remember mine—And so farewell, my dear son."

Roland returned his good wishes, and failed not to send his humble duty to his kind Lady, charging the falconer, at the same time, to express his regret that he should have offended her, and his determination so to bear him in the world that she would not be ashamed of the generous protection she had afforded him.

The falconer embraced his young friend, mounted his stout, round-made, trotting-nag, which the serving-man, who had attended him, held ready at the door, and took the road to the southward. A sullen and heavy sound echoed from the horse's feet, as if indicating the sorrow of the good-natured rider. Every hoof-tread seemed to tap upon Roland's heart as he heard his comrade withdraw with so little of his usual alert activity, and felt that he was once more alone in the world.

He was roused from his reverie by Michael Wing-the-wind, who reminded him that it was necessary they should instantly return to the palace, as my Lord Regent went to the Sessions early in the morning. They went thither accordingly, and Wing-the-wind, a favourite old domestic, who was admitted nearer to the Regent's person and privacy, than many whose posts were more ostensible, soon introduced Graeme into a small matted chamber, where he had an audience of the present head of the troubled State of Scotland. The Earl of Murray was clad in a sad-coloured morning-gown, with a cap and slippers of the same cloth, but, even in this easy deshabillé, held his sheathed rapier in his hand, a precaution which he adopted when receiving strangers, rather in compliance with the earnest remonstrances of his friends and partisans, than from any personal apprehensions of his own. He answered with a silent nod the respectful obeisance of the page, and took one or two turns through the small apartment in silence, fixing his keen eye on Roland, as if he wished to penetrate into his very soul. At length he broke silence.

"Your name is, I think, Julian Graeme?"

"Roland Graeme, my lord, not Julian," replied the page.

"Right—I was misled by some trick of my memory—Roland Graeme, from the Debateable Land.—Roland, thou knowest the duties which belong to a lady's service?"

"I should know them, my lord," replied Roland, "having been bred so near the person of my Lady of Avenel; but I trust never more to practise them, as the Knight hath promised—"

"Be silent, young man," said the Regent, "I am to speak, and you to hear and obey. It is necessary that, for some space at least, you shall again enter into the service of a lady, who, in rank, hath no equal in Scotland; and this service accomplished, I give thee my word as Knight and Prince, that it shall open to you a course of ambition, such as may

SIR WALTER SCOTT

well gratify the aspiring wishes of one whom circumstances entitle to entertain much higher views than thou. I will take thee into my household and near to my person, or, at your own choice, I will give you the command of a foot-company—either is a preferment which the proudest laird in the land might be glad to ensure for a second son."

"May I presume to ask, my lord," said Roland, observing the Earl paused for a reply, "to whom my poor services are in the first place destined?"

"You will be told hereafter," said the Regent; and then, as if overcoming some internal reluctance to speak farther himself, he added, "or why should I not myself tell you, that you are about to enter into the service of a most illustrious—most unhappy lady—into the service of Mary of Scotland."

"Of the Queen, my lord!" said the page, unable to suppress his surprise.

"Of her who was the Queen!" said Murray, with a singular mixture of displeasure and embarrassment in his tone of voice. "You must be aware, young man, that her son reigns in her stead."

He sighed from an emotion, partly natural, perhaps, and partly assumed.

"And am I to attend upon her Grace in her place of imprisonment, my lord?" again demanded the page, with a straightforward and hardy simplicity, which somewhat disconcerted the sage and powerful statesman.

"She is not imprisoned," answered Murray, angrily; "God forbid she should—she is only sequestered from state affairs, and from the business of the public, until the world be so effectually settled, that she may enjoy her natural and uncontrolled freedom, without her royal disposition being exposed to the practices of wicked and designing men. It is for this purpose," he added, "that while she is to be furnished, as right is, with such attendance as may befit her present secluded state, it becomes necessary that those placed around her, are persons on whose prudence I can have reliance. You see, therefore, you are at once called on to discharge an office most honourable in itself, and so to discharge it that you may make a friend of the Regent of Scotland. Thou art, I have been told, a singularly apprehensive youth; and I perceive by thy look, that thou dost already understand what I would say on this matter. In this schedule your particular points of duty are set down at length—but the sum required of you is fidelity—I mean fidelity to myself and to the state. You are, therefore, to watch every attempt which is made, or inclination displayed, to open any communication with any of the lords who have become banders in the west—with Hamilton, Seyton, with Fleming, or the like. It is true that my gracious sister, reflecting upon the ill chances that have happened to the state of this poor kingdom, from evil counsellors who have abused her royal nature in time past, hath determined to sequestrate herself from state affairs in future. But it is our duty, as acting for and in the name of our infant nephew, to guard against the evils which may arise from any mutation or vacillation in her royal resolutions. Wherefore, it will be thy duty to watch, and report to our lady mother, whose guest our sister is for the present, whatever may infer a disposition to withdraw her person from the place of security in which she is lodged, or to open communication with those without. If, however, your observation should detect any thing of weight, and which may exceed mere suspicion, fail not to send notice by an especial messenger to me directly, and this ring shall be thy warrant to order horse and men on such service.—And now begone. If there be half the wit in thy head that there is apprehension in thy look, thou fully comprehendest all that I would say—Serve me faithfully, and sure as I am belted earl, thy reward shall be great."

Roland Graeme made an obeisance, and was about to depart.

The Earl signed to him to remain. "I have trusted thee deeply," he said, "young man, for thou art the only one of her suite who has been sent to her by my own recommendation. Her gentlewomen are of her own nomination—it were too hard to have barred her that privilege, though some there were who reckoned it inconsistent with sure policy. Thou art young and handsome. Mingle in their follies, and see they cover not deeper designs under the appearance of female levity—if they do mine, do thou countermine. For the rest, bear all decorum and respect to the person of thy mistress—she is a princess, though a most unhappy one, and hath been a queen! though now, alas! no longer such! Pay, therefore, to her all honour and respect, consistent with thy fidelity to the King and me—and now, farewell.—Yet stay—you travel with Lord Lindesay, a man of the old world, rough and honest, though untaught; see that thou offend him not, for he is not patient of raillery, and thou, I have heard, art a crack-halter." This he said with a smile, then added, "I could have wished the Lord Lindesay's mission had been intrusted to some other and more gentle noble."

"And wherefore should you wish that, my lord?" said Morton, who even then entered the apartment; "the council have decided for the best—we have had but too many proofs of this lady's stubbornness of mind, and the oak that resists the sharp steel axe, must be riven with the rugged iron wedge.—And this is to be her page?—My Lord Regent hath doubtless instructed you, young man, how you shall guide yourself in these matters; I will add but a little hint on my part. You are going to the castle of a Douglas, where treachery never thrives—the first moment of suspicion will be the last of your life. My kinsman, William Douglas, understands no raillery, and if he once have cause to think you false, you will waver in the wind from the castle battlements ere the sun set upon his anger.—And is the lady to have an almoner withal?"

"Occasionally, Douglas," said the Regent; "it were hard to deny the spiritual consolation which she thinks essential to her salvation."

"You are ever too soft hearted, my lord—What! a false priest to communicate her lamentations, not only to our unfriends in Scotland, but to the Guises, to Rome, to Spain, and I know not where!"

"Fear not," said the Regent, "we will take such order that no treachery shall happen."

"Look to it then." said Morton; "you know my mind respecting the wench you have consented she shall receive as a waiting-woman—one of a family, which, of all others, has ever been devoted to her, and inimical to us. Had we not been wary, she would have been purveyed of a page as much to her purpose as her waiting-damsel. I hear a rumour that an old mad Romish pilgrimer, who passes for at least half a saint among them, was employed to find a fit subject."

"We have escaped that danger at least," said Murray, "and converted it into a point of advantage, by sending this boy of Glendinning's— and for her waiting-damsel, you cannot grudge her one poor maiden instead of her four noble Marys and all their silken train?"

"I care not so much for the waiting-maiden," said Morton, "but I cannot brook the almoner—I think priests of all persuasions are much like each other—Here is John Knox, who made such a noble puller-down, is ambitious of becoming a setter-up, and a founder of schools and colleges out of the Abbey lands, and bishops' rents, and other spoils of Rome, which the nobility of Scotland have won with their sword and bow, and with which he would endow new hives to sing the old drone."

"John is a man of God," said the Regent, "and his scheme is a devout imagination."

The sedate smile with which this was spoken, left it impossible to conjecture whether the words were meant in approbation, or in derision, of the plan of the Scottish Reformer. Turning then to Roland Graeme, as if he thought he had been long enough a witness of this conversation, he bade him get him presently to horse, since my Lord of Lindesay was already mounted. The page made his reverence, and left the apartment.

Guided by Michael Wing-the-wind, he found his horse ready saddled and prepared for the journey, in front of the palace porch, where hovered about a score of men-at-arms, whose leader showed no small symptoms of surly impatience.

"Is this the jackanape page for whom we have waited thus long?" said he to Wing-the-wind.—"And my Lord Ruthven will reach the castle long before us."

Michael assented, and added, that the boy had been detained by the Regent to receive some parting instructions. The leader made an inarticulate sound in his throat, expressive of sullen acquiescence, and calling to one of his domestic attendants, "Edward," said he, "take the gallant into your charge, and let him speak with no one else."

He then addressed, by the title of Sir Robert, an elderly and respectable-looking gentleman, the only one of the party who seemed above the rank of a retainer or domestic, and observed, that they must get to horse with all speed.

During this discourse, and while they were riding slowly along the street of the suburb, Roland had time to examine more accurately the looks and figure of the Baron, who was at their head.

Lord Lindesay of the Byres was rather touched than stricken with years. His upright stature and strong limbs, still showed him fully equal to all the exertions and fatigues of war. His thick eyebrows, now partially grizzled, lowered over large eyes full of dark fire, which seemed yet darker from the uncommon depth at which they were set in his head. His features, naturally strong and harsh, had their sternness exaggerated by one or two scars received in battle. These features, naturally calculated to express the harsher passions, were shaded by an open steel cap, with a projecting front, but having no visor, over the gorget of which fell the black and grizzled beard of the grim old Baron, and totally hid the lower part of his face. The rest of his dress was a loose buff-coat, which had once been lined with silk and adorned with embroidery, but which seemed much stained with travel, and damaged with cuts, received probably in battle. It covered a corslet, which had once been of polished steel, fairly gilded, but was now somewhat injured with rust. A sword of antique make and uncommon size, framed to be wielded with both hands, a kind of weapon which was then beginning to go out of use, hung from his neck in a baldrick, and was so disposed as to traverse his whole person, the huge hilt appearing over his left shoulder, and the point reaching well-nigh to the right heel, and jarring against his spur as he walked. This unwieldy weapon could only be unsheathed by pulling the handle over the left shoulder—for no human arm was long enough to draw it in the usual manner. The whole equipment was that of a rude warrior, negligent of his exterior even to misanthropical sullenness; and the short, harsh, haughty tone, which he used towards his attendants, belonged to the same unpolished character.

The personage who rode with Lord Lindesay, at the head of the party, was an absolute contrast to him, in manner, form, and features. His thin and silky hair was already white, though he seemed not above forty-five or fifty years old. His tone of voice was soft and insinuating—his form thin, spare, and bent by an habitual stoop—his pale cheek was expressive of shrewdness and intelligence—his eye was quick though placid, and his whole demeanour mild and conciliatory. He rode an ambling nag, such as were used by ladies, clergymen, or others of peaceful professions—wore a riding habit of black velvet, with a cap and feather of the same hue, fastened up by a golden medal—and for show, and as a mark of rank rather than for use, carried a walking-sword, (as the short light rapiers were called,) without any other arms, offensive or defensive.

The party had now quitted the town, and proceeded, at a steady trot, towards the west.—As they prosecuted their journey, Roland Graeme would gladly have learned something of its purpose and tendency, but the countenance of the personage next to whom he had been placed in the train, discouraged all approach to familiarity. The Baron himself did not look more grim and inaccessible than his feudal retainer, whose grisly beard fell over his mouth like the portcullis before the gate of a castle, as if for the purpose of preventing the escape of any word, of which absolute necessity did not demand the utterance. The rest of the train seemed under the same taciturn influence, and journeyed on without a word being exchanged amongst them—more like a troop of Carthusian friars than a party of military retainers. Roland Graeme was surprised at this extremity of discipline; for even in the household of the Knight of Avenel, though somewhat distinguished for the accuracy with which decorum was enforced, a journey was a period of license, during which jest and song, and every thing within the limits of becoming mirth and pastime were freely permitted. This unusual silence was, however, so far acceptable, that it gave him time to bring any shadow of judgment which he possessed to council on his own situation and prospects, which would have appeared to any reasonable person in the highest degree dangerous and perplexing.

It was quite evident that he had, through various circumstances not under his own control, formed contradictory connexions with both the contending factions, by whose strife the kingdom was distracted, without being properly an adherent of either. It seemed also clear, that the same situation in the household of the deposed Queen, to which he was now promoted by the influence of the Regent, had been destined to him by his enthusiastic grandmother, Magdalen Graeme; for on this subject, the words which Morton had dropped had been a ray of light; yet it was no less clear that these two persons, the one the declared enemy, the other the enthusiastic votary, of the Catholic religion,—the one at the head of the King's new government, the other, who regarded that government as a criminal usurpation—must have required and expected very different services from the individual whom they had thus united in recommending. It required very little reflection to foresee that these contradictory claims on his services might speedily place him in a situation where his honour as well as his life might be endangered. But it was not in Roland Graeme's nature to anticipate evil before it came, or to prepare to combat difficulties before they arrived. "I will see this beautiful and unfortunate Mary Stewart," said he, "of whom we have heard so much, and then there will be time enough to determine whether I will be kingsman or queensman. None of them can say I have given word or promise to either of their factions; for they have led me up and down like a blind Billy, without giving me any light into what I was to do. But it was lucky that grim Douglas came into the Regent's closet this morning, otherwise I had never got free of him without plighting my troth to do all the Earl would have me, which seemed, after all, but foul play to the poor imprisoned lady, to place her page as an espial on her."

Skipping thus lightly over a matter of such consequence, the thoughts of the hare-brained boy went a wool-gathering after more agreeable topics. Now he admired the Gothic towers of Barnbougle, rising from the seabeaten rock, and overlooking one of the most glorious landscapes in Scotland—and now he began to consider what notable sport for the hounds and the hawks must be afforded by the variegated ground over which they travelled—and now he compared the steady and dull trot at which they were then prosecuting their journey, with the delight of sweeping over hill and dale in pursuit of his favourite sports. As, under the influence of these joyous recollections, he gave his horse the spur, and made him execute a gambade, he instantly incurred the censure of his grave neighbour, who hinted to him to keep the pace, and move quietly and in order, unless he wished such notice to be taken of his eccentric movements as was likely to be very displeasing to him.

The rebuke and the restraint under which the youth now found himself, brought back to his recollection his late good-humoured and accommodating associate and guide, Adam Woodcock; and from that topic his imagination made a short flight to Avenel Castle, to the quiet and unconfined life of its inhabitants, the goodness of his early protectress, not forgetting the denizens of its stables, kennels, and hawk-mews. In a brief space, all these subjects of meditation gave way to the resemblance of that riddle of womankind, Catherine Seyton, who appeared before the eye of his mind—now in her female form, now in her male attire—now in both at once—like some strange dream, which presents to us the same individual under two different characters at the same instant. Her mysterious present also recurred to his recollection—the sword which he now wore at his side, and which he was not to draw save by command of his legitimate Sovereign! But the key of this mystery he judged he was likely to find in the issue of his present journey.

With such thoughts passing through his mind, Roland Graeme accompanied the party of Lord Lindesay to the Queen's-Ferry, which they passed in vessels that lay in readiness for them. They encountered no adventure whatever in their passage, excepting one horse being lamed in getting into the boat, an accident very common on such occasions, until a few years ago, when the ferry was completely regulated. What was more peculiarly characteristic of the olden age, was the discharge of a culverin at the party from the battlements of the old castle of Rosythe, on the north side of the Ferry, the lord of which happened to have some public or private quarrel with the Lord Lindesay, and took this mode of expressing his resentment. The insult, however, as it was harmless, remained unnoticed and unavenged, nor did any thing else occur worth notice until the band had come where Lochleven spread its magnificent sheet of waters to the beams of a bright summer's sun.

The ancient castle, which occupies an island nearly in the centre of the lake, recalled to the page that of Avenel, in which he had been nurtured. But the lake was much larger, and adorned with several islets besides that on which the fortress was situated; and instead of being embosomed in hills like that of Avenel, had upon the southern side only a splendid mountainous screen, being the descent of one of the Lomond hills, and on the other was surrounded by the extensive and fertile plain of Kinross. Roland Graeme looked with some degree of dismay on the water-girdled fortress, which then, as now, consisted only of one large donjon-keep, surrounded with a court-yard, with two round flanking-towers at the angles, which contained within its circuit some other buildings of inferior importance. A few old trees, clustered together near the castle, gave some relief to the air of desolate seclusion; but yet the page, while he gazed upon a building so sequestrated, could not but feel for the situation of a captive Princess doomed to dwell there, as well as for his own. "I must have been born," he thought, "under the star that presides over ladies and lakes of water, for I cannot by any means escape from the service of the one, or from dwelling in the other. But if they allow me not the fair freedom of my sport and exercise, they shall find it as hard to confine a wild-drake, as a youth who can swim like one."

The band had now reached the edge of the water, and one of the party advancing displayed Lord Lindesay's pennon, waving it repeatedly to and fro, while that Baron himself blew a clamorous blast on his bugle. A banner was presently displayed from the roof of the castle in reply to these signals, and one or two figures were seen busied as if unmooring a boat which lay close to the islet.

"It will be some time ere they can reach us with the boat," said the companion of Lord Lindesay; "should we not do well to proceed to the town, and array ourselves in some better order, ere we appear before—"

"You may do as you list, Sir Robert," replied Lindesay, "I have neither time nor temper to waste on such vanities. She has cost me many a hard ride, and must not now take offence at the threadbare cloak and soiled doublet that I am arrayed in. It is the livery to which she has brought all Scotland."

"Do not speak so harshly," said Sir Robert; "if she hath done wrong, she hath dearly abied it; and in losing all real power, one would not deprive her of the little external homage due at once to a lady and a princess."

SIR WALTER SCOTT

"I say to you once more, Sir Robert Melville," replied Lindesay, "do as you will—for me, I am now too old to dink myself as a gallant to grace the bower of dames."

"The bower of dames, my lord!" said Melville, looking at the rude old tower—"is it yon dark and grated castle, the prison of a captive Queen, to which you give so gay a name?"

"Name it as you list," replied Lindesay; "had the Regent desired to send an envoy capable to speak to a captive Queen, there are many gallants in his court who would have courted the occasion to make speeches out of Amadis of Gaul, or the Mirror of Knighthood. But when he sent blunt old Lindesay, he knew he would speak to a misguided woman, as her former misdoings and her present state render necessary. I sought not this employment—it has been thrust upon me; and I will not cumber myself with more form in the discharge of it, than needs must be tacked to such an occupation."

So saying, Lord Lindesay threw himself from horseback, and wrapping his riding-cloak around him, lay down at lazy length upon the sward, to await the arrival of the boat, which was now seen rowing from the castle towards the shore. Sir Robert Melville, who had also dismounted, walked at short turns to and fro upon the bank, his arms crossed on his breast, often looking to the castle, and displaying in his countenance a mixture of sorrow and of anxiety. The rest of the party sate like statues on horseback, without moving so much as the points of their lances, which they held upright in the air.

As soon as the boat approached a rude quay or landing-place, near to which they had stationed themselves, Lord Lindesay started up from his recumbent posture, and asked the person who steered, why he had not brought a larger boat with him to transport his retinue.

"So please you," replied the boatman, "because it is the order of our lady, that we bring not to the castle more than four persons."

"Thy lady is a wise woman," said Lindesay, "to suspect me of treachery!—Or, had I intended it, what was to hinder us from throwing you and your comrades into the lake, and filling the boat with my own fellows?"

The steersman, on hearing this, made a hasty signal to his men to back their oars, and hold off from the shore which they were approaching.

"Why, thou ass," said Lindesay, "thou didst not think that I meant thy fool's head serious harm? Hark thee, friend—with fewer than three servants I will go no whither—Sir Robert Melville will require at least the attendance of one domestic; and it will be at your peril and your lady's to refuse us admission, come hither as we are, on matters of great national concern."

The steersman answered with firmness, but with great civility of expression, that his orders were positive to bring no more than four into the island, but he offered to row back to obtain a revisal of his orders.

"Do so, my friend," said Sir Robert Melville, after he had in vain endeavoured to persuade his stubborn companion to consent to a temporary abatement of his train, "row back to the castle, sith it will be no better, and obtain thy lady's orders to transport the Lord Lindesay, myself, and our retinue hither."

"And hearken," said Lord Lindesay, "take with you this page, who comes as an attendant on your lady's guest.—Dismount, sirrah," said he, addressing Roland, "and embark with them in that boat."

"And what is to become of my horse?" said Graeme; "I am answerable for him to my master."

"I will relieve you of the charge," said Lindesay; "thou wilt have little enough to do with horse, saddle, or bridle, for ten years to come—Thou mayst take the halter an thou wilt—it may stand thee in a turn."

"If I thought so," said Roland—but he was interrupted by Sir Robert Melville, who said to him good-humouredly, "Dispute it not, young friend—resistance can do no good, but may well run thee into danger."

Roland Graeme felt the justice of what he said, and, though neither delighted with the matter or manner of Lindesay's address, deemed it best to submit to necessity, and to embark without farther remonstrance. The men plied their oars. The quay, with the party of horse stationed near it, receded from the page's eyes—the castle and the islet seemed to draw near in the same proportion, and in a brief space he landed under the shadow of a huge old tree which overhung the landing place. The steersman and Graeme leaped ashore; the boatmen remained lying on their oars ready for further service.

XXI

Could valour aught avail or people's love,
France had not wept Navarre's brave Henry slain;
If wit or beauty could compassion move,
The rose of Scotland had not wept in vain.
Elegy in a Royal Mausoleum.

—Lewis

At the gate of the court-yard of Lochleven appeared the stately form of the Lady Lochleven, a female whose early charms had captivated James V, by whom she became mother of the celebrated Regent Murray. As she was of noble birth (being a daughter of the house of Mar) and of great beauty, her intimacy with James did not prevent her being afterwards sought in honourable marriage by many gallants of the time, among whom she had preferred Sir William Douglas of Lochleven. But well has it been said

—*"Our pleasant vices*
Are made the whips to scourge us"—

The station which the Lady of Lochleven now held as the wife of a man of high rank and interest, and the mother of a lawful family, did not prevent her nourishing a painful sense of degradation, even while she was proud of the talents, the power, and the station of her son, now prime ruler of the state, but still a pledge of her illicit intercourse. "Had James done to her," she said, in her secret heart, "the justice he owed her, she had seen in her son, as a source of unmixed delight and of unchastened pride, the lawful monarch of Scotland, and one of the ablest who ever swayed the sceptre." The House of Mar, not inferior in antiquity or grandeur to that of Drummond, would then have also boasted a Queen among its daughters, and escaped the stain attached to female frailty, even when it has a royal lover for its apology. While such feelings preyed on a bosom naturally proud and severe, they had a corresponding effect on her countenance, where, with the remains of great beauty, were mingled traits of inward discontent and peevish melancholy. It perhaps contributed to increase this habitual temperament, that the Lady Lochleven had adopted uncommonly rigid and severe views of religion, imitating in her ideas of reformed faith the very worst errors of the Catholics, in limiting the benefit of the gospel to those who profess their own speculative tenets.

In every respect, the unfortunate Queen Mary, now the compulsory guest, or rather prisoner, of this sullen lady, was obnoxious to her hostess. Lady Lochleven disliked her as the daughter of Mary of Guise, the legal possessor of those rights over James's heart and hand, of which she conceived herself to have been injuriously deprived; and yet more so as the professor of a religion which she detested worse than Paganism.

Such was the dame, who, with stately mien, and sharp yet handsome features, shrouded by her black velvet coif, interrogated the domestic who steered her barge to the shore, what had become of Lindesay and Sir Robert Melville. The man related what had passed, and she smiled scornfully as she replied, "Fools must be flattered, not foughten with.— Row back—make thy excuse as thou canst—say Lord Ruthven hath already reached this castle, and that he is impatient for Lord Lindesay's presence. Away with thee, Randal—yet stay—what galopin is that thou hast brought hither?"

"So please you, my lady, he is the page who is to wait upon—"

"Ay, the new male minion," said the Lady Lochleven; "the female attendant arrived yesterday. I shall have a well-ordered house with this lady and her retinue; but I trust they will soon find some others to undertake such a charge. Begone, Randal—and you" (to Roland Graeme) "follow me to the garden."

She led the way with a slow and stately step to the small garden, which, enclosed by a stone wall ornamented with statues, and an artificial fountain in the centre, extended its dull parterres on the side of the court-yard, with which it communicated by a low and arched portal. Within the narrow circuit of its formal and limited walks, Mary Stewart was now learning to perform the weary part of a prisoner, which, with little interval, she was doomed to sustain during the remainder of her life. She was followed in her slow and melancholy exercise by two female attendants; but in the first glance which Roland Graeme bestowed upon one so illustrious by birth, so distinguished by her beauty, accomplishments, and misfortunes, he was sensible of the presence of no other than the unhappy Queen of Scotland.

Her face, her form, have been so deeply impressed upon the imagination, that even at the distance of nearly three centuries, it is

SIR WALTER SCOTT

unnecessary to remind the most ignorant and uninformed reader of the striking traits which characterize that remarkable countenance, which seems at once to combine our ideas of the majestic, the pleasing, and the brilliant, leaving us to doubt whether they express most happily the queen, the beauty, or the accomplished woman. Who is there, that, at the very mention of Mary Stewart's name, has not her countenance before him, familiar as that of the mistress of his youth, or the favourite daughter of his advanced age? Even those who feel themselves compelled to believe all, or much, of what her enemies laid to her charge, cannot think without a sigh upon a countenance expressive of anything rather than the foul crimes with which she was charged when living, and which still continue to shade, if not to blacken, her memory. That brow, so truly open and regal—those eyebrows, so regularly graceful, which yet were saved from the charge of regular insipidity by the beautiful effect of the hazel eyes which they overarched, and which seem to utter a thousand histories—the nose, with all its Grecian precision of outline—the mouth, so well proportioned, so sweetly formed, as if designed to speak nothing but what was delightful to hear—the dimpled chin—the stately swan-like neck, form a countenance, the like of which we know not to have existed in any other character moving in that class of life, where the actresses as well as the actors command general and undivided attention. It is in vain to say that the portraits which exist of this remarkable woman are not like each other; for, amidst their discrepancy, each possesses general features which the eye at once acknowledges as peculiar to the vision which our imagination has raised while we read her history for the first time, and which has been impressed upon it by the numerous prints and pictures which we have seen. Indeed we cannot look on the worst of them, however deficient in point of execution, without saying that it is meant for Queen Mary; and no small instance it is of the power of beauty, that her charms should have remained the subject not merely of admiration, but of warm and chivalrous interest, after the lapse of such a length of time. We know that by far the most acute of those who, in latter days, have adopted the unfavourable view of Mary's character, longed, like the executioner before his dreadful task was performed, to kiss the fair hand of her on whom he was about to perform so horrible a duty.

Dressed, then, in a deep mourning robe, and with all those charms of face, shape, and manner, with which faithful tradition has made each reader familiar, Mary Stewart advanced to meet the Lady of Lochleven, who, on her part, endeavoured to conceal dislike and apprehension under the appearance of respectful indifference. The truth was, that she had experienced repeatedly the Queen's superiority in that species of disguised yet cutting sarcasm, with which women can successfully avenge themselves, for real and substantial injuries. It may be well doubted, whether this talent was not as fatal to its possessor as the many others enjoyed by that highly gifted, but most unhappy female; for, while it often afforded her a momentary triumph over her keepers, it failed not to exasperate their resentment; and the satire and sarcasm in which she had indulged were frequently retaliated by the deep and bitter hardships which they had the power of inflicting. It is well known that her death was at length hastened by a letter which she wrote to Queen Elizabeth, in which she treated her jealous rival, and the Countess of Shrewsbury, with the keenest irony and ridicule.

As the ladies met together, the Queen said, bending her head at the same time, in return to the obeisance of the Lady Lochleven, "We are this day fortunate—we enjoy the company of our amiable hostess at an unusual hour, and during a period which we have hitherto been permitted to give to our private exercise. But our good hostess knows well she has at all times access to our presence, and need not observe the useless ceremony of requiring our permission."

"I am sorry my presence is deemed an intrusion by your Grace," said the Lady of Lochleven. "I came but to announce the arrival of an addition to your train," motioning with her hand towards Roland Graeme; "a circumstance to which ladies are seldom indifferent."

"Oh! I crave your ladyship's pardon; and am bent to the earth with obligations for the kindness of my nobles—or my sovereigns, shall I call them?—who have permitted me such a respectable addition to my personal retinue."

"They have indeed studied, Madam," said the Lady of Lochleven, "to show their kindness towards your Grace—something at the risk perhaps of sound policy, and I trust their doings will not be misconstrued."

"Impossible!" said the Queen; "the bounty which permits the daughter of so many kings, and who yet is Queen of the realm, the attendance of two waiting-women and a boy, is a grace which Mary Stewart can never sufficiently acknowledge. Why! my train will be equal to that of any country dame in this your kingdom of Fife, saving but the lack of a gentleman-usher, and a pair or two of blue-coated serving-men. But I must not forget, in my selfish joy, the additional trouble and

SIR WALTER SCOTT

charges to which this magnificent augmentation of our train will put our kind hostess, and the whole house of Lochleven. It is this prudent anxiety, I am aware, which clouds your brows, my worthy lady. But be of good cheer; the crown of Scotland has many a fair manor, and your affectionate son, and my no less affectionate brother, will endow the good knight your husband with the best of them, ere Mary should be dismissed from this hospitable castle from your ladyship's lack of means to support the charges."

"The Douglasses of Lochleven, madam," answered the lady, "have known for ages how to discharge their duty to the State, without looking for reward, even when the task was both irksome and dangerous."

"Nay! but, my dear Lochleven," said the Queen, "you are over scrupulous—I pray you accept of a goodly manor; what should support the Queen of Scotland in this her princely court, saving her own crown-lands—and who should minister to the wants of a mother, save an affectionate son like the Earl of Murray, who possesses so wonderfully both the power and inclination?—Or said you it was the danger of the task which clouded your smooth and hospitable brow?—No doubt, a page is a formidable addition to my body-guard of females; and I bethink me it must have been for that reason that my Lord of Lindesay refused even now to venture within the reach of a force so formidable, without being attended by a competent retinue."

The Lady Lochleven started, and looked something surprised; and Mary suddenly changing her manner from the smooth ironical affectation of mildness to an accent of austere command, and drawing up at the same time her fine person, said, with the full majesty of her rank, "Yes! Lady of Lochleven; I know that Ruthven is already in the castle, and that Lindesay waits on the bank the return of your barge to bring him hither along with Sir Robert Melville. For what purpose do these nobles come—and why am I not in ordinary decency apprised of their arrival?"

"Their purpose, madam," replied the Lady of Lochleven, "they must themselves explain—but a formal annunciation were needless, where your Grace hath attendants who can play the espial so well."

"Alas! poor Fleming," said the Queen, turning to the elder of the female attendants, "thou wilt be tried, condemned, and gibbeted, for a spy in the garrison, because thou didst chance to cross the great hall while my good Lady of Lochleven was parleying at the full pitch of her voice with her pilot Randal. Put black wool in thy ears, girl, as you value the wearing of them longer. Remember, in the Castle of Lochleven, ears and tongues are matters not of use, but for show merely. Our good hostess can hear, as well as speak, for us all. We excuse your farther attendance, my lady hostess," she said, once more addressing the object of her resentment, "and retire to prepare for an interview with our rebel lords. We will use the ante-chamber of our sleeping apartment as our hall of audience. You, young man," she proceeded, addressing Roland Graeme, and at once softening the ironical sharpness of her manner into good-humoured raillery, "you, who are all our male attendance, from our Lord High Chamberlain down to our least galopin, follow us to prepare our court."

She turned, and walked slowly towards the castle. The Lady of Lochleven folded her arms, and smiled in bitter resentment, as she watched her retiring steps.

"The whole male attendance!" she muttered, repeating the Queen's last words, "and well for thee had it been had thy train never been larger;" then turning to Roland, in whose way she had stood while making this pause, she made room for him to pass, saying at the same time, "Art thou already eaves-dropping? follow thy mistress, minion, and, if thou wilt, tell her what I have now said."

Roland Graeme hastened after his royal mistress and her attendants, who had just entered a postern-gate communicating betwixt the castle and the small garden. They ascended a winding-stair as high as the second story, which was in a great measure occupied by a suite of three rooms, opening into each other, and assigned as the dwelling of the captive Princess. The outermost was a small hall or ante-room, within which opened a large parlour, and from that again the Queen's bedroom. Another small apartment, which opened into the same parlour, contained the beds of the gentlewomen in waiting.

Roland Graeme stopped, as became his station, in the outermost of these apartments, there to await such orders as might be communicated to him. From the grated window of the room he saw Lindesay, Melville, and their followers disembark; and observed that they were met at the castle gate by a third noble, to whom Lindesay exclaimed, in his loud harsh voice, "My Lord of Ruthven, you have the start of us!"

At this instant, the page's attention was called to a burst of hysterical sobs from the inner apartment, and to the hurried ejaculations of the terrified females, which led him almost instantly to hasten to their assistance. When he entered, he saw that the Queen had thrown herself into the large chair which stood nearest the door, and was sobbing for breath in a strong fit of hysterical affection. The elder female supported her in her arms, while the younger bathed her face with water and with tears alternately.

"Hasten, young man!" said the elder lady, in alarm, "fly—call in assistance—she is swooning!"

But the Queen exclaimed in a faint and broken voice, "Stir not, I charge you!—call no one to witness—I am better—I shall recover instantly." And, indeed, with an effort which seemed like that of one struggling for life, she sate up in her chair, and endeavoured to resume her composure, while her features yet trembled with the violent emotion of body and mind which she had undergone. "I am ashamed of my weakness, girls," she said, taking the hands of her attendants; "but it is over—and I am Mary Stewart once more. The savage tone of that man's voice—my knowledge of his insolence—the name which he named—the purpose for which they come—may excuse a moment's weakness, and it shall be a moment's only." She snatched from her head the curch or cap, which had been disordered during her hysterical agony, shook down the thick clustered tresses of dark brown which had been before veiled under it—and, drawing her slender fingers across the labyrinth which they formed, she arose from the chair, and stood like the inspired image of a Grecian prophetess in a mood which partook at once of sorrow and pride, of smiles and of tears. "We are ill appointed," she said, "to meet our rebel subjects; but, as far as we may, we will strive to present ourselves as becomes their Queen. Follow me, my maidens," she said; "what says thy favourite song, my Fleming?

> 'My maids, come to my dressing-bower,
> And deck my nut-brown hair;
> Where'er ye laid a plait before,
> Look ye lay ten times 'mair.'

"Alas!" she added, when she had repeated with a smile these lines of an old ballad, "violence has already robbed me of the ordinary decorations of my rank; and the few that nature gave me have been destroyed by sorrow and by fear." Yet while she spoke thus, she again let her slender fingers stray through the wilderness of the beautiful tresses which veiled her kingly neck and swelling bosom, as if, in her agony of mind, she had not altogether lost the consciousness of her unrivalled charms. Roland Graeme, on whose youth, inexperience, and ardent sense of what was dignified and lovely, the demeanour of so fair and high-born a lady wrought like the charm of a magician, stood rooted to the spot with surprise and interest, longing to hazard his life in a quarrel so fair as that which Mary Stewart's must needs be. She had been bred in France—she was possessed of the most distinguished beauty—she had reigned a Queen and a Scottish Queen, to whom knowledge of character was as essential as the use of vital air. In all these capacities, Mary was, of all women on the earth, most alert at perceiving and using the advantages which her charms gave her over almost all who came within the sphere of their influence. She cast on Roland a glance which might have melted a heart of stone. "My poor boy," she said, with a feeling partly real, partly politic, "thou art a stranger to us—sent to this doleful captivity from the society of some tender mother, or sister, or maiden, with whom you had freedom to tread a gay measure round the Maypole. I grieve for you; but you are the only male in my limited household—wilt thou obey my orders?"

"To the death, madam," said Graeme, in a determined tone.

"Then keep the door of mine apartment," said the Queen; "keep it till they offer actual violence, or till we shall be fitly arrayed to receive these intrusive visiters."

"I will defend it till they pass over my body," said Roland Graeme; any hesitation which he had felt concerning the line of conduct he ought to pursue being completely swept away by the impulse of the moment.

"Not so, my good youth," answered Mary; "not so, I command. If I have one faithful subject beside me, much need, God wot, I have to care for his safety. Resist them but till they are put to the shame of using actual violence, and then give way, I charge you. Remember my commands." And, with a smile expressive at once of favour and of authority, she turned from him, and, followed by her attendants, entered the bedroom.

The youngest paused for half a second ere she followed her companion, and made a signal to Roland Graeme with her hand. He had been already long aware that this was Catherine Seyton—a circumstance which could not much surprise a youth of quick intellects, who recollected the sort of mysterious discourse which had passed betwixt the two matrons at the deserted nunnery, and on which his meeting with Catherine in this place seemed to cast so much light. Yet such was the engrossing effect of Mary's presence, that it surmounted for the moment even the feelings of a youthful lover; and it was not until

Catherine Seyton had disappeared, that Roland began to consider in what relation they were to stand to each other. "She held up her hand to me in a commanding manner," he thought; "perhaps she wanted to confirm my purpose for the execution of the Queen's commands; for I think she could scarce purpose to scare me with the sort of discipline which she administered to the groom in the frieze-jacket, and to poor Adam Woodcock. But we will see to that anon; meantime, let us do justice to the trust reposed in us by this unhappy Queen. I think my Lord of Murray will himself own that it is the duty of a faithful page to defend his lady against intrusion on her privacy."

Accordingly, he stepped to the little vestibule, made fast, with lock and bar, the door which opened from thence to the large staircase, and then sat himself down to attend the result. He had not long to wait—a rude and strong hand first essayed to lift the latch, then pushed and shook the door with violence, and, when it resisted his attempt to open it, exclaimed, "Undo the door there, you within!"

"Why, and at whose command," said the page, "am I to undo the door of the apartments of the Queen of Scotland?"

Another vain attempt, which made hinge and bolt jingle, showed that the impatient applicant without would willingly have entered altogether regardless of his challenge; but at length an answer was returned.

"Undo the door, on your peril—the Lord Lindesay comes to speak with the Lady Mary of Scotland."

"The Lord Lindesay, as a Scottish noble," answered the page, "must await his Sovereign's leisure."

An earnest altercation ensued amongst those without, in which Roland distinguished the remarkable harsh voice of Lindesay in reply to Sir Robert Melville, who appeared to have been using some soothing language—"No! no! no! I tell thee, no! I will place a petard against the door rather than be baulked by a profligate woman, and bearded by an insolent footboy."

"Yet, at least," said Melville, "let me try fair means in the first instance. Violence to a lady would stain your scutcheon for ever. Or await till my Lord Ruthven comes."

"I will await no longer," said Lindesay; "it is high time the business were done, and we on our return to the council. But thou mayest try thy fair play, as thou callest it, while I cause my train to prepare the petard. I came hither provided with as good gunpowder as blew up the Kirk of Field."

"For God's sake, be patient," said Melville; and, approaching the door, he said, as speaking to those within, "Let the Queen know, that I, her faithful servant, Robert Melville, do entreat her, for her own sake, and to prevent worse consequences, that she will undo the door, and admit Lord Lindesay, who brings a mission from the Council of State."

"I will do your errand to the Queen," said the page, "and report to you her answer."

He went to the door of the bedchamber, and tapping against it gently, it was opened by the elderly lady, to whom he communicated his errand, and returned with directions from the Queen to admit Sir Robert Melville and Lord Lindesay. Roland Graeme returned to the vestibule, and opened the door accordingly, into which the Lord Lindesay strode, with the air of a soldier who has fought his way into a conquered fortress; while Melville, deeply dejected, followed him more slowly.

"I draw you to witness, and to record," said the page to this last, "that, save for the especial commands of the Queen, I would have made good the entrance, with my best strength, and my best blood, against all Scotland."

"Be silent, young man," said Melville, in a tone of grave rebuke; "add not brands to fire—this is no time to make a flourish of thy boyish chivalry."

"She has not appeared even yet," said Lindesay, who had now reached the midst of the parlour or audience-room; "how call you this trifling?"

"Patience, my lord," replied Sir Robert, "time presses not—and Lord Ruthven hath not as yet descended."

At this moment the door of the inner apartment opened, and Queen Mary presented herself, advancing with an air of peculiar grace and majesty, and seeming totally unruffled, either by the visit, or by the rude manner in which it had been enforced. Her dress was a robe of black velvet; a small ruff, open in front, gave a full view of her beautifully formed chin and neck, but veiled the bosom. On her head she wore a small cap of lace, and a transparent white veil hung from her shoulders over the long black robe, in large loose folds, so that it could be drawn at pleasure over the face and person. She wore a cross of gold around her neck, and had her rosary of gold and ebony hanging from her girdle. She was closely followed by her two ladies, who remained standing behind her during the conference. Even Lord Lindesay, though the rudest noble of that rude age, was surprised into something like respect by the unconcerned and majestic mien of her, whom he had expected to find frantic with impotent passion, or dissolved in useless and vain sorrow, or overwhelmed with the fears likely in such a situation to assail fallen royalty.

"We fear we have detained you, my Lord of Lindesay," said the Queen, while she curtsied with dignity in answer to his reluctant obeisance; "but a female does not willingly receive her visiters without some minutes spent at the toilette. Men, my lord, are less dependant on such ceremonies."

Lord Lindesay, casting his eye down on his own travel-stained and disordered dress, muttered something of a hasty journey, and the Queen paid her greeting to Sir Robert Melville with courtesy, and even, as it seemed, with kindness. There was then a dead pause, during which Lindesay looked towards the door, as if expecting with impatience the colleague of their embassy. The Queen alone was entirely unembarrassed, and, as if to break the silence, she addressed Lord Lindesay, with a glance at the large and cumbrous sword which he wore, as already mentioned, hanging from his neck.

"You have there a trusty and a weighty travelling companion, my lord. I trust you expected to meet with no enemy here, against whom such a formidable weapon could be necessary? it is, methinks, somewhat a singular ornament for a court, though I am, as I well need to be, too much of a Stuart to fear a sword."

"It is not the first time, madam," replied Lindesay, bringing round the weapon so as to rest its point on the ground, and leaning one hand on the huge cross-handle, "it is not the first time that this weapon has intruded itself into the presence of the House of Stewart."

"Possibly, my lord," replied the Queen, "it may have done service to my ancestors—Your ancestors were men of loyalty"

"Ay, madam," replied he, "service it hath done; but such as kings love neither to acknowledge nor to reward. It was the service which the knife renders to the tree when trimming it to the quick, and depriving it of the superfluous growth of rank and unfruitful suckers, which rob it of nourishment."

"You talk riddles, my lord," said Mary; "I will hope the explanation carries nothing insulting with it."

"You shall judge, madam," answered Lindesay. "With this good sword was Archibald Douglas, Earl of Angus, girded on the memorable day when he acquired the name of Bell-the-Cat, for dragging from the presence of your great grandfather, the third James of the race, a crew of minions, flatterers, and favourites whom he hanged over the bridge of Lauder, as a warning to such reptiles how they approach a Scottish throne. With this same weapon, the same inflexible champion of Scottish honour and nobility slew at one blow Spens of Kilspindie, a courtier of your grandfather, James the fourth, who had dared to speak lightly of him in the royal presence. They fought near the brook of Fala; and Bell-the-Cat, with this blade, sheared through the thigh of his opponent, and lopped the limb as easily as a shepherd's boy slices a twig from a sapling."

"My lord," replied the Queen, reddening, "my nerves are too good to be alarmed even by this terrible history—May I ask how a blade so illustrious passed from the House of Douglas to that of Lindesay?—Methinks it should have been preserved as a consecrated relic, by a family who have held all that they could do against their king, to be done in favour of their country."

"Nay, madam," said Melville, anxiously interfering, "ask not that question of Lord Lindesay—And you, my lord, for shame—for decency—forbear to reply to it."

"It is time that this lady should hear the truth," replied Lindesay.

"And be assured," said the Queen, "that she will be moved to anger by none that you can tell her, my lord. There are cases in which just scorn has always the mastery over just anger."

"Then know," said Lindesay, "that upon the field of Carberry-hill, when that false and infamous traitor and murderer, James, sometime Earl of Bothwell, and nicknamed Duke of Orkney, offered to do personal battle with any of the associated nobles who came to drag him to justice, I accepted his challenge, and was by the noble Earl of Morton gifted with his good sword that I might therewith fight it out—Ah! so help me Heaven, had his presumption been one grain more, or his cowardice one grain less, I should have done such work with this good steel on his traitorous corpse, that the hounds and carrion-crows should have found their morsels daintily carved to their use !"

The Queen's courage well-nigh gave way at the mention of Bothwell's name—a name connected with such a train of guilt, shame, and disaster. But the prolonged boast of Lindesay gave her time to rally herself, and to answer with an appearance of cold contempt—"It is easy to slay an enemy who enters not the lists. But had Mary Stewart inherited her father's sword as well as his sceptre, the boldest of her rebels should not upon that day have complained that they had no one to cope withal. Your lordship will forgive me if I abridge this conference. A brief description of a bloody fight is long enough to satisfy a lady's curiosity; and unless my Lord of Lindesay has something more important to tell us than of the deeds which old Bell-the-Cat achieved, and how he would himself have emulated them, had time and tide permitted, we will retire to our private apartment, and you, Fleming, shall finish reading to us yonder little treatise *Des Rodomontades Espagnolles.*"

"Tarry, madam," said Lindesay, his complexion reddening in his turn, "I know your quick wit too well of old to have sought an interview that you might sharpen its edge at the expense of my honour. Lord Ruthven and myself, with Sir Robert Melville as a concurrent, come to your Grace on the part of the Secret Council, to tender to you what much concerns the safety of your own life and the welfare of the State."

"The Secret Council?" said the Queen; "by what powers can it subsist or act, while I, from whom it holds its character, am here detained under unjust restraint? But it matters not—what concerns the welfare of Scotland shall be acceptable to Mary Stewart, come from whatever quarter it will—and for what concerns her own life, she has lived long enough to be weary of it, even at the age of twenty-five.—Where is your colleague, my lord?—why tarries he?"

"He comes, madam," said Melville, and Lord Ruthven entered at the instant, holding in his hand a packet. As the Queen returned his salutation she became deadly pale, but instantly recovered herself by dint of strong and sudden resolution, just as the noble, whose appearance seemed to excite such emotions in her bosom, entered the apartment in company with George Douglas, the youngest son of the Knight of Lochleven, who, during the absence of his father and brethren, acted as Seneschal of the Castle, under the direction of the elder Lady Lochleven, his father's mother.

XXII

I give this heavy weight from off my head,
And this unwieldy sceptre from my hand;
With mine own tears I wash away my balm,
With mine own hand I give away my crown,
With mine own tongue deny my sacred state,
With mine own breath release all duteous oaths.

—RICHARD II

L ord Ruthven had the look and bearing which became a soldier and a statesman, and the martial cast of his form and features procured him the popular epithet of Greysteil, by which he was distinguished by his intimates, after the hero of a metrical romance then generally known. His dress, which was a buff-coat embroidered, had a half-military character, but exhibited nothing of the sordid negligence which distinguished that of Lindesay. But the son of an ill-fated sire, and the father of a yet more unfortunate family, bore in his look that cast of inauspicious melancholy, by which the physiognomists of that time pretended to distinguish those who were predestined to a violent and unhappy death.

The terror which the presence of this nobleman impressed on the Queen's mind, arose from the active share he had borne in the slaughter of David Rizzio; his father having presided at the perpetration of that abominable crime, although so weak from long and wasting illness, that he could not endure the weight of his armour, having arisen from a sick-bed to commit a murder in the presence of his Sovereign. On that occasion his son also had attended and taken an active part. It was little to be wondered at, that the Queen, considering her condition when such a deed of horror was acted in her presence, should retain an instinctive terror for the principal actors in the murder. She returned, however, with grace the salutation of Lord Ruthven, and extended her hand to George Douglas, who kneeled, and kissed it with respect; the first mark of a subject's homage which Roland Graeme had seen any of them render to the captive Sovereign. She returned his greeting in silence, and there was a brief pause, during which the steward of the castle, a man of a sad brow and a severe eye, placed, under George Douglas's

SIR WALTER SCOTT'S

directions, a table and writing materials; and the page, obedient to his mistress's dumb signal, advanced a large chair to the side on which the Queen stood, the table thus forming a sort of bar which divided the Queen and her personal followers from her unwelcome visitors. The steward then withdrew after a low reverence. When he had closed the door behind him, the Queen broke silence—"With your favour, my lords, I will sit—my walks are not indeed extensive enough at present to fatigue me greatly, yet I find repose something more necessary than usual."

She sat down accordingly, and, shading her cheek with her beautiful hand, looked keenly and impressively at each of the nobles in turn. Mary Fleming applied her kerchief to her eyes, and Catherine Seyton and Roland Graeme exchanged a glance, which showed that both were too deeply engrossed with sentiments of interest and commiseration for their royal mistress, to think of any thing which regarded themselves.

"I wait the purpose of your mission, my lords," said the Queen, after she had been seated for about a minute without a word-being spoken,— "I wait your message from those you call the Secret Council.-I trust it is a petition of pardon, and a desire that I will resume my rightful throne, without using with due severity my right of punishing those who have dispossessed me of it."

"Madam," replied Ruthven, "it is painful for us to speak harsh truths to a Princess who has long ruled us. But we come to offer, not to implore, pardon. In a word, madam, we have to propose to you on the part of the Secret Council, that you sign these deeds, which will contribute greatly to the pacification of the State, the advancement of God's word, and the welfare of your own future life."

"Am I expected to take these fair words on trust, my lord? or may I hear the contents of these reconciling papers, ere I am asked to sign them?"

"Unquestionably, madam; it is our purpose and wish, you should read what you are required to sign," replied Ruthven.

"Required?" replied the Queen, with some emphasis; "but the phrase suits well the matter-read, my lord."

The Lord Ruthven proceeded to read a formal instrument, running in the Queen's name, and setting forth that she had been called, at an early age, to the administration of the crown and realm of Scotland, and had toiled diligently therein, until she was in body and spirit so wearied out and disgusted, that she was unable any longer to endure the travail and pain of State affairs; and that since God had blessed her with a fair and hopeful son, she was desirous to ensure to him, even while she yet lived, his succession to the crown, which was his by right of hereditary descent. "Wherefore," the instrument proceeded, "we, of the motherly affection we bear to our said son, have renounced and demitted, and by these our letters of free good-will, renounce and demit, the Crown, government, and guiding of the realm of Scotland, in favour of our said son, that he may succeed to us as native Prince thereof, as much as if we had been removed by disease, and not by our own proper act. And that this demission of our royal authority may have the more full and solemn effect, and none pretend ignorance, we give, grant, and commit, fall and free and plain power to our trusty cousins, Lord Lindesay of the Byres, and William Lord Ruthven, to appear in our name before as many of the nobility, clergy, and burgesses, as may be assembled at Stirling, and there, in our name and behalf, publicly, and in their presence, to renounce the Crown, guidance, and government of this our kingdom of Scotland."

The Queen here broke in with an air of extreme surprise. "How is this, my lords?" she said: "Are my ears turned rebels, that they deceive me with sounds so extraordinary?—And yet it is no wonder that, having conversed so long with rebellion, they should now force its language upon my understanding. Say I am mistaken, my lords—say, for the honour of yourselves and the Scottish nobility, that my right trusty cousins of Lindesay and Ruthven, two barons of warlike fame and ancient line, have not sought the prison-house of their kind mistress for such a purpose as these words seem to imply. Say, for the sake of honour and loyalty, that my ears have deceived me."

"No, madam," said Ruthven gravely, "your ears do *not* deceive you— they deceived you when they were closed against the preachers of the evangele, and the honest advice of your faithful subjects; and when they were ever open to flattery of pickthanks and traitors, foreign cubiculars and domestic minions. The land may no longer brook the rule of one who cannot rule herself; wherefore, I pray you to comply with the last remaining wish of your subjects and counsellors, and spare yourself and us the farther agitation of matter so painful."

"And is this *all* my loving subjects require of me, my lord?" said Mary, in a tone of bitter irony. "Do they really stint themselves to the easy boon that I should yield up the crown, which is mine by birthright, to an infant which is scarcely more than a year old—fling down my sceptre, and take up a distaff—Oh no! it is too little for them to ask—That other roll of parchment contains something harder to be complied with, and which may more highly task my readiness to comply with the petitions of my lieges."

"This parchment," answered Ruthven, in the same tone of inflexible gravity, and unfolding the instrument as he spoke, "is one by which your grace constitutes your nearest in blood, and the most honourable and trustworthy of your subjects, James, Earl of Murray, Regent of the kingdom during the minority of the young King. He already holds the appointment from the Secret Council."

The Queen gave a sort of shriek, and, clapping her hands together, exclaimed, "Comes the arrow out of his quiver?—out of my brother's bow?—Alas! I looked for his return from France as my sole, at least my readiest, chance of deliverance.—And yet, when I heard he had assumed the government, I guessed he would shame to wield it in my name."

"I must pray your answer, madam," said Lord Ruthven, "to the demand of the Council."

"The demand of the Council!" said the Queen; "say rather the demand of a set of robbers, impatient to divide the spoil they have seized. To such a demand, and sent by the mouth of a traitor, whose scalp, but for my womanish mercy, should long since have stood on the city gates, Mary of Scotland has no answer."

"I trust, madam," said Lord Ruthven, "my being unacceptable to your presence will not add to your obduracy of resolution. It may become you to remember that the death of the minion, Rizzio, cost the house of Ruthven its head and leader. My father, more worthy than a whole province of such vile sycophants, died in exile, and broken-hearted."

The Queen clasped her hands on her face, and, resting her arms on the table, stooped down her head and wept so bitterly, that the tears were seen to find their way in streams between the white and slender fingers with which she endeavoured to conceal them.

"My lords," said Sir Robert Melville, "this is too much rigour. Under your lordship's favour, we came hither, not to revive old griefs, but to find the mode of avoiding new ones."

"Sir Robert Melville," said Ruthven, "we best know for what purpose we were delegated hither, and wherefore you were somewhat unnecessarily sent to attend us."

"Nay, by my hand," said Lord Lindesay, "I know not why we were cumbered with the good knight, unless he comes in place of the lump of sugar which pothicars put into their wholesome but bitter medicaments, to please a froward child—a needless labour, methinks, where men have the means to make them swallow the physic otherwise."

"Nay, my lords," said Melville, "ye best know your own secret instructions. I conceive I shall best obey mine in striving to mediate between her Grace and you."

"Be silent, Sir Robert Melville," said the Queen, arising, and her face still glowing with agitation as she spoke. "My kerchief, Fleming—I shame that traitors should have power to move me thus.—Tell me, proud lords," she added, wiping away the tears as she spoke, "by what earthly warrant can liege subjects pretend to challenge the rights of an anointed Sovereign—to throw off the allegiance they have vowed, and to take away the crown from the head on which Divine warrant hath placed it?"

"Madam," said Ruthven, "I will deal plainly with you. Your reign, from the dismal field of Pinkie-cleugh, when you were a babe in the cradle, till now that ye stand a grown dame before us, hath been such a tragedy of losses, disasters, civil dissensions, and foreign wars, that the like is not to be found in our chronicles. The French and English have, with one consent, made Scotland the battle-field on which to fight out their own ancient quarrel.—For ourselves every man's hand hath been against his brother, nor hath a year passed over without rebellion and slaughter, exile of nobles, and oppressing of the commons. We may endure it no longer, and therefore, as a prince, to whom God hath refused the gift of hearkening to wise counsel, and on whose dealings and projects no blessing hath ever descended, we pray you to give way to other rule and governance of the land, that a remnant may yet be saved to this distracted realm."

"My lord," said Mary, "it seems to me that you fling on my unhappy and devoted head those evils, which, with far more justice, I may impute to your own turbulent, wild, and untameable dispositions—the frantic violence with which you, the Magnates of Scotland, enter into feuds against each other, sticking at no cruelty to gratify your wrath, taking deep revenge for the slightest offences, and setting at defiance those wise laws which your ancestors made for stanching of such cruelty, rebelling against the lawful authority, and bearing yourselves as if there were no king in the land; or rather as if each were king in his own premises. And now you throw the blame on me—on me, whose life has

SIR WALTER SCOTT

been embittered—whose sleep has been broken—whose happiness has been wrecked by your dissensions. Have I not myself been obliged to traverse wilds and mountains, at the head of a few faithful followers, to maintain peace and put down oppression? Have I not worn harness on my person, and carried pistols at my saddle; fain to lay aside the softness of a woman, and the dignity of a Queen, that I might show an example to my followers?"

"We grant, madam," said Lindesay, "that the affrays occasioned by your misgovernment, may sometimes have startled you in the midst of a masque or galliard; or it may be that such may have interrupted the idolatry of the mass, or the jesuitical counsels of some French ambassador. But the longest and severest journey which your Grace has taken in my memory, was from Hawick to Hermitage Castle; and whether it was for the weal of the state, or for your own honour, rests with your Grace's conscience."

The Queen turned to him with inexpressible sweetness of tone and manner, and that engaging look which Heaven had assigned her, as if to show that the choicest arts to win men's affections may be given in vain. "Lindesay," she said, "you spoke not to me in this stern tone, and with such scurril taunt, yon fair summer evening, when you and I shot at the butts against the Earl of Mar and Mary Livingstone, and won of them the evening's collation, in the privy garden of Saint Andrews. The Master of Lindesay was then my friend, and vowed to be my soldier. How I have offended the Lord of Lindesay I know not, unless honours have changed manners."

Hardhearted as he was, Lindesay seemed struck with this unexpected appeal, but almost instantly replied, "Madam, it is well known that your Grace could in those days make fools of whomever approached you. I pretend not to have been wiser than others. But gayer men and better courtiers soon jostled aside my rude homage, and I think your Grace cannot but remember times, when my awkward attempts to take the manners that pleased you, were the sport of the court-popinjays, the Marys and the Frenchwomen."

"My lord, I grieve if I have offended you through idle gaiety," said the Queen; "and can but say it was most unwittingly done. You are fully revenged; for through gaiety," she said with a sigh, "will I never offend any one more."

"Our time is wasting, madam," said Lord Ruthven; "I must pray your decision on this weighty matter which I have submitted to you."

"What, my lord!" said the Queen, "upon the instant, and without a moment's time to deliberate?—Can the Council, as they term themselves, expect this of me?"

"Madam," replied Ruthven, "the Council hold the opinion, that since the fatal term which passed betwixt the night of King Henry's murder and the day of Carberry-hill, your Grace should have held you prepared for the measure now proposed, as the easiest escape from your numerous dangers and difficulties."

"Great God!" exclaimed the Queen; "and is it as a boon that you propose to me, what every Christian king ought to regard as a loss of honour equal to the loss of life!—You take from me my crown, my power, my subjects, my wealth, my state. What, in the name of every saint, can you offer, or do you offer, in requital of my compliance?"

"We give you pardon," answered Ruthven, sternly—"we give you space and means to spend your remaining life in penitence and seclusion—we give you time to make your peace with Heaven, and to receive the pure Gospel, which you have ever rejected and persecuted."

The Queen turned pale at the menace which this speech, as well as the rough and inflexible tones of the speaker, seemed distinctly to infer—"And if I do not comply with your request so fiercely urged, my lord, what then follows?"

She said this in a voice in which female and natural fear was contending with the feelings of insulted dignity.—There was a pause, as if no one cared to return to the question a distinct answer. At length Ruthven spoke: "There is little need to tell to your Grace, who are well read both in the laws and in the chronicles of the realm, that murder and adultery are crimes for which ere now queens themselves have suffered death."

"And where, my lord, or how, found you an accusation so horrible, against her who stands before you?" said Queen Mary. "The foul and odious calumnies which have poisoned the general mind of Scotland, and have placed me a helpless prisoner in your hands, are surely no proof of guilt?"

"We need look for no farther proof," replied the stern Lord Ruthven, "than the shameless marriage betwixt the widow of the murdered and the leader of the band of murderers!—They that joined hands in the fated month of May, had already united hearts and counsel in the deed which preceded that marriage but a few brief weeks."

"My lord, my lord!" said the Queen, eagerly, "remember well there were more consents than mine to that fatal union, that most unhappy act of a most unhappy life. The evil steps adopted by sovereigns are often the suggestion of bad counsellors; but these counsellors are worse than fiends who tempt and betray, if they themselves are the first to call their unfortunate princes to answer for the consequences of their own advice.—Heard ye never of a bond by the nobles, my lords, recommending that ill-fated union to the ill-fated Mary? Methinks, were it carefully examined, we should see that the names of Morton and of Lindesay, and of Ruthven, may be found in that bond, which pressed me to marry that unhappy man.—Ah! stout and loyal Lord Herries, who never knew guile or dishonour, you bent your noble knee to me in vain, to warn me of my danger, and wert yet the first to draw thy good sword in my cause when I suffered for neglecting thy counsel! Faithful knight and true noble, what a difference betwixt thee and those counsellors of evil, who now threaten my life for having fallen into the snares they spread for me!"

"Madam," said Ruthven, "we know that you are an orator; and perhaps for that reason the Council has sent hither men, whose converse hath been more with the wars, than with the language of the schools or the cabals of state. We but desire to know if, on assurance of life and honour, ye will demit the rule of this kingdom of Scotland?"

"And what warrant have I," said the Queen, "that ye will keep treaty with me, if I should barter my kingly estate for seclusion, and leave to weep in secret?"

"Our honour and our word, madam," answered Ruthven.

"They are too slight and unsolid pledges, my lord," said the Queen; "add at least a handful of thistle-down to give them weight in the balance."

"Away, Ruthven," said Lindesay; "she was ever deaf to counsel, save of slaves and sycophants; let her remain by her refusal, and abide by it!"

"Stay, my lord," said Sir Robert Melville, "or rather permit me to have but a few minutes' private audience with her Grace. If my presence with you could avail aught, it must be as a mediator—do not, I conjure you, leave the castle, or break off the conference, until I bring you word how her Grace shall finally stand disposed."

"We will remain in the hall," said Lindesay, "for half an hour's space; but in despising our words and our pledge of honour, she has touched the honour of my name—let her look herself to the course she has to pursue. If the half hour should pass away without her determining to comply with the demands of the nation, her career will be brief enough."

With little ceremony the two nobles left the apartment, traversed the vestibule, and descended the winding-stairs, the clash of Lindesay's huge sword being heard as it rang against each step in his descent. George Douglas followed them, after exchanging with Melville a gesture of surprise and sympathy.

As soon as they were gone, the Queen, giving way to grief, fear, and agitation, threw herself into the seat, wrung her hands, and seemed to abandon herself to despair. Her female attendants, weeping themselves, endeavoured yet to pray her to be composed, and Sir Robert Melville, kneeling at her feet, made the same entreaty. After giving way to a passionate burst of sorrow, she at length said to Melville, "Kneel not to me, Melville—mock me not with the homage of the person, when the heart is far away—Why stay you behind with the deposed, the condemned? her who has but few hours perchance to live? You have been favoured as well as the rest; why do you continue the empty show of gratitude and thankfulness any longer than they?"

"Madam," said Sir Robert Melville, "so help me Heaven at my need, my heart is as true to you as when you were in your highest place."

"True to me! true to me!" repeated the Queen, with some scorn; "tush, Melville, what signifies the truth which walks hand in hand with my enemies' falsehood?—thy hand and thy sword have never been so well acquainted that I can trust thee in aught where manhood is required—Oh, Seyton, for thy bold father, who is both wise, true, and valiant!"

Roland Graeme could withstand no longer his earnest desire to offer his services to a princess so distressed and so beautiful. "If one sword," he said, "madam, can do any thing to back the wisdom of this grave counsellor, or to defend your rightful cause, here is my weapon, and here is my hand ready to draw and use it." And raising his sword with one hand, he laid the other upon the hilt.

As he thus held up the weapon, Catherine Seyton exclaimed, "Methinks I see a token from my father, madam;" and immediately crossing the apartment, she took Roland Graeme by the skirt of the cloak, and asked him earnestly whence he had that sword.

The page answered with surprise, "Methinks this is no presence in which to jest—Surely, damsel, you yourself best know whence and how I obtained the weapon."

"Is this a time for folly?" said Catherine Seyton; "unsheathe the sword instantly!"

"If the Queen commands me," said the youth, looking towards his royal mistress.

SIR WALTER SCOTT

"For shame, maiden!" said the Queen; "wouldst thou instigate the poor boy to enter into useless strife with the two most approved soldiers in Scotland?"

"In your Grace's cause," replied the page, "I will venture my life upon them!" And as he spoke, he drew his weapon partly from the sheath, and a piece of parchment, rolled around the blade, fell out and dropped on the floor. Catherine Seyton caught it up with eager haste.

"It is my father's hand-writing," she said, "and doubtless conveys his best duteous advice to your Majesty; I know that it was prepared to be sent in this weapon, but I expected another messenger."

"By my faith, fair one," thought Roland, "and if you knew not that I had such a secret missive about me, I was yet more ignorant."

The Queen cast her eye upon the scroll, and remained a few minutes wrapped in deep thought. "Sir Robert Melville," she at length said, "this scroll advises me to submit myself to necessity, and to subscribe the deeds these hard men have brought with them, as one who gives way to the natural fear inspired by the threats of rebels and murderers. You, Sir Robert, are a wise man, and Seyton is both sagacious and brave. Neither, I think, would mislead me in this matter."

"Madam," said Melville, "if I have not the strength of body of the Lord Herries or Seyton, I will yield to neither in zeal for your Majesty's service. I cannot fight for you like these lords, but neither of them is more willing to die for your service."

"I believe it, my old and faithful counsellor," said the Queen, "and believe me, Melville, I did thee but a moment's injustice. Read what my Lord Seyton hath written to us, and give us thy best counsel."

He glanced over the parchment, and instantly replied,—"Oh! my dear and royal mistress, only treason itself could give you other advice than Lord Seyton has here expressed. He, Herries, Huntly, the English ambassador Throgmorton, and others, your friends, are all alike of opinion, that whatever deeds or instruments you execute within these walls, must lose all force and effect, as extorted from your Grace by duresse, by sufferance of present evil, and fear of men, and harm to ensue on your refusal. Yield, therefore, to the tide, and be assured, that in subscribing what parchments they present to you, you bind yourself to nothing, since your act of signature wants that which alone can make it valid, the free will of the granter."

"Ay, so says my Lord Seyton," replied Mary; "yet methinks, for the daughter of so long a line of sovereigns to resign her birthright, because rebels press upon her with threats, argues little of royalty, and will read ill for the fame of Mary in future chronicles. Tush! Sir Robert Melville, the traitors may use black threats and bold words, but they will not dare to put their hands forth on our person."

"Alas! madam, they have already dared so far and incurred such peril by the lengths which they have gone, that they are but one step from the worst and uttermost."

"Surely," said the Queen, her fears again predominating, "Scottish nobles would not lend themselves to assassinate a helpless woman?"

"Bethink you, madam," he replied, "what horrid spectacles have been seen in our day; and what act is so dark, that some Scottish hand has not been found to dare it? Lord Lindesay, besides his natural sullenness and hardness of temper, is the near kinsman of Henry Darnley, and Ruthven has his own deep and dangerous plans. The Council, besides, speak of proofs by writ and word, of a casket with letters—of I know not what."

"Ah! good Melville," answered the Queen, "were I as sure of the even-handed integrity of my judges, as of my own innocence—and yet—"

"Oh! pause, madam," said Melville; "even innocence must sometimes for a season stoop to injurious blame. Besides, you are here—"

He looked round, and paused.

"Speak out, Melville," said the Queen, "never one approached my person who wished to work me evil; and even this poor page, whom I have to-day seen for the first time in my life, I can trust safely with your communication."

"Nay, madam," answered Melville, "in such emergence, and he being the bearer of Lord Seyton's message, I will venture to say, before him and these fair ladies, whose truth and fidelity I dispute not—I say I will venture to say, that there are other modes besides that of open trial, by which deposed sovereigns often die; and that, as Machiavel saith, there is but one step betwixt a king's prison and his grave."

"Oh I were it but swift and easy for the body," said the unfortunate Princess, "were it but a safe and happy change for the soul, the woman lives not that would take the step so soon as I—But, alas! Melville, when we think of death, a thousand sins, which we have trod as worms beneath our feet, rise up against us as flaming serpents. Most injuriously do they accuse me of aiding Darnley's death; yet, blessed Lady! I afforded too open occasion for the suspicion—I espoused Bothwell."

"Think not of that now, madam," said Melville, "think rather of the immediate mode of saving yourself and son. Comply with the present unreasonable demands, and trust that better times will shortly arrive."

"Madam," said Roland Graeme, "if it pleases you that I should do so, I will presently swim through the lake, if they refuse me other conveyance to the shore; I will go to the courts successively of England, France, and Spain, and will show you have subscribed these vile instruments from no stronger impulse than the fear of death, and I will do battle against them that say otherwise."

The Queen turned her round, and with one of those sweet smiles which, during the era of life's romance, overpay every risk, held her hand towards Roland, but without "speaking a word. He kneeled reverently, and kissed it, and Melville again resumed his plea.

"Madam," he said, "time presses, and you must not let those boats, which I see they are even now preparing, put forth on the lake. Here are enough of witnesses—your ladies—this bold youth—myself, when it can serve your cause effectually, for I would not hastily stand committed in this matter—but even without me here is evidence enough to show, that you have yielded to the demands of the Council through force and fear, but from no sincere and unconstrained assent. Their boats are already manned for their return—oh! permit your old servant to recall them."

"Melville," said the Queen, "thou art an ancient courtier—when didst thou ever know a Sovereign Prince recall to his presence subjects who had parted from him on such terms as those on which these envoys of the Council left us, and who yet were recalled without submission or apology?—Let it cost me both life and crown, I will not again command them to my presence."

"Alas! madam, that empty form should make a barrier! If I rightly understand, you are not unwilling to listen to real and advantageous counsel—but your scruple is saved—I hear them returning to ask your final resolution. Oh! take the advice of the noble Seyton, and you may once more command those who now usurp a triumph over you. But hush! I hear them in the vestibule."

As he concluded speaking, George Douglas opened the door of the apartment, and marshalled in the two noble envoys.

"We come, madam," said the Lord Ruthven, "to request your answer to the proposal of the Council."

"Your final answer," said Lord Lindesay; "for with a refusal you must couple the certainty that you have precipitated your fate, and renounced the last opportunity of making peace with God, and ensuring your longer abode in the world."

"My lords," said Mary, with inexpressible grace and dignity, "the evils we cannot resist we must submit to—I will subscribe these parchments with such liberty of choice as my condition permits me. Were I on yonder shore, with a fleet jennet and ten good and loyal knights around me, I would subscribe my sentence of eternal condemnation as soon as the resignation of my throne. But here, in the Castle of Lochleven, with deep water around me—and you, my lords, beside me,—I have no freedom of choice.—Give me the pen, Melville, and bear witness to what I do, and why I do it."

"It is our hope your Grace will not suppose yourself compelled by any apprehensions from us," said the Lord Ruthven, "to execute what must be your own voluntary deed."

The Queen had already stooped towards the table, and placed the parchment before her, with the pen between her fingers, ready for the important act of signature. But when Lord Ruthven had done speaking, she looked up, stopped short, and threw down the pen. "If," she said, "I am expected to declare I give away my crown of free will, or otherwise than because I am compelled to renounce it by the threat of worse evils to myself and my subjects, I will not put my name to such an untruth—not to gain full possession of England, France, and Scotland!—all once my own, in possession, or by right."

"Beware, madam," said Lindesay, and, snatching hold of the Queen's arm with his own gauntleted hand, he pressed it, in the rudeness of his passion, more closely, perhaps, than he was himself aware of,—"beware how you contend with those who are the stronger, and have the mastery of your fate!"

He held his grasp on her arm, bending his eyes on her with a stern and intimidating look, till both Ruthven and Melville cried shame; and Douglas, who had hitherto remained in a state of apparent apathy, had made a stride from the door, as if to interfere. The rude Baron then quitted his hold, disguising the confusion which he really felt at having indulged his passion to such extent, under a sullen and contemptuous smile.

The Queen immediately began, with an expression of pain, to bare the arm which he had grasped, by drawing up the sleeve of her gown,

SIR WALTER SCOTT

and it appeared that his gripe had left the purple marks of his iron fingers upon her flesh—"My lord," she said, "as a knight and gentleman, you might have spared my frail arm so severe a proof that you have the greater strength on your side, and are resolved to use it—But I thank you for it—it is the most decisive token of the terms on which this day's business is to rest.—I draw you to witness, both lords and ladies," she said, showing the marks of the grasp on her arm, "that I subscribe these instruments in obedience to the sign manual of my Lord of Lindsay, which you may see imprinted on mine arm."*

Lindesay would have spoken, but was restrained by his colleague Ruthven, who said to him, "Peace, my lord. Let the Lady Mary of Scotland ascribe her signature to what she will, it is our business to procure it, and carry it to the Council. Should there be debate hereafter on the manner in which it was adhibited, there will be time enough for it."

Lindesay was silent accordingly, only muttering within his beard, "I meant not to hurt her; but I think women's flesh be as tender as new-fallen snow."

---

* The details of this remarkable event are, as given in the preceding chapter, imaginary; but the outline of the events is historical. Sir Robert Lindesay, brother to the author of the Memoirs, was at first intrusted with the delicate commission of persuading the imprisoned queen to resign her crown. As he flatly refused to interfere, they determined to send the Lord Lindesay, one of the rudest and most violent of their own faction, with instructions, first to use fair persuasions, and if these did not succeed, to enter into harder terms. Knox associates Lord Ruthven with Lindesay in this alarming commission. He was the son of that Lord Ruthven who was prime agent in the murder of Rizzio; and little mercy was to be expected from his conjunction with Lindesay.

The employment of such rude tools argued a resolution on the part of those who had the Queen's person in their power, to proceed to the utmost extremities, should they find Mary obstinate. To avoid this pressing danger, Sir Robert Melville was despatched by them to Lochleven, carrying with him, concealed in the scabbard of his sword, letters to the Queen from the Earl of Athole, Maitland of Lethington, and even from Throgmorton, the English Ambassador, who was then favourable to the unfortunate Mary, conjuring her to yield to the necessity of the times, and to subscribe such deeds as Lindesay should lay before her, without being startled by their tenor; and assuring her that her doing so, in the state of captivity under which she was placed, would neither, in law, honour, nor conscience, be binding upon her when she should obtain her liberty. Submitting by the advice of one part of her subjects to the menace of the others, and learning that Lindesay was arrived in a boasting, that is, threatening humour, the Queen, "with some reluctancy, and with tears," saith Knox, subscribed one deed resigning her crown to her infant son, and another establishing the Earl of Murray regent. It seems agreed by historians that Lindesay behaved with great brutality on the occasion. The deeds were signed 24th July, 1567.

The Queen meanwhile subscribed the rolls of parchment with a hasty indifference, as if they had been matters of slight consequence, or of mere formality. When she had performed this painful task, she arose, and, having curtsied to the lords, was about to withdraw to her chamber. Ruthven and Sir Robert Melville made, the first a formal reverence, the second an obeisance, in which his desire to acknowledge his sympathy was obviously checked by the fear of appearing in the eyes of his colleagues too partial to his former mistress. But Lindesay stood motionless, even when they were preparing to withdraw. At length, as if moved by a sudden impulse, he walked round the table which had hitherto been betwixt them and the Queen, kneeled on one knee, took her hand, kissed it, let it fall, and arose—"Lady," he said, "thou art a noble creature, even though thou hast abused God's choicest gifts. I pay that devotion to thy manliness of spirit, which I would not have paid to the power thou hast long undeservedly wielded—I kneel to Mary Stewart, not to the Queen."

"The Queen and Mary Stewart pity thee alike, Lindesay," said Mary—"alike thee pity, and they forgive thee. An honoured soldier hadst thou been by a king's side—leagued with rebels, what art thou but a good blade in the hands of a ruffian?—Farewell, my Lord Ruthven, the smoother but the deeper traitor.—Farewell, Melville—Mayest thou find masters that can understand state policy better, and have the means to reward it more richly, than Mary Stewart.—Farewell, George of Douglas—make your respected grand-dame comprehend that we would be alone for the remainder of the day—God wot, we have need to collect our thoughts."

All bowed and withdrew; but scarce had they entered the vestibule, ere Ruthven and Lindesay were at variance. "Chide not with me, Ruthven," Lindesay was heard to say, in answer to something more indistinctly urged by his colleague—"Chide not with me, for I will not brook it! You put the hangman's office on me in this matter, and even the very hangman hath leave to ask some pardon of those on whom he does his office. I would I had as deep cause to be this lady's friend as I have to be her enemy—thou shouldst see if I spared limb and life in her quarrel."

"Thou art a sweet minion," said Ruthven, "to fight a lady's quarrel, and all for a brent brow and a tear in the eye! Such toys have been out of thy thoughts this many a year."

"Do me right, Ruthven," said Lindesay. "You are like a polished corslet of steel; it shines more gaudily, but it is not a whit softer—nay, it is five times harder than a Glasgow breastplate of hammered iron. Enough. We know each other."

They descended the stairs, were heard to summon their boats, and the Queen signed to Roland Graeme to retire to the vestibule, and leave her with her female attendants.

XXIII

Give me a morsel on the greensward rather,
Coarse as you will the cooking—Let the fresh spring
Bubble beside my napkin—and the free birds
Twittering and chirping, hop from bough to bough,
To claim the crumbs I leave for perquisites—
Your prison feasts I like not.

—THE WOODSMAN, A DRAMA

A recess in the vestibule was enlightened by a small window, at which Roland Graeme stationed himself to mark the departure of the lords. He could see their followers mustering on horseback under their respective banners—the western sun glancing on their corslets and steel-caps as they moved to and fro, mounted or dismounted, at intervals. On the narrow space betwixt the castle and the water, the Lords Ruthven and Lindesay were already moving slowly to their boats, accompanied by the Lady of Lochleven, her grandson, and their principal attendants. They took a ceremonious leave of each other, as Roland could discern by their gestures, and the boats put oft from their landing-place; the boatmen stretched to their oars, and they speedily diminished upon the eye of the idle gazer, who had no better employment than to watch their motions. Such seemed also the occupation of the Lady Lochleven and George Douglas, who, returning from the landing-place, looked frequently back to the boats, and at length stopped as if to observe their progress under the window at which Roland Graeme was stationed.— As they gazed on the lake, he could hear the lady distinctly say, "And she has bent her mind to save her life at the expense of her kingdom?"

"Her life, madam!" replied her son; "I know not who would dare to attempt it in the castle of my father. Had I dreamt that it was with such purpose that Lindesay insisted on bringing his followers hither, neither he nor they should have passed the iron gate of Lochleven castle."

"I speak not of private slaughter, my son, but of open trial, condemnation, and execution; for with such she has been threatened, and to such threats she has given way. Had she not more of the false Gusian blood than of the royal race of Scotland in her veins, she had bidden them defiance to their teeth—But it is all of the same complexion, and meanness is

SIR WALTER SCOTT

the natural companion of profligacy.—I am discharged, forsooth, from intruding on her gracious presence this evening. Go thou, my son, and render the usual service of the meal to this unqueened Queen."

"So please you, lady mother," said Douglas, "I care not greatly to approach her presence."

"Thou art right, my son; and therefore I trust thy prudence, even because I have noted thy caution. She is like an isle on the ocean, surrounded with shelves and quicksands; its verdure fair and inviting to the eye, but the wreck of many a goodly vessel which hath approached it too rashly. But for thee, my son, I fear nought; and we may not, with our honour, suffer her to eat without the attendance of one of us. She may die by the judgment of Heaven, or the fiend may have power over her in her despair; and then we would be touched in honour to show that in our house, and at our table, she had had all fair play and fitting usage."

Here Roland was interrupted by a smart tap on the shoulders, reminding him sharply of Adam Woodcock's adventure of the preceding evening. He turned round, almost expecting to see the page of Saint Michael's hostelry. He saw, indeed, Catherine Seyton; but she was in female attire, differing, no doubt, a great deal in shape and materials from that which she had worn when they first met, and becoming her birth as the daughter of a great baron, and her rank as the attendant on a princess. "So, fair page," said she, "eaves-dropping is one of your page-like qualities, I presume."

"Fair sister," answered Roland, in the same tone, "if some friends of mine be as well acquainted with the rest of our mystery as they are with the arts of swearing, swaggering, and switching, they need ask no page in Christendom for farther insight into his vocation."

"Unless that pretty speech infer that you have yourself had the discipline of the switch since we last met, the probability whereof I nothing doubt, I profess, fair page, I am at a loss to conjecture your meaning. But there is no time to debate it now—they come with the evening meal. Be pleased, Sir Page, to do your duty."

Four servants entered bearing dishes, preceded by the same stern old steward whom Roland had already seen, and followed by George Douglas, already mentioned as the grandson of the Lady of Lochleven, and who, acting as seneschal, represented, upon this occasion, his father, the Lord of the Castle. He entered with his arms folded on his bosom, and his looks bent on the ground. With the assistance of Roland Graeme, a table was suitably covered in the next or middle apartment, on which the domestics placed their burdens with great reverence, the steward and Douglas bending low when they had seen the table properly adorned, as if their royal prisoner had sat at the board in question. The door opened, and Douglas, raising his eyes hastily, cast them again on the earth, when he perceived it was only the Lady Mary Fleming who entered.

"Her Grace," she said, "will not eat to-night."

"Let us hope she may be otherwise persuaded," said Douglas; "meanwhile, madam, please to see our duty performed."

A servant presented bread and salt on a silver plate, and the old steward carved for Douglas a small morsel in succession from each of the dishes presented, which he tasted, as was then the custom at the tables of princes, to which death was often suspected to find its way in the disguise of food.

"The Queen will not then come forth to-night?" said Douglas.

"She has so determined," replied the lady.

"Our farther attendance then is unnecessary—we leave you to your supper, fair ladies, and wish you good even."

He retired slowly as he came, and with the same air of deep dejection, and was followed by the attendants belonging to the castle. The two ladies sate down to their meal, and Roland Graeme, with ready alacrity, prepared to wait upon them. Catherine Seyton whispered to her companion, who replied with the question spoken in a low tone, but looking at the page—"Is he of gentle blood and well nurtured?"

The answer which she received seemed satisfactory, for she said to Roland, "Sit down, young gentleman, and eat with your sisters in captivity."

"Permit me rather to perform my duty in attending them," said Roland, anxious to show he was possessed of the high tone of deference prescribed by the rules of chivalry towards the fair sex, and especially to dames and maidens of quality.

"You will find, Sir Page," said Catherine, "you will have little time allowed you for your meal; waste it not in ceremony, or you may rue your politeness ere to-morrow morning."

"Your speech is too free, maiden," said the elder lady; "the modesty of the youth may teach you more fitting fashions towards one whom to-day you have seen for the first time."

Catherine Seyton cast down her eyes, but not till she had given a single glance of inexpressible archness towards Roland, whom her more grave companion now addressed in a tone of protection.

"Regard her not, young gentleman—she knows little of the world, save the forms of a country nunnery—take thy place at the board-end, and refresh thyself after thy journey."

Roland Graeme obeyed willingly, as it was the first food he had that day tasted; for Lindesay and his followers seemed regardless of human wants. Yet, notwithstanding the sharpness of his appetite, a natural gallantry of disposition, the desire of showing himself a well-nurtured gentleman, in all courtesies towards the fair sex, and, for aught I know, the pleasure of assisting Catherine Seyton, kept his attention awake, during the meal, to all those nameless acts of duty and service which gallants of that age were accustomed to render. He carved with neatness and decorum, and selected duly whatever was most delicate to place before the ladies. Ere they could form a wish, he sprung from the table, ready to comply with it—poured wine—tempered it with water—removed the exchanged trenchers, and performed the whole honours of the table, with an air at once of cheerful diligence, profound respect, and graceful promptitude.

When he observed that they had finished eating, he hastened to offer to the elder lady the silver ewer, basin, and napkin, with the ceremony and gravity which he would have used towards Mary herself. He next, with the same decorum, having supplied the basin with fair water, presented it to Catherine Seyton. Apparently, she was determined to disturb his self-possession, if possible; for, while in the act of bathing her hands, she contrived, as it were by accident, to flirt some drops of water upon the face of the assiduous assistant. But if such was her mischievous purpose she was completely disappointed; for Roland Graeme, internally piquing himself on his self-command, neither laughed nor was discomposed; and all that the maiden gained by her frolic was a severe rebuke from her companion, taxing her with mal-address and indecorum. Catherine replied not, but sat pouting, something in the humour of a spoilt child, who watches the opportunity of wreaking upon some one or other its resentment for a deserved reprimand.

The Lady Mary Fleming, in the mean-while, was naturally well pleased with the exact and reverent observance of the page, and said to Catherine, after a favourable glance at Roland Graeme,—"You might well say, Catherine, our companion in captivity was well born and gentle nurtured. I would not make him vain by my praise, but his services enable us to dispense with those which George Douglas condescends not to afford us, save when the Queen is herself in presence."

"Umph! I think hardly," answered Catherine. "George Douglas is one of the most handsome gallants in Scotland, and 'tis pleasure to see him even still, when the gloom of Lochleven Castle has shed the same melancholy over him, that it has done over every thing else. When he was at Holyrood who would have said the young sprightly George Douglas would have been contented to play the locksman here in Lochleven, with no gayer amusement than that of turning the key on two or three helpless women?—a strange office for a Knight of the Bleeding Heart—why does he not leave it to his father or his brothers?"

"Perhaps, like us, he has no choice," answered the Lady Fleming. "But, Catherine, thou hast used thy brief space at court well, to remember what George Douglas was then."

"I used mine eyes, which I suppose was what I was designed to do, and they were worth using there. When I was at the nunnery, they were very useless appurtenances; and now I am at Lochleven, they are good for nothing, save to look over that eternal work of embroidery."

"You speak thus, when you have been but a few brief hours amongst us—was this the maiden who would live and die in a dungeon, might she but have permission to wait on her gracious Queen?"

"Nay, if you chide in earnest, my jest is ended," said Catherine Seyton. "I would not yield in attachment to my poor god-mother, to the gravest dame that ever had wise saws upon her tongue, and a double-starched ruff around her throat—you know I would not, Dame Mary Fleming, and it is putting shame on me to say otherwise."

"She will challenge the other court lady," thought Roland Graeme; "she will to a certainty fling down her glove, and if Dame Mary Fleming hath but the soul to lift it, we may have a combat in the lists!"—but the answer of Lady Mary Fleming was such as turns away wrath.

"Thou art a good child," she said, "my Catherine, and a faithful; but Heaven pity him who shall have one day a creature so beautiful to delight him, and a thing so mischievous to torment him—thou art fit to drive twenty husbands stark mad."

"Nay," said Catherine, resuming the full career of her careless good-humour, "he must be half-witted beforehand, that gives me such an opportunity. But I am glad you are not angry with me in sincerity," casting herself as she spoke into the arms of her friend, and continuing, with a tone of apologetic fondness, while she kissed her on either side of the face; "you know, my dear Fleming, that I have to contend with both my father's lofty pride, and with my mother's high spirit—God bless them! they have left me these good qualities, having small portion to give besides, as times go—and so I am wilful and saucy; but let me remain only a week in this castle, and oh, my dear Fleming, my spirit will be as chastised and humble as thine own."

Dame Mary Fleming's sense of dignity, and love of form, could not resist this affectionate appeal. She kissed Catherine Seyton in her turn affectionately; while, answering the last part of her speech, she said, "Now Our Lady forbid, dear Catherine, that you should lose aught that is beseeming of what becomes so well your light heart and lively humour. Keep but your sharp wit on this side of madness, and it cannot but be a blessing to us. But let me go, mad wench—I hear her Grace touch her silver call." And, extricating herself from Catherine's grasp, she went towards the door of Queen Mary's apartment, from which was heard the low tone of a silver whistle, which, now only used by the boatswains in the navy, was then, for want of bells, the ordinary mode by which ladies, even of the very highest rank, summoned their domestics. When she had made two or three steps towards the door, however, she turned back, and advancing to the young couple whom she left together, she said, in a very serious though a low tone, "I trust it is impossible that we can, any of us, or in any circumstances, forget, that, few as we are, we form the household of the Queen of Scotland; and that, in her calamity, all boyish mirth and childish jesting can only serve to give a great triumph to her enemies, who have already found their account in objecting to her the lightness of every idle folly, that the young and the gay practised in her court." So saying, she left the apartment.

Catherine Seyton seemed much struck with this remonstrance— She suffered herself to drop into the seat which she had quitted when she went to embrace Dame Mary Fleming, and for some time rested her brow upon her hands; while Roland Graeme looked at her earnestly, with a mixture of emotions which perhaps he himself could neither have analysed nor explained. As she raised her face slowly from the posture to which a momentary feeling of self-rebuke had depressed it, her eyes encountered those of Roland, and became gradually animated with their usual spirit of malicious drollery, which not unnaturally excited a similar expression in those of the equally volatile page. They sat for the space of two minutes, each looking at the other with great seriousness on their features, and much mirth in their eyes, until at length Catherine was the first to break silence.

"May I pray you, fair sir," she began, very demurely, "to tell me what you see in my face to arouse looks so extremely sagacious and knowing as those with which it is your worship's pleasure to honour me? It would seem as if there were some wonderful confidence and intimacy betwixt us, fair sir, if one is to judge from your extremely cunning looks; and so help me, Our Lady, as I never saw you but twice in my life before."

"And where were those happy occasions," said Roland, "if I may be bold enough to ask the question?"

"At the nunnery of St. Catherine's," said the damsel, "in the first instance; and, in the second, during five minutes of a certain raid or foray which it was your pleasure to make into the lodging of my lord and father, Lord Seyton, from which, to my surprise, as probably to your own, you returned with a token of friendship and favour, instead of broken bones, which were the more probable reward of your intrusion, considering the prompt ire of the house of Seyton. I am deeply mortified," she added, ironically, "that your recollection should require refreshment on a subject so important; and that my memory should be stronger than yours on such an occasion, is truly humiliating."

"Your own, memory is not so exactly correct, fair mistress," answered the page, "seeing you have forgotten meeting the third, in the hostelrie of St. Michael's, when it pleased you to lay your switch across the face of my comrade, in order, I warrant, to show that, in the house of Seyton, neither the prompt ire of its descendants, nor the use of the doublet and hose, are subject to Salique law, or confined to the use of the males."

"Fair sir," answered Catherine, looking at him with great steadiness, and some surprise, "unless your fair wits have forsaken you, I am at a loss what to conjecture of your meaning."

"By my troth, fair mistress," answered Roland, "and were I as wise a warlock as Michael Scott, I could scarce riddle the dream you read me. Did I not see you last night in the hostelrie of St. Michael's?—Did you not bring me this sword, with command not to draw it save at the command of my native and rightful Sovereign? And have I not done as you required me? Or is the sword a piece of lath—my word a bulrush— my memory a dream—and my eyes good for nought—espials which corbies might pick out of my head?"

"And if your eyes serve you not more truly on other occasions than in your vision of St. Michael," said Catherine, "I know not, the pain apart, that the corbies would do you any great injury in the deprivation—But hark, the bell—hush, for God's sake, we are interrupted.—"

The damsel was right; for no sooner had the dull toll of the castle bell begun to resound through the vaulted apartment, than the door of the vestibule flew open, and the steward, with his severe countenance, his gold chain, and his white rod, entered the apartment, followed by the same train of domestics who had placed the dinner on the table, and who now, with the same ceremonious formality, began to remove it.

The steward remained motionless as some old picture, while the domestics did their office; and when it was accomplished, every thing removed from the table, and the board itself taken from its tressels and disposed against the wall, he said aloud, without addressing any one in particular, and somewhat in the tone of a herald reading a proclamation, "My noble lady, Dame Margaret Erskine, by marriage Douglas, lets the Lady Mary of Scotland and her attendants to wit, that a servant of the true evangele, her reverend chaplain, will to-night, as usual, expound, lecture, and catechise, according to the forms of the congregation of gospellers."

"Hark you, my friend, Mr. Dryfesdale," said Catherine, "I understand this announcement is a nightly form of yours. Now, I pray you to remark, that the Lady Fleming and I—for I trust your insolent invitation concerns us only—have chosen Saint Peter's pathway to Heaven, so I see no one whom your godly exhortation, catechise, or lecture, can benefit, excepting this poor page, who, being in Satan's hand as well as yourself, had better worship with you than remain to cumber our better-advised devotions."

The page was well-nigh giving a round denial to the assertions which this speech implied, when, remembering what had passed betwixt him and the Regent, and seeing Catherine's finger raised in a monitory fashion, he felt himself, as on former occasions at the Castle of Avenel, obliged to submit to the task of dissimulation, and followed Dryfesdale down to the castle chapel, where he assisted in the devotions of the evening.

The chaplain was named Elias Henderson. He was a man in the prime of life, and possessed of good natural parts, carefully improved by the best education which those times afforded. To these qualities were added a faculty of close and terse reasoning; and, at intervals, a flow of happy illustration and natural eloquence. The religious faith of Roland Graeme, as we have already had opportunity to observe, rested on no secure basis, but was entertained rather in obedience to his grandmother's behests, and his secret desire to contradict the chaplain of Avenel Castle, than from any fixed or steady reliance which he placed on the Romish creed. His ideas had been of late considerably enlarged by the scenes he had passed through; and feeling that there was shame in not understanding something of those political disputes betwixt the professors of the ancient and the reformed faith, he listened with more attention than it had hitherto been in his nature to yield on such occasions, to an animated discussion of some of the principal points of difference betwixt the churches. So passed away the first day in the Castle of Lochleven; and those which followed it were, for some time, of a very monotonous and uniform tenor.

XXIV

'Tis a weary life this—
Vaults overhead, and grates and bars around me,
And my sad hours spent with as sad companions,
Whose thoughts are brooding: o'er their own mischances,
Far, far too deeply to take part in mine.

—THE WOODSMAN

The course of life to which Mary and her little retinue were doomed, was in the last degree secluded and lonely, varied only as the weather permitted or rendered impossible the Queen's usual walk in the garden or on the battlements. The greater part of the morning she wrought with her ladies at those pieces of needlework, many of which still remain proofs of her indefatigable application. At such hours the page was permitted the freedom of the castle and islet; nay, he was sometimes invited to attend George Douglas when he went a-sporting upon the lake, or on its margin; opportunities of diversion which were only clouded by the remarkable melancholy which always seemed to brood on that gentleman's brow, and to mark his whole demeanour,—a sadness so profound, that Roland never observed him to smile, or to speak any word unconnected with the immediate object of their exercise.

The most pleasant part of Roland's day, was the occasional space which he was permitted to pass in personal attendance on the Queen and her ladies, together with the regular dinner-time, which he always spent with Dame Mary Fleming and Catharine Seyton. At these periods, he had frequent occasion to admire the lively spirit and inventive imagination of the latter damsel, who was unwearied in her contrivances to amuse her mistress, and to banish, for a time at least, the melancholy which preyed on her bosom. She danced, she sung, she recited tales of ancient and modern times, with that heartfelt exertion of talent, of which the pleasure lies not in the vanity of displaying it to others, but in the enthusiastic consciousness that we possess it ourselves. And yet these high accomplishments were mixed with an air of rusticity and harebrained vivacity, which seemed rather to belong to some village maid, the coquette of the ring around the Maypole, than to the high-bred descendant of an ancient baron. A touch of audacity, altogether short of effrontery, and far less approaching to vulgarity, gave as it were a wildness to all that she did; and Mary, while defending her from some of the occasional censures of her grave companion, compared her to a trained singing-bird escaped from a cage, which practises in all the luxuriance of freedom, and in full possession of the greenwood bough, the airs which it had learned during its earlier captivity.

The moments which the page was permitted to pass in the presence of this fascinating creature, danced so rapidly away, that, brief as they were, they compensated the weary dulness of all the rest of the day. The space of indulgence, however, was always brief, nor were any private interviews betwixt him and Catharine permitted, or even possible. Whether it were some special precaution respecting the Queen's household, or whether it were her general ideas of propriety, Dame Fleming seemed particularly attentive to prevent the young people from holding any separate correspondence together, and bestowed, for Catharine's sole benefit in this matter, the full stock of prudence and experience which she had acquired, when mother of the Queen's maidens of honour, and by which she had gained their hearty hatred. Casual meetings, however, could not be prevented, unless Catherine had been more desirous of shunning, or Roland Graeme less anxious in watching for them. A smile, a gibe, a sarcasm, disarmed of its severity by the arch look with which it was accompanied, was all that time permitted to pass between them on such occasions. But such passing interviews neither afforded means nor opportunity to renew the discussion of the circumstances attending their earlier acquaintance, nor to permit Roland to investigate more accurately the mysterious apparition of the page in the purple velvet cloak at the hostelrie of Saint Michael's.

The winter months slipped heavily away, and spring was already advanced, when Roland Graeme observed a gradual change in the manners of his fellow-prisoners. Having no business of his own to attend to, and being, like those of his age, education, and degree, sufficiently curious concerning what passed around, he began by degrees to suspect, and finally to be convinced, that there was something in agitation among his companions in captivity, to which they did not desire that he should be privy. Nay, he became almost certain that, by some means unintelligible to him, Queen Mary held correspondence beyond the walls and waters which surrounded her prison-house, and that she nourished some secret hope of deliverance or escape. In the conversations betwixt her and her attendants, at which he was necessarily present, the

Queen could not always avoid showing that she was acquainted with the events which were passing abroad in the world, and which he only heard through her report. He observed that she wrote more and worked less than had been her former custom, and that, as if desirous to lull suspicion asleep, she changed her manner towards the Lady Lochleven into one more gracious, and which seemed to express a resigned submission to her lot. "They think I am blind," he said to himself, "and that I am unfit to be trusted because I am so young, or it may be because I was sent hither by the Regent. Well!—be it so—they may be glad to confide in me in the long run; and Catherine Seyton, for as saucy as she is, may find me as safe a confidant as that sullen Douglas, whom she is always running after. It may be they are angry with me for listening to Master Elias Henderson; but it was their own fault for sending me there, and if the man speaks truth and good sense, and preaches only the word of God, he is as likely to be right as either Pope or Councils."

It is probable that in this last conjecture, Roland Graeme had hit upon the real cause why the ladies had not intrusted him with their councils. He had of late had several conferences with Henderson on the subject of religion, and had given him to understand that he stood in need of his instructions, although he had not thought there was either prudence or necessity for confessing that hitherto he had held the tenets of the Church of Rome.

Elias Henderson, a keen propagator of the reformed faith, had sought the seclusion of Lochleven Castle, with the express purpose and expectation of making converts from Rome amongst the domestics of the dethroned Queen, and confirming the faith of those who already held the Protestant doctrines. Perhaps his hopes soared a little higher, and he might nourish some expectation of a proselyte more distinguished in the person of the deposed Queen. But the pertinacity with which she and her female attendants refused to see or listen to him, rendered such hope, if he nourished it, altogether abortive.

The opportunity, therefore, of enlarging the religious information of Roland Graeme, and bringing him to a more due sense of his duties to Heaven, was hailed by the good man as a door opened by Providence for the salvation of a sinner. He dreamed not, indeed, that he was converting a Papist, but such was the ignorance which Roland displayed upon some material points of the reformed doctrine, that Master Henderson, while praising his docility to the Lady Lochleven and her grandson, seldom failed to add, that his venerable brother,

Henry Warden, must be now decayed in strength and in mind, since he found a catechumen of his flock so ill-grounded in the principles of his belief. For this, indeed, Roland Graeme thought it was unnecessary to assign the true reason, which was his having made it a point of honour to forget all that Henry Warden taught him, as soon as he was no longer compelled to read it over as a lesson acquired by rote. The lessons of his new instructor, if not more impressively delivered, were received by a more willing ear, and a more awakened understanding, and the solitude of Lochleven Castle was favourable to graver thoughts than the page had hitherto entertained. He wavered yet, indeed, as one who was almost persuaded; but his attention to the chaplain's instructions procured him favour even with the stern old dame herself; and he was once or twice, but under great precaution, permitted to go to the neighbouring village of Kinross, situated on the mainland, to execute some ordinary commission of his unfortunate mistress.

For some time Roland Graeme might be considered as standing neuter betwixt the two parties who inhabited the water-girdled Tower of Lochleven; but, as he rose in the opinion of the Lady of the Castle and her chaplain, he perceived, with great grief, that he lost ground in that of Mary and her female allies.

He came gradually to be sensible that he was regarded as a spy upon their discourse, and that, instead of the ease with which they had formerly conversed in his presence, without suppressing any of the natural feelings of anger, of sorrow, or mirth, which the chance topic of the moment happened to call forth, their talk was now guardedly restricted to the most indifferent subjects, and a studied reserve observed even in their mode of treating these. This obvious want of confidence was accompanied with a correspondent change in their personal demeanor towards the unfortunate page. The Queen, who had at first treated him with marked courtesy, now scarce spoke to him, save to convey some necessary command for her service. The Lady Fleming restricted her notice to the most dry and distant expressions of civility, and Catherine Seyton became bitter in her pleasantries, and shy, cross, and pettish, in any intercourse they had together. What was yet more provoking, he saw, or thought he saw, marks of intelligence betwixt George Douglas and the beautiful Catherine Seyton; and, sharpened by jealousy, he wrought himself almost into a certainty, that the looks which they exchanged, conveyed matters of deep and serious import. "No wonder," he thought, "if, courted by the son of a proud and powerful baron, she can no longer spare a word or look to the poor fortuneless page."

In a word, Roland Graeme's situation became truly disagreeable, and his heart naturally enough rebelled against the injustice of this treatment, which deprived him of the only comfort which he had received for submitting to a confinement in other respects irksome. He accused Queen Mary and Catherine Seyton (for concerning the opinion of Dame Fleming he was indifferent) of inconsistency in being displeased with him on account of the natural consequences of an order of their own. Why did they send him to hear this overpowering preacher? The Abbot Ambrosius, he recollected, understood the weakness of their Popish cause better, when he enjoined him to repeat within his own mind, *aves*, and *credos*, and *paters*, all the while old Henry Warden preached or lectured, that so he might secure himself against lending even a momentary ear to his heretical doctrine. "But I will endure this life no longer," said he to himself, manfully; "do they suppose I would betray my mistress, because I see cause to doubt of her religion?—that would be a serving, as they say, the devil for God's sake. I will forth into the world—he that serves fair ladies, may at least expect kind looks and kind words; and I bear not the mind of a gentleman, to submit to cold treatment and suspicion, and a life-long captivity besides. I will speak to George Douglas to-morrow when we go out a-fishing."

A sleepless night was spent in agitating this magnanimous resolution, and he arose in the morning not perfectly decided in his own mind whether he should abide by it or not. It happened that he was summoned by the Queen at an unusual hour, and just as he was about to go out with George Douglas. He went to attend her commands in, the garden; but as he had his angling-rod in his hand, the circumstance announced his previous intention, and the Queen, turning to the Lady Fleming, said, "Catherine must devise some other amusement for us, *ma bonnie amie*; our discreet page has already made his party for the day's pleasure."

"I said from the beginning," answered the Lady Fleming, "that your Grace ought not to rely on being favoured with the company of a youth who has so many Huguenot acquaintances, and has the means of amusing himself far more agreeably than with us."

"I wish," said Catherine, her animated features reddening with mortification, "that his friends would sail away with him for good, and bring us in return a page (if such a thing can be found) faithful to his Queen and to his religion."

"One part of your wishes may be granted, madam," said Roland Graeme, unable any longer to restrain his sense of the treatment which he received on all sides; and he was about to add, "I heartily wish you a companion in my room, if such can be found, who is capable of enduring women's caprices without going distracted." Luckily, he recollected the remorse which he had felt at having given way to the vivacity of his temper upon a similar occasion; and, closing his lips, imprisoned, until it died on his tongue, a reproach so misbecoming the presence of majesty.

"Why do you remain there," said the Queen, "as if you were rooted to the parterre?"

"I but attend your Grace's commands," said the page.

"I have none to give you—Begone, sir."

As he left the garden to go to the boat, he distinctly heard Mary upbraid one of her attendants in these words:—"You see to what you have exposed us!"

This brief scene at once determined Roland Graeme's resolution to quit the castle, if it were possible, and to impart his resolution to George Douglas without loss of time. That gentleman, in his usual mood of silence, sate in the stern of the little skiff which they used on such occasions, trimming his fishing-tackle, and, from time to time, indicating by signs to Graeme, who pulled the oars, which way he should row. When they were a furlong or two from the castle, Roland rested on the oars, and addressed his companion somewhat abruptly,— "I have something of importance to say to you, under your pleasure, fair sir."

The pensive melancholy of Douglas's countenance at once gave way to the eager, keen, and startled look of one who expects to hear something of deep and alarming import.

"I am wearied to the very death of this Castle of Lochleven," continued Roland.

"Is that all?" said Douglas; "I know none of its inhabitants who are much better pleased with it."

"Ay, but I am neither a native of the house, nor a prisoner in it, and so I may reasonably desire to leave it."

"You might desire to quit it with equal reason," answered Douglas, "if you were both the one and the other."

"But," said Roland Graeme, "I am not only tired of living in Lochleven Castle, but I am determined to quit it."

"That is a resolution more easily taken than executed," replied Douglas.

"Not if yourself, sir, and your Lady Mother, choose to consent," answered the page.

"You mistake the matter, Roland," said Douglas; "you will find that the consent of two other persons is equally essential—that of the Lady Mary your mistress, and that of my uncle the Regent, who placed you about her person, and who will not think it proper that she should change her attendants so soon."

"And must I then remain whether I will or no?" demanded the page, somewhat appalled at a view of the subject, which would have occurred sooner to a person of more experience.

"At least," said George Douglas, "you must will to remain till my uncle consents to dismiss you."

"Frankly," said the page, "and speaking to you as a gentleman who is incapable of betraying me, I will confess, that if I thought myself a prisoner here, neither walls nor water should confine me long."

"Frankly," said Douglas, "I could not much blame you for the attempt; yet, for all that, my father, or uncle, or the earl, or any of my brothers, or in short any of the king's lords into whose hands you fell, would in such a case hang you like a dog, or like a sentinel who deserts his post; and I promise you that you will hardly escape them. But row towards Saint Serf's island—there is a breeze from the west, and we shall have sport, keeping to windward of the isle, where the ripple is strongest. We will speak more of what you have mentioned when we have had an hour's sport."

Their fishing was successful, though never did two anglers pursue even that silent and unsocial pleasure with less of verbal intercourse.

When their time was expired, Douglas took the oars in his turn, and by his order Roland Graeme steered the boat, directing her course upon the landing-place at the castle. But he also stopped in the midst of his course, and, looking around him, said to Graeme, "There is a thing which I could mention to thee; but it is so deep a secret, that even here, surrounded as we are by sea and sky, without the possibility of a listener, I cannot prevail on myself to speak it out."

"Better leave it unspoken, sir," answered Roland Graeme, "if you doubt the honour of him who alone can hear it."

"I doubt not your honour," replied George Douglas; "but you are young, imprudent, and changeful."

"Young," said Roland, "I am, and it may be imprudent—but who hath informed you that I am changeful?"

"One that knows you, perhaps, better than you know yourself," replied Douglas.

"I suppose you mean Catherine Seyton," said the page, his heart rising as he spoke; "but she is herself fifty times more variable in her humour than the very water which we are floating upon."

"My young acquaintance," said Douglas, "I pray you to remember that Catherine Seyton is a lady of blood and birth, and must not be lightly spoken of."

"Master George of Douglas," said Graeme, "as that speech seemed to be made under the warrant of something like a threat, I pray you to observe, that I value not the threat at the estimation of a fin of one of these dead trouts; and, moreover, I would have you to know that the champion who undertakes the defence of every lady of blood and birth, whom men accuse of change of faith and of fashion, is like to have enough of work on his hands."

"Go to," said the Seneschal, but in a tone of good-humour, "thou art a foolish boy, unfit to deal with any matter more serious than the casting of a net, or the flying of a hawk."

"If your secret concern Catherine Seyton," said the page, "I care not for it, and so you may tell her if you will. I wot she can shape you opportunity to speak with her, as she has ere now."

The flush which passed over Douglas's face, made the page aware that he had alighted on a truth, when he was, in fact, speaking at random; and the feeling that he had done so, was like striking a dagger into his own heart. His companion, without farther answer, resumed the oars, and pulled lustily till they arrived at the island and the castle. The servants received the produce of their spoil, and the two fishers, turning from each other in silence, went each to his several apartment.

Roland Graeme had spent about an hour in grumbling against Catherine Seyton, the Queen, the Regent, and the whole house of Lochleven, with George Douglas at the head of it, when the time approached that his duty called him to attend the meal of Queen Mary. As he arranged his dress for this purpose, he grudged the trouble, which, on similar occasions, he used, with boyish foppery, to consider as one of the most important duties of his day; and when he went to take his place behind the chair of the Queen, it was with an air of offended dignity, which could not escape her observation, and probably appeared to her ridiculous enough, for she whispered something in French to her ladies, at which the lady Fleming laughed, and Catherine appeared half diverted and half disconcerted. This pleasantry, of which the subject was concealed from him, the unfortunate page received, of course, as a new offence, and called an additional degree of sullen dignity into his mien, which might have exposed him to farther raillery, but that Mary appeared disposed to make allowance for and compassionate his feelings.

With the peculiar tact and delicacy which no woman possessed in greater perfection, she began to soothe by degrees the vexed spirit of her magnanimous attendant. The excellence of the fish which he had taken in his expedition, the high flavour and beautiful red colour of the trouts, which have long given distinction to the lake, led her first to express her thanks to her attendant for so agreeable an addition to her table, especially upon a *jour de jeune*; and then brought on inquiries into the place where the fish had been taken, their size, their peculiarities, the times when they were in season, and a comparison between the Lochleven trouts and those which are found in the lakes and rivers of the south of Scotland. The ill humour of Roland Graeme was never of an obstinate character. It rolled away like mist before the sun, and he was easily engaged in a keen and animated dissertation about Lochleven trout, and sea trout, and river trout, and bull trout, and char, which never rise to a fly, and par, which some suppose infant salmon, and *herlings*, which frequent the Nith, and *vendisses*, which are only found in the Castle-Loch of Lochmaben; and he was hurrying on with the eager impetuosity and enthusiasm of a young sportsman, when he observed that the smile with which the Queen at first listened to him died languidly away, and that, in spite of her efforts to suppress them, tears rose to her eyes. He stopped suddenly short, and, distressed in his turn, asked, "If he had the misfortune unwittingly to give displeasure to her Grace?"

"No, my poor boy," replied the Queen; "but as you numbered up the lakes and rivers of my kingdom, imagination cheated me, as it will do, and snatched me from these dreary walls away to the romantic streams of Nithsdale, and the royal towers of Lochmaben.—O land, which my fathers have so long ruled! of the pleasures which you extend so freely, your Queen is now deprived, and the poorest beggar, who may wander free from one landward town to another, would scorn to change fates with Mary of Scotland!"

"Your highness," said the Lady Fleming, "will do well to withdraw."

"Come with me, then, Fleming," said the Queen, "I would not burden hearts so young as these are, with the sight of my sorrows."

She accompanied these words with a look of melancholy compassion towards Roland and Catherine, who were now left alone together in the apartment.

The page found his situation not a little embarrassing; for, as every reader has experienced who may have chanced to be in such a situation, it is extremely difficult to maintain the full dignity of an offended person in the presence of a beautiful girl, whatever reason we may have for being angry with her. Catherine Seyton, on her part, sate still like a lingering ghost, which, conscious of the awe which its presence imposes, is charitably disposed to give the poor confused mortal whom it visits, time to recover his senses, and comply with the grand rule of demonology by speaking first. But as Roland seemed in no hurry to avail himself of her condescension, she carried it a step farther, and herself opened the conversation.

"I pray you, fair sir, if it may be permitted me to disturb your august reverie by a question so simple,—what may have become of your rosary?"

"It is lost, madam—lost some time since," said Roland, partly embarrassed and partly indignant.

"And may I ask farther, sir," said Catherine, "why you have not replaced it with another?—I have half a mind," she said, taking from her pocket a string of ebony beads adorned with gold, "to bestow one upon you, to keep for my sake, just to remind you of former acquaintance."

There was a little tremulous accent in the tone with which these words were delivered, which at once put to flight Roland Graeme's resentment, and brought him to Catherine's side; but she instantly resumed the bold and firm accent which was more familiar to her. "I did not bid you," she said, "come and sit so close by me; for the acquaintance that I spoke of, has been stiff and cold, dead and buried, for this many a day."

"Now Heaven forbid!" said the page, "it has only slept, and now that you desire it should awake, fair Catherine, believe me that a pledge of your returning favour—"

"Nay, nay," said Catherine, withholding the rosary, towards which, as he spoke, he extended his hand, "I have changed my mind on better reflection. What should a heretic do with these holy beads, that have been blessed by the father of the church himself?"

Roland winced grievously, for he saw plainly which way the discourse was now likely to tend, and felt that it must at all events be embarrassing. "Nay, but," he said, "it was as a token of your own regard that you offered them."

"Ay, fair sir, but that regard attended the faithful subject, the loyal and pious Catholic, the individual who was so solemnly devoted at the same time with myself to the same grand duty; which, you must now understand, was to serve the church and Queen. To such a person, if you ever heard of him, was my regard due, and not to him who associates with heretics, and is about to become a renegade."

"I should scarce believe, fair mistress," said Roland, indignantly, "that the vane of your favour turned only to a Catholic wind, considering that it points so plainly to George Douglas, who, I think, is both kingsman and Protestant."

"Think better of George Douglas," said Catherine, "than to believe—" and then checking herself, as if she had spoken too much, she went on, "I assure you, fair Master Roland, that all who wish you well are sorry for you."

"Their number is very few, I believe," answered Roland, "and their sorrow, if they feel any, not deeper than ten minutes' time will cure."

"They are more numerous, and think more deeply concerning you, than you seem to be aware," answered Catherine. "But perhaps they think wrong—You are the best judge in your own affairs; and if you prefer gold and church-lands to honour and loyalty, and the faith of your fathers, why should you be hampered in conscience more than others?"

"May Heaven bear witness for me," said Roland, "that if I entertain any difference of opinion—that is, if I nourish any doubts in point of religion, they have been adopted on the conviction of my own mind, and the suggestion of my own conscience!"

"Ay, ay, your conscience—your conscience!" repeated she with satiric emphasis; "your conscience is the scape-goat; I warrant it an able one—it will bear the burden of one of the best manors of the Abbey of Saint Mary of Kennaquhair, lately forfeited to our noble Lord the King, by the Abbot and community thereof, for the high crime of fidelity to their religious vows, and now to be granted by the High and Mighty Traitor, and so forth, James Earl of Murray, to the good squire of dames Roland Graeme, for his loyal and faithful service as under-espial, and deputy-turnkey, for securing the person of his lawful sovereign, Queen Mary."

"You misconstrue me cruelly," said the page; "yes, Catherine, most cruelly—God knows I would protect this poor lady at the risk of my life, or with my life; but what can I do—what can any one do for her?"

"Much may be done—enough may be done—all may be done—if men will be but true and honourable, as Scottish men were in the days of Bruce and Wallace. Oh, Roland, from what an enterprise you are now withdrawing your heart and hand, through mere fickleness and coldness of spirit!"

"How can I withdraw," said Roland, "from an enterprise which has never been communicated to me?—Has the Queen, or have you, or has any one, communicated with me upon any thing for her service which I have refused? Or have you not, all of you, held me at such distance from your counsels, as if I were the most faithless spy since the days of Ganelon?"*

"And who," said Catherine Seyton, "would trust the sworn friend, and pupil, and companion, of the heretic preacher Henderson? ay—a proper tutor you have chosen, instead of the excellent Ambrosius, who is now turned out of house and homestead, if indeed he is not languishing in a dungeon, for withstanding the tyranny of Morton, to whose brother the temporalities of that noble house of God have been gifted away by the Regent."

"Is it possible?" said the page; "and is the excellent Father Ambrose in such distress?"

"He would account the news of your falling away from the faith of your fathers," answered Catherine, "a worse mishap than aught that tyranny can inflict on himself."

"But why," said Roland, very much moved, "why should you suppose that—that—that it is with me as you say?"

"Do you yourself deny it?" replied Catherine; "do you not admit that you have drunk the poison which you should have dashed from your lips?—Do you deny that it now ferments in your veins, if it has not altogether corrupted the springs of life?—Do you deny that you have your doubts, as you proudly term them, respecting what popes and councils have declared it unlawful to doubt of?—Is not your faith wavering, if not overthrown?—Does not the heretic preacher boast his

* Gan, Gano, or Ganelon of Mayence, is in the Romances on the subject of Charlemagne and his Paladins, always represented as the traitor by whom the Christian champions are betrayed.

conquest?—Does not the heretic woman of this prison-house hold up thy example to others?—Do not the Queen and the Lady Fleming believe in thy falling away?—And is there any except one—yes, I will speak it out, and think as lightly as you please of my good-will—is there one except myself that holds even a lingering hope that you may yet prove what we once all believed of you?"

"I know not," said our poor page, much embarrassed by the view which was thus presented to him of the conduct he was expected to pursue, and by a person in whom he was not the less interested that, though long a resident in Lochleven Castle, with no object so likely to attract his undivided attention, no lengthened interview had taken place since they had first met,—"I know not what you expect of me, or fear from me. I was sent hither to attend Queen Mary, and to her I acknowledge the duty of a servant through life and death. If any one had expected service of another kind, I was not the party to render it. I neither avow nor disclaim the doctrines of the reformed church.—Will you have the truth?—It seems to me that the profligacy of the Catholic clergy has brought this judgment on their own heads, and, for aught I know, it may be for their reformation. But, for betraying this unhappy Queen, God knows I am guiltless of the thought. Did I even believe worse of her, than as her servant I wish—as her subject I dare to do—I would not betray her—far from it—I would aid her in aught which could tend to a fair trial of her cause."

"Enough! enough!" answered Catherine, clasping her hands together; "then thou wilt not desert us if any means are presented, by which, placing our Royal Mistress at freedom, this case may be honestly tried betwixt her and her rebellious subjects?"

"Nay—but, fair Catherine," replied the page, "hear but what the Lord of Murray said when he sent me hither."—

"Hear but what the devil said," replied the maiden, "rather than what a false subject, a false brother, a false counsellor, a false friend, said! A man raised from a petty pensioner on the crown's bounty, to be the counsellor of majesty, and the prime distributor of the bounties of the state;—one with whom rank, fortune, title, consequence, and power, all grew up like a mushroom, by the mere warm good-will of the sister, whom, in requital, he hath mewed up in this place of melancholy seclusion—whom, in farther requital, he has deposed, and whom, if he dared, he would murder!"

"I think not so ill of the Earl of Murray," said Roland Graeme; "and sooth to speak," he added, with a smile, "it would require some bribe to make me embrace, with firm and desperate resolution, either one side or the other."

"Nay, if that is all," replied Catherine Seyton, in a tone of enthusiasm, "you shall be guerdoned with prayers from oppressed subjects—from dispossessed clergy—from insulted nobles—with immortal praise by future ages—with eager gratitude by the present—with fame on earth, and with felicity in heaven! Your country will thank you—your Queen will be debtor to you—you will achieve at once the highest from the lowest degree in chivalry—all men will honour, all women will love you—and I, sworn with you so early to the accomplishment of Queen Mary's freedom, will—yes, I will—love you better than—ever sister loved brother!" "Say on—say on!" whispered Roland, kneeling on one knee, and taking her hand, which, in the warmth of exhortation, Catherine held towards him.

"Nay," said she, pausing, "I have already said too much—far too much, if I prevail not with you—far too little if I do. But I prevail," she continued, seeing that the countenance of the youth she addressed returned the enthusiasm of her own—"I prevail; or rather the good cause prevails through its own strength—thus I devote thee to it." And as she spoke she approached her finger to the brow of the astonished youth, and, without touching it, signed the cross over his forehead—stooped her face towards him, and seemed to kiss the empty space in which she had traced the symbol; then starting up, and extricating herself from his grasp, darted into the Queen's apartment.

Roland Graeme remained as the enthusiastic maiden had left him, kneeling on one knee, with breath withheld, and with eyes fixed upon the space which the fairy form of Catherine Seyton had so lately occupied. If his thoughts were not of unmixed delight, they at least partook of that thrilling and intoxicating, though mingled sense of pain and pleasure, the most over-powering which life offers in its blended cup. He rose and retired slowly; and although the chaplain Mr. Henderson preached on that evening his best sermon against the errors of Popery, I would not engage that he was followed accurately through the train of his reasoning by the young proselyte, with a view to whose especial benefit he had handled the subject.

SIR WALTER SCOTT

XXV

And when love's torch hath set the heart in flame,
Comes Seignor Reason, with his saws and cautions,
Giving such aid as the old gray-beard Sexton,
Who from the church-vault drags the crazy engine,
To ply its dribbling ineffectual streamlet
Against a conflagration.

—OLD PLAY

In a musing mood, Roland Graeme upon the ensuing morning betook himself to the battlements of the Castle, as a spot where he might indulge the course of his thick-coming fancies with least chance of interruption. But his place of retirement was in the present case ill chosen, for he was presently joined by Mr. Elias Henderson.

"I sought you, young man," said the preacher, "having to speak of something which concerns you nearly."

The page had no pretence for avoiding the conference which the chaplain thus offered, though he felt that it might prove an embarrassing one.

"In teaching thee, as far as my feeble knowledge hath permitted, thy duty towards God," said the chaplain, "there are particulars of your duty towards man, upon which I was unwilling long or much to insist. You are here in the service of a lady, honourable as touching her birth, deserving of all compassion as respects her misfortunes, and garnished with even but too many of those outward qualities which win men's regard and affection. Have you ever considered your regard to this Lady Mary of Scotland, in its true light and bearing?"

"I trust, reverend sir," replied Roland Graeme, "that I am well aware of the duties a servant in my condition owes to his royal mistress, especially in her lowly and distressed condition."

"True," answered the preacher; "but it is even that honest feeling which may, in the Lady Mary's case, carry thee into great crime and treachery."

"How so, reverend sir?" replied the page; "I profess I understand you not."

"I speak to you not of the crimes of this ill-advised lady," said the preacher; "they are not subjects for the ears of her sworn servant. But it is enough to say, that this unhappy person hath rejected more offers of grace, and more hopes of glory, than ever were held out to earthly princes; and that she is now, her day of favour being passed, sequestered in this lonely castle, for the common weal of the people of Scotland, and it may be for the benefit of her own soul."

"Reverend sir," said Roland, somewhat impatiently, "I am but too well aware that my unfortunate mistress is imprisoned, since I have the misfortune to share in her restraint myself—of which, to speak sooth, I am heartily weary."

"It is even of that which I am about to speak," said the chaplain, mildly; "but, first, my good Roland, look forth on the pleasant prospect of yonder cultivated plain. You see, where the smoke arises, yonder village standing half hidden by the trees, and you know it to be the dwelling-place of peace and industry. From space to space, each by the side of its own stream, you see the gray towers of barons, with cottages interspersed; and you know that they also, with their household, are now living in unity; the lance hung upon the wall, and the sword resting in its sheath. You see, too, more than one fair church, where the pure waters of life are offered to the thirsty, and where the hungry are refreshed with spiritual food.—What would he deserve, who should bring fire and slaughter into so fair and happy a scene—who should bare the swords of the gentry and turn them against each other—who should give tower and cottage to the flames, and slake the embers with the blood of the indwellers?—What would he deserve who should lift up again that ancient Dagon of Superstition, whom the worthies of the time have beaten down, and who should once more make the churches of God the high places of Baal?"

"You have limned a frightful picture, reverend sir," said Roland Graeme; "yet I guess not whom you would charge with the purpose of effecting a change so horrible."

"God forbid," replied the preacher, "that I should say to thee, Thou art the man.—Yet beware, Roland Graeme, that thou, in serving thy mistress, hold fast the still higher service which thou owest to the peace of thy country, and the prosperity of her inhabitants; else, Roland Graeme, thou mayest be the very man upon whose head will fall the curses and assured punishment due to such work. If thou art won by the song of these sirens to aid that unhappy lady's escape from this place of penitence and security, it is over with the peace of Scotland's cottages, and with the prosperity of her palaces—and the babe unborn shall curse the name of the man who gave inlet to the disorder which will follow the war betwixt the mother and the son."

"I know of no such plan, reverend sir," answered the page, "and therefore can aid none such.—My duty towards the Queen has been simply that of an attendant; it is a task, of which, at times, I would willingly have been freed; nevertheless—"

"It is to prepare thee for the enjoyment of something more of liberty," said the preacher, "that I have endeavoured to impress upon you the deep responsibility under which your office must be discharged. George Douglas hath told the Lady Lochleven that you are weary of this service, and my intercession hath partly determined her good ladyship, that, as your discharge cannot be granted, you shall, instead, be employed in certain commissions on the mainland, which have hitherto been discharged by other persons of confidence. Wherefore, come with me to the lady, for even to-day such duty will be imposed on you."

"I trust you will hold me excused, reverend sir," said the page, who felt that an increase of confidence on the part of the Lady of the Castle and her family would render his situation in a moral view doubly embarrassing, "one cannot serve two masters—and I much fear that my mistress will not hold me excused for taking employment under another."

"Fear not that," said the preacher; "her consent shall be asked and obtained. I fear she will yield it but too easily, as hoping to avail herself of your agency to maintain correspondence with her friends, as those falsely call themselves, who would make her name the watchword for civil war."

"And thus," said the page, "I shall be exposed to suspicion on all sides; for my mistress will consider me as a spy placed on her by her enemies, seeing me so far trusted by them; and the Lady Lochleven will never cease to suspect the possibility of my betraying her, because circumstances put it into my power to do so—I would rather remain as I am."

There followed a pause of one or two minutes, during which Henderson looked steadily in Roland's countenance, as if desirous to ascertain whether there was not more in the answer than the precise words seemed to imply. He failed in this point, however; for Roland, bred a page from childhood, knew how to assume a sullen pettish cast of countenance, well enough calculated to hide all internal emotions.

"I understand thee not, Roland," said the preacher, "or rather thou thinkest on this matter more deeply than I apprehended to be in thy nature. Methought, the delight of going on shore with thy bow, or thy gun, or thy angling-rod, would have borne away all other feelings."

"And so it would," replied Roland, who perceived the danger of suffering Henderson's half-raised suspicions to become fully awake,—"I would have thought of nothing but the gun and the oar, and the wild water-fowl that tempt me by sailing among the sedges yonder so far out of flight-shot, had you not spoken of my going on shore as what was to occasion burning of town and tower, the downfall of the evangele, and the upsetting of the mass."

"Follow me, then," said Henderson, "and we will seek the Lady Lochleven."

They found her at breakfast with her grandson George Douglas.— "Peace be with your ladyship!" said the preacher, bowing to his patroness; "Roland Graeme awaits your order."

"Young man," said the lady, "our chaplain hath warranted for thy fidelity, and we are determined to give you certain errands to do for us in our town of Kinross."

"Not by my advice," said Douglas, coldly.

"I said not that it was," answered the lady, something sharply. "The mother of thy father may, I should think, be old enough to judge for herself in a matter so simple.—Thou wilt take the skiff, Roland, and two of my people, whom Dryfesdale or Randal will order out, and fetch off certain stuff of plate and hangings, which should last night be lodged at Kinross by the wains from Edinburgh."

"And give this packet," said George Douglas, "to a servant of ours, whom you will find in waiting there.—It is the report to my father," he added, looking towards his grandmother, who acquiesced by bending her head.

"I have already mentioned to Master Henderson," said Roland Graeme, "that as my duty requires my attendance on the Queen, her Grace's permission for my journey ought to be obtained before I can undertake your commission."

"Look to it, my son," said the old lady, "the scruple of the youth is honourable."

"Craving your pardon, madam, I have no wish to force myself on her presence thus early," said. Douglas, in an indifferent tone; "it might displease her, and were no way agreeable to me."

"And I," said the Lady Lochleven, "although her temper hath been more gentle of late, have no will to undergo, without necessity, the rancour of her wit."

"Under your permission, madam," said the chaplain, "I will myself render your request to the Queen. During my long residence in this house she hath not deigned to see me in private, or to hear my doctrine; yet so may Heaven prosper my labours, as love for her soul, and desire to bring her into the right path, was my chief desire for coming hither."

"Take care, Master Henderson," said Douglas, in a tone which seemed almost sarcastic, "lest you rush hastily on an adventure to which you have no vocation—you are learned, and know the adage, *Ne accesseris in consilium nisi vocatus*.—Who hath required this at your hand?"

"The Master to whose service I am called," answered the preacher, looking upward,—"He who hath commanded me to be earnest in season and out of season."

"Your acquaintance hath not been much, I think, with courts or princes," continued the young Esquire.

"No, sir," replied Henderson, "but like my Master Knox, I see nothing frightful in the fair face of a pretty lady."

"My son," said the Lady of Lochleven, "quench not the good man's zeal—let him do the errand to this unhappy Princess."

"With more willingness than I would do it myself," said George Douglas. Yet something in his manner appeared to contradict his words.

The minister went accordingly, followed by Roland Graeme, and, demanding an audience of the imprisoned Princess, was admitted. He found her with her ladies engaged in the daily task of embroidery. The Queen received him with that courtesy, which, in ordinary cases, she used towards all who approached her, and the clergyman, in opening his commission, was obviously somewhat more embarrassed than he had expected to be.—"The good Lady of Lochleven—may it please your Grace—"

He made a short pause, during which Mary said, with a smile, "My Grace would, in truth, be well pleased, were the Lady Lochleven our *good* lady—But go on—what is the will of the good Lady of Lochleven?"

"She desires, madam," said the chaplain, "that your Grace will permit this young gentleman, your page, Roland Graeme, to pass to Kinross, to look after some household stuff and hangings, sent hither for the better furnishing your Grace's apartments."

"The Lady of Lochleven," said the Queen, "uses needless ceremony, in requesting our permission for that which stands within her own pleasure. We well know that this young gentleman's attendance on us had not been so long permitted, were he not thought to be more at the command of that good lady than at ours.—But we cheerfully yield consent that he shall go on her errand—with our will we would doom no living creature to the captivity which we ourselves must suffer."

"Ay, madam," answered the preacher, "and it is doubtless natural for humanity to quarrel with its prison-house. Yet there have been those, who have found, that time spent in the house of temporal captivity may be so employed as to redeem us from spiritual slavery."

"I apprehend your meaning, sir," replied the Queen, "but I have heard your apostle—I have heard Master John Knox; and were I to be perverted, I would willingly resign to the ablest and most powerful of heresiarchs, the poor honour he might acquire by overcoming my faith and my hope."

"Madam," said the preacher, "it is not to the talents or skill of the husbandman that God gives the increase—the words which were offered in vain by him whom you justly call our apostle, during the bustle and gaiety of a court, may yet find better acceptance during the leisure for reflection which this place affords. God knows, lady, that I speak in singleness of heart, as one who would as soon compare himself to the immortal angels, as to the holy man whom you have named. Yet would you but condescend to apply to their noblest use, those talents and that learning which all allow you to be possessed of—would you afford us but the slightest hope that you would hear and regard what can be urged against the blinded superstition and idolatry in which you are brought up, sure am I, that the most powerfully-gifted of my brethren, that even John Knox himself, would hasten hither, and account the rescue of your single soul from the nets of Romish error—"

"I am obliged to you and to them for their charity," said Mary; "but as I have at present but one presence-chamber, I would reluctantly see it converted into a Huguenot synod."

"At least, madam, be not thus obstinately blinded in your errors! Hear one who has hungered and thirsted, watched and prayed, to undertake the good work of your conversion, and who would be content to die the instant that a work so advantageous for yourself and so beneficial to Scotland were accomplished—Yes, lady, could I but shake the remaining pillar of the heathen temple in this land—and that permit

SIR WALTER SCOTT

me to term your faith in the delusions of Rome—I could be content to die overwhelmed in the ruins!"

"I will not insult your zeal, sir," replied Mary, "by saying you are more likely to make sport for the Philistines than to overwhelm them—your charity claims my thanks, for it is warmly expressed and may be truly purposed—But believe as well of me as I am willing to do of you, and think that I may be as anxious to recall you to the ancient and only road, as you are to teach me your new by-ways to paradise."

"Then, madam, if such be your generous purpose," said Henderson, eagerly, "—what hinders that we should dedicate some part of that time, unhappily now too much at your Grace's disposal, to discuss a question so weighty? You, by report of all men, are both learned and witty; and I, though without such advantages, am strong in my cause as in a tower of defence. Why should we not spend some space in endeavouring to discover which of us hath the wrong side in this important matter?"

"Nay," said Queen Mary, "I never alleged my force was strong enough to accept of a combat *en champ clos*, with a scholar and a polemic. Besides, the match is not equal. You, sir, might retire when you felt the battle go against you, while I am tied to the stake, and have no permission to say the debate wearies me.—I would be alone."

She curtsied low to him as she uttered these words; and Henderson, whose zeal was indeed ardent, but did not extend to the neglect of delicacy, bowed in return, and prepared to withdraw.

"I would," he said, "that my earnest wish, my most zealous prayer, could procure to your Grace any blessing or comfort, but especially that in which alone blessing or comfort is, as easily as the slightest intimation of your wish will remove me from your presence."

He was in the act of departing, when Mary said to him with much courtesy, "Do me no injury in your thoughts, good sir; it may be, that if my time here be protracted longer—as surely I hope it will not, trusting that either my rebel subjects will repent of their disloyalty, or that my faithful lieges will obtain the upper hand—but if my time be here protracted, it may be I shall have no displeasure in hearing one who seems so reasonable and compassionate as yourself, and I may hazard your contempt by endeavouring to recollect and repeat the reasons which schoolmen and councils give for the faith that is in me,—although I fear that, God help me! my Latin has deserted me with my other possessions. This must, however, be for another day. Meanwhile, sir, let the Lady of Lochleven employ my page as she lists—I will not afford suspicion by speaking a word to him before he goes.—Roland Graeme, my friend, lose not an opportunity of amusing thyself—dance, sing, run, and leap—all may be done merrily on the mainland; but he must have more than quicksilver in his veins who would frolic here."

"Alas! madam," said the preacher, "to what is it you exhort the youth, while time passes, and eternity summons? Can our salvation be insured by idle mirth, or our good work wrought out without fear and trembling?"

"I cannot fear or tremble," replied the Queen; "to Mary Stewart such emotions are unknown. But if weeping and sorrow on my part will atone for the boy's enjoying an hour of boyish pleasure, be assured the penance shall be duly paid."

"Nay, but, gracious lady," said the preacher, "in this you greatly err;—our tears and our sorrows are all too little for our own faults and follies, nor can we transfer them, as your church falsely teaches, to the benefit of others."

"May I pray you, sir," answered the Queen, "with as little offence as such a prayer may import, to transfer yourself elsewhere? We are sick at heart, and may not now be disposed with farther controversy—and thou, Roland, take this little purse;" (then, turning to the divine, she said, showing its contents,) "Look, reverend sir,—it contains only these two or three gold testoons, a coin which, though bearing my own poor features, I have ever found more active against me than on my side, just as my subjects take arms against me, with my own name for their summons and signal.—Take this purse, that thou mayest want no means of amusement. Fail not—fail not to bring met back news from Kinross; only let it be such as, without suspicion or offence, may be told in the presence of this reverend gentleman, or of the good Lady Lochleven herself."

The last hint was too irresistible to be withstood; and Henderson withdrew, half mortified, half pleased, with his reception; for Mary, from long habit, and the address which was natural to her, had learned, in an extraordinary degree, the art of evading discourse which was disagreeable to her feelings or prejudices, without affronting those by whom it was proffered.

Roland Graeme retired with the chaplain, at a signal from his lady; but it did not escape him, that as he left the room, stepping backwards, and making the deep obeisance due to royalty, Catherine Seyton held up her slender forefinger, with a gesture which he alone could witness, and which seemed to say, "Remember what has passed betwixt us."

The young page had now his last charge from the Lady of Lochleven. "There are revels," she said, "this day at the village—my son's authority is, as yet, unable to prevent these continued workings of the ancient leaven of folly which the Romish priests have kneaded into the very souls of the Scottish peasantry. I do not command thee to abstain from them—that would be only to lay a snare for thy folly, or to teach thee falsehood; but enjoy these vanities with moderation, and mark them as something thou must soon learn to renounce and contemn. Our chamberlain at Kinross, Luke Lundin,—Doctor, as he foolishly calleth himself,—will acquaint thee what is to be done in the matter about which thou goest. Remember thou art trusted—show thyself, therefore, worthy of trust."

When we recollect that Roland Graeme was not yet nineteen, and that he had spent his whole life in the solitary Castle of Avenel, excepting the few hours he had passed in Edinburgh, and his late residence at Lochleven, (the latter period having very little served to enlarge his acquaintance with the gay world.) we cannot wonder that his heart beat, high with hope and curiosity, at the prospect of partaking the sport even of a country wake. He hastened to his little cabin, and turned over the wardrobe with which (in every respect becoming his station) he had been supplied from Edinburgh, probably by order of the Earl of Murray. By the Queen's command he had hitherto waited upon her in mourning, or at least in sad-coloured raiment. Her condition, she said, admitted of nothing more gay. But now he selected the gayest dress his wardrobe afforded; composed of scarlet slashed with black satin, the royal colours of Scotland—combed his long curled hair—disposed his chain and medal round a beaver hat of the newest block; and with the gay falchion which had reached him in so mysterious a manner, hung by his side in an embroidered belt, his apparel, added to his natural frank mien and handsome figure, formed a most commendable and pleasing specimen of the young gallant of the period. He sought to make his parting reverence to the Queen and her ladies, but old Dryfesdale hurried him to the boat.

"We will have no private audiences," he said, "my master; since you are to be trusted with somewhat, we will try at least to save thee from the temptation of opportunity. God help thee, child," he added, with a glance of contempt at his gay clothes, "an the bear-ward be yonder from Saint Andrews, have a care thou go not near him."

"And wherefore, I pray you?" said Roland.

"Lest he take thee for one of his runaway jackanapes," answered the steward, smiling sourly.

"I wear not my clothes at thy cost," said Roland indignantly.

"Nor at thine own either, my son" replied the steward, "else would thy garb more nearly resemble thy merit and thy station."

Roland Graeme suppressed with difficulty the repartee which arose to his lips, and, wrapping his scarlet mantle around him, threw himself into the boat, which two rowers, themselves urged by curiosity to see the revels, pulled stoutly towards the west end of the lake. As they put off, Roland thought he could discover the face of Catherine Seyton, though carefully withdrawn from observation, peeping from a loophole to view his departure. He pulled off his hat, and held it up as a token that he saw and wished her adieu. A white kerchief waved for a second across the window, and for the rest of the little voyage, the thoughts of Catherine Seyton disputed ground in his breast with the expectations excited by the approaching revel. As they drew nearer and nearer the shore, the sounds of mirth and music, the laugh, the halloo, and the shout, came thicker upon the ear, and in a trice the boat was moored, and Roland Graeme hastened in quest of the chamberlain, that, being informed what time he had at his own disposal, he might lay it out to the best advantage.

XXVI

Room for the master of the ring, ye swains,
Divide your crowded ranks—before him march
The rural minstrelsy, the rattling drum,
The clamorous war-pipe, and far-echoing horn.

—*Rural Sports*, SOMERVILLE

No long space intervened ere Roland Graeme was able to discover among the crowd of revellers, who gambolled upon the open space which extends betwixt the village and the lake, a person of so great importance as Dr. Luke Lundin, upon whom devolved officially the charge of representing the lord of the land, and who was attended for support of his authority by a piper, a drummer, and four sturdy clowns armed with rusty halberds, garnished with party-coloured ribbons; myrmidons who, early as the day was, had already broken more than one head in the awful names of the Laird of Lochleven and his chamberlain.[*]

As soon as this dignitary was informed that the castle skiff had arrived, with a gallant, dressed like a lord's son at the least, who desired presently to speak to him, he adjusted his ruff and his black coat, turned round his girdle till the garnished hilt of his long rapier became visible, and walked with due solemnity towards the beach. Solemn indeed he was entitled to be, even on less important occasions, for he had been bred to the venerable study of medicine, as those acquainted with the science very soon discovered from the aphorisms which ornamented

---

[*] At Scottish fairs, the bailie, or magistrate, deputed by the lord in whose name the meeting is held, attends the fair with his guard, decides trifling disputes, and punishes on the spot any petty delinquencies. His attendants are usually armed with halberds, and sometimes, at least, escorted by music. Thus, in the "Life and Death of Habbie Simpson," we are told of that famous minstrel,—

> *"At fairs he play'd before the spear-men,*
> *And gaily graithed in their gear-men;—*
> *Steel bonnets, jacks, and swords shone clear then,*
> *Like ony bead;*
> *Now wha shall play before sic weir-men,*
> *Since Habbie's dead!*

his discourse. His success had not been equal to his pretensions; but as he was a native of the neighbouring kingdom of Fife, and bore distant relation to, or dependence upon, the ancient family of Lundin of that Ilk, who were bound in close friendship with the house of Lochleven, he had, through their interest, got planted comfortably enough in his present station upon the banks of that beautiful lake. The profits of his chamberlainship being moderate, especially in those unsettled times, he had eked it out a little with some practice in his original profession; and it was said that the inhabitants of the village and barony of Kinross were not more effectually thirled (which may be translated enthralled) to the baron's mill, than they were to the medical monopoly of the chamberlain. Wo betide the family of the rich boor, who presumed to depart this life without a passport from Dr. Luke Lundin! for if his representatives had aught to settle with the baron, as it seldom happened otherwise, they were sure to find a cold friend in the chamberlain. He was considerate enough, however, gratuitously to help the poor out of their ailments, and sometimes out of all their other distresses at the same time.

Formal, in a double proportion, both as a physician and as a person in office, and proud of the scraps of learning which rendered his language almost universally unintelligible, Dr. Luke Lundin approached the beach, and hailed the page as he advanced towards him.—"The freshness of the morning upon you, fair sir—You are sent, I warrant me, to see if we observe here the regimen which her good ladyship hath prescribed, for eschewing all superstitious observances and idle anilities in these our revels. I am aware that her good ladyship would willingly have altogether abolished and abrogated them—But as I had the honour to quote to her from the works of the learned Hercules of Saxony, *omnis curatio est vel canonica vel coacta*,—that is, fair sir, (for silk and velvet have seldom their Latin *ad unguem*,) every cure must be wrought either by art and induction of rule, or by constraint; and the wise physician chooseth the former. Which argument her ladyship being pleased to allow well of, I have made it my business so to blend instruction and caution with delight—*fiat mixtio*, as we say—that I can answer that the vulgar mind will be defecated and purged of anile and Popish fooleries by the medicament adhibited, so that the *primae vice* being cleansed, Master Henderson, or any other able pastor, may at will throw in tonics, and effectuate a perfect moral cure, *tuto, cito, jucunde*."

"I have no charge, Dr. Lundin," replied the page—

"Call me not doctor," said the chamberlain, "since I have laid aside my furred gown and bonnet, and retired me into this temporality of chamberlainship."

"Oh, sir," said the page, who was no stranger by report to the character of this original, "the cowl makes not the monk, neither the cord the friar—we have all heard of the cures wrought by Dr. Lundin."

"Toys, young sir—trifles," answered the leech with grave disclamation of superior skill; "the hit-or-miss practice of a poor retired gentleman, in a short cloak and doublet—Marry, Heaven sent its blessing—and this I must say, better fashioned mediciners have brought fewer patients through—*lunga roba corta scienzia*, saith the Italian—ha, fair sir, you have the language?"

Roland Graeme did not think it necessary to expound to this learned Theban whether he understood him or no; but, leaving that matter uncertain, he told him he came in quest of certain packages which should have arrived at Kinross, and been placed under the chamberlain's charge the evening before.

"Body o' me!" said Doctor Lundin, "I fear our common carrier, John Auchtermuchty, hath met with some mischance, that he came not up last night with his wains—bad land this to journey in, my master; and the fool will travel by night too, although, (besides all maladies from your *tussis* to your *pestis*, which walk abroad in the night-air,) he may well fall in with half a dozen swash-bucklers, who will ease him at once of his baggage and his earthly complaints. I must send forth to inquire after him, since he hath stuff of the honourable household on hand— and, by our Lady, he hath stuff of mine too—certain drugs sent me from the city for composition of my alexipharmics—this gear must be looked to.—Hodge," said he, addressing one of his redoubted body- guard, "do thou and Toby Telford take the mickle brown aver and the black cut-tailed mare, and make out towards the Kerry-craigs, and see what tidings you can have of Auchtermuchty and his wains—I trust it is only the medicine of the pottle-pot, (being the only *medicamentum* which the beast useth,) which hath caused him to tarry on the road. Take the ribbons from your halberds, ye knaves, and get on your jacks, plate-sleeves, and knapskulls, that your presence may work some terror if you meet with opposers." He then added, turning to Roland Graeme, "I warrant me, we shall have news of the wains in brief season. Meantime it will please you to look upon the sports; but first to enter my poor lodging and take your morning's cup. For what saith the school of Salerno?

Poculum, mane haustum,
Restaurat naturam exhaustam."

"Your learning is too profound for me," replied the page; "and so would your draught be likewise, I fear."

"Not a whit, fair sir—a cordial cup of sack, impregnated with wormwood, is the best anti-pestilential draught; and, to speak truth, the pestilential miasmata are now very rife in the atmosphere. We live in a happy time, young man," continued he, in a tone of grave irony, "and have many blessings unknown to our fathers—Here are two sovereigns in the land, a regnant and a claimant—that is enough of one good thing—but if any one wants more, he may find a king in every peel-house in the country; so if we lack government, it is not for want of governors. Then have we a civil war to phlebotomize us every year, and to prevent our population from starving for want of food—and for the same purpose we have the Plague proposing us a visit, the best of all recipes for thinning a land, and converting younger brothers into elder ones. Well, each man in his vocation. You young fellows of the sword desire to wrestle, fence, or so forth, with some expert adversary; and for my part, I love to match myself for life or death against that same Plague."

As they proceeded up the street of the little village towards the Doctor's lodgings, his attention was successively occupied by the various personages whom he met, and pointed out to the notice of his companion.

"Do you see that fellow with the red bonnet, the blue jerkin, and the great rough baton in his hand?—I believe that clown hath the strength of a tower—he has lived fifty years in the world, and never encouraged the liberal sciences by buying one penny-worth of medicaments.—But see you that man with the *facies hippocratica*?" said he, pointing out a thin peasant, with swelled legs, and a most cadaverous countenance; "that I call one of the worthiest men in the barony—he breakfasts, luncheons, dines, and sups by my advice, and not without my medicine; and, for his own single part, will go farther to clear out a moderate stock of pharmaceutics, than half the country besides.—How do you, my honest friend?" said he to the party in question, with a tone of condolence.

"Very weakly, sir, since I took the electuary," answered the patient; "it neighboured ill with the two spoonfuls of pease-porridge and the kirnmilk."

"Pease-porridge and kirnmilk! Have you been under medicine

these ten years, and keep your diet so ill?—the next morning take the electuary by itself, and touch nothing for six hours."—The poor object bowed, and limped off.

The next whom the Doctor deigned to take notice of, was a lame fellow, by whom the honour was altogether undeserved, for at sight of the mediciner, he began to shuffle away in the crowd as fast as his infirmities would permit.

"There is an ungrateful hound for you," said Doctor Lundin; "I cured him of the gout in his feet, and now he talks of the chargeableness of medicine, and makes the first use of his restored legs to fly from his physician. His *podagra* hath become a *chiragra*, as honest Martial hath it—the gout has got into his fingers, and he cannot draw his purse. Old saying and true,

Praemia cum poscit medicus, Sathan est.

We are angels when we come to cure—devils when we ask payment—but I will administer a purgation to his purse I warrant him. There is his brother too, a sordid chuff.—So ho, there! Saunders Darlet! you have been ill, I hear?"

"Just got the turn, as I was thinking to send to your honour, and I am brawly now again—it was nae great thing that ailed me."

"Hark you, sirrah," said the Doctor, "I trust you remember you are owing to the laird four stones of barleymeal, and a bow of oats; and I would have you send no more such kain-fowls as you sent last season, that looked as wretchedly as patients just dismissed from a plague-hospital; and there is hard money owing besides."

"I was thinking, sir," said the man, *more Scotico*, that is, returning no direct answer on the subject on which he was addressed, "my best way would be to come down to your honour, and take your advice yet, in case my trouble should come back."

"Do so, then, knave," replied Lundin, "and remember what Ecclesiasticus saith—'Give place to the physician-let him not go from thee, for thou hast need of him.'"

His exhortation was interrupted by an apparition, which seemed to strike the doctor with as much horror and surprise, as his own visage inflicted upon sundry of those persons whom he had addressed.

The figure which produced this effect on the Esculapius of the village, was that of a tall old woman, who wore a high-crowned hat and muffler. The first of these habiliments added apparently to her stature, and the other served to conceal the lower part of her face, and as the hat itself was slouched, little could be seen besides two brown cheek-bones, and the eyes of swarthy fire, that gleamed from under two shaggy gray eyebrows. She was dressed in a long dark-coloured robe of unusual fashion, bordered at the skirts, and on the stomacher, with a sort of white trimming resembling the Jewish phylacteries, on which were wrought the characters of some unknown language. She held in her hand a walking staff of black ebony.

"By the soul of Celsus," said Doctor Luke Lundin, "it is old Mother Nicneven herself—she hath come to beard me within mine own bounds, and in the very execution of mine office! Have at thy coat, Old Woman, as the song says—Hob Anster, let her presently be seized and committed to the tolbooth; and if there are any zealous brethren here who would give the hag her deserts, and duck her, as a witch, in the loch, I pray let them in no way be hindered."

But the myrmidons of Dr. Lundin showed in this case no alacrity to do his bidding. Hob Anster even ventured to remonstrate in the name of himself and his brethren. "To be sure he was to do his honour's bidding; and for a' that folks said about the skill and witcheries of Mother Nicneven, he would put his trust in God, and his hand on her collar, without dreadour. But she was no common spaewife, this Mother Nicneven, like Jean Jopp that lived in the Bricrie-baulk. She had lords and lairds that would ruffle for her. There was Moncrieff of Tippermalloch, that was Popish, and the laird of Carslogie, a kend Queen's man, were in the fair, with wha kend how mony swords and bucklers at their back; and they would be sure to make a break-out if the officers meddled with the auld Popish witch-wife, who was sae weel friended; mair especially as the laird's best men, such as were not in the castle, were in Edinburgh with him, and he doubted his honour the Doctor would find ower few to make a good backing, if blades were bare."

The doctor listened unwillingly to this prudential counsel, and was only comforted by the faithful promise of his satellite, that "the old woman should," as he expressed it, "be ta'en canny the next time she trespassed on the bounds."

"And in that event," said the Doctor to his companion, "fire and fagot shall be the best of her welcome."

This he spoke in hearing of the dame herself, who even then, and in passing the Doctor, shot towards him from under her gray eyebrows a look of the most insulting and contemptuous superiority.

"This way," continued the physician, "this way," marshalling his guest into his lodging,—"take care you stumble not over a retort, for it is hazardous for the ignorant to walk in the ways of art."

The page found all reason for the caution; for besides stuffed birds, and lizards, and snakes bottled up, and bundles of simples made up, and other parcels spread out to dry, and all the confusion, not to mention the mingled and sickening smells, incidental to a druggist's stock in trade, he had also to avoid heaps of charcoal crucibles, bolt-heads, stoves, and the other furniture of a chemical laboratory.

Amongst his other philosophical qualities, Doctor Lundin failed not to be a confused sloven, and his old dame housekeeper, whose life, as she said, was spent in "redding him up," had trotted off to the mart of gaiety with other and younger folks. Much chattering and jangling therefore there was among jars, and bottles, and vials, ere the Doctor produced the salutiferous potion which he recommended so strongly, and a search equally long and noisy followed, among broken cans and cracked pipkins, ere he could bring forth a cup out of which to drink it. Both matters being at length achieved, the Doctor set the example to his guest, by quaffing off a cup of the cordial, and smacking his lips with approbation as it descended his gullet.—Roland, in turn, submitted to swallow the potion which his host so earnestly recommended, but which he found so insufferably bitter, that he became eager to escape from the laboratory in search of a draught of fair water to expel the taste. In spite of his efforts, he was nevertheless detained by the garrulity of his host, till he gave him some account of Mother Nicneven.

"I care not to speak of her," said the Doctor, "in the open air, and among the throng of people; not for fright, like yon cowardly dog Anster, but because I would give no occasion for a fray, having no leisure to look to stabs, slashes, and broken bones. Men call the old hag a prophetess—I do scarce believe she could foretell when a brood of chickens will chip the shell—Men say she reads the heavens—my black bitch knows as much of them when she sits baying the moon—Men pretend the ancient wretch is a sorceress, a witch, and, what not—*Inter nos*, I will never contradict a rumour which may bring her to the stake which she so justly deserves; but neither will I believe that the tales of witches which they din into our ears are aught but knavery, cozenage, and old women's fables."

"In the name of Heaven, what is she then," said the page, "that you make such a stir about her?"

"She is one of those cursed old women," replied the Doctor, "who take currently and impudently upon themselves to act as advisers and curers of the sick, on the strength of some trash of herbs, some rhyme of spells, some julap or diet, drink or cordial."

"Nay, go no farther," said the page; "if they brew cordials, evil be their lot and all their partakers!"

"You say well, young man," said Dr. Lundin; "for mine own part, I know no such pests to the commonwealth as these old incarnate devils, who haunt the chambers of the brain-sick patients, that are mad enough to suffer them to interfere with, disturb, and let, the regular process of a learned and artificial cure, with their sirups, and their julaps, and diascordium, and mithridate, and my Lady What-shall-call'um's powder, and worthy Dame Trashem's pill; and thus make widows and orphans, and cheat the regular and well-studied physician, in order to get the name of wise women and skeely neighbours, and so forth. But no more on't—Mother Nicneven* and I will meet one day, and she shall know there is danger in dealing with the Doctor."

"It is a true word, and many have found it," said the page; "but under your favour, I would fain walk abroad for a little, and see these sports."

"It is well moved," said the Doctor, "and I too should be showing myself abroad. Moreover the play waits us, young man-to-day, *totus mundus agit histrionem*."—And they sallied forth accordingly into the mirthful scene.

---

* This was the name given to the grand Mother Witch, the very Hecate of Scottish popular superstition. Her name was bestowed, in one or two instances, upon sorceresses, who were held to resemble her by their superior skill in "Hell's black grammar."

XXVII

See on yon verdant lawn, the gathering crowd
Thickens amain; the buxom nymphs advance,
Usher'd by jolly clowns; distinctions cease,
Lost in the common joy, and the bold slave
Leans on his wealthy master unreproved.

—*Rural Games*, SOMERVILLLE

The re-appearance of the dignified Chamberlain on the street of the village was eagerly hailed by the revellers, as a pledge that the play, or dramatic representation, which had been postponed owing to his absence, was now full surely to commence. Any thing like an approach to this most interesting of all amusements, was of recent origin in Scotland, and engaged public attention in proportion. All other sports were discontinued. The dance around the Maypole was arrested—the ring broken up and dispersed, while the dancers, each leading his partner by the hand, tripped, off to the silvan theatre. A truce was in like manner achieved betwixt a huge brown bear and certain mastiffs, who were tugging and pulling at his shaggy coat, under the mediation of the bear-ward and half a dozen butchers and yeomen, who, by dint of *staving and tailing*, as it was technically termed, separated the unfortunate animals, whose fury had for an hour past been their chief amusement. The itinerant minstrel found himself deserted by the audience he had collected, even in the most interesting passage of the romance which he recited, and just as he was sending about his boy, with bonnet in hand, to collect their oblations. He indignantly stopped short in the midst of *Rosewal and Lilian*, and, replacing his three-stringed fiddle, or rebeck, in its leathern case, followed the crowd, with no good-will, to the exhibition which had superseded his own. The juggler had ceased his exertions of emitting flame and smoke, and was content to respire in the manner of ordinary mortals, rather than to play gratuitously the part of a fiery dragon. In short, all other sports were suspended, so eagerly did the revellers throng towards the place of representation.

They would err greatly, who should regulate their ideas of this dramatic exhibition upon those derived from a modern theatre; for the rude shows of Thespis were far less different from those exhibited by Euripides on the stage of Athens, with all its magnificent decorations and pomp of dresses and of scenery. In the present case, there were no scenes, no stage, no machinery, no pit, box, and gallery, no box-lobby; and, what might in poor Scotland be some consolation for other negations, there was no taking of money at the door. As in the devices of the magnanimous Bottom, the actors had a greensward plot for a stage, and a hawthorn bush for a greenroom and tiring-house; the spectators being accommodated with seats on the artificial bank which had been raised around three-fourths of the playground, the remainder being left open for the entrance and exit of the performers. Here sate the uncritical audience, the Chamberlain in the centre, as the person highest in office, all alive to enjoyment and admiration, and all therefore dead to criticism.

The characters which appeared and disappeared before the amused and interested audience, were those which fill the earlier stage in all nations—old men, cheated by their wives and daughters, pillaged by their sons, and imposed on by their domestics, a braggadocia captain, a knavish pardoner or quaestionary, a country bumpkin and a wanton city dame. Amid all these, and more acceptable than almost the whole put together, was the all-licensed fool, the Gracioso of the Spanish drama, who, with his cap fashioned into the resemblance of a coxcomb, and his bauble, a truncheon terminated by a carved figure wearing a fool's cap, in his hand, went, came, and returned, mingling in every scene of the piece, and interrupting the business, without having any share himself in the action, and ever and anon transferring his gibes from the actors on the stage to the audience who sate around, prompt to applaud the whole.

The wit of the piece, which was not of the most polished kind, was chiefly directed against the superstitious practices of the Catholic religion; and the stage artillery had on this occasion been levelled by no less a person than Doctor Lundin, who had not only commanded the manager of the entertainment to select one of the numerous satires which had been written against the Papists, (several of which were cast in a dramatic form,) but had even, like the Prince of Denmark, caused them to insert, or according to his own phrase, to infuse here and there, a few pleasantries of his own penning, on the same inexhaustible subject, hoping thereby to mollify the rigour of the Lady of Lochleven towards pastimes of this description. He failed not to jog Roland's elbow, who was sitting in state behind him, and recommend to his particular attention those favourite passages. As for the page, to whom, the very idea of such an exhibition, simple as it was, was entirely new, he beheld it with the undiminished and ecstatic delight with which men of all ranks look for the first time on dramatic representation, and laughed, shouted, and clapped his hands as the performance proceeded. An incident at length took place, which effectually broke off his interest in the business of the scene.

One of the principal personages in the comic part of the drama was, as we have already said, a quaestionary or pardoner, one of those itinerants who hawked about from place to place relics, real or pretended, with which he excited the devotion at once, and the charity of the populace, and generally deceived both the one and the other. The hypocrisy, impudence, and profligacy of these clerical wanderers, had made them the subject of satire from the time of Chaucer down to that of Heywood. Their present representative failed not to follow the same line of humour, exhibiting pig's bones for relics, and boasting the virtues of small tin crosses, which had been shaken in the holy porringer at Loretto, and of cockleshells, which had been brought from the shrine of Saint James of Compostella, all which he disposed of to the devout Catholics at nearly as high a price as antiquaries are now willing to pay for baubles of similar intrinsic value. At length the pardoner pulled from his scrip a small phial of clear water, of which he vaunted the quality in the following verses:—

> *Listneth, gode people, everiche one*
> *For in the londe of Babylone,*
> *Far eastward I wot it lyeth,*
> *And is the first londe the sonne espieth,*
> *Ther, as he cometh fro out the sé;*
> *In this ilk londe, as thinketh me,*
> *Right as holie legendes tell.*
> *Snottreth from a roke a well,*
> *And falleth into ane bath of ston,*
> *Where chaste Susanne, in times long gon,*

> *Wax wont to wash her bodie and lim*
> *Mickle vertue hath that streme,*
> *As ye shall se er that ye pas,*

Ensample by this little glas—
Through nightés cold and dayés hote
Hiderward I have it brought;
Hath a wife made slip or side,
Or a maiden stepp'd aside,
Putteth this water under her nese,
Wold she nold she, she shall snese.

The jest, as the reader skilful in the antique language of the drama must at once perceive, turned on the same pivot as in the old minstrel tales of the Drinking Horn of King Arthur, and the Mantle made Amiss. But the audience were neither learned nor critical enough to challenge its want of originality. The potent relic was, after such grimace and buffoonery as befitted the subject, presented successively to each of the female personages of the drama, not one of whom sustained the supposed test of discretion; but, to the infinite delight of the audience, sneezed much louder and longer than perhaps they themselves had counted on. The jest seemed at last worn threadbare, and the pardoner was passing on to some new pleasantry, when the jester or clown of the drama, possessing himself secretly of the phial which contained the wondrous liquor, applied it suddenly to the nose of a young woman, who, with her black silk muffler, or screen drawn over her face, was sitting in the foremost rank of the spectators, intent apparently upon the business of the stage. The contents of the phial, well calculated to sustain the credit of the pardoner's legend, set the damsel a-sneezing violently, an admission of frailty which was received with shouts of rapture by the audience. These were soon, however, renewed at the expense of the jester himself, when the insulted maiden extricated, ere the paroxysm was well over, one hand from the folds of her mantle, and bestowed on the wag a buffet, which made him reel fully his own length from the pardoner, and then acknowledge the favour by instant prostration.

No one pities a jester overcome in his vocation, and the clown met with little sympathy, when, rising from the ground, and whimpering forth his complaints of harsh treatment, he invoked the assistance and sympathy of the audience. But the Chamberlain, feeling his own dignity insulted, ordered two of his halberdiers to bring the culprit before him. When these official persons first approached the virago, she threw herself into an attitude of firm defiance, as if determined

SIR WALTER SCOTT

to resist their authority; and from the sample of strength and spirit which she had already displayed, they showed no alacrity at executing their commission. But on half a minute's reflection, the damsel changed totally her attitude and manner, folded her cloak around her arms in modest and maiden-like fashion, and walked of her own accord to the presence of the great man, followed and guarded by the two manful satellites. As she moved across the vacant space, and more especially as she stood at the footstool of the Doctor's judgment-seat, the maiden discovered that lightness and elasticity of step, and natural grace of manner, which connoisseurs in female beauty know to be seldom divided from it. Moreover, her neat russet-coloured jacket, and short petticoat of the same colour, displayed a handsome form and a pretty leg. Her features were concealed by the screen; but the Doctor, whose gravity did not prevent his pretensions to be a connoisseur of the school we have hinted at, saw enough to judge favourably of the piece by the sample.

He began, however, with considerable austerity of manner.—"And how now, saucy quean!" said the medical man of office; "what have you to say why I should not order you to be ducked in the loch, for lifting your hand to the man in my presence?"

"Marry," replied the culprit, "because I judge that your honour will not think the cold bath necessary for my complaints."

"A pestilent jade," said the Doctor, whispering to Roland Graeme; "and I'll warrant her a good one—her voice is as sweet as sirup.—But, my pretty maiden," said he, "you show us wonderful little of that countenance of yours—be pleased to throw aside your muffler."

"I trust your honour will excuse me till we are more private," answered the maiden; "for I have acquaintance, and I should like ill to be known in the country as the poor girl whom that scurvy knave put his jest upon."

"Fear nothing for thy good name, my sweet little modicum of candied manna," replied the Doctor, "for I protest to you, as I am Chamberlain of Lochleven, Kinross, and so forth, that the chaste Susanna herself could not have snuffed that elixir without sternutation, being in truth a curious distillation of rectified *acetum*, or vinegar of the sun, prepared by mine own hands—Wherefore, as thou sayest thou wilt come to me in private, and express thy contrition for the offence whereof thou hast been guilty, I command that all for the present go forward as if no such interruption of the prescribed course had taken place."

The damsel curtsied and tripped back to her place. The play proceeded, but it no longer attracted the attention of Roland Graeme.

The voice, the figure, and what the veil permitted to be seen of the neck and tresses of the village damsel, bore so strong a resemblance to those of Catherine Seyton, that he felt like one bewildered in the mazes of a changeful and stupifying dream. The memorable scene of the hostelrie rushed on his recollection, with all its doubtful and marvellous circumstances. Were the tales of enchantment which he had read in romances realized in this extraordinary girl? Could she transport herself from the walled and guarded Castle of Lochleven, moated with its broad lake, (towards which he cast back a look as if to ascertain it was still in existence,) and watched with such scrupulous care as the safety of a nation demanded?—Could she surmount all these obstacles, and make such careless and dangerous use of her liberty, as to engage herself publicly in a quarrel in a village fair? Roland was unable to determine whether the exertions which it must have cost her to gain her freedom or the use to which she had put it, rendered her the most unaccountable creature.

Lost in these meditations, he kept his gaze fixed on the subject of them; and in every casual motion, discovered, or thought he discovered, something which reminded him still more strongly of Catherine Seyton. It occurred to him more than once, indeed, that he might be deceiving himself by exaggerating some casual likeness into absolute identity. But then the meeting at the hostelrie of Saint Michael's returned to his mind, and it seemed in the highest degree improbable, that, under such various circumstances, mere imagination should twice have found opportunity to play him the selfsame trick. This time, however, he determined to have his doubts resolved, and for this purpose he sate during the rest of the play like a greyhound in the slip, ready to spring upon the hare the instant that she was started. The damsel, whom he watched attentively lest she should escape in the crowd when the spectacle was closed, sate as if perfectly unconscious that she was observed. But the worthy Doctor marked the direction of his eyes, and magnanimously suppressed his own inclination to become the Theseus to this Hippolyta, in deference to the rights of hospitality, which enjoined him to forbear interference with the pleasurable pursuits of his young friend. He passed one or two formal gibes upon the fixed attention which the page paid to the unknown, and upon his own jealousy; adding, however, that if both were to be presented to the patient at once, he had little doubt she would think the younger man the sounder prescription. "I fear me," he added, "we shall have no news of the knave Auchtermuchty for some time, since the vermin whom I sent after him seem to have proved corbie-messengers. So you have an hour or two on your hands, Master Page; and as the minstrels are beginning to strike up, now the play is ended, why, an you incline for a dance, yonder is the green, and there sits your partner—I trust you will hold me perfect in my diagnostics, since I see with half an eye what disease you are sick of, and have administered a pleasing remedy.

"Discernit sapiens res *(as Chambers hath it)* quas confundit asellus."

The page hardly heard the end of the learned adage, or the charge which the Chamberlain gave him to be within reach, in case of the wains arriving suddenly, and sooner than expected—so eager he was at once to shake himself free of his learned associate, and to satisfy his curiosity regarding the unknown damsel. Yet in the haste with which he made towards her he found time to reflect, that, in order to secure an opportunity of conversing with her in private, he must not alarm her at first accosting her. He therefore composed his manner and gait, and advancing with becoming self-confidence before three or four country-fellows who were intent on the same design, but knew not so well how to put their request into shape, he acquainted her that he, as the deputy of the venerable Chamberlain, requested the honour of her hand as a partner.

"The venerable Chamberlain," said the damsel frankly, reaching the page her hand, "does very well to exercise this part of his privilege by deputy; and I suppose the laws of the revels leave me no choice but to accept of his faithful delegate."

"Provided, fair damsel," said the page, "his choice of a delegate is not altogether distasteful to you."

"Of that, fair sir," replied the maiden, "I will tell you more when we have danced the first measure."

Catherine Seyton had admirable skill in gestic lore, and was sometimes called on to dance for the amusement of her royal mistress. Roland Graeme had often been a spectator of her skill, and sometimes, at the Queen's command, Catherine's partner on such occasions. He was, therefore, perfectly acquainted with Catherine's mode of dancing; and observed that his present partner, in grace, in agility, in quickness of ear, and precision of execution, exactly resembled her, save that the Scottish jig, which he now danced with her, required a more violent and rapid motion, and more rustic agility, than the stately pavens, lavoltas, and courantoes, which he had seen her execute in the chamber of Queen Mary. The active duties of the dance left him little time for reflection, and none for conversation; but when their *pas de deux* was finished, amidst the acclamations of the villagers, who had seldom witnessed such an exhibition, he took an opportunity, when they yielded up the green to another couple, to use the privilege of a partner and enter into conversation with the mysterious maiden, whom he still held by the hand.

"Fair partner, may I not crave the name of her who has graced me thus far?"

"You may," said the maiden; "but it is a question whether I shall answer you."

"And why?" asked Roland.

"Because nobody gives anything for nothing—and you can tell me nothing in return which I care to hear."

"Could I not tell you my name and lineage, in exchange for yours?" returned Roland.

"No!" answered the maiden, "for you know little of either."

"How?" said the page, somewhat angrily.

"Wrath you not for the matter," said the damsel; "I will show you in an instant that I know more of you than you do of yourself."

"Indeed," answered Graeme; "for whom then do you take me?"

"For the wild falcon," answered she, "whom a dog brought in his mouth to a certain castle, when he was but an unfledged eyas—for the hawk whom men dare not fly, lest he should check at game, and pounce on carrion—whom folk must keep hooded till he has the proper light of his eyes, and can discover good from evil."

"Well—be it so," replied Roland Graeme; "I guess at a part of your parable, fair mistress mine—and perhaps I know as much of you as you do of me, and can well dispense with the information which you are so niggard in giving."

"Prove that," said the maiden, "and I will give you credit for more penetration than I judged you to be gifted withal."

"It shall be proved instantly," said Roland Graeme. "The first letter of your name is S, and the last N."

"Admirable," said his partner, "guess on."

"It pleases you to-day," continued Roland, "to wear the snood and kirtle, and perhaps you may be seen to-morrow in hat and feather, hose and doublet."

"In the clout! in the clout! you have hit the very white," said the damsel, suppressing a great inclination to laugh.

"You can switch men's eyes out of their heads, as well as the heart out of their bosoms."

These last words were uttered in a low and tender tone, which, to Roland's great mortification, and somewhat to his displeasure, was so far from allaying, that it greatly increased, his partner's disposition to laughter. She could scarce compose herself while she replied, "If you had thought my hand so formidable," extricating it from his hold, "you would not have grasped it so hard; but I perceive you know me so fully, that there is no occasion to show you my face."

"Fair Catherine," said the page, "he were unworthy ever to have seen you, far less to have dwelt so long in the same service, and under the same roof with you, who could mistake your air, your gesture, your step in walking or in dancing, the turn of your neck, the symmetry of your form—none could be so dull as not to recognize you by so many proofs; but for me, I could swear even to that tress of hair that escapes from under your muffler."

"And to the face, of course, which that muffler covers," said the maiden, removing her veil, and in an instant endeavouring to replace it. She showed the features of Catherine; but an unusual degree of petulant impatience inflamed them, when, from some awkwardness in her management of the muffler, she was unable again to adjust it with that dexterity which was a principal accomplishment of the coquettes of the time.

"The fiend rive the rag to tatters!" said the damsel, as the veil fluttered about her shoulders, with an accent so earnest and decided, that it made the page start. He looked again at the damsel's face, but the information which his eyes received, was to the same purport as before. He assisted her to adjust her muffler, and both were for an instant silent. The damsel spoke first, for Roland Graeme was overwhelmed with surprise at the contrarieties which Catherine Seyton seemed to include in her person and character.

"You are surprised," said the damsel to him, "at what you see and hear—But the times which make females men, are least of all fitted for men to become women; yet you yourself are in danger of such a change."

"I in danger of becoming effeminate!" said the page.

"Yes, you, for all the boldness of your reply," said the damsel. "When you should hold fast your religion, because it is assailed on all sides by rebels, traitors, and heretics, you let it glide out of your breast like water grasped in the hand. If you are driven from the faith of your fathers from fear of a traitor, is not that womanish?—If you are cajoled by the cunning arguments of a trumpeter of heresy, or the praises of a puritanic old woman, is not that womanish?—If you are bribed by the hope of spoil and preferment, is not that womanish?—And when you wonder at my venting a threat or an execration, should you not wonder at yourself, who, pretending to a gentle name and aspiring to knighthood, can be at the same time cowardly, silly, and self-interested!"

"I would that a man would bring such a charge," said the page; "he should see, ere his life was a minute older, whether he had cause to term me coward or no."

"Beware of such big words," answered the maiden; "you said but anon that I sometimes wear hose and doublet."

"But remain still Catharine Seyton, wear what you list," said the page, endeavouring again to possess himself of her hand.

"You indeed are pleased to call me so," replied the maiden, evading his intention, "but I have many other names besides."

"And will you not reply to that," said the page, "by which you are distinguished beyond every other maiden in Scotland?"

The damsel, unallured by his praises, still kept aloof, and sung with gaiety a verse from an old ballad,

> "Oh, some do call me Jack, sweet love,
> And some do call me Gill;
> But when I ride to Holyrood,
> My name is Wilful Will."

"Wilful Will" exclaimed the page, impatiently; "say rather Will o' the Wisp—Jack with the Lantern—for never was such a deceitful or wandering meteor!"

"If I be such," replied the maiden, "I ask no fools to follow me—If they do so, it is at their own pleasure, and must be on their own proper peril."

"Nay, but, dearest Catherine," said Roland Graeme, "be for one instant serious."

"If you will call me your dearest Catherine, when I have given you so many names to choose upon," replied the damsel, "I would ask you how, supposing me for two or three hours of my life escaped from yonder tower, you have the cruelty to ask me to be serious during the only merry moments I have seen perhaps for months?"

"Ay, but, fair Catherine, there are moments of deep and true feeling, which are worth ten thousand years of the liveliest mirth; and such was that of yesterday, when you so nearly—"

"So nearly what?" demanded the damsel, hastily.

"When you approached your lips so near to the sign you had traced on my forehead."

"Mother of Heaven!" exclaimed she, in a yet fiercer tone, and with a more masculine manner than she had yet exhibited,—"Catherine Seyton approach her lips to a man's brow, and thou that man!—vassal, thou liest!"

The page stood astonished; but, conceiving he had alarmed the damsel's delicacy by alluding to the enthusiasm of a moment, and the manner in which she had expressed it, he endeavoured to falter forth an apology. His excuses, though he was unable to give them any regular shape, were accepted by his companion, who had indeed suppressed her indignation after its first explosion—"Speak no more on't," she said. "And now let us part; our conversation may attract more notice than is convenient for either of us."

"Nay, but allow me at least to follow you to some sequestered place."

"You dare not," replied the maiden.

"How," said the youth, "dare not? where is it you dare go, where I dare not follow?"

"You fear a Will o' the Wisp," said the damsel; "how would you face a fiery dragon, with an enchantress mounted on its back?"

"Like Sir Eger, Sir Grime, or Sir Greysteil," said the page; "but be there such toys to be seen here?"

"I go to Mother Nicneven's," answered the maid; "and she is witch enough to rein the horned devil, with a red silk thread for a bridle, and a rowan-tree switch for a whip."

"I will follow you," said the page.

"Let it be at some distance," said the maiden.

And wrapping her mantle round her with more success than on her former attempt, she mingled with the throng, and walked towards the village, heedfully followed by Roland Graeme at some distance, and under every precaution which he could use to prevent his purpose from being observed.

XXVIII

Yes, it is he whose eyes look'd on thy childhood,
And watch'd with trembling hope thy dawn of youth,
That now, with these same eyeballs dimm'd with age,
And dimmer yet with tears, sees thy dishonour.

—OLD PLAY

A t the entrance of the principal, or indeed, so to speak, the only street in Kinross, the damsel, whose steps were pursued by Roland Graeme, cast a glance behind her, as if to be certain he had not lost trace of her and then plunged down a very narrow lane which ran betwixt two rows of poor and ruinous cottages. She paused for a second at the door of one of those miserable tenements, again cast her eye up the lane towards Roland, then lifted the latch, opened the door, and disappeared from his view.

With whatever haste the page followed her example, the difficulty which he found in discovering the trick of the latch, which did not work quite in the usual manner, and in pushing open the door, which did not yield to his first effort, delayed for a minute or two his entrance into the cottage. A dark and smoky passage led, as usual, betwixt the exterior wall of the house, and the *hallan*, or clay wall, which served as a partition betwixt it and the interior. At the end of this passage, and through the partition, was a door leading into the *ben*, or inner chamber of the cottage, and when Roland Graeme's hand was upon the latch of this door, a female voice pronounced, *"Benedictus qui veniat in nomine Domini, damnandus qui in nomine inimici."* On entering the apartment, he perceived the figure which the chamberlain had pointed out to him as Mother Nicneven, seated beside the lowly hearth. But there was no other person in the room. Roland Graeme gazed around in surprise at the disappearance of Catherine Seyton, without paying much regard to the supposed sorceress, until she attracted and riveted his regard by the tone in which she asked him—"What seekest thou here?"

"I seek," said the page, with much embarrassment; "I seek—"

But his answer was cut short, when the old woman, drawing her huge gray eyebrows sternly together, with a frown which knitted her brow into a thousand wrinkles, arose, and erecting herself up to her full natural size, tore the kerchief from her head, and seizing Roland by the arm, made two strides across the floor of the apartment to a small window through which the light fell full on her face, and showed the astonished youth the countenance of Magdalen Graeme.—"Yes, Roland," she said, "thine eyes deceive thee not; they show thee truly the features of her whom thou hast thyself deceived, whose wine thou hast turned into gall, her bread of joyfulness into bitter poison, her hope into the blackest despair—it is she who now demands of thee, what seekest thou here?—She whose heaviest sin towards Heaven hath been, that she loved thee even better than the weal of the whole church, and could not without reluctance surrender thee even in the cause of God— she now asks you, what seekest thou here?"

While she spoke, she kept her broad black eye riveted on the youth's face, with the expression with which the eagle regards his prey ere he tears it to pieces. Roland felt himself at the moment incapable either of reply or evasion. This extraordinary enthusiast had preserved over him in some measure the ascendency which she had acquired during his childhood; and, besides, he knew the violence of her passions and her impatience of contradiction, and was sensible that almost any reply which he could make, was likely to throw her into an ecstasy of rage. He was therefore silent; and Magdalen Graeme proceeded with increasing enthusiasm in her apostrophe—"Once more, what seek'st thou, false boy?—seek'st thou the honour thou hast renounced, the faith thou hast abandoned, the hopes thou hast destroyed?—Or didst thou seek me, the sole protectress of thy youth, the only parent whom thou hast known, that thou mayest trample on my gray hairs, even as thou hast already trampled on the best wishes of my heart?"

"Pardon me, mother," said Roland Graeme; "but, in truth and reason, I deserve not your blame. I have been treated amongst you—even by yourself, my revered parent, as well as by others—as one who lacked the common attributes of free-will and human reason, or was at least deemed unfit to exercise them. A land of enchantment have I been led into, and spells have been cast around me—every one has met me in disguise—every one has spoken to me in parables—I have been like one who walks in a weary and bewildering dream; and now you blame me that I have not the sense, and judgment, and steadiness of a waking, and a disenchanted, and a reasonable man, who knows what he is doing, and wherefore he does it. If one must walk with masks and spectres, who waft themselves from place to place as it were in vision rather than reality, it might shake the soundest faith and turn the wisest head. I sought, since I must needs avow my folly, the same Catherine Seyton with whom you made me first acquainted, and whom I most strangely find in this village of Kinross, gayest among the revellers, when I had but just left her in the well-guarded castle of Lochleven, the sad attendant of an imprisoned Queen-I sought her, and in her place I find you, my mother, more strangely disguised than even she is."

"And what hadst thou to do with Catherine Seyton?" said the matron, sternly; "is this a time or a world to follow maidens, or to dance around a Maypole? When the trumpet summons every true-hearted Scotsman around the standard of the true sovereign, shalt thou be found loitering in a lady's bower?"

"No, by Heaven, nor imprisoned in the rugged walls of an island castle!" answered Roland Graeme: "I would the blast were to sound even now, for I fear that nothing less loud will dispel the chimerical visions by which I am surrounded."

"Doubt not that it will be winded," said the matron, "and that so fearfully loud, that Scotland will never hear the like until the last and loudest blast of all shall announce to mountain and to valley that time is no more. Meanwhile, be thou but brave and constant—Serve God and honour thy sovereign—Abide by thy religion—I cannot—I will not—I dare not ask thee the truth of the terrible surmises I have heard touching thy falling away—perfect not that accursed sacrifice—and yet, even at this late hour, thou mayest be what I have hoped for the son of my dearest hope—what say I? the son of *my* hope—thou shalt be the hope of Scotland, her boast and her honour!—Even thy wildest and most foolish wishes may perchance be fulfilled—I might blush to mingle meaner motives with the noble guerdon I hold out to thee—It shames me, being such as I am, to mention the idle passions of youth, save with contempt and the purpose of censure. But we must bribe children to wholesome medicine by the offer of cates, and youth to honourable achievement with the promise of pleasure. Mark me, therefore, Roland. The love of Catherine Seyton will follow him only who shall achieve the freedom of her mistress; and believe, it may be one day in thine own power to be that happy lover. Cast, therefore, away doubt and fear, and prepare to do what religion calls for, what thy country demands of thee, what thy duty as a subject and as a servant alike require at your hand; and be assured, even the idlest or wildest wishes of thy heart will be most readily attained by following the call of thy duty."

As she ceased speaking, a double knock was heard against the inner door. The matron hastily adjusting her muffler, and resuming her chair by the hearth, demanded who was there.

"*Salve in nomine sancto*," was answered from without.

"*Salvete et vos*," answered Magdalen Graeme.

And a man entered in the ordinary dress of a nobleman's retainer, wearing at his girdle a sword and buckler—"I sought you," said he, "my mother, and him whom I see with you." Then addressing himself to Roland Graeme, he said to him, "Hast thou not a packet from George Douglas?"

"I have," said the page, suddenly recollecting that which had been committed to his charge in the morning, "but I may not deliver it to any one without some token that they have a right to ask it."

"You say well," replied the serving-man, and whispered into his ear, "The packet which I ask is the report to his father—will this token suffice?"

"It will," replied the page, and taking the packet from his bosom, gave it to the man.

"I will return presently," said the serving-man, and left the cottage.

Roland had now sufficiently recovered his surprise to accost his relative in turn, and request to know the reason why he found her in so precarious a disguise, and a place so dangerous—"You cannot be ignorant," he said, "of the hatred that the Lady of Lochleven bears to those of your—that is of our religion—your present disguise lays you open to suspicion of a different kind, but inferring no less hazard; and whether as a Catholic, or as a sorceress, or as a friend to the unfortunate Queen, you are in equal danger, if apprehended within the bounds of the Douglas; and in the chamberlain who administers their authority, you have, for his own reasons, an enemy, and a bitter one."

"I know it," said the matron, her eyes kindling with triumph; "I know that, vain of his school-craft, and carnal wisdom, Luke Lundin views with jealousy and hatred the blessings which the saints have conferred on my prayers, and on the holy relics, before the touch, nay, before the bare presence of which, disease and death have so often been known to retreat.—I know he would rend and tear me; but there is a chain and a muzzle on the ban dog that shall restrain his fury, and the Master's servant shall not be offended by him until the Master's work is wrought. When that hour comes, let the shadows of the evening descend on me in thunder and in tempest; the time shall be welcome that relieves my eyes from seeing guilt, and my ears from listening to blasphemy. Do thou but be constant—play thy part as I have played and will play mine, and my release shall be like that of a blessed martyr whose ascent to heaven angels hail with psalm and song, while earth pursues him with hiss and with execration."

As she concluded, the serving-man again entered the cottage, and said, "All is well! the time holds for to-morrow night."

"What time? what holds?" exclaimed Roland Graeme; "I trust I have given the Douglas's packet to no wrong—"

"Content yourself, young man," answered the serving-man; "thou hast my word and token."

"I know not if the token be right," said the page; "and I care not much for the word of a stranger."

"What," said the matron, "although thou mayest have given a packet delivered to thy charge by one of the Queen's rebels into the hand of a loyal subject—there were no great mistake in that, thou hot-brained boy!"

"By Saint Andrew, there were foul mistake, though," answered the page; "it is the very spirit of my duty, in this first stage of chivalry, to be faithful to my trust; and had the devil given me a message to discharge, I would not (so I had plighted my faith to the contrary) betray his counsel to an angel of light."

"Now, by the love I once bore thee," said the matron, "I could slay thee with mine own hand, when I hear thee talk of a dearer faith being due to rebels and heretics, than thou owest to thy church and thy prince!"

"Be patient, my good sister," said the serving-man; "I will give him such reasons as shall counterbalance the scruples which beset him-—the spirit is honourable, though now it may be mistimed and misplaced.— Follow me, young man."

"Ere I go to call this stranger to a reckoning," said the page to the matron, "is there nothing I can do for your comfort and safety?"

"Nothing," she replied, "nothing, save what will lead more to thine own honour;—the saints who have protected me thus far, will lend me succour as I need it. Tread the path of glory that is before thee, and only think of me as the creature on earth who will be most delighted to hear of thy fame.—Follow the stranger—he hath tidings for you that you little expect."

The stranger remained on the threshold as if waiting for Roland, and as soon as he saw him put himself in motion, he moved on before at a quick pace. Diving still deeper down the lane, Roland perceived that it was now bordered by buildings upon the one side only, and that the other was fenced by a high old wall, over which some trees extended their branches. Descending a good way farther, they came to a small door in the wall. Roland's guide paused, looked around an instant to see if any one were within sight, then taking a key from his pocket, opened the door and entered, making a sign to Roland Graeme to follow him. He did so, and the stranger locked the door carefully on the inside. During this operation the page had a moment to look around, and perceived that he was in a small orchard very trimly kept.

The stranger led him through an alley or two, shaded by trees loaded with summer-fruit, into a pleached arbour, where, taking the turf-seat which was on the one side, he motioned to Roland to occupy that which was opposite to him, and, after a momentary silence, opened the conversation as follows: "You have asked a better warrant than the word of a mere stranger, to satisfy you that I have the authority of George of Douglas for possessing myself of the packet intrusted to your charge."

"It is precisely the point on which I demand reckoning of you," said Roland. "I fear I have acted hastily; if so, I must redeem my error as I best may."

"You hold me then as a perfect stranger?" said the man. "Look at my face more attentively, and see if the features do not resemble those of a man much known to you formerly."

Roland gazed attentively; but the ideas recalled to his mind were so inconsistent with the mean and servile dress of the person before him, that he did not venture to express the opinion which he was irresistibly induced to form.

"Yes, my son," said the stranger, observing his embarrassment, "you do indeed see before you the unfortunate Father Ambrosius, who once accounted his ministry crowned in your preservation from the snares of heresy, but who is now condemned to lament thee as a castaway!"

Roland Graeme's kindness of heart was at least equal to his vivacity of temper—he could not bear to see his ancient and honoured master and spiritual guide in a situation which inferred a change of fortune so melancholy, but throwing himself at his feet, grasped his knees and wept aloud.

"What mean these tears, my son?" said the Abbot; "if they are shed for your own sins and follies, surely they are gracious showers, and may avail thee much—but weep not, if they fall on my account. You indeed see the Superior of the community of Saint Mary's in the dress of a poor sworder, who gives his master the use of his blade and buckler, and, if needful, of his life, for a coarse livery coat and four marks by the year. But such a garb suits the time, and, in the period of the church militant, as well becomes her prelates, as staff, mitre, and crosier, in the days of the church's triumph."

"By what fate," said the page—"and yet why," added he, checking himself, "need I ask? Catherine Seyton in some sort prepared me for this. But that the change should be so absolute—the destruction so complete!"—

"Yes, my son," said the Abbot Ambrosius, "thine own eyes beheld, in my unworthy elevation to the Abbot's stall, the last especial act of holy solemnity which shall be seen in the church of Saint Mary's, until it shall please Heaven to turn back the captivity of the church. For the present, the shepherd is smitten—ay, well-nigh to the earth—the flock are scattered, and the shrines of saints and martyrs, and pious benefactors to the church, are given to the owls of night, and the satyrs of the desert."

"And your brother, the Knight of Avenel—could he do nothing for your protection?"

"He himself hath fallen under the suspicion of the ruling powers," said the Abbot, "who are as unjust to their friends as they are cruel to their enemies. I could not grieve at it, did I hope it might estrange him from his cause; but I know the soul of Halbert, and I rather fear it will drive him to prove his fidelity to their unhappy cause, by some deed which may be yet more destructive to the church, and more offensive to Heaven. Enough of this; and now to the business of our meeting.—I trust you will hold it sufficient if I pass my word to you that the packet of which you were lately the bearer, was designed for my hands by George of Douglas?"

"Then," said the page, "is George of Douglas—"

"A true friend to his Queen, Roland; and will soon, I trust, have his eyes opened to the errors of his (miscalled) church."

"But what is he to his father, and what to the Lady of Lochleven, who has been as a mother to him?" said the page impatiently.

"The best friend to both, in time and through eternity," said the Abbot, "if he shall prove the happy instrument for redeeming the evil they have wrought, and are still working."

"Still," said the page, "I like not that good service which begins in breach of trust."

"I blame not thy scruples, my son," said the Abbot; "but the time which has wrenched asunder the allegiance of Christians to the church, and of subjects to their king, has dissolved all the lesser bonds of society; and, in such days, mere human ties must no more restrain our progress, than the brambles and briers which catch hold of his garments, should delay the path of a pilgrim who travels to pay his vows."

"But, my father,"—said the youth, and then stopt short in a hesitating manner.

"Speak on, my son," said the Abbot; "speak without fear."

"Let me not offend you then," said Roland, "when I say, that it is even this which our adversaries charge against us; when they say that, shaping the means according to the end, we are willing to commit great moral evil in order that we may work out eventual good."

"The heretics have played their usual arts on you, my son," said the Abbot; "they would willingly deprive us of the power of acting wisely and secretly, though their possession of superior force forbids our contending with them on terms of equality. They have reduced us to a state of exhausted weakness, and now would fain proscribe the means by which weakness, through all the range of nature, supplies the lack of strength and defends itself against its potent enemies. As well might the hound say to the hare, use not these wily turns to escape me, but contend with me in pitched battle, as the armed and powerful heretic demand of the down-trodden and oppressed Catholic to lay aside the wisdom of the serpent, by which alone they may again hope to raise up the Jerusalem over which they weep, and which it is their duty to rebuild—But more of this hereafter. And now, my son, I command thee on thy faith to tell me truly and particularly what has chanced to thee since we parted, and what is the present state of thy conscience. Thy relation, our sister Magdalen, is a woman of excellent gifts, blessed with a zeal which neither doubt nor danger can quench; but yet it is not a zeal altogether according to knowledge; wherefore, my son, I would willingly be myself thy interrogator, and thy counsellor, in these days of darkness and stratagem."

With the respect which he owed to his first instructor, Roland Graeme went rapidly through the events which the reader is acquainted with; and while he disguised not from the prelate the impression which had been made on his mind by the arguments of the preacher

Henderson, he accidentally and almost involuntarily gave his Father Confessor to understand the influence which Catherine Seyton had acquired over his mind.

"It is with joy I discover, my dearest son," replied the Abbot, "that I have arrived in time to arrest thee on the verge of the precipice to which thou wert approaching. These doubts of which you complain, are the weeds which naturally grow up in a strong soil, and require the careful hand of the husbandman to eradicate them. Thou must study a little volume, which I will impart to thee in fitting time, in which, by Our Lady's grace, I have placed in somewhat a clearer light than heretofore, the points debated betwixt us and these heretics, who sow among the wheat the same tares which were formerly privily mingled with the good seed by the Albigenses and the Lollards. But it is not by reason alone that you must hope to conquer these insinuations of the enemy: It is sometimes by timely resistance, but oftener by timely flight. You must shut your ears against the arguments of the heresiarch, when circumstances permit you not to withdraw the foot from his company. Anchor your thoughts upon the service of Our Lady, while he is expending in vain his heretical sophistry. Are you unable to maintain your attention on heavenly objects—think rather on thine own earthly pleasures, than tempt Providence and the Saints by giving an attentive ear to the erring doctrine—think of thy hawk, thy hound, thine angling rod, thy sword and buckler—think even of Catherine Seyton, rather than give thy soul to the lessons of the tempter. Alas! my son, believe not that, worn out with woes, and bent more by affliction than by years, I have forgotten the effect of beauty over the heart of youth. Even in the watches of the night, broken by thoughts of an imprisoned Queen, a distracted kingdom, a church laid waste and ruinous, come other thoughts than these suggest, and feelings which belonged to an earlier and happier course of life. Be it so—we must bear our load as we may: and not in vain are these passions implanted in our breast, since, as now in thy case, they may come in aid of resolutions founded upon higher grounds. Yet beware, my son—this Catherine Seyton is the daughter of one of Scotland's proudest, as well as most worthy barons; and thy state may not suffer thee, as yet, to aspire so high. But thus it is—Heaven works its purposes through human folly; and Douglas's ambitious affection, as well as thine, shall contribute alike to the desired end."

"How, my father," said the page, "my suspicions are then true!—Douglas loves—"

SIR WALTER SCOTT

"He does; and with a love as much misplaced as thine own; but beware of him—cross him not—thwart him not."

"Let him not cross or thwart me," said the page; "for I will not yield him an inch of way, had he in his body the soul of every Douglas that has lived since the time of the Dark Gray Man."*

"Nay, have patience, idle boy, and reflect that your suit can never interfere with his.—But a truce with these vanities, and let us better employ the little space which still remains to us to spend together. To thy knees, my son, and resume the long-interrupted duty of confession, that, happen what may, the hour may find in thee a faithful Catholic, relieved from the guilt of his sins by authority of the Holy Church. Could I but tell thee, Roland, the joy with which I see thee once more put thy knee to its best and fittest use! *Quid dicis, mi fili?*"

"*Culpas meas*" answered the youth; and according to the ritual of the Catholic Church, he confessed and received absolution, to which was annexed the condition of performing certain enjoined penances.

When this religious ceremony was ended, an old man, in the dress of a peasant of the better order, approached the arbour, and greeted the Abbot.—"I have waited the conclusion of your devotions," he said, "to tell you the youth is sought after by the chamberlain, and it were well he should appear without delay. Holy Saint Francis, if the halberdiers were to seek him here, they might sorely wrong my garden-plot—they are in office, and reck not where they tread, were each step on jessamine and clovegilly-flowers."

"We will speed him forth, my brother," said the Abbot; "but alas! is it possible that such trifles should live in your mind at a crisis so awful as that which is now impending?"

"Reverend father," answered the proprietor of the garden, for such he was, "how oft shall I pray you to keep your high counsel for high minds like your own? What have you required of me, that I have not granted unresistingly, though with an aching heart?"

"I would require of you to be yourself, my brother," said the Abbot Ambrosius; "to remember what you were, and to what your early vows have bound you."

---

* By an ancient, though improbable tradition, the Douglasses are said to have derived their name from a champion who had greatly distinguished himself in an action. When the king demanded by whom the battle had been won, the attendants are said to have answered, "Sholto Douglas, sir;" which is said to mean, "Yonder dark gray man." But the name is undoubtedly territorial, and taken from Douglas river and vale.

"I tell thee, Father Ambrosius," replied the gardener, "the patience of the best saint that ever said pater-noster, would be exhausted by the trials to which you have put mine—What I have been, it skills not to speak at present-no one knows better than yourself, father, what I renounced, in hopes to find ease and quiet during the remainder of my days—and no one better knows how my retreat has been invaded, my fruit-trees broken, my flower-beds trodden down, my quiet frightened away, and my very sleep driven from my bed, since ever this poor Queen, God bless her, hath been sent to Lochleven.—I blame her not; being a prisoner, it is natural she should wish to get out from so vile a hold, where there is scarcely any place even for a tolerable garden, and where the water-mists, as I am told, blight all the early blossoms—I say, I cannot blame her for endeavouring for her freedom; but why I should be drawn into the scheme—why my harmless arbours, that I planted with my own hands, should become places of privy conspiracy-why my little quay, which I built for my own fishing boat, should have become a haven for secret embarkations—in short, why I should be dragged into matters where both heading and hanging are like to be the issue, I profess to you, reverend father, I am totally ignorant."

"My brother," answered the Abbot, "you are wise, and ought to know—"

"I am not—I am not—I am not wise," replied the horticulturist, pettishly, and stopping his ears with his fingers—"I was never called wise but when men wanted to engage me in some action of notorious folly."

"But, my good brother," said the Abbot—

"I am not good neither," said the peevish gardener; "I am neither good nor wise—Had I been wise, you would not have been admitted here; and were I good, methinks I should send you elsewhere to hatch plots for destroying the quiet of the country. What signifies disputing about queen or king,—when men may sit at peace—*sub umbra vitis sui?* and so would I do, after the precept of Holy Writ, were I, as you term me, wise or good. But such as I am, my neck is in the yoke, and you make me draw what weight you list.—Follow me, youngster. This reverend father, who makes in his jackman's dress nearly as reverend a figure as I myself, will agree with me in one thing at least, and that is, that you have been long enough here."

"Follow the good father, Roland," said the Abbot, "and remember my words—a day is approaching that will try the temper of all true Scotsmen—may thy heart prove faithful as the steel of thy blade!"

The page bowed in silence, and they parted; the gardener, notwithstanding his advanced age, walking on before him very briskly, and muttering as he went, partly to himself, partly to his companion, after the manner of old men of weakened intellects—"When I was great," thus ran his maundering, "and had my mule and my ambling palfrey at command, I warrant you I could have as well flown through the air as have walked at this pace. I had my gout and my rheumatics, and an hundred things besides, that hung fetters on my heels; and, now, thanks to Our Lady, and honest labour, I can walk with any good man of my age in the kingdom of Fife—Fy upon it, that experience should be so long in coming!"

As he was thus muttering, his eye fell upon the branch of a pear-tree which drooped down for want of support, and at once forgetting his haste, the old man stopped and set seriously about binding it up. Roland Graeme had both readiness, neatness of hand, and good nature in abundance; he immediately lent his aid, and in a minute or two the bough was supported, and tied up in a way perfectly satisfactory to the old man, who looked at it with great complaisance. "They are bergamots," he said, "and if you will come ashore in autumn, you shall taste of them—the like are not in Lochleven Castle—the garden there is a poor pin-fold, and the gardener, Hugh Houkham, hath little skill of his craft—so come ashore, Master Page, in autumn, when you would eat pears. But what am I thinking of—ere that time come, they may have given thee sour pears for plums. Take an old man's advice, youth, one who hath seen many days, and sat in higher places than thou canst hope for—bend thy sword into a pruning-hook, and make a dibble of thy dagger—thy days shall be the longer, and thy health the better for it,—and come to aid me in my garden, and I will teach thee the real French fashion of *imping*, which the Southron call graffing. Do this, and do it without loss of time, for there is a whirlwind coming over the land, and only those shall escape who lie too much beneath the storm to have their boughs broken by it."

So saying, he dismissed Roland Graeme, through a different door from that by which he had entered, signed a cross, and pronounced a benedicite as they parted, and then, still muttering to himself, retired into the garden, and locked the door on the inside.

XXIX

Pray God she prove not masculine ere long!

—King Henry VI

Dismissed from the old man's garden, Roland Graeme found that a grassy paddock, in which sauntered two cows, the property of the gardener, still separated him from the village. He paced through it, lost in meditation upon the words of the Abbot. Father Ambrosius had, with success enough, exerted over him that powerful influence which the guardians and instructors of our childhood possess over our more mature youth. And yet, when Roland looked back upon what the father had said, he could not but suspect that he had rather sought to evade entering into the controversy betwixt the churches, than to repel the objections and satisfy the doubts which the lectures of Henderson had excited. "For this he had no time," said the page to himself, "neither have I now calmness and learning sufficient to judge upon points of such magnitude. Besides, it were base to quit my faith while the wind of fortune sets against it, unless I were so placed, that my conversion, should it take place, were free as light from the imputation of self-interest. I was bred a Catholic—bred in the faith of Bruce and Wallace—I will hold that faith till time and reason shall convince me that it errs. I will serve this poor Queen as a subject should serve an imprisoned and wronged sovereign—they who placed me in her service have to blame themselves—who sent me hither, a gentleman trained in the paths of loyalty and honour, when they should have sought out some truckling, cogging, double-dealing knave, who would have been at once the observant page of the Queen, and the obsequious spy of her enemies. Since I must choose betwixt aiding and betraying her, I will decide as becomes her servant and her subject; but Catherine Seyton—Catherine Seyton, beloved by Douglas and holding me on or off as the intervals of her leisure or caprice will permit—how shall I deal with the coquette?— By heaven, when I next have an opportunity, she shall render me some reason for her conduct, or I will break with her for ever!"

As he formed this doughty resolution, he crossed the stile which led out of the little enclosure, and was almost immediately greeted by Dr. Luke Lundin.

SIR WALTER SCOTT

"Ha! my most excellent young friend," said the Doctor, "from whence come you?—but I note the place.—Yes, neighbour Blinkhoolie's garden is a pleasant rendezvous, and you are of the age when lads look after a bonny lass with one eye, and a dainty plum with another. But hey! you look subtriste and melancholic—I fear the maiden has proved cruel, or the plums unripe; and surely I think neighbour Blinkhoolie's damsons can scarcely have been well preserved throughout the winter—he spares the saccharine juice on his confects. But courage, man, there are more Kates in Kinross; and for the immature fruit, a glass of my double distilled *aqua mirabilis—probatum est.*"

The page darted an ireful glance at the facetious physician; but presently recollecting that the name Kate, which had provoked his displeasure, was probably but introduced for the sake of alliteration, he suppressed his wrath, and only asked if the wains had been heard of?

"Why, I have been seeking for you this hour, to tell you that the stuff is in your boat, and that the boat waits your pleasure. Auchtermuchty had only fallen into company with an idle knave like himself, and a stoup of aquavitae between them. Your boatmen lie on their oars, and there have already been made two wefts from the warder's turret to intimate that those in the castle are impatient for your return. Yet there is time for you to take a slight repast; and, as your friend and physician, I hold it unfit you should face the water-breeze with an empty stomach."

Roland Graeme had nothing for it but to return, with such cheer as he might, to the place where his boat was moored on the beach, and resisted all offer of refreshment, although the Doctor promised that he should prelude the collation with a gentle appetizer—a decoction of herbs, gathered and distilled by himself. Indeed, as Roland had not forgotten the contents of his morning cup, it is possible that the recollection induced him to stand firm in his refusal of all food, to which such an unpalatable preface was the preliminary. As they passed towards the boat, (for the ceremonious politeness of the worthy Chamberlain would not permit the page to go thither without attendance,) Roland Graeme, amidst a group who seemed to be assembled around a party of wandering musicians, distinguished, as he thought, the dress of Catherine Seyton. He shook himself clear from his attendant, and at one spring was in the midst of the crowd, and at the side of the damsel. "Catherine," he whispered, "is it well for you to be still here?—will you not return to the castle?"

"To the devil with your Catherines and your castles!" answered the maiden, snappishly; "have you not had time enough already to get rid of your follies? Begone! I desire not your farther company, and there will be danger in thrusting it upon me."

"Nay—but if there be danger, fairest Catherine," replied Roland; "why will you not allow me to stay and share it with you?"

"Intruding fool," said the maiden, "the danger is all on thine own side—the risk in, in plain terms, that I strike thee on the mouth with the hilt of my dagger." So saying, she turned haughtily from him, and moved through the crowd, who gave way in some astonishment at the masculine activity with which she forced her way among them.

As Roland, though much irritated, prepared to follow, he was grappled on the other side by Doctor Luke Lundin, who reminded him of the loaded boat, of the two wefts, or signals with the flag, which had been made from the tower, of the danger of the cold breeze to an empty stomach, and of the vanity of spending more time upon coy wenches and sour plums. Roland was thus, in a manner, dragged back to his boat, and obliged to launch her forth upon his return to Lochleven Castle.

That little voyage was speedily accomplished, and the page was greeted at the landing-place by the severe and caustic welcome of old Dryfesdale. "So, young gallant, you are come at last, after a delay of six hours, and after two signals from the castle? But, I warrant, some idle junketing hath occupied you too deeply to think of your service or your duty. Where is the note of the plate and household stuff?—Pray Heaven it hath not been diminished under the sleeveless care of so young a gad-about!"

"Diminished under my care, Sir Steward!" retorted the page angrily; "say so in earnest, and by Heaven your gray hair shall hardly protect your saucy tongue!"

"A truce with your swaggering, young esquire," returned the steward; "we have bolts and dungeons for brawlers. Go to my lady, and swagger before her, if thou darest—she will give thee proper cause of offence, for she has waited for thee long and impatiently."

"And where then is the Lady of Lochleven?" said the page; "for I conceive it is of her thou speakest."

"Ay—of whom else?" replied Dryfesdale; "or who besides the Lady of Lochleven hath a right to command in this castle?"

"The Lady of Lochleven is thy mistress," said Roland Graeme; "but mine is the Queen of Scotland."

The steward looked at him fixedly for a moment, with an air in which suspicion and dislike were ill concealed by an affectation of contempt. "The bragging cock-chicken," he said, "will betray himself by his rash crowing. I have marked thy altered manner in the chapel of late—ay, and your changing of glances at meal-time with a certain idle damsel, who, like thyself, laughs at all gravity and goodness. There is something about you, my master, which should be looked to. But, if you would know whether the Lady of Lochleven, or that other lady, hath a right to command thy service, thou wilt find them together in the Lady Mary's ante-room."

Roland hastened thither, not unwilling to escape from the ill-natured penetration of the old man, and marvelling at the same time what peculiarity could have occasioned the Lady of Lochleven's being in the Queen's apartment at this time of the afternoon, so much contrary to her usual wont. His acuteness instantly penetrated the meaning. "She wishes," he concluded, "to see the meeting betwixt the Queen and me on my return, that she may form a guess whether there is any private intelligence or understanding betwixt us—I must be guarded."

With this resolution he entered the parlour, where the Queen, seated in her chair, with the Lady Fleming leaning upon the back of it, had already kept the Lady of Lochleven standing in her presence for the space of nearly an hour, to the manifest increase of her very visible bad humour. Roland Graeme, on entering the apartment, made a deep obeisance to the Queen, and another to the Lady, and then stood still as if to await their farther question. Speaking almost together, the Lady Lochleven said, "So, young man, you are returned at length?"

And then stopped indignantly short, while the Queen went on without regarding her—"Roland, you are welcome home to us—you have proved the true dove and not the raven—Yet I am sure I could have forgiven you, if, once dismissed, from this water-circled ark of ours, you had never again returned to us. I trust you have brought back an olive-branch, for our kind and worthy hostess has chafed herself much on account of your long absence, and we never needed more some symbol of peace and reconciliation."

"I grieve I should have been detained, madam," answered the page; "but from the delay of the person intrusted with the matters for which I was sent, I did not receive them till late in the day."

"See you there now," said the Queen to the Lady Lochleven; "we could not persuade you, our dearest hostess, that your household goods were in all safe keeping and surety. True it is, that we can excuse your anxiety, considering that these august apartments are so scantily furnished, that we have not been able to offer you even the relief of a stool during the long time you have afforded us the pleasure of your society."

"The will, madam," said the lady, "the will to offer such accommodation was more wanting than the means."

"What!" said the Queen, looking round, and affecting surprise, "there are then stools in this apartment—one, two—no less than four, including the broken one—a royal garniture!—We observed them not—will it please your ladyship to sit?"

"No, madam, I will soon relieve you of my presence," replied the Lady Lochleven; "and while with you, my aged limbs can still better brook fatigue, than my mind stoop to accept of constrained courtesy."

"Nay, Lady of Lochleven, if you take it so deeply," said the Queen, rising and motioning to her own vacant chair, "I would rather you assumed my seat—you are not the first of your family who has done so."

The Lady of Lochleven curtsied a negative, but seemed with much difficulty to suppress the angry answer which rose to her lips.

During this sharp conversation, the page's attention had been almost entirely occupied by the entrance of Catherine Seyton, who came from the inner apartment, in the usual dress in which she attended upon the Queen, and with nothing in her manner which marked either the hurry or confusion incident to a hasty change of disguise, or the conscious fear of detection in a perilous enterprise. Roland Graeme ventured to make her an obeisance as she entered, but she returned it with an air of the utmost indifference, which, in his opinion, was extremely inconsistent with the circumstances in which they stood towards each other.—"Surely," he thought, "she cannot in reason expect to bully me out of the belief due to mine own eyes, as she tried to do concerning the apparition in the hostelry of Saint Michael's—I will try if I cannot make her feel that this will be but a vain task, and that confidence in me is the wiser and safer course to pursue."

These thoughts had passed rapidly through his mind, when the Queen, having finished her altercation with the Lady of the castle, again addressed him—"What of the revels at Kinross, Roland Graeme? Methought they were gay, if I may judge from some faint sounds of mirth and distant music, which found their way so far as these grated windows, and died when they entered them, as all that is mirthful

SIR WALTER SCOTT

must—But thou lookest as sad as if thou hadst come from a conventicle of the Huguenots!"

"And so perchance he hath, madam," replied the Lady of Lochleven, at whom this side-shaft was lanched. "I trust, amid yonder idle fooleries, there wanted not some pouring forth of doctrine to a better purpose than that vain mirth, which, blazing and vanishing like the crackling of dry thorns, leaves to the fools who love it nothing but dust and ashes."

"Mary Fleming," said the Queen, turning round and drawing her mantle about her, "I would that we had the chimney-grate supplied with a fagot or two of these same thorns which the Lady of Lochleven describes so well. Methinks the damp air from the lake, which stagnates in these vaulted rooms, renders them deadly cold."

"Your Grace's pleasure shall be obeyed," said the Lady of Lochleven; "yet may I presume to remind you that we are now in summer?"

"I thank you for the information, my good lady," said the Queen; "for prisoners better learn their calender from the mouth of their jailor, than from any change they themselves feel in the seasons.—Once more, Roland Graeme, what of the revels?"

"They were gay, madam," said the page, "but of the usual sort, and little worth your Highness's ear."

"Oh, you know not," said the Queen, "how very indulgent my ear has become to all that speaks of freedom and the pleasures of the free. Methinks I would rather have seen the gay villagers dance their ring round the Maypole, than have witnessed the most stately masques within the precincts of a palace. The absence of stone-wall—the sense that the green turf is under the foot which may tread it free and unrestrained, is worth all that art or splendour can add to more courtly revels."

"I trust," said the Lady Lochleven, addressing the page in her turn, "there were amongst these follies none of the riots or disturbances to which they so naturally lead?"

Roland gave a slight glance to Catherine Seyton, as if to bespeak her attention, as he replied,—"I witnessed no offence, madam, worthy of marking—none indeed of any kind, save that a bold damsel made her hand somewhat too familiar with the cheek of a player-man, and ran some hazard of being ducked in the lake."

As he uttered these words he cast a hasty glance at Catherine; but she sustained, with the utmost serenity of manner and countenance, the hint which he had deemed could not have been thrown out before her without exciting some fear and confusion.

"I will cumber your Grace no longer with my presence," said the Lady Lochleven, "unless you have aught to command me."

"Nought, our good hostess," answered the Queen, "unless it be to pray you, that on another occasion you deem it not needful to postpone your better employment to wait so long upon us."

"May it please you," added the Lady Lochleven, "to command this your gentleman to attend us, that I may receive some account of these matters which have been sent hither for your Grace's use?"

"We may not refuse what you are pleased to require, madam," answered the Queen. "Go with the lady, Roland, if our commands be indeed necessary to thy doing so. We will hear to-morrow the history of thy Kinross pleasures. For this night we dismiss thy attendance."

Roland Graeme went with the Lady of Lochleven, who failed not to ask him many questions concerning what had passed at the sports, to which he rendered such answers as were most likely to lull asleep any suspicions which she might entertain of his disposition to favour Queen Mary, taking especial care to avoid all allusion to the apparition of Magdalen Graeme, and of the Abbot Ambrosius. At length, after undergoing a long and somewhat close examination, he was dismissed with such expressions, as, coming from the reserved and stern Lady of Lochleven, might seem to express a degree of favour and countenance.

His first care was to obtain some refreshment, which was more cheerfully afforded him by a good-natured pantler than by Dryfesdale, who was, on this occasion, much disposed to abide by the fashion of Pudding-burn House, where

> *They who came not the first call.*
> *Gat no more meat till the next meal.*

When Roland Graeme had finished his repast, having his dismissal from the Queen for the evening, and being little inclined for such society as the castle afforded, he stole into the garden, in which he had permission to spend his leisure time, when it pleased him. In this place, the ingenuity of the contriver and disposer of the walks had exerted itself to make the most of little space, and by screens, both of stone ornamented with rude sculpture, and hedges of living green, had endeavoured to give as much intricacy and variety as the confined limits of the garden would admit.

Here the young man walked sadly, considering the events of the day, and comparing what had dropped from the Abbot with what he had himself noticed of the demeanour of George Douglas. "It must be so," was the painful but inevitable conclusion at which he arrived. "It must be by his aid that she is thus enabled, like a phantom, to transport herself from place to place, and to appear at pleasure on the mainland or on the islet.—It must be so," he repeated once more; "with him she holds a close, secret, and intimate correspondence, altogether inconsistent with the eye of favour which she has sometimes cast upon me, and destructive to the hopes which she must have known these glances have necessarily inspired." And yet (for love will hope where reason despairs) the thought rushed on his mind, that it was possible she only encouraged Douglas's passion so far as might serve her mistress's interest, and that she was of too frank, noble, and candid a nature, to hold out to himself hopes which she meant not to fulfil. Lost in these various conjectures, he seated himself upon a bank of turf which commanded a view of the lake on the one side, and on the other of that front of the castle along which the Queen's apartments were situated.

The sun had now for some time set, and the twilight of May was rapidly fading into a serene night. On the lake, the expanded water rose and fell, with the slightest and softest influence of a southern breeze, which scarcely dimpled the surface over which it passed. In the distance was still seen the dim outline of the island of Saint Serf, once visited by many a sandalled pilgrim, as the blessed spot trodden by a man of God—now neglected or violated, as the refuge of lazy priests, who had with justice been compelled to give place to the sheep and the heifers of a Protestant baron.

As Roland gazed on the dark speck, amid the lighter blue of the waters which surrounded it, the mazes of polemical discussion again stretched themselves before the eye of the mind. Had these men justly suffered their exile as licentious drones, the robbers, at once, and disgrace, of the busy hive? or had the hand of avarice and rapine expelled from the temple, not the ribalds who polluted, but the faithful priests who served the shrine in honour and fidelity? The arguments of Henderson, in this contemplative hour, rose with double force before him; and could scarcely be parried by the appeal which the Abbot Ambrosius had made from his understanding to his feelings,—an appeal which he had felt more forcibly amid the bustle of stirring life, than now when his reflections were more undisturbed. It required an effort to divert his mind from this embarrassing topic; and he found that he best succeeded by turning his eyes to the front of the tower, watching where a twinkling light still streamed from the casement of Catherine Seyton's apartment, obscured by times for a moment as the shadow of the fair inhabitant passed betwixt the taper and the window. At length the light was removed or extinguished, and that object of speculation was also withdrawn from the eyes of the meditative lover. Dare I confess the fact, without injuring his character for ever as a hero of romance? These eyes gradually became heavy; speculative doubts on the subject of religious controversy, and anxious conjectures concerning the state of his mistress's affections, became confusedly blended together in his musings; the fatigues of a busy day prevailed over the harassing subjects of contemplation which occupied his mind, and he fell fast asleep.

Sound were his slumbers, until they were suddenly dispelled by the iron tongue of the castle-bell, which sent its deep and sullen sounds wide over the bosom of the lake, and awakened the echoes of Bennarty, the hill which descends steeply on its southern bank. Roland started up, for this bell was always tolled at ten o'clock, as the signal for locking the castle gates, and placing the keys under the charge of the seneschal. He therefore hastened to the wicket by which the garden communicated with the building, and had the mortification, just as he reached it, to hear the bolt leave its sheath with a discordant crash, and enter the stone groove of the door-lintel. "Hold, hold," cried the page, "and let me in ere you lock the wicket." The voice of Dryfesdale replied from within, in his usual tone of embittered sullenness, "The hour is passed, fair master—you like not the inside of these walls—even make it a complete holiday, and spend the night as well as the day out of bounds."

"Open the door," exclaimed the indignant page, "or by Saint Giles I will make thy gold chain smoke for it!"

"Make no alarm here," retorted the impenetrable Dryfesdale, "but keep thy sinful oaths and silly threats for those that regard them—I do mine office, and carry the keys to the seneschal.—Adieu, my young master! the cool night air will advantage your hot blood."

The steward was right in what he said; for the cooling breeze was very necessary to appease the feverish fit of anger which Roland experienced, nor did the remedy succeed for some time. At length, after some hasty turns made through the garden, exhausting his passion in vain vows of vengeance, Roland Graeme began to be sensible that his situation ought rather to be held as matter of laughter than of serious resentment.

To one bred a sportsman, a night spent in the open air had in it little of hardship, and the poor malice of the steward seemed more worthy of his contempt than his anger. "I would to God," he said, "that the grim old man may always have contented himself with such sportive revenge. He often looks as he were capable of doing us a darker turn." Returning, therefore, to the turf-seat which he had formerly occupied, and which was partially sheltered by a trim fence of green holly, he drew his mantle around him, stretched himself at length on the verdant settle, and endeavoured to resume that sleep which the castle bell had interrupted to so little purpose.

Sleep, like other earthly blessings, is niggard of its favours when most courted. The more Roland invoked her aid, the farther she fled from his eyelids. He had been completely awakened, first, by the sounds of the bell, and then by his own aroused vivacity of temper, and he found it difficult again to compose himself to slumber. At length, when his mind—was wearied out with a maze of unpleasing meditation, he succeeded in coaxing himself into a broken slumber. This was again dispelled by the voices of two persons who were walking in the garden, the sound of whose conversation, after mingling for some time in the page's dreams, at length succeeded in awaking him thoroughly. He raised himself from his reclining posture in the utmost astonishment, which the circumstance of hearing two persons at that late hour conversing on the outside of the watchfully guarded Castle of Lochloven, was so well calculated to excite. His first thought was of supernatural beings; his next, upon some attempt on the part of Queen Mary's friends and followers; his last was, that George of Douglas, possessed of the keys, and having the means of ingress and egress at pleasure, was availing himself of his office to hold a rendezvous with Catherine Seyton in the castle garden. He was confirmed in this opinion by the tone of the voice, which asked in a low whisper, "whether all was ready?"

XXX

Roland Graeme, availing himself of a breach in the holly screen, and of the assistance of the full moon, which was now arisen, had a perfect opportunity, himself unobserved, to reconnoitre the persons and the motions of those by whom his rest had been thus unexpectedly disturbed; and his observations confirmed his jealous apprehensions. They stood together in close and earnest conversation within four yards of the place of his retreat, and he could easily recognize the tall form and deep voice of Douglas, and the no less remarkable dress and tone of the page at the hostelry of Saint Michael's.

"I have been at the door of the page's apartment," said Douglas, "but he is not there, or he will not answer. It is fast bolted on the inside, as is the custom, and we cannot pass through it—and what his silence may bode I know not."

"You have trusted him too far," said the other; "a feather-headed coxcomb, upon whose changeable mind and hot brain there is no making an abiding impression."

"It was not I who was willing to trust him," said Douglas, "but I was assured he would prove friendly when called upon—for—" Here he spoke so low that Roland lost the tenor of his words, which was the more provoking, as he was fully aware that he was himself the subject of their conversation.

"Nay," replied the stranger, more aloud, "I have on my side put him off with fair words, which make fools vain—but now, if you distrust him at the push, deal with him with your dagger, and so make open passage."

"That were too rash," said Douglas; "and besides, as I told you, the door of his apartment is shut and bolted. I will essay again to waken him."

Graeme instantly comprehended, that the ladies, having been somehow made aware of his being in the garden, had secured the

SIR WALTER SCOTT

door of the outer room in which he usually slept, as a sort of sentinel upon that only access to the Queen's apartments. But then, how came Catherine Seyton to be abroad, if the Queen and the other lady were still within their chambers, and the access to them locked and bolted?—"I will be instantly at the bottom of these mysteries," he said, "and then thank Mistress Catherine, if this be really she, for the kind use which she exhorted Douglas to make of his dagger—they seek me, as I comprehend, and they shall not seek me in vain."

Douglas had by this time re-entered the castle by the wicket, which was now open. The stranger stood alone in the garden walk, his arms folded on his breast, and his eyes cast impatiently up to the moon, as if accusing her of betraying him by the magnificence of her lustre. In a moment Roland Graeme stood before him—"A goodly night," he said, "Mistress Catherine, for a young lady to stray forth in disguise, and to meet with men in an orchard!"

"Hush!" said the stranger page, "hush, thou foolish patch, and tell us in a word if thou art friend or foe."

"How should I be friend to one who deceives me by fair words, and who would have Douglas deal with me with his poniard?" replied Roland.

"The fiend receive George of Douglas and thee too, thou born madcap and sworn marplot!" said the other; "we shall be discovered, and then death is the word."

"Catherine," said the page, "you have dealt falsely and cruelly with me, and the moment of explanation is now come—neither it nor you shall escape me."

"Madman!" said the stranger, "I am neither Kate nor Catherine—the moon shines bright enough surely to know the hart from the hind."

"That shift shall not serve you, fair mistress," said the page, laying hold on the lap of the stranger's cloak; "this time, at least, I will know with whom I deal."

"Unhand me," said she, endeavouring to extricate herself from his grasp; and in a tone where anger seemed to contend with a desire to laugh, "use you so little discretion towards a daughter of Seyton?"

But as Roland, encouraged perhaps by her risibility to suppose his violence was not unpardonably offensive, kept hold on her mantle, she said, in a sterner tone of unmixed resentment,—"Madman! let me go!— there is life and death in this moment—I would not willingly hurt thee, and yet beware!"

As she spoke she made a sudden effort to escape, and, in doing so, a pistol, which she carried in her hand or about her person, went off.

This warlike sound instantly awakened the well-warded castle. The warder blew his horn, and began to toll the castle bell, crying out at the same time, "Fie, treason! treason! cry all! cry all!"

The apparition of Catherine Seyton, which the page had let loose in the first moment of astonishment, vanished in darkness; but the plash of oars was heard, and, in a second or two, five or six harquebuses and a falconet were fired from the battlements of the castle successively, as if levelled at some object on the water. Confounded with these incidents, no way for Catherine's protection (supposing her to be in the boat which he had heard put from the shore) occurred to Roland, save to have recourse to George of Douglas. He hastened for this purpose towards the apartment of the Queen, whence he heard loud voices and much trampling of feet. When he entered, he found himself added to a confused and astonished group, which, assembled in that apartment, stood gazing upon each other. At the upper end of the room stood the Queen, equipped as for a journey, and—attended not only by the Lady Fleming, but by the omnipresent Catherine Seyton, dressed in the habit of her own sex, and bearing in her hand the casket in which Mary kept such jewels as she had been permitted to retain. At the other end of the hall was the Lady of Lochleven, hastily dressed, as one startled from slumber by the sudden alarm, and surrounded by domestics, some bearing torches, others holding naked swords, partisans, pistols, or such other weapons as they had caught up in the hurry of a night alarm. Betwixt these two parties stood George of Douglas, his arms folded on his breast, his eyes bent on the ground, like a criminal who knows not how to deny, yet continues unwilling to avow, the guilt in which he has been detected.

"Speak, George of Douglas," said the Lady of Lochleven; "speak, and clear the horrid suspicion which rests on thy name. Say, 'A Douglas was never faithless to his trust, and I am a Douglas.' Say this, my dearest son, and it is all I ask thee to say to clear thy name, even under, such a foul charge. Say it was but the wile of these unhappy women, and this false boy, which plotted an escape so fatal to Scotland—so destructive to thy father's house."

"Madam," said old Dryfesdale the steward, "this much do I say for this silly page, that he could not be accessary to unlocking the doors, since I myself this night bolted him out of the castle. Whoever limned this night-piece, the lad's share in it seems to have been small."

"Thou liest, Dryfesdale," said the Lady, "and wouldst throw the blame on thy master's house, to save the worthless life of a gipsy boy."

"His death were more desirable to me than his life," answered the steward, sullenly; "but the truth is the truth."

At these words Douglas raised his head, drew up his figure to its full height, and spoke boldly and sedately, as one whose resolution was taken. "Let no life be endangered for me. I alone——"

"Douglas," said the Queen, interrupting him, "art thou mad? Speak not, I charge you."

"Madam," he replied, bowing with the deepest respect, "gladly would I obey your commands, but they must have a victim, and let it be the true one.—Yes, madam," he continued, addressing the Lady of Lochleven, "I alone am guilty in this matter. If the word of a Douglas has yet any weight with you, believe me that this boy is innocent; and on your conscience I charge you, do him no wrong; nor let the Queen suffer hardship for embracing the opportunity of freedom which sincere loyalty—which a sentiment yet deeper—offered to her acceptance. Yes! I had planned the escape of the most beautiful, the most persecuted of women; and far from regretting that I, for a while, deceived the malice of her enemies, I glory in it, and am most willing to yield up life itself in her cause."

"Now may God have compassion on my age," said the Lady of Lochleven, "and enable me to bear this load of affliction! O Princess, born in a luckless hour, when will you cease to be the instrument of seduction and of ruin to all who approach you? O ancient house of Lochleven, famed so long for birth and honour, evil was the hour which brought the deceiver under thy roof!"

"Say not so, madam," replied her grandson; "the old honours of the Douglas line will be outshone, when one of its descendants dies for the most injured of queens—for the most lovely of women."

"Douglas," said the Queen, "must I at this moment—ay, even at this moment, when I may lose a faithful subject for ever, chide thee for forgetting what is due to me as thy Queen?"

"Wretched boy," said the distracted Lady of Lochleven, "hast thou fallen even thus far into the snare of this Moabitish woman?—hast thou bartered thy name, thy allegiance, thy knightly oath, thy duty to thy parents, thy country, and thy God, for a feigned tear, or a sickly smile, from lips which flattered the infirm Francis—lured to death the idiot Darnley—read luscious poetry with the minion Chastelar—mingled in the lays of love which were sung by the beggar Rizzio—and which were joined in rapture to those of the foul and licentious Bothwell?"

"Blaspheme not, madam!" said Douglas;—"nor you, fair Queen, and virtuous as fair, chide at this moment the presumption of thy vassal!—Think not that the mere devotion of a subject could have moved me to the part I have been performing. Well you deserve that each of your lieges should die for you; but I have done more—have done that to which love alone could compel a Douglas—I have dissembled. Farewell, then, Queen of all hearts, and Empress of that of Douglas!—When you are freed from this vile bondage—as freed you shall be, if justice remains in Heaven—and when you load with honours and titles the happy man who shall deliver you, cast one thought on him whose heart would have despised every reward for a kiss of your hand—cast one thought on his fidelity, and drop one tear on his grave." And throwing himself at her feet, he seized her hand, and pressed it to his lips.

"This before my face!" exclaimed the Lady of Lochleven—"wilt thou court thy adulterous paramour before the eyes of a parent?—Tear them asunder, and put him under strict ward! Seize him, upon your lives!" she added, seeing that her attendants looked at each other with hesitation.

"They are doubtful," said Mary. "Save thyself, Douglas, I command thee!"

He started up from the floor, and only exclaiming, "My life or death are yours, and at your disposal!"—drew his sword, and broke through those who stood betwixt him and the door. The enthusiasm of his onset was too sudden and too lively to have been opposed by any thing short of the most decided opposition; and as he was both loved and feared by his father's vassals, none of them would offer him actual injury.

The Lady of Lochleven stood astonished at his sudden escape—"Am I surrounded," she said, "by traitors? Upon him, villains!—pursue, stab, cut him down."

"He cannot leave the island, madam," said Dryfesdale, interfering; "I have the key of the boat-chain."

But two or three voices of those who pursued from curiosity, or command of their mistress, exclaimed from below, that he had cast himself into the lake.

"Brave Douglas still!" exclaimed the Queen—"Oh, true and noble heart, that prefers death to imprisonment!"

"Fire upon him!" said the Lady of Lochleven; "if there be here a true servant of his father, let him shoot the runagate dead, and let the lake cover our shame!"

The report of a gun or two was heard, but they were probably shot rather to obey the Lady, than with any purpose of hitting the mark; and Randal immediately entering, said that Master George had been taken up by a boat from the castle, which lay at a little distance.

"Man a barge, and pursue them!" said the Lady.

"It were quite vain," said Randal; "by this time they are half way to shore, and a cloud has come over the moon."

"And has the traitor then escaped?" said the Lady, pressing her hands against her forehead with a gesture of despair; "the honour of our house is for ever gone, and all will be deemed accomplices in this base treachery."

"Lady of Lochleven," said Mary, advancing towards her, "you have this night cut off my fairest hopes—You have turned my expected freedom into bondage, and dashed away the cup of joy in the very instant I was advancing it to my lips—and yet I feel for your sorrow the pity that you deny to mine—Gladly would I comfort you if I might; but as I may not, I would at least part from you in charity."

"Away, proud woman!" said the Lady; "who ever knew so well as thou to deal the deepest wounds under the pretence of kindness and courtesy?—Who, since the great traitor, could ever so betray with a kiss?"

"Lady Douglas of Lochleven," said the Queen, "in this moment thou canst not offend me—no, not even by thy coarse and unwomanly language, held to me in the presence of menials and armed retainers. I have this night owed so much to one member of the house of Lochleven, as to cancel whatever its mistress can do or say in the wildness of her passion."

"We are bounden to you, Princess," said Lady Lochleven, putting a strong constraint on herself, and passing from her tone of violence to that of bitter irony; "our poor house hath been but seldom graced with royal smiles, and will hardly, with my choice, exchange their rough honesty for such court-honour as Mary of Scotland has now to bestow."

"They," replied Mary, "who knew so well how to *take*, may think themselves excused from the obligation implied in receiving. And that I have now little to offer, is the fault of the Douglasses and their allies."

"Fear nothing, madam," replied the Lady of Lochleven, in the same bitter tone, "you retain an exchequer which neither your own prodigality can drain, nor your offended country deprive you of. While you have fair words and delusive smiles at command, you need no other bribes to lure youth to folly."

The Queen cast not an ungratified glance on a large mirror, which, hanging on one side of the apartment, and illuminated by the torchlight, reflected her beautiful face and person. "Our hostess grows complaisant," she said, "my Fleming; we had not thought that grief and captivity had left us so well stored with that sort of wealth which ladies prize most dearly."

"Your Grace will drive this severe woman frantic," said Fleming, in a low tone. "On my knees I implore you to remember she is already dreadfully offended, and that we are in her power."

"I will not spare her, Fleming," answered the Queen; "it is against my nature. She returned my honest sympathy with insult and abuse, and I will gall her in return,—if her words are too blunt for answer, let her use her poniard if she dare!"

"The Lady Lochleven," said the Lady Fleming aloud, "would surely do well now to withdraw, and to leave her Grace to repose."

"Ay," replied the Lady, "or to leave her Grace, and her Grace's minions, to think what silly fly they may next wrap their meshes about. My eldest son is a widower—were he not more worthy the flattering hopes with which you have seduced his brother?—True, the yoke of marriage has been already thrice fitted on—but the church of Rome calls it a sacrament, and its votaries may deem it one in which they cannot too often participate."

"And the votaries of the church of Geneva," replied Mary, colouring with indignation, "as they deem marriage *no* sacrament, are said at times to dispense with the holy ceremony."—Then, as if afraid of the consequences of this home allusion to the errors of Lady Lochleven's early life, the Queen added, "Come, my Fleming, we grace her too much by this altercation; we will to our sleeping apartment. If she would disturb us again to-night, she must cause the door to be forced." So saying, she retired to her bed-room, followed by her two women.

Lady Lochleven, stunned as it were by this last sarcasm, and not the less deeply incensed that she had drawn it upon herself, remained like a statue on the spot which she had occupied when she received an affront so flagrant. Dryfesdale and Randal endeavoured to rouse her to recollection by questions.

"What is your honourable Ladyship's pleasure in the premises?"

"Shall we not double the sentinels, and place one upon the boats and another in the garden?" said Randal.

"Would you that despatches were sent to Sir William at Edinburgh, to acquaint him with what has happened?" demanded Dryfesdale; "and ought not the place of Kinross to be alarmed, lest there be force upon the shores of the lake?"

"Do all as thou wilt," said the Lady, collecting herself, and about to depart. "Thou hast the name of a good soldier, Dryfesdale, take all precautions.—Sacred Heaven! that I should be thus openly insulted!"

"Would it be your pleasure," said Dryfesdale, hesitating, "that this person—this Lady—be more severely restrained?"

"No, vassal!" answered the Lady, indignantly, "my revenge stoops not to so low a gratification. But I will have more worthy vengeance, or the tomb of my ancestors shall cover my shame!"

"And you shall have it, madam," replied Dryfesdale—"ere two suns go down, you shall term yourself amply revenged."

The Lady made no answer—perhaps did not hear his words, as she presently left the apartment. By the command of Dryfesdale, the rest of the attendants were dismissed, some to do the duty of guard, others to their repose. The steward himself remained after they had all departed; and Roland Graeme, who was alone in the apartment, was surprised to see the old soldier advance towards him with an air of greater cordiality than he had ever before assumed to him, but which sat ill on his scowling features.

"Youth," he said, "I have done thee some wrong—it is thine own fault, for thy behaviour hath seemed as light to me as the feather thou wearest in thy hat; and surely thy fantastic apparel, and idle humour of mirth and folly, have made me construe thee something harshly. But I saw this night from my casement, (as I looked out to see how thou hadst disposed of thyself in the garden,) I saw, I say, the true efforts which thou didst make to detain the companion of the perfidy of him who is no longer worthy to be called by his father's name, but must be cut off from his house like a rotten branch. I was just about to come to thy assistance when the pistol went off; and the warder (a false knave, whom I suspect to be bribed for the nonce) saw himself forced to give the alarm, which, perchance, till then he had wilfully withheld. To atone, therefore, for my injustice towards you, I would willingly render you a courtesy, if you would accept of it from my hands."

"May I first crave to know what it is?" replied the page.

"Simply to carry the news of this discovery to Holyrood, where thou mayest do thyself much grace, as well with the Earl of Morton and the Regent himself, as with Sir William Douglas, seeing thou hast seen the matter from end to end, and borne faithful part therein. The making thine own fortune will be thus lodged in thine own hand, when I trust thou wilt estrange thyself from foolish vanities, and learn to walk in this world as one who thinks upon the next."

"Sir Steward," said Roland Graeme, "I thank you for your courtesy, but I may not do your errand. I pass that I am the Queen's sworn servant, and may not be of counsel against her. But, setting this apart, methinks it were a bad road to Sir William of Lochleven's favour, to be the first to tell him of his son's defection—neither would the Regent be over well pleased to hear the infidelity of his vassal, nor Morton to learn the falsehood of his kinsman."

"Um!" said the steward, making that inarticulate sound which expresses surprise mingled with displeasure. "Nay, then, even fly where ye list; for, giddy-pated as ye may be, you know how to bear you in the world."

"I will show you my esteem is less selfish than ye think for," said the page; "for I hold truth and mirth to be better than gravity and cunning—ay, and in the end to be a match for them.—You never loved me less, Sir Steward, than you do at this moment. I know you will give me no real confidence, and I am resolved to accept no false protestations as current coin. Resume your old course—suspect me as much and watch me as closely as you will, I bid you defiance—you have met with your match."

"By Heaven, young man," said the steward, with a look of bitter malignity, "if thou darest to attempt any treachery towards the House of Lochleven, thy head shall blacken in the sun from the warder's turret!"

"He cannot commit treachery who refuses trust," said the page; "and for my head, it stands as securely on my shoulders, as on any turret that ever mason built."

"Farewell, thou prating and speckled pie," said Dryfesdale, "that art so vain of thine idle tongue and variegated coat! Beware trap and lime-twig."

"And fare thee well, thou hoarse old raven," answered the page; "thy solemn flight, sable hue, and deep croak, are no charms against bird-bolt or hail-shot, and that thou mayst find—it is open war betwixt us, each for the cause of our mistress, and God show the right!"

SIR WALTER SCOTT

"Amen, and defend his own people!" said the steward. "I will let my mistress know what addition thou hast made to this mess of traitors. Good night, Monsieur Featherpate."

"Good-night, Seignior Sowersby," replied the page; and, when the old man departed, he betook himself to rest.

XXXI

Poison'd—ill fare!—dead, forsook, cast off!—

—King John

However weary Roland Graeme might be of the Castle of Lochleven—however much he might wish that the plan for Mary's escape had been perfected, I question if he ever awoke with more pleasing feelings than on the morning after George Douglas's plan for accomplishing her deliverance had been frustrated. In the first place, he had the clearest conviction that he had misunderstood the innuendo of the Abbot, and that the affections of Douglas were fixed, not on Catherine Seyton, but on the Queen; and in the second place, from the sort of explanation which had taken place betwixt the steward and him, he felt himself at liberty, without any breach of honour towards the family of Lochleven, to contribute his best aid to any scheme which should in future be formed for the Queen's escape; and, independently of the good-will which he himself had to the enterprise, he knew he could find no surer road to the favour of Catherine Seyton. He now sought but an opportunity to inform her that he had dedicated himself to this task, and fortune was propitious in affording him one which was unusually favourable.

At the ordinary hour of breakfast, it was introduced by the steward with his usual forms, who, as soon as it was placed on the board in the inner apartment, said to Roland Graeme, with a glance of sarcastic import, "I leave you, my young sir, to do the office of sewer—it has been too long rendered to the Lady Mary by one belonging to the house of Douglas."

"Were it the prime and principal who ever bore the name," said Roland, "the office were an honour to him."

The steward departed without replying to this bravade, otherwise than by a dark look of scorn. Graeme, thus left alone, busied himself as one engaged in a labour of love, to imitate, as well as he could, the grace and courtesy with which George of Douglas was wont to render his ceremonial service at meals to the Queen of Scotland. There was more than youthful vanity—there was a generous devotion in the feeling with which he took up the task, as a brave soldier assumes the place of a

SIR WALTER SCOTT

comrade who has fallen in the front of battle. "I am now," he said, "their only champion: and, come weal, come wo, I will be, to the best of my skill and power, as faithful, as trustworthy, as brave, as any Douglas of them all could have been."

At this moment Catherine Seyton entered alone, contrary to her custom; and not less contrary to her custom, she entered with her kerchief at her eyes. Roland Graeme approached her with beating heart and with down-cast eyes, and asked her, in a low and hesitating voice, whether the Queen were well?

"Can you suppose it?" said Catherine. "Think you her heart and body are framed of steel and iron, to endure the cruel disappointment of yester even, and the infamous taunts of yonder puritanic hag?—Would to God that I were a man, to aid her more effectually!"

"If those who carry pistols, and batons, and poniards," said the page, "are not men, they are at least Amazons; and that is as formidable."

"You are welcome to the flash of your wit, sir," replied the damsel; "I am neither in spirits to enjoy, nor to reply to it."

"Well, then," said the page, "list to me in all serious truth. And, first, let me say, that the gear last night had been smoother, had you taken me into your counsels."

"And so we meant; but who could have guessed that Master Page should choose to pass all night in the garden, like some moon-stricken knight in a Spanish romance—instead of being in his bed-room, when Douglas came to hold communication with him on our project."

"And why," said the page, "defer to so late a moment so important a confidence?"

"Because your communications with Henderson, and—with pardon— the natural impetuosity and fickleness of your disposition, made us dread to entrust you with a secret of such consequence, till the last moment."

"And why at the last moment?" said the page, offended at this frank avowal; "why at that, or any other moment, since I had the misfortune to incur so much suspicion?"

"Nay—now you are angry again," said Catherine; "and to serve you aright I should break off this talk; but I will be magnanimous, and answer your question. Know, then, our reason for trusting you was twofold. In the first place, we could scarce avoid it, since you slept in the room through which we had to pass. In the second place—"

"Nay," said the page, "you may dispense with a second reason, when the first makes your confidence in me a case of necessity."

"Good now, hold thy peace," said Catherine. "In the second place, as I said before, there is one foolish person among us, who believes that Roland Graeme's heart is warm, though his head is giddy—that his blood is pure, though it boils too hastily—and that his faith and honour are true as the load-star, though his tongue sometimes is far less than discreet."

This avowal Catherine repeated in a low tone, with her eye fixed on the floor, as if she shunned the glance of Roland while she suffered it to escape her lips—"And this single friend," exclaimed the youth in rapture; "this only one who would do justice to the poor Roland Graeme, and whose own generous heart taught her to distinguish between follies of the brain and faults of the heart—Will you not tell me, dearest Catherine, to whom I owe my most grateful, my most heartfelt thanks?"

"Nay," said Catherine, with her eyes still fixed on the ground, "if your own heart tell you not—"

"Dearest Catherine!" said the page, seizing upon her hand, and kneeling on one knee.

"If your own heart, I say, tell you not," said Catherine, gently disengaging her hand, "it is very ungrateful; for since the maternal kindness of the Lady Fleming—"

The page started on his feet. "By Heaven, Catherine, your tongue wears as many disguises as your person! But you only mock me, cruel girl. You know the Lady Fleming has no more regard for any one, than hath the forlorn princess who is wrought into yonder piece of old figured court tapestry."

"It may be so," said Catherine Seyton, "but you should not speak so loud."

"Pshaw!" answered the page, but at the same time lowering his voice, "she cares for no one but herself and the Queen. And you know, besides, there is no one of you whose opinion I value, if I have not your own. No—not that of Queen Mary herself."

"The more shame for you, if it be so," said Catherine, with great composure.

"Nay, but, fair Catherine," said the page, "why will you thus damp my ardour, when I am devoting myself, body and soul, to the cause of your mistress?"

"It is because in doing so," said Catherine, "you debase a cause so noble, by naming along with it any lower or more selfish motive. Believe me," she said, with kindling eyes, and while the blood mantled on her cheek, "they think vilely and falsely of women—I mean of those who deserve the name—who deem that they love the gratification of their vanity, or the mean purpose of engrossing a lover's admiration and affection, better than they love the virtue and honour of the man they may be brought to prefer. He that serves his religion, his prince, and his country, with ardour and devotion, need not plead his cause with the commonplace rant of romantic passion—the woman whom he honours with his love becomes his debtor, and her corresponding affection is engaged to repay his glorious toil."

"You hold a glorious prize for such toil," said the youth, bending his eyes on her with enthusiasm.

"Only a heart which knows how to value it," said Catherine. "He that should free this injured Princess from these dungeons, and set her at liberty among her loyal and warlike nobles, whose hearts are burning to welcome her—where is the maiden in Scotland whom the love of such a hero would not honour, were she sprung from the blood royal of the land, and he the offspring of the poorest cottager that ever held a plough?"

"I am determined," said Roland, "to take the adventure. Tell me first, however, fair Catherine, and speak it as if you were confessing to the priest—this poor Queen, I know she is unhappy—but, Catherine, do you hold her innocent? She is accused of murder."

"Do I hold the lamb guilty, because it is assailed by the wolf?" answered Catherine; "do I hold yonder sun polluted, because an earth-damp sullies his beams?"

The page sighed and looked down. "Would my conviction were as deep as thine! But one thing is clear, that in this captivity she hath wrong—She rendered herself up, on a capitulation, and the terms have been refused her—I will embrace her quarrel to the death!"

"Will you—will you, indeed?" said Catherine, taking his hand in her turn. "Oh, be but firm in mind, as thou art bold in deed and quick in resolution; keep but thy plighted faith, and after ages shall honour thee as the saviour of Scotland!"

"But when I have toiled successfully to win that Leah, Honour, thou wilt not, my Catherine," said the page, "condemn me to a new term of service for that Rachel, Love?"

"Of that," said Catherine, again extricating her hand from his grasp, "we shall have full time to speak; but Honour is the elder sister, and must be won the first."

"I may not win her," answered the page; "but I will venture fairly for her, and man can do no more. And know, fair Catherine,—for you shall see the very secret thought of my heart,—that not Honour only—not only that other and fairer sister, whom you frown on me for so much as mentioning—but the stern commands of duty also, compel me to aid the Queen's deliverance."

"Indeed!" said Catherine; "you were wont to have doubts on that matter."

"Ay, but her life was not then threatened," replied Roland.

"And is it now more endangered than heretofore?" asked Catherine Seyton, in anxious terror.

"Be not alarmed," said the page; "but you heard the terms on which your royal mistress parted with the Lady of Lochleven?"

"Too well—but too well," said Catherine; "alas! that she cannot rule her princely resentment, and refrain from encounters like these!"

"That hath passed betwixt them," said Roland, "for which woman never forgives woman. I saw the Lady's brow turn pale, and then black, when, before all the menzie, and in her moment of power, the Queen humbled her to the dust by taxing her with her shame. And I heard the oath of deadly resentment and revenge which she muttered in the ear of one, who by his answer will, I judge, be but too ready an executioner of her will."

"You terrify me," said Catherine.

"Do not so take it—call up the masculine part of your spirit—we will counteract and defeat her plans, be they dangerous as they may. Why do you look upon me thus, and weep?"

"Alas!" said Catherine, "because you stand there before me a living and breathing man, in all the adventurous glow and enterprise of youth, yet still possessing the frolic spirits of childhood—there you stand, full alike of generous enterprise and childish recklessness; and if to-day, or to-morrow, or some such brief space, you lie a mangled and lifeless corpse upon the floor of these hateful dungeons, who but Catherine Seyton will be the cause of your brave and gay career being broken short as you start from the goal? Alas! she whom you have chosen to twine your wreath, may too probably have to work your shroud!"

"And be it so, Catherine," said the page, in the full glow of youthful enthusiasm; "and *do* thou work my shroud! and if thou grace it with such tears as fall now at the thought, it will honour my remains more than an earl's mantle would my living body. But shame on this faintness of heart! the time craves a firmer mood—Be a woman, Catherine, or rather be a man—thou canst be a man if thou wilt."

Catherine dried her tears, and endeavoured to smile.

"You must not ask me," she said, "about that which so much disturbs your mind; you shall know all in time—nay, you should know all now, but that—Hush! here comes the Queen."

Mary entered from her apartment, paler than usual, and apparently exhausted by a sleepless night, and by the painful thoughts which had ill supplied the place of repose; yet the languor of her looks was so far from impairing her beauty, that it only substituted the frail delicacy of the lovely woman for the majestic grace of the Queen. Contrary to her wont, her toilette had been very hastily despatched, and her hair, which was usually dressed by Lady Fleming with great care, escaping from beneath the headtire, which had been hastily adjusted, fell in long and luxuriant tresses of Nature's own curling, over a neck and bosom which were somewhat less carefully veiled than usual.

As she stepped over the threshold of her apartment, Catherine, hastily drying her tears, ran to meet her royal mistress, and having first kneeled at her feet, and kissed her hand, instantly rose, and placing herself on the other side of the Queen, seemed anxious to divide with the Lady Fleming the honour of supporting and assisting her. The page, on his part, advanced and put in order the chair of state, which she usually occupied, and having placed the cushion and footstool for her accommodation, stepped back, and stood ready for service in the place usually occupied by his predecessor, the young Seneschal. Mary's eye rested an instant on him, and could not but remark the change of persons. Hers was not the female heart which could refuse compassion, at least, to a gallant youth who had suffered in her cause, although he had been guided in his enterprise by a too presumptuous passion; and the words "Poor Douglas!" escaped from her lips, perhaps unconsciously, as she leant herself back in her chair, and put the kerchief to her eyes.

"Yes, gracious madam," said Catherine, assuming a cheerful manner, in order to cheer her sovereign, "our gallant Knight is indeed banished—the adventure was not reserved for him; but he has left behind him a youthful Esquire, as much devoted to your Grace's service, and who, by me, makes you tender of his hand and sword."

"If they may in aught avail your Grace," said Roland Graeme, bowing profoundly.

"Alas!" said the Queen, "what needs this, Catherine?—why prepare new victims to be involved in, and overwhelmed by, my cruel fortune?—were we not better cease to struggle, and ourselves sink in the tide without farther resistance, than thus drag into destruction with us every generous heart which makes an effort in our favour?—I have had but too much of plot and intrigue around me, since I was stretched an orphan child in my very cradle, while contending nobles strove which should rule in the name of the unconscious innocent. Surely time it were that all this busy and most dangerous coil should end. Let me call my prison a convent, and my seclusion a voluntary sequestration of myself from the world and its ways."

"Speak not thus, madam, before your faithful servants," said Catherine, "to discourage their zeal at once, and to break their hearts. Daughter of Kings, be not in this hour so unkingly—Come, Roland, and let us, the youngest of her followers, show ourselves worthy of her cause—let us kneel before her footstool, and implore her to be her own magnanimous self." And leading Roland Graeme to the Queen's seat, they both kneeled down before her. Mary raised herself in her chair, and sat erect, while, extending one hand to be kissed by the page, she arranged with the other the clustering locks which shaded the bold yet lovely brow of the high-spirited Catherine.

"Alas! *ma mignóne*," she said, for so in fondness she often called her young attendant, "that you should thus desperately mix with my unhappy fate the fortune of your young lives!—Are they not a lovely couple, my Fleming? and is it not heart-rending to think that I must be their ruin?"

"Not so," said Roland Graeme, "it is we, gracious Sovereign, who will be your deliverers."

"*Ex oribus parvulorum!*" said the Queen, looking upward; "if it is by the mouth of these children that Heaven calls me to resume the stately thoughts which become my birth and my rights, thou wilt grant them thy protection, and to me the power of rewarding their zeal!"—Then turning to Fleming, she instantly added,—"Thou knowest, my friend, whether to make those who have served me happy, was not ever Mary's favourite pastime. When I have been rebuked by the stern preachers of the Calvinistic heresy—when I have seen the fierce countenances of my nobles averted from me, has it not been because I mixed in the harmless pleasures of the young and gay, and rather for the sake of their happiness than my own, have mingled in the masque, the song, or the dance, with the youth of my household? Well, I repent not of it—though Knox termed it sin, and Morton degradation—I was happy, because I saw happiness around me; and woe betide the wretched jealousy that can extract guilt out of the overflowings of an unguarded gaiety!—Fleming, if we are restored to our throne, shall we not have one blithesome day at a blithesome bridal, of which we must now name neither the bride nor the bridegroom? but that bridegroom shall have the barony of Blairgowrie, a fair gift even for a Queen to give, and that bride's chaplet shall be twined with the fairest pearls that ever were found in the depths of Lochlomond; and thou thyself, Mary Fleming, the best dresser of tires that ever busked the tresses of a Queen, and who would scorn to touch those of any woman of lower rank,—thou thyself shalt, for my love, twine them into the bride's tresses.—Look, my Fleming, suppose them such clustered locks as those of our Catherine, they would not put shame upon thy skill."

So saying, she passed her hand fondly over the head of her youthful favourite, while her more aged attendant replied despondently, "Alas! madam, your thoughts stray far from home."

"They do, my Fleming," said the Queen; "but is it well or kind in you to call them back?—God knows, they have kept the perch this night but too closely—Come, I will recall the gay vision, were it but to punish them. Yes, at that blithesome bridal, Mary herself shall forget the weight of sorrows, and the toil of state, and herself once more lead a measure.—At whose wedding was it that we last danced, my Fleming? I think care has troubled my memory—yet something of it I should remember—canst thou not aid me?—I know thou canst."

"Alas! madam," replied the lady—

"What!" said Mary, "wilt thou not help us so far? this is a peevish adherence to thine own graver opinion, which holds our talk as folly. But thou art court-bred, and wilt well understand me when I say, the Queen *commands* Lady Fleming to tell her where she led the last *branle*."

With a face deadly pale, and a mien as if she were about to sink into the earth, the court-bred dame, no longer daring to refuse obedience, faltered out—"Gracious Lady—if my memory err not—it was at a masque in Holyrood—at the marriage of Sebastian."

The unhappy Queen, who had hitherto listened with a melancholy smile, provoked by the reluctance with which the Lady Fleming brought out her story, at this ill-fated word interrupted her with a shriek so wild and loud that the vaulted apartment rang, and both Roland and Catherine sprang to their feet in the utmost terror and alarm. Meantime, Mary seemed, by the train of horrible ideas thus suddenly excited, surprised not only beyond self-command, but for the moment beyond the verge of reason.

"Traitress!" she said to the Lady Fleming, "thou wouldst slay thy sovereign—Call my French guards—*a moi! a moi! mes Français!*—I am beset with traitors in mine own palace—they have murdered my husband—Rescue! rescue for the Queen of Scotland!" She started up from her chair—her features, late so exquisitely lovely in their paleness, now inflamed with the fury of frenzy, and resembling those of a Bellona. "We will take the field ourself," she said; "warn the city—warn Lothian and Fife—saddle our Spanish barb, and bid French Paris see our petronel be charged!—Better to die at the head of our brave Scotsmen, like our grandfather at Flodden, than of a broken heart, like our ill-starred father!"

"Be patient—be composed, dearest Sovereign," said Catherine: and then addressing Lady Fleming angrily, she added, "How could you say aught that reminded her of her husband?"

The word reached the ear of the unhappy Princess, who caught it up, speaking with great rapidity. "Husband!—what husband?—Not his most Christian Majesty—he is ill at ease—he cannot mount on horseback.—Not him of the Lennox—but it was the Duke of Orkney thou wouldst say."

"For God's love, madam, be patient!" said the Lady Fleming.

But the Queen's excited imagination could by no entreaty be diverted from its course. "Bid him come hither to our aid," she said, "and bring with him his lambs, as he calls them—Bowton, Hay of Talla, Black Ormiston, and his kinsman Hob—Fie! how swart they are, and how they smell of sulphur! What! closeted with Morton? Nay, if the Douglas and the Hepburn hatch the complot together, the bird, when it breaks the shell, will scare Scotland. Will it not, my Fleming?"

"She grows wilder and wilder," said Fleming; "we have too many hearers for these strange words."

"Roland," said Catherine, "in the name of God, begone! You cannot aid us here—Leave us to deal with her alone—Away—away!"

She thrust him to the door of the anteroom; yet even when he had entered that apartment, and shut the door, he could still hear the Queen talk in a loud and determined tone, as if giving forth orders, until at length the voice died away in a feeble and continued lamentation.

SIR WALTER SCOTT

At this crisis Catherine entered the anteroom. "Be not too anxious," she said, "the crisis is now over; but keep the door fast—let no one enter until she is more composed."

"In the name of God, what does this mean?" said the page; "or what was there in the Lady Fleming's words to excite so wild a transport?"

"Oh, the Lady Fleming, the Lady Fleming," said Catherine, repeating the words impatiently; "the Lady Fleming is a fool—she loves her mistress, yet knows so little how to express her love, that were the Queen to ask her for very poison, she would deem it a point of duty not to resist her commands. I could have torn her starched head-tire from her formal head—The Queen should have as soon had the heart out of my body, as the word Sebastian out of my lips—That that piece of weaved tapestry should be a woman, and yet not have wit enough to tell a lie!"

"And what was this story of Sebastian?" said the page. "By Heaven, Catherine, you are all riddles alike!"

"You are as great a fool as Fleming," returned the impatient maiden; "know ye not, that on the night of Henry Darnley's murder, and at the blowing up of the Kirk of Field, the Queen's absence was owing to her attending on a masque at Holyrood, given by her to grace the marriage of this same Sebastian, who, himself a favoured servant, married one of her female attendants, who was near to her person?"

"By Saint Giles," said the page, "I wonder not at her passion, but only marvel by what forgetfulness it was that she could urge the Lady Fleming with such a question."

"I cannot account for it," said Catherine; "but it seems as if great and violent grief and horror sometimes obscure the memory, and spread a cloud like that of an exploding cannon, over the circumstances with which they are accompanied. But I may not stay here, where I came not to moralize with your wisdom, but simply to cool my resentment against that unwise Lady Fleming, which I think hath now somewhat abated, so that I shall endure her presence without any desire to damage either her curch or vasquine. Meanwhile, keep fast that door—I would not for my life that any of these heretics saw her in the unhappy state, which, brought on her as it has been by the success of their own diabolical plottings, they would not stick to call, in their snuffling cant, the judgment of Providence."

She left the apartment just as the latch of the outward door was raised from without. But the bolt which Roland had drawn on the inside, resisted the efforts of the person desirous to enter. "Who is there?" said Graeme aloud.

"It is I," replied the harsh and yet slow voice of the steward Dryfesdale.

"You cannot enter now," returned the youth.

"And wherefore?" demanded Dryfesdale, "seeing I come but to do my duty, and inquire what mean the shrieks from the apartment of the Moabitish woman. Wherefore, I say, since such is mine errand, can I not enter?"

"Simply," replied the youth, "because the bolt is drawn, and I have no fancy to undo it. I have the right side of the door to-day, as you had last night."

"Thou art ill-advised, thou malapert boy," replied the steward, "to speak to me in such fashion; but I shall inform my Lady of thine insolence."

"The insolence," said the page, "is meant for thee only, in fair guerdon of thy discourtesy to me. For thy Lady's information, I have answer more courteous—you may say that the Queen is ill at ease, and desires to be disturbed neither by visits nor messages."

"I conjure you, in the name of God," said the old man, with more solemnity in his tone than he had hitherto used, "to let me know if her malady really gains power on her!"

"She will have no aid at your hand, or at your Lady's—wherefore, begone, and trouble us no more—we neither want, nor will accept of, aid at your hands."

With this positive reply, the steward, grumbling and dissatisfied, returned down stairs.

XXXII

It is the curse of kings to be attended
By slaves, who take their humours for a warrant
To break into the bloody house of life,
And on the winking of authority
To understand a law.

—KING JOHN

The Lady of Lochleven sat alone in her chamber, endeavouring with sincere but imperfect zeal, to fix her eyes and her attention on the black-lettered Bible which lay before her, bound in velvet and embroidery, and adorned with massive silver clasps and knosps. But she found her utmost efforts unable to withdraw her mind from the resentful recollection of what had last night passed betwixt her and the Queen, in which the latter had with such bitter taunt reminded her of her early and long-repented transgression.

"Why," she said, "should I resent so deeply that another reproaches me with that which I have never ceased to make matter of blushing to myself? and yet, why should this woman, who reaps—at least, has reaped—the fruits of my folly, and has jostled my son aside from the throne, why should she, in the face of all my domestics, and of her own, dare to upbraid me with my shame? Is she not in my power? Does she not fear me? Ha! wily tempter, I will wrestle with thee strongly, and with better suggestions than my own evil heart can supply!"

She again took up the sacred volume, and was endeavouring to fix her attention on its contents, when she was disturbed by a tap at the door of the room. It opened at her command, and the steward Dryfesdale entered, and stood before her with a gloomy and perturbed expression on his brow.

"What has chanced, Dryfesdale, that thou lookest thus?" said his mistress—"Have there been evil tidings of my son, or of my grandchildren?"

"No, Lady," replied Dryfesdale, "but you were deeply insulted last night, and I fear me thou art as deeply avenged this morning—Where is the chaplain?"

"What mean you by hints so dark, and a question so sudden? The chaplain, as you well know, is absent at Perth upon an assembly of the brethren."

"I care not," answered the steward; "he is but a priest of Baal."

"Dryfesdale," said the Lady, sternly, "what meanest thou? I have ever heard, that in the Low Countries thou didst herd with the Anabaptist preachers, those boars which tear up the vintage—But the ministry which suits me and my house must content my retainers."

"I would I had good ghostly counsel, though," replied the steward, not attending to his mistress's rebuke, and seeming to speak to himself. "This woman of Moab—"

"Speak of her with reverence," said the Lady; "she is a king's daughter."

"Be it so," replied Dryfesdale; "she goes where there is little difference betwixt her and a beggar's child—Mary of Scotland is dying."

"Dying, and in my castle!" said the Lady, starting up in alarm; "of what disease, or by what accident?"

"Bear patience, Lady. The ministry was mine."

"Thine, villain and traitor!—how didst thou dare—"

"I heard you insulted, Lady—I heard you demand vengeance—I promised you should have it, and I now bring tidings of it."

"Dryfesdale, I trust thou ravest?" said the Lady.

"I rave not," replied the steward. "That which was written of me a million of years ere I saw the light, must be executed by me. She hath that in her veins that, I fear me, will soon stop the springs of life." "Cruel villain," exclaimed the Lady, "thou hast not poisoned her?" "And if I had," said Dryfesdale, "what does it so greatly merit? Men bane vermin—why not rid them of their enemies so? in Italy they will do it for a cruizuedor."

"Cowardly ruffian, begone from my sight!"

"Think better of my zeal, Lady," said the steward, "and judge not without looking around you. Lindesay, Ruthven, and your kinsman Morton, poniarded Rizzio, and yet you now see no blood on their embroidery—the Lord Semple stabbed the Lord of Sanquhar—does his bonnet sit a jot more awry on his brow? What noble lives in Scotland who has not had a share, for policy or revenge, in some such dealing?— and who imputes it to them? Be not cheated with names—a dagger or a draught work to the same end, and are little unlike—a glass phial imprisons the one, and a leathern sheath the other—one deals with the brain, the other sluices the blood—Yet, I say not I gave aught to this lady."

"What dost thou mean by thus dallying with me?" said the Lady; "as thou wouldst save thy neck from the rope it merits, tell me the whole truth of this story-thou hast long been known a dangerous man."

"Ay, in my master's service I can be cold and sharp as my sword. Be it known to you, that when last on shore, I consulted with a woman of skill and power, called Nicneven, of whom the country has rung for some brief time past. Fools asked her for charms to make them beloved, misers for means to increase their store; some demanded to know the future—an idle wish, since it cannot be altered; others would have an explanation of the past—idler still, since it cannot be recalled. I heard their queries with scorn, and demanded the means of avenging myself of a deadly enemy, for I grow old, and may trust no longer to Bilboa blade. She gave me a packet—'Mix that,' said she, 'with any liquid, and thy vengeance is complete.'"

"Villain! and you mixed it with the food of this imprisoned Lady, to the dishonour of thy master's house?"

"To redeem the insulted honour of my master's house, I mixed the contents of the packet with the jar of succory-water: They seldom fail to drain it, and the woman loves it over all."

"It was a work of hell," said the Lady Lochleven, "both the asking and the granting.—Away, wretched man, let us see if aid be yet too late!"

"They will not admit us, madam, save we enter by force—I have been twice at the door, but can obtain no entrance."

"We will beat it level with the ground, if needful—And, hold—summon Randal hither instantly.—Randal, here is a foul and evil chance befallen—send off a boat instantly to Kinross, the Chamberlain Luke Lundin is said to have skill—Fetch off, too, that foul witch Nicneven; she shall first counteract her own spell, and then be burned to ashes in the island of Saint Serf. Away, away—Tell them to hoist sail and ply oar, as ever they would have good of the Douglas's hand!"

"Mother Nicneven will not be lightly found, or fetched hither on these conditions," answered Dryfesdale.

"Then grant her full assurance of safety—Look to it, for thine own life must answer for this lady's recovery."

"I might have guessed that," said Dryfesdale, sullenly; "but it is my comfort I have avenged mine own cause, as well as yours. She hath scoffed and scripped at me, and encouraged her saucy minion of a page to ridicule my stiff gait and slow speech. I felt it borne in upon me that I was to be avenged on them."

"Go to the western turret," said the Lady, "and remain there in ward until we see how this gear will terminate. I know thy resolved disposition—thou wilt not attempt escape."

"Not were the walls of the turret of egg-shells, and the lake sheeted ice," said Dryfesdale. "I am well taught, and strong in belief, that man does nought of himself; he is but the foam on the billow, which rises, bubbles, and bursts, not by its own effort, but by the mightier impulse of fate which urges him. Yet, Lady, if I may advise, amid this zeal for the life of the Jezebel of Scotland, forget not what is due to thine own honour, and keep the matter secret as you may."

So saying, the gloomy fatalist turned from her, and stalked off with sullen composure to the place of confinement allotted to him.

His lady caught at his last hint, and only expressed her fear that the prisoner had partaken of some unwholesome food, and was dangerously ill. The castle was soon alarmed and in confusion. Randal was dispatched to the shore to fetch off Lundin, with such remedies as could counteract poison; and with farther instructions to bring mother Nicneven, if she could be found, with full power to pledge the Lady of Lochleven's word for her safety.

Meanwhile the Lady of Lochleven herself held parley at the door of the Queen's apartment, and in vain urged the page to undo it.

"Foolish boy!" she said, "thine own life and thy Lady's are at stake—Open, I say, or we will cause the door to be broken down."

"I may not open the door without my royal mistress's orders," answered Roland; "she has been very ill, and now she slumbers—if you wake her by using violence, let the consequence be on you and your followers."

"Was ever woman in a strait so fearful!" exclaimed the Lady of Lochleven—"At least, thou rash boy, beware that no one tastes the food, but especially the jar of succory-water."

She then hastened to the turret, where Dryfesdale had composedly resigned himself to imprisonment. She found him reading, and demanded of him, "Was thy fell potion of speedy operation?"

"Slow," answered the steward. "The hag asked me which I chose—I told her I loved a slow and sure revenge. 'Revenge,' said I, 'is the highest-flavoured draught which man tastes upon earth, and he should sip it by little and little—not drain it up greedily at once."

"Against whom, unhappy man, couldst thou nourish so fell a revenge?"

"I had many objects, but the chief was that insolent page."

"The boy!—thou inhuman man!" exclaimed the lady; "what could he do to deserve thy malice?"

"He rose in your favour, and you graced him with your commissions— that was one thing. He rose in that of George Douglas's also—that was another. He was the favourite of the Calvinistic Henderson, who hated me because my spirit disowns a separated priesthood. The Moabitish Queen held him dear—winds from each opposing point blew in his favour—the old servitor of your house was held lightly among ye— above all, from the first time I saw his face, I longed to destroy him."

"What fiend have I nurtured in my house!" replied the Lady. "May God forgive me the sin of having given thee food and raiment!"

"You might not choose, Lady," answered the steward. "Long ere this castle was builded—ay, long ere the islet which sustains it reared its head above the blue water, I was destined to be your faithful slave, and you to be my ungrateful mistress. Remember you not when I plunged amid the victorious French, in the time of this lady's mother, and brought off your husband, when those who had hung at the same breasts with him dared not attempt the rescue?—Remember how I plunged into the lake when your grandson's skiff was overtaken by the tempest, boarded, and steered her safe to the land. Lady—the servant of a Scottish baron is he who regards not his own life, or that of any other, save his master. And, for the death of the woman, I had tried the potion on her sooner, had not Master George been her taster. Her death—would it not be the happiest news that Scotland ever heard? Is she not of the bloody Guisian stock, whose sword was so often red with the blood of God's saints? Is she not the daughter of the wretched tyrant James, whom Heaven cast down from his kingdom, and his pride, even as the king of Babylon was smitten?"

"Peace, villain!" said the Lady—a thousand varied recollections thronging on her mind at the mention of her royal lover's name; "Peace, and disturb not the ashes of the dead—of the royal, of the unhappy dead. Read thy Bible; and may God grant thee to avail thyself better of its contents than thou hast yet done!" She departed hastily, and as she reached the next apartment, the tears rose in her eyes so hastily, that she was compelled to stop and use her kerchief to dry them. "I expected not this," she said, "no more than to have drawn water from the dry flint, or sap from a withered tree. I saw with a dry eye the apostacy and shame of George Douglas, the hope of my son's house—the child of my love; and yet I now weep for him who has so long lain in his grave—for him to whom I owe it that his daughter can make a scoffing and a jest of my name! But she is *his* daughter—my heart, hardened against her for so many causes, relents when a glance of her eye places her father unexpectedly before me—and as often her likeness to that true daughter of the house of Guise, her detested mother, has again confirmed my resolution. But she must not—must not die in my house, and by so foul a practice. Thank God, the operation of the potion is slow, and may be counteracted. I will to her apartment once more. But oh! that hardened villain, whose fidelity we held in such esteem, and had such high proof of! What miracle can unite so much wickedness and so much truth in one bosom!"

The Lady of Lochleven was not aware how far minds of a certain gloomy and determined cast by nature, may be warped by a keen sense of petty injuries and insults, combining with the love of gain, and sense of self-interest, and amalgamated with the crude, wild, and indigested fanatical opinions which this man had gathered among the crazy sectaries of Germany; or how far the doctrines of fatalism, which he had embraced so decidedly, sear the human conscience, by representing our actions as the result of inevitable necessity.

During her visit to the prisoner, Roland had communicated to Catherine the tenor of the conversation he had had with her at the door of the apartment. The quick intelligence of that lively maiden instantly comprehended the outline of what was believed to have happened, but her prejudices hurried her beyond the truth.

"They meant to have poisoned us," she exclaimed in horror, "and there stands the fatal liquor which should have done the deed!—Ay, as soon as Douglas ceased to be our taster, our food was likely to be fatally seasoned. Thou, Roland, who shouldst have made the essay, wert readily doomed to die with us. Oh, dearest Lady Fleming, pardon, pardon, for the injuries I said to you in my anger—your words were prompted by Heaven to save our lives, and especially that of the injured Queen. But what have we now to do? that old crocodile of the lake will be presently back to shed her hypocritical tears over our dying agonies.—Lady Fleming, what shall we do?"

"Our Lady help us in our need!" she replied; "how should I tell?—unless we were to make our plaint to the Regent."

"Make our plaint to the devil," said Catherine impatiently, "and accuse his dam at the foot of his burning throne!—The Queen still sleeps—we must gain time. The poisoning hag must not know her

　　　　　　　　　　　SIR WALTER SCOTT

scheme has miscarried; the old envenomed spider has but too many ways of mending her broken web. The jar of succory-water," said she—"Roland, if thou be'st a man, help me—empty the jar on the chimney or from the window—make such waste among the viands as if we had made our usual meal, and leave the fragments on cup and porringer, but taste nothing as thou lovest thy life. I will sit by the Queen, and tell her at her waking, in what a fearful pass we stand. Her sharp wit and ready spirit will teach us what is best to be done. Meanwhile, till farther notice, observe, Roland, that the Queen is in a state of torpor—that Lady Fleming is indisposed—that character" (speaking in a lower tone) "will suit her best, and save her wits some labour in vain. I am not so much indisposed, thou understandest."

"And I?" said the page—

"You?" replied Catherine, "you are quite well—who thinks it worth while to poison puppy-dogs or pages?"

"Does this levity become the time?" asked the page.

"It does, it does," answered Catherine Seyton; "if the Queen approves, I see plainly how this disconcerted attempt may do us good service."

She went to work while she spoke, eagerly assisted by Roland. The breakfast table soon displayed the appearance as if the meal had been eaten as usual; and the ladies retired as softly as possible into the Queen's sleeping apartment. At a new summons of the Lady Lochleven, the page undid the door, and admitted her into the anteroom, asking her pardon for having withstood her, alleging in excuse, that the Queen had fallen into a heavy slumber since she had broken her fast.

"She has eaten and drunken, then?" said the Lady of Lochleven.

"Surely," replied the page, "according to her Grace's ordinary custom, unless upon the fasts of the church."

"The jar," she said, hastily examining it, "it is empty—drank the Lady Mary the whole of this water?"

"A large part, madam; and I heard the Lady Catherine Seyton jestingly upbraid the Lady Mary Fleming with having taken more than a just share of what remained, so that but little fell to her own lot."

"And are they well in health?" said the Lady of Lochleven.

"Lady Fleming," said the page, "complains of lethargy, and looks duller than usual; and the Lady Catherine of Seyton feels her head somewhat more giddy than is her wont."

He raised his voice a little as he said these words, to apprise the ladies of the part assigned to each of them, and not, perhaps, without the wish of conveying to the ears of Catherine the page-like jest which lurked in the allotment.

"I will enter the Queen's bedchamber," said the Lady of Lochleven; "my business is express."

As she advanced to the door, the voice of Catherine Seyton was heard from within—"No one can enter here—the Queen sleeps."

"I will not be controlled, young lady," replied the Lady of Lochleven; "there is, I wot, no inner bar, and I will enter in your despite."

"There is, indeed, no inner bar," answered Catherine, firmly, "but there are the staples where that bar should be; and into those staples have I thrust mine arm, like an ancestress of your own, when, better employed than the Douglasses of our days, she thus defended the bedchamber of her sovereign against murderers. Try your force, then, and see whether a Seyton cannot rival in courage a maiden of the house of Douglas."

"I dare not attempt the pass at such risk," said the Lady of Lochleven: "Strange, that this Princess, with all that justly attaches to her as blameworthy, should preserve such empire over the minds of her attendants.—Damsel, I give thee my honour that I come for the Queen's safety and advantage. Awaken her, if thou lovest her, and pray her leave that I may enter—I will retire from the door the whilst."

"Thou wilt not awaken the Queen?" said the Lady Fleming.

"What choice have we?" said the ready-witted maiden, "unless you deem it better to wait till the Lady Lochleven herself plays lady of the bedchamber. Her fit of patience will not last long, and the Queen must be prepared to meet her."

"But thou wilt bring back her Grace's fit by thus disturbing her."

"Heaven forbid!" replied Catherine; "but if so, it must pass for an effect of the poison. I hope better things, and that the Queen will be able when she wakes to form her own judgment in this terrible crisis. Meanwhile, do thou, dear Lady Fleming, practise to look as dull and heavy as the alertness of thy spirit will permit."

Catherine kneeled by the side of the Queen's bed, and, kissing her hand repeatedly, succeeded at last in awakening without alarming her. She seemed surprised to find that she was ready dressed, but sate up in her bed, and appeared so perfectly composed, that Catherine Seyton, without farther preamble, judged it safe to inform her of the predicament in which they were placed. Mary turned pale, and crossed herself again and again, when she heard the imminent danger in which she had stood. But, like the Ulysses of Homer,

—Hardly waking yet,
Sprung in her mind the momentary wit,

and she at once understood her situation, with the dangers and advantages that attended it.

"We cannot do better," she said, after her hasty conference with Catherine, pressing her at the same time to her bosom, and kissing her forehead; "we cannot do better than to follow the scheme so happily devised by thy quick wit and bold affection. Undo the door to the Lady Lochleven—She shall meet her match in art, though not in perfidy. Fleming, draw close the curtain, and get thee behind it—thou art a better tire-woman than an actress; do but breathe heavily, and, if thou wilt, groan slightly, and it will top thy part. Hark! they come. Now, Catherine of Medicis, may thy spirit inspire me, for a cold northern brain is too blunt for this scene!"

Ushered by Catherine Seyton, and stepping as light as she could, the Lady Lochleven was shown into the twilight apartment, and conducted to the side of the couch, where Mary, pallid and exhausted from a sleepless night, and the subsequent agitation of the morning, lay extended so listlessly as might well confirm the worst fears of her hostess.

"Now, God forgive us our sins!" said the Lady of Lochleven, forgetting her pride, and throwing herself on her knees by the side of the bed; "It is too true—she is murdered!"

"Who is in the chamber?" said Mary, as if awaking from a heavy sleep. "Seyton, Fleming, where are you? I heard a strange voice. Who waits?—Call Courcelles."

"Alas! her memory is at Holyrood, though her body is at Lochleven.—Forgive, madam," continued the Lady, "if I call your attention to me—I am Margaret Erskine, of the house of Mar, by marriage Lady Douglas of Lochleven."

"Oh, our gentle hostess," answered the Queen, "who hath such care of our lodgings and of our diet—We cumber you too much and too long, good Lady of Lochleven; but we now trust your task of hospitality is well-nigh ended."

"Her words go like a knife through my heart," said the Lady of Lochleven—"With a breaking heart, I pray your Grace to tell me what is your ailment, that aid may be had, if there be yet time."

"Nay, my ailment," replied the Queen, "is nothing worth telling, or worth a leech's notice—my limbs feel heavy—my heart feels cold—a prisoner's limbs and heart are rarely otherwise—fresh air, methinks, and freedom, would soon revive me; but as the Estates have ordered it, death alone can break my prison-doors."

"Were it possible, madam," said the Lady, "that your liberty could restore your perfect health, I would myself encounter the resentment of the Regent—of my son, Sir William—of my whole friends, rather than you should meet your fate in this castle."

"Alas! madam," said the Lady Fleming, who conceived the time propitious to show that her own address had been held too lightly of; "it is but trying what good freedom may work upon us; for myself, I think a free walk on the greensward would do me much good at heart."

The Lady of Lochleven rose from the bedside, and darted a penetrating look at the elder valetudinary. "Are you so evil-disposed, Lady Fleming?"

"Evil-disposed indeed, madam," replied the court dame, "and more especially since breakfast."

"Help! help!" exclaimed Catherine, anxious to break off a conversation which boded her schemes no good; "help! I say, help! the Queen is about to pass away. Aid her, Lady Lochleven, if you be a woman!"

The Lady hastened to support the Queen's head, who, turning her eyes towards her with an air of great languor, exclaimed, "Thanks, my dearest Lady of Lochleven—notwithstanding some passages of late, I have never misconstrued or misdoubted your affection to our house. It was proved, as I have heard, before I was born."

The Lady Lochleven sprung from the floor, on which she had again knelt, and, having paced the apartment in great disorder, flung open the lattice, as if to get air.

"Now, Our Lady forgive me!" said Catherine to herself. "How deep must the love of sarcasm, be implanted in the breasts of us women, since the Queen, with all her sense, will risk ruin rather than rein in her wit!" She then adventured, stooping over the Queen's person, to press her arm with her hand, saying, at the same time, "For God's sake, madam, restrain yourself!"

"Thou art too forward, maiden," said the Queen; but immediately added, in a low whisper, "Forgive me, Catherine; but when I felt the hag's murderous hands busy about my head and neck, I felt such disgust and hatred, that I must have said something, or died. But I will be schooled to better behaviour—only see that thou let her not touch me."

"Now, God be praised!" said the Lady Lochleven, withdrawing her head from the window, "the boat comes as fast as sail and oar can send wood through water. It brings the leech and a female—certainly, from the appearance, the very person I was in quest of. Were she but well out of this castle, with our honour safe, I would that she were on the top of the wildest mountain in Norway; or I would I had been there myself, ere I had undertaken this trust."

While she thus expressed herself, standing apart at one window, Roland Graeme, from the other, watched the boat bursting through the waters of the lake, which glided from its side in ripple and in foam. He, too, became sensible, that at the stern was seated the medical Chamberlain, clad in his black velvet cloak; and that his own relative, Magdalen Graeme, in her assumed character of Mother Nieneven, stood in the bow, her hands clasped together, and pointed towards the castle, and her attitude, even at that distance, expressing enthusiastic eagerness to arrive at the landing-place. They arrived there accordingly, and while the supposed witch was detained in a room beneath, the physician was ushered to the Queen's apartment, which he entered with all due professional solemnity. Catherine had, in the meanwhile, fallen back from the Queen's bed, and taken an opportunity to whisper to Roland, "Methinks, from the information of the threadbare velvet cloak and the solemn beard, there would be little trouble in haltering yonder ass. But thy grandmother, Roland—thy grandmother's zeal will ruin us, if she get not a hint to dissemble."

Roland, without reply, glided towards the door of the apartment, crossed the parlour, and safely entered the antechamber; but when he attempted to pass farther, the word "Back! Back!" echoed from one to the other, by two men armed with carabines, convinced him that the Lady of Lochleven's suspicions had not, even in the midst of her alarms, been so far lulled to sleep as to omit the precaution of stationing sentinels on her prisoners. He was compelled, therefore, to return to the parlour, or audience-chamber, in which he found the Lady of the castle in conference with her learned leech.

"A truce with your cant phrase and your solemn foppery, Lundin," in such terms she accosted the man of art, "and let me know instantly, if thou canst tell, whether this lady hath swallowed aught that is less than wholesome?"

"Nay, but, good lady—honoured patroness—to whom I am alike bonds-man in my medical and official capacity, deal reasonably with me. If this, mine illustrious patient, will not answer a question, saving with sighs and moans—if that other honourable lady will do nought but yawn in my face when I inquire after the diagnostics—and if that other young damsel, who I profess is a comely maiden—"

"Talk not to me of comeliness or of damsels," said the Lady of Lochleven, "I say, are they evil-disposed?—In one word, man, have they taken poison, ay or no?"

"Poisons, madam," said the learned leech, "are of various sorts. There is your animal poison, as the lepus marinus, as mentioned by Dioscorides and Galen—there are mineral and semi-mineral poisons, as those compounded of sublimate regulus of antimony, vitriol, and the arsenical salts—there are your poisons from herbs and vegetables, as the aqua cymbalariae, opium, aconitum, cantharides, and the like—there are also—"

"Now, out upon thee for a learned fool! and I myself am no better for expecting an oracle from such a log," said the Lady.

"Nay, but if your ladyship will have patience—if I knew what food they have partaken of, or could see but the remnants of what they have last eaten—for as to the external and internal symptoms, I can discover nought like; for, as Galen saith in his second book *de Antidotis*—"

"Away, fool!" said the Lady; "send me that hag hither; she shall avouch what it was that she hath given to the wretch Dryfesdale, or the pilniewinks and thumbikins shall wrench it out of her finger joints!"

"Art hath no enemy unless the ignorant," said the mortified Doctor; veiling, however, his remark under the Latin version, and stepping apart into a corner to watch the result.

In a minute or two Magdalen Graeme entered the apartment, dressed as we have described her at the revel, but with her muffler thrown back, and all affectation of disguise. She was attended by two guards, of whose presence she did not seem even to be conscious, and who followed her with an air of embarrassment and timidity, which was probably owing to their belief in her supernatural power, coupled with the effect produced by her bold and undaunted demeanour. She confronted the Lady of Lochleven, who seemed to endure with high disdain the confidence of her air and manner.

"Wretched woman!" said the Lady, after essaying for a moment to bear her down, before she addressed her, by the stately severity of her look, "what was that powder which thou didst give to a servant of this house, by name Jasper Dryfesdale, that he might work out with it some slow and secret vengeance?—Confess its nature and properties, or, by the honour of Douglas, I give thee to fire and stake before the sun is lower!"

"Alas!" said Magdalen Graeme in reply, "and when became a Douglas or a Douglas's man so unfurnished in his revenge, that he should seek them at the hands of a poor and solitary woman? The towers in which your captives pine away into unpitied graves, yet stand fast on their foundation—the crimes wrought in them have not yet burst their vaults asunder—your men have still their cross-bows, pistolets, and daggers—why need you seek to herbs or charms for the execution of your revenges?"

"Hear me, foul hag," said the Lady Lochleven,—"but what avails speaking to thee?—Bring Dryfesdale hither, and let them be confronted together."

"You may spare your retainers the labour," replied Magdalen Graeme. "I came not here to be confronted with a base groom, nor to answer the interrogatories of James's heretical leman—I came to speak with the Queen of Scotland—Give place there!"

And while the Lady Lochleven stood confounded at her boldness, and at the reproach she had cast upon her, Magdalen Graeme strode past her into the bedchamber of the Queen, and, kneeling on the floor, made a salutation as if, in the Oriental fashion, she meant to touch the earth with her forehead.

"Hail, Princess!" she said, "hail, daughter of many a King, but graced above them all in that thou art called to suffer for the true faith—hail to thee, the pure gold of whose crown has been tried in the seven-times heated furnace of affliction—hear the comfort which God and Our Lady send thee by the mouth of thy unworthy servant.—But first"— and stooping her head she crossed herself repeatedly, and, still upon her knees, appeared to be rapidly reciting some formula of devotion.

"Seize her, and drag her to the massy-more!—to the deepest dungeon with the sorceress, whose master, the Devil, could alone have inspired her with boldness enough to insult the mother of Douglas in his own castle!"

Thus spoke the incensed Lady of Lochleven, but the physician presumed to interpose.

"I pray of you, honoured madam, she be permitted to take her course without interruption. Peradventure we shall learn something concerning the nostrum she hath ventured, contrary to law and the rules of art, to adhibit to these ladies, through the medium of the steward Dryfesdale."

"For a fool," replied the Lady of Lochleven, "thou hast counselled wisely—I will bridle my resentment till their conference be over."

"God forbid, honoured Lady," said Doctor Lundin, "that you should suppress it longer—nothing may more endanger the frame of your honoured body; and truly, if there be witchcraft in this matter, it is held by the vulgar, and even by solid authors on Demonology, that three scruples of the ashes of the witch, when she hath been well and carefully burned at a stake, is a grand Catholicon in such matter, even as they prescribe *crinis canis rabidi*, a hair of the dog that bit the patient, in cases of hydrophobia. I warrant neither treatment, being out of the regular practice of the schools; but, in the present case, there can be little harm in trying the conclusion upon this old necromancer and quacksalver-*fiat experimentum* (as we say) *in corpore vili*."

"Peace, fool!" said the Lady, "she is about to speak."

At that moment Magdalen Graeme arose from her knees, and turned her countenance on the Queen, at the same time advancing her foot, extending her arm, and assuming the mien and attitude of a Sibyl in frenzy. As her gray hair floated back from beneath her coif, and her eye gleamed fire from under its shaggy eyebrow, the effect of her expressive though emaciated features, was heightened by an enthusiasm approaching to insanity, and her appearance struck with awe all who were present. Her eyes for a time glanced wildly around as if seeking for something to aid her in collecting her powers of expression, and her lips had a nervous and quivering motion, as those of one who would fain speak, yet rejects as inadequate the words which present themselves. Mary herself caught the infection as if by a sort of magnetic influence, and raising herself from her bed, without being able to withdraw her eyes from those of Magdalen, waited as if for the oracle of a Pythoness. She waited not long, for no sooner had the enthusiast collected herself, than her gaze became instantly steady, her features assumed a determined energy, and when she began to speak, the words flowed from her with a profuse fluency, which might have passed for inspiration, and which, perhaps, she herself mistook for such.

"Arise," she said, "Queen of France and of England! Arise, Lioness of Scotland, and be not dismayed though the nets of the hunters have encircled thee! Stoop not to feign with the false ones, whom thou shall soon meet in the field. The issue of battle is with the God of armies, but by battle thy cause shall be tried. Lay aside, then, the arts of lower mortals, and assume those which become a Queen! True defender of the only true faith, the armoury of heaven is open to thee! Faithful daughter of the Church, take the keys of St. Peter, to bind and to loose!—Royal Princess of the land, take the sword of St. Paul, to smite and to shear! There is darkness in thy destiny;—but not in these towers, not under the rule of their haughty mistress, shall that destiny be closed—In other lands the lioness may crouch to the power of the tigress, but not in her own—not in Scotland shall the Queen of Scotland long remain captive—nor is the fate of the royal Stuart in the hands of the traitor Douglas. Let the Lady of Lochleven double her bolts and deepen her dungeons, they shall not retain thee—each element shall give thee its assistance ere thou shalt continue captive—the land shall lend its earthquakes, the water its waves, the air its tempests, the fire its devouring flames, to desolate this house, rather than it shall continue the place of thy captivity.—Hear this, and tremble, all ye who fight against the light, for she says it, to whom it hath been assured!"

She was silent, and the astonished physician said, "If there was ever an *Energumene,* or possessed demoniac, in our days, there is a devil speaking with that woman's tongue!"

"Practice," said the Lady of Lochleven, recovering her surprise; "here is all practice and imposture—To the dungeon with her!"

"Lady of Lochleven," said Mary, arising from her bed, and coming forward with her wonted dignity, "ere you make arrest on any one in our presence, hear me but one word. I have done you some wrong—I believed you privy to the murderous purpose of your vassal, and I deceived you in suffering you to believe it had taken effect. I did you wrong, Lady of Lochleven, for I perceive your purpose to aid me was sincere. We tasted not of the liquid, nor are we now sick, save that we languish for our freedom."

"It is avowed like Mary of Scotland," said Magdalen Graeme; "and know, besides, that had the Queen drained the drought to the dregs, it was harmless as the water from a sainted spring. Trow ye, proud woman," she added, addressing herself to the Lady of Lochleven, "that I—I—would have been the wretch to put poison into the hands of a servant or vassal of the house of Lochleven, knowing whom that house contained? as soon would I have furnished drug to slay my own daughter!"

"Am I thus bearded in mine own castle?" said the Lady; "to the dungeon with her!—she shall abye what is due to the vender of poisons and practiser of witchcraft."

"Yet hear me for an instant, Lady of Lochleven," said Mary; "and do you," to Magdalen, "be silent at my command.—Your steward, lady, has by confession attempted my life, and those of my household, and this woman hath done her best to save them, by furnishing him with what was harmless, in place of the fatal drugs which he expected. Methinks I propose to you but a fair exchange when I say I forgive your vassal with all my heart, and leave vengeance to God, and to his conscience, so that you also forgive the boldness of this woman in your presence; for we trust you do not hold it as a crime, that she substituted an innocent beverage for the mortal poison which was to have drenched our cup."

"Heaven forfend, madam," said the Lady, "that I should account that a crime which saved the house of Douglas from a foul breach of honour and hospitality! We have written to our son touching our vassal's delict, and he must abide his doom, which will most likely be death. Touching this woman, her trade is damnable by Scripture, and is mortally punished by the wise laws of our ancestry—she also must abide her doom."

"And have I then," said the Queen, "no claim on the house of Lochleven for the wrong I have so nearly suffered within their walls? I ask but in requital, the life of a frail and aged woman, whose brain, as yourself may judge, seems somewhat affected by years and suffering."

"If the Lady Mary," replied the inflexible Lady of Lochleven, "hath been menaced with wrong in the house of Douglas, it may be regarded as some compensation, that her complots have cost that house the exile of a valued son."

"Plead no more for me, my gracious Sovereign," said Magdalen Graeme, "nor abase yourself to ask so much as a gray hair of my head at her hands. I knew the risk at which I served my Church and my Queen, and was ever prompt to pay my poor life as the ransom. It is a comfort to think, that in slaying me, or in restraining my freedom, or even in injuring that single gray hair, the house, whose honour she boasts so highly, will have filled up the measure of their shame by the breach of their solemn written assurance of safety."—And taking from her bosom a paper, she handed it to the Queen.

"It is a solemn assurance of safety in life and limb," said Queen Mary, "with space to come and go, under the hand and seal of the Chamberlain of Kinross, granted to Magdalen Graeme, commonly called Mother Nicneven, in consideration of her consenting to put herself, for the space of twenty-four hours, if required, within the iron gate of the Castle of Lochleven."

SIR WALTER SCOTT

"Knave!" said the Lady, turning to the Chamberlain, "how dared you grant her such a protection?"

"It was by your Ladyship's orders, transmitted by Randal, as he can bear witness," replied Doctor Lundin; "nay, I am only like the pharmacopolist, who compounds the drugs after the order of the mediciner."

"I remember—I remember," answered the Lady; "but I meant the assurance only to be used in case, by residing in another jurisdiction, she could not have been apprehended under our warrant."

"Nevertheless," said the Queen, "the Lady of Lochleven is bound by the action of her deputy in granting the assurance."

"Madam," replied the Lady, "the house of Douglas have never broken their safe-conduct, and never will—too deeply did they suffer by such a breach of trust, exercised on themselves, when your Grace's ancestor, the second James, in defiance of the rights of hospitality, and of his own written assurance of safety, poniarded the brave Earl of Douglas with his own hand, and within two yards of the social board, at which he had just before sat the King of Scotland's honoured guest."

"Methinks," said the Queen, carelessly, "in consideration of so very recent and enormous a tragedy, which I think only chanced some six-score years agone, the Douglasses should have shown themselves less tenacious of the company of their sovereigns, than you, Lady of Lochleven, seem to be of mine."

"Let Randal," said the Lady, "take the hag back to Kinross, and set her at full liberty, discharging her from our bounds in future, on peril of her head.—And let your wisdom," to the Chamberlain, "keep her company. And fear not for your character, though I send you in such company; for, granting her to be a witch, it would be a waste of fagots to burn you for a wizard."

The crest-fallen Chamberlain was preparing to depart; but Magdalen Graeme, collecting herself, was about to reply, when the Queen interposed, saying, "Good mother, we heartily thank you for your unfeigned zeal towards our person, and pray you, as our liege-woman, that you abstain from whatever may lead you into personal danger; and, farther, it is our will that you depart without a word of farther parley with any one in this castle. For thy present guerdon, take this small reliquary—it was given to us by our uncle the Cardinal, and hath had the benediction of the Holy Father himself;—and now depart in peace and in silence.—For you, learned sir," continued the Queen, advancing to the Doctor, who made his reverence in a manner doubly embarrassed by the awe of the Queen's presence, which made him fear to do too little, and by the apprehension of his lady's displeasure, in case he should chance to do too much—"for you, learned sir, as it was not your fault, though surely our own good fortune, that we did not need your skill at this time, it would not become us, however circumstanced, to suffer our leech to leave us without such guerdon as we can offer."

With these words, and with the grace which never forsook her, though, in the present case, there might lurk under it a little gentle ridicule, she offered a small embroidered purse to the Chamberlain, who, with extended hand and arched back, his learned face stooping until a physiognomist might have practised the metoposcopical science upon it, as seen from behind betwixt his gambadoes, was about to accept of the professional recompense offered by so fair as well as illustrious a hand. But the Lady interposed, and, regarding the Chamberlain, said aloud, "No servant of our house, without instantly relinquishing that character, and incurring withal our highest displeasure, shall dare receive any gratuity at the hand of the Lady Mary."

Sadly and slowly the Chamberlain raised his depressed stature into the perpendicular attitude, and left the apartment dejectedly, followed by Magdalen Graeme, after, with mute but expressive gesture, she had kissed the reliquary with which the Queen had presented her, and, raising her clasped hands and uplifted eyes towards Heaven, had seemed to entreat a benediction upon the royal dame. As she left the castle, and went towards the quay where the boat lay, Roland Graeme, anxious to communicate with her if possible, threw himself in her way, and might have succeeded in exchanging a few words with her, as she was guarded only by the dejected Chamberlain and his halberdiers, but she seemed to have taken, in its most strict and literal acceptation, the command to be silent which she had received from the Queen; for, to the repeated signs of her grandson, she only replied by laying her finger on her lip. Dr. Lundin was not so reserved. Regret for the handsome gratuity, and for the compulsory task of self-denial imposed on him, had grieved the spirit of that worthy officer and learned mediciner—"Even thus, my friend," said he, squeezing the page's hand as he bade him farewell, "is merit rewarded. I came to cure this unhappy Lady—and I profess she well deserves the trouble, for, say what they will of her, she hath a most winning manner, a sweet voice, a gracious smile, and a most majestic wave of her hand. If she was not poisoned, say, my dear Master Roland, was that fault of mine, I being ready to cure her if she had?—and now I am denied the permission to accept my well-earned honorarium—O Galen! O Hippocrates! is the graduate's cap and doctor's scarlet brought to this pass! *Frustra fatigamus remediis aegros!*"

He wiped his eyes, stepped on the gunwale, and the boat pushed off from the shore, and went merrily across the lake, which was dimpled by the summer wind.*

---

* A romancer, to use a Scottish phrase, wants but a hair to make a tether of. The whole detail of the steward's supposed conspiracy against the life of Mary, is grounded upon an expression in one of her letters, which affirms, that Jasper Dryfesdale, one of the Laird of Lochleven's servants, had threatened to murder William Douglas, (for his share in the Queen's escape,) and averred that he would plant a dagger in Mary's own heart.— CHALMER's *Life of Queen Mary*, vol. i. p. 278.

XXXIII

Death distant?—No, alas! he's ever with us,
And shakes the dart at us in all our actings:
He lurks within our cup, while we're in health;
Sits by our sick-bed, mocks our medicines;
We cannot walk, or sit, or ride, or travel,
But Death is by to seize us when he lists.

—The Spanish Father

From the agitating scene in the Queen's presence-chamber, the Lady of Lochleven retreated to her own apartment, and ordered the steward to be called before her.

"Have they not disarmed thee, Dryfesdale?" she said, on seeing him enter, accoutred, as usual, with sword and dagger.

"No!" replied the old man; "how should they?—Your ladyship, when you commanded me to ward, said nought of laying down my arms; and, I think none of your menials, without your order, or your son's, dare approach Jasper Dryfesdale for such a purpose.—Shall I now give up my sword to you?—it is worth little now, for it has fought for your house till it is worn down to old iron, like the pantler's old chipping knife."

"You have attempted a deadly crime—poison under trust."

"Under trust?—hem!—I know not what your ladyship thinks of it, but the world without thinks the trust was given you even for that very end; and you would have been well off had it been so ended as I proposed, and you neither the worse nor the wiser."

"Wretch!" exclaimed the lady, "and fool as well as villain, who could not even execute the crime he had planned!"

"I bid as fair for it as man could," replied Dryfesdale; "I went to a woman—a witch and a Papist—If I found not poison, it was because it was otherwise predestined. I tried fair for it; but the half-done job may be clouted, if you will."

"Villain! I am even now about to send off an express messenger to my son, to take order how thou shouldst be disposed of. Prepare thyself for death, if thou canst."

"He that looks on death, Lady," answered Dryfesdale, "as that which he may not shun, and which has its own fixed and certain hour, is ever prepared for it. He that is hanged in May will eat no flaunes* in midsummer—so there is the moan made for the old serving-man. But whom, pray I, send you on so fair an errand?"

"There will be no lack of messengers," answered his mistress.

"By my hand, but there will," replied the old man; "your castle is but poorly manned, considering the watches that you must keep, having this charge—There is the warder, and two others, whom you discarded for tampering with Master George; then for the warder's tower, the bailie, the donjon—five men mount each guard, and the rest must sleep for the most part in their clothes. To send away another man, were to harass the sentinels to death—unthrifty misuse for a household. To take in new soldiers were dangerous, the charge requiring tried men. I see but one thing for it—I will do your errand to Sir William Douglas myself."

"That were indeed a resource!—And on what day within twenty years would it be done?" said the Lady.

"Even with the speed of man and horse," said Dryfesdale; "for though I care not much about the latter days of an old serving-man's life, yet I would like to know as soon as may be, whether my neck is mine own or the hangman's."

"Holdest thou thy own life so lightly?" said the Lady.

"Else I had reckoned more of that of others," said the predestinarian— "What is death?—it is but ceasing to live—And what is living?—a weary return of light and darkness, sleeping and waking, being hungered and eating. Your dead man needs neither candle nor can, neither fire nor feather-bed; and the joiner's chest serves him for an eternal frieze-jerkin."

"Wretched man! believest thou not that after death comes the judgment?"

"Lady," answered Dryfesdale, "as my mistress, I may not dispute your words; but, as spiritually speaking, you are still but a burner of bricks in Egypt, ignorant of the freedom of the saints; for, as was well shown to me by that gifted man, Nicolaus Schoefferbach, who was martyred by the bloody Bishop of Munster, he cannot sin who doth but execute that which is predestined, since—"

"Silence!" said the Lady, interrupting him,—"Answer me not with thy bold and presumptuous blasphemy, but hear me. Thou hast been long the servant of our house—"

---

* Pancakes.

"The born servant of the Douglas—they have had the best of me—I served them since I left Lockerbie: I was then ten years old, and you may soon add the threescore to it."

"Thy foul attempt has miscarried, so thou art guilty only in intention. It were a deserved deed to hang thee on the warder's tower; and yet in thy present mind, it were but giving a soul to Satan. I take thine offer, then—Go hence—here is my packet—I will add to it but a line, to desire him to send me a faithful servant or two to complete the garrison. Let my son deal with you as he will. If thou art wise, thou wilt make for Lockerbie so soon as thy foot touches dry land, and let the packet find another bearer; at all rates, look it miscarries not."

"Nay, madam," replied he—"I was born, as I said, the Douglas's servant, and I will be no corbie-messenger in mine old age—your message to your son shall be done as truly by me as if it concerned another man's neck. I take my leave of your honour."

The Lady issued her commands, and the old man was ferried over to the shore, to proceed on his extraordinary pilgrimage. It is necessary the reader should accompany him on his journey, which Providence had determined should not be of long duration.

On arriving at the village, the steward, although his disgrace had transpired, was readily accommodated with a horse, by the Chamberlain's authority; and the roads being by no means esteemed safe, he associated himself with Auchtermuchty, the common carrier, in order to travel in his company to Edinburgh.

The worthy waggoner, according to the established customs of all carriers, stage-coachmen, and other persons in public authority, from the earliest days to the present, never wanted good reasons for stopping upon the road, as often as he would; and the place which had most captivation for him as a resting-place was a change-house, as it was termed, not very distant from a romantic dell, well known by the name of Keirie Craigs. Attractions of a kind very different from those which arrested the progress of John Auchtermuchty and his wains, still continue to hover round this romantic spot, and none has visited its vicinity without a desire to remain long and to return soon.

Arrived near his favourite *howss*, not all the authority of Dryfesdale (much diminished indeed by the rumours of his disgrace) could prevail on the carrier, obstinate as the brutes which he drove, to pass on without his accustomed halt, for which the distance he had travelled furnished little or no pretence. Old Keltie, the landlord, who had bestowed his name on a bridge in the neighbourhood of his quondam dwelling, received the carrier with his usual festive cordiality, and adjourned with him into the house, under pretence of important business, which, I believe, consisted in their emptying together a mutchkin stoup of usquebaugh. While the worthy host and his guest were thus employed, the discarded steward, with a double portion of moroseness in his gesture and look, walked discontentedly into the kitchen of the place, which was occupied but by one guest. The stranger was a slight figure, scarce above the age of boyhood, and in the dress of a page, but bearing an air of haughty aristocratic boldness and even insolence in his look and manner, that might have made Dryfesdale conclude he had pretensions to superior rank, had not his experience taught him how frequently these airs of superiority were assumed by the domestics and military retainers of the Scottish nobility.—"The pilgrim's morning to you, old sir," said the youth; "you come, as I think, from Lochleven Castle—What news of our bonny Queen?—a fairer dove was never pent up in so wretched a dovecot."

"They that speak of Lochleven, and of those whom its walls contain," answered Dryfesdale, "speak of what concerns the Douglas; and they who speak of what concerns the Douglas, do it at their peril."

"Do you speak from fear of them, old man, or would you make a quarrel for them?—I should have deemed your age might have cooled your blood."

"Never, while there are empty-pated coxcombs at each corner to keep it warm."

"The sight of thy gray hairs keeps mine cold," said the boy, who had risen up and now sat down again.

"It is well for thee, or I had cooled it with this holly-rod," replied the steward. "I think thou be'st one of those swash-bucklers, who brawl in alehouses and taverns; and who, if words were pikes, and oaths were Andrew Ferraras, would soon place the religion of Babylon in the land once more, and the woman of Moab upon the throne."

"Now, by Saint Bennet of Seyton," said the youth, "I will strike thee on the face, thou foul-mouthed old railing heretic!"

"Saint Bennet of Seyton," echoed the steward; "a proper warrant is Saint Bennet's, and for a proper nest of wolf-birds like the Seytons!—I will arrest thee as a traitor to King James and the good Regent.—Ho! John Auchtermuchty, raise aid against the King's traitor!"

So saying, he laid his hand on the youth's collar, and drew his sword. John Auchtermuchty looked in, but, seeing the naked weapon, ran faster out than he entered. Keltie, the landlord, stood by and helped neither party, only exclaiming, "Gentlemen! gentlemen! for the love of Heaven!" and so forth. A struggle ensued, in which the young man, chafed at Dryfesdale's boldness, and unable, with the ease he expected, to extricate himself from the old man's determined grasp, drew his dagger, and with the speed of light, dealt him three wounds in the breast and body, the least of which was mortal. The old man sunk on the ground with a deep groan, and the host set up a piteous exclamation of surprise.

"Peace, ye brawling hound!" said the wounded steward; "are dagger-stabs and dying men such rarities in Scotland, that you should cry as if the house were falling?—Youth, I do not forgive thee, for there is nought betwixt us to forgive. Thou hast done what I have done to more than one—And I suffer what I have seen them suffer—it was all ordained to be thus and not otherwise. But if thou wouldst do me right, thou wilt send this packet safely to the hands of Sir William Douglas; and see that my memory suffer not, as if I would have loitered on mine errand for fear of my life."

The youth, whose passion had subsided the instant he had done the deed, listened with sympathy and attention, when another person, muffled in his cloak, entered the apartment, and exclaimed—"Good God! Dryfesdale, and expiring!"

"Ay, and Dryfesdale would that he had been dead," answered the wounded man, "rather than that his ears had heard the words of the only Douglas that ever was false—but yet it is better as it is. Good my murderer, and the rest of you, stand back a little, and let me speak with this unhappy apostate.—Kneel down by me, Master George—You have heard that I failed in my attempt to take away that Moabitish stumbling-block and her retinue—I gave them that which I thought would have removed the temptation out of thy path—and this, though I had other reasons to show to thy mother and others, I did chiefly purpose for love of thee."

"For the love of me, base poisoner!" answered Douglas, "wouldst thou have committed so horrible, so unprovoked a murder, and mentioned my name with it?"

"And wherefore not, George of Douglas?" answered Dryfesdale. "Breath is now scarce with me, but I would spend my last gasp on this argument. Hast thou not, despite the honour thou owest to thy parents, the faith that is due to thy religion, the truth that is due to thy king, been so carried away by the charms of this beautiful sorceress, that thou wouldst have helped her to escape from her prison-house, and lent her thine arm again to ascend the throne, which she had made a place of abomination?—Nay, stir not from me—my hand, though fast stiffening, has yet force enough to hold thee—What dost thou aim at?—to wed this witch of Scotland?—I warrant thee, thou mayest succeed—her heart and hand have been oft won at a cheaper rate, than thou, fool that thou art, would think thyself happy to pay. But, should a servant of thy father's house have seen thee embrace the fate of the idiot Darnley, or of the villain Bothwell—the fate of the murdered fool, or of the living pirate—while an ounce of ratsbane would have saved thee?"

"Think on God, Dryfesdale," said George Douglas, "and leave the utterance of those horrors—Repent, if thou canst—if not, at least be silent.—Seyton, aid me to support this dying wretch, that he may compose himself to better thoughts, if it be possible."

"Seyton!" answered the dying man; "Seyton! Is it by a Seyton's hand that I fall at last?—There is something of retribution in that—since the house had nigh lost a sister by my deed." Fixing his fading eyes on the youth, he added, "He hath her very features and presence!—Stoop down, youth, and let me see thee closer—I would know thee when we meet in yonder world, for homicides will herd together there, and I have been one." He pulled Seyton's face, in spite of some resistance, closer to his own, looked at him fixedly, and added, "Thou hast begun young—thy career will be the briefer—ay, thou wilt be met with, and that anon—a young plant never throve that was watered with an old man's blood.—Yet why blame I thee? Strange turns of fate," he muttered, ceasing to address Seyton; "I designed what I could not do, and he has done what he did not perchance design.—Wondrous, that our will should ever oppose itself to the strong and uncontrollable tide of destiny—that we should strive with the stream when we might drift with the current! My brain will serve me to question it no farther—I would Schoefferbach were here—yet why?—I am on a course which the vessel can hold without a pilot.—Farewell, George of Douglas—I die true to thy father's house." He fell into convulsions at these words, and shortly after expired.

Seyton and Douglas stood looking on the dying man, and when the scene was closed, the former was the first to speak. "As I live, Douglas, I meant not this, and am sorry; but he laid hands on me, and compelled me to defend my freedom, as I best might, with my dagger. If he were ten times thy friend and follower, I can but say that I am sorry."

"I blame thee not, Seyton," said Douglas, "though I lament the chance. There is an overruling destiny above us, though not in the sense in which it was viewed by that wretched man, who, beguiled by some foreign mystagogue, used the awful word as the ready apology for whatever he chose to do—we must examine the packet."

They withdrew into an inner room, and remained deep in consultation, until they were disturbed by the entrance of Keltie, who, with an embarrassed countenance, asked Master George Douglas's pleasure respecting the disposal of the body. "Your honour knows," he added, "that I make my bread by living men, not by dead corpses; and old Mr. Dryfesdale, who was but a sorry customer while he was alive, occupies my public room now that he is deceased, and can neither call for ale nor brandy."

"Tie a stone round his neck," said Seyton, "and when the sun is down, have him to the Loch of Ore, heave him in, and let him alone for finding out the bottom."

"Under your favour, sir," said George Douglas, "it shall not be so.—Keltie, thou art a true fellow to me, and thy having been so shall advantage thee. Send or take the body to the chapel at Scotland's wall, or to the church of Ballanry, and tell what tale thou wilt of his having fallen in a brawl with some unruly guests of thine. Auchtermuchty knows nought else, nor are the times so peaceful as to admit close-looking into such accounts."

"Nay, let him tell the truth," said Seyton, "so far as it harms not our scheme.—Say that Henry Seyton met with him, my good fellow;—I care not a brass bodle for the feud."

"A feud with the Douglas was ever to be feared, however," said George, displeasure mingling with his natural deep gravity of manner.

"Not when the best of the name is on my side," replied Seyton.

"Alas! Henry, if thou meanest me, I am but half a Douglas in this emprize—half head, half heart, and half hand.—But I will think on one who can never be forgotten, and be all, or more, than any of my ancestors was ever.—Keltie, say it was Henry Seyton did the deed; but beware, not a word of me!—Let Auchtermuchty carry this packet" (which he had resealed with his own signet) "to my father at Edinburgh; and here is to pay for the funeral expenses, and thy loss of custom."

"And the washing of the floor," said the landlord, "which will be an extraordinary job; for blood they say, will scarcely ever cleanse out."

SIR WALTER SCOTT

"But as for your plan," said George of Douglas, addressing Seyton, as if in continuation of what they had been before treating of, "it has a good face; but, under your favour, you are yourself too hot and too young, besides other reasons which are much against your playing the part you propose."

"We will consult the Father Abbot upon it," said the youth. "Do you ride to Kinross to-night?"

"Ay—so I purpose," answered Douglas; "the night will be dark, and suits a muffled man.* —Keltie, I forgot, there should be a stone laid on that man's grave, recording his name, and his only merit, which was being a faithful servant to the Douglas."

"What religion was the man of?" said Seyton; "he used words, which make me fear I have sent Satan a subject before his time."

"I can tell you little of that," said George Douglas; "he was noted for disliking both Rome and Geneva, and spoke of lights he had learned among the fierce sectaries of Lower Germany—an evil doctrine it was, if we judge by the fruits. God keep us from presumptuously judging of Heaven's secrets!"

"Amen!" said the young Seyton, "and from meeting any encounter this evening."

"It is not thy wont to pray so," said George Douglas.

"No! I leave that to you," replied the youth, "when you are seized with scruples of engaging with your father's vassals. But I would fain have this old man's blood off these hands of mine ere I shed more—I will confess to the Abbot to-night, and I trust to have light penance for ridding the earth of such a miscreant. All I sorrow for is, that he was not a score of years younger—He drew steel first, however, that is one comfort."

---

* Generally, a disguised man; originally one who wears the cloak or mantle muffled round the lower part of the face to conceal his countenance. I have on an ancient, piece of iron the representation of a robber thus accoutred, endeavouring to make his way into a house, and opposed by a mastiff, to whom he in vain offers food. The motto is *spernit dona fides*. It is part of a fire-grate said to have belonged to Archbishop Sharpe.

XXXIV

Ay, Pedro,—Come you here with mask and lantern.
Ladder of ropes and other moonshine tools—
Why, youngster, thou mayst cheat the old Duenna,
Flatter the waiting-woman, bribe the valet;
But know, that I her father play the Gryphon,
Tameless and sleepless, proof to fraud or bribe,
And guard the hidden, treasure of her beauty.

—THE SPANISH FATHER

The tenor of our tale carries us back to the Castle of Lochleven, where we take up the order of events on the same remarkable day on which Dryfesdale had been dismissed from the castle. It was past noon, the usual hour of dinner, yet no preparations seemed made for the Queen's entertainment. Mary herself had retired into her own apartment, where she was closely engaged in writing. Her attendants were together in the presence-chamber, and much disposed to speculate on the delay of the dinner; for it may be recollected that their breakfast had been interrupted. "I believe in my conscience," said the page, "that having found the poisoning scheme miscarry, by having gone to the wrong merchant for their deadly wares, they are now about to try how famine will work upon us."

Lady Fleming was somewhat alarmed at this surmise, but comforted herself by observing that the chimney of the kitchen had reeked that whole day in a manner which contradicted the supposition.—Catherine Seyton presently exclaimed, "They were bearing the dishes across the court, marshalled by the Lady Lochleven herself, dressed out in her highest and stiffest ruff, with her partlet and sleeves of cyprus, and her huge old-fashioned farthingale of crimson velvet."

"I believe on my word," said the page, approaching the window also, "it was in that very farthingale that she captivated the heart of gentle King Jamie, which procured our poor Queen her precious bargain of a brother."

"That may hardly be, Master Roland," answered the Lady Fleming, who was a great recorder of the changes of fashion, "since the farthingales came first in when the Queen Regent went to Saint Andrews, after the battle of Pinkie, and were then called *Vertugardins*—"

She would have proceeded farther in this important discussion, but was interrupted by the entrance of the Lady of Lochleven, who preceded the servants bearing the dishes, and formally discharged the duty of tasting each of them. Lady Fleming regretted, in courtly phrase, "that the Lady of Lochleven should have undertaken so troublesome an office."

"After the strange incident of this day, madam," said the Lady, "it is necessary for my honour and that of my son, that I partake whatever is offered to my involuntary guest. Please to inform the Lady Mary that I attend her commands."

"Her Majesty," replied Lady Fleming, with due emphasis on the word, "shall be informed that the Lady Lochleven waits."

Mary appeared instantly, and addressed her hostess with courtesy, which even approached to something more cordial. "This is nobly done, Lady Lochleven," she said; "for though we ourselves apprehend no danger under your roof, our ladies have been much alarmed by this morning's chance, and our meal will be the more cheerful for your presence and assurance. Please you to sit down."

The Lady Lochleven obeyed the Queen's commands, and Roland performed the office of carver and attendant as usual. But, notwithstanding what the Queen had said, the meal was silent and unsocial; and every effort which Mary made to excite some conversation, died away under the solemn and chill replies of the Lady of Lochleven. At length it became plain that the Queen, who had considered these advances as a condescension on her part, and who piqued herself justly on her powers of pleasing, became offended at the repulsive conduct of her hostess. After looking with a significant glance at Lady Fleming and Catherine, she slightly shrugged her shoulders, and remained silent. A pause ensued, at the end of which the Lady Douglas spoke:—"I perceive, madam, I am a check on the mirth of this fair company. I pray you to excuse me—I am a widow—alone here in a most perilous charge-—deserted by my grandson—betrayed by my servant—I am little worthy of the grace you do me in offering me a seat at your table, where I am aware that wit and pastime are usually expected from the guests."

"If the Lady Lochleven is serious," said the Queen, "we wonder by what simplicity she expects our present meals to be seasoned with mirth. If she is a widow, she lives honoured and uncontrolled, at the head of her late husband's household. But I know at least of one widowed woman in the world, before whom the words desertion and betrayal ought never to be mentioned, since no one has been made so bitterly acquainted with their import."

"I meant not, madam, to remind you of your misfortunes, by the mention of mine," answered the Lady Lochleven, and there was again a deep silence.

Mary at length addressed Lady Fleming. "We can commit no deadly sins here, *ma bonne*, where we are so well warded and looked to; but if we could, this Carthusian silence might be useful as a kind of penance. If thou hast adjusted my wimple amiss, my Fleming, or if Catherine hath made a wry stitch in her broidery, when she was thinking of something else than her work, or if Roland Graeme hath missed a wild-duck on the wing, and broke a quarrel-pane* of glass in the turret window, as chanced to him a week since, now is the time to think on your sins and to repent of them."

"Madam, I speak with all reverence," said the Lady Lochleven; "but I am old, and claim the privilege of age. Methinks your followers might find fitter subjects for repentance than the trifles you mention, and so mention—once more, I crave your pardon—as if you jested with sin and repentance both."

"You have been our taster, Lady Lochleven," said the Queen, "I perceive you would eke out your duty with that of our Father Confessor—and since you choose that our conversation should be serious, may I ask you why the Regent's promise—since your son so styles himself—has not been kept to me in that respect? From time to time this promise has been renewed, and as constantly broken. Methinks those who pretend themselves to so much gravity and sanctity, should not debar from others the religious succours which their consciences require."

"Madam, the Earl of Murray was indeed weak enough," said the Lady Lochleven, "to give so far way to your unhappy prejudices, and a religioner of the Pope presented himself on his part at our town of Kinross. But the Douglass is Lord of his own castle, and will not permit his threshold to be darkened, no not for a single moment, by an emissary belonging to the Bishop of Rome."

"Methinks it were well, then," said Mary, "that my Lord Regent would send me where there is less scruple and more charity."

"In this, madam," answered the Lady Lochleven, "you mistake the nature both of charity and of religion. Charity giveth to those who are

---

* Diamond-shaped; literally, formed like the head of a *quarrel*, or arrow for the crossbow.

in delirium the medicaments which may avail their health, but refuses those enticing cates and liquors which please the palate, but augment the disease."

"This your charity, Lady Lochleven, is pure cruelty, under the hypocritical disguise of friendly care. I am oppressed amongst you as if you meant the destruction both of my body and soul; but Heaven will not endure such iniquity for ever, and they who are the most active agents in it may speedily expect their reward."

At this moment Randal entered the apartment, with a look so much perturbed, that the Lady Fleming uttered a faint scream, the Queen was obviously startled, and the Lady of Lochleven, though too bold and proud to evince any marked signs of alarm, asked hastily what was the matter?

"Dryfesdale has been slain, madam," was the reply; "murdered as soon as he gained the dry land by young Master Henry Seyton."

It was now Catherine's turn to start and grow pale—"Has the murderer of the Douglas's vassal escaped?" was the Lady's hasty question.

"There was none to challenge him but old Keltie, and the carrier Auchtermuchty," replied Randal; "unlikely men to stay one of the frackest* youths in Scotland of his years, and who was sure to have friends and partakers at no great distance."

"Was the deed completed?" said the Lady.

"Done, and done thoroughly," said Randal; "a Seyton seldom strikes twice—But the body was not despoiled, and your honour's packet goes forward to Edinburgh by Auchtermuchty, who leaves Keltie-Bridge early to-morrow—marry, he has drunk two bottles of aquavitae to put the fright out of his head, and now sleeps them off beside his cart-avers."†

There was a pause when this fatal tale was told. The Queen and Lady Douglas looked on each other, as if each thought how she could best turn the incident to her own advantage in the controversy, which was continually kept alive betwixt them—Catherine Seyton kept her kerchief at her eyes and wept.

"You see, madam, the bloody maxims and practice of the deluded Papists," said Lady Lochleven.

"Nay, madam," replied the Queen, "say rather you see the deserved judgment of Heaven upon a Calvinistical poisoner."

* Boldest—most forward.
† Cart-horses.

"Dryfesdale was not of the Church of Geneva, or of Scotland," said the Lady of Lochleven, hastily.

"He was a heretic, however," replied Mary; "there is but one true and unerring guide; the others lead alike into error."

"Well, madam, I trust it will reconcile you to your retreat, that this deed shows the temper of those who might wish you at liberty. Blood-thirsty tyrants, and cruel men-quellers are they all, from the Clan-Ranald and Clan-Tosach in the north, to the Ferniherst and Buccleuch in the south—the murdering Seytons in the east, and—"

"Methinks, madam, you forget that I am a Seyton?" said Catherine, withdrawing her kerchief from her face, which was now coloured with indignation.

"If I had forgot it, fair mistress, your forward bearing would have reminded me," said Lady Lochleven.

"If my brother has slain the villain that would have poisoned his Sovereign, and his sister," said Catherine, "I am only so far sorry that he should have spared the hangman his proper task. For aught farther, had it been the best Douglas in the land, he would have been honoured in falling by the Seyton's sword."

"Farewell, gay mistress," said the Lady of Lochleven, rising to withdraw; "it is such maidens as you, who make giddy-fashioned revellers and deadly brawlers. Boys must needs rise, forsooth, in the grace of some sprightly damsel, who thinks to dance through life as through a French galliard." She then made her reverence to the Queen, and added, "Do you also, madam, fare you well, till curfew time, when I will make, perchance, more bold than welcome in attending upon your supper board.—Come with me, Randal, and tell me more of this cruel fact."

"'Tis an extraordinary chance," said the Queen, when she had departed; "and, villain as he was, I would this man had been spared time for repentance. We will cause something to be done for his soul, if we ever attain our liberty, and the Church will permit such grace to a heretic.—But, tell me, Catherine, *ma mignóne*—this brother of thine, who is so *frack*, as the fellow called him, bears he the same wonderful likeness to thee as formerly?"

"If your Grace means in temper, you know whether I am so *frack* as the serving-man spoke him."

"Nay, thou art prompt enough in all reasonable conscience," replied the Queen; "but thou art my own darling notwithstanding—But I meant, is this thy twin-brother as like thee in form and features as formerly? I remember thy dear mother alleged it as a reason for destining thee to the veil, that, were ye both to go at large, thou wouldst surely get the credit of some of thy brother's mad pranks."

"I believe, madam," said Catherine, "there are some unusually simple people even yet, who can hardly distinguish betwixt us, especially when, for diversion's sake, my brother hath taken a female dress,"—and as she spoke, she gave a quick glance at Roland Graeme, to whom this conversation conveyed a ray of light, welcome as ever streamed into the dungeon of a captive through the door which opened to give him freedom.

"He must be a handsome cavalier this brother of thine, if he be so like you," replied Mary. "He was in France, I think, for these late years, so that I saw him not at Holyrood."

"His looks, madam, have never been much found fault with," answered Catherine Seyton; "but I would he had less of that angry and heady spirit which evil times have encouraged amongst our young nobles. God knows, I grudge not his life in your Grace's quarrel; and love him for the willingness with which he labours for your rescue. But wherefore should he brawl with an old ruffianly serving-man, and stain at once his name with such a broil, and his hands with the blood of an old and ignoble wretch?"

"Nay, be patient, Catherine; I will not have thee traduce my gallant young knight. With Henry for my knight, and Roland Graeme for my trusty squire, methinks I am like a princess of romance, who may shortly set at defiance the dungeons and the weapons of all wicked sorcerers.— But my head aches with the agitation of the day. Take me *La Mer Des Histoires*, and resume where we left off on Wednesday.—Our Lady help thy head, girl, or rather may she help thy heart!—I asked thee for the Sea of Histories, and thou hast brought *La Cronique d'Amour*."

Once embarked upon the Sea of Histories, the Queen continued her labours with her needle, while Lady Fleming and Catherine read to her alternately for two hours.

As to Roland Graeme, it is probable that he continued in secret intent upon the Chronicle of Love, notwithstanding the censure which the Queen seemed to pass upon that branch of study. He now remembered a thousand circumstances of voice and manner, which, had his own prepossession been less, must surely have discriminated the brother from the sister; and he felt ashamed, that, having as it were by heart every particular of Catherine's gestures, words, and manners, he should have thought her, notwithstanding her spirits and levity, capable of assuming the bold step, loud tones, and forward assurance, which accorded well enough with her brother's hasty and masculine character. He endeavoured repeatedly to catch a glance of Catherine's eye, that he might judge how she was disposed to look upon him since he had made the discovery, but he was unsuccessful; for Catherine, when she was not reading herself, seemed to take so much interest in the exploits of the Teutonic knights against the Heathens of Esthonia and Livonia, that he could not surprise her eye even for a second. But when, closing the book, the Queen commanded their attendance in the garden, Mary, perhaps of set purpose, (for Roland's anxiety could not escape so practised an observer,) afforded him a favourable opportunity of accosting his mistress. The Queen commanded them to a little distance, while she engaged Lady Fleming in a particular and private conversation; the subject whereof we learn, from another authority, to have been the comparative excellence of the high standing ruff and the falling band. Roland must have been duller, and more sheepish than ever was youthful lover, if he had not endeavoured to avail himself of this opportunity.

"I have been longing this whole evening to ask of you, fair Catherine," said the page, "how foolish and unapprehensive you must have thought me, in being capable to mistake betwixt your brother and you?"

"The circumstance does indeed little honour to my rustic manners," said Catherine, "since those of a wild young man were so readily mistaken for mine. But I shall grow wiser in time; and with that view I am determined not to think of your follies, but to correct my own."

"It will be the lighter subject of meditation of the two," said Roland.

"I know not that," said Catherine, very gravely; "I fear we have been both unpardonably foolish."

"I have been mad," said Roland, "unpardonably mad. But you, lovely Catherine—"

"I," said Catherine, in the same tone of unusual gravity, "have too long suffered you to use such expressions towards me—I fear I can permit it no longer, and I blame myself for the pain it may give you."

"And what can have happened so suddenly to change our relation to each other, or alter, with such sudden cruelty, your whole deportment to me?"

"I can hardly tell," replied Catherine, "unless it is that the events of the day have impressed on my mind the necessity of our observing more distance to each other. A chance similar to that which betrayed to you the existence of my brother, may make known to Henry the terms you have used to me; and, alas! his whole conduct, as well as his deed, this day, makes me too justly apprehensive of the consequences."

"Fear nothing for that, fair Catherine," answered the page; "I am well able to protect myself against risks of that nature."

"That is to say," replied she, "that you would fight with my twin-brother to show your regard for his sister? I have heard the Queen say, in her sad hours, that men are, in love or in hate, the most selfish animals of creation; and your carelessness in this matter looks very like it. But be not so much abashed—you are no worse than others."

"You do me injustice, Catherine," replied the page, "I thought but of being threatened with a sword, and did not remember in whose hand your fancy had placed it. If your brother stood before me, with his drawn weapon in his hand, so like as he is to you in word, person, and favour, he might shed my life's blood ere I could find in my heart to resist him to his injury."

"Alas!" said she, "it is not my brother alone. But you remember only the singular circumstances in which we have met in equality, and I may say in intimacy. You think not, that whenever I re-enter my father's house, there is a gulf between us you may not pass, but with peril of your life.—Your only known relative is of wild and singular habits, of a hostile and broken clan* —the rest of your lineage unknown—forgive me that I speak what is the undeniable truth."

"Love, my beautiful Catherine, despises genealogies," answered Roland Graeme.

"Love may, but so will not the Lord Seyton," rejoined the damsel.

"The Queen, thy mistress and mine, she will intercede. Oh! drive me not from you at the moment I thought myself most happy!—and if I shall aid her deliverance, said not yourself that you and she would become my debtors?"

"All Scotland will become your debtors," said Catherine; "but for the active effects you might hope from our gratitude, you must remember I am wholly subjected to my father; and the poor Queen is, for a long time, more likely to be dependant on the pleasure of the nobles of her party, than possessed of power to control them."

---

* A broken clan was one who had no chief able to find security for their good behaviour—a clan of outlaws; And the Graemes of the Debateable Land were in that condition.

"Be it so," replied Roland; "my deeds shall control prejudice itself—it is a bustling world, and I will have my share. The Knight of Avenel, high as he now stands, rose from as obscure an origin as mine."

"Ay!" said Catherine, "there spoke the doughty knight of romance, that will cut his way to the imprisoned princess, through fiends and fiery dragons!"

"But if I can set the princess at large, and procure her the freedom of her own choice," said the page, "where, dearest Catherine, will that choice alight?"

"Release the princess from duresse, and she will tell you," said the damsel; and breaking off the conversation abruptly, she joined the Queen so suddenly, that Mary exclaimed, half aloud—

"No more tidings of evil import—no dissension, I trust, in my limited household?"—Then looking on Catherine's blushing cheek, and Roland's expanded brow and glancing eye—"No—no," she said, "I see all is well—*Ma petite mignone*, go to my apartment and fetch me down—let me see—ay, fetch my pomander box."

And having thus disposed of her attendant in the manner best qualified to hide her confusion, the Queen added, speaking apart to Roland, "I should at least have two grateful subjects of Catherine and you; for what sovereign but Mary would aid true love so willingly?—Ay, you lay your hand on your sword—your *petite flamberge à rien* there—Well, short time will show if all the good be true that is protested to us—I hear them toll curfew from Kinross. To our chamber—this old dame hath promised to be with us again at our evening meal. Were it not for the hope of speedy deliverance, her presence would drive me distracted. But I will be patient."

"I profess," said Catherine, who just then entered, "I would I could be Henry, with all a man's privileges, for one moment—I long to throw my plate at that confect of pride and formality, and ill-nature."

The Lady Fleming reprimanded her young companion for this explosion of impatience; the Queen laughed, and they went to the presence-chamber, where almost immediately entered supper, and the Lady of the castle. The Queen, strong in her prudent resolutions, endured her presence with great fortitude and equanimity, until her patience was disturbed by a new form, which had hitherto made no part of the ceremonial of the castle. When the other attendant had retired, Randal entered, bearing the keys of the castle fastened upon a chain, and, announcing that the watch was set, and the gates locked, delivered the keys with all reverence to the Lady of Lochleven.

SIR WALTER SCOTT

The Queen and her ladies exchanged with each other a look of disappointment, anger, and vexation; and Mary said aloud, "We cannot regret the smallness of our court, when we see our hostess discharge in person so many of its offices. In addition to her charges of principal steward of our household and grand almoner, she has to-night done duty as captain of our guard."

"And will continue to do so in future, madam," answered the Lady Lochleven, with much gravity; "the history of Scotland may teach me how ill the duty is performed, which is done by an accredited deputy—We have heard, madam, of favourites of later date, and as little merit, as Oliver Sinclair."*

"Oh, madam," replied the Queen, "my father had his female as well as his male favourites—there were the Ladies Sandilands and Olifaunt,† and some others, methinks; but their names cannot survive in the memory of so grave a person as you."

The Lady Lochleven looked as if she could have slain the Queen on the spot, but commanded her temper and retired from the apartment, bearing in her hand the ponderous bunch of keys.

"Now God be praised for that woman's youthful frailty!" said the Queen. "Had she not that weak point in her character, I might waste my words on her in vain—But that stain is the very reverse of what is said of the witch's mark—I can make her feel there, though she is otherwise insensible all over.—But how say you, girls—here is a new difficulty—How are these keys to be come by?—there is no deceiving or bribing this dragon, I trow."

"May I crave to know," said Roland, "whether, if your Grace were beyond the walls of the castle, you could find means of conveyance to the firm land, and protection when you are there?"

"Trust us for that, Roland," said the Queen; "for to that point our scheme is indifferent well laid."

"Then if your Grace will permit me to speak my mind, I think I could be of some use in this matter."

"As how, my good youth?—speak on," said the Queen, "and fearlessly."

"My patron the Knight of Avenel used to compel the youth educated in his household to learn the use of axe and hammer, and working in

---

* A favourite, and said to be an unworthy one, of James V.
† The names of these ladies, and a third frail favourite of James, are preserved in an epigram too *gaillard* for quotation.

wood and iron—he used to speak of old northern champions, who forged their own weapons, and of the Highland Captain, Donald nan Ord, or Donald of the Hammer, whom he himself knew, and who used to work at the anvil with a sledge-hammer in each hand. Some said he praised this art, because he was himself of churl's blood. However, I gained some practice in it, as the Lady Catherine Seyton partly knows; for since we were here, I wrought her a silver brooch."

"Ay," replied Catharine, "but you should tell her Grace that your workmanship was so indifferent that it broke to pieces next day, and I flung it away."

"Believe her not, Roland," said the Queen; "she wept when it was broken, and put the fragments into her bosom. But for your scheme—could your skill avail to forge a second set of keys?"

"No, madam, because I know not the wards. But I am convinced I could make a set so like that hateful bunch which the Lady bore off even now, that could they be exchanged against them by any means, she would never dream she was possessed of the wrong."

"And the good dame, thank Heaven, is somewhat blind," said the Queen; "but then for a forge, my boy, and the means of labouring unobserved?"

"The armourer's forge, at which I used sometimes to work with him, is the round vault at the bottom of the turret—he was dismissed with the warder for being supposed too much attached to George Douglas. The people are accustomed to see me work there, and I warrant I shall find some excuse that will pass current with them for putting bellows and anvil to work."

"The scheme has a promising face," said the Queen; "about it, my lad, with all speed, and beware the nature of your work is not discovered."

"Nay, I will take the liberty to draw the bolt against chance visitors, so that I will have time to put away what I am working upon, before I undo the door."

"Will not that of itself attract suspicion, in a place where it is so current already?" said Catherine.

"Not a whit," replied Roland; "Gregory the armourer, and every good hammerman, locks himself in when he is about some master piece of craft. Besides, something must be risked."

"Part we then to-night," said the Queen, "and God bless you my children!—If Mary's head ever rises above water, you shall all rise along with her."

XXXV

It is a time of danger, not of revel,
When churchmen turn to masquers.

—SPANISH FATHER

The enterprise of Roland Graeme appeared to prosper. A trinket or two, of which the work did not surpass the substance, (for the materials were silver, supplied by the Queen,) were judiciously presented to those most likely to be inquisitive into the labours of the forge and anvil, which they thus were induced to reckon profitable to others and harmless in itself. Openly, the page was seen working about such trifles. In private, he forged a number of keys resembling so nearly in weight and in form those which were presented every evening to the Lady Lochleven, that, on a slight inspection, it would have been difficult to perceive the difference. He brought them to the dark rusty colour by the use of salt and water; and, in the triumph of his art, presented them at length to Queen Mary in her presence-chamber, about an hour before the tolling of the curfew. She looked at them with pleasure, but at the same time with doubt.—"I allow," she said, "that the Lady Lochleven's eyes, which are not of the clearest, may be well deceived, could we pass those keys on her in place of the real implements of her tyranny. But how is this to be done, and which of my little court dare attempt this *tour de jongleur* with any chance of success? Could we but engage her in some earnest matter of argument—but those which I hold with her, always have been of a kind which make her grasp her keys the faster, as if she said to herself—Here I hold what sets me above your taunts and reproaches—And even for her liberty, Mary Stuart could not stoop to speak the proud heretic fair.—What shall we do? Shall Lady Fleming try her eloquence in describing the last new head-tire from Paris?—alas! the good dame has not changed the fashion of her head-gear since Pinkie-field for aught that I know. Shall my *mignóne* Catherine sing to her one of those touching airs, which draw the very souls out of me and Roland Graeme?—Alas! Dame Margaret Douglas would rather hear a Huguenot psalm of Clement Marrot, sung to the tune of *Reveillez vous, belle endormie.*—Cousins and liege counsellors, what is to be done, for our wits are really astray in this matter?—Must our man-at-arms and the champion of our body, Roland Graeme, manfully assault the old lady, and take the keys from her *par voie du fait?*"

"Nay! with your Grace's permission." said Roland, "I do not doubt being able to manage the matter with more discretion; for though, in your Grace's service, I do not fear—"

"A host of old women," interrupted Catherine, "each armed with rock and spindle, yet he has no fancy for pikes and partisans, which might rise at the cry of *Help! a Douglas, a Douglas!*"

"They that do not fear fair ladies' tongues," continued the page, "need dread nothing else.—But, gracious Liege, I am well-nigh satisfied that I could pass the exchange of these keys on the Lady Lochleven; but I dread the sentinel who is now planted nightly in the garden, which, by necessity, we must traverse."

"Our last advices from our friends on the shore have promised us assistance in that matter," replied the Queen.

"And is your Grace well assured of the fidelity and watchfulness of those without?"

"For their fidelity, I will answer with my life, and for their vigilance, I will answer with my life—I will give thee instant proof, my faithful Roland, that they are ingenuous and trusty as thyself. Come hither— Nay, Catherine, attend us; we carry not so deft a page into our private chamber alone. Make fast the door of the parlour, Fleming, and warn us if you hear the least step—or stay, go thou to the door, Catherine," (in a whisper, "thy ears and thy wits are both sharper.)—Good Fleming, attend us thyself"—(and again she whispered, "her reverend presence will be as safe a watch on Roland as thine can—so be not jealous, *mignone*.")

Thus speaking, they were lighted by the Lady Fleming into the Queen's bedroom, a small apartment enlightened by a projecting window.

"Look from that window, Roland," she said; "see you amongst the several lights which begin to kindle, and to glimmer palely through the gray of the evening from the village of Kinross-seest thou, I say, one solitary spark apart from the others, and nearer it seems to the verge of the water?—It is no brighter at this distance than the torch of the poor glowworm, and yet, my good youth, that light is more dear to Mary Stuart, than every star that twinkles in the blue vault of heaven. By that signal, I know that more than one true heart is plotting my deliverance; and without that consciousness, and the hope of freedom it gives me,

I had long since stooped to my fate, and died of a broken heart. Plan after plan has been formed and abandoned, but still the light glimmers; and while it glimmers, my hope lives.—Oh! how many evenings have I sat musing in despair over our ruined schemes, and scarce hoping that I should again see that blessed signal; when it has suddenly kindled, and, like the lights of Saint Elmo in a tempest, brought hope and consolation, where there, was only dejection and despair!"

"If I mistake not," answered Roland, "the candle shines from the house of Blinkhoolie, the mail-gardener."

"Thou hast a good eye," said the Queen; "it is there where my trusty lieges—God and the saints pour blessings on them!—hold consultation for my deliverance. The voice of a wretched captive would die on these blue waters, long ere it could mingle in their councils; and yet I can hold communication—I will confide the whole to thee—I am about to ask those faithful friends if the moment for the great attempt is nigh.—Place the lamp in the window, Fleming."

She obeyed, and immediately withdrew it. No sooner had she done so, than the light in the cottage of the gardener disappeared.

"Now count," said Queen Mary, "for my heart beats so thick that I cannot count myself."

The Lady Fleming began deliberately to count one, two, three, and when she had arrived at ten, the light on the shore showed its pale twinkle.

"Now, our Lady be praised!" said the Queen; "it was but two nights since, that the absence of the light remained while I could tell thirty. The hour of deliverance approaches. May God bless those who labour in it with such truth to me!—alas! with such hazard to themselves—and bless you, too, my children!—Come, we must to the audience-chamber again. Our absence might excite suspicion, should they serve supper."

They returned to the presence-chamber, and the evening concluded as usual.

The next morning, at dinner-time, an unusual incident occurred. While Lady Douglas of Lochleven performed her daily duty of assistant and taster at the Queen's table, she was told a man-at-arms had arrived, recommended by her son, but without any letter or other token than what he brought by word of mouth.

"Hath he given you that token?" demanded the Lady.

"He reserved it, as I think, for your Ladyship's ear," replied Randal.

"He doth well," said the Lady; "tell him to wait in the hall—But no—with your permission, madam," (to the Queen) "let him attend me here."

"Since you are pleased to receive your domestics in my presence," said the Queen, "I cannot choose—"

"My infirmities must plead my excuse, madam," replied the Lady; "the life I must lead here ill suits with the years which have passed over my head, and compels me to waive ceremonial."

"Oh, my good Lady," replied the Queen, "I would there were nought in this your castle more strongly compulsive than the cobweb chains of ceremony; but bolts and bars are harder matters to contend with."

As she spoke, the person announced by Randal entered the room, and Roland Graeme at once recognized in him the Abbot Ambrosius.

"What is your name, good fellow?" said the Lady.

"Edward Glendinning," answered the Abbot, with a suitable reverence.

"Art thou of the blood of the Knight of Avenel?" said the Lady of Lochleven.

"Ay, madam, and that nearly," replied the pretended soldier.

"It is likely enough," said the Lady, "for the Knight is the son of his own good works, and has risen from obscure lineage to his present high rank in the Estate—But he is of sure truth and approved worth, and his kinsman is welcome to us. You hold, unquestionably, the true faith?"

"Do not doubt of it, madam," said the disguised churchman.

"Hast thou a token to me from Sir William Douglas?" said the Lady.

"I have, madam," replied he; "but it must be said in private."

"Thou art right," said the Lady, moving towards the recess of a window; "say in what does it consist?"

"In the words of an old bard," replied the Abbot.

"Repeat them," answered the Lady; and he uttered, in a low tone, the lines from an old poem, called The Howlet,—

> *"O Douglas! Douglas!*
> *Tender and true."*

"Trusty Sir John Holland!"* said the Lady Douglas, apostrophizing the poet, "a kinder heart never inspired a rhyme, and the Douglas's honour was ever on thy heart-string! We receive you among our followers, Glendinning—But, Randal, see that he keep the outer ward

---

* Sir John Holland's poem of the Howlet is known to collectors by the beautiful edition presented to the Bannatyne Club, by Mr. David Laing.

SIR WALTER SCOTT

only, till we shall hear more touching him from our son.—Thou fearest not the night air. Glendinning?"

"In the cause of the Lady before whom I stand, I fear nothing, madam," answered the disguised Abbot.

"Our garrison, then, is stronger by one trustworthy soldier," said the matron—"Go to the buttery, and let them make much of thee."

When the Lady Lochleven had retired, the Queen said to Roland Graeme, who was now almost constantly in her company, "I spy comfort in that stranger's countenance; I know not why it should be so, but I am well persuaded he is a friend."

"Your Grace's penetration does not deceive you," answered the page; and he informed her that the Abbot of St. Mary's himself played the part of the newly arrived soldier.

The Queen crossed herself and looked upwards. "Unworthy sinner that I am," she said, "that for my sake a man so holy, and so high in spiritual office, should wear the garb of a base sworder, and run the risk of dying the death of a traitor!"

"Heaven will protect its own servant, madam," said Catherine Seyton; "his aid would bring a blessing on our undertaking, were it not already blest for its own sake."

"What I admire in my spiritual father," said Roland, "was the steady front with which he looked on me, without giving the least sign of former acquaintance. I did not think the like was possible, since I have ceased to believe that Henry was the same person with Catherine."

"But marked you not how astuciously the good father," said the Queen, "eluded the questions of the woman Lochleven, telling her the very truth, which yet she received not as such?"

Roland thought in his heart, that when the truth was spoken for the purpose of deceiving, it was little better than a lie in disguise. But it was no time to agitate such questions of conscience.

"And now for the signal from the shore," exclaimed Catherine; "my bosom tells me we shall see this night two lights instead of one gleam from that garden of Eden—And then, Roland, do you play your part manfully, and we will dance on the greensward like midnight fairies!"

Catherine's conjecture misgave not, nor deceived her. In the evening two beams twinkled from the cottage, instead of one; and the page heard, with beating heart, that the new retainer was ordered to stand sentinel on the outside of the castle. When he intimated this news to the Queen, she held her hand out to him—he knelt, and when he raised it to his lips in all dutiful homage, he found it was damp and cold as marble. "For God's sake, madam, droop not now,—sink not now!"

"Call upon our Lady, my Liege," said the Lady Fleming—"call upon your tutelar saint."

"Call the spirits of the hundred kings you are descended from," exclaimed the page; "in this hour of need, the resolution of a monarch were worth the aid of a hundred saints."

"Oh! Roland Graeme," said Mary, in a tone of deep despondency, "be true to me—many have been false to me. Alas! I have not always been true to myself. My mind misgives me that I shall die in bondage, and that this bold attempt will cost all our lives. It was foretold me by a soothsayer in France, that I should die in prison, and by a violent death, and here comes the hour—Oh, would to God it found me prepared!"

"Madam," said Catherine Seyton, "remember you are a Queen. Better we all died in bravely attempting to gain our freedom, than remained here to be poisoned, as men rid them of the noxious vermin that haunt old houses."

"You are right, Catherine," said the Queen; "and Mary will bear her like herself. But alas! your young and buoyant spirit can ill spell the causes which have broken mine. Forgive me, my children, and farewell for a while—I will prepare both mind and body for this awful venture."

They separated, till again called together by the tolling of the curfew. The Queen appeared grave, but firm and resolved; the Lady Fleming, with the art of an experienced courtier, knew perfectly how to disguise her inward tremors; Catherine's eye was fired, as if with the boldness of the project, and the half smile which dwelt upon her beautiful mouth seemed to contemn all the risk and all the consequences of discovery; Roland, who felt how much success depended on his own address and boldness, summoned together his whole presence of mind, and if he found his spirits flag for a moment, cast his eye upon Catherine, whom he thought he had never seen look so beautiful.—"I may be foiled," he thought, "but with this reward in prospect, they must bring the devil to aid them ere they cross me." Thus resolved, he stood like a greyhound in the slips, with hand, heart, and eye intent upon making and seizing opportunity for the execution of their project.

The keys had, with the wonted ceremonial, been presented to the Lady Lochleven. She stood with her back to the casement, which, like that of the Queen's apartment, commanded a view of Kinross, with the church, which stands at some distance from the town, and nearer to the lake, then connected with the town by straggling cottages. With her back to this casement, then, and her face to the table, on which the keys lay for an instant while she tasted the various dishes which were placed there, stood the Lady of Lochleven, more provokingly intent than usual—so at least it seemed to her prisoners—upon the huge and heavy bunch of iron, the implements of their restraint. Just when, having finished her ceremony as taster of the Queen's table, she was about to take up the keys, the page, who stood beside her, and had handed her the dishes in succession, looked sideways to the churchyard, and exclaimed he saw corpse-candles in the churchyard. The Lady of Lochleven was not without a touch, though a slight one, of the superstitions of the time; the fate of her sons made her alive to omens, and a corpse-light, as it was called, in the family burial-place boded death. She turned her head towards the casement—saw a distant glimmering—forgot her charge for one second, and in that second were lost the whole fruits of her former vigilance. The page held the forged keys under his cloak, and with great dexterity exchanged them for the real ones. His utmost address could not prevent a slight clash as he took up the latter bunch. "Who touches the keys?" said the Lady; and while the page answered that the sleeve of his cloak had stirred them, she looked round, possessed herself of the bunch which now occupied the place of the genuine keys, and again turned to gaze on the supposed corpse-candles.

"I hold these gleams," she said, after a moment's consideration, "to come, not from the churchyard, but from the hut of the old gardener Blinkhoolie. I wonder what thrift that churl drives, that of late he hath ever had light in his house till the night grew deep. I thought him an industrious, peaceful man—If he turns resetter of idle companions and night-walkers, the place must be rid of him."

"He may work his baskets perchance," said the page, desirous to stop the train of her suspicion.

"Or nets, may he not?" answered the Lady.

"Ay, madam," said Roland, "for trout and salmon."

"Or for fools and knaves," replied the Lady: "but this shall be looked after to-morrow.—I wish your Grace and your company a good evening.—Randal, attend us." And Randal, who waited in the antechamber after having surrendered his bunch of keys, gave his escort to his mistress as usual, while, leaving the Queen's apartments, she retired to her own (End of paragraph missing in original)

"To-morrow" said the page, rubbing his hands with glee as he repeated the Lady's last words, "fools look to-morrow, and wise folk use to-night.—May I pray you, my gracious Liege, to retire for one half hour, until all the castle is composed to rest? I must go and rub with oil these blessed implements of our freedom. Courage and constancy, and all will go well, provided our friends on the shore fail not to send the boat you spoke of."

"Fear them not," said Catherine, "they are true as steel—if our dear mistress do but maintain her noble and royal courage."[*]

"Doubt not me, Catherine," replied the Queen; "a while since I was overborne, but I have recalled the spirit of my earlier and more sprightly days, when I used to accompany my armed nobles, and wish to be myself a man, to know what life it was to be in the fields with sword and buckler, jack, and knapscap."

"Oh, the lark lives not a gayer life, nor sings a lighter and gayer song than the merry soldier," answered Catherine. "Your Grace shall be in the midst of them soon, and the look of such a liege Sovereign will make each of your host worth three in the hour of need:—but I must to my task."

"We have but brief time," said Queen Mary; "one of the two lights in the cottage is extinguished—that shows the boat is put off."

---

[*] In the dangerous expedition to Aberdeenshire, Randolph, the English Ambassador, gives Cecil the following account of Queen Mary's demeanour:—

"In all those garbulles, I assure your honour, I never saw the Queen merrier, never dismayed; nor never thought I that stomache to be in her that I find. She repented nothing but, when the Lords and others, at Inverness, came in the morning from the watches, that she was not a man, to know what life it was to lye all night in the fields, or to walk upon the causeway with a jack and a knaps-cap, a Glasgow buckler, and a broadsword."—RANDOLPH *to* CECIL, *September* 18, 1562.

The writer of the above letter seems to have felt the same impression which Catherine Seyton, in the text, considered as proper to the Queen's presence among her armed subjects.

"Though we neither thought nor looked for other than on that day to have fought or never-what desperate blows would not have been given, when every man should have fought in the sight of so noble a Queen, and so many fair ladies, our enemies to have taken them from us, and we to save our honours, not to be reft of them, your honour can easily judge."

—*The same to the same, September* 24, 1562

SIR WALTER SCOTT

"They will row very slow," said the page, "or kent where depth permits, to avoid noise.—To our several tasks—I will communicate with the good Father."

At the dead hour of midnight, when all was silent in the castle, the page put the key into the lock of the wicket which opened into the garden, and which was at the bottom of a staircase which descended from the Queen's apartment. "Now, turn smooth and softly, thou good bolt," said he, "if ever oil softened rust!" and his precautions had been so effectual, that the bolt revolved with little or no sound of resistance. He ventured not to cross the threshold, but exchanging a word with the disguised Abbot, asked if the boat were ready?

"This half hour," said the sentinel. "She lies beneath the wall, too close under the islet to be seen by the warder, but I fear she will hardly escape his notice in putting off again."

"The darkness," said the page, "and our profound silence, may take her off unobserved, as she came in. Hildebrand has the watch on the tower—a heavy-headed knave, who holds a can of ale to be the best headpiece upon a night-watch. He sleeps, for a wager."

"Then bring the Queen," said the Abbot, "and I will call Henry Seyton to assist them to the boat."

On tiptoe, with noiseless step and suppressed breath, trembling at every rustle of their own apparel, one after another the fair prisoners glided down the winding stair, under the guidance of Roland Graeme, and were received at the wicket-gate by Henry Seyton and the churchman. The former seemed instantly to take upon himself the whole direction of the enterprise. "My Lord Abbot," he said, "give my sister your arm—I will conduct the Queen—and that youth will have the honour to guide Lady Fleming."

This was no time to dispute the arrangement, although it was not that which Roland Graeme would have chosen. Catherine Seyton, who well knew the garden path, tripped on before like a sylph, rather leading the Abbot than receiving assistance—the Queen, her native spirit prevailing over female fear, and a thousand painful reflections, moved steadily forward, by the assistance of Henry Seyton—while the Lady Fleming, encumbered with her fears and her helplessness Roland Graeme, who followed in the rear, and who bore under the other arm a packet of necessaries belonging to the Queen. The door of the garden, which communicated with the shore of the islet, yielded to one of the keys of which Roland had possessed himself, although not until he had tried several,—a moment of anxious terror and expectation. The ladies were then partly led, partly carried, to the side of the lake, where a boat with six rowers attended them, the men couched along the bottom to secure them from observation. Henry Seyton placed the Queen in the stern; the Abbot offered to assist Catherine, but she was seated by the Queen's side before he could utter his proffer of help; and Roland Graeme was just lifting Lady Fleming over the boat-side, when a thought suddenly occurred to him, and exclaiming, "Forgotten, forgotten! wait for me but one half-minute," he replaced on the shore the helpless Lady of the bed-chamber, threw the Queen's packet into the boat, and sped back through the garden with the noiseless speed of a bird on the wing.

"By Heaven, he is false at last!" said Seyton; "I ever feared it!"

"He is as true," said Catherine, "as Heaven itself, and that I will maintain."

"Be silent, minion," said her brother, "for shame, if not for fear— Fellows, put off, and row for your lives!"

"Help me, help me on board!" said the deserted Lady Fleming, and that louder than prudence warranted.

"Put off—put off!" cried Henry Seyton; "leave all behind, so the Queen is safe."

"Will you permit this, madam?" said Catherine, imploringly; "you leave your deliverer to death."

"I will not," said the Queen.—"Seyton I command you to stay at every risk."

"Pardon me, madam, if I disobey," said the intractable young man; and with one hand lifting in Lady Fleming, he began himself to push off the boat.

She was two fathoms' length from the shore, and the rowers were getting her head round, when Roland Graeme, arriving, bounded from the beach, and attained the boat, overturning Seyton, on whom he lighted. The youth swore a deep but suppressed oath, and stopping Graeme as he stepped towards the stern, said, "Your place is not with high-born dames—keep at the head and trim the vessel—Now give way—give way—Row, for God and the Queen!"

The rowers obeyed, and began to pull vigorously.

"Why did ye not muffle the oars?" said Roland Graeme; "the dash must awaken the sentinel—Row, lads, and get out of reach of shot; for had not old Hildebrand, the warder, supped upon poppy-porridge, this whispering must have waked him."

"It was all thine own delay," said Seyton; "thou shalt reckon, with me hereafter for that and other matters."

But Roland's apprehension was verified too instantly to permit him to reply. The sentinel, whose slumbering had withstood the whispering, was alarmed by the dash of the oars. His challenge was instantly heard. "A boat——a boat!—bring to, or I shoot!" And, as they continued to ply their oars, he called aloud, "Treason! treason!" rung the bell of the castle, and discharged his harquebuss at the boat. The ladies crowded on each other like startled wild foul, at the flash and report of the piece, while the men urged the rowers to the utmost speed. They heard more than one ball whiz along the surface of the lake, at no great distance from their little bark; and from the lights, which glanced like meteors from window to window, it was evident the whole castle was alarmed, and their escape discovered.

"Pull!" again exclaimed Seyton; "stretch to your oars, or I will spur you to the task with my dagger—they will launch a boat immediately."

"That is cared for," said Roland; "I locked gate and wicket on them when I went back, and no boat will stir from the island this night, if doors of good oak and bolts of iron can keep men within stone-walls.— And now I resign my office of porter of Lochleven, and give the keys to the Kelpie's keeping."

As the heavy keys plunged in the lake, the Abbot,—who till then had been repeating his prayers, exclaimed, "Now, bless thee, my son! for thy ready prudence puts shame on us all."*

---

* It is well known that the escape of Queen Mary from Lochleven was effected by George Douglas, the youngest brother of Sir William Douglas, the lord of the castle; but the minute circumstances of the event have been a good deal confused, owing to two agents having been concerned in it who bore the same name. It has been always supposed that George Douglas was induced to abet Mary's escape by the ambitions hope that, by such service, he might merit her hand. But his purpose was discovered by his brother Sir William, and he was expelled from the castle. He continued, notwithstanding, to hover in the neighbourhood, and maintain a correspondence with the royal prisoner and others in the fortress.

If we believe the English ambassador Drury, the Queen was grateful to George Douglas, and even proposed a marriage with him; a scheme which could hardly be serious, since she was still the wife of Bothwell, but which, if suggested at all, might be with a purpose of gratifying the Regent Murray's ambition, and propitiating his favour; since he was, it must be remembered, the brother uterine of George Douglas, for whom such high honour was said to be designed.

The proposal, if seriously made, was treated as inadmissible, and Mary again resumed her purpose of escape. Her failure in her first attempt has some picturesque particulars,

"I knew," said Mary, drawing her breath more freely, as they were now out of reach of the musketry—"I knew my squire's truth, promptitude, and sagacity.—I must have him my dear friends—with my no less true knights, Douglas and Seyton—but where, then, is Douglas?"

---

which might have been advantageously introduced in fictitious narrative. Drury sends Cecil the following account of the matter:—

"But after, upon the 25th of the last, (April 1567,) she interprised an escape, and was the rather near effect, through her accustomed long lying in bed all the morning. The manner of it was thus: there cometh in to her the laundress early as other times before she was wanted, and the Queen according to such a secret practice putteth on her the hood of the laundress, and so with the fardel of clothes and the muffler upon her face, passeth, out and entereth the boat to pass the Loch; which, after some space, one of them that rowed said merrily, 'Let us see what manner of dame this is,' and therewith offered to pull down her muffler, which to defend, she put up her hands, which they spied to be very fair and white; wherewith they entered into suspicion whom she was, beginning to wonder at her enterprise. Whereat she was little dismayed, but charged them, upon danger of their lives, to row her over to the shore, which they nothing regarded, but eftsoons rowed her back again, promising her it should be secreted, and especially from the lord of the house, under whose guard she lyeth. It seemeth she knew her refuge, and—where to have found it if she had once landed; for there did, and yet do linger, at a little village called Kinross, hard at the Loch side, the same George Douglas, one Sempel and one Beton, the which two were sometime her trusty servants, and, as yet appeareth, they mind her no less affection."—*Bishop Keith's History of the Affairs of Church and State in Scotland*, p. 490.

Notwithstanding this disappointment, little spoke of by historians, Mary renewed her attempts to escape. There was in the Castle of Lochleven a lad, named William Douglas, some relation probably of the baron, and about eighteen years old. This youth proved as accessible to Queen Mary's prayers and promises, as was the brother of his patron, George Douglas, from whom this William must be carefully kept distinct. It was young William who played the part commonly assigned to his superior, George, stealing the keys of the castle from the table on which they lay, while his lord was at supper. He let the Queen and a waiting woman out of the apartment where they were secured, and out of the tower itself, embarked with them in a small skiff, and rowed them to the shore. To prevent instant pursuit, he, for precaution's sake, locked the iron grated door of the tower, and threw the keys into the lake. They found George Douglas and the Queen's servant, Beton, waiting for them, and Lord Seyton and James Hamilton of Orbeiston in attendance, at the head of a party of faithful followers, with whom they fled to Niddrie Castle, and from thence to Hamilton.

In narrating this romantic story, both history and tradition confuse the two Douglasses together, and confer on George the successful execution of the escape from the castle, the merit of which belongs, in reality, to the boy called William, or, more frequently, the Little Douglas, either from his youth or his slight stature. The reader will observe, that in the romance, the part of the Little Douglas has been assigned to Roland Graeme. In another case, it would be tedious to point out in a work of amusement such minute points of historical fact; but the general interest taken in the fate of Queen Mary, renders every thing of consequence which connects itself with her misfortunes.

SIR WALTER SCOTT

"Here, madam," answered the deep and melancholy voice of the boatman who sat next her, and who acted as steersman.

"Alas! was it you who stretched your body before me," said the Queen, "when the balls were raining around us?"

"Believe you," said he, in a low tone, "that Douglas would have resigned to any one the chance of protecting his Queen's life with his own?"

The dialogue was here interrupted by a shot or two from one of those small pieces of artillery called falconets, then used in defending castles. The shot was too vague to have any effect, but the broader flash, the deeper sound, the louder return which was made by the midnight echoes of Bennarty, terrified and imposed silence on the liberated prisoners. The boat was alongside of a rude quay or landing place, running out from a garden of considerable extent, ere any of them again attempted to speak. They landed, and while the Abbot returned thanks aloud to Heaven,—which had thus far favoured their enterprise, Douglas enjoyed the best reward of his desperate undertaking, in conducting the Queen to the house of the gardener.

Yet, not unmindful of Roland Graeme even in that moment of terror and exhaustion, Mary expressly commanded Seyton to give his assistance to Fleming, while Catherine voluntarily, and without bidding, took the arm of the page. Seyton presently resigned Lady Fleming to the care of the Abbot, alleging, he must look after their horses; and his attendants, disencumbering themselves of their boat-cloaks, hastened to assist him.

While Mary spent in the gardener's cottage the few minutes which were necessary to prepare the steeds for their departure, she perceived, in a corner, the old man to whom the garden belonged, and called him to approach. He came as it were with reluctance.

"How, brother," said the Abbot, "so slow to welcome thy royal Queen and mistress to liberty and to her kingdom!"

The old man, thus admonished, came forward, and, in good terms of speech, gave her Grace joy of her deliverance. The Queen returned him thanks in the most gracious manner, and added, "It will remain to us to offer some immediate reward for your fidelity, for we wot well your house has been long the refuge in which our trusty servants have met to concert measures for our freedom." So saying, she offered gold, and added, "We will consider your services more fully hereafter."

"Kneel, brother," said the Abbot, "kneel instantly, and thank her Grace's kindness."

"Good brother, that wert once a few steps under me, and art still many years younger," replied the gardener, pettishly, "let me do mine acknowledgments in my own way. Queens have knelt to me ere now, and in truth my knees are too old and stiff to bend even to this lovely-faced lady. May it please your Grace, if your Grace's servants have occupied my house, so that I could not call it mine own—if they have trodden down my flowers in the zeal of their midnight comings and goings, and destroyed the hope of the fruit season, by bringing their war-horses into my garden, I do but crave of your Grace in requital, that you will choose your residence as far from me as possible. I am an old man who would willingly creep to my grave as easily as I can, in peace, good-will, and quiet labour."

"I promise you fairly, good man," said the Queen, "I will not make yonder castle my residence again, if I can help it. But let me press on you this money—it will make some amends for the havoc we have made in your little garden and orchard."

"I thank your Grace, but it will make me not the least amends," said the old man. "The ruined labours of a whole year are not so easily replaced to him who has perchance but that one year to live; and besides, they tell me I must leave this place and become a wanderer in mine old age—I that have nothing on earth saving these fruit-trees, and a few old parchments and family secrets not worth knowing. As for gold, if I had loved it, I might have remained Lord Abbot of St. Mary's—and yet, I wot not—for, if Abbot Boniface be but the poor peasant Blinkhoolie, his successor, the Abbot Ambrosius, is still transmuted for the worse into the guise of a sword-and-buckler-man."

"Is this indeed the Abbot Boniface of whom I have heard?" said the Queen. "It is indeed I who should have bent the knee for your blessing, good Father."

"Bend no knee to me, Lady! The blessing of an old man, who is no longer an Abbot, go with you over dale and down—I hear the trampling of your horses."

"Farewell, Father," said the Queen. "When we are once more seated at Holyrood, we will neither forget thee nor thine injured garden."

"Forget us both," said the Ex-Abbot Boniface, "and may God be with you!"

As they hurried out of the house, they heard the old man talking and muttering to himself, as he hastily drew bolt and bar behind them.

SIR WALTER SCOTT

"The revenge of the Douglasses will reach the poor old man," said the Queen. "God help me, I ruin every one whom I approach!"

"His safety is cared for," said Seyton; "he must not remain here, but will be privately conducted to a place of greater security. But I would your Grace were in the saddle.—To horse! to horse!"

The party of Seyton and of Douglas were increased to about ten by those attendants who had remained with the horses. The Queen and her ladies, with all the rest who came from the boat, were instantly mounted; and holding aloof from the village, which was already alarmed by the firing from the castle, with Douglas acting as their guide, they soon reached the open ground and began to ride as fast as was consistent with keeping together in good order.

XXXVI

The influence of the free air, the rushing of the horses over high and low, the ringing of the bridles, the excitation at once arising from a sense of freedom and of rapid motion, gradually dispelled the confused and dejected sort of stupefaction by which Queen Mary was at first overwhelmed. She could not at last conceal the change of her feelings to the person who rode at her rein, and who she doubted not was the Father Ambrosius; for Seyton, with all the heady impetuosity of a youth, proud, and justly so, of his first successful adventure, assumed all the bustle and importance of commander of the little party, which escorted, in the language of the time, the Fortune of Scotland. He now led the van, now checked his bounding steed till the rear had come up, exhorted the leaders to keep a steady, though rapid pace, and commanded those who were hindmost of the party to their spurs, and allow no interval to take place in their line of march; and anon he was beside the Queen, or her ladies, inquiring how they brooked the hasty journey, and whether they had any commands for him. But while Seyton thus busied himself in the general cause with some advantage to the regular order of the march, and a good deal of personal ostentation, the horseman who rode beside the Queen gave her his full and undivided attention, as if he had been waiting upon some superior being. When the road was rugged and dangerous, he abandoned almost entirely the care of his own horse, and kept his hand constantly upon the Queen's bridle; if a river or larger brook traversed their course, his left arm retained her in the saddle, while his right held her palfrey's rein.

"I had not thought, reverend Father," said the Queen, when they reached the other bank, "that the convent bred such good horsemen."— The person she addressed sighed, but made no other answer.—"I know not how it is," said Queen Mary, "but either the sense of freedom, or the pleasure of my favourite exercise, from which I have been so long debarred, or both combined, seem to have given wings to me—no fish ever shot through the water, no bird through the air, with the hurried feeling of liberty and rapture with which I sweep through, this night-wind, and over these wolds. Nay, such is the magic of feeling myself once more in the saddle, that I could almost swear I am at this moment mounted on my own favourite Rosabelle, who was never matched in Scotland for swiftness, for ease of motion, and for sureness of foot."

"And if the horse which bears so dear a burden could speak," answered the deep voice of the melancholy George of Douglas, "would she not reply, who but Rosabelle ought at such an emergence as this to serve her beloved mistress, or who but Douglas ought to hold her bridle-rein?"

Queen Mary started; she foresaw at once all the evils like to arise to herself and him from the deep enthusiastic passion of this youth; but her feelings as a woman, grateful at once and compassionate, prevented her assuming the dignity of a Queen, and she endeavoured to continue the conversation in an indifferent tone.

"Methought," she said, "I heard that, at the division of my spoils, Rosabelle had become the property of Lord Morton's paramour and ladye-love Alice."

"The noble palfrey had indeed been destined to so base a lot," answered Douglas; "she was kept under four keys, and under the charge of a numerous crew of grooms and domestics—but Queen Mary needed Rosabelle, and Rosabelle is here."

"And was it well, Douglas," said Queen Mary, "when such fearful risks of various kinds must needs be encountered, that you should augment their perils to yourself for a subject of so little moment as a palfrey?"

"Do you call that of little moment," answered Douglas, "which has afforded you a moment's pleasure?—Did you not start with joy when I first said you were mounted on Rosabelle?—And to purchase you that pleasure, though it were to last no longer than the flash of lightning doth, would not Douglas have risked his life a thousand times?"

"Oh, peace, Douglas, peace," said the Queen, "this is unfitting language; and, besides, I would speak," said she, recollecting herself, "with the Abbot of Saint Mary's—Nay, Douglas, I will not let you quit my rein in displeasure."

"Displeasure, lady!" answered Douglas: "alas! sorrow is all that I can feel for your well-warranted contempt—I should be as soon displeased with Heaven for refusing the wildest wish which mortal can form."

"Abide by my rein, however," said Mary, "there is room for my Lord Abbot on the other side; and, besides, I doubt if his assistance would be so useful to Rosabelle and me as yours has been, should the road again require it."

The Abbot came up on the other side, and she immediately opened a conversation with him on the topic of the state of parties, and the plan fittest for her to pursue inconsequence of her deliverance. In this conversation Douglas took little share, and never but when directly applied to by the Queen, while, as before, his attention seemed entirely engrossed by the care of Mary's personal safety. She learned, however, she had a new obligation to him, since, by his contrivance, the Abbot, whom he had furnished with the family pass-word, was introduced into the castle as one of the garrison.

Long before daybreak they ended their hasty and perilous journey before the gates of Niddrie, a castle in West Lothian, belonging to Lord Seyton. When the Queen was about to alight, Henry Seyton, preventing Douglas, received her in his arms, and, kneeling down, prayed her Majesty to enter the house of his father, her faithful servant.

"Your Grace," he added, "may repose yourself here in perfect safety— it is already garrisoned with good men for your protection; and I have sent a post to my father, whose instant arrival, at the head of five hundred men, may be looked for. Do not dismay yourself, therefore, should your sleep be broken by the trampling of horse; but only think that here are some scores more of the saucy Seytons come to attend you."

"And by better friends than the Saucy Seytons, a Scottish Queen cannot be guarded," replied Mary. "Rosabelle went fleet as the summer breeze, and well-nigh as easy; but it is long since I have been a traveller, and I feel that repose will be welcome.—Catherine, *ma mignone*, you must sleep in my apartment to-night, and bid me welcome to your noble father's castle.—Thanks, thanks to all my kind deliverers—thanks, and a good night is all I can now offer; but if I climb once more to the upper side of Fortune's wheel, I will not have her bandage. Mary Stewart will keep her eyes open, and distinguish her friends.—Seyton, I need scarcely recommend the venerable Abbot, the Douglas, and my page, to your honourable care and hospitality."

Henry Seyton bowed, and Catherine and Lady Fleming attended the Queen to her apartment; where, acknowledging to them that she should have found it difficult in that moment to keep her promise of

SIR WALTER SCOTT

holding her eyes open, she resigned herself to repose, and awakened not till the morning was advanced.

Mary's first feeling when she awoke, was the doubt of her freedom; and the impulse prompted her to start from bed, and hastily throwing her mantle over her shoulders, to look out at the casement of her apartment. Oh, sight of joy! instead of the crystal sheet of Lochleven, unaltered save by the influence of the wind, a landscape of wood and moorland lay before her, and the park around the castle was occupied by the troops of her most faithful and most favourite nobles.

"Rise, rise, Catherine," cried the enraptured Princess; "arise and come hither!—here are swords and spears in true hands, and glittering armour on loyal breasts. Here are banners, my girl, floating in the wind, as lightly as summer clouds—Great God! what pleasure to my weary eyes to trace their devices—thine own brave father's—the princely Hamilton's—the faithful Fleming's—See—see—they have caught a glimpse of me, and throng towards the window!"

She flung the casement open, and with her bare head, from which the tresses flew back loose and dishevelled, her fair arm slenderly veiled by her mantle, returned by motion and sign the exulting shouts of the warriors, which echoed for many a furlong around. When the first burst of ecstatic joy was over, she recollected how lightly she was dressed, and, putting her hands to her face, which was covered with blushes at the recollection, withdrew abruptly from the window. The cause of her retreat was easily conjectured, and increased the general enthusiasm for a Princess, who had forgotten her rank in her haste to acknowledge the services of her subjects. The unadorned beauties of the lovely woman, too, moved the military spectators more than the highest display of her regal state might; and what might have seemed too free in her mode of appearing before them, was more than atoned for by the enthusiasm of the moment and by the delicacy evinced in her hasty retreat. Often as the shouts died away, as often were they renewed, till wood and hill rung again; and many a deep path was made that morning on the cross of the sword, that the hand should not part with the weapon, till Mary Stewart was restored to her rights. But what are promises, what the hopes of mortals? In ten days, these gallant and devoted votaries were slain, were captives, or had fled.

Mary flung herself into the nearest seat, and still blushing, yet half smiling, exclaimed, "*Ma mignone*, what will they think of me?—to show myself to them with my bare feet hastily thrust into the slippers—only this loose mantle about me—my hair loose on my shoulders—my arms and neck so bare—Oh, the best they can suppose is, that her abode in yonder dungeon has turned their Queen's brain! But my rebel subjects saw me exposed when I was in the depth of affliction, why should I hold colder ceremony with these faithful and loyal men?—Call Fleming, however—I trust she has not forgotten the little mail with my apparel—We must be as brave as we can, *mignóne.*"

"Nay, madam, our good Lady Fleming was in no case to remember any thing."

"You jest, Catherine," said the Queen, somewhat offended; "it is not in her nature surely, to forget her duty so far as to leave us without a change of apparel?"

"Roland Graeme, madam, took care of that," answered Catherine; "for he threw the mail, with your highness's clothes and jewels, into the boat, ere he ran back to lock the gate—I never saw so awkward a page as that youth—the packet well-nigh fell on my head."

"He shall make thy heart amends, my girl," said Queen Mary, laughing, "for that and all other offences given. But call Fleming, and let us put ourselves into apparel to meet our faithful lords."

Such had been the preparations, and such was the skill of Lady Fleming, that the Queen appeared before her assembled nobles in such attire as became, though it could not enhance, her natural dignity. With the most winning courtesy, she expressed to each individual her grateful thanks, and dignified not only every noble, but many of the lesser barons by her particular attention.

"And whither now, my lords?" she said; "what way do your counsels determine for us?"

"To Draphane Castle," replied Lord Arbroath, "if your Majesty is so pleased; and thence to Dunbarton, to place your Grace's person in safety, after which we long to prove if these traitors will abide us in the field."

"And when do we journey?"

"We propose," said Lord Seyton, "if your Grace's fatigue will permit, to take horse after the morning's meal."

"Your pleasure, my Lords, is mine," replied the Queen; "we will rule our journey by your wisdom now, and hope hereafter to have the advantage of governing by it our kingdom.—You will permit my ladies and me, my good lords, to break our fasts along with you—We must be half soldiers ourselves, and set state apart."

SIR WALTER SCOTT

Low bowed many a helmeted head at this gracious proffer, when the Queen, glancing her eyes through the assembled leaders, missed both Douglas and Roland Graeme, and inquired for them in a whisper to Catherine Seyton.

"They are in yonder oratory, madam, sad enough," replied Catherine; and the Queen observed that her favourite's eyes were red with weeping.

"This must not be," said the Queen. "Keep the company amused—I will seek them, and introduce them myself."

She went into the oratory, where the first she met was George Douglas, standing, or rather reclining, in the recess of a window, his back rested against the wall, and his arms folded on his breast. At the sight of the Queen he started, and his countenance showed, for an instant, an expression of intense delight, which was instantly exchanged for his usual deep melancholy.

"What means this?" she said; "Douglas, why does the first deviser and bold executor of the happy scheme for our freedom, shun the company of his fellow-nobles, and of the Sovereign whom he has obliged?"

"Madam," replied Douglas, "those whom you grace with your presence bring followers to aid your cause, wealth to support your state,—can offer you halls in which to feast, and impregnable castles for your defence. I am a houseless and landless man—disinherited by my mother, and laid under her malediction—disowned by my name and kindred—who bring nothing to your standard but a single sword, and the poor life of its owner."

"Do you mean to upbraid me, Douglas," replied the Queen, "by showing what you have lost for my sake?"

"God forbid, madam!" interrupted the young man, eagerly; "were it to do again, and had I ten times as much rank and wealth, and twenty times as many friends to lose, my losses would be overpaid by the first step you made, as a free princess, upon the soil of your native kingdom."

"And what then ails you, that you will not rejoice with those who rejoice upon the same joyful occasion?" said the Queen.

"Madam," replied the youth," though exheridated and disowned, I am yet a Douglas: with most of yonder nobles my family have been in feud for ages—a cold reception amongst them, were an insult, and a kind one yet more humiliating."

"For shame, Douglas," replied the Queen, "shake off this unmanly gloom!—I can make thee match for the best of them in title and fortune, and, believe me, I will.—Go then amongst them, I command you."

"That word," said Douglas, "is enough—I go. This only let me say, that not for wealth or title would I have done that which I have done—Mary Stewart will not, and the Queen cannot, reward me."

So saying, he left the oratory, mingled with the nobles, and placed himself at the bottom of the table. The Queen looked after him, and put her kerchief to her eyes.

"Now, Our Lady pity me," she said, "for no sooner are my prison cares ended, than those which beset me as a woman and a Queen again thicken around me.—Happy Elizabeth! to whom political interest is every thing, and whose heart never betrays thy head.—And now must I seek this other boy, if I would prevent daggers-drawing betwixt him and the young Seyton."

Roland Graeme was in the same oratory, but at such a distance from Douglas, that he could not overhear what passed betwixt the Queen and him. He also was moody and thoughtful, but cleared his brow at the Queen's question, "How now, Roland? you are negligent in your attendance this morning. Are you so much overcome with your night's ride?"

"Not so, gracious madam," answered Graeme; "but I am told the page of Lochleven is not the page of Niddrie Castle; and so Master Henry Seyton hath in a manner been pleased to supersede my attendance."

"Now, Heaven forgive me," said the Queen, "how soon these cock-chickens begin to spar!—with children and boys, at least, I may be a queen.—I will have you friends.—Some one send me Henry Seyton hither." As she spoke the last words aloud, the youth whom she had named entered the apartment. "Come hither," she said, "Henry Seyton—I will have you give your hand to this youth, who so well aided in the plan of my escape."

"Willingly, madam," answered Seyton, "so that the youth will grant me, as a boon, that he touch not the hand of another Seyton whom he knows of. My hand has passed current for hers with him before now—and to win my friendship, he must give up thoughts of my sister's love."

"Henry Seyton," said the Queen, "does it become you to add any condition to my command?"

"Madam," said Henry, "I am the servant of your Grace's throne, son to the most loyal man in Scotland. Our goods, our castles, our blood, are yours: Our honour is in our own keeping. I could say more, but—"

"Nay, speak on, rude boy," said the Queen; "what avails it that I am released from Lochleven, if I am thus enthralled under the yoke of my pretended deliverers, and prevented from doing justice to one who has deserved as well of me as yourself?"

"Be not in this distemperature for me, sovereign Lady," said Roland; "this young gentleman, being the faithful servant of your Grace, and the brother of Catherine Seyton, bears that about him which will charm down my passion at the hottest."

"I warn thee once more," said Henry Seyton, haughtily, "that you make no speech which may infer that the daughter of Lord Seyton can be aught to thee beyond what she is to every churl's blood in Scotland."

The Queen was again about to interfere, for Roland's complexion rose, and it became somewhat questionable how long his love for Catherine would suppress the natural fire of his temper. But the interposition of another person, hitherto unseen, prevented Mary's interference. There was in the oratory a separate shrine, enclosed with a high screen of pierced oak, within which was placed an image of Saint Bennet, of peculiar sanctity. From this recess, in which she had been probably engaged in her devotions, issued suddenly Magdalen Graeme, and addressed Henry Seyton, in reply to his last offensive expressions,—"And of what clay, then, are they moulded these Seytons, that the blood of the Graemes may not aspire to mingle with theirs? Know, proud boy, that when I call this youth my daughter's child, I affirm his descent from Malise Earl of Strathern, called Malise with the Bright Brand; and I trow the blood of your house springs from no higher source."

"Good mother," said Seyton, "methinks your sanctity should make you superior to these worldly vanities; and indeed it seems to have rendered you somewhat oblivious touching them, since, to be of gentle descent, the father's name and lineage must be as well qualified as the mother's."

"And if I say he comes of the blood of Avenel by the father's side," replied Magdalen Graeme, "name I not blood as richly coloured as thine own?"

"Of Avenel?" said the Queen; "is my page descended of Avenel?"

"Ay, gracious Princess, and the last male heir of that ancient house—Julian Avenel was his father, who fell in battle against the Southron."

"I have heard the tale of sorrow," said the Queen; "it was thy daughter, then, who followed that unfortunate baron to the field, and died on his body? Alas! how many ways does woman's affection find to work out her own misery! The tale has oft been told and sung in hall and bower—And thou, Roland, art that child of misfortune, who was left among the dead and dying? Henry Seyton, he is thine equal in blood and birth."

"Scarcely so," said Henry Seyton, "even were he legitimate; but if the tale be told and sung aright, Julian Avenel was a false knight, and his leman a frail and credulous maiden."

"Now, by Heaven, thou liest!" said Roland Graeme, and laid his hand on his sword. The entrance of Lord Seyton, however, prevented violence.

"Save me, my lord," said the Queen, "and separate these wild and untamed spirits."

"How, Henry," said the Baron, "are my castle, and the Queen's presence, no checks on thine insolence and impetuosity?—And with whom art thou brawling?—unless my eyes spell that token false, it is with the very youth who aided me so gallantly in the skirmish with the Leslies—Let me look, fair youth, at the medal which thou wearest in thy cap. By Saint Bennet, it is the same!—Henry, I command thee to forbear him, as thou lovest my blessing—"

"And as you honour my command," said the Queen; "good service hath he done me."

"Ay, madam," replied young Seyton, "as when he carried the billet enclosed in the sword-sheath to Lochleven—marry, the good youth knew no more than a pack-horse what he was carrying."

"But I who dedicated him to this great work," said Magdalen Graeme—"I, by whose advice and agency this just heir hath been unloosed from her thraldom—I, who spared not the last remaining hope of a falling house in this great action—I, at least, knew and counselled; and what merit may be mine, let the reward, most gracious Queen, descend upon this youth. My ministry here is ended; you are free—a sovereign Princess, at the head of a gallant army, surrounded by valiant barons—My service could avail you no farther, but might well prejudice you; your fortune now rests upon men's hearts and men's swords. May they prove as trusty as the faith of women!"

"You will not leave us, mother," said the Queen—"you whose practices in our favour were so powerful, who dared so many dangers, and wore so many disguises, to blind our enemies and to confirm our friends—you will not leave us in the dawn of our reviving fortunes, ere we have time to know and to thank you?"

"You cannot know her," answered Magdalen Graeme, "who knows not herself—there are times, when, in this woman's frame of mine, there is the strength of him of Gath—in this overtoiled brain, the wisdom of the most sage counsellor—and again the mist is on me, and my strength is weakness, my wisdom folly. I have spoken before princes and cardinals—ay, noble Princess, even before the princes of thine own house of Lorraine; and I know not whence the words of persuasion came which flowed from my lips, and were drunk in by their ears.—And now, even when I most need words of persuasion, there is something which chokes my voice, and robs me of utterance."

"If there be aught in my power to do thee pleasure," said the Queen, "the barely naming it shall avail as well as all thine eloquence."

"Sovereign Lady," replied the enthusiast, "it shames me that at this high moment something of human frailty should cling to one, whose vows the saints have heard, whose labours in the rightful cause Heaven has prospered. But it will be thus while the living spirit is shrined in the clay of mortality—I will yield to the folly," she said, weeping as she spoke, "and it shall be the last." Then seizing Roland's hand, she led him to the Queen's feet, kneeling herself upon one knee, and causing him to kneel on both. "Mighty Princess," she said, "look on this flower—it was found by a kindly stranger on a bloody field of battle, and long it was ere my anxious eyes saw, and my arms pressed, all that was left of my only daughter. For your sake, and for that of the holy faith we both profess, I could leave this plant, while it was yet tender, to the nurture of strangers—ay, of enemies, by whom, perchance, his blood would have been poured forth as wine, had the heretic Glendinning known that he had in his house the heir of Julian Avenel. Since then I have seen him only in a few hours of doubt and dread, and now I part with the child of my love—for ever—for ever!—Oh, for every weary step I have made in your rightful cause, in this and in foreign lands, give protection to the child whom I must no more call mine!"

"I swear to you, mother," said the Queen, deeply affected, "that, for your sake and his own, his happiness and fortunes shall be our charge!"

"I thank you, daughter of princes," said Magdalen, and pressed her lips, first to the Queen's hand, then to the brow of her grandson. "And now," she said, drying her tears, and rising with dignity, "Earth has had its own, and Heaven claims the rest.—Lioness of Scotland, go forth and conquer! and if the prayers of a devoted votaress can avail thee, they will rise in many a land, and from many a distant shrine. I will glide like a ghost from land to land, from temple to temple; and where the very name of my country is unknown, the priests shall ask who is the Queen of that distant northern land, for whom the aged pilgrim was so fervent in prayer. Farewell! Honour be thine, and earthly prosperity, if it be the will of God—if not, may the penance thou shalt do here ensure thee happiness hereafter!—Let no one speak or follow me—my resolution is taken—my vow cannot be cancelled."

She glided from their presence as she spoke, and her last look was upon her beloved grandchild. He would have risen and followed, but the Queen and Lord Seyton interfered.

"Press not on her now," said Lord Seyton, "if you would not lose her for ever. Many a time have we seen the sainted mother, and often at the most needful moment; but to press on her privacy, or to thwart her purpose, is a crime which she cannot pardon. I trust we shall yet see her at her need—a holy woman she is for certain, and dedicated wholly to prayer and penance; and hence the heretics hold her as one distracted, while true Catholics deem her a saint."

"Let me then hope," said the Queen, "that you, my lord, will aid me in the execution of her last request."

"What! in the protection of my young second?—cheerfully—that is, in all that your majesty can think it fitting to ask of me.—Henry, give thy hand upon the instant to Roland Avenel, for so I presume he must now be called."

"And shall be Lord of the Barony," said the Queen, "if God prosper our rightful arms."

"It can only be to restore it to my kind protectress, who now holds it," said young Avenel. "I would rather be landless, all my life, than she lost a rood of ground by me."

"Nay," said the Queen, looking to Lord Seyton, "his mind matches his birth—Henry, thou hast not yet given thy hand."

"It is his," said Henry, giving it with some appearance of courtesy, but whispering Roland at the same time,—"For all this, thou hast not my sister's."

"May it please your Grace," said Lord Seyton, "now that these passages are over, to honour our poor meal. Time it were that our banners were reflected in the Clyde. We must to horse with as little delay as may be."

XXXVII

Ay, sir—our ancient crown, in these wild times,
Oft stood upon a cast—the gamester's ducat,
So often staked, and lost, and then regain'd,
Scarce knew so many hazards.

—The Spanish Father

It is not our object to enter into the historical part of the reign of the ill-fated Mary, or to recount how, during the week which succeeded her flight from Lochleven, her partisans mustered around her with their followers, forming a gallant army, amounting to six thousand men. So much light has been lately thrown on the most minute details of the period, by Mr. Chalmers, in his valuable history of Queen Mary, that the reader may be safely referred to it for the fullest information which ancient records afford concerning that interesting time. It is sufficient for our purpose to say, that while Mary's head-quarters were at Hamilton, the Regent and his adherents had, in the King's name, assembled a host at Glasgow, inferior indeed to that of the Queen in numbers, but formidable from the military talents of Murray, Morton, the Laird of Grange, and others, who had been trained from their youth in foreign and domestic wars.

In these circumstances, it was the obvious policy of Queen Mary to avoid a conflict, secure that were her person once in safety, the number of her adherents must daily increase; whereas, the forces of those opposed to her must, as had frequently happened in the previous history of her reign, have diminished, and their spirits become broken. And so evident was this to her counsellors, that they resolved their first step should be to place the Queen in the strong castle of Dunbarton, there to await the course of events, the arrival of succours from France, and the levies which were made by her adherents in every province of Scotland. Accordingly, orders were given, that all men should be on horseback or on foot, apparelled in their armour, and ready to follow the Queen's standard in array of battle, the avowed determination being to escort her to the Castle of Dunbarton in defiance of her enemies.

The muster was made upon Hamilton-Moor, and the march commenced in all the pomp of feudal times. Military music sounded, banners and pennons waved, armour glittered far and wide, and spears glanced and twinkled like stars in a frosty sky. The gallant spectacle of warlike parade was on this occasion dignified by the presence of the Queen herself, who, with a fair retinue of ladies and household attendants, and a special guard of gentlemen, amongst whom young Seyton and Roland were distinguished, gave grace at once and confidence to the army, which spread its ample files before, around, and behind her. Many churchmen also joined the cavalcade, most of whom did not scruple to assume arms, and declare their intention of wielding them in defence of Mary and the Catholic faith. Not so the Abbot of Saint Mary's. Roland had not seen this prelate since the night of their escape from Lochleven, and he now beheld him, robed in the dress of his order, assume his station near the Queen's person. Roland hastened to pull off his basnet, and beseech the Abbot's blessing.

"Thou hast it, my son!" said the priest; "I see thee now under thy true name, and in thy rightful garb. The helmet with the holly branch befits your brows well—I have long waited for the hour thou shouldst assume it."

"Then you knew of my descent, my good father?" said Roland.

"I did so, but it was under seal of confession from thy grandmother; nor was I at liberty to tell the secret, till she herself should make it known."

"Her reason for such secrecy, my father?" said Roland Avenel.

"Fear, perchance of my brother—a mistaken fear, for Halbert would not, to ensure himself a kingdom, have offered wrong to an orphan; besides that, your title, in quiet times, even had your father done your mother that justice which I well hope he did, could not have competed with that of my brother's wife, the child of Julian's elder brother."

"They need fear no competition from me," said Avenel. "Scotland is wide enough, and there are many manors to win, without plundering my benefactor. But prove to me, my reverend father, that my father was just to my mother—show me that I may call myself a legitimate Avenel, and make me your bounden slave for ever."

"Ay," replied the Abbot, "I hear the Seytons hold thee cheap for that stain on thy shield. Something, however, I have learnt from the late Abbot Boniface, which, if it prove sooth, may redeem that reproach."

"Tell me that blessed news," said Roland, "and the future service of my life—"

"Rash boy!" said the Abbot, "I should but madden thine impatient temper, by exciting hopes that may never be fulfilled—and is this a time for them? Think on what perilous march we are bound, and if thou hast a sin unconfessed, neglect not the only leisure which Heaven may perchance afford thee for confession and absolution."

"There will be time enough for both, I trust, when we reach Dunbarton," answered the page.

"Ay," said the Abbot, "thou crowest as loudly as the rest—but we are not yet at Dunbarton, and there is a lion in the path."

"Mean you Murray, Morton, and the other rebels at Glasgow, my reverend father? Tush! they dare not look on the royal banner."

"Even so," replied the Abbot, "speak many of those who are older, and should be wiser, than thou.—I have returned from the southern shires, where I left many a chief of name arming in the Queen's interest—I left the lords here wise and considerate men—I find them madmen on my return—they are willing, for mere pride and vain-glory, to brave the enemy, and to carry the Queen, as it were in triumph, past the walls of Glasgow, and under the beards of the adverse army.—Seldom does Heaven smile on such mistimed confidence. We shall be encountered, and that to the purpose."

"And so much the better," replied Roland; "the field of battle was my cradle."

"Beware it be not thy dying bed," said the Abbot. "But what avails it whispering to young wolves the dangers of the chase? You will know, perchance, ere this day is out, what yonder men are, whom you hold in rash contempt."

"Why, what are they?" said Henry Seyton, who now joined them: "have they sinews of wire, and flesh of iron?—Will lead pierce and steel cut them?—If so, reverend father, we have little to fear."

"They are evil men," said the Abbot, "but the trade of war demands no saints.—Murray and Morton are known to be the best generals in Scotland. No one ever saw Lindesay's or Ruthven's back—Kirkaldy of Grange was named by the Constable Montmorency the first soldier in Europe—My brother, too good a name for such a cause, has been far and wide known for a soldier."

"The better, the better!" said Seyton, triumphantly; "we shall have all these traitors of rank and name in a fair field before us. Our cause is the best, our numbers are the strongest, our hearts and limbs match theirs—Saint Bennet, and set on!"

The Abbot made no reply, but seemed lost in reflection; and his anxiety in some measure communicated itself to Roland Avenel, who ever, as their line of march led over a ridge or an eminence, cast an anxious look towards the towers of Glasgow, as if he expected to see symptoms of the enemy issuing forth. It was not that he feared the fight, but the issue was of such deep import to his country, and to himself, that the natural fire of his spirit burned with a less lively, though with a more intense glow. Love, honour, fame, fortune, all seemed to depend on the issue of one field, rashly hazarded perhaps, but now likely to become unavoidable and decisive.

When, at length, their march came to be nearly parallel with the city of Glasgow, Roland became sensible that the high grounds before them were already in part occupied by a force, showing, like their own, the royal banner of Scotland, and on the point of being supported by columns of infantry and squadrons of horse, which the city gates had poured forth, and which hastily advanced to sustain those troops who already possessed the ground in front of the Queen's forces. Horseman after horseman galloped in from the advanced guard, with tidings that Murray had taken the field with his whole army; that his object was to intercept the Queen's march, and his purpose unquestionable to hazard a battle. It was now that the tempers of men were subjected to a sudden and a severe trial; and that those who had too presumptuously concluded that they would pass without combat, were something disconcerted, when, at once, and with little time to deliberate, they found themselves placed in front of a resolute enemy.—Their chiefs immediately assembled around the Queen, and held a hasty council of war. Mary's quivering lip confessed the fear which she endeavoured to conceal under a bold and dignified demeanour. But her efforts were overcome by painful recollections of the disastrous issue of her last appearance in arms at Carberry-hill; and when she meant to have asked them their advice for ordering the battle, she involuntarily inquired whether there were no means of escaping without an engagement?

"Escaping?" answered the Lord Seyton; "when I stand as one to ten of your Highness's enemies, I may think of escape—but never while I stand with three to two!"

"Battle! battle!" exclaimed the assembled lords; "we will drive the rebels from their vantage ground, as the hound turns the hare on the hill side."

"Methinks, my noble lords," said the Abbot, "it were as well to prevent his gaining that advantage.—Our road lies through yonder hamlet on the brow, and whichever party hath the luck to possess it, with its little gardens and enclosures, will attain a post of great defence."

"The reverend father is right," said the Queen. "Oh, haste thee, Seyton, haste, and get thither before them—they are marching like the wind."

Seyton bowed low, and turned his horse's head.—"Your Highness honours me," he said; "I will instantly press forward, and seize the pass."

"Not before me, my lord, whose charge is the command of the vanguard," said the Lord of Arbroath.

"Before you, or any Hamilton in Scotland," said the Seyton, "having the Queen's command—Follow me, gentlemen, my vassals and kinsmen—Saint Bennet, and set on!"

"And follow me," said Arbroath, "my noble kinsmen, and brave mentenants, we will see which will first reach the post of danger. For God and Queen Mary!"

"Ill-omened haste, and most unhappy strife," said the Abbot, who saw them and their followers rush hastily and emulously to ascend the height without waiting till their men were placed in order.—"And you, gentlemen," he continued, addressing Roland and Seyton, who were each about to follow those who hastened thus disorderly to the conflict, "will you leave the Queen's person unguarded?"

"Oh, leave me not, gentlemen!" said the Queen—"Roland and Seyton, do not leave me—there are enough of arms to strike in this fell combat—withdraw not those to whom I trust for my safety."

"We may not leave her Grace," said Roland, looking at Seyton, and turning his horse.

"I ever looked when thou wouldst find out that," rejoined the fiery youth.

Roland made no answer, but bit his lip till the blood came, and spurring his horse up to the side of Catherine Seyton's palfrey, he whispered in a low voice, "I never thought to have done aught to deserve you; but this day I have heard myself upbraided with cowardice, and my sword remained still sheathed, and all for the love of you."

"There is madness among us all," said the damsel; "my father, my brother, and you, are all alike bereft of reason. Ye should think only of this poor Queen, and you are all inspired by your own absurd jealousies— The monk is the only soldier and man of sense amongst you all.—My lord Abbot," she cried aloud, "were it not better we should draw to the westward, and wait the event that God shall send us, instead of remaining here in the highway, endangering the Queen's person, and cumbering the troops in their advance?"

"You say well, my daughter," replied the Abbot; "had we but one to guide us where the Queen's person may be in safety—Our nobles hurry to the conflict, without casting a thought on the very cause of the war."

"Follow me," said a knight, or man-at-arms, well mounted, and attired completely in black armour, but having the visor of his helmet closed, and bearing no crest on his helmet, or device upon his shield.

"We will follow no stranger," said the Abbot, "without some warrant of his truth."

"I am a stranger and in your hands," said the horseman; "if you wish to know more of me, the Queen herself will be your warrant."

The Queen had remained fixed to the spot, as if disabled by fear, yet mechanically smiling, bowing, and waving her hand, as banners were lowered and spears depressed before her, while, emulating the strife betwixt Seyton and Arbroath, band on band pressed forward their march towards the enemy. Scarce, however, had the black rider whispered something in her ear, than she assented to what he said; and when he spoke aloud, and with an air of command, "Gentlemen, it is the Queen's pleasure that you should follow me," Mary uttered, with something like eagerness, the word "Yes."

All were in motion in an instant; for the black horseman, throwing off a sort of apathy of manner, which his first appearance indicated, spurred his horse to and fro, making him take such active bounds and short turns, as showed the rider master of the animal; and getting the Queen's little retinue in some order for marching, he led them to the left, directing his course towards a castle, which, crowning a gentle yet commanding eminence, presented an extensive view over the country beneath, and in particular, commanded a view of those heights which both armies hastened to occupy, and which it was now apparent must almost instantly be the scene of struggle and dispute.

"Yonder towers," said the Abbot, questioning the sable horseman, "to whom do they belong?—and are they in the hands of friends?"

"They are untenanted," replied the stranger, "or, at least, they have no hostile inmates.—But urge these youths. Sir Abbot, to make more haste—this is but an evil time to satisfy their idle curiosity, by peering out upon the battle in which they are to take no share."

"The worse luck mine," said Henry Seyton, who overheard him—"I would rather be under my father's banner at this moment than be made Chamberlain of Holyrood, for this my present duty of peaceful ward well and patiently discharged."

"Your place under your father's banner will shortly be right dangerous," said Roland Avenel, who, pressing his horse towards the westward, had still his look reverted to the armies; "for I see yonder body of cavalry, which presses from the eastward, will reach the village ere Lord Seyton can gain it."

"They are but cavalry," said Seyton, looking attentively; "they cannot hold the village without shot of harquebuss."

"Look more closely," said Roland; "you will see that each of these horseman who advance so rapidly from Glasgow, carries a footman behind him."

"Now, by Heaven, he speaks well!" said the black cavalier; "one of you two must go carry the news to Lord Seyton and Lord Arbroath, that they hasten not their horsemen on before the foot, but advance more regularly."

"Be that my errand," said Roland, "for I first marked the stratagem of the enemy."

"But, by your leave," said Seyton, "yonder is my father's banner engaged, and it best becomes me to go to the rescue."

"I will stand by the Queen's decision," said Roland Avenel.

"What new appeal?—what new quarrel?" said Queen Mary—"Are there not in yonder dark host enemies enough to Mary Stewart, but must her very friends turn enemies to each other?"

"Nay, madam," said Roland, "the young master of Seyton and I did but dispute who should leave your person to do a most needful message to the host. He thought his rank entitled him, and I deemed that the person of least consequence, being myself, were better perilled—"

"Not so," said the Queen; "if one must leave me, be it Seyton."

Henry Seyton bowed till the white plumes on his helmet mixed with the flowing mane of his gallant war-horse, then placed himself firm in the saddle, shook his lance aloft with an air of triumph and determination, and striking his horse with the spurs, made towards his father's banner, which was still advancing up the hill, and dashed his steed over every obstacle that occurred in his headlong path.

"My brother! my father!" exclaimed Catherine, with an expression of agonized apprehension—"they are in the midst of peril, and I in safety!"

"Would to God," said Roland, "that I were with them, and could ransom every drop of their blood by two of mine!"

"Do I not know thou dost wish it?" said Catherine—"Can a woman say to a man what I have well-nigh said to thee, and yet think that he could harbour fear or faintness of heart?—There is that in yon distant sound of approaching battle that pleases me even while it affrights me. I would I were a man, that I might feel that stern delight, without the mixture of terror!"

"Ride up, ride up, Lady Catherine Seyton," cried the Abbot, as they still swept on at a rapid pace, and were now close beneath the walls of the castle—"ride up, and aid Lady Fleming to support the Queen—she gives way more and more."

They halted and lifted Mary from the saddle, and were about to support her towards the castle, when she said faintly, "Not there—not there—these walls will I never enter more!"

"Be a Queen, madam," said the Abbot, "and forget that you are a woman."

"Oh, I must forget much, much more," answered the unfortunate Mary, in an under tone, "ere I can look with steady eyes on these well-known scenes!—I must forget the days which I spent here as the bride of the lost—the murdered—"

"This is the Castle of Crookstone," said the Lady Fleming, "in which the Queen held her first court after she was married to Darnley."

"Heaven," said the Abbot, "thy hand is upon us!—Bear yet up, madam—your foes are the foes of Holy Church, and God will this day decide whether Scotland shall be Catholic or heretic."

A heavy and continued fire of cannon and musketry, bore a tremendous burden to his words, and seemed far more than they to recall the spirits of the Queen.

"To yonder tree," she said, pointing to a yew-tree which grew on a small mount close to the castle; "I know it well—from thence you may see a prospect wide as from the peaks of Schehallion."

And freeing herself from her assistants, she walked with a determined, yet somewhat wild step, up to the stem of the noble yew. The Abbot, Catherine, and Roland Avenel followed her, while Lady Fleming kept back the inferior persons of her train. The black horseman also followed the Queen, waiting on her as closely as the shadow upon the light, but ever remaining at the distance of two or three yards-—he folded his arms on his bosom, turned his back to the battle, and seemed solely occupied by gazing on Mary, through the bars of his closed visor. The Queen regarded him not, but fixed her eyes upon the spreading yew."

"Ay, fair and stately tree," she said, as if at the sight of it she had been rapt away from the present scene, and had overcome the horror

SIR WALTER SCOTT

which had oppressed her at the first approach to Crookstone, "there thou standest, gay and goodly as ever, though thou hearest the sounds of war, instead of the vows of love. All is gone since I last greeted thee—love and lover—vows and vower—king and kingdom.—How goes the field, my Lord Abbot?—with us, I trust—yet what but evil can Mary's eyes witness from this spot?"

Her attendants eagerly bent their eyes on the field of battle, but could discover nothing more than that it was obstinately contested. The small enclosures and cottage gardens in the village, of which they had a full and commanding view, and which shortly before lay, with their lines of sycamore and ash-trees, so still and quiet in the mild light of a May sun, were now each converted into a line of fire, canopied by smoke; and the sustained and constant report of the musketry and cannon, mingled with the shouts of meeting combatants, showed that as yet neither party had given ground.

"Many a soul finds its final departure to heaven or hell, in these awful thunders," said the Abbot; "let those that believe in the Holy Church, join me in orisons for victory in this dreadful combat."

"Not here—not here," said the unfortunate Queen; "pray not here, father, or pray in silence—my mind is too much torn between the past and the present, to dare to approach the heavenly throne—Or, if we will pray, be it for one whose fondest affections have been her greatest crimes, and who has ceased to be a queen, only because she was a deceived and a tender-hearted woman."

"Were it not well," said Roland, "that I rode somewhat nearer the hosts, and saw the fate of the day?"

"Do so, in the name of God," said the Abbot; "for if our friends are scattered, our flight must be hasty—but beware thou approach not too nigh the conflict; there is more than thine own life depends on thy safe return."

"Oh, go not too nigh," said Catherine; "but fail not to see how the Seytons fight, and how they bear themselves."

"Fear nothing, I will be on my guard," said Roland Avenel; and without waiting farther answer, rode towards the scene of conflict, keeping, as he rode, the higher and unenclosed ground, and ever looking cautiously around him, for fear of involving himself in some hostile party. As he approached, the shots rung sharp and more sharply on his ear, the shouts came wilder and wilder, and he felt that thick beating of the heart, that mixture of natural apprehension, intense curiosity, and anxiety for the dubious event, which even the bravest experience when they approach alone to a scene of interest and of danger.

At length he drew so close, that from a bank, screened by bushes and underwood, he could distinctly see where the struggle was most keenly maintained. This was in a hollow way, leading to the village, up which the Queen's vanguard had marched, with more hasty courage than well-advised conduct, for the purpose of possessing themselves of that post of advantage. They found their scheme anticipated, and the hedges and enclosures already occupied by the enemy, led by the celebrated Kirkaldy of Grange and the Earl of Morton; and not small was the loss which they sustained while struggling forward to come to close with the men-at-arms on the other side. But, as the Queen's followers were chiefly noblemen and barons, with their kinsmen and followers, they had pressed onward, contemning obstacles and danger, and had, when Roland arrived on the ground, met hand to hand at the gorge of the pass with the Regent's vanguard, and endeavoured to bear them out of the village at the spear-point; while their foes, equally determined to keep the advantage which they had attained, struggled with the like obstinacy to drive back the assailants. Both parties were on foot, and armed in proof; so that, when the long lances of the front ranks were fixed in each other's shields, corslets, and breastplates, the struggle resembled that of two bulls, who fixing their frontlets hard against each other, remain in that posture for hours, until the superior strength or obstinacy of the one compels the other to take to flight, or bears him down to the earth. Thus locked together in the deadly struggle, which swayed slowly to and fro, as one or other party gained the advantage, those who fell were trampled on alike by friends and foes; those whose weapons were broken, retired from the front rank, and had their place supplied by others; while the rearward ranks, unable otherwise to share in the combat, fired their pistols, and hurled their daggers, and the points and truncheons of the broken weapons, like javelins against the enemy.

"God and the Queen!" resounded from the one party; "God and the King!" thundered from the other; while, in the name of their sovereign, fellow-subjects on both sides shed each other's blood, and, in the name of their Creator, defaced his image. Amid the tumult was often heard the voices of the captains, shouting their commands; of leaders and chiefs, crying their gathering words; of groans and shrieks from the falling and the dying.

SIR WALTER SCOTT

The strife had lasted nearly an hour. The strength of both parties seemed exhausted; but their rage was unabated, and their obstinacy unsubdued, when Roland, who turned eye and ear to all around him, saw a column of infantry, headed by a few horsemen, wheel round the base of the bank where he had stationed himself, and, levelling their long lances, attack the Queen's vanguard, closely engaged as they were in conflict on their front. The very first glance showed him that the leader who directed this movement was the Knight of Avenel, his ancient master; and the next convinced him, that its effects would be decisive. The result of the attack of fresh and unbroken forces upon the flank of those already wearied with a long and obstinate struggle, was, indeed, instantaneous.

The column of the assailants, which had hitherto shown one dark, dense, and united line of helmets, surmounted with plumage, was at once broken and hurled in confusion down the hill, which they had so long endeavoured to gain. In vain were the leaders heard calling upon their followers to stand to the combat, and seen personally resisting when all resistance was evidently vain. They were slain, or felled to the earth, or hurried backwards by the mingled tide of flight and pursuit. What were Roland's feelings on beholding the rout, and feeling that all that remained for him was to turn bridle, and endeavour to ensure the safety of the Queen's person! Yet, keen as his grief and shame might be, they were both forgotten, when, almost close beneath the bank which he occupied, he saw Henry Seyton forced away from his own party in the tumult, covered with dust and blood, and defending himself desperately against several of the enemy who had gathered around him, attracted by his gay armour. Roland paused not a moment, but pushing his steed down the bank, leaped him amongst the hostile party, dealt three or four blows amongst them, which struck down two, and made the rest stand aloof; then reaching Seyton his hand, he exhorted him to seize fast on his horse's mane.

"We live or die together this day," said he; "keep but fast hold till we are out of the press, and then my horse is yours."

Seyton heard and exerted his remaining strength, and, by their joint efforts, Roland brought him out of danger, and behind the spot from whence he had witnessed the disastrous conclusion of the fight. But no sooner were they under shelter of the trees, than Seyton let go his hold, and, in spite of Roland's efforts to support him, fell at length on the turf. "Trouble yourself no more with me," he said; "this is my first and my last battle—and I have already seen too much to wish to see the close. Hasten to save the Queen—and commend me to Catherine—she will never more be mistaken for me nor I for her—the last sword-stroke has made an eternal distinction."

"Let me aid you to mount my horse," said Roland, eagerly, "and you may yet be saved—I can find my own way on foot—turn but my horse's head westward, and he will carry you fleet and easy as the wind."

"I will never mount steed more," said the youth; "farewell—I love thee better dying, than ever I thought to have done while in life—I would that old man's blood were not on my hand!—*Sancte Benedicte, ora pro me*—Stand not to look on a dying man, but haste to save the Queen!"

These words were spoken with the last effort of his voice, and scarce were they uttered ere the speaker was no more. They recalled Roland to a sense of the duty which he had well-nigh forgotten, but they did not reach his ears only.

"The Queen—where is the Queen?" said Halbert Glendinning, who, followed by two or three horsemen, appeared at this instant. Roland made no answer, but, turning his horse, and confiding in his speed, gave him at once rein and spur, and rode over height and hollow towards the Castle of Crookstone. More heavily armed, and mounted upon a horse of less speed, Sir Halbert Glendinning followed with couched lance, calling out as he rode, "Sir, with the holly-branch, halt, and show your right to bear that badge—fly not thus cowardly, nor dishonour the cognizance thou deservest not to wear!—Halt, sir coward, or by Heaven, I will strike thee with my lance on the back, and slay thee like a dastard—I am the Knight of Avenel—I am Halbert Glendinning."

But Roland, who had no purpose of encountering his old master, and who, besides, knew the Queen's safety depended on his making the best speed he could, answered not a word to the defiances and reproaches which Sir Halbert continued to throw out against him; but making the best use of his spurs, rode yet harder than before, and had gained about a hundred yards upon his pursuer, when, coming near to the yew-tree where he had left the Queen, he saw them already getting to horse, and cried out as loud as he could, "Foes! foes!—Ride for it, fair ladies—Brave gentlemen, do your devoir to protect them!"

So saying, he wheeled his horse, and avoiding the shock of Sir Halbert Glendinning, charged one of that Knight's followers, who was nearly on a line with him, so rudely with his lance, that he overthrew horse and man. He then drew his sword and attacked the second, while the black man-at-arms, throwing himself in the way of Glendinning, they rushed on each other so fiercely, that both horses were overthrown, and the riders lay rolling on the plain. Neither was able to arise, for the black horseman was pierced through with Glendinning's lance, and the Knight of Avenel, oppressed with the weight of his own horse and sorely bruised besides, seemed in little better plight than he whom he had mortally wounded.

"Yield thee, Sir Knight of Avenel, rescue or no rescue," said Roland, who had put a second antagonist out of condition to combat, and hastened to prevent Glendinning from renewing the conflict.

"I may not choose but yield," said Sir Halbert, "since I can no longer fight; but it shames me to speak such a word to a coward like thee!"

"Call me not coward," said Roland, lifting his visor, and helping his prisoner to rise, "since but for old kindness at thy hands, and yet more at thy lady's, I had met thee as a brave man should."

"The favourite page of my wife!" said Sir Halbert, astonished; "Ah! wretched boy, I have heard of thy treason at Lochleven."

"Reproach him not, my brother," said the Abbot, "he was but an agent in the hands of Heaven."

"To horse, to horse!" said Catherine Seyton; "mount and begone, or we are all lost. I see our gallant army flying for many a league—To horse, my Lord Abbot—To horse, Roland—my gracious Liege, to horse! Ere this, we should have ridden many a mile."

"Look on these features," said Mary, pointing to the dying knight, who had been unhelmed by some compassionate hand; "look there, and tell me if she who ruins all who love her, ought to fly a foot farther to save her wretched life!"

The reader must have long anticipated the discovery which the Queen's feelings had made before her eyes confirmed it. It was the features of the unhappy George Douglas, on which death was stamping his mark.

"Look—look at him well," said the Queen, "thus has it been with all who loved Mary Stewart!—The royalty of Francis, the wit of Chastelar, the power and gallantry of the gay Gordon, the melody of Rizzio, the portly form and youthful grace of Darnley, the bold address and courtly manners of Bothwell—and now the deep-devoted passion of the noble Douglas—nought could save them!—they looked on the wretched Mary, and to have loved her was crime enough to deserve early death! No sooner had the victim formed a kind thought of me, than the poisoned cup, the axe and block, the dagger, the mine, were ready to punish them for casting away affection on such a wretch as I am!—Importune me not—I will fly no farther—I can die but once, and I will die here."

While she spoke, her tears fell fast on the face of the dying man, who continued to fix his eyes on her with an eagerness of passion, which death itself could hardly subdue.—"Mourn not for me," he said faintly, "but care for your own safety—I die in mine armour as a Douglas should, and I die pitied by Mary Stewart!"

He expired with these words, and without withdrawing his eyes from her face; and the Queen, whose heart was of that soft and gentle mould, which in domestic life, and with a more suitable partner than Darnley, might have made her happy, remained weeping by the dead man, until recalled to herself by the Abbot, who found it necessary to use a style of unusual remonstrance. "We also, madam," he said, "we, your Grace's devoted followers, have friends and relatives to weep for. I leave a brother in imminent jeopardy—the husband of the Lady Fleming—the father and brothers of the Lady Catherine, are all in yonder bloody field, slain, it is to be feared, or prisoners. We forget the fate of our nearest and dearest, to wait on our Queen, and she is too much occupied with her own sorrows to give one thought to ours."

"I deserve not your reproach, father," said the Queen, checking her tears; "but I am docile to it—where must we go—what must we do?"

"We must fly, and that instantly," said the Abbot; "whither is not so easily answered, but we may dispute it upon the road—Lift her to her saddle, and set forward."*

---

* I am informed in the most polite manner, by D. MacVean, Esq. of Glasgow, that I have been incorrect in my locality, in giving an account of the battle of Langside. Crookstone Castle, he observes, lies four miles west from the field of battle, and rather in the rear of Murray's army. The real place from which Mary saw the rout of her last army, was Cathcart Castle, which, being a mile and a half east from Langside, was, situated in the rear of the Queen's own army. I was led astray in the present case, by the authority of my deceased friend, James Grahame the excellent and amiable author of the Sabbath, in his drama on the subject of Queen Mary; and by a traditionary report of Mary having seen the battle from the Castle of Crookstone, which seemed so much to increase the interest of the scene, that I have been unwilling to make, in this particular instance, the fiction give way to the fact, which last is undoubtedly in favour of Mr. MacVean's system.

It is singular how tradition, which is sometimes a sure guide to truth, is, in other cases, prone to mislead us. In the celebrated field of battle at Killiecrankie, the traveller is struck with one of those rugged pillars of rough stone, which indicate the scenes of ancient conflict. A friend of the author, well acquainted with the circumstances of the battle,

SIR WALTER SCOTT

They set off accordingly—Roland lingered a moment to command the attendants of the Knight of Avenel to convey their master to the Castle of Crookstone, and to say that he demanded from him no other condition of liberty, than his word, that he and his followers would keep secret the direction in which the Queen fled. As he turned his

---

was standing near this large stone, and looking on the scene around, when a highland shepherd hurried down from the hill to offer his services as cicerone, and proceeded to inform him, that Dundee was slain at that stone, which was raised to his memory. "Fie, Donald." answered my friend, "how can you tell such a story to a stranger? I am sure you know well enough that Dundee was killed at a considerable distance from this place, near the house of Fascally, and that this stone was here long before the battle, in 1688."—"Oich! oich!" said Donald, no way abashed, "and your honour's in the right, and I see you ken a' about it. And he wasna killed on the spot neither, but lived till the next morning; but a' the Saxon gentlemen like best to hear he was killed at the great stane." It is on the same principle of pleasing my readers, that I retain Crookstone Castle instead of Cathcart.

If, however, the author has taken a liberty in removing the actual field of battle somewhat to the eastward, he has been tolerably strict in adhering to the incidents of the engagement, as will appear from it comparison of events in the novel, with the following account from an old writer.

"The Regent was out on foot and all his company, except the Laird of Grange, Alexander Hume of Manderston, and some borderers to the number of two hundred. The Laird of Grange had already viewed the ground, and with all imaginable diligence caused every horseman to take behind him a footman of the Regent's, to guard behind them, and rode with speed to the head of Langside-hill, and set down the footmen with their culverins at the head of a straight lane, where there were some cottage houses and yards of great advantage. Which soldiers with their continual shot killed divers of the vaunt guard, led by the Hamiltons, who, courageously and fiercely ascending up the hill, were already out of breath, when the Regent's vaunt guard joined with them. Where the worthy Lord Hume fought on foot with his pike in his hand very manfully, assisted by the Laird of Cessford, his brother-in-law, who helped him up again when he was strucken to the ground by many strokes upon his face, through the throwing pistols at him after they had been discharged. He was also wounded with staves, and had many strokes of spears through his legs; for he and Grange, at the joining, cried to let their adversaries first lay down their spears, to bear up theirs; which spears were so thick fixed in the others' jacks, that some of the pistols and great staves that were thrown by them which were behind, might be seen lying upon the spears.

"Upon the Queen's side the Earl of Argyle commanded the battle, and the Lord of Arbroth the vaunt guard. But the Regent committed to the Laird of Grange the special care, as being an experimented captain, to oversee every danger, and to ride to every wing, to encourage and make help where greatest need was. He perceived, at the first joining, the right wing of the Regent's vaunt guard put back and like to fly, whereof the greatest part were commons of the barony of Renfrew; whereupon he rode to them, and told them that their enemy was already turning their backs, requesting them to stay and debate till he should bring them fresh men forth of the battle. Whither at full speed he did ride alone, and told the Regent that the enemy were shaken and flying away behind

rein to depart, the honest countenance of Adam Woodcock stared upon him with an expression of surprise, which, at another time, would have excited his hearty mirth. He had been one of the followers who had experienced the weight of Roland's arm, and they now knew each other, Roland having put up his visor, and the good yeoman having thrown away his barret-cap, with the iron bars in front, that he might the more readily assist his master. Into this barret-cap, as it lay on the ground, Roland forgot not to drop a few gold pieces, (fruits of the Queen's liberality,) and with a signal of kind recollection and enduring friendship, he departed at full gallop to overtake the Queen, the dust raised by her train being already far down the hill.

"It is not fairy-money," said honest Adam, weighing and handling the gold—"And it was Master Roland himself, that is a certain thing— the same open hand, and, by our Lady!" (shrugging his shoulders)— "the same ready fist!—My Lady will hear of this gladly, for she mourns for him as if he were her son. And to see how gay he is! But these light lads are as sure to be uppermost as the froth to be on the top of the quart-pot—Your man of solid parts remains ever a falconer." So saying, he went to aid his comrades, who had now come up in greater numbers, to carry his master into the Castle of Crookstone.

---

the little village, and desired a few number of fresh men to go with him. Where he found enough willing, as the Lord Lindesay, the Laird of Lochleven, Sir James Balfour, and all the Regent's servants, who followed him with diligence, and reinforced that wing which was beginning to fly; which fresh men with their loose weapons struck the enemies in their flank and faces, which forced them incontinent to give place and turn back after long fighting and pushing others to and fro with their spears. There were not many horsemen to pursue after them, and the Regent cried to save and not to kill, and Grange was never cruel, so that there were few slain and taken. And the only slaughter was at the first rencounter by the shot of the soldiers, which Grange had planted at the lane head behind some dikes."

It is remarkable that, while passing through the small town of Renfrew, some partisans, adherents of the House of Lennox, attempting to arrest Queen Mary and her attendants, were obliged to make way for her not without slaughter.

XXXVIII

My native land, good night!

—BYRON

M any a bitter tear was shed, during the hasty flight of Queen Mary, over fallen hopes, future prospects, and slaughtered friends. The deaths of the brave Douglas, and of the fiery but gallant young Seyton, seemed to affect the Queen as much as the fall from the throne, on which she had so nearly been again seated. Catherine Seyton devoured in secret her own grief, anxious to support the broken spirits of her mistress; and the Abbot, bending his troubled thoughts upon futurity, endeavoured in vain to form some plan which had a shadow of hope. The spirit of young Roland—for he also mingled in the hasty debates held by the companions of the Queen's flight—continued unchecked and unbroken.

"Your Majesty," he said, "has lost a battle—Your ancestor, Bruce, lost seven successively, ere he sat triumphant on the Scottish throne, and proclaimed with the voice of a victor, in the field of Bannockburn, the independence of his country. Are not these heaths, which we may traverse at will, better than the locked, guarded, and lake-moated Castle of Lochleven?—We are free—in that one word there is comfort for all our losses."

He struck a bold note, but the heart of Mary made no response.

"Better," she said, "I had still been in Lochleven, than seen the slaughter made by rebels among the subjects who offered themselves to death for my sake. Speak not to me of farther efforts—they would only cost the lives of you, the friends who recommend them! I would not again undergo what I felt, when I saw from yonder mount the swords of the fell horsemen of Morton raging among the faithful Seytons and Hamiltons, for their loyalty to their Queen—I would not again feel what I felt when Douglas's life-blood stained my mantle for his love to Mary Stewart—not to be empress of all that Britain's seas enclose. Find for me some place where I can hide my unhappy head, which brings destruction on all who love it—it is the last favour that Mary asks of her faithful followers."

In this dejected mood, but still pursuing her flight with unabated rapidity, the unfortunate Mary, after having been joined by Lord

Herries and a few followers, at length halted, for the first time, at the Abbey of Dundrennan, nearly sixty miles distant from the field of battle. In this remote quarter of Galloway, the Reformation not having yet been strictly enforced against the monks, a few still lingered in their cells unmolested; and the Prior, with tears and reverence, received the fugitive Queen at the gate of his convent.

"I bring you ruin, my good father," said the Queen, as she was lifted from her palfrey.

"It is welcome," said the Prior, "if it comes in the train of duty."

Placed on the ground, and supported by her ladies, the Queen looked for an instant at her palfrey, which, jaded and drooping its head, seemed as if it mourned the distresses of its mistress.

"Good Roland," said the Queen, whispering, "let Rosabelle be cared for—ask thy heart, and it will tell thee why I make this trifling request even in this awful hour."

She was conducted to her apartment, and in the hurried consultation of her attendants, the fatal resolution of the retreat to England was finally adopted. In the morning it received her approbation, and a messenger was despatched to the English warden, to pray him for safe-conduct and hospitality, on the part of the Queen of Scotland. On the next day the Abbot Ambrose walked in the garden of the Abbey with Roland, to whom he expressed his disapprobation of the course pursued. "It is madness and ruin," he said; "better commit herself to the savage Highlanders or wild Bordermen, than to the faith of Elizabeth. A woman to a rival woman—a presumptive successor to the keeping of a jealous and childless Queen!—Roland, Herries is true and loyal, but his counsel has ruined his mistress."

"Ay, ruin follows us every where," said an old man, with a spade in his hand, and dressed like a lay-brother, of whose presence, in the vehemence of his exclamation, the Abbot had not been aware—"Gaze not on me with such wonder!—I am he who was the Abbot Boniface at Kennaquhair, who was the gardener Blinkhoolie at Lochleven, hunted round to the place in which I served my noviciate, and now ye are come to rouse me up again!—A weary life I have had for one to whom peace was ever the dearest blessing!"

"We will soon rid you of our company, good father," said the Abbot; "and the Queen will, I fear, trouble your retreat no more."

"Nay, you said as much before," said the querulous old man, "and yet I was put forth from Kinross, and pillaged by troopers on the road.—

They took from me the certificate that you wot of—that of the Baron—ay, he was a moss-trooper like themselves—You asked me of it, and I could never find it, but they found it—it showed the marriage of—of—my memory fails me—Now see how men differ! Father Nicholas would have told you an hundred tales of the Abbot Ingelram, on whose soul God have mercy!—He was, I warrant you, fourscore and six, and I am not more than—let me see—"

"Was not Avenel the name you seek, my good father?" said Roland, impatiently, yet moderating his tone for fear of alarming or offending the infirm old man.

"Ay, right—Avenel, Julian Avenel—You are perfect in the name—I kept all the special confessions, judging it held with my vow to do so—I could not find it when my successor, Ambrosius, spoke on't—but the troopers found it, and the Knight who commanded the party struck his breast, till the target clattered like an empty watering-can."

"Saint Mary!" said the Abbot, "in whom could such a paper excite such interest! What was the appearance of the knight, his arms, his colours?"

"Ye distract me with your questions—I dared hardly look at him—they charged me with bearing letters for the Queen, and searched my mail—This was all along of your doings at Lochleven."

"I trust in God," said the Abbot to Roland, who stood beside him, shivering and trembling "with impatience," the paper has fallen into the hands of my brother—I heard he had been with his followers on the scout betwixt Stirling and Glasgow.—Bore not the Knight a holly-bough on his helmet?—Canst thou not remember?"

"Oh, remember—remember," said the old man pettishly; "count as many years as I do, if your plots will let you, and see what, and how much, you remember.—Why, I scarce remember the pear-mains which I graffed here with my own hands some fifty years since."

At this moment a bugle sounded loudly from the beach.

"It is the death-blast to Queen Mary's royalty," said Ambrosius; "the English warden's answer has been received, favourable doubtless, for when was the door of the trap closed against the prey which it was set for?—Droop not, Roland—this matter shall be sifted to the bottom—but we must not now leave the Queen—follow me—let us do our duty, and trust the issue with God—Farewell, good Father—I will visit thee again soon."

He was about to leave the garden, followed by Roland, with half-reluctant steps. The Ex-Abbot resumed his spade.

"I could be sorry for these men," he said, "ay, and for that poor Queen, but what avail earthly sorrows to a man of fourscore?—and it is a rare dropping morning for the early colewort."

"He is stricken with age," said Ambrosius, as he dragged Roland down to the sea-beach; "we must let him take his time to collect himself—nothing now can be thought on but the fate of the Queen."

They soon arrived where she stood, surrounded by her little train, and by her side the sheriff of Cumberland, a gentleman of the house of Lowther, richly dressed and accompanied by soldiers. The aspect of the Queen exhibited a singular mixture of alacrity and reluctance to depart. Her language and gestures spoke hope and consolation to her attendants, and she seemed desirous to persuade even herself that the step she adopted was secure, and that the assurance she had received of kind reception was altogether satisfactory; but her quivering lip, and unsettled eye, betrayed at once her anguish at departing from Scotland, and her fears of confiding herself to the doubtful faith of England.

"Welcome, my Lord Abbot," she said, speaking to Ambrosius, "and you, Roland Avenel, we have joyful news for you—our loving sister's officer proffers us, in her name, a safe asylum from the rebels who have driven us from our home—only it grieves me we must here part from you for a short space."

"Part from us, madam!" said the Abbot. "Is your welcome in England, then, to commence with the abridgment of your train, and dismissal of your counsellors?"

"Take it not thus, good Father," said Mary; "the Warden and the Sheriff, faithful servants of our Royal Sister, deem it necessary to obey her instructions in the present case, even to the letter, and can only take upon them to admit me with my female attendants. An express will instantly be despatched from London, assigning me a place of residence; and I will speedily send to all of you whenever my Court shall be formed."

"Your Court formed in England! and while Elizabeth lives and reigns?" said the Abbot—"that will be when we shall see two suns in one heaven!"

"Do not think so," replied the Queen; "we are well assured of our sister's good faith. Elizabeth loves fame—and not all that she has won by her power and her wisdom will equal that which she will acquire by extending her hospitality to a distressed sister!—not all that she may hereafter do of good, wise, and great, would blot out the reproach of abusing our confidence.—Farewell, my page—now my knight—farewell for a brief season. I will dry the tears of Catherine, or I will weep with her till neither of us can weep longer."—She held out her hand to Roland, who flinging himself on his knees, kissed it with much emotion. He was about to render the same homage to Catherine, when the Queen, assuming an air of sprightliness, said, "Her lips, thou foolish boy! and, Catherine, coy it not—these English gentlemen should see, that, even in our cold clime, Beauty knows how to reward Bravery and Fidelity!"

"We are not now to learn the force of Scottish beauty, or the mettle of Scottish valour," said the Sheriff of Cumberland, courteously—"I would it were in my power to bid these attendants upon her who is herself the mistress of Scottish beauty, as welcome to England as my poor cares would make them. But our Queen's orders are positive in case of such an emergence, and they must not be disputed by her subject.—May I remind your Majesty that the tide ebbs fast?"

The Sheriff took the Queen's hand, and she had already placed her foot on the gangway, by which she was to enter the skiff, when the Abbot, starting from a trance of grief and astonishment at the words of the Sheriff, rushed into the water, and seized upon her mantle.

"She foresaw it!—She foresaw it!"—he exclaimed—"she foresaw your flight into her realm; and, foreseeing it, gave orders you should be thus received. Blinded, deceived, doomed—Princess! your fate is sealed when you quit this strand.—Queen of Scotland, thou shalt not leave thine heritage!" he continued, holding a still firmer grasp upon her mantle; "true men shall turn rebels to thy will, that they may save thee from captivity or death. Fear not the bills and bows whom that gay man has at his beck—we will withstand him by force. Oh, for the arm of my warlike brother!—Roland Avenel, draw thy sword."

The Queen stood irresolute and frightened; one foot upon the plank, the other on the sand of her native shore, which she was quitting for ever.

"What needs this violence, Sir Priest?" said the Sheriff of Cumberland; "I came hither at your Queen's command, to do her service; and I will depart at her least order, if she rejects such aid as I can offer. No marvel is it if our Queen's wisdom foresaw that such chance as this might happen amidst the turmoils of your unsettled State; and, while willing to afford fair hospitality to her Royal Sister, deemed it wise to prohibit the entrance of a broken army of her followers into the English frontier."

"You hear," said Queen Mary, gently unloosing her robe from the Abbot's grasp, "that we exercise full liberty of choice in leaving this shore; and, questionless, the choice will remain free to us in going to France, or returning to our own dominions, as we shall determine—Besides, it is too late—Your blessing, Father, and God speed thee!"

"May He have mercy on thee, Princess, and speed thee also!" said the Abbot, retreating. "But my soul tells me I look on thee for the last time!" The sails were hoisted, the oars were plied, the vessel went freshly on her way through the firth, which divides the shores of Cumberland from those of Galloway; but not till the vessel diminished to the size of a child's frigate, did the doubtful, and dejected, and dismissed followers of the Queen cease to linger on the sands; and long, long could they discern the kerchief of Mary, as she waved the oft-repeated signal of adieu to her faithful adherents, and to the shores of Scotland.

If good tidings of a private nature could have consoled Roland for parting with his mistress, and for the distresses of his sovereign, he received such comfort some days subsequent to the Queen's leaving Dundrennan. A breathless post—no other than Adam Woodcock—brought despatches from Sir Halbert Glendinning to the Abbot, whom he found with Roland, still residing at Dundrennan, and in vain torturing Boniface with fresh interrogations. The packet bore an earnest invitation to his brother to make Avenel Castle for a time his residence. "The clemency of the Regent," said the writer, "has extended pardon both to Roland and to you, upon condition of your remaining a time under my wardship. And I have that to communicate respecting the parentage of Roland, which not only you will willingly listen to, but which will be also found to afford me, as the husband of his nearest relative, some interest in the future course of his life."

The Abbot read this letter, and paused, as if considering what were best for him to do. Meanwhile, Woodcock took Roland side, and addressed him as follows:—"Now, look, Mr. Roland, that you do not let any papestrie nonsense lure either the priest or you from the right quarry. See you, you ever bore yourself as a bit of a gentleman. Read that, and thank God that threw old Abbot Boniface in our way, as two of the Seyton's men were conveying him towards Dundrennan here.—We searched him for intelligence concerning that fair exploit of yours at Lochleven, that has cost many a man his life, and me a set of sore bones—and we found what is better for your purpose than ours."

The paper which he gave, was, indeed, an attestation by Father Philip, subscribing himself unworthy Sacristan, and brother of the House of

Saint Mary's, stating, "that under a vow of secrecy he had united, in the holy sacrament of marriage, Julian Avenel and Catherine Graeme; but that Julian having repented of his union, he, Father Philip, had been sinfully prevailed on by him to conceal and disguise the same, according to a complot devised betwixt him and the said Julian Avenel, whereby the poor damsel was induced to believe that the ceremony had been performed by one not in holy orders, and having no authority to that effect. Which sinful concealment the undersigned conceived to be the cause why he was abandoned to the misguiding of a water-fiend, whereby he had been under a spell, which obliged him to answer every question, even touching the most solemn matters, with idle snatches of old songs, besides being sorely afflicted with rheumatic pains ever after. Wherefore he had deposited this testificate and confession with the day and date of the said marriage, with his lawful superior Boniface, Abbot of Saint Mary's, *sub sigillo confessionis*."

It appeared by a letter from Julian, folded carefully up with the certificate, that the Abbot Boniface had, in effect, bestirred himself in the affair, and obtained from the Baron a promise to avow his marriage; but the death of both Julian and his injured bride, together with the Abbot's resignation, his ignorance of the fate of their unhappy offspring, and above all, the good father's listless and inactive disposition, had suffered the matter to become totally forgotten, until it was recalled by some accidental conversation with the Abbot Ambrosius concerning the fortunes of the Avenel family. At the request of his successor, the quondam Abbot made search for it; but as he would receive no assistance in looking among the few records of spiritual experiences and important confessions, which he had conscientiously treasured, it might have remained for ever hidden amongst them, but for the more active researches of Sir Halbert Glendinning.

"So that you are like to be heir of Avenel at last, Master Roland, after my lord and lady have gone to their place," said Adam; "and as I have but one boon to ask, I trust you will not nick me with nay."

"Not if it be in my power to say yes, my trusty friend."

"Why then, I must needs, if I live to see that day, keep on feeding the eyases with unwashed flesh," said Woodcock sturdily, as if doubting the reception that his request might meet with.

"Thou shalt feed them with what you list for me," said Roland, laughing; "I am not many months older than when I left the Castle, but I trust I have gathered wit enough to cross no man of skill in his own vocation."

"Then I would not change places with the King's falconer," said Adam Woodcock, "nor with the Queen's neither—but they say she will be mewed up and never need one.—I see it grieves you to think of it, and I could grieve for company; but what help for it?—Fortune will fly her own flight, let a man hollo himself hoarse."

The Abbot and Roland journeyed to Avenel, where the former was tenderly received by his brother, while the lady wept for joy to find that in her favourite orphan she had protected the sole surviving branch of her own family. Sir Halbert Glendinning and his household were not a little surprised at the change which a brief acquaintance with the world had produced in their former inmate, and rejoiced to find, in the pettish, spoiled, and presuming page, a modest and unassuming young man, too much acquainted with his own expectations and character, to be hot or petulant in demanding the consideration which was readily and voluntarily yielded to him. The old Major Domo Wingate was the first to sing his praises, to which Mistress Lilias bore a loud echo, always hoping that God would teach him the true gospel.

To the true gospel the heart of Roland had secretly long inclined, and the departure of the good Abbot for France, with the purpose of entering into some house of his order in that kingdom, removed his chief objection to renouncing the Catholic faith. Another might have existed in the duty which he owed to Magdalen Graeme, both by birth and from gratitude. But he learned, ere he had been long a resident in Avenel, that his grandmother had died at Cologne, in the performance of a penance too severe for her age, which she had taken upon herself in behalf of the Queen and Church of Scotland, as soon as she heard of the defeat at Langside. The zeal of the Abbot Ambrosius was more regulated; but he retired into the Scottish convent of—, and so lived there, that the fraternity were inclined to claim for him the honours of canonization. But he guessed their purpose, and prayed them, on his death-bed, to do no honours to the body of one as sinful as themselves; but to send his body and his heart to be buried in Avenel burial-aisle, in the monastery of Saint Mary's, that the last Abbot of that celebrated house of devotion might sleep among its ruins.*

---

* This was not the explanation of the incident of searching for the heart, mentioned in the introduction to the tale, which the author originally intended. It was designed to refer to the heart of Robert Bruce. It is generally known that that great monarch, being on his death-bed, bequeathed to the good Lord James of Douglas, the task of carrying his heart to the Holy Land, to fulfil in a certain degree his own desire to perform a crusade. Upon

SIR WALTER SCOTT

Long before that period arrived, Roland Avenel was wedded to Catherine Seyton, who, after two years' residence with her unhappy mistress, was dismissed upon her being subjected to closer restraint than had been at first exercised. She returned to her father's house, and as Roland was acknowledged for the successor and lawful heir of

---

Douglas's death, fighting against the Moors in Spain, a sort of military hors d'oeuvre to which he could have pleaded no regular call of duty, his followers brought back the Bruce's heart, and deposited it in the Abbey church of Melrose, the Kennaquhair of the tale.

This Abbey has been always particularly favoured by the Bruce. We have already seen his extreme anxiety that each of the reverend brethren should be daily supplied with a service of boiled almonds, rice and milk, pease, or the like, to be called the King's mess, and that without the ordinary service of their table being either disturbed in quantity or quality. But this was not the only mark of the benignity of good King Robert towards the monks of Melrose, since, by a charter of the dale 29th May, 1326, he conferred on the Abbot of Melrose the sum of two thousand pounds sterling, for rebuilding: the church of St. Mary's, ruined by the English; and there is little or no doubt that the principal part of the remains which now display such exquisite specimens of Gothic architecture, at its very purest period, had their origin in this munificent donation. The money was to be paid out of crown lands, estates forfeited to the King, and other property or demesnes of the crown.

A very curious letter written to his son about three weeks before his death, has been pointed out to me by my friend Mr. Thomas Thomson, Deputy-Register for Scotland. It enlarges so much on the love of the royal writer to the community of Melrose, that it is well worthy of being inserted in a work connected in some degree with Scottish History.

Litera Domini Regis Roberti Ad Filium Suum David.

"Robertius dei gratia Rex Scottorum, David precordialissimo filio suo, ac ceteris successoribus suis; Salutem, et sic ejus precepta tenere, ut cum sua benedictione possint regnare. Fili carissime, digne censeri videtur filius, qui, paternos in bonis mores imitans, piam ejus nititur exequi voluntatem; nec proprie sibi sumit nomen heredis, qui salubribus predecessoris affectibus non adherit: Cupientes igitur, ut piam affectionem et scinceram delectionem, quam erga monasterium de Melros, ubi cor nostrum ex speciali devotione disposuimus tumularidum, et erga Religiosos ibidem Deo servientes, ipsorum vita sanctissima nos ad hoc excitante, concepimus; Tu ceterique successores mei pia scinceritate prosequarimi, ut, ex vestre dilectionis affectu dictis Religiosis nostri causa post mortem nostrum ostenso, ipsi pro nobis ad orandum ferveucius et forcius animentur: Vobis precipimus quantum possumus, instanter supplicamus, et ex toto corde injungimus, Quatinus assignacionibus quas eisdem yiris Religiosis et fabrica Ecclesie sue de novo fecimus ac eciam omnibus aliis donacionibus nostris, ipsos libere gaudere permittatis, Easdem potius si necesse fuerit augmentantes quam diminuentes, ipsorum peticiones auribus benevolis admittentes, ac ipsos contra suos invasores et emuios pia defensione protegentes. Hanc autem exhortacionem supplicacionem et preceptum tu, fili ceterique successores nostri prestanti animo complere curetis, si nostram benedictionem habere velitis, una cum benedictione filii summi Regis, qui filios docuit patrum voluntates

the ancient house of Avenel, greatly increased as the estate was by the providence of Sir Halbert Gleninning, there occurred no objections to the match on the part of her family. Her mother was recently dead when she first entered the convent; and her father, in the unsettled times which followed Queen Mary's flight to England, was not averse to an alliance with a youth, who, himself loyal to Queen Mary, still held some influence, through means of Sir Halbert Glendinning, with the party in power.

Roland and Catherine, therefore, were united, spite of their differing faiths; and the White Lady, whose apparition had been infrequent when the house of Avenel seemed verging to extinction, was seen to sport by her haunted well, with a zone of gold around her bosom as broad as the baldrick of an Earl.

END OF THE ABBOT

---

in bono perficere, asserens in mundum se venisse non ut suam voluntatem faceret sed paternam. In testimonium autem nostre devotionis ergra locum predictum sic a nobis dilectum et electum concepte, presentem literam Religiosis predictis dimittimus, nostris successoribus in posterum ostendendam. Data apud Cardros, undecimo die Maij, Anno Regni nostri vicesimo quarto."

If this charter be altogether genuine, and there is no appearance of forgery, it gives rise to a curious doubt in Scottish History. The letter announces that the King had already destined his heart to be deposited at Melrose. The resolution to send it to Palestine, under the charge of Douglas, must have been adopted betwixt 11th May 1329, the date of the letter, and 7th June of the same year, when the Bruce died; or else we must suppose that the commission of Douglas extended not only to taking the Bruce's heart to Palestine, but to bring it safe back to its final place of deposit in the Abbey of Melrose.

It would not be worth inquiring: by what caprice the author was induced to throw the incident of the Bruce's heart entirely out of the story, save merely to say, that he found himself unable to fill up the canvass he had sketched, and indisposed to prosecute the management of the supernatural machinery with which his plan, when it was first rough-hewn, was connected and combined.

A Note About the Author

Sir Walter Scott (1771–1832) was a Scottish novelist, poet, playwright, and historian who also worked as a judge and legal administrator. Scott's extensive knowledge of history and his exemplary literary technique earned him a role as a prominent author of the romantic movement and innovator of the historical fiction genre. After rising to fame as a poet, Scott started to venture into prose fiction as well, which solidified his place as a popular and widely-read literary figure, especially in the 19th century. Scott left behind a legacy of innovation, and is praised for his contributions to Scottish culture.

A Note from the Publisher

Spanning many genres, from non-fiction essays to literature classics to children's books and lyric poetry, Mint Edition books showcase the master works of our time in a modern new package. The text is freshly typeset, is clean and easy to read, and features a new note about the author in each volume. Many books also include exclusive new introductory material. Every book boasts a striking new cover, which makes it as appropriate for collecting as it is for gift giving. Mint Edition books are only printed when a reader orders them, so natural resources are not wasted. We're proud that our books are never manufactured in excess and exist only in the exact quantity they need to be read and enjoyed. To learn more and view our library, go to minteditionbooks.com

bookfinity & ◼ MINT EDITIONS

Enjoy more of your favorite classics with Bookfinity,
a new search and discovery experience for readers.
With Bookfinity, you can discover more vintage
literature for your collection, find your Reader Type,
track books you've read or want to read,
and add reviews to your favorite books.
Visit www.bookfinity.com, and click on
Take the Quiz to get started.

Don't forget to follow us
@bookfinityofficial and @mint_editions

CPSIA information can be obtained
at www.ICGtesting.com
Printed in the USA
BVHW041456060621
608895BV00010B/621

9 781513 280448